MW01172069

Cerberus MC Collection 3

Marie James

Snatch
A Very Cerberus Christmas
Lawson
Hound

Snatch

Copyright

Synopsis:

I've been Jaxon Donovan since the day I was born, obviously. My road name, Snatch, came years later due to my ability to literally snatch up any woman I set my sights on. I've always been a connoisseur of the opposite sex. Tall, short, thin, thick and juicy, my tastes knew no limitations.

I didn't think there was a limitation to my sexuality, and I found out just how true that actually was the night my best friend took it upon himself to take me in his mouth. Sure, there'd been close calls before, the slip of a hand or misplaced lips. With our propensity to share women, it's bound to happen. That fateful night, I was met with pure intention and an experience I never want to forget.

How do you explain to your friends, your brother's in arms, that your extremely active sexuality has led you to your best friend's doorstep? How do you admit, after twenty-six years of heterosexuality, that you're into something else?

I'll soon find out that what happens in the dark will always come to light.

Dedication

To those who can't be their self because society has a different expectation of normal.

Note to Readers

First, let me start by apologizing for the unfortunate name choices. Snatch: I'll be honest. I LOVE the name, and it fits him to a T, but I had no idea the direction these characters would take me, so the unfortunate part is Itchy's name. Even to me, Itchy Snatch is pretty cringe-worthy. But, it is what it is, and there's no going back at this point!

Also, this story runs parallel to all of the other books in the series, starting when Darby was rescued from the SINdicate brothel. This means a lot of the things that happens herein, have happened from other's points of view. You'll get the guys' POV and a ton extra stuff!!

I hope you enjoy!

Prologue

Snatch

Blackness surrounds me when the power to the building we're infiltrating is cut. Somehow tipped off, the insurgents knew we were coming and prepared in advance. Back to the nearest wall, I'm so pissed I want to kick my own ass. Both Itchy and Kincaid urged me to wear night vision, but I waved them off. The green tint, even with the infrared gives me a headache that lasts for days. Besides, we've been watching this place for almost a week, and it has always been lit up like the fucking Christmas tree in Rockefeller Center.

"I'm blind," I whisper yell into my mic.

"Fucking told you," Itchy taunts. "Just stay against the wall, pretty boy. Let the men handle this sh—"

His word is cut off the exact moment gunfire echoes around us. I crouch low to the ground tucking my chin to my chest, so my Kevlar helmet is facing the action, making myself as small as possible, and hold. I'm no use to them, having to wait until the dust settles before I can move without risking getting my head blown off.

The sound of bullets hitting the concrete walls as well as small explosions to my left reverberate off the walls. The guys communicate through their mics on where the threats are and systematically take each one out. I know I'm going to catch shit over this once they're done, and Kincaid will never let me opt out of the night vision headset again.

The same sense of calm I always feel in these situations is with me even without being able to see what's going on. The only difference is the guilt I feel because I know that they're taking care of the combatants as well as making sure I don't get a bullet in my melon since I'm practically a sitting duck. It leaves them distracted; Itchy especially.

I shake my head, refusing to run the last two years through my head, refusing to let my own stubbornness take hold while in the middle of deadly combat.

I don't initially freak out when I hear Kincaid come over the mic. "Itchy's been hit."

We sometimes take a shot to the chest, that's why we wear the best Kevlar money can buy. It isn't until Shadow yells out that my blood runs cold.

"Right leg!" Shadow screams. "He's down, Snatch. Eight meters up and six to your left. I'll cover you, but you have to go now."

Without thought, without consideration of my own safety, I crawl toward him. I slip and nearly face plant when I get within a foot. I realize immediately when I pull my hand from the wetness that it's covered in blood. My best friend is fucking bleeding out, and I'm blind, wrapped in a darkness that grows more ominous with each passing second.

"Stay with me," I beg. "I got you."

I run my hand up his right leg, looking for the wound. Finding the tear in his cammies, I shove my finger into the bullet hole. *Goddamn it*, I think but barely keep the words inside. Inside of his right leg, he's been hit in the femoral artery. I hate the feel of his pulse as each burst pushes more blood past my finger, and I struggle to keep the injury plugged against the force I'm working with.

"Fuck," he hisses.

"Sorry, man," I mutter as I use my free hand to pull my belt off.

It isn't until it's wrapped high around his leg and pulled as tight as I can get it that I pull my finger from the bullet hole and reach for his night vision.

"You're crying," he whispers, voice already growing weak and ragged from the blood loss.

My eyes flutter closed when his fingers reach up and caress my cheek.

"Don't get all soft on me now," I tease as I situate the headset.

I told myself not to react, no matter how bad he looked, but I can't help the cuss word that slips from my mouth when I look down at his leg. What I had assumed was a small puddle is actually a full on pool of his blood.

"I'm cold," he says, and I can hear the shiver in his voice.

"Don't," I hiss. "Save your energy."

"I love you," he whispers. "I'm so sorry I couldn't be what you needed."

In the green haze of the goggles, I see his eyes close. I did the same thing when my back was against the wall earlier because it's easier to zero in on your other senses that way. The pained look on Itchy's face, however, tells me his eyes are closed due to loss of strength.

"Please," I beg him. "Stay with me. You're all I'll ever need. I love you, too. Please open your eyes."

They flutter, but he no longer has the strength to obey my order. Before resting my head on his chest, I tug on the belt-turned-tourniquet around his leg and get it a quarter inch tighter. His breaths are shallow and intermittent, and his pulse is thready.

"I love you. I love you." I chant over and over. I confess the words for the first time out loud with each compression of his chest.

I'm repeating it still when I feel someone's hand on my shoulders. I'm still saying it when the lights are turned on, and I'm staring down at the ashen gray body of my best friend, lover, and the greatest man I'll ever know.

Chapter 1

Itchy

Two Years Prior

"Get a load of this fucker," I say angling my head closer to Snatch as Kid walks into the room.

"Whose fucking jalopy is that out front?" he asks as he walks in.

I look over at my best friend to find him smiling in the youngest member's direction. Kid is in running gear, soaked through from one of the runs he's been taking more often recently.

"Sad asshole," Snatch mutters with a laugh. "I bet his nuts are so blue they're purple by now."

Kid used to fuck anything that walks, but after saving Khloe from a prescription pill overdose a little while back, she's all he seems to see now. The problem is that pretty little girl is only seventeen, and he's doing his best to keep his horny hands to himself until her birthday.

I grin, trying to mask the irritation at my best friend. I'd give anything to only focus on the one person I can picture spending the rest of my life with. The only problem with my obsession is he's sitting beside me and as straight as they come.

The overhead light glints off of the small stud that's centered in the tattooed star on his cheek, and I lose my ability to stay mad. It's how it's always been. I can't get mad at him for not returning my feelings, especially since I'd never even hint at them out loud.

I can't tell him and expect my heterosexual best friend to just suddenly be attracted to men, myself in particular. My sexuality is more fluid than anyone else in the clubhouse. I haven't tried to get with any of the men here, but then again Snatch is the only one I've found myself even picturing getting on my knees for. I haven't been with a man since high school, and even then it was more childlike petting, fumbling to fuck than actually getting anywhere.

Snatch laughs again, and I look up to find Kid glaring at us with his middle finger turned up in our direction. We tease him about Khloe not to really piss him off, but to agitate him a little. From the look on his face right now, I fully comprehend that he's in no mood to be fucked with. The glare in his eyes actually makes it seem like he's reached his breaking point, which concerns me because we're all well aware of just how wild Kid can be. For Khloe's sake, I hope it works out in their favor, and he doesn't fuck it all up.

I didn't catch what Shadow said to him, but I'm certain it was a jab. We're all assholes, and given the opportunity to do the same to us, Kid would be all over that shit.

The meeting begins, and Bryan, our guest and old friend, lays out his dilemma. A girl he knows was abducted from Florida, and after speaking with her father, she's being held in Vegas. This should be a pretty simple recon and extraction. Having known Bryan from when Blade was in Walter Reed years ago, Shadow assures him we'll do everything in our power to get her back.

I can't help but cackle when Kid argues about going to Vegas and continues to bitch as he leaves the room.

"He's afraid he'll fuck a hooker," I mutter as we watch him leave the room like a petulant child who has had his favorite toy taken away.

"He better not," Snatch says in Khloe's defense. "But, maybe it's best she finds out how he is now before she goes all in and gets fucked over."

"People can change, asshole. Kid has already proven he can forgo the other women in the club." Snatch's doubt filled blue eyes meet mine. "Seriously. He turned down Snapper the other night. When was the last time he's done something like that?"

Kincaid waves at us as we stand, letting us know that we need to stick around. Shadow follows Bryan out of the room, presumably to show him where he can rack up for the night.

My grin falters when Kincaid turns in our direction. "You guys are driving Kid crazy."

Snatch points at me like an eight-year-old, rather than the twenty-seven-year-old he actually is. "He started it."

Rolling his eyes, Kincaid takes a seat at the head of the table. Hanging his head into his open palms, he grumbles, "I have a house full of fucking children."

"Khloe is the only child here," I correct, earning me a slap on the arm from Snatch.

"She's not a child you idiot. She's seventeen. That's technically legal to fuck in New Mexico," Snatch says.

Kincaid's head snaps up, and he glares at him.

Snatch holds his hands up in mock surrender. "I mean, I wouldn't fuck a seventeen-year-old," he backpedals.

"And neither will Kid. Just," he shakes his head as he searches for the words. "Just leave him the fuck alone. This is hard enough for him."

Snatch snickers when our President says the word *hard*. His laugh actually pulls a grin from Kincaid before he grows serious again.

"Kid and Bryan are heading to Vegas, and I need you two to go with Shadow. I know there's got to be something he missed in Tampa before he bolted out of there. He's not trained the way you are." The pointed look in my direction tells me everything I need to know. Bryan is emotionally involved in this and not seeing the full picture. The concern in his eyes also means this may be a little more dangerous than Bryan thinks.

Snatch and I both nod, but I can't help the grin that spreads on my face. Tampa? Girls wearing bikinis and down for just about anything. I'm already picturing the tan, thick ass Cuban woman who will no doubt be sinking down on my cock. I look over at Snatch, checking to see if he has the same reaction. The sparkle in his eyes is all I need to see.

"No," Kincaid says cutting into the oiled up fantasy of Snatch and I double teaming a beautiful woman. "There's no time to play, guys."

Snatch's head shifts back a few inches, affronted at the implication. "We'd never play before all of the work was done, Prez. You know that."

I cock an eyebrow over at him. *Speak for yourself.* My cock is twitching in my jeans at the thought of what kind of pussy we could get into while out of town.

Kincaid stands and leaves the conference room without another word.

Snatch turns to me. "Whatcha wanna do tonight?"

I shrug. He knows I'm pretty much up for anything.

"I don't really feel like leaving the clubhouse," he says as we walk toward the door. "We could see if Snapper wants to play."

I chuckle. "All of the girls were literally drawing straws on who got to fuck Bryan tonight. No sooner was he ten feet through the door, and they were in the kitchen. Snapper was leading the crew, so my guess is she cheated to win."

"Jake's?" he asks.

I scan the living room, finding a couple of the members just hanging around, shooting the shit, and drinking some beer, pretty calm compared to the way things were before Emmalyn and Khloe showed up. It's still a pretty decent party once they go to bed for the night, but we've been instructed to keep things tame in their presence.

I don't see Bryan anywhere, but Snapper is sitting at the end of the couch, frustration pulling at her brow as she inspects her fingernails. Seeing the exact same thing, Snatch slaps me in the chest. We grin at each other before he calls out to her.

"Hey, Red."

Excitement fills her eyes, the disappointment fading as if it were never there, to begin with. She scurries off of the couch and makes her way across the room to where we're standing. I bite my bottom lip as I watch her hips sway.

"Boys," she purrs placing a hand on each of our chests. "Wanna play?"

My eyes can't be bothered to leave the expanse of her chest. The ripped tank top she's wearing sans bra has every ounce of my concentration.

"Can you handle both of us tonight, doll?" The gravel of Snatch's voice fills my ears until I can't distinguish if it's Snapper or him that's making my cock throb in my jeans.

She giggles as if his question is the silliest thing she's ever heard. "I'm going to drain both of you dry."

She steps between us, heading toward the hall that leads to the rooms.

"Fuck," Snatch mutters as we both turn to see the cheeks of her ass hanging out of the bottom of her cutoff shorts.

"Grab a couple bottles of water and some snacks, fellas. It's going to be a long night."

Chapter 2

Snatch

The putrid smell hits us before we clear the landing on the second floor. Death, but more distinctively, decay, is something Itchy, Shadow, and I encounter more often than we'd like to. Today is no exception.

"How long has it been since Bryan spoke with this girl's dad?" Itchy asks as Shadow toes the door open with the tip of his boot.

"Less than a week," Shadow says as we all file into the tiny apartment.

"He must've died not long after," I say resisting the urge to cover my mouth and nose with my forearm. There's only so much about the smell that you can get accustomed to.

"Overdose," Itchy says pointing at the drug paraphernalia near the body.

"Sad," I mutter as we all stand just inside.

"Probably for the best," Shadow adds. "Let's back out of here, call the cops, and let them deal with this. We'll come back this evening after they've removed the body."

It goes without saying that he'll call the police anonymously to report the smell. We don't need Tampa PD on our asses asking questions about an abduction they won't even bother to work. The neighborhood is shit, and they have bigger cases to work on, but we'd get the third degree because they'll no doubt feel like we're here stepping on their toes. Jurisdiction wars aren't something we ever want to involve ourselves with since we have no type of authority here in Florida, and this isn't a case we'd need to call favors in for anyways.

Shadow makes the call as we head back out to the SUV. There's no sense in checking the littered parking lot for evidence. It's been days since she was taken, and with the amount of trash all around, we'd never be able to determine what is related to her case and what isn't.

"This place is ridiculous," Itchy mutters as we stand beside the SUV and wait for Shadow to get off of the phone.

"Yeah," I agree looking around the area. "Crazy that slums like this exist in America. I'd expect this in Ecuador or Cuba."

"Don't even get me started on how our government doesn't take care of domestic issues before sticking their nose in other country's business."

"Preaching to the choir," Shadow says after hanging up and tugging open the driver's side door.

We drive in silence to the hotel room, something we hadn't planned on having to do. We'd expected to show up, find what we need, and hop right back on the jet by nightfall. The dead body on the sofa threw a wrench in that plan. Now we have to bunk up for the night, wait for the police to finish up at the apartment, and pray they don't spend all damn night.

"It's pretty open and shut," Itchy says as if he can read my mind. "Shouldn't take them long. They've got bigger shit to deal with than spending all day on some junkie who couldn't handle his heroin."

I nod in agreement. "Did Bryan say how close this girl is to her dad?"

"I don't think he knows her that well. My impression is they had like one date and she was snatched up after she left his place. He didn't have many details," Shadow answers as we pull up to the hotel.

"What's the game plan?" Itchy asks as we pile out of the SUV and grab our bags from the back. We may not have anticipated staying, but we always pack just in case.

"Well," Shadow says with a smirk so familiar I already know what's coming. "I'm going back to New Mexico tonight. You guys will head back to the apartment tonight or first thing in the morning."

"What are you expecting we'll find?" Itchy asks.

Shadow shrugs. "I'll be honest. I don't expect much, but due diligence means we at least check it out. Maybe you guys can get her stuff into storage. I don't imagine she'll want to go back to that shit hole once she gets back home."

"No doubt," Itchy agrees.

Ten minutes later, after grabbing a room and tossing our shit on the beds, we're headed back to the airport to drop Shadow off with the promise he'll send the jet back for us to return home tomorrow.

"Wanna grab something to eat?" I ask as we pull off the tarmac before Shadow has even climbed the short set of stairs into the plane.

"I could eat," Itchy mutters looking out the window.

"Something on your mind?" I prod in reaction to his sudden sullen mood.

He shakes his head but says nothing more. He's been rather broody lately, which is completely unlike the guy who quickly became my best friend after he joined Cerberus a couple of years ago.

We're both known to be the jokesters and clowns of the MC, but he's acting more like Kincaid's brother Dominic, all short answers and shitty attitude.

I don't bother asking him what he wants to eat. I know everything he likes and what he doesn't.

"Tacos," I say with honest enthusiasm. All food in Tampa is seasoned with a Cuban flare and beyond delicious.

"Perfect," he responds, genuine contentment in his voice as he looks up at the hole-in-the-wall restaurant tucked behind a strip center.

"So what?" Itchy begins as we make our way into the near-empty building. "We eat, find some hot chick to plow, and then go back and deal with this girl's apartment?"

I look down at my watch. "It might be a little early in the day to find a chick."

It's just after one in the afternoon, and Tampa is known for its nightlife.

He gives me a look over his shoulder as he steps up to the counter to order. "Really? Doubting my skills?"

I laugh at his egotistical attitude. "I have no doubt you could find a chick to hook up with, but I question the quality of what you're going to end up with in the middle of the afternoon on a Tuesday."

His devious challenge of a grin is all I get, and an hour later we're sitting at a small table in an open air mall as he has his pick of women.

One woman, sitting only two tables away with two friends can't keep her eyes off of us or her teeth from biting her bottom lip.

"What do you think?" Itchy asks just before bringing the glass rim of his beer to his lips.

I wink at the woman, almost groaning when her legs inch apart a fraction at my attention, hating that the shadow from her short skirt is hiding what I desire to see most. "I think she's perfect for a little afternoon fun."

"Think we can convince her friends also?" His hopeful voice pulls my eyes from the tanned goddess and back to his.

"I think she'll do fine." He knows orgies aren't really my thing. I'm known to dabble some with larger groups, but a plain Jane three-way is always my go-to form of entertainment.

He hitches his head, his overly long hair falling into his eyes. He doesn't even bother to push it away, and it only adds to the mystique.

It's the beard; I think keeping my eyes on him rather than the woman I can see sauntering up to our table from my peripheral vision.

"Hey guys," she coos when she's less than a foot away from my arm. Golden skin, long dark hair, and legs that lead up to the thickest ass I've seen in a long time.

"Hey," Itchy says, scooting his chair away from the table a few inches.

Brazenly, she doesn't bother with the chair but sits right in his lap. I'll never question his ability to score again. Hell, at this point I would agree with him if he told me he could fuck a preacher's wife in the middle of Sunday service.

"You boys in town for long?" The thick accent flows from her plump lips shooting straight to my cock. She's well aware of how the afternoon is going to go, and from the way she's running her long red fingernail down Itchy's chest while eye-fucking me, I can tell we're not going to have to do much convincing when she finds out we're both going to take pleasure in her.

"Just long enough to fuck you so good you'll beg us to take you along when we leave," Itchy whispers against her neck.

Her teeth scrape over her bottom lip again as she cups his thick cock on top of his jeans.

"Is that so?" she purrs, eyes sparking with a fierce lust.

"Guaranteed," I respond, speaking for the first time since she joined us.

"My apartment is right around the corner," she offers, standing from my friend's lap and reaching for both of our hands. "Don't want to waste any time, do we?"

I don't miss the wink she throws to her two friends a couple of tables away. They both roll their eyes but smile at her as she leads us back to her apartment. We allow it for the time being. Once we get her in private, the dominance and power exchange will flip.

"I fucking love Tampa," Itchy says as he adjusts his cock while waiting for her to unlock her door.

Chapter 3

Itchy

"They didn't say," I tell Snatch as he assembles his weapon.

"That sucks," Snatch says shaking his head slightly before going back to work on his weapon.

Kid was hurt in Vegas because of the bastards we're about to take down. His short-term memory is wiped, and he fucked his relationship up with Khloe by fucking Snapper the day he got back to the clubhouse. I'd assumed he'd fuck a hooker while in Vegas, but he got hurt before he had the chance. The asshole waited until he got back, right in front Khloe's face and chose one of the club girls. Snapper is a hell of a lay, but she's about as devious as they come.

We just arrived in Vegas on Thursday, and it's Tuesday now, the night everything is supposed to go down. At the command center a couple of miles away from The Golden Dragon where Aviana Maguire is being held with at least a half-dozen other women, we're getting ready to take over SINdicate tonight.

The FBI is also on the case. Apparently, Vincent "Vinnie" Sinclair has been on their radar for some time. The girls in the glorified whore house have been less of a concern for them because their focus has been on the weapons, drugs, and murders they're suspected of.

Shadow ran into them while doing re-con earlier this week. They weren't very happy when they realized Cerberus was on the scene, but after a phone call to the Director, there was a sudden shift in the focus of their investigation. Begrudgingly, they're now on board with the direction tonight needs to go. Shadow has ceded pseudo control to them, since they have jurisdiction, and from the outside, Cerberus looks like some rogue, vigilante group. There are three places the teams are split to raid tonight: The floor where Aviana is being kept, a place referred to as The Cat House, where they house the hookers Sinclair forces on the street, and the warehouse where we've discovered the cache of weapons and drugs are being kept.

All Cerberus members will be involved in the raid on The Golden Dragon, Aviana Maguire is our sole purpose for being in Vegas, and that's where our resources will lie.

"These are some of the main players," Shadow says slapping down a paper with twelve mugshots on them. He walks around and hands some of the other guys a copy of the same sheet. "We don't anticipate Sinclair being up there tonight. Last report said he was at the warehouse prepping a shipment of coke for delivery."

I feel the warmth of Snatch's body as he leans over my back to study the photo lineup.

"They all look like douches," he mutters, unaware of how his hot breath on my neck makes my cock twitch in my jeans.

I clear my throat, doing my best to push images of our time in Tampa from my mind. As much as I'd like to ruminate on the way his muscular thighs felt against mine while we double-teamed that sexy as fuck woman for hours, now isn't the time or place.

"I recognize this motherfucker," Snatch says as he reaches up and points to the scarred face of a guy identified as Franklin "Frankie" Moretti. "He's on one of our watch lists."

I grunt, the only response I can muster as his hand brushes against my arm.

"This one too," he adds pointing at another guy.

I hand him the paper over my shoulder and take a step away, unable to handle the contact and closeness any longer.

How fucked up is it that I'm standing here fantasizing about my straight best friend when we're supposed to be preparing for a raid on assholes who deal in the flesh trade? I resign myself to only feeling the slide of his cock against mine while we fuck a chick together and finish getting my gear ready.

"You need to pull your head out of your ass," he mutters catching onto my sudden change in attitude.

"I'm fine," I grumble popping a clip into my HK416. "These types of guys just piss me off."

"Same for all of us, brother," he says slapping my back before going over to talk to Shadow and the FBI Agent who identified himself as Jones earlier.

I've always been attracted to the tattooed motherfucker, but recently it's begun to interfere with our friendship. I avoid him as much as I can, which isn't much because staying to myself will only raise questions I'm not sure I'll ever be able to answer. When we do hang out, if there's not a girl between us I'm in a shitty mood, and he's picking up on it more lately.

I need something to refocus on, or I need to get the fuck away from Cerberus for a while. It's the thought of never seeing him that makes my chest ache.

"Anything serious we need to worry about with these assholes?" Ace asks from the other side of the room.

Jones speaks up since he knows more about them. "They're all Family rejects, associates to a couple of Made Men."

"Which Family?" Ace interjects.

"All of them," Jones answers. "They're like the melting pot of mafia rejects. Sinclair's only at the top because he's got some legit Family blood in him and weak ties to Chicago. We haven't figured out why the extended families in Vegas haven't given them their walking papers yet."

"No shit," Snatch mutters.

"We suspect," Jones continues, "that SINdicate is a front for the bigger families here, but that's just speculation. We hope to know more once the dust settles tonight."

Shadow's phone rings and all sound in the small room ceases. He's been waiting for the call to confirm that Bryan is inside which is our queue to enter. He hangs up, gives us the signal that it's time to roll out, and we jump into action.

We caravan, three Suburbans deep, to the front doors of The Golden Dragon. Tactical assaults on high rise buildings are a nightmare. Getting inside unnoticed, with as many men as we need, is an impossibility. Agent Jones sends two guys dressed in civvies in first to take over their command room. The last thing we need is to be ambushed in the stairwell.

I commit myself to taking my time at the gym more seriously as we reach the landing to the top floor. I'm more winded than I ever should be for this type of job, but not so much that I can't function.

"Need to lay off those cigars," Snatch snips playfully.

I'd flip him the finger, but training keeps both of my hands on my rifle, and if I'm honest, I don't have the breath to waste on him. His bright blue eyes shine with mirth that can be seen through the shield of his tactical goggles. I despise the black masks we wear when we do domestic jobs to maintain anonymity because it blocks the smile I've come to love.

"Asshole," I hiss as we get into position at the only entrance to SINdicate's glorified whore house.

"Not my fault you're turning into an old man," he teases back.

"I'm a year youn—"

My words are cut off when the door is kicked in, and the concussion grenade reverberates all around us.

"You're only as young as you feel, old man," he continues as we push inside and make our way down the hall to clear all of the rooms.

"I don't feel old, mother fucker," I hiss into my mic. Snatch enters a room, and I go past him to the next one.

"Can you children kindly shut the fuck up?" Shadow's voice booms into my ear.

"RAH!" I narrow my eyes at Ace's agreement with Shadow's command, but soon my attention is turned to the door I just kicked in.

"Get dressed," I command the woman who's standing in the center of the room, naked as the day she was born, with her hands on her hips like I'm not standing here in full tactical gear with a rifle in my hands.

"No," she hisses. "Vito is on his way to see me, and I'll be damned if I'm leaving without seeing him."

Vito Barzini is Vinnie Sinclair's right-hand man and the one we were told to be most cautious of. He's quick to pull the trigger and has had enough arrests that they fear he'll fight to the death before getting arrested again.

My eyes dart around the room, looking for a robe to throw at her, and I spot the prepared lines of coke on a large mirror beside the bed. Several streaks of residue let me know she's been in here partying on her own for a while. It explains her defiance and lack of fear. Powered by powder.

"Vito's tied up at the moment." It's not really a lie. I know the room Snatch was meant to go into after he grabbed McKinley was a woman by the name of Darby. She's one of his favorites, and it was speculated he'd be with her. "Grab some clothes, and I'll take you to him."

Her eyes narrow as she tries to assess whether or not I'm being truthful. I tap the side of my rifle with my trigger finger, annoyed that my time is being wasted in the room with this chick. She's hot, no doubt, but coke heads and whores really aren't my thing. We were told the women are here voluntarily. They are contracted hookers, and even though they have limited access to the outside world, it isn't unheard of for them to go to parties and high society functions on the arms of SINdicate soldiers.

I won't however, take the risk of speaking down to her or roughing her up to get compliance because there's always a chance the women here are either forced, manipulated into being here or are suffering from Stockholm Syndrome. We see it a lot in our missions overseas.

"I'm Courtney," she purrs as she throws on a slinky little dress. "What's your name?"

I let her walk past me into the hallway but follow close behind.

"Fred," I mutter.

She stops when she sees all of the men in tactical gear and runs to the guy I recognize from the photo lineup as Vito. He's knocked out cold, slumped in a pile on the floor in the middle of what's being used by the women as the living room.

"Are we clear?" I ask Snatch, identifiable by his choice of weapon and the fact that he insists on wearing a tactical vest that he had custom painted to match his inked skin below.

"Yep," he answers as we watch two FBI agents wrestle with Courtney and place her in handcuffs when she wouldn't stop clinging to the unconscious Vito. "Fuck, she's hot, too."

I let my eyes rove over all the half-naked women. They look more agitated to have their night interrupted than thankful we've rescued them from indentured labor.

"If they're working here of their own free will, and prostitution is legal just a couple of miles outside the city limits, what's the big deal?"

"They abducted Aviana Maguire, fuckface," Snatch answers the question I don't even realize I said out loud. "There's a good chance some of these women got here the same way. Besides, Jones said earlier that they think there's money in the bank for them. Like some type of ledger is kept tallying all the things they've been doing with these guys."

I nod. "That could be incentive enough to stick around for a couple of years."

Snatch shakes his head, sighing, the nonverbal *you idiot* clear in his stance. "There's no fucking accounts. Jones said they couldn't find anything concerning the women here. Not a list of names, or services provided. They tapped into their computer system last month and have been keeping close tabs on it, but there's nothing. It's why they didn't know this place even existed. So unless they find some hand written book with all this shit in it, there's no money for these women."

"I wonder if they know that and that's why they're pissed. At least here they were provided for."

"We've seen much worse," Snatch says with another look around the room.

Our conversation halts when Shadow waves us over to help the FBI escort the handful of men in custody out of the room and back down to be transported to a holding area until they can be interrogated.

I grumble to myself when I reach down to tug one of the assholes up from the floor.

"Don't worry," I hear Snatch's voice in my ear. "You can take the elevator this time old man."

This time I hear Shadow's and Ace's laughter in my ear.

Chapter 4

Snatch

"We got nine of the twelve we were hoping to capture tonight," Jones says from the head of the long table at the FBI office. "The three we didn't get our hands on are some of the lower ranking guys. They'll either try to join ranks with some of the other influences in town, or they'll scatter like the rats they are."

We all nod in understanding. We don't anticipate the guys who couldn't even gain rank in such a shoddy organization to be much trouble from here on out. They just happened to luck out tonight. Knowing they'll be caught eventually just means it's likely they high-tail it out of town.

"Vinnie?" Shadow inquires.

Jones shakes his head. "He pulled on my guys the second they came through the door of the warehouse. They plugged him full."

"Good," Shadow says, voicing what everyone else in the room is feeling. He pulls out his phone when it chimes with a text.

"We have to figure out what to do with all of those women out there," Jones says with clear frustration in his voice. "With the exception of Aviana Maguire and a friend she made, not one of them is happy about what went down tonight."

"Do they know they weren't making any money?" I ask. "That they were being lied to the entire time they were there?"

Jones shrugs while he taps the edge of a stack of paper. "When we told them they were even more pissed at us. Not one of them has anything to fall back on. They weren't very talkative, but the ones that were willing to share a little told us they're mostly from the streets. SINdicate providing for them was the best life they've had for years. It all crumbled when we blasted in there tonight."

"We'll take care of that," Shadow murmurs not pulling his eyes from his cell phone as his fingers skate over the keys with quick precision.

Jones cocks an eyebrow at him. "Take care of that?"

I chuckle at the Agent, which draws his attention from my VP.

"I'm not sure what you boys are planning on doing with thirteen whores, but I'm not sure the FBI is just going to let you waltz out of here with them."

I chuckle again and his eyes narrow. We get this a lot. Many people we work with who aren't privileged to the work we do question our intentions. When you're saving women, giving them new identifications, and protecting them from asshole scumbags, sharing exactly what we plan isn't something we advertise.

Several long minutes tick by as Shadow ignores the obvious anger building in the misinformed agent. He doesn't raise his eyes to the red-faced Jones until he's completed his text message, no doubt to Blade, who does most of our organizing.

"First," he begins with an edge to his voice that means business. "I think for a man who makes his living in Sin City, the use of the word whores is a little extreme. Everything in this city is just legalized skin. Second, it's not like we're going to take them back to our clubhouse and put them to work on their backs."

I slide closer to Itchy because we both enjoy a good show when Shadow has been offended and feels the need to put an asshole in his place. I grin over at him, only to find him not watching but ignoring me. I sigh and turn my head back to the current entertainment.

"Arrangements have been made to house all of them in Kingman," Shadow says before the chime of his cell phone pulls his attention from the now seething Agent Jones.

Kingman, Arizona is just about two hours away, and it gets the girls out of the craziness of the city. We've used one of the hotels down there before.

"We need to dig deeper into their backgrounds," he counters.

Shadow shakes his head. "You ran every one of them. Besides the two with petty theft from years ago, they all came back clean."

"They may be able to give us info on those assholes we have in custody," he argues further.

It's Shadow's turn to laugh at his straw grasping. Itchy even drops the new asshole attitude he's adopted over the last several weeks and laughs beside me.

"I don't think those *whores* are going to give you any more than you've already gotten," Shadow says just as Jones' phone rings. "Might want to answer that. It's your boss's boss."

Shadow walks out, but like usual, Itchy and I stick around and listen to him 'yes, sir' whoever is on the other line. He mumbles about jurisdiction and something about 'whose dick do I need to suck to get that kind of pull' before he walks out and leaves us in the room alone.

"That never gets old," I say as I grip Itchy's shoulder and turn him toward the door.

He shrugs me off, and I ignore the shitty mood that has already returned. That smoking hot girl that was in with Vito flashes in my mind. I'm not into the drug scene but seeing that douche bag snort a line of coke off her tits made my dick hard right in the middle of the fucking raid.

Exiting the room, paying no mind to Itchy who walks right out the front of the building, I find the blonde beauty across the room sitting with Aviana. She notices me immediately, speaking to her friend, but never pulls her eyes from mine.

She doesn't seem fearful, which is nice. Many women are intimidated by the tats and piercings, assuming I'm a thug or criminal at first glance.

I walk toward her, reminding myself not to appear too anxious and overly excited at her response.

"Temptress," I whisper offering my hand.

She takes it in hers, a sly smile playing on her pouty lips. "Darby," she answers with a huskiness that makes my nuts ache.

"Snatch," I say in introduction without releasing her hand.

Aware of Aviana beside her, I only stroke the back of her hand with a single, tattooed finger when I want nothing more than to pull my cock out and offer it to her on a silver fucking platter.

"I'm sure," Darby says her voice laced with innuendo.

I smile down at her, barely keeping my tongue from snaking out and sliding over my bottom lip.

Satisfaction warms me when she turns to look at Aviana and says, "I think New Mexico is a perfect place to go."

She offers the chair beside hers but never lets go of my hand.

"You're coming along to the clubhouse?"

She nods, but it's Aviana who answers. "We're going to go there with you guys and after that head to Tampa. Darby's never been to Florida."

Darby bites her lip when she notices my inability to pull my eyes from her luscious tits. I nearly groan. "So I get a couple of days with you."

"Looks that way." God, I love a woman with a husky voice. It tells me just how rough it's going to be after she's been begging me to fuck her harder all night.

"You just made my year, baby." She smiles and leans closer to me.

"What about your friend?" She tilts her head toward the exit.

I see Itchy coming back in, the last bit of smoke from one of his disgusting cigars trailing behind him. For a split second, I want to keep her to myself, knowing with his shit demeanor he doesn't deserve someone this amazing, but I concede. I'd never deny him the chance to fuck a girl together. Honestly, sex is always better when we're both in a room playing with a woman.

"Itchy?" I lean in closer to her ear as we both watch him run his hand over his thick beard. "Itchy will worship your pussy while I spend days reveling in your amazing tits."

"Sounds like a great time," she answers almost breathless as she squirms in her seat. "I can't wait."

Aviana has moved her attention from Darby as Bryan comes up and sits her in his lap, and I'm grateful not to have her listening in on our conversation. She doesn't seem like the type that would be okay with a threesome, and I don't need judgmental friends talking Darby out the fun we can have back home.

I'd be concerned about coercion, but Darby is the one who suggested we bring Itchy into the mix.

Trust but verify. "Only if it's something you want to do, baby. We wouldn't force you into anything. That's not what Cerberus is about."

"Are you going make me beg?" Her finger trails over my name patch on my cut. "I will."

I lean back just a bit, suddenly uneasy without facts.

"Why were you at SINdicate?"

Her eyes find mine, and she shrugs. "Vito found me on the street. Made me an offer I couldn't refuse."

"He had you tied to a bed only hours ago. I'm fucked up for even thinking about fucking you."

She chuckles a humorless laugh. "You were one of the guys that came in?"

I nod.

"He gets angry sometimes. The coke makes him a little aggressive."

"You were crying." I push up the sleeve of the sweatshirt she's wearing, turning her hand over, so the marks on her wrists are visible. "He did this. I saw all the other welts on your body. You were terrified when we came in there. He was hurting you."

She bites her lip again before speaking. "I asked him to tie me up. He went a little far with the cane tonight, but it wasn't past my limits. I was terrified because that's a natural reaction when men with guns barge in on an intimate experience." I shake my head and look away, but she reaches up, clutching my chin until I look at her. "I was crying because he wouldn't let me come."

I swallow the thickness in my throat.

"That's so fucking wrong," I tell her.

She hangs her head, ashamed and reading my words wrong. "That I asked him to do those things?"

It's my turn to grip her chin. I shake my head when her eyes meet mine. "That he wouldn't let you come. I promise you, sweet girl. You'll always come like a train with me."

Her eyes sparkle at my vow, and I once again hate being so far from home.

Chapter 5

Itchy

Wooing. There was no other name for what Snatch is doing with the woman across the room. My eyes find his the second I walk back in, and hers only a fraction of a second later. The smile playing on his lips is one I know all too well, one that speaks of the depraved things we'll be doing later.

Only it's taking longer than we expect as several of the girls from SINdicate refuse to get in the SUVs that are heading to Kingman. Courtney, the girl I evacuated, is the leader of the small group, who seem to have plotted and planned while we were debriefing with the FBI.

"I won't," she refuses once again, and I can see the pink at the top of Shadow's ears, the only sign that he's growing increasingly frustrated with her. "I want to go back to the hotel."

He shakes his head, running an aggravated hand over the top of his dark blond hair. "I've told you more than once ma'am, SINdicate fell tonight. The organization no longer exists."

"You should've just left us the fuck alone." She points across the room to Bryan and Aviana, but they're too snuggled up with each other, heads lowered, and talking softly to even be aware of the argument across the room. "You should have gotten that bitch out and left the rest of us alone. I want the money they've been saving for me."

The other girls mumble their agreements.

"We can see about getting that for you," Shadow agrees. "But it isn't going to happen here, and it isn't going to happen tonight."

Not every woman we encounter feels like they need to be rescued, and from the way the hotel rooms looked that she came from, she was living a fairly decent life, if you take out the abuse, drugs, and inability to come and go as she pleased.

"Assholes," she sneers, but she weighs her options and stomps out the front to the waiting SUV.

The other girls scramble after her, all piling into the same vehicle.

"Women," Shadow mutters. "It's chicks like her that keep me from settling down. I bet she used to be a sweet girl. I bet all women turn bitter like that as they get older."

"Shut the fuck up," I say with a clap on his back. "Your parents are still together."

"And my dad fishes every chance he gets," he says with a rueful smile.

"We about ready to head out?" Snatch's voice makes me flinch. I didn't even realize he'd made it across the room, and usually, I'm all too aware of his proximity to me.

"Wheels up in sixty," Shadow mutters before disappearing through the heavy wooden door leading back to Jones' office.

"Hey, man." I feel the jab to my shoulder just as the words leave Snatch's mouth.

I turn, planning to give him my full attention but the dark haired beauty beside him garners it all.

"I'm Darby," she says holding her hand out to me.

I clasp it and immediately bring it to my mouth.

"Itchy," I offer, knowing my beard abrades her skin and loving the feel of her shiver from the contact.

"Snatch tells me we're going to have some fun later." Brazen little thing.

My eyes find my best friend's shining bright with anticipation. He waggles his eyebrows, and I can tell he's even more excited than he was in Tampa. It brings an honest smile to my face as my blood hums with the prospect of spending a few hours with him and Darby.

"We can't get home soon enough," I whisper and offer the crook of my arm. She takes it and slides her arm into Snatch's as well. We walk out of the FBI, Las Vegas division as one unit.

***

The plane ride back to New Mexico is a stressful exercise in sexual control. I count no less than a half dozen times seeing Snatch adjust his hard-on in his jeans at Darby's whispers in his ear. I know exactly what he's struggling with. She's sandwiched between the two of us, one of her wandering hands on each of our thighs.

"We can get started here, can't we?" she whispers in my ear reaching for my zipper.

"Fuck, I wish," Snatch growls from two seats over.

I stop her hand from pulling my throbbing cock from my jeans as I look across the private plane toward Bryan and Aviana. He gives me a quick grin and an amused shake of his head, but then quickly turns his attention back to the sleeping girl in his lap.

"Probably not the best place," I chide but ease the rejection with a soft kiss to her fingertips.

If it were only the three of us, she would've been pinned to the floor with two holes filled and fingers in her mouth. Hell, even with the other guys with us that would've been a real possibility, but Bryan and Aviana are wild cards, and I have enough respect for them to keep my clothes on, even if my cock doesn't agree.

The pretty pout of her lips has me questioning my decision, but Snatch whispers something in her ear. I watch her nod at his words, lay her head on his shoulder, and close her eyes.

He looks over the top of her head and gives me a wink. That simple gesture, filled with sexual intent for only her, makes my mind race. Having desired him for so long, my mind makes plans, imagining fantasies that will never come to fruition. My cock is straining in my jeans, leaking from the tip in anticipation by the time we make it to the clubhouse.

"Wow," Darby and Aviana both whisper as they make it inside.

Club members are spread out everywhere, our club girls half, if not fully nude, give cheers when we all make it inside. Darby is in awe, but Aviana's look is one of pure shock. I commend myself internally for keeping it PG on the plane. Both Shadow and Kincaid speak with Bryan before they make a quick retreat to their rooms.

"What do you think?" I ask, leaning close enough to Darby's ear that my beard touches her chin.

Her grin spreads wide as she takes in the scene. I try to see, with new eyes, the scene in front of us. Members, all in cuts, surrounded by eager women. Even Snapper keeps her eyes on us as she leans down and swipes her tongue over the tip of Snake's exposed cock.

I notice her attention has paused on the sight.

"I'm told she eats pussy better than Itchy," Snatch says in a low grumble. I side eye him. "And I've seen Itchy make a girl come in under a minute with his oral skills."

"Oh God," she pants, longing in her tone. "Will she join us tonight?"

"No, gorgeous," I say. "But soon, if that's what you want."

She nods almost violently at the prospect. "Yes, please."

Snatch chuckles reaching for her hand and dragging her further into the room. "Drink?"

She assents with a quick dip of her head but never pulls her eyes from the red superstar who's deep throating across the room. Snatch lines up at least ten shot glasses on the small bar top and overfills them with tequila.

"She's pretty," she praises.

"You're prettier," I counter, but turn my eyes to the public sex that's got her rapt attention.

I see Snake bite his lip as his fingers tangle in Snapper's red hair, but it's the way he's eyeing Darby that makes the unfamiliar possessiveness strum just below my skin.

In a proprietary move, I wrap my arm around her shoulder, finding Snatch has just done the same thing, his eyes hot on the other MC member. Snake smirks and raises his hands in defeat, finally lowering his eyes back down to Snapper as he groans loud enough to pull even more attention from around the room. Darby jumps slightly when some of the other guys and the girls whose mouths aren't full cheer at his release.

"You want him?" Snatch asks as we all watch Snake lean back on the couch so Snapper can clean him up with her mouth.

She bites her lip. "I want *her*."

"Fuck, you're perfect," I tell her as Snatch pulls away to line up more shots.

The tequila eases the tension in my shoulders that built up on the plane ride over but does nothing to calm the sexual need rushing to my cock.

"You want to stay and watch or head to the back?" I finally ask after downing the additional shots Snatch shoved into my hands.

"Let's head back," she answers. "I'm ready to play."

Chapter 6

Snatch

My body is tingling all over, part from the need to sink into Darby's pussy and part from the tequila we downed in record time.

Once in Itchy's room, we're a tangle of arms and mouths. Mentioning the skill of his mouth was my offering to Itchy. We've been doing this long enough to use mere context clues to hash out our plans before the women even agree to the action.

He works on getting her lower half naked as I pull her sweatshirt and tank top over her head. The unbelievable tits I'd seen hours ago at the hotel are now fully exposed. Unable to resist a minute longer, my head lowers, mouth wrapping around one nipple. Normally off-putting, the salty twang from the cocaine that asshole was snorting off her tits, only serves to make my cock harder.

Itchy, in control of everything from the waist down, guides her until she's walking toward the bed. At the edge, we stop because no clothing is going to be involved tonight. I feel her shift as her pants are pulled down, shoes are removed, and she's stepping out one leg at a time, my mouth never leaving her body.

She whimpers, the familiar sound letting me know that Itchy already has his mouth on her pussy. Mine waters, jealous of my best friend. I'm hoping the offering, that first sweet taste of a new pussy, the one thing we argue most over when negotiating, is enough to pull him from whatever has caused his recent shitty mood.

As promised, Darby is trembling in my arms less than a minute later as the first of many orgasms she's going to have tonight rushes through her body. I hold her up as her knees almost give out, knowing Itchy is nowhere close to being done. The first one is always just the ice breaker before he gets serious.

"Take me out," I urge her, and her hands work to get my jeans open and down my tense thighs.

I watch Itchy as he rises from his knees and gets to work on stripping out of his restrictive clothing. He's in absolute heaven, beard wet from Darby's release. My tongue sneaks out, wetting my bottom lip, wishing that slickness was on my own face. I watch his mouth, enthralled as Darby takes me in both hands.

"Holy shit," she gasps as I fall heavily into her hands.

Itchy smiles, just as he always does when a woman gets her hands on me for the very first time. My cock is long, thick, and throbbing in her small, cool hands. My dick is a masterpiece, the slight curve perfect for finding a woman's G-spot like its only mission in life.

Itchy grabs her hips, resting his equally magnificent cock against her ass. She startles, jumping an inch at the reminder that he's in the room. I hear him chuckle before he steps back and positions himself on his back.

"Up here, gorgeous. I haven't gotten my fill of that pussy yet." His voice is husky, filled so full with yearning, it echoes in my dick as she looks from him and back to me, torn between my cock and his mouth.

"Go on," I urge with a sharp slap to her ass. "I'm coming too."

She scampers on the bed, and Itchy shows her just how he wants her, kneeled down on his mouth facing his cock. I tug off my t-shirt while kicking my boots off. My jeans follow soon after. I pull a strip of condoms from the bedside table and quickly get into position. We're experts at this, having perfected three-way sex down to a fucking science. I straddle my best friend's legs, letting my cock hang close to his, the perfect position for her to choose between which one is going in her mouth.

The moment she whimpers and grinds down on Itchy's mouth, my hand is on the back of her head, guiding her hot mouth to my cock. This is another part of the rules. If he gets the first lick of her slit; I get the first sweep of her tongue, the very first suck of her mouth. Some guys may argue over which one of us is the luckiest. Itchy always wants his mouth on them first, and most days I would agree that's the true winner. Today? As Darby sucks me down her throat without so much as an explorative lick to the thick crown, I'd defend my current position as the champion.

"Goddamn it," I groan, the anticipation that has been building all night drawing my nuts up tight to my body.

Itchy chuckles at my exquisite pain, knowing full well what my sudden outburst is from. Darby, mindful of the tension I'm feeling gives me a quick reprieve and moves her mouth to his cock. Hand on the back of her head, I urge her to take him deeper. They hiss in unison, and I feel Itchy's thighs jump against my legs. When her mouth is on me again, I'm not even bothered that Itchy's hands are on my legs rather than her body.

The tingle hits too soon, creeping down my spine long before I'm ready for this to be over. Leaning back, I pull from her mouth with a satisfying slurp. Unaffected, she just moves a few inches lower to take Itchy back down her throat.

Grabbing a condom from beside me on the mattress, I slide it down my erection as I climb off the bed and walk around, so I'm behind her. They're too far away to take her standing, so I climb up and straddle Itchy's head. I watch for a few long minutes while he attacks her with vigor. Her near boneless legs are splayed open so wide Itchy doesn't even have to extend his neck to reach her hot cunt.

"Perfect," I praise as I hook a thumb inside of her.

"She's ready," Itchy says, urging me on before he attacks her clit once more.

I thrust, slamming into her in one fluid motion. She tries to buck away from my intrusion, but the grip Itchy has on her hips doesn't allow much forward movement.

"Fuck, she feels good man." I swivel my hips, enticing her to push back against me, and giving myself a second to adjust to the grip of her slick heat.

"Darby, your lips are clinging to him like you never want to let him go," Itchy says, the warmth of his breath spreading from my sac and cooling her arousal on my cock. It's unfamiliar, but not altogether unpleasant.

It borders on sensation overload, and I can't help but want him to keep talking so I can feel it again. He doesn't, opting instead to lick and bite her hardened bud until she's a quivering mess.

The tip of his nose, covered in her slickness, or his tongue rubs the underside of my cock, and I shudder, feeling more aroused than I have in as long as I can remember. I'm going to blow soon, and I'm grateful Itchy is below, paying her body attention because every nasty thing I whispered to her on the plane is never going to find its way into this room tonight. The end is coming so fast, I know I'm going to be embarrassed and probably catch flak from Itchy once we're through.

"Wait," I grunt, pulling from her and ripping the condom off of my cock. "I need a minute."

"No," Itchy hisses just before the suction of his mouth is engulfing my cock.

I still immediately, but the buildup is too much, the burn in my nuts too sharp to make him stop now. With a bruising grip, I cling to Darby's hips and push my cock further down my best friend's throat. I can't even question what the fuck is going on or remind myself this has never fucking happened before.

Darby shifts forward several inches, and I lose the grip on her, but the bed shifts as Itchy begins to reposition himself.

Unable to resist, I look down and watch him suck my cock with so much enthusiasm my thighs begin to tremble, threatening to give up under my weight. His head is now at the perfect angle as he pushes up on one elbow to gain better access to my straining cock. His long, skilled fingers replace my cock in Darby's hot pussy. The sight of her fucking herself on and off of them combined with my dick disappearing down Itchy's throat is the grandest sight I've never even had the inclination to imagine before.

When his eyes roll into the back of his head, I realize Darby never stopped sucking his cock. The rumble in his chest as he comes rolls down my cock and sets off my own orgasm. Relentless bursts of come land on his tongue and chin, coating his beard.

The warm shiver of possibly the best fucking orgasm I've ever had covers my entire body, but my eyes never pull from Itchy as he swallows and licks the over-sensitized triangle at the base of my crown. My hips jerk back at the surfeit of sensation, and I shiver again when his head turns as if chasing it, needing more. My lips part, panting breaths escaping my lungs, my eyes locked on the sight of my come wetting his beard. A satisfied smirk tugs at the corners of his mouth, lips still swollen from his effort.

What the fuck did we just do?

"That was so fucking hot," Darby pants. It isn't until I look over at her, seeing her sitting on the bed wiping Itchy's come from her lips with the back of her hand that I realize she was a witness to what happened. Fear sits heavy in my gut.

It isn't the fact that I loved my best friend's mouth wrapped around my cock or the glorious way he received the offering my body gave him that had me shuffling back and standing at the end of the bed.

It had even less to do with the fact that a woman we don't even know participated in the first homosexual act I've ever been involved in. It had nothing to do with the expectant look in his eyes, and the way his cock was still standing tall and proud, ready for more.

What had me freaking out and running from the room without even bothering to get dressed was the way my mouth watered, the tingle on my tongue telling me I wanted to do the exact same fucking thing to him.

Chapter 7

Itchy

I'm still reveling, flying high from the night before when my eyes open. Darby snuggles deeper into my side, and I hug her closer, knowing she was the catalyst, part of the reason I had the courage to follow through last night.

We didn't chase after Snatch when he high-tailed it out of here last night. We didn't talk, didn't discuss what happened. My cock was still throbbing, and she was so wet from it all, we spent hours devouring each other. This morning has to be different. The conversations we should've had last night have to happen before she leaves this room. I know she's leaving this morning, heading to Tampa with Bryan and Aviana, and the chances of ever seeing her again are slim, but I don't want her saying anything at breakfast or even hinting about the secrets only the three of us and these four walls should ever know.

"Hey, sleepy head," I whisper when she looks up at me.

"Hey, yourself." Am I just now noticing the huskiness of her voice?

I decide to jump right in. "So about last night."

She smiles sleepily. "Last night was perfect. I hate that Snatch was so eager to leave. He promised me so many things."

Eager. That's one way to put it. My pulse picks up thinking about the aftermath I'm going to have to deal with shortly. I enjoyed the fuck out of last night, and I know he did too, while it was happening. After though? This morning? Extremely different feelings.

"Next time, I want to watch." She bites her lip, and my already hard cock jumps under her thigh. "It was over by the time I turned around."

"You like that sort of thing?" I test the waters.

"Last night was the first time I've ever had the two guys I was fucking go after each other. It turned me on more than I ever thought it could." Her fingernail brushes over my nipple, pulling a hiss from my lips. "I think I could've come just watching you suck his cock."

"There may not be a next time," I tell her unable to hide the disappointment in my own voice. "We've never messed around before." Her eyes widen. "He didn't just up and leave because he was done, he freaked out because I sucked his cock and he liked it."

"Wow," is all she can manage.

I look up at the ceiling, freaking out even more about what today may bring.

"So it just happened?"

I nod. "I've..." I pause, unsure if I should be telling her anything. I barely know her, but she seems like the type of person who's keeping many secrets. "You can't tell anyone what happened in here last night."

She shakes her head against my chest. "I wouldn't, promise."

I swallow the fear that's increasing exponentially in my throat.

"I've wanted to, for longer than I've ever had the right, but last night was the first time I've mustered the courage."

We hold each other, surrounded by silence and our own thoughts before she speaks again.

"You're afraid he's going to freak out?"

"He freaked out last night. I saw it all in his eyes. The fear of someone finding out, the disgust at what he'd let me do, the repulsion that I'm the type of man who enjoyed sucking his cock and swallowing his come." I tremble at picturing it all again.

"What are you going to do?"

I shrug, jostling her head on my shoulder. "I've got to run an errand for Kid this morning, and when I get back, I'm going to pretend it never happened. Then I'll pray that he will let it go and I won't lose my best friend over my own impulsive sexual desire."

"I think this goes a little deeper than desire."

I huff a humorless laugh. "Yeah."

"You have to talk to him," she urges.

"There's not a fucking chance of that happening."

She shifts, pulling her body away from mine as she sits beside me.

"If you care about him, you have to tell him how you feel."

Maybe telling her anything was a bad idea. I sit up, facing away from her on the edge of the bed. My fingers shake as they sweep over the top of my head.

I jump when her hand touches my back. She pulls it away immediately.

"You don't understand," I mutter.

"I understand love," she begins. "Well, I understand the concept of love, anyway."

I laugh at the ridiculousness of her words. "Believe me, babe. It isn't love. I may want him to fuck me, but the idea of some sort of fucked up happily-ever-after has never entered my mind."

"I won't tell anyone," she promises as I walk into the bathroom and leave her sitting on the bed.

Love?

Only in my wildest dreams, and even then the idea makes my heart pound. I didn't have to lie to her, but honesty out in the open, confessions that will never gain any ground are pointless.

I sucked my straight best friend's cock. He loved it and a minute later freaked the fuck out. How can I think about love when at a minimum I hope he doesn't hate me and kill me in my sleep?

***

The high from last night filled my blood all the way across town and back to grab some paperwork Kincaid texted about while on the plane. That bliss ended the second I stepped into the kitchen.

It turns to dread as I walk to the coffee pot and overfill a mug. Unsure of what to do next, for the first time since joining Cerberus, I take my time cleaning up the mess I made on the counter. When I turn, facing the animated groups of people, all enjoying their breakfast and talking amongst themselves, I debate just walking out and hiding in my room like the pussy I've suddenly become.

Darby doesn't allow it, waving me over when our eyes meet. She's perched in Snatch's lap, looking as beautiful as she did last night. Tight tank top and tiny shorts, she's possibly the most gorgeous woman in the room.

"Morning," I say keeping my eyes on my coffee.

I ignore the stiffening in Snatch's leg as my thigh brushes his. I scoot a few inches away, hating the broken contact, but knowing that he needs it. The tension in the air surrounding the three of us is thick and more stressful than I would've anticipated.

Darby must also notice because she lifts her legs and lays them across mine, joining the three of us once again. Being included by even half of them is a mild relief, soothing the ache in my chest that has been building since I saw the look in Snatch's eyes just before he left my room last night. I close my eyes, hearing the click of the lock between our joined rooms all over again, the deadbolt having never been activated until last night. The action said everything that ever needs to be said about the situation.

"I'm going to miss you boys," Darby says.

"We'll miss you, too," Snatch says with a nip at her earlobe.

We'll.

He actually includes me in his statements. I wonder immediately if it's just a habit he plans on breaking soon.

"You should stay," I offer.

Snatch doesn't look at me, but he also doesn't argue.

"I made a lot of promises," I hear him whisper in her ear. "I'm not near done with you."

"Let me go see what Aviana plans," she shifts her weight, pulling her legs from my lap but doesn't stand immediately. Her eyes find mine as she rolls her hips, grinding down on Snatch's crotch. He groans, leaning back a few inches, giving her free reign.

"Not in here, babe," he grunts before clasping her hips and effectively ceasing her teasing.

"I can't wait until you're both inside me at the same time."

She licks Snatch's mouth before dipping her delicate tongue inside. The second she pulls away from him, she grips the front of my cut and pulls me to her mouth. The motion forces me to put my hand out to prevent me from crashing into both of them. Her lips find mine, and I'm not certain if it's her, or the placement of my hand on my friend's thigh that causes the moan to escape my throat.

"I'll be right back boys," she whispers against my lips but loud enough for us both to hear.

My hand leaves the only place I want it the second she pops up from Snatch's lap. We both watch as she saunters away. Hell, every single man in the room is watching her as she sits down beside her friend.

The unfamiliar tension between us goes up like a black wall of despair almost immediately.

"Hey, man," I begin, needing just to put that shit out there. "About last night."

He gets up from the table, so fast his chair scrapes the dining area tile. My eyes find my coffee once more.

"Fuck," I mutter, lifting my eyes just in time to see Snatch clasp Darby's hand and pull her from the room.

Chapter 8

Snatch

About last night.

Three simple words, spoken with no sexual innuendo. A segue into a conversation about something I prayed he'd never mention while in the same second hoping he'd beg me to let happen again. All night I laid awake in my bed, listening to him fuck Darby over and over. My cock pulsed and throbbed in rhythm to the banging of his headboard.

That throbbing renewed when he placed his hand on my thigh and pounded relentlessly when he turned toward me to discuss what we did last night.

I can't spend a second more sitting here, exposed, in the open, around a group of men who would never be okay with the things we did, no matter how enjoyable it was. It doesn't matter if our dalliances affect no one else, Marines don't fuck other Marines, with the exception of wooks. It's an unspoken rule. That's a lie, the rule is pretty much written in stone, and not much has changed people's way of thinking even after 'Don't Ask, Don't Tell' was repealed in 2011.

Darby is just standing from the table having spoken with Aviana. The grin on her face is all I need to be sure she's staying.

"Where are we going?" she asks as I take her hand and pull her out of the kitchen.

"My room," I grunt. "Seems I missed out on some fun last night."

She sighs loudly as we hit the back hallway. "You made that choice, big guy, not us."

Us. Not me. She's including Itchy as if we're some sort of unspoken team.

I shake my head, even knowing it's not going to keep the images from last night out of my head. Honestly, I don't want them gone. I've stroked my cock to numerous unsatisfying orgasms already thinking about last night.

Her lips are on my neck by the time I get the door closed, and we're secluded in the room. I guide her, first to the locked door leading into Itchy's room and then to the edge of the bed, where I strip her out of her clothes. My nose trails down the delicate curve of her neck as her hands find and release my zipper. The relief of pressure on my cock is immediate, my groan the proof of my need.

I breathe in her scent, hating that she showered. She now smells like Itchy's shower gel, a rich masculine, woodsy scent, but I'd hoped the heady scent of his body on hers after fucking all night was what I would find. Knowing he loves to rip condoms off and ejaculate on stomachs and tits, I was anticipating the taste of his come on her skin.

"Can we talk first?" The timidness in her voice has my hand stopping low on her belly. It's almost as if she's unsure if I will do as she asks.

"Of course," I tell her taking a half-step back. "So long as I can still get naked."

She beams up at me, reaching for my t-shirt.

"Nope," I chastise with another half-step back. "If we're going to talk you're going to have to keep your hands to yourself. I only have so much control here."

She pouts, but drops her hands to her side, watching mine with a fierce lust as I make the most of her eyes on me, undressing slowly and piece by piece. Once naked, I angle my head, indicating for her to climb on my bed. She obliges, and I follow after her.

"What do you want to talk about, gorgeous? The weather? Sleeping arrangements?"

She laughs. "Tell me more about the club."

"Like what?" My hackles rise slightly, and for the first time since meeting her, I question her motives and intentions.

"That pretty redhead," she says dreamily.

"She goes by Snapper. She's been with the club just about as long as it's been in existence. She can be trouble, but she's also a hell of a good time," I explain.

"She's with that biker from last night?"

"She was last night. Tonight she may be with someone else." I watch her eyes, waiting for her to put it all together.

"She's a whore?"

"She's a club girl," I emphasize.

"So she's here to fuck the guys?"

I laugh. Not many people understand or even take the chance to understand what goes on in a clubhouse. Their judgments and assumptions cloud their minds before someone even has a chance to explain how Cerberus operates.

"She's here because she wants to be here. She's very open about her sexuality." I pause, and she waits patiently for me to continue. "She isn't sleeping with anyone because she's obligated. Some of the girls just like to have sex."

"All the girls here?"

I shake my head but continue to talk because confusion is pulling her brow tight. "Rose is married to Doc, you haven't met them yet, but they're the older couple, sort of like the club parents. Khloe and Emmalyn who were sitting at the table with Aviana are spoken for."

I don't bother mentioning the bullshit with Kid and Khloe right now. We'll have to touch on that later.

"Other than those three, the rest are club girls. They stay here because they want to be here. They help out around the clubhouse. They cook, clean, sometimes laundry if you ask really nicely." I wink at her.

"And the guys? They sleep with all of the girls."

I smile at the hopefulness in her voice. "They're pretty liberal and equally opportunistic with their time."

A devious grin turns up the corners of her mouth.

"Kid, the young biker and Kincaid, the club President are off limits." Her frown turns into a pout. "I'm serious, Darby. You will be out on your ass. I advise you don't even look in their direction."

She looks affronted, pulling her head back a couple of inches at my words. "I'm not a rude person, Snatch."

"Darlin', I'm not telling you to be rude. Be nice, cordial, friendly even, but it may be best if you just give those guys a wide berth. Sex appeal and the need to fuck just rolls off of you. I don't want Khloe and Emmalyn misinterpreting that."

She nods. "But Snapper is okay?"

The half-hearted look on my face confuses her even more. "Snapper isn't okay?"

"She's... a damn wildcat. She's pulled some shit around the clubhouse that has made her quite unpopular, and I don't see that changing anytime soon. If you choose to hang out with her, it's fine, but don't expect the warmest welcome from the other girls. They're not mean, but they won't be as confident in your trust if you spend most of your time with Snapper."

"But Snapper is my people?" She's contemplative for a second. "I know I'll be more comfortable around her."

"Just don't let her get you into trouble," I warn. "If it has anything to do with the taken guys, or in your gut, it doesn't seem like a good idea, ask Itchy or me for some guidance."

She nods in understanding. "Let's talk about Itchy."

Her nail abrades my nipple as languid strokes trace the tattoos on my chest.

"I want to watch you guys together. I can't imagine a hotter fantasy."

I shake my head, rejecting the idea outright.

"Please?" she begs as if asking for something as simple as a new purse or a ride to the movies. "Last night was so fucking hot."

I grip her hips when she moves to straddle my legs. Thankfully, she's keeping my erect cock between us rather than trying to mount it. I'm all for loads of fucking, but going unwrapped isn't something anyone will catch me participating in anytime soon.

"I was drunk," I counter.

She leans in, her warm breath on my neck and ear. The gooseflesh that spreads down my arm is a welcome diversion to the thoughts in my head.

"I'll never forget the sounds his mouth made as he worked you." A groan rumbles in my chest.

"Me either," I confess.

"The sounds you made when you came is what set me off. My only regret is that he got it all and I didn't get a taste."

I'd never confess to her that I was jealous she got all Itchy had to offer.

"How often do you guys do threesomes?"

"More often than not," I answer honestly. "We like to play together."

"But nothing like last night?"

I shake my head no.

"You didn't like it?" she presses with her words as her nails scrape my short Mohawk. "It seemed like you liked it. Your orgasm shook the bed."

I know it did. I felt it all the way to my core, from the top of my head to the tips of my toes, and every damn thing in between. My cock jumps between us, eager for a repeat of the sensations.

"I was drunk," I reiterate.

"You're sober now, and your cock seems to think it's a good idea," she urges, never changing the tone of her voice.

I can't deny any of what she's saying, and my free will, my right to choose is the only thing I have left, but Goddamn it if I don't want to give in. I want to chase those feelings I had last night. I need to feel his lips tugging on my erection, the roughness of his beard against my thighs.

I groan and hiss in tandem when she grips me in her fist and cups my sac in her other hand.

I open my mouth to deny her but, "I'll text him," comes out instead.

Chapter 9

Itchy

Snatch: My room NOW

I stare down at the text, dread filling my gut. I knew this moment would come. I knew last night before I ever opened my mouth to take that first lick of his cock that it would come to this. I rise from the table, deciding at the threshold of the kitchen to go ahead and face the situation like a man, even though my eyes do dart to the front door.

Cracking my knuckles, preparing my fists for the brawl I know I'm about to face, I make my way down the short hall to Snatch's room. I don't bother knocking. He summoned me, so he knows I'm the next one coming through his door.

Opening it and stepping inside, my brain scrambles the first few seconds at finding both of them naked, Darby's mouth wrapped around Snatch's proud cock. I'm hard as stone before the door even clicks shut. Anticipating what could happen in this room, I'm mindful of making sure the lock is activated. Getting interrupted by anyone in the clubhouse will bring questions I'm sure none of us will ever be ready to answer.

"You wanted me?" My voice rolls out in a rough, scratchy tone, my eyes never diverting from the skill of Darby's mouth.

She grins up at me, a scheming tilt to her puffy lips. "I want you both."

Snatch doesn't even look at me as he places his hand on the back of her head, guiding her back down on his cock.

"Get naked," she orders before sucking him in again.

I look up at Snatch for confirmation or guidance that he actually wants to get involved again, but he continues to deny me his eyes. I need a clue or something to tell me which direction this is going to go. Is this going to be a normal three-way, like we've done countless times or are we going to take things further like I did last night?

"You heard the lady," he finally grunts out, attention still on the dark head bobbing up and down his shaft.

Unsure hands pull my t-shirt over my head as I kick my boots off. My jeans and boxers are shed last, just as Darby reaches her hand out to me. I take it and climb on the bed, making sure not to touch Snatch.

"I want to watch you suck him," she whispers with her hand still at the base of his cock.

I want to tell her his gorgeous cock doesn't need assistance because it stands up on its own but that's giving away more than I want right now. I don't want to freak him out, and the knowledge that I study his cock more than the girls we've been with has the power to do just that.

I reach for it, needing to replace her hand with mine, her mouth with mine.

"No," Snatch grumbles, and I pull back instantly.

Suddenly, I feel like a voyeur, someone who's not been invited. Heart pounding in my ears at his rejection I begin to slide off the bed.

"Stop," Darby says with a lust-filled voice, refusing to give up.

She's looking at Snatch, but I can tell by the inflection that she's directing the word at both of us.

"You're leaking at the thought," she tells him purposely running her fingers through the slickness at his tip.

Snatch shakes his head but still remains silent.

"I have an idea," she says and reaches for the stack of folded bandannas on his bedside table.

"Close your eyes," she purrs as she begins folding the navy fabric into a blindfold. "Just enjoy the sensations. It doesn't matter who's doing what so long as it feels good."

"Darby," he chastises but closes his eyes as she lifts the fabric.

His mouth finds her taut nipple when she reaches up to tie it behind his head.

"Do I need to tie your hands too?"

He shakes his head. Blinded by the fabric around his head, he finally looks in my direction.

"Don't stick... you know," he clears his throat. "Don't do that to me."

I can't help but laugh. Fucking Snatch in the ass hadn't even crossed my mind. Well, not today anyways.

"I won't," I vow.

"Where are you going?" Snatch asks as Darby crawls off of the bed.

She grins up at me, standing by my side. Her hand finds my cock, and I want to ask her what her plans are. Snatch and I have perfected the choreography of fucking women with simple hand gestures, code words, and familiar looks. With Darby, I'm in total darkness on how to do this.

"Mr. Impatient," she chides. "Hold your horses. We have to pregame."

Her idea of pregaming is dropping her knees to the carpet and taking me in her mouth.

"Fuck," I groan as I strike at the back of her throat. "Jesus, your mouth."

Snatch groans, and I see his head look down, directly at the back of Darby's.

"Can you see?" I ask, and his head snaps up in the direction of my voice.

"No," he answers. "But the slurping is so fucking loud there's no way not to know where it's coming from."

I don't know how well this is going to work. He's a Marine, trained to catch on to sounds, shifts in air pressure, even the slightest movement can be tracked. I realize then, the blindfold is only to make him more comfortable, a way to block out a little bit of the world to give him the courage to do something he's dying to let happen but can't do so with his eyes wide open.

I regret the absence of Darby's mouth the second she pulls off of me.

Snatch chuckles on the bed. "Sucks when she stops right?"

She stands, taking my hand and pulling me beside my best friend. Our joined hands find Snatch's thick cock, circling it together. Her other hand finds the back of my head, and she guides my mouth to the tip. Unlike last night, when urgency was the only thing driving my courage, I take a slow swipe at the tip.

"Mmm," Darby moans as if she's tasting him herself.

Her hands cup his nuts while I work him with my mouth. His hands clench the sheets at his hips, either from the overwhelming sensation or as a way to keep from reaching out. He loves to guide a woman down his cock, angling her head exactly how he wants it. He's never been afraid to take his pleasure, but he's hesitant today. He has to know I'm the one wrapped around him. Every mouth is different, and after having Darby sucking him only moments earlier, he has to be able to distinguish the change.

"My turn," Darby whispers in my ear, tilting her head indicating his top half.

I shake my head violently. Nothing will end this little party quicker than taking this farther than something he's already done. The blowjob is as far as I should take things, no matter how bad I want my mouth on every inch of his body.

Her eyes narrow, and she mouths 'go' before wrapping her lips around his cock.

Against better judgment, I make my way up his body, nipping licking, sucking, tracing every dark line of his tattoo. I'm rougher than I would be with a woman, my teeth leaving behind indentions in his painted skin. There's nothing I can do about the scratch of my beard as it drags behind my mouth, but he hasn't once flinched away. If anything he's arching his back, lifting it to my mouth.

He hisses, pained and full of need when my teeth toy with the barbell in his nipple. I bite down, part in desperation for him to know it's me, but also to cause him some amount of pain. It's retaliatory for the way he looked at me last night, the way he ran out without so much as a word. If he's going to freak out and regret today as well, he'll have to look at my marks on his skin in the mirror.

He doesn't push me away; rather his trembling hand grips my muscled back. His first contact with my skin seers me to the bone. His whispered, "please" near my ear sets me on fire.

Testing his limits, I release his injured nipple and trail my tongue over the diamonds on his chest to the stars canvassing his neck. His strong hand releases my back going back to fist the sheets. It's a small step back but not full blown rejection. I smile against his skin, moving over his neck closer to the pierced lips I've wanted on mine for months now. A breath away he turns his head, denying me the one thing I want most. I feel Darby lick up my back. I turn my head as she makes her way over my shoulder, capturing her mouth in mine. She eases his rejection slightly, and I try to remind myself that we have to take this one step at a time and I can't get pissed at him for not just jumping my bones.

Yesterday morning he woke up straight as an arrow, today he's exploring the fluidity of his sexuality. It's more than I could've ever asked for.

I watch, dejected, when she moves her mouth from mine and straight to Snatch's. He kisses her without reservation, licking into her mouth feverishly before they both pull away panting.

I move to run my hand down her back, but her hand finds mine instead, in it is a small bottle of lube. When she pulled it from the bedside table, where I know it always is, I have no clue, but I'm grateful for it.

Snatch tenses when the sound of the lid popping open echoes around the otherwise silent room.

"It's for me," she soothes him. "He's going to get me ready."

I lean in close to his ear but maintain my eye contact with Darby. "Then you're going to fuck her ass and pretend it's mine."

She smiles, and I realize I got her intent correct.

"Fuck," Snatch groans shifting his restless hips under Darby's body.

Goddamn, I wish there was some way to trick him into taking me that way.

With lubed fingers, I tease the tight pucker of her ass, biting my lip when she whimpers with need and pushes herself back against my hand.

"Touch me," she begs Snatch, and he responds immediately.

This is nothing new for us. His hand waits patiently for me to pour lube on it, and together we enter her. Our mouths both find her neck.

"No," she objects. "This isn't about me."

She shifts so her mouth can reach Snatch's neck and I do the same. His finger, sliding in and out of her tight ass beside mine, moves faster at our contact.

"You'll have to turn around," I urge Darby. "There's no way I can keep my cock out of you for much longer."

While Darby scrambles to put her back against Snatch's chest, I take one more opportunity to wrap my lips around his cock. This time, enraptured in the moment, his hand fists my hair as his hips jolt, shoving further into my mouth. With punishing strokes, he doesn't afford me the same relief he would if a woman was gagging around him. Almost vindictive, like he's penalizing me for liking his cock in my mouth, he thrusts into my mouth, only pulling me off when Darby begs to be filled.

Lots of firsts going on today, I think as I grab a condom and roll it down the length of my best friend's cock.

"You want his ass?" she teases as I line his cock against the tight ring of muscle. She slowly slides down him, fluid and in one long glide. "Take him."

"Oh God," he hisses, the sound of his pained pleasure making my nuts tighten.

I grab another rubber and sheath my cock, grunting when I slide into her tightness.

"Shit," she nearly screams.

We both settle, allowing her to adjust to both of us. A light sheen of sweat blooms on my skin as my cock urges me to move.

"Fuck him," she pants at Snatch, who obliges and begins to move his hips.

This has to be the weirdest, yet most erotic three-way of my life.

"Damn it," Snatch mutters. "I won't last."

"Is he tight?" she pants.

"So fucking tight," he answers with a sharp jab that presses his nuts against my own. God, I'm going to come soon.

"Fuck me," I beg, unsure if I'm speaking to him or her. They both groan. "Fuck me hard!"

My fingers find her clit, bright red, filled with blood, and I stroke it until she's got every bit of her weight against Snatch. Her head rolls on his shoulder, so I lean in closer, knowing he can feel my panting breaths over her shoulder. With more courage than I have a right to feel, I reach up and pull the blindfold from his eyes.

He blinks several times to allow his eyes to adjust, but then his gaze locks on mine.

"Fuck me," I whisper again, staring into his bright blue irises.

A slow haze, one of euphoria glazes his eyes. My best friend comes, with one hand on my thigh and the other on Darby's. I follow him only one pulse of his cock later.

Chapter 10

Snatch

"The fuck is your problem?" The man to my right knocks my boot off the bottom rung of my barstool.

I glare at Ace, running scenarios of how I can kick his meddling ass through my head.

"But seriously though," Snake says, smart enough to keep his face back out of reach. "Something has been off since that Darby chick showed up."

I ignore both of them as best I can, but they're relentless.

"She's a sweet fucking piece of ass," Ace adds. "We got ahold of her the other night, and I'm almost willing to fight you for her."

My head snaps up. "You and Itchy fucked her?"

My pulse pounds in my ears at the thought.

He shakes his head. "Me and Skid. Don't be pissed."

"I'm not mad," I answer honestly. Why doesn't the idea of Darby fucking everyone in the club not bother me, but the sheer hint that she and Itchy are hooking up in three-ways that don't include me is enough to make me spit fire?

Snake chuckles when Ace gets an almost orgasmic, far away look in his eyes.

"Here we go again," he mutters.

"What?" Ace asks snapping out of it.

"The fuck is going on?" I feel like the outsider of some fucked up joke.

Snake crosses his arms over his chest and stares at his best friend. The playful way they joke with each other is reminiscent of the way Itchy and I were before Darby came along. I bet Snake has never let his best friend suck his dick though.

I tilt my beer back, draining the last half of it down my throat.

"Ok," Ace says leaning in conspiratorially. "She does this thing where she sticks her finger in your ass while she's sucking your cock."

Snake full on laughs when my eyes go wide at his confession. Ace shudders at his own memory.

"I came so fucking hard I nearly broke the fucking bed. Like, no shit, my jizz came out of her damn nose." He sits back, proud as can be taking a long pull on his own beer.

"You like that sort of thing?" There's no judgment in my tone, just curiosity.

"Fuck yeah," he says after a long swallow.

"You've done this?" I ask looking over at Snake.

He shakes his head with a wide grin. "No, but the more he talks about it, the more I want to experience it. It just weirds me out a little."

I nod in understanding.

Ace slaps him across the chest with the back of his hand. "I'm telling you, man. If that makes me gay or some shit." Fuck here we go. "Stick a saddle on my back, pony boy, and ride me into the sunset. It was *that* fucking good."

Not at all what I was expecting.

I know they're talking about Darby and all of her amazing skills, and she's very talented, but when I close my eyes for the briefest of seconds, it's the bearded fucker I can't get out of my head that flashed through my mind.

After the last time, with the blindfold on my eyes, I had to take a step back from both of them. I haven't talked to him or given into any of her suggestive invitations. Yeah, I was a little freaked out by the whole thing, but what concerned me more is how much I liked it and how much I wanted to do it again. I was floored by the need I felt in my gut to return the favor, knowing full well he'd be okay with letting me do to him what he did to me and what I was doing to Darby.

Fuck me.

I squeeze my eyes closed, the thought of fucking my best friend making my cock strain against my tight jeans.

His begging has echoed in my ears for weeks. The door joining our rooms has remained unlocked, taunting me with the access I wish some days wasn't even an option.

"You're gonna take it for a spin, aren't you?" Ace asks from the other side of the table.

I grin over at him. "I just might."

"Think Gypsy or Snapper could pull off something like that?" Snake asks. Snapper is his favorite go-to girl because she's down for just about anything. It honestly surprises me that she hasn't pulled something like this. A finger in the ass may be something none of the guys had thought of before Darby bestowed that little gem on Ace, though.

"You may want to have the professional give it a go first," Ace says, his tone marked with seriousness. "I don't think I'd leave something like that up to Snapper."

We all laugh, knowing Snapper could get over-zealous and hurt one of them.

"Where's Itchy tonight?" Snake asks as he flags down the waitress for another round.

I shrug. "Couldn't tell you."

"Is that what your shitty mood is about?" Ace asks without pulling his eyes off of the nearly exposed ass of the waitress.

"Hey," Snake says after an endless minute. "Don't let some chick come between you and your brother. No woman is worth that, even if she has the mouth like a vacuum and a golden pussy."

"It's not," I begin but shake my head, the temptation to explain the real reason I'm in a shit mood fading as quickly as it showed up. "I'm ready for a job. I need to get out of this damn town."

They both nod in understanding, holding their beers up in a mock salute.

Maybe leaving town, getting some distance from the door that taunts me nightly, combined with being able to kill some seriously demented men would set my mind right.

I'm lost in my own thoughts when I feel Snake nudge my arm. I look at him to find his eyes focused across the bar. Looking over my shoulder, I see the woman that's caught his eyes.

"Fuck, she's perfect," he all but pants.

I chuckle and turn my attention back to the guys at the table.

"Every girl you see is perfect," I mutter, making eye contact with the waitress and holding my empty bottle up. She winks at me, and I know I'll have a refill shortly.

"She looks disappointed," Ace observes.

"All your damned fault," Snake spits in my direction.

I shrug. I get that type of attention all the time. Most nights I'd be all over her, proving to her that my tattoos and piercing do in fact mean I'm a nasty mother fucker and will give them a night they'll never forget, but my heart's just not in it right now.

"We could have a four-way," Ace offers as if the thought of fucking in a group would entice me more than a one-on-one session with some chick. I know her type. The kind that wants to take a walk on the wild side but knowing she's safe since I'm wearing my cut and the club has a reputation for being decent guys.

"You can have a threesome," I counter.

They both groan.

Snake sits back in his chair and takes a long pull on his beer, but Ace doesn't know when to give up.

"She won't fuck us if you're not part of the package." I look up at him, his attempt at a guilt trip having no effect on me.

"You really want to fuck a chick who's only willing to fuck you because I'm there?"

He shrugs. "Pussy is pussy man."

"There are girls at the clubhouse for that," I say and thank the waitress when she drops off my fresh beer and grabs the empties from the table.

"New pussy is new pussy," he corrects with a grin.

I look back over my shoulder, having no fucking clue why I'm even considering fucking some chick just so these assholes can get a fresh piece of ass.

She bites her bottom lip, going for seductive, but falling short in my book.

"No thanks," I tell them. "Besides, she's fucking tiny and couldn't begin to handle the three of us. That requires someone sturdier than that hundred and fifteen-pound little pixie."

Ace narrows his eyes at me. "I think she can decide for herself what she can handle."

"Really?" I take a sip from my ice cold beer and watch his head bob up and down in response. "You ever had a foursome with a woman that small?"

It's Snake's turn to laugh. "He's never had a four-way. He got lucky with Darby and Skid."

The table jolts and Snake glares at his best friend.

"Kick me again fucker, and the only thing you'll be fucking is some chick in your dreams because I will break your arms and legs," Snake snaps at him.

Ace's eyes light up, a strange reaction to the threat of losing his limbs, but I smell the pungent scent of too much perfume a second before I feel heat at my back. I'm always cognizant of my surroundings, but the men at the table with me keep an eye out behind me just as I do for them. Besides, this is Jake's, and no one here is smart enough to fuck with us here.

"Hey boys." The seductive purr hits my ear a half second before the whiskey saturated breath warms my cheeks.

A chill runs down my spine, and not one of the good kind. The eagerness to fuck I found so intoxicating with Darby isn't anywhere to be found tonight. I twist in my chair to see two women who had to have split an entire can of hairspray to get their hair as high as it is standing beside me.

"Hey," Ace growls, hunger clear as day in his tone.

The taller thinner blonde lays her hand on my thigh, dark red fingernails digging into my jeans.

"Don't," I warn, giving her the opportunity to move it on her own. When she doesn't, probably because of the copious amount of alcohol she's consumed which is evident in the redness of her eyes and inability to stand there without swaying, I clasp it as gently as I can manage and place it on the table in front of us.

She pouts, an attempt to look sexy. I resist the urge to tell her it might work any other night, but the smear of her lipstick on her teeth really isn't doing it for me.

"Pissy," she whispers. "Nothing a blowjob won't fix."

Her friend is already cozied up next to Ace, standing between his open thighs and running her hand and over his cut, tracing his patches with an overly long fingernail. If he's not careful, he'll lose an eye to one of those damned things by tomorrow.

"How about you?" my admirer says to Snake, thankfully giving up any idea she might have had about us hooking up.

"I love blowjobs," he says with a smile around the mouth of his beer bottle.

I stand, drop some cash on the table, and rap my knuckles on the top. "See you guys back at the clubhouse."

I hear one of the girls giggle and mention always wanting to go to a real MC clubhouse. Snake cuts her off, explaining that not just anyone can go inside, but promises to fuck her with his cut on. I walk away from the train wreck, thankful the three beers I drank tonight is way below my limit to safely drive away from this shit show without having to call someone to come pick me up.

Chapter 11

Itchy

"What a fucking nightmare," Shadow says leaning back on the bar stool, back against the wall.

We're in a shitty bar, in a shitty hotel, in a shitty town in Costa Rica, needing a little time to wind down after a brutal week.

"It went better than we expected," Kincaid says, keeping his eyes on the locals who don't seem very happy we're here.

"A dead girl and an American who won't even talk because she's afraid we just signed her entire family's death certificates?" Snatch asks from beside me. I'm honestly surprised he willingly chose to sit next to me. I'm grateful, don't get me wrong but the heat from his legs is burning a fire through mine that's almost enough to make me combust. His eyes have followed me all week, but each night we fall into bed exhausted from eighteen hour days, so he hasn't made a move. Not that I expect him to.

"We pulled four girls from that building," Kincaid says to Snatch. "Including the one we came to get. That's a win in my book."

"She'll never be the same," I lament. She was brutalized beyond what most people could even imagine without copious amounts of searching in some seedy ass corners of the internet.

"They never are," Kincaid agrees, taking his eyes from the crowd to meet those of my best friend. "They never are."

I turn my attention back to my beer as Kincaid and Shadow talk for a few minutes. I'm peeling the label, arms on the table in front of us when I see Shadow stand and make his way across the bar to a tiny, albeit smoking hot woman.

I shake my head, watching her look up at him like he's her savior. Every one of us is well aware that the chick Misty from Denver has him all twisted up. They didn't have a relationship or anything, but she won't text him back or answer when he calls. I'm certain it's the rejection and not actually her that's got him so fucked up. Prez may be all wrapped up in Em, trying to get pregnant, and Kid is head over fucking heels for Khloe, but Shadow will never settle down. It's not in his DNA.

Snatch's leg hits mine, a sign that something, or rather someone has caught his eye. Rather than look at him, I look up and find not one, not two, but three beautiful South American women looking in our direction.

I'm ecstatic, more because he's actually interested in fucking even if it involves women. It's been over a month since the night of the blindfold and him pretending to fuck my ass while he was pounding into Darby. Just the thought makes my cock start to thicken.

"Three?" I ask not taking my eyes from the women across the bar, each one beautiful on their own, but a sweet fucking enticement together.

"You up for it?" he challenges.

I side eye him but keep track of the big fucker in the corner who is none too pleased with the attention we're getting from the women in the bar.

"You know how I feel about being outnumbered," I mutter.

His hearty laugh washes over me and I know I'd agree to whatever the fuck he wants right now.

"Afraid you'll get rolled by those Latin beauties?"

I scoff. "Hardly, but that's more holes than dicks, and you know how I feel about eating foreign pussy."

He nods. The rule is, don't put your mouth on anything you can't personally account for, especially when you're on international soil, in a country that has second-rate medical care.

"I don't think you'll have to worry about it," he says.

I pull my eyes from the sneering asshole in the corner back to the three women who are working very hard to get our attention. I raise an eyebrow as one woman runs her hand up the thigh of the one in the middle. It disappears under her dress, and my skin heats as I imagine the sound of her gasp as it leaves her mouth even though we're too far away to actually hear it.

"I think she'll be easy enough to convince to eat pussy all night long." The sound of his beer bottle hitting the table in front of us with an echoing thud pulls my mind from the dirty things I plan to do with them, the dirty things I picture doing to Snatch. "Let's go."

I stand when he does, barely stopping the urge to reach down, grab his hand, and insist it should just be us tonight. A tilt of his head toward the door is all it takes for the women to start sauntering our way. Five minutes later we're upstairs in the hotel room, with the promise of so many orgasms we're sure to be sore as fuck tomorrow.

***

My internal alarm clock wakes me just as the sun is peeking over the horizon. I look around the room as the first hints of daylight filter through the thin ass curtains. Snatch's bed is empty, the girls having been shuffled out before we closed our eyes less than five hours ago. The water running and an occasional grunt from the bathroom tells me exactly where he's at.

I groan, turning over, feeling the tightness of my muscles in my legs. It's as if I did squats for hours, and added an extreme ab workout, but good fucking should always leave you a little spent the next day.

I close my eyes, picture the way he touched me last night. It wasn't overtly obvious, but the graze of his hand against my arm when he was showing one of the girls how I liked my cock sucked, and the way he gripped my thigh as he came while we were both going at one of the women didn't go unnoticed either.

My spent cock has the gumption to twitch at the memory, but it's the familiar grunt from the bathroom that has it flagging at damn near attention. I know what he's doing before I get off the bed and confirm it with my eyes.

I stand in the doorway, watching my frustrated friend as he leans over, one forearm against the shower wall as he jerks his cock with a tight grip.

"Damn it," he mutters.

I watch, unabashedly for several long minutes. Water cascades down his muscular back, his tattoos rippling with each frustrated jerk.

"Leave me alone," he hisses, never opening his eyes, but sensing my presence.

I don't move a muscle, other than the ones in my face pulling my lips up in a grin. "You came three times last night, and yet here you are stroking another one out in the shower? It's going to fucking fall off if you don't let it rest."

His hand slows, but his need is too much to remove his hand completely. Silently, I close the distance between us. The hotel is so shitty, there isn't even a shower curtain in here, but going along with the shitty accommodations is the rough concrete floor, so slipping while it's wet isn't a concern.

"It wasn't enough," he complains.

"That's not true, and you know it," I say startling him now that I'm so close I could reach out and touch him.

"Those women," he begins, but I interrupt.

"Were amazing, and you damn well know it."

"Yet, I wake up with a raging hard on," he spits, his exasperation growing by the second.

"It wasn't what you needed," I explain as I step into the shower with him.

I keep my distance, but he knows I'm in here with him.

"I came three times," he says repeating my words from a minute ago.

His eyes fly open when my hand wraps around his, but he doesn't deck me. His mouth opens on a pleasure-filled gasp as his eyes race back and forth between mine.

"It wasn't what you needed." I sink to my knees, hating Central America and their harsh fucking concrete, but loving being alone with him in this shower over three thousand miles from home.

His fist strikes the wall with a thud, and he mumbles obscenities when my lips wrap around the angry red crown of his cock. I look up, expecting to find his eyes clenched tight, taking what I'm offering but refusing to visually acknowledge that it's coming from a man. Rather, I find his bright blue eyes, wide awake, half-lidden and watching every stroke of my tongue down his shaft. My own dick hardens painfully at his attention. My grunt of approval can be felt in the tremble of his thighs against my hands.

"Fuck, that's good," he praises, hips moving his cock deeper.

Doubling my efforts at the sound of his panting breaths, I no longer feel the bite of the rough texture ripping into my knees. It's overpowered by the silky slide of his cock against my tongue and the coarse hair under my hands at his thighs.

"Stroke yourself," he commands, my fist obeying before the words fully leave his mouth.

My eyes find his once more after long minutes of giving the most enthusiastic blowjob of my life with no completion on his part. It isn't saying much, considering I can count them all on one hand. I'm sure he overexerted himself last night.

I nearly come when his hand finds the back of my head, but whimper at the loss as fear sinks heavy in my gut when he pulls himself from my mouth.

"This isn't what I need either," he says with such conviction, I scramble to my feet, fully prepared to take his fist to my jaw since he's clearly seen the light.

He reaches for one of the bottles in the shower squirting some of the product into his palm. I turn to leave, swallowing the rage I feel at his blatant rejection. He's going to finish his fucking shower and pretend I didn't just have his dick down my throat.

"The fuck are you going?" he growls just as his rough hand finds my arms.

Before I can answer, I'm spun to face the wall, and I feel his fingers run down my back, stopping a mere inch from my asshole.

"Tell me to stop," he hisses in my ear. "Tell me that fucking your ass in the shower is taking it too far. Tell me you don't want it."

My eyes flutter closed when his fingers tease me, lubricated by the conditioner he poured into his hand.

"I—I," I grunt when he pushes past the first tight ring, only to withdraw and enter again with two thick fingers. "I can't."

"You can't what?" he taunts.

His fingers never stop. He's working them, scissoring them, preparing me to take his cock, and I'm in bliss with the thought of giving myself to him that way.

"I can't tell you to stop," I finally manage to answer. "I want you to fuck me."

"Jesus." He takes a step closer, chest against my back, rock hard cock sandwiched between us. "You sure?"

I nod, face scraping against the roughly tiled wall. His free hand is inches from my face, palm flat against the wall and I want to beg him to fist my cock the same way he was working his earlier, but I can't find the courage, afraid if I ask too much from him it will all stop. I have to be content with the contact at my spine, especially since it's the most skin on skin we've ever shared.

As if he can read my thoughts and they're too complicated for him, he takes a step back, and the loss of his warmth makes my heart pound as if it's trying to escape my chest.

"Please," I beg, unsure at this point if I'm asking for him to fill me or just leave me alone to mourn his loss.

His fingers never stop probing, but his hand near my face is gone, and a second later I feel the tip of his cock replace his fingers, toying exactly where I need him.

My eyes widen when he pushes a fraction of an inch deeper.

Fuck this was a bad idea.

Every muscle in my body tenses at his intrusion, rejecting the invasion of his length.

"Relax." The word hits my ear on a groan of his own.

"Snatch," I hiss, the burn from the stretch ten times greater than his fingers, the tremble in my legs almost too much to keep me standing.

"*This* is what I need." He pulls back before sliding back in. "*This* is what those women couldn't give me."

I almost argue with him knowing he fucked two of the three in the ass last night. I'd groaned last night seeing him fight his way inside of them. When he closed his eyes, I had imagined he was doing it so it would be easier to pretend they were me.

"Nothing compares," he adds.

My balls tighten painfully when his hand travels from my chest, over my abdomen to fist my cock.

"Fuck," I spit, the pleasure from his grip alleviating some of the burn from his invasion.

It isn't until I feel the scratch of his thigh hair against the back of my own legs that I realize he's fully seated inside of me. His moans build an energy so low and intense in my gut. I know the release I'm going to find is going to be vicious, ripping from me with a fury I've never experienced before.

His hips move back as his hand strokes down my length until it's against my belly. When he pushes back inside, his hand works up to my tip. He's a machine, cock and hand operating in perfect synchronicity.

I don't know how long we've been like this, seconds feel like a millennia, yet all the time in the world with him like this would not even come close to being enough.

"Damn," he says awe filling his voice when my body clamps down on him as the tingle traveling down my spine draws my nuts up.

His fist works faster, coaxing my release with the expert precision only a man who works his own cock on a regular basis can.

"I'm gonna..." I never finish my sentence as my cock begins pulsing my release on the wall of the shower.

"Shit." His hips move faster, driving deeper for several strokes before his own release hits. The jolts and kicks of his own cock blends with mine.

We're both panting, breaths coming harsh and too fast, mine against the wall since I'm still pinned, his against my back since his forehead is resting there.

"Fuck," he says, taking a step back and slowly pulling out. "I came inside of you."

I can't help but laugh. I was certain he was going to freak out that he just fucked a guy in a shower in a shitty hotel in Costa Rica while he was completely sober. His concern for the mess is something I can handle.

"Don't worry," I say turning around and catching water in my cupped hands so I can rinse the shower wall. I wink at him. "I'm on the pill."

"Asshole," he says, punching me on the shoulder before walking out of the bathroom soaking wet.

I catch his smile in the mirror on the wall as he crosses the threshold. I can only hope that his jovial mood sticks around this time. I'd rather none of this shit happened in the first place if it meant avoiding his silent treatment for weeks.

Chapter 12

Snatch

"I'm coming," Darby gasps as if we can't tell by the rippling squeeze of her body on both our cocks.

"That's right," Itchy hisses, voice nearly gone from our wild night as he pushes into her from below.

With trembling legs and a racing heart, I pound into her with relentless thrusts, enjoying her moans as much as the slide of my best friend's cock against my own when he drills into her pussy, and I take her ass.

Looking for a better grip on her hips for the finale, my wandering hand brushes against the calloused fingertips of Itchy's hand. Rather than move a few inches higher or lower like would've been protocol a few months ago, I twine my fingers in his, the simple point of contact saying things my mouth hasn't found the courage to utter.

Looking over Darby's shoulder, my drowsy morning eyes find his just as his other hand clamps down on my thigh.

"Come for me," he commands.

Mouth opening on a harsh pant, my head nods ever so slightly, acknowledging his order. His words, combined with the rough grasp of his hand on my leg send me careening over the edge.

"Fuck," I murmur as I pulse inside of Darby, feeling like an asshole because, for the first time since we've shared her, I wish she wasn't in between us.

His teeth dig into his bottom lip as his orgasm takes root, and I feel his cock jerk against mine.

"That's a perfect way to wake up," Darby says with a chuckle and deep roll of her hips.

The way his eyes dart from me to her, makes me wonder if he'd forgotten she was there as well.

"It's gonna be a great day," Itchy says with a sharp slap to her ass cheek as she shifts forward and we fall free of her.

"Always," she whispers against his lips before climbing off the bed and heading to the bathroom.

What seems like an eternity later I realize that not only am I still straddling his legs, but our hands are clasped together, and our latex covered, softening cocks are resting against each other.

My eyes follow his to our dicks, the attention enough to make me twitch in anticipation even after an orgasm that should've left me drained.

"Let me help you with that," he says, his fingers pulling free from mine and reaching for my cock that begins to thicken, meeting his hand half way.

Humming from the bathroom as Darby turns on the shower barely registers in my ears as Itchy pulls the condom from my cock. My hips jolt as his thumb sweeps the sensitive underside.

Tossing the used rubber on the floor, he finds my cock once again.

"Messy." Without releasing me, he shifts from between my legs, turning, so his mouth is so close, I can feel the warmth of his breath on my come covered cock. "Let me clean you up."

The initial sweep of his tongue is a live wire of sensation. I can fuck all night, and it never feels as good as his mouth on me. We've been back from Costa Rica for just over a week, but our mutual shower plays on a constant loop in my mind. I pray I never forget the way his cock pulsed in my hand as he came with me buried in his ass.

"Beautiful fucking cock," he mutters before taking me to the back of his throat.

With no shame or embarrassment, his eyes watch mine as I struggle to breathe in regular rhythm. Pulling back, his tongue flicks against the head.

"Dude," I say with incredulity. "Don't call my cock beautiful."

"It is," he counters.

"It's manly," I correct. I mean, how can cock be anything but masculine?

"That too," he concedes. His tongue traces the throbbing vein from the head until I lose sight of his eyes. "This part is my favorite."

"Do I need to leave the shower going?" Darby asks from the other side of the half-open door.

On instinct, I rip from his mouth wondering if the nip from his teeth as I pull out is intentional.

"Yeah, doll," I say, ignoring the disappointment in my lover's eyes as I climb off the bed and will my cock to deflate.

I stand, back to him at the edge of the bed, giving myself the minute I need to calm my racing heart. He doesn't touch me, but he's close enough that his whispered words are all I can hear.

"You can touch me; fuck me even in front of her."

How do I explain to him that sharing him with her is the last thing I want?

"We can tell her what happened in Costa Rica; she'll love it." I sigh and take a couple more steps closer to the shower. "We don't have to hide anything from her."

I turn then to look at him, search his eyes for the answers I can't seem to find on my own. Hell, at this point I don't even know what the questions are anymore.

"Can I trust you to keep your mouth shut? With her and everyone else?"

His eyes narrow at my tone, anger tugging the corners of his mouth into a sneer. "Sure thing, brother. It's our dirty little secret."

"All yours," Darby says walking out of the bathroom with a cloud of steam following behind her.

Without another word, I head into the bathroom, closing and locking the door behind me. The last thing I want is Darby following me for more attention than we gave her all night and then again this morning. As a self-proclaimed nympho, she's rarely satisfied unless she's got dicks buried in her. 'The more, the merrier.' Her words, not mine.

By the time I step out of the shower and walk back into the room, I find Itchy gone and Darby in my bed as if she owns the place. She doesn't have a room to herself, but she seems to enjoy bouncing around the clubhouse. No room of her own means she never sleeps alone, and I know she loves the shit out of that.

"He thinks you're ashamed," she says unprompted as I tug a pair of jeans out of the dresser.

"He tell you that?" I know he didn't say a word to her. He'd never betray the trust I've placed in him, just as I would never do it to him, especially over a woman.

"He didn't have to," she answers. "I can see it in his eyes."

I scoff at her diagnosis of the situation. "I didn't realize you got a degree in psychology while I was in the shower."

"Don't be an asshole to me," she hisses.

Sighing, I drop my ass to the edge of the bed to tug on my socks and boots.

"Listen," I begin. "I'm sorry. This just isn't something I want everyone knowing."

She chuckles at that. "You wouldn't believe what some of the guys in this clubhouse are interested in. Believe me when I say you liking your dick sucked by Itchy is far from devious."

My mind flashes to the story Ace told about blowjobs and fingers in assholes. If she knew what I did to my best friend in Costa Rica, she'd change her fucking tune really fast.

"You can't tell anyone, Darby." I look up at her, eyes pleading.

"I won't," she promises. "It's just not something to be ashamed of."

Shame? Is that what I feel? The reason I don't want my MC brothers knowing I suddenly have an urge for gay sex?

"Your secret is safe with me," she vows again before walking toward the door.

I know she can't be trusted with something as epic as this. She was seconds away from spilling the beans on what the other guys like. She has no loyalty to Itchy and me, no real faithfulness to the club or anyone in it.

I have no reason to explain to her Marine mentality or shit as simple as Don't Ask, Don't Tell, but I find myself wanting if only to cement my need to keep this under wraps.

"Darby," I call out just as her hand reaches for the door joining mine and Itchy's room.

She turns toward me with a lost look in her eyes. "I know I haven't been here long, but I've spent a lot of time with the other guys in the club. Well, not all of them because I know Kincaid and Kid are off limits and Shadow won't even look my direction, but homophobia isn't a trait I've noticed in a single one of them. They're not going to care that you're gay."

I shake my head, automatically rejecting her words. "I'm not gay."

She nods, an appeasement only since the look in her eyes tell a different reality.

"You don't know them like I do." I'm referring to Marines in general, not just my brothers in the club.

"True," she says softly. "But I know homophobic assholes. I was a hooker for the mob, remember? The men here are incredible, Snatch. They'd never turn their backs on you because of your sexual preferences."

I run a frustrated hand over my hair, exasperated that she's just not understanding. "The last thing I need is them treating me different, wondering every time we hit the showers on a mission that I'm checking them out or thirsting after their dicks."

"Would you?" she asks.

"What?" I look up at her.

"Would you want to fuck them?"

My neck snaps back at her question. "Fuck no. I'm not attracted to men."

She raises an eyebrow at me. "So just Itchy then."

Not a question, obvious fact assessed from our interactions together.

"I can't explain it," I begin, but pull my words back before admitting anything else to her. "I just... I like his mouth on my cock."

"Right," she says. "And holding his hand when you fuck me, the scratch of his beard on your thighs. Maintaining eye contact with him when you come."

It appears we haven't been as secretive as I'd hoped. The incredible passion I feel with him is to blame for my inability to separate fucking her from wanting to fuck him.

"No shame," she whispers before the door clicks softly behind her.

Chapter 13

Itchy

I hitch my head at Kincaid, acknowledging him on my way out to my bike. I shouldn't be pissed that Snatch has once again shut down any idea of letting even Darby in on what we're doing, but that doesn't keep the emotion from sitting heavy in my gut.

"You busy?" Kincaid asks as I walk past.

"Not really," I reply, hoping for a distraction from my thoughts.

"Hoping you could head into town for a beer run. Couple of the guys want to play some poker later. Fridge is all but empty, and the bar has about run dry," he says adjusting the ball cap on his head.

I shrug. "No problem."

"Thanks, man," he says with a slap on my back before disappearing down the corridor to his and Em's room.

Grabbing a set of keys from the hook near the door, I step outside into the dry New Mexico heat. The weather here is so much nicer than that coastal humid shit we had for over a week in Costa Rica.

"Hey," Snapper says looking up as I walk out on the small porch.

Smiling around a deep drag of her cigarette pulls a similar grin from my mouth. I've been so focused on Snatch, I realize I haven't spent time with her lately. She's devious as hell, but at the same time she's funny and a wildcat in the sack.

"Hey, Red," I greet taking a seat beside her on the concrete steps.

"Heading out?" She stubs the tip of her smoke out in the small ashtray at her hip.

"Beer run. Guys are playing poker later," I answer. "Wanna go?"

She huffs a humorless laugh. "Sure you don't want to take Darby?"

My skin prickles at her jealous jab, but I choose to ignore it. "Even if she was going, sweetheart, you could still come along."

Silence settles between us as she looks out over the parking lot filled with bikes and a handful of SUVs, cages not many of us ever enjoy being trapped in.

"Are you feeling neglected?" I bump my shoulder with hers, thankful my playfulness pulls a small grin from her lips.

"A little," she admits.

"I thought you and Darby were friends."

"We are." More silence. "I just haven't spent much time with you and Snatch lately."

"You're welcome anytime," I lie. Snatch isn't interested in Snapper other than the fact that she's down for double penetration more often than some of the other girls.

"I guess I'm just worried you guys are going to go gaga over her pussy and stop fucking everyone else."

I don't correct her. I would never tell Snapper anything about my preference is leaning more to my best friend these days than any particular woman in the clubhouse, including Darby.

"Kincaid barely tolerates my presence since Emmalyn showed up." I blink at her, trying to think of a way to handle this situation.

"Come on, Red. Kincaid wasn't interested in club pussy long before Em came along. He's happy, you should be happy for him. He's your President."

I don't miss the quick shake of her head as if she's rejecting his leadership.

"Bunny sucked his cock once," she counters. "Kid hates me. It's like fucking him when he wanted it is all my fault."

Funny how her memories are different from everyone else's.

"Snapper, you knew he had amnesia. How he felt about Khloe was clear long before he left for Vegas."

She turns her head, looking me in the eye, hers shining with tears. "You're turning on me, too?"

I shake my head, wrapping an arm around her shoulder and pulling her to my chest. "I'm not turning on anyone. You both fucked up that night. What's done is done, but I'm not going to placate you and minimize the situation. Khloe is his soul mate. They've moved on. You should too."

She nods, but there's no telling what's going on in her head. Snapper isn't one to think in a straight line like most people. She had a rough childhood and even worse teen years. Fending for herself, even at the expense of others will always be her go-to tactic, even to the detriment of herself at a later time.

"Let's go grab some beer. The guys are dangerously close to running out, and the last thing we need is a clubhouse full of sober bikers."

She laughs and follows me to the nearest SUV. I open the door for her, making my way around to the driver's side once she's settled in.

"I get it," she says quietly a couple of minutes later, keeping her eyes on the tree line outside of her window.

"What's that," I ask turning down the radio so I can hear her better.

"Darby's appeal. She's pretty perfect." Her head turns to look at me, smile on her red lips. "She's got a mouth on her like no other."

"Oh yeah?" I can't help but smile. Darby could make me come in less than a minute, so I know exactly what she's talking about. "You gals sneaking around?"

She laughs, but it's laced with something I just can't quite put my finger on. "Believe me, baby. I'm not the one sneaking around."

My pulse pounds in my ears, hands turning clammy as I grip the steering wheel until my knuckles turn white. She doesn't say another word until we're pulling into the parking lot of the liquor store.

She doesn't make to move out of the vehicle, so neither do I.

"You said earlier that Kid found his soul mate, and it's obvious that Kincaid has done the same. Do you ever want to find that one woman who makes you stop all of your wild ways? The one who is so fucking incredible you can't imagine yourself touching any other pussy but hers?" Her eyes follow a man with a case of beer to his car.

"Nothing against anyone I've met thus far, but I'm certain there isn't a single woman in the world that would make me want to stop fucking the way I do," I answer honestly. A man covered in tattoos with a pierced cock so perfect I want it in my ass every day for the rest of my life? Now that's not what she asked, is it?

"Playboy for life," she mutters opening her door and finally climbing out.

"Maybe when we get back, we can grab her and head to your room." I nod in agreement as she switches gears back to our conversation on Darby. I grab a flat cart from the row where they're lined up against the outside of the building keeping my back to her so she can't see the fear still in my eyes from her elusive comment about sneaking around. "She can give you a few pointers on how to please a woman."

She's turned playful once again, slapping my ass as she walks ahead of me into the store. I laugh at her words, exactly what she expects at the moment.

"Are you saying I don't know how to please you?" I tease, hoping she can't hear the tremble in my voice. I can't be sure she honestly knows anything, but you never know with Snapper. She always has something up her sleeve, always planning the self-destructive act.

"Not at all, baby," she answers with a wide grin.

She holds the cart while I start piling on cases of beer before we head to the bottle shop in the back.

"You sure?" I help her as she struggles to push the cart to the next brand. "Sounds like I don't please you."

She shrugs, mood shifting ever so slightly once again. I wonder if she's bi-polar but I'm pretty sure second to second changes from manic to depressed isn't a characteristic of the disease.

"It's been so long since we fucked, I can't even remember what skills you have."

I grin, thankful for the opening for distraction she's just given me.

Wrapping my arms around her waist, I look around, thankfully finding the store sparsely populated this early in the back. One hand cups her braless tit while the other wanders down to the jean covered V between her legs.

"Sounds like you need a reminder," I say in her ear, already feeling like I've won when she sighs and leans back against my chest. "And you know I love a challenge."

She pants, worked up almost immediately at my embrace. "We can fuck in the bathroom before we leave."

As appealing as the chance to reroute our conversation is, I know it won't be enough to satisfy her need to feel wanted, and short-lived distraction isn't going to help me in the long run.

"And miss the opportunity for Darby to teach me how to properly take care of you?" I hiss when her hips rotate against my thickening cock. I may be freaking out, mind racing to figure out just what the hell she hinted at earlier, but I'm still a man with a warm pussy and big tit in my hand.

"We can do both," she offers.

I laugh in her ear, pride filling my chest when goose bumps race down her arm. She may have something planned, but at the end of the day, she just wants to be fucked. She's almost Darby's twin in that sense. Fill her with cock and show her enough attention and she's as happy as can be. Unlike Darby though, Snapper has the potential to ruin lives when she's feeling neglected.

"You'll wait," I say releasing her breast and cupping my hand at her throat, the mild pressure making her pulse thrum against my fingertips. "And you'll take my cock however I want to give it to you."

She nods as a longing filled whimper escapes her mouth.

I've got her right where I want her. The problem is Snapper never does what she's told.

Chapter 14

Snatch

"You keep playing shit hands like that, and you'll never sit down at this table again," I snip at Kid as he throws down another winning set.

My words don't even make sense. Not much does for me these days. If he was playing like shit, he wouldn't be scraping another pile of chips across the table toward his even larger pile. The urgency to slap the smirk off his damn face hits me hard, but I can't blame his winning ass on my bad mood. The cards I've been dealt, both literally and figuratively are what's shitty. The four beers I've drank since we sat down to play half an hour ago are doing nothing to ease my mind after the conversation I had with Darby earlier.

I look around the table. Shadow, Kincaid, Ace, and even the smug ass Kid sitting across from me does nothing for me. I'm secure enough in my manhood that I can acknowledge they're a great looking group of guys, but I don't have an ounce of sexual attraction to a single one of them. It's what's fucking with my head the most, not knowing exactly what it is about Itchy's bearded ass that makes my cock swell anytime he's within eye sight of me, and why now? Why after years of friendship, after sharing hundreds of women does the thought of his lips wrapped around my cock or the tightness of his ass make me want to forsake all women and spend my days inside his body in one way or another? And why the fuck does the thought of him bending me over in the shower and taking me like I took him a week ago make my nuts ache more than they ever have?

"You're just pissed you're losing," Kid taunts as he separates the chips by color and piles them higher than necessary before scooping up the cards to shuffle.

I feel Shadow's eyes focused on the side of my face, but I keep my eyes on Kid's hands as he works the deck. I know he wants an explanation for my outburst, but how do I bring up the fact that I'm fucking another member of the club at the poker table with four other guys? Doesn't really seem like a proper poker conversation right now... or ever.

Leave it to Kid to bring up the words Shadow would never confront me with in front of the other guys. I would die for the fucker, but Kid's an asshole with no damn decorum at all, so I should expect nothing less from him.

"Besides, asshole," he begins not bothering to look up from his less than skilled shuffle. "What's crawled up your ass? Where's Darby?" Only now does he look up and around the room with an exaggeration that makes my blood begin to boil. "She's usually out here on your dick by now."

My chair scrapes back an inch or so, as I begin to stand from my chair. I know I'm being an asshole, but Kid is normally more laid back than he's acting right now. Kid grins, unaffected and begins to deal the deck. I could pop him on the chin for taunting me, and we'd be fine by tomorrow. It's just how we operate, and even if he would hold a grudge, it's a chance I'm ready to take.

"Boys," Kincaid says, the one-word chastisement enough to make my ass fall back into my chair.

It doesn't, however, keep my middle finger from flicking up at him as he tosses cards around the table.

"Where's Khloe?" Shadow asks, and I'm grateful they begin talking about her and Em's college classes if only to pull the attention away from me.

"Em studying, too?" Kid asks, his voice pulling my attention back to the game.

"Naw. She's taking a nap." Kincaid answers with a knowing grin on his lips.

I laugh at the love-struck look on his face, readying to say something sexually explicit to Kincaid about Em, but the challenging arch of his eyebrow is enough to make me swallow my words. I hide my smile behind my hand as Kid tosses away his first shitty hand of the evening. I sometimes forget that Kincaid and Kid are no longer part of the single crowd, and they'd never give up salacious details about their women. I guess we all have secrets in that respect; only their relationships only have one cock in the equation.

I hear footsteps at my back, and from the look on Kid's face, I can easily predict it's Snapper. He doesn't do well at hiding his resentment of the woman, after the shit she pulled when he came back from Vegas with a hit so hard he lost his short term memory for a while. The hairs standing up on my neck are a clear indication that Itchy is with her as well. I don't even bother to look up from my cards as they walk past going deeper into the living room. The fingernail traveling down my chest isn't a surprise either because I can smell the sex permeating Darby's skin when she's within a foot of me.

Scowl still on my face at my quasi-argument with Kid, I push my chair back a couple of inches so Darby can curl up in my lap. When Itchy huffs at something from across the room as she settles on my lap, I don't bother to look in his direction, terrified it will raise even more suspicion. Shadow is watching me like a hawk trying to figure out what the fuck is going on in my head. My eyes do dart up to find Shadow's who, as suspected, is glaring at me as if he can read me like a book.

"You're mad at me," she whispers, tilting my head up to look at her with a finger under my chin. Clear concern and sympathy are in her eyes making me feel like shit for not feeling more for her than I do. "Please don't be mad."

She kisses my lips, and I groan into her mouth as her tongue strokes over mine. The saltiness still in her mouth from what I can only assume is Itchy's come shoots an arrow of desire straight to my cock. I harden against her ass, and she squirms acknowledging my readiness.

"You smell like pussy," I whisper before taking her mouth again. "And taste like come."

She gives me a weak smile, a tear on her lower lash threatening to roll down her cheek. I cup her face in my hands grateful for the gift she's just given to me, something I'd never have the courage to ask for or take myself. My thumb sweeps the plumpness of her cock swollen lips just before I lean my forehead against hers. "Thank you."

"You're welcome," she returns, her mouth finding mine once more. She moans, allowing my exploration into her mouth as I seek out every hint of his taste.

It isn't until I feel Shadow shift beside me and stand that I become aware that we're having this intimate moment in front of half of the club. My mind races, trying to remember if I said anything incriminating in front the guys.

I don't have long to spend questioning my own actions, because when I look up, I see Shadow frozen in the doorway, back stiff as if a ghost has just appeared before his eyes.

He bends, reaching down for something, as he speaks, but he's too far away for me to hear the conversation. When he turns back around followed by the familiar face of Misty, the chick he was banging from Denver, I'm shocked, but when I look down and see his hand clinging to the handle of a fucking car seat, I nearly fall out of my fucking chair.

"What the hell is that?" I ask before I catch myself.

"Kincaid," Shadow grunts, the first word he's said loud enough since he stood from the table.

I already know what's coming, so I grip Darby's hips and guide her to standing before I rise to my feet as well.

"Everyone out," Kincaid says, but Darby and I are already making our way to the hallway leading to the rooms.

Darby stops me with a hand on my arm. "What's going on? Who is that woman?"

My eyes find Kid's as we stand in the hallway, far enough out of sight but still within earshot. Kincaid can't actually expect us not to stick around and wait to find out exactly what the fuck is going on.

"Did Shadow get some chick pregnant?" Snapper hisses. She's upset, as if that's the actual situation, she's just proved some point she's been trying to get everyone to understand.

"Shhh," Darby chastises her friend. "I can't hear anything."

None of us can, other than the rapid breathing of half a dozen idiots standing together in the narrow hallway. I don't think Shadow's stupid enough to knock some chick up, but I can't say I'm not grateful for the distraction. At this point, I'll take anything to keep the eyes and suspicions out of my life, and a baby showing up on the doorsteps of the clubhouse is sure to do just that.

"What's going on?" Em's voice comes up from behind us. We part like the Red Sea as our untitled queen steps out into the hallway.

Luckily the women stay quiet, and I know it has everything to do with Snapper not liking her and Darby keeping her distance just like she was instructed.

"Misty is here." Em smiles brightly at my words.

"From Denver?" she asks. "I've always wanted to meet her. Kincaid thinks the world of her."

She makes to move out into the open from the hallway but I grasp her arms just as she steps past and the baby's cries can be heard.

"She has a baby with her, Em" Her eyes widen, and she walks past us, free range to go anywhere she wants even though Kincaid commanded the rest of us to vacate the common area.

Chapter 15

Itchy

"Fuck," I yell as my fist meets the drywall just inside the door of my room.

Feeling like a complete idiot, I pull my hand from the hole knowing I'll be tasked with fixing it later.

I pace around at the end of my bed like a caged animal waiting for a chance to escape. The sight of Darby crawling up in Snatch's lap isn't what set me off, but the fact that they can be open, a kiss between the two of them means nothing as far as the guys are concerned. Anyone paying attention would either smile at their public display of affection or wish they could tag team her. I know that's what was on Ace's mind when he couldn't pull his eyes from them.

Even if I thought anyone in Cerberus would have a problem if I walked up and planted a kiss on his lips I wouldn't give a shit. I seriously don't think one single guy here would say a damn word, but I'd never risk it because it's not what Snatch wants.

Thinking about it only pisses me off more. Stripping out of my clothes and leaving them in a pile on my floor I head to the shower. I can't lie, fucking Darby and Snapper for the last two hours was a great fucking time, but just like Snatch admitted last week in Central America, something was missing. Hot, tight pussy and two talented mouths are no longer enough to make me feel satiated.

With angry swipes of a wash rag, I scrub my skin until it feels as if I've been out in the sun for too long. As pissed as I am at the situation, staying away from him isn't something I can tolerate either. I dry so ineffectively in my haste to get back out to the group, my t-shirt sticks to my wet back as I struggle to pull it on. Same goes for my damn socks and jeans. It does nothing but piss me off even more.

The anger ebbs away when I step out into the hallway to see everyone huddled together with heads bent around the door frame.

"The fuck is going on?" I ask stepping up behind Darby, but making sure not to touch Snatch while this close to other members of the club.

It isn't until Snatch looks over his shoulder at me, concern etching wrinkles in his forehead. "Misty just showed up from Denver with a fucking baby."

"No shit?" I ask watching his hand settle at the small of Darby's back when she leans against his shoulder to get a better look.

Taking a chance I know I never should, but not giving a fuck either way, I place my hand over his. Instead of rejecting me and jerking his hand away, he spreads his fingers so I can slide mine between them, a small victory all things considered.

I can't see shit, being at the far back of the small group, but my focus in on the warmth at my palm until all hell breaks loose in the living room. I hear Shadow and Kincaid barking orders over the wail of a baby with brand new and very efficient lungs.

I can't even be mad when Snatch releases my hand to move himself and Darby out of Shadow's way as he barrels into the hall with an ashen Misty in his arms.

"Fuck," I mutter as he walks past.

Kincaid follows close behind instructing Snatch to wait out front for Doc Davison to arrive. Next is Em, holding a car seat close to her face as she tries to soothe the wailing baby. It's like the fucking twilight zone in this mother fucker today.

Unsure if I'm needed or not, I stay in the hallway, waiting for instruction of some kind. Darby leans into my side, and instinctively I wrap her in my arms.

"Does this happen a lot?" she whispers as the other members begin to clear out and head back into the living room.

"Do women show up unannounced claiming to have gotten pregnant by one of our guys?" Kid asks as he holds his arms open to Khloe who has exited her room after the commotion.

Darby nods. "Never," Kid and I say at the same time.

Action in the doorway to Shadow's room draws our attention. Our VP steps a couple inches into the hallway.

"Ace-Itchy, go to fucking Target or something and get some formula and diapers." His order leaves no room for argument.

"How the fuck do we know what to get?" I hear Ace ask causing me to look over my shoulder because I was sure he'd left the hallway with everyone else.

"I don't know shit about babies," I add.

"Just get one of everything," Shadow says as he reaches into his wallet and hands Ace a credit card.

"Come on fucker," Ace says to me as he turns to head to the front door.

My eyes catch Darby's, pleading for help.

"Don't look at me," she says holding her hands up and stepping out of my embrace. "I don't know shit about babies either."

Something about the idea scares her, and it's written all over her face, but I don't have the time to investigate her weird ass reaction right now.

"Go find Snatch, babe. I'll be back in a little while." I give her forehead a swift kiss and follow Ace out the front.

I nod at Doc Davison on my way down the front steps, grateful we have him as a resource when shit goes down at the club.

* * *

"Seriously?" I ask Ace as he walks up to me.

I'm scouring the sixteen million different kinds of baby formula at Walmart, knowing Shadow would expect the best for that tiny baby even if he isn't the father.

"What?" He looks down at the stupid fucking Tonka truck. "It's a boy. He was wrapped in a blue blanket, asshole."

The woman loading her cart with jars of disgusting looking baby food a few feet away gasps and disappears around the end of the aisle. Honestly, I'm surprised she didn't leave sooner, seeing as two bearded bikers were within a few feet of her. She didn't look like the type that we'd ever run into socially.

"He said diapers and formula," I sneer, frustrated over the endless choices in front of me. "And you're wasting your damn time in the toy section."

"Don't be a dick," he snaps tossing the truck into the cart. "I got the diapers, and the toy section is right over there. You're the one holding this ride up not me."

"You found diapers that quick?"

He beams like he's just solved an algebraic equation. "Yep. Heard Shadow say she had a C-section four days ago, so I got the package with a big four on it."

"Fucking idiot," I mutter walking past him and shoving a can of formula that touts brain health and has breastmilk like qualities into his hands. "Size four in diapers is for like really damn big kids, not newborn babies."

"How the fuck am I supposed to know that?"

I grab the diapers out of the shopping cart and head to the other aisle.

He's easily distracted, like an excitable Chihuahua on crack, so it doesn't surprise me that he's nowhere to be found when I swap out the diapers for a familiar brand I've seen commercials for labeled with NB.

I head to the front, only to find him nose to nose with a woman who, although would fit right in at the clubhouse, looks like a hooker in the middle of Walmart.

"For fuck's sake," I mutter, closing the short distance between us. The way she's smiling, popping her gum, and pushing her tits further in his face, if it weren't for the size of the place, I'd swear we were in the damn dollar store.

"You like babies?" he asks leaning further over the shopping cart, which I'm sure is the only thing keeping his mouth off of her skin.

She grins wide. "Yeah, but my pimp thought sterilization was best after the last pregnancy scare."

Where the fuck do these people come from?

"Down boy," I say and thump his ear after tossing the correct sized diapers into the cart. "You know the doctor said no sex during a herpes flare-up, even if you are on the meds."

He glares at me, but Hooker Barbie doesn't miss a beat. "Which medicine? I've had the best luck with Valtrex."

I nearly gag as I pull the cart out of his grip and head to the front. It takes less than half a minute for him to catch up with me.

"Fuck, thanks, man. You really saved me back there."

I shake my head at his idiocy. "You've got to be joking."

I pull the items from the cart and place them on the short conveyor belt, rolling my eyes at the little rubber duck he's tossed in there but add it to the small pile nonetheless.

"Yeah, man. I don't know how you know which girls aren't right, but I appreciate it."

I huff a laugh at his ridiculousness. "You didn't notice the burns from her crack pipe on her lips?"

How this man survived numerous combat tours, I'll never know.

"I never got past her tits," he admits.

"Leave it to a set of tits to be the fall of mankind," I mutter stepping out of the way so Ace can pay for the items.

Chapter 16

Snatch

"You sure you left anything in the store?" I ask Emmalyn as we climb out of the SUV and head to the back.

"Probably not," she answers without hesitation and full seriousness.

"Really?" I open the back hatch of the Tahoe, barely catching a bag before it falls to the ground. It's stuffed to the max.

"Babies require a lot of stuff." She reaches for the bags, but I stop her. "All Ace and Itchy managed to get last night was a can of formula, diapers, a Tonka truck, and a rubber duck."

I shrug because it seems like legitimate shit to buy for a baby. I'll have to commend Ace on the rubber duck. There's no way Itchy thought of that, and it's a nice touch.

"I'll bring it all in, Em." She laughs, shoves past me and grabs a couple of bags.

"You sure you want to take Misty feminine products?" She waves a package of pads so big in my face, I'm certain they're adult diapers.

"Hell no." I step out of her way like I'll be tainted if I get within arm's reach of that shit.

She laughs, sifting through the back before tugging a couple more bags free. "If you could bring the rest in that'd be great, and I'd love you forever if you can put that bassinet together for Griffin."

"I'm gonna tell Prez you're hitting on me." She winks at me before turning to head into the clubhouse.

"He'd never believe it. Thanks for going with me even though you hung out in electronics the entire time."

"What can I say? I'm a guy. I don't mind shopping, but the bike shop is more my speed than Target."

"Hey, Em?" I catch her before she disappears inside. "What the hell is a bassinet?"

"The bed thing, Snatch." I hear her laughter until it fades away inside.

It takes four trips to get all of Em's purchases into Shadow's room. I saved the bed thing for last, planning to lay everything out in the living room and toss it together really quick. Just as my ass hits the floor and I papercut the shit out of my finger trying to get into the box, my phone chimes a text.

I grumble, typing out my response to Itchy's text asking where I am with one hand because my injured finger is in my mouth.

"You sure know how to turn me on, sucking on your finger like that."

My eyes snap up to my best friend, agitated he'd say some shit like that outside of the sanctuary of one of our rooms. It doesn't, however, prevent my cock from thickening, a rather uncomfortable situation considering I'm in jeans on the damn floor.

"I've had less painful injuries in the fucking war zone," I complain around my finger.

"Please stop," he grunts.

I look up, smiling around my finger when his heated glare stays pinned to my mouth.

With a quick shake of his head, he snaps himself out of whatever fantasy was playing in his mind. My eyes dart to the erection straining against his jeans.

He clears his throat and sits on the other side of the box.

"You're covered in fucking tattoos and piercings, sitting here complaining about a paper cut? Nut the fuck up, man."

I circle my tongue around the tip of my finger before releasing it with a pop that's pulled his eyes back to my mouth for good measure. I'm sure the haze clouding his eyes matches mine.

"You going to help me with this shit or not?" I ask after watching his Adam's apple bob on a rough swallow.

"Huh?"

"The bed thing, Itchy. Em said they need it for Griffin."

He nods, the mention of the baby pulling his mind from illicit thoughts.

"Shadow has a fucking baby," he mutters cutting open the end of the box with his pocket knife.

"Fucking crazy right? I can't even imagine."

We work in silence for over an hour, both refusing to look at the instructions and complaining about the fall of America to products made in China.

"Oh, thanks, by the way," I mutter after snapping the last wheel in place. "If you and Idiot Biker had gotten more shit last night, I wouldn't have sliced my finger open."

"Papercut," he chides.

"Cardboard cut," I correct. "Ten times fucking worse."

"Maybe," he agrees. "I had a hard enough time keeping him from picking up a crack head and bringing her back to the clubhouse to worry about more than we were told to get. Shadow asked for diapers and formula, and that's what he got."

"Well, I got roped into shopping at the Bull's Eye for three fucking hours," I complain. "You can only look at new release DVDs and TVs for so long before you want to stab yourself in the eye."

"I spent the last two hours cleaning out Kid's old room so Shadow can stay in there while Misty recovers from her C-section. Besides, you were supposed to help Em shop for the baby shit," he says stuffing the extra packaging into the empty box.

"I did. I helped her push three carts of baby crap out to the truck and pack-muled all that shit to Shadow's room." I hold my hand up for proof. "And I have the injuries to prove it."

He laughs at my inability to forget about the cut on my hand.

"You want me to kiss it and make it better?" He's asking about my hand, but his eyes never leave my mouth.

It's my turn to swallow past the sudden dryness in my throat. I take a quick look around the room, pleased to find us still alone. "You can kiss something else."

He smiles, flashing white teeth before they sink into his lip. "I'm pretty sure sucking it would feel better."

Are we really doing this in the middle of the living room? My cock urges me on like a wingman at a sorority party.

"You want to suck my cock, Itchy?" I haven't verbalized my wishes since the hotel shower.

"So fucking bad." The gravel and need in his voice echoes in my rock hard dick.

My back stiffens, and Itchy's eyes dart to the front door when the knob turns. Snapper and Snake laugh their way into the clubhouse, none the wiser to the conversation we were just having, but it doesn't stop the freak out from starting.

"Don't," Itchy hisses, his eyes following the happy twosome to the sofa twenty feet away. Eventually, his eyes find mine. "Don't shut down on me."

Before I can respond, Shadow converges on us. "Is it ready?"

He's exhausted, dark circles under his eyes only the first clue he probably hasn't slept since Misty showed up yesterday.

"Yeah," Itchy says collecting a stray bolt from the ground.

Shadow's eyes follow it until it disappears into the box with the rest of the trash. "Did you put it together right? Why are there pieces left over? I can't have my son sleeping in some rigged up piece of shit."

"Calm down," Itchy says with a chuckle. "It's safe, promise."

"Son?" I ask. "You're sure he's yours."

Shadow runs a hand over his beard. "He looks just like me."

Itchy laughs. "He looks like a wrinkled old man."

Shadow takes a menacing step in his direction. "He has my eyes."

Itchy holds his hands up indicating he doesn't want any trouble, but he still can't manage to keep his damn mouth shut. "Snatch has your eyes, man. Doesn't mean you're his daddy."

I glare at my best friend and back to Shadow, wondering if he thinks it's weird that Itchy notices things like the color of my eyes.

"Yeah, well," Shadow says with another rough grab at his beard. "The DNA test will be back in a few days."

"Cool," Itchy mutters, standing from the floor wiping down the front of his jeans and disappears down the hallway.

"I need a few minutes," Shadow says looking past me at the front door. "Can you get this to Misty?"

"Sure, man," I agree, but his back is already to me heading out the front door.

My cell dings, once again a text from Itchy.

Itchy: My room. 30 minutes. Darby and I will be ready for you.

I take my time delivering the bassinet to Shadow's old room dragging the empty packaging out to the dumpster on the edge of the property.

My blood hums with the prospect of the planned clandestine meeting, and I realize thirty minutes is a long ass fucking time when it's leading up to something you want so fucking bad. It's as if I'm a kid again, waiting in my room until my parents come get me on Christmas morning.

"Hey," Ace calls out from the front of the garage before I can make it back up the front steps of the clubhouse. "So Shadow's the first daddy in the house, huh?"

I look around, noticing Shadow's bike is gone. "Looks that way."

He tilts back a beer even though it's only noon. "I seriously thought Kid would knock Khloe up before Shadow would fuck up and have a baby show up on the front porch."

"I'd keep your opinions to yourself, Ace. Shadow is on edge these days, and Kid's not going to let any bullshit about Khloe slide." He grumbles some bullshit about the club being taken over by unavailable women and babies before turning around and disappearing into the garage.

I can't be bothered by his disgruntled attitude over Misty showing up with a baby; I have a guy inside waiting to suck my dick. My priorities are straight. Besides, bitching about something beyond my control is pointless.

Chapter 17

Itchy

"Fuck," I hiss when Darby takes me to the back of her throat. "You have an amazing mouth."

Coming up for air, she grins at the tip, licking the underside with a roll of her tongue so skilled I'd bet she took classes. "Shouldn't we wait for Snatch?"

With fingers tangled in her messy blonde hair, I guide her back down my cock. "He'll be here eventually."

She pops again, playfulness sparkling in her eyes. "Maybe he wants to be the one sucking you off."

I nearly blow in her mouth at the thought, but I know better. Snatch wants my mouth, my ass, but returning the favor isn't something I anticipate ever happening.

I'm about to close my eyes, ignoring her words when the door into Snatch's room opens and he walks inside. His eyes sweep to the door leading out of my room into the hallway, verifying that it's locked. The notion sends a chill up my spine, anticipation going up a hundred levels. He wouldn't be worried about getting walked in on unless he's afraid of getting caught doing something he doesn't want others to know. My mouth waters at the thought of sucking his cock.

"You couldn't even wait for me?" His words are teasing, but his eyes never leave Darby's head as it bobs down my cock.

"She's eager," I placate.

Cold rushes the length of my dick when Darby pulls her mouth off. I relish the reprieve. Now that Snatch has joined us, his pleasure and the thrill I get from giving it to him is my only concern.

My eyes stay on him as his clothes disappear and hundreds of tattoos are revealed. God, he's a work of art.

"He's ready for your mouth," Darby coos.

Snatch's cock jerks at her words, and he fists it, squeezing hard. When I look down at her, I realize she's said the words to Snatch, not me. Looking back at him, my sac tightens when I see his eyes on her mouth as she licks the weeping tip of my cock. His tongue sweeping his lower lip is almost my undoing.

"Come here," she says holding her arm out and offering him her hand.

My heart stops when he closes the distance to the bed, eyes never leaving my cock.

I will fucking die if he even so much as breathes on my dick. I know cardiac arrest is in my future, but what a fucking way to go.

The bed dips under his weight, knee touching my thigh but he pauses, making no further attempt at contact.

Darby, always the one to keep things from getting awkward and the one to encourage whatever this shit is that's building between Snatch and I, releases my cock and sucks the head of his in her mouth.

His eyes lock on mine, trapping me in his stare until his gaze lowers to my mouth. Having been with him, fucking countless women, I can tell by the stiffness in his spine and the way his hands hang loosely at his sides that Darby sucking his cock isn't what he wants. He's allowing it, not encouraging it. As skillful as her mouth is, we're losing his focus, and she doesn't even have a clue.

It's not what I need.

His words from Costa Rica fill the room as if he's transferring them to me telepathically. I nod in understanding, knowing I've guessed right when the tightness at the corners of his eyes relax.

"Let me," I offer with a gentle touch to the back of her head.

"He couldn't get enough of your taste yesterday," she says softly before sucking one of his balls into her mouth. Her eyes meet mine. "He kissed me until the taste of your come was gone."

Instinct and unfulfilled need make my hips roll against the mattress, grinding my erection into the tousled sheets.

"He wants to suck your cock, but he just doesn't know how to ask for it," she assures.

I close my eyes, working his cock exactly how I'd love him to work mine and push her words away.

"What are you guys whispering about?" Snatch grumbles.

After a final swipe of his balls, Darby pulls her head back a few inches to speak. "I was telling Itchy that you..."

I pinch her nipple until she yelps. There's no way I can take the chance that she's reading him wrong.

She glares at me, clears her throat and continues. "You should grab a condom from the drawer so Itchy can fuck me while he's sucking you off."

I give her a weak smile, thanking her for not telling him the truth.

Even she knows that Snatch would rather come in my mouth than inside of her, and the pain in her eyes is evident even though her words are contradictory. She's well aware how one-sided this situation is, and it makes me feel like shit.

We reposition, Darby on her back ankles being held aloft in Snatch's hands, exposing her beautiful pussy to me. He's straddling her head, legs spread wide enough for her to still be able to suck and lick his sac without having to strain her neck. I position myself at her entrance, loving the slide of my cock into her heat before bending forward and reclaiming Snatch's cock.

"Oh fuck," he grunts as we lavish him with attention.

I don't realize my hips are static until Darby's abdomen flexes and bunches. She's taking her own pleasure, fucking herself on me.

Sensation overload is an understatement as Snatch's rough hand grips the back of my head, fingers flexing at my scalp. I suck harder, take him deeper, only come up for a breath of air when he allows it.

"He wants you, too," she whispers licking her finger.

I watch, entranced, as her hand disappears behind his sac. His cock kicks so hard he nearly falls from my mouth.

"Holy shit," Snatch groans. "Oh God."

"Suck," she urges.

I double my efforts, nearly coming myself when I watch her hand work inside of him. I hate that the minuscule movement of her hand is all I can see. I'd sell my soul for a front seat of the actual act.

"Fuck, fuck, fuuuck." Snatch's voice echoes in the room just before his cock thickens further and he orgasms.

I nearly choke on the heated flood but manage to swallow his offering. Darby's pussy clenches around me as she claims her own release.

"Jesus," I hiss pulling my mouth off of Snatch and my cock out of Darby.

My hand trembles when I rip the latex free of my cock, my orgasm barely holding back long enough to move my hand.

Jet after jet of come streaks Darby's pussy and lower belly, and I'm amazed at how damned fast we all peaked.

Darby smiles up at me, her face half hidden in the shadows under Snatch's body. I look up at him to see his eyes clenched tight and his chest struggling with uneven breaths.

"Let me get you a wash rag," I offer climbing off the bed and heading into the bathroom.

I grip the edge of the sink, doing my best to regain my composure, the knowledge that Darby's fingers were inside my best friend almost more than I can bare.

I stop cold in my tracks when I head back into the room. I hardly notice the warmth of the wash rag as it falls from my hand and lands on my foot. Half-mast cock, now fully erect, I stand in the doorway and watch Snatch as he devours Darby's pussy like a gourmet meal.

Her eyes are closed, head tilted back digging into the pillow, but that's not what makes me creep closer to the bed to get a better look.

The come I'd spurted onto her body is gone, licked and cleaned away by Snatch's mouth. Normally the way he's devouring her, fingers plunging deep would be what got my libido to an all-time high, but today it's the clean milky expanse of her lower stomach.

My only regret is that I left the room and didn't get the chance to see it on his tongue.

***

"This is nice," Darby says sleepily.

We're all three still in my room, never having left the bed after Snatch made Darby come twice more with his mouth. I watched, unable to look away as he took care of her like she'd given him a new house for his birthday and he was repaying her kindness. We didn't talk about it of course, and I hate that Darby is in the middle rather than tucked into my side with Snatch on the other. But, beggars and choosers and all that.

My eyes look up at the door to the hallway when I hear Griffin cry as someone carries him toward the kitchen.

"That's so fucking strange," Snatch mutters, his eyes looking the same direction as mine.

"Tell me about it," I agree.

"Not used to babies being around?" Darby asks one hand on each of our thighs under the blanket that covers us from the waist down but leaves her gorgeous tits exposed to the chilly air.

I huff a laugh. "Never. I mean Kincaid and Em are trying to get pregnant. That we'd be prepared for. Misty showing up with a baby after lying and pretty much tricking Shadow into knocking her up? We never saw that shit coming."

Her fingers grip my thigh harder before she pulls her hand away completely.

"You guys don't eventually want kids?"

"Fuck no," Snatch hisses, answering my sentiments before I can get the words out.

I laugh at his response. "No babies for us, Darby. Our lives are too crazy, too dangerous for children."

"Besides," Snatch adds. "We'd never settle down long enough to raise a kid. We got too much fucking to do."

He reaches over her head, fist clenched, expecting to bump with mine. I give him what he needs, just like I always will, but his confession of never settling down weighs heavy on my heart.

"I'd fucking die if some chick showed up with my kid," he mumbles before climbing out of bed and pulling his jeans up his tattooed thighs. "Y'all hungry? Let's go find something to eat."

Darby sits up, eyes searching for mine, almost as if she wants to say something but can't find the words. I'm the asshole who climbs off the bed, relieved she stays silent because the only thing I can think of is following Snatch to the kitchen.

Chapter 18

Snatch

"I'm not carrying your beer for you, asshole." I look over at Snake whose arms are full of long necks.

"I can't carry anymore," he whines like a child despite being almost thirty years old.

"You can do one of two things. You can choose not to drink so much, or you can make two trips."

I hear him grumble behind me, but I leave him to figure it out and head to the garage. A lot of us guys hang out there now that the house has been overrun with women. Brighton, Shadow's older sister was at the clubhouse when we got home from a mission a couple of weeks ago. He said she was tasked with helping Misty with Griffin while he was gone, but it was quickly discovered that although in her mid-thirties she doesn't know shit about kids.

Her arrival along with Misty still being around has created even more tension with the club girls. They've become snippy as hell, so us guys leave them to their shit and stay outside most of the time.

"Hey, man." I clap Shadow on the back and take the empty chair beside him.

He doesn't even acknowledge me, too busy working the label off of his beer bottle.

"His dog die?" I ask Kid.

"Woman trouble," he mutters before taking a long swig from his beer.

"Fuck," Shadow says pulling his eyes from his bottle and leaning back in his chair. "Women are nothing but trouble."

Itchy and I raise our beers in silent salute. Kincaid and Kid look at both of us like we're idiots. No way will they ever be caught dead toasting when they have amazing women just inside the clubhouse.

"Anything in particular? Or are we hating the fairer sex in general?" I look around the group, but no one seems to want to discuss the issue Shadow is having with him sitting right there.

A long stretch of silence fills the garage; only crickets chirping can be heard through the open bay door. That is until Snake's ass comes barging in with an empty diaper box filled with beer bottles. The glass bottles clank against each other until he finally sets it down beside the only empty chair left. He smirks at me, ecstatic he figured out how to get them out here without using either one of my suggestions.

"Misty wants to get a job," Shadow says after tossing his empty bottle in the trash can with a loud bang.

I stay silent because I don't have a problem with women working.

"Shit," Kid says as if it's a travesty the woman wants to work.

"I went through the same thing with Em," Kincaid adds with commiseration.

My eyes cut to Itchy, wondering what part of this strange shit is so bad. He shrugs blissfully unaware.

"I'm afraid if she works she'll leave." Snake grumbles but doesn't refuse him when Shadow reaches over and pulls one of his beers from the diaper box. "I won't let her take my son away from me."

"That's not going to happen," Kid interjects. "Khloe is going to school, but I know she'd want to work if she didn't have anything else to do."

Shadow rips the top off of the fresh beer but doesn't raise it to his lips. "Khloe isn't going anywhere."

"Damn straight she's not," Kid says with confidence.

Shadow scowls at him.

"I don't think she has any plans to take Griff, man," Itchy adds.

Shadow raises an eyebrow at him, and for the first time since walking in here, I'm glad I'm not sitting right beside my best friend.

"The fuck do you know about my... Misty," Shadow quickly catches his word slip. "Has she said something to you?"

I look over at Itchy, just as curious about his answer.

He shakes his head. "Naw, man. She just doesn't seem like the single mother type."

Shadow scoots closer to the edge of his chair, and I cuss under my breath. Itchy should know better than to make assumptions, and should be even more aware that they should never leave his mouth. Shadow has been on a hair trigger since Misty showed up over a month ago, and right now I'm concerned for his safety.

I'm also an asshole for worrying if Shadow breaks his jaw, he won't be able to suck my cock later.

"Are you saying the mother of my child can't handle raising that little boy on her own? That if, God forbid, something happens to me on a mission, she won't make it without me?" Shadow is gripping his beer bottle so hard his knuckles are turning white.

"That's not what he means," Kincaid says as he places his hand on Shadow's shoulder. "Misty is more than capable of keeping him safe."

Itchy leans forward, not menacingly, but a face full of anger. I can kiss that blowjob goodbye since he can't just leave well enough alone. "First off, you need to calm the fuck down and stop putting words in my mouth."

If he knew how good your blowjobs were, he'd want to stick something else there.

"Second," he continues, not privileged to my thoughts. "Don't put anything like, 'if something happens to you' into words. You can't fuck with cosmic shit like that. Third, you know that boy will never want for anything if you weren't around. I'd raise that boy like he was my own if it came down to anything fucked up like that. You know that we all would."

Everyone raises their beer in solidarity. The round of "here, here" enough to make Shadow calm if only for a minute.

"I know you would," he concedes.

"She said she wants to be able to take care of herself. It just struck a chord with me. She should know that I'll always take care of them." He huffs and finally takes a long pull on his beer.

"Does she?" Kid asks, tempting the devil like an idiot. "Does she know you'll take care of her? Or does she somehow have it in her head that your only concern is for Griff?"

Before Shadow can rip his head off, Kincaid cuts in. "Em needed her independence when she first got here too. She needed to know that if push came to shove, she'd be okay. I think that's where Misty is at also."

Shadow is still glaring at Kid even though I know he heard what Kincaid just said. He's itching for a fight and doesn't seem to want to walk out of this garage without one.

"Women," Snake says as if the word is a curse.

"I'm just saying," Kid says, hands open palm up on his lap. "If you didn't tell her in as many words, you can't assume that she knows."

"Complicated creatures," Snake laments.

Shadow closes his eyes, something someone has said in the last half hour actually sinking in.

"Fuck," he grunts.

"On that note," I say slapping my legs before standing up. "I'm going to bed. The shit is too deep out here for me."

I give Itchy a quick glance wanting him to read my mind and meet me in his room in a while, but his eyes are on the bottle in his hands.

"Night," Kincaid says before talking more to Shadow about the similarities between Misty and Emmalyn.

I have no idea where Ace is as I walk through the house, not that I'm very concerned about his extracurriculars, but the clubhouse is eerily quiet as I make my way to my room.

Closing myself into my room, I lean against the door, eyes closed, just needing a break from everyone else's drama. I have enough to worry about not trying to get caught in the fucking closet I've apparently been enjoying too much the last couple of months.

A sniffle coming from my bathroom snaps my eyes open and has my feet moving before I can even evaluate the situation. Toeing the door open with my boot, I see Darby curled up in the corner by the shower. Her red-rimmed eyes look up at me when the light from the doorway washes over her.

"Hey," I say with a softness I rarely use.

"I'm sorry," she says with hasty wipes at the tears rolling down her cheeks. "I didn't think you'd be back so soon. You guys usually stay in the garage until the roosters are crowing."

"Anything I can help with?" What is it about crying women that makes me want to turn tail and run? Well, women who are crying and you don't know the reason more specifically. We deal with crying women a lot, but being abducted, raped, and tortured will make anyone cry.

She huffs a humorless laugh and my hackles immediately go up.

Her eyes search mine, head dropping back down to her bent knees when she doesn't find what she's looking for.

"Darby," I begin, but she cuts me off.

"I'm tired of hiding," she whispers, barely audible.

"You don't have to stay in the bathroom," I respond immediately.

She shakes her head. "I'm tired of hiding our relationship. Tired of having to sneak around and pretend that we aren't a triad."

"Triad?" *What is this woman smoking?*

"The three of us. I don't want to hide our relationship any longer." She sniffles again, looking up at me with hope in her eyes.

She's got another thing coming if she thinks getting upset and a few tears are enough for me just to march outside and tell men who put their lives in my hands on a regular basis that I like to fuck my best friend in the ass and have him suck my dick on occasion.

"That's not what this is," I tell her, knowing she doesn't want to hear it, but I'm trying to do my best not to be a complete asshole.

"You don't have to be ashamed," she challenges.

"I'm not fucking ashamed!" I roar, the lie tasting like shit in my mouth.

"You are!" she rages back. "They'll all see how much we love each other, and welcome our relationship with open arms."

I glare at her dumbfounded, unable to break down all of the stupid shit she's spitting at me.

Love? Relationship? Open arms?

I start from the beginning. "Love?"

She nods, eyes pleading. "I love you both."

"You shouldn't," I mutter, crossing my arms over my chest, rejecting her feelings outright.

"You don't love me? Don't love Itchy?"

"I don't love you." The answer to her first question comes easy. The second question is so convoluted; it's not something I'm delving into right now, especially not with her.

"But you love Itchy." A statement, not a question.

"He's my best friend," I say as if it explains everything.

"I thought you were different."

I rake my hands over my short Mohawk, frustrated beyond belief and wishing I would've stayed outside to listen to Shadow whining about his woman.

"Than what, Darby? I don't understand how great sex turned into love. Have I ever implied or made you believe there would be anything more than what we've had?"

"You're just like the men back in Vegas, taking all that you want but giving nothing in return."

I bristle at the comparison.

"I promised you nothing other than incredible orgasms, which I'm pretty sure I delivered. You're the one changing the game and expecting me to be okay with the new rules. I'm nothing like those pieces of shit in Vegas. You're free to come and go as you wish. Not one person will stop you from leaving." My pulse is racing, hating the new level of prick I've become.

"You want me gone?" Tears begin streaming down her face again.

"Fuck," I hiss. "That's not what I said."

"But you won't try to stop me if I leave?"

What the fuck is she fishing for?

"You're not a prisoner here, Darby." I know what she wants, and I refuse to give it to her. I don't lie to women. Not to get them to fuck me and not to get them to stick around, no matter how incredible they are in bed.

"Okay," she says wiping her nose on the back of her hand and standing from the floor. "I know exactly where I stand."

The same place you've always stood, I want to tell her but keep my mouth shut.

I turn sideways so she can walk past me.

"Darby?" Her back stiffens, but she stops to listen to me. "You won't tell anyone, will you? About Itchy and me?"

When she looks over her shoulder, her face is a solid mask of hatred, and I know I'm fucked.

"Your precious fucking secret is safe with me," she spits before disappearing into Itchy's room.

I jolt when the door slams, even though I knew it was coming. The click of the lock echoes through the room, and I can't help but wonder how much I just fucked things up.

Chapter 19

Itchy

"Hey, doll," I say to Darby as I walk into my room. Her body shifted slightly when I stepped in so I know she's awake.

Unsteady on my feet is an understatement. Somehow, a couple of beers in the garage turned into shots as war stories we'd never discuss in front of civilians began to spew from our mouths. Some were funny; some weren't. Once the liquor was flowing though, they were easier to tell, sort of like our own brand of therapy, the counselors being our brothers in arms because they'd lived through the shit too.

Even in my inebriated state, I can tell she's upset. Soft sniffles and the slight tremble of her shoulders are hard to ignore.

"What's wrong?" I ask sliding in behind her and wrapping my arm around her waist.

Normally, she'd melt into my embrace. Tonight she's stiff as a board. Once pliable muscles and innate sexuality have morphed into tension and nonverbal rejection.

"Talk to me," I urge.

She shakes her head, refusing, but I stay silent. Most women, left to stew will eventually speak. They want to be heard, need to articulate what's bothering them. Darby is different from many women I've met, but at the end of the day, those feminine traits are there.

"He hates me," she sobs.

I don't have to ask her who she means. We don't discuss her play times with the other members. Not that it's a rule or anything, but our only conversations include us and the tattooed man who tends to be an asshole when he's deflecting.

I cringe, knowing she probably spoke with him about the things I have been trying to ignore for weeks. When we're together sans Snatch, she's been grasping, reaching for information and opinions on stuff she's playing off as pure curiosity.

It started shortly after Misty and Griff showed up, questions about having children. It's progressed more recently with questions of whether we'd ever leave the MC to settle down. She's expressed an urge to live in a house in the country where it's quiet, and no one is around. She's been smart enough to not mention Snatch and me in her visions, but we're not idiots. Well, at least I caught on to her little ploy. With the way she's acting now, I imagine she's said something to my best friend, and he shut her down like a crack house that's popped up beside a police station.

I never should've let her talk. I should've told her weeks ago, that the thoughts she was having weren't something she'd ever get from either of us, but Snatch especially. Holding her, though, feeling her warmth against my skin after an illicit night of three-way fun, was nice, needed even. Snatch would get up and leave, not take the chance of getting caught in the bed with us, and she'd remain, giving me what I wished I'd get from him.

"He doesn't hate you," I counter, finally finding my voice. I'm not one hundred percent sure, even as the words flow easily from my mouth, that I'm actually telling the truth. I know he doesn't hate her; if he did he wouldn't give her the time of day, but we've not discussed her. He's made sure we aren't ever seen alone. In his mind, this will rid everyone of any suspicion of whatever the hell is going on between us.

"I told him I loved you guys and he shut me down."

I stiffen behind her, praying she doesn't notice.

Jesus, what a fucking mess.

"That probably wasn't the best idea," I mutter. "He's not capable of love or settling down. The world is nothing but a playground for him."

It takes all of my strength not to remind her that both of us have been nothing but honest about our expectations, or lack of them specifically, with her, but I know now isn't the time. I also know, having been friends with Snatch for so long and seeing how he's dealt with clingy women before, that unless he was pushed past his breaking point, he never would've been outright rude to her.

"He loves you," she mutters.

The wave of gooseflesh that covers every exposed inch of my skin is unnerving. Squeezing my eyes shut, I push the possibility out of my head. Allowing it to stay will only give me the same expectations Darby is struggling with, and that's not good for anyone involved.

"We're best friends," I say. "It's a different kind of care. It's not based on emotions, but an investment born of trial and tribulation."

"You may have explained it better, but he said the same thing." She buries her head in her pillow when the rattle of the locked door knob between mine and Snatch's can be heard. "I don't want to see him."

"I'll be back," I mutter, spine stiff and ready to fight.

I get he comes off as brusk and overly rude sometimes, but leaving her alone when she's upset, forcing me to deal with his mess, does nothing but piss me off.

Picking the words I plan to use with him in my mind when I leave my room, I'm startled when I see him leaving his own room at the same time.

He knows I'm seething just by looking at me when we make eye contact.

"I guess she's in there, huh?" He hitches his thumb in the direction of my closed bedroom door.

"I realize," I whisper-hiss only inches from his face, "that you're a complete asshole, even on your best day, but treating her like shit is an all-time low, even for you."

"Is that what she said?" he challenges, voice low enough as to not draw attention to us.

Not in so many words, but the end result is still the same.

"She's extremely upset," I inform him.

"Her emotional state is not my responsibility."

I close more of the distance between us, agitated beyond belief, cock hard with the need to turn my status quo submission into full-on domination.

"Do you really think pissing her off while she's holding your secret in her hands is the smartest thing?"

The corner of his lip twitches, a giant fuck-you to any contrition I'd hoped to find for upsetting her.

"Your secret, too," he mutters.

His words set a fire in my blood, pissing me off and somehow bringing joy at the same time. I step into him, hating how his eyes dart down the hall, checking to make sure we aren't being watched. It takes every ounce of self-control not to groan when his stiff cock presses against my own.

"I'm in the same boat as her," I say, voice filled with unspoken truths. "This isn't *our* secret; it's solely yours. I would walk out there, living room full of members and ride your cock just like I'd fuck one of the girls in front of them."

His eyelids go heavy, the bright pools of blue focused on my mouth.

"She needs to understand that this isn't a relationship," he states.

My pulse pounds in my ears, not knowing if he's just going to shut the whole thing down now. Instantly, I regret coming out here to confront him. From his tone, I can only presume that he's not only talking about his interactions with her but also the times we've been intimate.

"She says she loves us."

He nods, finally pulling his eyes from my mouth but making no attempt to shift his cock away from mine. "So she says."

"Would it be so bad," I offer.

He laughs. "Bad? Would it be bad to be in some fucked up, labeled, relationship with a club girl?"

"She's pretty awesome," I offer. "I know you enjoy fucking her."

"I fuck her," he responds immediately, "because that's what you want."

Not possible. Is he saying he's only with her because he thinks *I* need her around? I shake my head, unable to trudge through those possibilities right now.

Both our heads snap down the hall at a noise. He shoves against my chest when he realizes he can't move back because I've practically got him pinned to the wall. I turn back to him, hating the relief I see in his eyes when no one rounds the corner. It makes me as angry as I imagine Darby feels right now at his rejection.

"I don't think giving it a try with her is such a bad thing," I tell him, walking forward and lining my cock right back against him since the coast in now clear.

"You can't be serious. She fucks everyone in the clubhouse, Itchy."

I know this. She's very open about her sexuality, and shame isn't something I think she's ever felt. She's become a fan favorite with both Snake and Snapper.

I give him a look that says: *So? We fuck a lot too.*

"Really? When was the last time you fucked someone other than us? Other than the women we've tagged together?"

I search my memory. "I doubled with Darby and Snapper a while back, but only because I thought Snap was getting suspicious."

"Exactly," he mutters. "I hate to state the obvious man, but there's no such thing as love or being in a relationship when the woman who's asking for it is fucking anyone she can get between her legs. You can't turn a club girl into a housewife, Itchy. There's no sense in even trying."

I scowl at him.

"I know it's fucking harsh, but it's also fucking reality. Prove me wrong, and I'll admit that I'm mistaken."

I stare at him, knowing he's right but terrified of losing what we have with her. Without her means waiting until he loses control while we're out of the country, and those trips don't come as often as I need him.

"You haven't fucked anyone either," I tell him.

"I haven't. The only person I've been inside of outside of these two rooms is when I was buried deep in you in that shower."

Both of our cocks jerk in our jeans at the memory. I open my mouth to ask how he feels about us just going solo, leaving Darby to her own devices, but his words stop not only what I was planning to say, but also shuts down any idea I might have about a relationship with him.

"We fuck, the three of us. This isn't some fucking love fest thing going on. The last thing I need is anyone getting the wrong idea about where it's heading. If she can't separate orgasmic euphoria from love, that's her problem, not mine." His face hardens. "I won't fucking touch her again. I'm in no mood to have to deal with that crying shit in my room like I had to tonight."

Before I can ask, if he includes me in his 'banished from his cock' list, he shoves at my chest and disappears into his room.

Chapter 20

Snatch

"Hey, handsome."

I can barely keep my eyes from rolling at the purr Snapper emits the second I sat two places down from her on the sofa. I just want to relax, drink a beer in peace, but not in complete solitude. I'm an idiot for thinking that could be done around the red-headed demon of the clubhouse.

"Hey," I mutter back. I may not particularly like the woman, but I'm hardly ever just outright rude to anyone.

"Darby left," she says unprompted.

"Yeah," I respond, still not wanting to engage her.

I hadn't seen Darby since the argument we had in my bathroom several days ago. Club girls come and go, sometimes disappear for weeks at a time then show back up. Darby not being here the last couple of days isn't a rare occurrence.

"She said she wanted a different life," Snapper continues when I don't respond.

I nod and take a sip of my beer.

"She seemed really sad." Now this chick is just fishing. I can't stand people who dance around hard conversations. It's manipulative, almost as if she's trying to figure out what I know without divulging what info she's privileged to. The second the thought enters my head, I know how much of a hypocrite I am. I haven't spoken to Itchy since our argument in the hall. I'm too busy avoiding him to know if he's avoiding me too.

"Clubhouse life isn't for everyone," I give as my only answer.

"True," she whispers looking down at her hands.

My eye twitches, watching her out-of-character response. Snapper isn't one to get upset that female competition is lowered. Now, pull one of the male members, and she throws a shit fit. Neither she nor Gypsy were very happy when Misty showed up, even though Shadow hadn't touched either one of them in a long ass time if he ever did to begin with.

Snapper is devious on her best day, but she must think we're idiots if she's convinced herself we don't see right through her.

"Dude," Snake says walking into the room. "You forget where you're supposed to be?"

I look up at him like he's lost his mind.

"Jake's?" He angles his head even further. "I don't have a fucking clue what's got your head all fucked up, but you have been off the last couple of days."

"Fuck off man," I mutter, turning my beer back up to my lips.

"Ok," he says walking toward the door. "I'll let Shadow know you couldn't be bothered to keep an eye on Misty during her shift tonight. No big deal, not like you promised him yesterday when he asked or anything."

The light bulb goes off in my head, yesterday's memories flooding back in. I fucking hate it when Snake, of all people, is right about something. I grumble my displeasure and stand up from the sofa, ready to slap the smirk off his damn face when I pass him to climb on my bike.

"Asshole."

He chuckles and climbs on his bike as well. I look around the lot before cranking the engine on my Harley.

"The fuck is everybody?" The parking lot is all but empty. The SUVs are parked off to the side, never getting much use besides grocery shopping and Griffin's doctor's appointments. Kincaid's bike is in the lot, and so is Kid's, but that's the norm.

"Probably Jake's," Snake says with a shrug before cranking his bike and drowning out all ability to hear.

If everyone is at Jake's, why the hell am I heading there to keep an eye on Misty? I know the answer, and keeping your word even when what you promised is no longer necessary is crucial. I now recall speaking with Shadow yesterday, and he'll expect me there even if all but two members of the MC are sardined into Jake's.

The freedom I feel every time my bike is rumbling between my thighs doesn't fail me tonight. Years of riding and the sensation is always the same. Power yet limited control, and faith in the road are all present in the ten-minute ride over to Jake's.

I recognize a handful of bikes belonging to Cerberus, but as always, there are another couple of motorcycles that belong to locals. They're not club affiliated, but some decent guys who just stop in for a beer or two and sometimes chat with one of our guys. They aren't angling for intel or a chance to join our ranks. Everyone in town is well aware of our membership requirements, and unless you've served with us in the sand, you'll never wear a Cerberus patch on your back.

I sigh, the heavy rush of breath from my lips unavoidable when I see Itchy's bike tucked into his normal corner. Any other day I would've parked near him, but I opt to keep my distance here as well. With every intention of checking in with Shadow and confirming he doesn't need me, I don't plan to be here even long enough to order a beer.

Doug, the younger, beefed up brother of the bar's owner, greets me when I step inside.

"Busy tonight," he says when I start to walk past. "Jake loves it when you guys have a girl here."

I narrow my eyes at him, ready to defend Misty's honor even though I know nothing about her. Shadow has kept most of her info close to his chest. He may speak to Kid and Kincaid, but I've been so busy with my own shit, I haven't paid much attention to him.

"Yeah?" I close some of the distance, going for intimidation, but Doug is a little on the stupid side, so it doesn't even register with him. "Why's that?"

He points in the direction of the other MC members. "They drink a lot of beer and tip really well."

I nod, willing myself to calm down when I realize he doesn't mean anything derogatory about Misty or Em when she worked here months ago.

"Plus," he says conspiratorially as he leans in a little. "The other assholes who always break shit stay away when they see your bikes out front. That saves Jake money too."

I give him a goodhearted slap on the back. "Sounds like your big brother should be paying us to drink here."

He laughs, knowing how ridiculous the idea is. Jake's a penny pincher if I ever saw one. So much so, I'm surprised you don't have to feed the bathroom door a dollar before you can step inside.

The simple sound of Doug's laughter follows me further into the bar until it's drowned out by some sad ass country song blaring from the jukebox in the corner. I look at the end of the bar, confirming that Stephen, the saddest town drunk Farmington has ever seen, is here. The only time dance tunes and fast-paced country aren't playing is when his depressed ass manages to get to the selection list before anyone else.

Mostly filled with locals, the music playing doesn't deter anyone from having a good time. High top tables scattered all around are crowded with bar flies and one larger group of women, here for a bachelorette party judging by the sash and ridiculous veil one of them is wearing. All the women in that particular party are looking and giggling in the direction of my boys, attempting to entice them to have some fun or at least give them a little of their attention. Ace, Snake, Shadow, and Skid are all in our usual spot, paying no mind to the frisky wedding party.

I'm not surprised Itchy isn't at the table with the guys. He normally can't keep from trolling anytime he's outside of the walls of the clubhouse. Not wanting to stay, but unable to leave without seeing him, I order a beer from Misty when she walks up just as I'm sitting down.

I don't even bother talking to Shadow. The way he's glaring across the bar at Misty as she smiles at another patron while taking his drink order is not something I'm going to get in the middle of. I pull my eyes from my VP who can't admit he has major feelings for the mother of his child and scan the bar looking for the guy who's causing me just as many problems.

Itchy's not hard to find. Leather cut over his normal bright white shirt and perfectly groomed beard, he's across the bar leaning in whispering to a petite little brunette. His back is facing our direction, and I hate and love all at the same time the way his jeans stretch over the backs of his thighs. The need to run my hand over the tautness of his ass hits me hard.

"You're not armed are you?" My hand grazes the gun always at my back on instinct as I look up at Ace.

"What?"

"The way you're staring at him makes me wonder if you're going to shoot his ass before the night is over with."

I don't bother to respond to his nonsense, but my eyes catch Itchy as he stands to his full height at the bar. His arm goes around the shoulder of the pixie-like woman, and when they turn, I see her face for the first time. Nothing remarkable, other than the award winning smile spanning her face. She's beyond excited to be leaving with him as if she's won a raffle or an auction she's been saving all year to participate in.

I shoot daggers at him, our conversation coming to mind from a few days ago. I was an asshole, but I'm always an asshole. It's not my fault that Darby left. He knows I don't lie to women to placate them, so I don't understand what he's doing right now.

He avoids looking in our direction as they walk past Doug at the front door and leave. I really fucked things up with him. Had I known he was so attached to Darby, I might have handled things differently. Yet, here I sit, with an empty beer and Misty nowhere to be found as my best friend, my lover, the only person I can think of being intimate with walks out with a woman he probably isn't even attracted to but one he never bothered to offer to me. The game has changed, and I'm the asshole who is so fucked in the head I don't even know what the new rules are.

Chapter 21

Itchy

"It's amazing how quick the fucking sex traffickers pop up," Snake says with a sigh. He leans back in his chair, seeming to relax but keeping his eyes on his surroundings.

"It's like gray hairs, man. You take one out and three more pop up in their place." I run a hand over my beard.

I have no clue why we're even here tonight. Kincaid stayed back home, something to do with Em and a doctor's appointment. Shadow is heading up this mission, and he's been an asshole since our boots hit the ground in the rain forest days ago. He's got some kind of baby momma drama going on back home and seems intent to take it all out on us.

I slap the back of my neck, missing the damn mosquito that's been buzzing around my head for the last half hour. We're sitting, drinking beer, but relaxation isn't even an option when a larger percentage of the people in this bar would rather see us dead than succeed. We were able to this time. The twin girls we came after luckily had super slow traffickers and didn't have the chance to move them before we were on them. We discovered they were less than a couple of hours from getting the twenty-two-year-old women to their secondary purchaser, who possibly would've left the continent with them.

"Too close of a call," I mutter, keeping my eyes on Snatch across the bar. He seems hell bent on picking someone up tonight.

I can't really be mad. He's seen me walk out of numerous places in the last two months with my arm around a woman. Things have been off between us since Darby left. Fifty-four days since our argument in the hall, not that I'm counting or anything. Nearly eight weeks since he made it clear that fuck buddies are all Darby and I were to him. It's what he's relegated every sexual partner to. I can't argue with him. If this is how he wants to live his life, I have to accept it.

I sneer in his direction, hating the caramel-skinned woman even though I've never seen her before.

Sure I've walked out of half a dozen places wrapped around a woman, letting everyone believe I'm going home with them. Truth is, I drive them home or part ways in the parking lot. I guarantee when Snatch walks out of this bar with that woman, he'll have her on her back within minutes of getting her to a bed. Pretending to take women home may be what I do, but he's not the type.

I feel a nudge on my shoulder, so I cut my eyes in Snake's direction, refusing to give him one hundred percent of my attention. I don't want to miss watching Snatch walk out of here with her. I've been holding out hope, praying that eventually, he'd miss me as much as I miss him. I've lain awake at night waiting for the door knob joining our rooms to turn. I've waited to catch his eye across the room, knowing if he looks at me he'll know exactly what I'm feeling. I know when I see him walk out of here, just like I've done recently, I'll finally be able to start letting go.

"You don't seem very interested in pussy tonight," Snake observes.

I snort and take another long pull of my beer. "Last time I fucked a chick in Guatemala, I got crabs."

Snake, for the first time ever, looks contemplative rather than laughing at my reasoning. I figured I'd have to explain it was over six years ago, and the very reason everyone now calls me Itchy, but after the day we've had he either doesn't catch on or he's suffered the devastation a bad case of crotch crickets can bring. My bet is on the latter.

"You know," he says with all seriousness. "You can just keep your shit shaved and don't have to worry about that crap."

True, and if he were anyone else, I could easily explain just how well-groomed I am, but he's not the one to open up to with shit like that.

"How you haven't gone blind or insane from a raging case of syphilis is beyond me." I smile around the top of my beer.

"Or," he continues with a sparkle in his eye. "You can visit Amy down at the salon, and she can wax you."

My mouth gapes at his words. This guy looks like he hasn't showered in a month, but he goes to get salon treatments on his sac? No way.

"Seriously," he adds. "She's really gentle. After the second or third time, it doesn't even hurt anymore."

"You know this because Snapper went and told you about it?"

He shakes his head. "I go. Twice a month. They have this cream they rub on your..."

I hold my hand up stopping him. "Nope. Don't. Keep that shit to yourself. I'm not interested in Amy or the wondrous services she offers downtown."

"You need to loosen up. Maybe if you had your asshole bleached, you wouldn't walk around all uptight and pissed off at the world."

"The fuck are you talking about?"

He points across the bar, my eyes following the direction of his finger. My lip twitches in irritation at the sight of Snatch working the girl across the room.

"See? Something is fucking going on. You guys were best friends, practically stuck up each other's asses." I stiffen at his words because he has no idea how true his statement is. "Darby did something to ruin that, but listen, man. She's gone, and you guys need to get that friendship back. Everyone in the clubhouse is talking about how different you guys are. I feel like I'm living inside an episode of Dr. Phil or Oprah or some shit."

I force my eyes away from Snatch even though I can tell by the way the chick is responding that they'll be leaving soon. I turn toward Snake, ready to tell him to mind his own business, but in the split second I was stuck in my own damn head, he's started up a conversation with Ace.

My eyes glance over at Shadow, who looks about ready to spit fucking nails. Even Kid can't seem to calm him down, but I can tell by his posture that even as mad as he is at Misty for whatever the hell is going on, there's not one woman in the bar that's enough to pull his attention from his thoughts. He may be livid and pissed beyond belief, but he values whatever is going on with Misty, even when he doesn't have the courage to admit it to himself, much less her.

In my head, I tip my beer to him because I'm in the same spot. I'd hoped Snatch and I could at least get our friendship back, but the last couple of months have been brutal. I don't know what's worse. Having him in some capacity and losing him or if my life would've been easier just pining after him from a distance but maintaining our friendship.

When I look up to track down the waitress for another beer, I can't keep my eyes from sweeping the side of the bar where Snatch is.

Was.

He's gone. My head snaps to the only exit, not seeing them, I slide off my stool, unsure of what I'll do or say if I find them. I can always ask to participate, prove to him we can go back to the way things were. I'm willing to do that.

I wave off Snake when he begins to talk and make my way to the restroom. The chick Snatch was chatting up didn't look like the type that would require a bed or special attention. If I were a gambling man, I'd say she was a sure thing. I head to the long, dark hallway leading to the latrine. Several couples are full-on fucking down the corridor but Snatch and his conquest for the night aren't a part of the public lewdness.

I know one of the guys will cover my tab, so I head out the front, not bothering to stop back by the table on my way out. Our hotel is only a couple of blocks down, but I make sure not to rush. My full attention is on everything going on around me. The muggy, thick warmth of the night air sticks to my skin and clothes, leaving me agitated and too hot as I reach the outside entry of his hotel room.

I stand, waiting, for no other reason than I have no idea what to say after I knock. Hell, he could have gone back to her place. He could be fucking her in the alleyway that I didn't bother to check on my way out. My eyes dart to my door right next to his, wondering just how bad things will be if I push this issue with him.

I wipe my hands down the front of my jeans, a last ditch effort to build the courage that's nowhere to be found right now. I figure I have nothing to lose. Two months of not one single word, after years of everyday interaction, has been absolute torture. A punishment, if I'm going to suffer, I'm going to earn.

I clear my throat and bang on the door, making sure to take a step back so he can see me through the peephole. I may want to confront him about whatever the hell we had a few months ago, but I don't need to fucking get shot outside of some nasty ass hotel in Central America. My pockets would be empty and boots would be stripped off my feet before my lifeless body hit the concrete.

The knock goes unanswered, so I step up and pound on the door harder. I don't care if he's balls fucking deep in that chick from the bar, we're having this conversation tonight. Twice more I pound on the door, desperation filling my fists each time.

When the door is finally pulled open, I shove past him and step into his room.

"This shit ends tonight," I mutter, rounding on him as he closes and locks the door.

I expect a fist to the face, an argument at a minimum. What I don't expect is to see my best friend standing in his room, soaking wet and only wrapped in the thinnest of towels.

Chapter 22

Snatch

This shit ends tonight.

I almost want to laugh at his words.

He does his best to keep his eyes from my soaked torso. His efforts are futile, darting from the corners of the room and back repeatedly, without another word from him.

"Where's your company?" he asks with a thick swallow, not even hiding the fact he's lost his battle with looking away.

I stand, ignoring his question for the time being, willing my cock to stay in control, but I lose my own struggle as well.

"The chick?"

He nods. I want to ask him why he's worried now. I want to remind him of all of the times I watched him leave a bar or club with some chick. Let him know how much sleep I lost imagining what he was doing to them, what he was letting them do to him.

"Don't worry about it," I mutter.

"Don't," he hisses with more backbone than I'd ever expect from him. Itchy isn't a push over on any level, but there's a definite dominant personality between the two of us and it sure as hell isn't him.

I cock an eyebrow at him, daring him to challenge me, but the look in his eyes says he's willing to face off with me, go head to head, and fuck if it doesn't make my cock throb behind the thin, scratchy material of the hotel towel.

Defiance is twisting the corner of his mouth into a sneer, he takes another step closer to me. I stand my ground if only to lessen the time when our bodies touch.

"Did you send her away?" he asks, close enough that I can smell his cologne mixed with the tangy sweet from the beer he drank back at the bar. "Or did you fuck her in the alley and send her on her way?"

I get lost momentarily, drowning almost in the fire in his eyes. An audible groan filters out of me when his tongue inches out and wets his lips.

"Neither," I answer with a huskiness in my voice I barely recognize. "I sent her on her way the second we stepped outside."

I hate that he's drawing this confession from me with no effort at all. I hate that I'm not indifferent enough to just take some random chick home and fuck her until I feel better, plow into her until sinking into her body erases the memories of sinking into his.

"You didn't want her." The statement doesn't even surprise me. Intuition being one of his special skills, he's reading me like a fucking book. "Why not?"

"I didn't want *her*," I answer without hesitation. I clutch my fingers into fists repeatedly, the tips tingling with an unnerving urge to touch him.

"No?" I shake my head in the negative. "Who then?"

"You," I croak as his fingers tease the edge of my towel below my navel.

"That so?"

Warmth covers every inch of my skin when his deft fingers untangle the towel from my body, and it flutters to the ground. My cock, proud and thick jumps, reaching up toward the hand still resting on my stomach. Labored breathing rushes past my lips in harsh, uneven pants.

"Please," I beg when he makes no move to ease the need flowing through my body. The simple grip of his fist around my straining cock would solve a litany of problems, every one of them in fact.

I shudder when his fingers trace the stars tattooed on my abdomen.

"That's not how tonight is going to go," he says close enough to my mouth that I feel the heat of his breath on my lips.

"What do you want?" I ask, stopping short of telling him I'll give him anything he desires.

My breathing hitches when his lips brush against mine with the slightest pressure, enough to let me know he's there but leaving me wanting so much more. I've licked his come from Darby's skin, he's sucked my cock, and taken my release into his own body, but that gentle sweep of his lips on mine seems infinitely more intimate than any other touch we've shared. I didn't realize how much I needed the simple action until he had the courage to take that step.

"I'm going to fuck your mouth." His tongue breaches his own lips, tracing the outline of mine.

It sets me on fire, the slow burn of every other interaction finally blazing with the force of a thousand forest fires. A half step forward on my part has my chest against his t-shirt and my cock resting against his own erection that's straining in his jeans.

Our lips meet with deliberation and need like I've never felt before. My hands find the tangle of his hair, beard brushing against my chin. The coarseness, I realize, is something I've needed all along. The rough grip of his hands, one at my naked hip and the other clawing at the back of my head, only fuels the urgency of our lips as they tangle together.

"On your knees," he insists, nipping at my bottom lip and leaving a sting sharp enough to make my breath catch.

At his command, my body buckles and I'm resting at his feet as if I've always belonged there. Surprise lights up his face, crinkling the skin at the corners of his eyes. He's as shocked as I am to be in this position, but my mouth waters for him. It has for months. Fear of his rejection, no matter how unfounded, and my own stupidity at trying to fight what was going on between us kept me from this exact situation. I'm done fighting it. I'm done listening to the tiny voice in my head telling me to fight against the urgency I feel in my gut to own him, to be owned *by* him. I can no longer ignore the need my body demands to be fed. I refuse to give into the part of my past, the whispers I heard as a child that instilled the thought that what we've been doing is depraved and an act against God himself. I've got other sins I'll need to atone for that don't hold a candle to what I'm about to do right now.

I reach for his zipper, mouth continuing to flood with anticipation, only to have my hands knocked away.

"Your mouth," he hisses as his zipper lowers and his strong hands pull his cock from its fabric confines.

My body trembles with near seizure like convulsions as my tongue tastes him for the first time. His body responds in kind nearly jerking from my mouth when I wrap my lips around him. The feral rumble in his chest at my eagerness as I take him too far down my throat urges me on even though I'm gagging around him.

With strength I don't possess, he shifts his hips back allowing the relief I need.

"Fuck, so eager," he grunts. "Go slower."

I shake my head before muttering, "I can't."

I swallow him again, the pressure of my fingers digging into his thighs sure to leave marks. I work him in and out of my mouth, more with enthusiasm than skill I possess, but I can't be fucking it up too much because he's moaning foul, disgusting things that he wants to do to me and pumping his hips, stroking his cock along my tongue and lips as I hold my head static. He insisted he wanted to fuck my mouth, so I'm giving him the chance to take what he needs.

Unlike my reaction to him, he doesn't take advantage, but he doesn't ease into my waiting mouth either. There is no doubt right now who is in control. Not only is he taking from me; I'm relinquishing everything I have to him.

"Oh fuck," he hisses just as I begin to choke on his heated flood.

My eyes water when he grips the back of my head and holds me in place, the pulse of his cock jetting his come down my throat. Greedy swallows of my working throat take all he has, feeling near bereft when he's through. It wasn't enough just now, and I have a sinking feeling mixing with absolute joy that it may never be enough.

"Damn it. I could fuck your mouth for hours." Husky and barely sated, his voice and declaration make me smile as his still semi-hard cock falls wetly from my mouth.

"Yet you busted in three minutes flat."

I remain on my knees because this is his show and I don't know what he expects from me. Waiting for his next command, however, does not keep my hand from finding and stroking the rock hard length between my thighs.

"How do I taste?" he asks sweeping his thumb at the corner of my mouth, swiping some of his wetness. He presses his thumb against my lips, and on instinct, I open for him.

"Amazing," I answer against his thumb.

"I hated not seeing you lick my come off of Darby's stomach. I would've fed it to you directly," he adds. "All you had to do was ask."

His digit slips free of my mouth. "I couldn't. I didn't know how."

He frowns down at me but doesn't say anything about the lost opportunities that have plagued us for months.

"What are we going to do with that?" I follow his finger as it points to my cock, my hands still stroking it.

I grin up at him, still unsure of asking for what I need.

"Quid pro quo?" I raise my eyebrows in heated anticipation of his answer, the Latin easier to say.

"This for that, huh?" I nod. "You don't want me to suck your cock."

I tilt my head in confusion as he takes a step back and indicates for me to stand. I oblige, only to take another step toward him. I reach for the hem of his t-shirt and pull it over his head as he kicks off his boots and jeans, something he didn't bother discarding while I sucked him off.

His lips meet the piercing through my nipple. The scorching heat of his mouth arrowing to my cock at the prospect of him using it there soon. Lips and teeth kiss and nip over my pectoral to my neck. I moan and ease my head to the side, giving him the access he needs to bite at the tense muscles in my neck.

"You want me to start with your cock in my mouth." His devious words cause a cold chill to race over every exposed inch of my body. "But you want to finish buried deep in my ass."

Fuck. I nearly come just at his words.

"Are you a mind reader now?" I chuckle when I feel his lips turn up into a smile against my skin.

"I know you, Snatch," he pants near my mouth, his lips ghosting on the edge. "I know you'd always rather come buried deep than inside a mouth."

I grip the back of his head, holding him against me when his lips kiss mine in earnest. My tongue sweeps his, dueling, tangling, fighting to taste every inch of his mouth. He pulls away long before I'm ready, smiling when I groan in agitation against his lips.

He breaks contact with me, and I watch as he walks to his jeans and grabs a small packet I recognize as lube from his discarded jeans.

"Prepared?" I ask as he lays it on the bedside table.

"A man can hope," he answers, and my cock jumps at the knowledge that he's been wanting me exactly where I've longed to be since Costa Rica. "The conditioner wasn't quite enough last time."

I frown at the thought that I may have hurt him.

"Don't overthink it," he mutters against my stomach, tracing my tattoos with the tip of his tongue as he lowers to his knees. "I loved every second of it."

I groan when his tongue tastes the sensitive triangle on the underside of my cock. "I've been waiting, praying, hoping it would happen again."

He punctuates each word with a heated swipe of his talented tongue. I know where I want this night to end, but if he doesn't relinquish my cock soon, I'll end up finishing in his mouth.

"I can't," I moan, still unable to move back, still unable to ask him to stop.

As if being controlled by the devil himself, he cups my sac in one hand and his other trails along my upper thigh between my legs. I nearly crumble on top of him when his finger toys with my taint and even further until he's teasing the puckered opening an inch higher.

"Oh God," I mutter, reaching behind me to clasp the edge of the nightstand. "I'm gonna come."

Akin to being doused in cold water, he releases me immediately. The cool air surrounding us spreads over the wetness left by his mouth. My body wars with the change of sensation.

"That's not what you want is it?" The devious look in his eyes informs me he's somehow maintained his control where mine has not only waned but disappeared altogether.

I scrub at my blurry eyes with the palms of my hands. "Fuck, I don't know what I want."

He stands, hand still stroking my cock, enough to know he's there but not enough to finish me off.

"Yes you do," he whispers against my lips.

His lips and his hand leave me, and I reach for him as he turns to bend over.

"No," I manage. "On your back, on the bed."

Swift confusion marks his brow.

"I want my mouth on yours," I explain grabbing the mini packet of lube and tearing the top off of it with my mouth.

"I want that, too," he says climbing on the bed.

Stroking the lube up and down my cock, I position myself between his thighs. My free hand runs up and down the length of his rock hard cock at first before he takes over and my fingers begin their exploration of where I want to be.

"Let me in," I mumble as his body resists my initial intrusion.

Finally, after some gentle coaxing, he relaxes. One finger is eventually joined with another and a third.

"Damn it," he pants. "That feels amazing. I can come just from that."

"Not until I'm inside of you," I plead.

"Hurry," he begs, rubbing his hand up and down his length faster.

The laugh that was trying to escape turns into a hiss when my cock replaces my fingers.

"Fuck, you're so hot." In one slow, but uninterrupted push I invade his body, unable to control the depth of the delivery. My thighs against his, I look down and marvel at the sight of myself fully seated inside of him. I didn't get this glorious of a view in Costa Rica.

"Move," he demands. "Please."

"I'll come," I complain, not wanting it to end anytime soon, if ever.

His hand squeezes his cock even harder, the angry head glistening with his need to come. "That's the point."

I huff out a laugh at his reasoning but pull my hips back. Four inches is all I allow myself to leave his body, my cock sliding against his sensitive tissues.

"Snatch!" he practically screams when my eyes stay on my unmoving cock a little too long.

Urged into action, I slide back in and out several times. The grunt that leaves his lips pulls my eyes to his. Heavy with lust, they plead with me to put us both out of our misery, so I do. I slam into him repeatedly until he's a mess of sensation wiggling under me.

"I'm going to come for you," he confesses. Just like in Costa Rica, the throb of his own orgasm rips mine to the surface.

"For you," I cry out as my release rips from my body in an almost satanic explosion.

Still inside of him, I lean forward and brush my lips against his, my first initiation of a kiss, one I couldn't resist even if I wanted to, which I don't.

"I wanted to kiss you while I fucked you," I say with an apology.

"Yet, you busted in less than two minutes," he says playfully, not only throwing my words from earlier back at me but reminding me that I came even faster than he did.

I smile against his lips before we once again become a tangle of arms and tongues.

With reluctance, we pull away from each other, grab a quick shower and crawl back into bed. I'm so thankful that this is my room and not his. I wouldn't have known what to do with myself after, but Itchy being Itchy he just crawled in the bed like he owned the damn place.

"I've missed spending time with you," he confesses fifteen minutes later into the darkness.

The tiny stream of light filtering through the curtains catches the corner of his eye and the small frown playing on his lips.

"You've been taking women home from bars, fucking everything that walks. Not once have you knocked on my door at the clubhouse. Not once have you indicated you wanted to keep doing this," I counter.

He sighs, and I feel the bed move enough to know he's turned his head and is looking in my direction even though my face is lost in the shadows.

"Did you have any intention of fucking that woman tonight?"

I run the events of the evening through my head. "Maybe at first, but the second we stepped outside, I knew no matter how hard I fucked her, I'd be unsatisfied when it was over."

Itchy's hand reaches out, caressing the hairless skin of my chest. It anchors me. "What you did tonight with that woman is the exact same thing I've done with every person I've left the bar with the last couple of months."

My head snaps in his direction, and I curse the lack of light I was so grateful for when we climbed into bed earlier.

"What?" I hiss.

"You and Darby are the last people I fucked."

I could strangle him and kiss him stupid at the same time.

"You were purposely trying to make me jealous?"

He laughs at my words, and I begin to lean more toward strangling. "You were jealous?"

I pause, knowing a confession of that magnitude has the ability to change the dynamic between us, so I refuse to verbalize what we both already know.

"I was hurting," he says when I don't respond to his question. "I was giving you space and what I thought you wanted."

What I wanted?

I turn my body, angling in his direction. His hand readjusts on my hip.

"This is what I want." His sharp intake of breath tells me he's just as surprised as I am at my words.

"You said in the hallway that we fuck, that sex is all it was, all it will ever be." The pain in his voice creates an ache in mine.

"I was talking about Darby," I mutter. "I can't deal with woman drama. You know that."

"You can't deal with relationship drama," he counters.

Fuck, that word freaks me out now, but for some reason, it doesn't cause as much stress as when Darby was asking for something I'd never been able to give before.

"I wasn't talking about you," I insist.

"You want this? You want an *us*?"

Damn it. He's going to make me actually say it.

"I like what we have, but I'm nowhere even near ready to tell anyone."

"I understand," he whispers.

"Is this enough for you?" I need to know the truth and pray he gives it to me straight.

"I'd rather have you in secret than not at all," he answers leaning in to take my mouth with such fever that I know we won't be going to sleep anytime soon.

Chapter 23

Itchy

"Worst fucking day ever," I grumble as I kick my boots off, shed my jeans, and crawl into the bed.

"Yep," Snatch agrees as he strips naked and climbs in with me. "Where's Ace?"

I shrug because who really knows where that man is? "He just told me not to wait up, and I got the impression he's not coming back tonight."

Snatch chuckles as his fist punches the pillow to situate it perfectly under his head. We're in Canada, sent out to find a set of missing, eight-year-old twin boys. We did find them. Unfortunately they'd snuck off in the middle of the night from their camping ground a few nights ago and fell to their death down a ravine.

"Did you see Shadow? I think today destroyed him." My words are soft, as they should be, talking about such a tragic outcome.

"Griff is only like seven months old, but I know he imagined himself in that situation, and it seriously fucked him up." He turns his body facing me but hasn't reached out to touch my skin yet. I long for that simple touch, a kind embrace after the horrific day.

"I don't think I'll ever get rid of the sound of the father crying when we returned with the bodies of his precious children." My throat is clogged with emotion, making my voice rough and barely audible. Tears burn the back of my eyes. I'm not much of a crier, but today was more than fucked up.

"I can't even imagine," Snatch agrees. "Fuck, I never want to be a parent. Just the chance of something like that happening is enough to keep me from fatherhood."

I nod in agreement. Unable to resist him being so close yet so far away, I run my hand over his shoulder. His tattooed hand covers mine as it settles above his beating heart.

In silence, we both stare at nothing in particular, running through the events of the day.

"The weather's so nice up here this time of year," Snatch says, breaking the quiet calm that has settled over us. "I really thought we'd find them alive."

"I know. Me, too." I scoot closer to him wanting the warmth of his body against mine.

Releasing my hand, his arm snakes around my back as he pulls me tighter to his chest. When I'd imagined us being together, my first thoughts were about all of the fantastic sex we'd be having, and believe me there's plenty of that when we can find time away with each other. I'd never allowed myself to consider that we'd be like this, snuggled against one another, talking like a regular couple. We normally get pretty fucking physical, our opportunities to be with one another so few and far between we tear into one another when the chance presents itself.

Tonight is different. Sexual electricity isn't crackling in the air; my cock isn't twitching against his leg in anticipation. The heaviness of the day is too much of a burden to increase expectations of sexual fulfillment. If I'm being honest, this right here, my arms wrapped around him, his heartbeat echoing in my ear is more than I could ever ask for from him.

"Speaking of Shadow," I mention trying to make some of the heartbreak dissipate. "He was watching you like a hawk at the bar the other day."

I grin against his jolting chest when he chuckles.

"When I left with those two women?"

"Yeah. I kept stealing glances at him, and I could practically see the cogs in his brain turning trying to figure it out. If he's suspicious then the others have to be wondering what's going on as well. We may need to tone down the hate in public a little bit."

His fingers begin to trail lightly up and down my spine, and it makes me want to rub against him, purr like a cat, and beg for more.

"You're the one who told them you wanted separate rooms a few months back when you were pissed at me." His voice is playful, but it's the edge of accusation that I focus on. We've missed numerous circumstances where we could be together while on missions, but my insistence on not staying in the room with him has carried over and become a pain in the ass rather than the reprieve I'd needed months ago.

I push off of his chest, so that I'm looking down at him. "I told you I was giving you the space you needed."

A small, sad smile tugs at the corners of his lips. "And I told you that what I said to Darby almost six months ago was not meant for you."

I could choke him for his stubbornness.

"Yes. You told me that, but it was after I'd requested separate rooms."

He sighs, his frustration obviously increasing as well.

I don't want to fight with him. I'm not interested in arguing points he's so unwilling to budge on. Every time the conversation steers in this direction we go days without speaking to each other, and we're both miserable assholes until one of us caves, usually me, and apologizes to the other. The only problem is no matter the number of times we fight about it, the outcome never changes.

His hand that was still resting against my back even after I sat up to face him falls away. Bringing it to his face, he scrubs over his eyes. Annoyance is evident in his long sigh, and most days I would care. Today is not that day. I hate the time we're forced to spend apart. I hate the plan we both decided would work best.

If we continued to pretend like we hated each other, suspicions would be kept low, but it's so different to how we were before that our staged discord and ambivalence with each other is throwing up more red flags than if we just acted like normal.

But, there's an issue with normal also. I catch myself watching him, following his movements with my eyes. I catch myself licking my lips when his muscles flex. I fucking groaned the other day when he bent over in my favorite pair of jeans to grab something out of the fridge. Snake was around when that slip up happened. So wrapped up in the sight of his ass, I wasn't able to play off my reaction very well.

I know if we go back to old hat, hanging out, fucking every chick who makes our cocks twitch, there will be no way for me to keep my hands off of him. My blood burns hotter just when he's in the room, making me feel like a teenage boy, not with sexual need and urges, but need for him alone. Never feeling like this about someone before is brand new, and I'm like an idiot who can't get enough, damn the consequences.

"Are we going to do this again?" His eyes dart between mine, asking, begging not to say a word. He hasn't pushed me away and climbed out of bed, which is a normal reaction, so I guess we're making progress.

"They won't care," I cajole, fingers tracing over the numerous tattoos on his abdomen.

His head tilts back, resting against the pillow. To anyone else, it would look relaxed albeit slightly annoyed, but the twitching muscle in his jaw and the tension in his corded neck muscles are enough to make me pull my hand from his skin.

"I care," he says finally. "I'm not ready to tell anyone."

Shit. I'm fucking this up. I hate that I push him, but I can't seem to help myself.

"Will you ever be ready?" I ask even though I know what's coming. I hope my insistence doesn't change what we have.

His eyes only find mine for the briefest of seconds before he stares off into the room, looking at nothing but unable to continue looking at me.

"I don't know," he mutters.

I nod, grateful for his honesty, happy that he's not placating me like some dirty little secret he wants to stay attached to so he lies to keep me by his side.

What we have is enough for now, but I don't know how long that will last for me. I'm terrified at the other guys finding out, fearful they will be unaccepting of what we have, but not so much that I want to sneak around, living in secret for all of eternity.

"Fair enough," I say, shooting for satisfied but falling short.

His eyes finally find mine, searching, trying to determine if I'm telling him the truth after his candor. He must find what he's looking for because he reaches for me, no words spoken, and pulls me back against his chest. I soak him in, take everything he's offering because I have no idea how much longer it will last.

Chapter 24

Snatch

My eyes jerk wide open when a shuffle at the end of the bed pulls me from a dead sleep. Getting lost in our time together is dangerous, but it's like my training and years of experience fly out the window when we're touching.

I track a stumbling Ace as he, for the second time, bumps into the end of the bed Itchy and I shared last night. He grumbles and curses, but his head never looks over at us, concentrating too hard on getting his clearly drunk ass into the restroom.

I groan as Itchy's sleepy hand trails down my abs and settles low on my stomach, the bottom of his palm resting against the tip of my rock hard cock. My dick has no fucks to give that someone who could blow this entire situation out of the water is nearby. It jerks with need and glistens for any attention, even in sleep, that Itchy's willing to give.

In a moment of surprising sanity, I grip his wrist and move it off of my body.

He grumbles, eyes peeking up at me, barely visible in the darkness when I begin to climb off of the bed.

"Don't leave me," he whispers.

My heart clenches, pulse pounding in my ears at his vulnerability. I want nothing more than to stay here with him, but I know it's not an option.

"Ace is in the shower," I warn against his mouth planting a quick kiss on his soft lips.

"You didn't fuck me," he practically whines stubbornly refusing to kiss me back.

"Just know that my cock is hard for you, always," I tell him.

Only then does he smile against my mouth and return my kiss.

I pull away, dress in record time, and head to the door when I hear his quiet voice again. "Back to hating the love of my life again."

Sadness washes over me, my heart breaking with every step I take away from his bed. All I want to do is wallow in self-pity and catch a little more sleep. Laying down and turning the world off is about the only thing that's going to keep me from saying *fuck it* and crawling back in bed with Itchy. I missed the brush of his warm skin against mine the second I pulled away, but it's the pain in his voice when I walked away that is pulling me to him the most.

"Hey," Kid mutters as I open the door to the small cabin we were assigned when we arrived in Canada.

I look to his right, out the window which gives him a clear damn view of the front door of Itchy's cabin.

"You guys must be getting along better," he says on a yawn scrubbing his hands down his face.

My quickening pulse pounds in my ears and a million scenarios and lies are already formulating on the tip of my tongue.

"What?" Simple enough right? Move along Kid, nothing to see here.

He angles his head at the window. "You must be getting along if you're banging chicks together again."

My eyes narrow at him, wondering if he's setting me up. He's not really the type, but stranger things have happened recently.

"Two actually," I lie with what I hope appears to be a mischievous glint in my eye.

He huffs a humorless laugh while shaking his head. "One of these days you'll find the one chick who turns your world upside down, and you won't even notice all the others around you."

It's my turn to laugh. "Sorry, Kid. I know you love Khloe and plan to spend the rest of your life with her, but there's not a woman in the world that would make me want to forsake all others."

With deliberate slowness I see his eyes look out the window one last time before turning back to me. "Yeah. I guess there's not a woman out there tempting enough to make you change your ways."

I'm granted a reprieve when he stands from the end of the bed and heads into the bathroom. Statue-like and unable to formulate an active thought, I stand in the middle of the room, eyes darting from the bathroom door to the window. If Kid doesn't know what's going on, he is making very educated guesses.

"The fuck?" he mutters pulling my attention from wherever my mind retreated.

I look over, finding him running a towel through his damn hair. He's shirtless but in jeans and socks.

"Have you been standing there the entire time I showered?" His lip twitches up, but he glances out of the window again. I know it's coming. No matter how unprepared I am, no matter how undecided I am to confess or lie, my world is going to come crashing down.

"No?" I answer it as a question because I'm not certain where my head was at or how long I've been standing here.

"Sure looks like," he persists as he sits on the edge of his bed to pull on his boots. "Want to talk about whatever is bothering you?"

"I'm fine, dude. Nothing to talk about." I busy myself grabbing a change of clean clothes out of my duffel bag. Keeping my back to him will make it easier to tell my truths no matter how bad I want to keep my secrets locked away from the world.

And I wait and wait. The silence drags on so long, I'm forced to turn around and look at him. Expecting to find a smirk on his lips as if I've fallen into his traps and he needs to gloat about it, I'm surprised to see him smiling and looking down at his phone, no doubt already texting Khloe this morning.

I take the opportunity his distraction provides and high-tail it to the bathroom for a quick shower. I ignore the ache in my balls I always get when I'm around Itchy and try to forget that we held each other all night, opting for closeness and comfort instead of orgasms and carnal bliss.

Still, I take my time, avoiding Kid and vowing to stay as far away from him as possible. My chest hurts by the time I turn off the water and climb out. I know Itchy and I have to double our efforts at being less suspicious. The entire time while showering I was going through the many interactions we've had, all the times we've been within arm's reach of each other and I can't pinpoint one single moment where either of us would've acted in a way that would make anyone suspect a sexual relationship other than one in which we fuck a woman together. Everyone in the clubhouse knows we do that, but as far as everyone else is concerned, we should just seem like two dudes who like to have three-ways.

I run the soft towel over my body, wiping away water droplets from my heavily inked skin before throwing on my clothes and leaving the bathroom.

"What time are we leaving?" I ask Kid as I pull socks from my duffel and sit down to get my boots on.

He takes his eyes off of his phone for the briefest of seconds before he returns his attention back to the small device he can't seem to go but a couple of minutes without looking at.

"We have to go back to the station and show them the location of the meth house we found yesterday while looking for the boys. I think after that we're heading out," he finally says after laughing at something on his phone.

"Meth house?" I ask.

We'd split up yesterday into two groups. The group I was in was unfortunate enough to locate the bodies. Afterward, we were all so upset the discovery of a meth house came secondary. If it was mentioned in my presence, I tuned it out.

"Yeah, about four miles in past that ridge we separated out," he confirms. "It wasn't top priority at the time, but we just can't let it go."

I nod in agreement.

"Where did you guys find chicks to fuck last night?"

I frown, shoving my dirty clothes into my bag and zipping the top. I should've known he wasn't going to leave the conversation alone.

"You looking for something on the side?" I ask knowing he isn't but any opportunity to pull attention away from Itchy's and my evening activities I'm going to take.

"You know better than that," he scoffs. "I just know Ace disappeared and so did you two."

"We ran into them at that little café after dinner last night. Seems Canadian women are similar to American women and have the hots for guys with tattoos and beards." I wink at him, taking it a step too far and wanting to kick my own ass for my cavalier attitude about non-existent women.

"Ace didn't join you?"

Why can't this fucker just leave it alone, or come right out and ask me?

"I wouldn't fuck Ace with your dick." I cringe at my word choice. "I mean I wouldn't share a woman with him if it was the last choice on Earth."

He laughs, catching my words if the smile playing at the corner of his mouth is any indication. "No, I guess you guys wouldn't."

"Ready?" I ask slinging the strap of my duffel over my shoulder and heading for the door.

He follows me out, and I distance myself immediately, choosing avoidance rather than sticking around and giving him the chance to dance around asking me what it's clear he wants to.

I pull out my phone on the way to the SUVs and type out a text to Itchy giving him the cover story I gave to Kid.

Fine, is the only text I get back from him.

I know he's upset I won't tell the others, but the fallout from that situation isn't one I'm planning on going through anytime soon.

Chapter 25

Itchy

Snatch: *I need you*

I stare down at my phone, smiling more than I should in mixed company, but I couldn't resist the emotion if I wanted to.

Looking around the living room, I formulate a plan to get up and make my exit. It's more difficult than it seems. We're all hanging out after returning from Canada yesterday. The sun hasn't even begun to sink low in the sky. If I feign not feeling well, Snapper is going to be on my dick trying to play nurse, so that's not an option. Saying I'm tired won't fly either because I'm usually one of the last ones to go to bed each night.

Fuck it. I'll just stand up and leave. That doesn't go over well either.

"Where are you going?" Snapper asks with a hand on my forearm, preventing me from leaving without giving a reason.

I'm agitated, annoyed that she's even questioning me but more because I hate having to hide. Not that I think it would ever happen, but even if we came out to everyone, I'd give up this club if it meant pursuing something real between Snatch and me.

I pull my arm from her grasp with more patience than I'm feeling and look down at her. "I got shit to do."

"I bet you do," she mutters.

The same trepidation I felt when she confronted me a couple of months ago sits heavy in my gut, but I walk away from her without another word. I can't confirm who is watching me as I leave because I don't turn back to see, but I can feel several pairs of eyes on my back as I hit the hallway leading to my room.

"Hey," Khloe says coming out of her room.

A genuine smile plays on my lips as I stop to talk to her.

"Long time no see," I tease.

"Ugh," she groans. "Mid-terms are going to kill me."

"Hardly," I counter. "You got this. I'm just glad to see you taking a breather."

"Kid is forcing me out, told me I have to socialize a little because people forgot what my face looked like." She smiles up at me, but I know she's glad for the break.

"No one could forget your beautiful face," I tell her shifting to the side so she can walk past me in the narrow hallway.

She laughs, her grin growing wider.

"Seriously," I say placing my hands on her shoulders, so she looks up at me. "We miss you, kiddo."

"I wanted to talk to you," she begins but is interrupted by Kid who no doubt thought she was avoiding leaving her school work and is coming to retrieve her.

He tilts his head, narrowing his possessive eyes as he closes the distance between us. "What's going on?"

I take a step back, the look on his face so questioning that I can't help but wonder if he's concerned about me trying to push up on Khloe.

She turns her attention to him, leaning on his shoulder when his greedy arm wraps around her back, and he pulls her against him.

"Itchy was giving me hell just like you have been about not showing my face around. Seems you're not the only one who misses me." She kisses his cheek, but his eyes stay trained on mine.

He's searching my face, and after not finding anything untoward going on, looks down at his girl. "I told you, Sweet Girl."

"You coming out there?" Khloe asks when Kid turns her toward the door leading into the living room.

Fuck.

"Umm." I do my best to think of a lie, but standing here on the spot like this no words come.

"You look tired," she says. "I figured you were going to grab a nap or something."

I nod but don't miss her eyes as they look at Snatch's door instead of mine. She winks at me and disappears with Kid.

Keeping up pretenses, I head into my room instead of his, making sure the door is locked and secure before heading straight to Snatch's door. The world is forgotten when I step into his room finding him in all of his naked glory, stretched out on the bed, huge hand already fisting his hard cock.

"Jesus, you're a sight," I say pulling my t-shirt over my head.

"I need your cock," he grunts with a hard downward stroke.

My hands still on the zipper of my jeans. "You're gonna let me..."

"In my mouth," he corrects at the implication of taking his ass for the first time.

"Will I ever?" I strip out of the rest of my clothes, needing him in any capacity so bad I don't care how this ends. I know we'll both come, and other than just actually spending time with him, that's what matters.

"Not tonight," he answers with no further information.

I climb on the bed, straddling his chest, cock pointed directly at his mouth.

"Fine," I say. "Suck my cock then."

He grins up at me but doesn't reach for the erection that's already glistening at the tip.

"So demanding." He reaches up and pulls me down by the shoulders until my mouth is hovering over his. "Kiss me."

Not even a fraction of a second passes before my mouth is on his and my tongue is swirling around. Both groaning, we dive into the action like we may never get to do it again. Intuition has my hips shifting back, my cock rubbing against his as we take each other's mouths.

"I love the scratch of your beard on my face," he confesses against my lips when we finally manage to come up for air.

I nip his bottom lip. "Never thought you'd be hard for someone with so much hair, huh?"

"This entire situation is something I never could've imagined happening." I grin down at him, but his words aren't playful. They've turned as serious as the hand that reaches up and cups my jaw, fingers tangling in my beard.

"Jaxon," I whisper.

His eyes soften at my use of his given name. I can't recall using it but a handful of times since we met in boot camp. Last names were always the norm in the military until his nickname took over. Right now though? They sound too impersonal, and there is nothing impersonal about the way he's looking up at me right now.

"If you call me that in front of the guys they're going to suspect something," he teases.

I nearly tell him about my weird interaction with Khloe in the hallway, which also reminds me about the suspicions I feel like Snapper has, but I know it will ruin the moment. A sinking feeling in my gut that things are going to take a turn for the worse soon keep my lips sealed tight.

"I won't," I promise, kissing his lips one last time before getting back up on my knees. "Now, suck my cock."

He chuckles, his warm breath ghosting over the tip, but it's followed by the scorching heat of his mouth. My hand finds the contour of his face, thumb rubbing over the pierced star on his cheek. I leave my hips static, forcing him to work his neck to take my cock. I seldom have control over our interactions, and I'm taking every inch he's willing to give, figuratively now and literally very soon.

For a guy who's only sucked cock less than a handful of times, he's like a Goddamn blowjob savant. His mouth works down my length, hand working over the base that he's unable to take at this angle. Twisting at the top, thumb stroking over that perfect spot on the underside on his upstroke. My thighs begin to tremble from the adept use of his lips and tongue.

"You want me to come in your mouth?"

He nods, never relenting his efforts.

"I'd rather come on your stomach while you're fucking my ass," I pant nearly failing at not spurting down his throat.

He releases me with pop, keen on my suggestion. I tilt to the edge, him holding my thighs, so I don't tumble to the floor and reach inside his nightstand, knowing he keeps lube stocked in there.

His hand is already extended in my direction by the time I pop the lid on the KY. A second later the cold liquid is spread from the bottom of my nuts to the eager pucker of my ass. He groans when I hiss as he breaches me for the first time in weeks.

I bite at the muscles of his chest and neck, licking at the pulse pounding below his ear. One finger gives way to two. The third coming shortly after is enough to arch my back as a pleasure filled gasp escapes my lips.

I actually whimper with need when he pulls his fingers free and teases me with the head of his cock.

"You ready?" he asks barely audible.

"Yes." My eyes slam shut as he slowly guides himself inside of me.

"I'll never get used to how fucking hot you are," he mutters sliding in another couple of inches. I lower as he pushes his hips up, meeting in the middle until he's fully seated.

My hands find his pecs, fingers splayed wide as I begin a slow rhythm, needing this to last. Tender, overstimulated tissue grips him, pulling him deeper refusing to let go. Pleasure and pain have always been a huge turn on for me, something I would seek in almost every sexual encounter, but this is beyond all of that.

I hiss, eyes going wide when Snatch's fist wraps around my cock, and I love that it's not soft and delicate. He knows how much I can take, unlike every woman who's ever touched me, worried they'd hurt me if they took control.

"Fuck," I grumble rolling my hips and taking him back inside.

"Go slow," he pleads, tension evident in his half-lidded eyes and straining muscles under my hands.

"I'm sorry," I say unable to slow down. Chasing my own orgasm prevents me from taking him into account.

"Fuck, Fuck, FUCK!" I pray no one heard him from the hallway since all other members and girls are accounted for out in the living room.

My come coats his stomach and chest in uneven jets as he pulses inside of me.

"Do you ever listen?" he asks as I swallow around the dryness in my throat.

His rough hands rub up and down my thighs as my index finger signs my name in the mess I left behind on him, my only claim to ownership.

I grin down at him. "I was already there when you asked me to slow down."

"I know," he whispers releasing my thighs and pulling me down to his waiting mouth by my shoulders.

Both groaning our displeasure when our phones simultaneously ding with a text, we pull our lips away. Our post orgasmic bliss is once again ruined by some unsuspecting person.

I lift off of Snatch, hating that we've probably being paged somewhere and a shower is required. I'd rather lay here for the rest of the evening, smelling like each other until the sun rose in the morning, but duty of some sort calls.

Snatch grabs his phone from the bedside table, reads the text, and turns it toward me to read, knowing I got the exact same one.

"What's that all about?" I ask climbing off the bed.

The text was from Shadow with an address and request to bring a trailer.

"When we got back yesterday, Shadow found out Misty moved while we were gone. He wasn't very happy. From the looks of that text, she's coming back."

I look up to find him grinning.

"Is she willing?" I ask.

He shrugs. "Who knows? Does it really matter?"

I laugh knowing exactly what he's talking about. Shadow never goes after something he doesn't get, but Misty, being the mother of his child may be different this time around. What the woman may not realize is he's going to fight even harder this time around because he actually has something to lose now.

"He's going to end up marrying that woman," Snatch predicts as we step inside of the shower together.

"Good for him," I say both happy and jealous of our VP for being able to have that.

Chapter 26

Snatch

Beers are flowing like water in the garage. Ace and Snake are the only fools willing to compromise their health with a continuous line of shots.

Dominic, Kincaid's older brother, is sitting off to the side. He's distant, always has been, but not in a way that makes you think he doesn't want to be here, but he definitely gives off a 'don't fuck with me' aura that's strong enough I don't even attempt to hold a conversation with the man until he speaks to me first.

Noise at the front of the garage pulls my eyes away from Ace and Snake acting like idiots. The fire that's always burning low in my gut flares to life at the sight of Itchy coming in with Shadow right behind him. He looks up sharing a quick, private smile before grabbing a beer from the fridge and sitting down next to the nitwit twins.

Ace is squeezing lime juice on Snake's knuckles he busted up earlier working on his bike.

"Don't even wince," Ace taunts before grinding the lime down on his fresh injuries.

"The fuck are you doing?" Shadow's booming voice pulls their attention momentarily from whatever damn game they've concocted.

"Nothing," Snake says with a grimace on his face.

"That counts," I hear Ace say near his best friend's ear.

"Damn it," Snake grumbles and tips three shots back one after the other.

Shadow shakes his head before twisting the top off of his beer bottle and sitting beside me.

"Don't expect much out of those fucking idiots tomorrow," I tell him as we both watch Snake return the torture to Ace's similarly injured hands.

"Never do," Shadow says with humor in his voice.

"Hey, guys," Kincaid says, the last one to join the group.

We all turn our attention in our president's direction.

The ear to ear grin can't be missed.

"Looks like prez just got laid!" Snake says before thinking. Fear fills his eyes the second the last word leaves his mouth.

Kincaid, out of character, just chuckles and shakes his head. He must have big news because his smile never falters. His minimal normal reaction would be a look that would bring Snake to his knees, the extreme being a couple of shots to his jaw.

"Spill," Shadow insists before Kincaid can even get his ass in the last remaining seat.

I know immediately. There's only one thing that will bring that type of happiness to a man.

He clears his throat, seeming to choke a little before he can get the words out.

"Em's pregnant."

If we had neighbors, I'm certain they would call the cops with all the yells and hollering that goes on with his amazing news. They've been trying for months, with no luck. A round of congrats, and much to Ace's insistence a round of shots filters through the garage.

"To babies and amazing women," Snake toasts.

We all tip back the tequila at the same time. The burn races down my throat, heating me from the inside out. Everyone but Ace declines as Snake attempts to refill our shot glasses.

"I don't mean to cast a shadow on your day, man," Kincaid says to Shadow as we finally all settle back in our seats.

"Fuck that, Diego. Em's pregnant, Misty and I are getting married tomorrow. It's the perfect time to celebrate all of it." They share a look, one of brotherhood, one of commiseration, having both come to the end of their own very long battles: Kincaid with infertility and the upward battle Shadow fought trying to win Misty's heart and sacrificing his own to her.

"Here, here," I boast holding my beer up high, an attempt to lighten the mood.

"Nice save," Shadow says with a quick smile. "Getting too serious for you?"

I take a long pull on my beer, purposely keeping my eyes away from Itchy's place in the room.

"You know me," I say pulling my phone from my pocket and hitting my favorite good-time playlist. Justin Bieber blares out of my phone, and all the guys around me groan. "I'm never serious."

I watch both men as they grin and chat with the others around the room. They've found their happiness, and I couldn't be more excited for them. I haven't spent much time with Misty, but I can tell just by our infrequent interactions that she's a wonderful mother and loves Shadow with an unprecedented fierceness. Emmalyn is amazing and has been since the day she showed up at the clubhouse with Kincaid after a trip to Denver over a year ago.

Kincaid is going to be a wreck for the next nine months. His knee is bouncing, not in nervousness but what I assume is eagerness to get back to his woman. Shadow notices too and grins at him around the mouth of his beer.

"Turn that shit off," Snake urges. "Or play some of his newer stuff at least."

I turn the music off, having no need for it now that everyone is settling into normal conversation.

"You don't seem nervous," I say to Shadow. "I thought men were supposed to be nervous before walking down the aisle."

"I wouldn't have asked her if I didn't want this day to come," he says his voice marked with nothing but seriousness. "She's the only person I want, the only woman I've ever considered spending the rest of my life with. I'm no fool. There's no way I'd walk away from someone as amazing as her."

Kincaid stands and tosses the empty bottle from the single beer he drank with us this evening as if Shadow's words are having an effect on him as well. "I'm going to hit the sack."

"Already?" Itchy asks, allowing me the chance to look in his direction without suspicion.

Shadow stands up a second later. "I'm going to go check on Griff."

My eyes stay on Itchy who follows both of them out with his eyes. I want to kiss the tiny grin on his lips.

"Those guys are suckers," Snake slurs once he makes sure Kincaid and Shadow are far enough away not to hear him. The tone he says it in is full of envy even though the words are a contradiction. It's clear Snake is jealous of what the other guys have. "Am I right?"

"More like lucky fuckers," Itchy mutters.

He catches my eyes for what feels like a flash and an endless moment all at the same time. I can't help but wonder if Ace would feel the same way if either one of the guys that just walked out were in a same-sex relationship. Would a homosexual relationship be enough to turn his opinion into something less complimentary?

My fingers wrap tighter around the beer bottle in my hands until they ache and turn white from the strain. If I were a good man, a strong man, I'd stand up now and take his mouth with the fierceness I feel in my soul, but I can't do that. I'm not that man. I'm a coward. I'm terrified of the fallout. I panic each time I catch Kid watching me from across the room, even though he hasn't even hinted at anything since our trip to Canada a couple of months ago.

"Let's go to Jake's." The harsh mumble from Snake's mouth echoes too loudly off of the walls around us. He has no volume control when he's been drinking as heavily as he has.

"Not a chance," I mutter turning up my beer to my mouth and emptying it.

"Give us a ride, Itchy," Ace urges.

I watch his face as he refuses to look my way. I hate we have to be like this around everyone. If he'd look over at me, he'd see the pleading in my eyes begging him to stay behind. He'd know exactly how I want tonight to go. Watching Kincaid's and Shadow's happiness left me feeling like I lacked something, a tiny hole in my chest that only Itchy is able to fill.

He agrees to take Ace and Snake to Jake's and never looks my way as he tosses his empty beer bottle into the trash and walks out toward the SUV parked to the side.

I wait, staying behind, alone in the garage until the red taillights disappear down the road. Crickets chirping and the occasional rustling of leaves from tree branches in the wind are all that can be heard. Listening to Shadow tonight, seeing that undying passion and love in his eyes forces me to think, urges me to take a step back and look at my own situation. For the first time since Itchy sucked my cock down his throat all those months ago, I take stock of what I have and the direction I want my life to go.

He's the only person that comes to mind when I think about my future. Other than the occasional good time, shared with him of course, I don't picture another woman between us. Our nights are much more fulfilling when it's only us in the bed.

I don't know if it's love, but what I feel for him hasn't been touched by another person, and I honestly don't know if it ever will. I can admit that. Now I just need to find the courage to tell the world that I'm pretty sure I want to spend the rest of my own forever with my best friend.

Chapter 27

Itchy

Frustrated hands scrub over my face and down my beard, which only serves to piss me off even more. My hands smell like sex from the hours Snatch and I spent in bliss until he was called away to work on some task Shadow and Kincaid needed help with. We aren't sent to do shit together anymore. The decision I made to distance us and pretend we hate each other has carried on now for over a year. Nobody in the clubhouse wants more discord than we already present to them, so we never get the chance to hang out other than the stolen moments late at night.

A cool breeze rushes over the empty land behind the clubhouse. The living room looked like an orgy when I finally stopped being pissed about being left alone in my bed. With no interest in joining the fun, I somehow ended up with a couple of beers, sitting alone on the covered back porch. We don't spend enough time out here if you ask me. The mountains in the distance serve as one amazing backdrop, but most of the guys opt for inside or the garage when they're trying to get away from the nagging women inside.

The sound of the door knob turning is followed by the soft whine of the screen door hinges, and I immediately regret not going to my room. At least there I'd be left alone.

"Hey." Khloe's soft voice is a relief.

Snapper was the one I worried would be coming out to pester me. No clue why I thought it'd be her. Fifteen minutes ago she was being spit-roasted by Ace and Skid on the living room carpet

"Hey," I return as she sits beside me on the porch swing.

I offer her one of the unopened beers I brought out with me, but the smirk on her lips forces me to realize just how distracted I've become.

"Sorry," I mutter.

"I should be the one apologizing." She shifts her weight, tucking her legs under her. "I wanted to take a break, but one look in the living room was enough to scar me for life."

"Fuck," I grumble. "They should take that shit to their rooms."

I turned around and walked out, which I regret now that Khloe has seen that shit. I should've told those horny bastards to move that shit somewhere else, but I was too caught up in my own shit to concern myself with them.

I shake my head. "Kid's gonna be pissed. Where is he?"

"Not the first time I walked in on something like that, Itchy. I'll be fine. Kid is off doing something with Shadow and your better half."

I narrow my eyes but keep my attention directed to the beer in my hands. We've been so adamant about keeping our relationship quiet that it's starting to make people talk. Men who piss each other off, especially us guys in Cerberus would normally just beat the shit out of each other and then go drink some beers. Once best friends, who have had some sort of unexplained falling out that drags on for as long as it has is suspicious.

"When did you know?" Her question is filled with genuine concern, not even taking on the slightest hint of judgment.

I huff a humorless laugh. "When did I know I wasn't one hundred percent straight? Or when did I know that I was in love with my best friend?"

"Either," she responds. "Both."

I turn my eyes to hers, scrutinizing, trying to find out what her intentions are for this out of the blue conversation. I want to talk to her about it all. Hell, I need to talk to someone.

"Tell me, Khloe. When did you figure it out?"

The gentle smile on her face almost pulls one from my own lips.

"You remember the fundraiser you guys had? The one for the soldier? It was the one Kid found me at when I..." she pauses and clears her throat, even after all this time emotional from the events that led up to that day. "When I took those pills?"

"I remember," I tell her. "I think that was the best and worst day of Kid's life. He's a lucky fucker to have you, sweetheart."

"I'm the lucky one," she whispers, but then gives her head a quick shake. "That's not why I'm bringing it up. That fundraiser was for my best friend, Alec, who was killed on his first tour."

I tilt my head in confusion. "I'm not sure I'm following."

"Alec was gay. What I'm trying to say is I've seen the signs for a while. The distance between you two, the looks you give him when you think no one is watching, the anger that follows because you're not getting what you want." Her hand rests on top of mine still wrapped around my near empty beer bottle. "Alec was the same way with the guy he was interested in."

"Is everyone talking about it? Like they already know, but are just choosing not to say anything about it?"

She shrugs. "Couldn't tell you. I haven't heard any direct chatter, but you know I keep to Misty and Em. They aren't really the gossip type. Nearly every one of their conversations is either about Griff or Em's pregnancy."

"I hate all of this," I confide.

"It's basic creation, Itchy. If he wasn't born with homosexual tendencies; there's not much of a chance of you guys being together."

I nearly laugh at her words. She has no idea what is going on between Snatch and me, but evidently, I'm as transparent as glass since she can read my feelings for him.

"I see," I agree, doing my best to keep the mirth off of my face and failing miserably.

"Did you tell him and that's why you guys hate each other now?"

I raise an eyebrow at her, finding her assumptions funny until I see the sadness in her eyes.

"I never saw Snatch as the type of guy who would turn his back on his best friend because of some conflicting feelings. I guess you just never know though. Same goes for racism. People say one thing until they're faced with diversity, and then their true colors shine through."

"Khloe." I place my beer at our feet and take her face in my hands. "Snatch is in no way shape or form homophobic."

"He's hurting you. I've seen it with my own eyes."

My thumb sweeps away a tear that was slowly making its way down her cheek. So much empathy and compassion. Kid is seriously one lucky fucker.

"He's hurting, too," I confess, knowing she's a smart girl and will know what I'm saying.

I don't know how much he's actually hurting, but I know he wants to spend more time together, just not at the risk of others knowing about us.

"You guys are... together?" Her eyes brighten when I nod my head.

"Kinda," I say with a grin.

"You guys are scared to come out?"

"He's not ready," I explain.

"I've never met more loving people than the ones living at this clubhouse." Her eyes search mine for correction. She doesn't find any because she's spot on. "I can't speak for everyone, but I don't think anyone will have a problem with it."

I release her face and pick up a fresh beer. She's not telling me anything I don't already know, things I've explained to Snatch only to be refused numerous times.

"I take that back," Khloe says quietly with a quick look at the back door to make sure no one is around. "Some of those club girls get pretty upset when the MC guys announce they're in committed relationships. Losing two at one time could lead to the cat fight of the century."

I sputter a laugh around the lip of my beer, even though I know she's completely serious. The non-committed men in the MC outnumber the women two to one, but Snapper and Gypsy have always been territorial and borderline psychotic when it came to giving up guys they'd staked some ownership over.

"How long have you guys... you know?"

"Darby was sort of the catalyst. She brought out things in both of us, encouraged the relationship. Gave me the courage to act on something I'd been wanting for a long time, but never had the balls to risk."

She peers off into the distance, looking at nothing now that the sun has finally sunk below the horizon.

"Why so contemplative?" I ask when she sighs loudly but doesn't speak.

"I'm just... I don't know. I'm happy for both of you but so terribly saddened that society has somehow managed to taint something as basic as love."

My heart sinks. "I'm not sure love is what he's feeling, Khloe. Love is supposed to be strong enough to conquer all, yet he's too afraid to tell his closest friends."

"But you love him?"

I nod. "More than I thought I could ever love someone."

"I'm just playing the devil's advocate here, but have you told him? Does he know how you feel?"

I laugh at the ridiculousness of it.

"I don't see anything I just said as being funny," she huffs.

"Seriously? We may be gay or bisexual men, Khloe, but at the end of the damn day, we're still men. Men don't just open up and confess their feelings."

She glares at me. "False, you misogynistic ass."

"Fine," I tell her with indigence. "Give me examples."

She holds her hand out in front of her, counting on her fingers as she speaks. "Kincaid, Shadow, and Kid. Kid tells me all the time how much he loves me, how much he needs me in his life, how grateful he is every day that he was able to get to me in time before I fell over the rail of the bridge."

I swallow and stare at her because she's made a very good point.

"And I'm not trying to be dirty and mean because you know that's not my thing," she pauses as her cheeks pink in the soft moonlight. "But Kid is all man and you sitting there saying that men don't act like that is almost like saying the beautiful words he's spoken to me, the promises he's made about our future are nothing but lies and manipulation. And that fucking pisses me off."

"Fuck," I mutter.

"Yeah, fuck," she says. "I can't tell you what to do, but you're my friend, and I hate seeing you hurting. It may not work out in the end, but you have to take risks in love."

I nod. She's the youngest person at the clubhouse and has somehow managed to be the most insightful.

She stands from the swing and kisses my forehead. Just as she's about to head back inside, she turns and speaks over her shoulder. "If you don't want people to stereotype you for who you love and the man you want to be in a relationship with, you have to stop stereotyping yourself. Men love just as fiercely, just as passionately as women. Somedays I wonder if they don't love harder than we do."

"Thanks, Khloe," I say, but the door is already clicking closed.

Chapter 28

Snatch

"How much longer?" My best friend hisses as he paces around my room. "It's been a year and a half. Will you ever be ready?"

He came at me again this morning, urging me to take the chance of telling everyone that we're together.

"Keep your fucking voice down," I whisper yell. "This is a damn clubhouse, not our own house out in the middle of nowhere. You want everyone to hear you?"

"Yes!" he yells even louder. "I want them all to know how much I want to suck your cock. How much I dream about you fucking me. They should know how much I love you!"

His eyes widen almost as much as mine do, but the shock only lasts a few seconds before he's back on his tirade.

"We shouldn't have to hide, shouldn't have to keep secrets." He shakes his head in frustration when I stand my ground in the middle of the room. "Khloe knows, she's happy for us."

He confessed that shit after one too many drinks a few months ago.

"Because you told her," I argue.

I'm pretty certain he's going to be bald if he keeps tugging on his hair.

"She told me," he says with an emphasized finger poking into his own chest. "I didn't have to say a damn thing. She could tell how much I cared for you."

I won't admit out loud that she's not the only one who has drawn conclusions. The verbal jab from Kid the other day at Dominic's while we were there dealing with a situation with Makayla comes to mind.

His words stop dead, pacing feet anchor to the floor.

"That's it isn't it?" I raise an eyebrow at him.

"What?" I ask genuinely confused.

"It's all one sided. You don't feel for me the way I feel for you. I'm a good time, a tight ass to fuck. That's it, nothing more. It has to be, especially since you've never let me fuck your ass."

My body responds to his words. The memories of the last eighteen months flooding back at the wrong time. My cock thickens and saliva pools in my greedy mouth.

"What?" he sneers. "You think you're less gay because my fingers are the only things that have been inside of you?"

He's pissed, that's apparent, but fuck if I can hold the smile back much longer.

"I got news for you, fucker," he hisses. "You sucking my dick any chance you get makes you pretty fucking gay."

I cross my arms over my chest, spreading my legs a few inches farther apart.

"Are you kidding me right now?" His eyes fall to the thick cock growing against the fabric of my boxer briefs. "We're fighting right now, why the fuck are you hard?"

"Suck my cock," I command, knowing it's only going to rile him up even more.

"Not a fucking chance," he counters, but he's the one who jumped out of bed this morning ranting about telling everyone. He does this every couple of months, and each time I get closer to giving him what he wants because deep down it's what I want also.

"Suck my cock or bend over, Itchy. One way or another, I'm coming in that body of yours."

"No thanks," he sputters.

My eyes glance from his handsome bearded face to the thick cock bobbing in the open air. At least I had my head on enough this morning to throw fucking underwear on. Fighting in the nude puts me at a disadvantage, but I'm not really complaining at the sight of him right now.

"You know you want to," I tease, grinning further when his own dick jerks.

"I don't," he argues, now mimicking my stance with his arms over his chest.

I take a step closer to him, but he doesn't back down. I fucking love it when he stands his ground.

I shrug when my chest bumps against his folded arms, ignoring the pissed off glare in his eyes. I hit my knees and suck the tip of his cock in my mouth without another word.

He grunts from the center of his chest when one hand grips the thick base of his cock and the other grips his heavy sac.

"I'm not gay," I say pulling my mouth off for the briefest of seconds. "I'm bisexual because the thought of a hot pink pussy still makes me hard as a rock."

I release the hand at his base, unable to ignore the throbbing in my own cock. I push my boxers down enough to fist my own cock, stroking it while I suck him deeper.

I hear him snort. "You get hard watching me fuck pussy. It's not the pussy itself that turns you on."

I smile around the tip of his magnificent cock and shrug again. "Semantics."

I'm about to shut him up quick by taking him to the back of my throat and swallowing around the head. I know he loves it and fuck if I don't long to hear the growl he emits every time I do it, but the sound of Kid knocking on his door and calling his name makes us both move into action.

He pulls out of my mouth so fucking fast, I'm certain my teeth caught the underside of his dick. We both look at my bedroom door and realize at the exact same second that we didn't lock it last night when we came in here in a tangle of arms, groping hands and twisting tongues.

"Fuck," I hiss.

He grabs for his strewn clothes all over my room. He's closing the door between our rooms just as I'm standing and Kid is knocking on my door. Unlike normal, he gives a quick knock and pushes the door open. If he'd come here first, he would have caught me on my knees with Itchy's cock down my throat.

"The fuck," I growl at the intrusion of my privacy. "You can wait until I answer."

He doesn't respond, but I follow his gaze after his eyebrow quirks up. Itchy's boots are still at the foot of my bed, forgotten last night and having not made it into his pile of shit he hightailed it out of here with a few seconds ago.

"We, ummm..." I don't have shit. On the spot. I can't come up with one fucking lie. I can't tell him Snapper or Gypsy were here because he's well aware neither Itchy nor I have messed around with one of them. Not that they pay much attention, but the girls have made it well known around the clubhouse that they aren't getting fucked as often as they used to.

"Save it," he says with an upturned hand. "Em's in labor. Kincaid is not handling it well. We need to get to the hospital."

"Fuck, it's too soon," I say walking toward him so we can head out. I was with them at the doctor's office a week or so ago, and she had over a month left.

"Kincaid said the same thing before he and Em left. You need to get dressed, fucker. Or at a minimum put your dick away."

He walks out and leaves me standing slack-jawed in the middle of my room. After a long minute, I look down to discover my cock is indeed hanging out. I never pulled my fucking boxers up during the frantic seconds before he opened my door.

I dress in a rush, leaving Itchy's boots sitting exactly where they got tossed last night. I know he's in his room waiting for the dust to settle before retrieving them. I startle, exiting my room to find Kid propped up against the wall waiting for me.

He angles his head back into my room, and I know what he's referencing without a word as we begin to walk toward the front of the clubhouse.

"Don't," I tell him, unable to face the birth of Kincaid's precious twin girls and have my life crumble at the same time.

"Why are you hiding?"

"I'm not," I counter, even though we both know it's another lie. My life has been nothing but lies for longer than I care to admit.

"You have to know you don't have to." His words are sincere, but I don't risk looking up at his face.

"Leave it," I argue. "Just forget about it."

"I can't forget," he offers quietly.

I stop him with a hand on his forearm before we cross over from the hallway into the living room. "Are you going to tell them?"

"Are you?" he asks.

"Not today," I say.

"It's not my story to tell, but if this shit continues to carry over into missions, putting us at risk, I'll scream it from the fucking rooftops." The sincerity on his face hits me in the gut. "I won't risk one of us not coming home to the ones we love over some bullshit you got going on."

"I can't believe Khloe told you," I say absently.

"She didn't have to asshole. You don't think I'm going to start paying more attention when my girl always has her head down whispering with Itchy?"

I chuckle. Itchy and Khloe have grown closer over the last couple of months. I think he's taken solace in knowing that he can discuss us with her.

"Itchy would never try," I begin but he cuts me off.

"I know he wouldn't, but it still made me pay more attention." He looks in the direction of Shadow and Misty's room. "Can you grab Dominic? I'll let Shadow know."

I nod and turn toward Dominic's temporary room. He and Makayla have been staying here for safety reasons since some shit is going down with her brother's club. I give the door a couple of hard knocks, knowing Makayla is in there with him, and having just been interrupted with my dick out, I don't want to do the same to them.

"This better be fucking important," Dominic hollers from inside the room. He's far enough away I can tell his response is coming from the bathroom.

"Sorry, man," I apologize. "Em's gone into labor, and Kincaid is freaking the fuck out. He says it's too early. They're already headed to the hospital. Thought you'd like to know. I'm heading out if you want to ride with me."

Chapter 29

Itchy

The sucky thing about pretending to fight with your best friend to keep all of your straight friends from knowing you're in a closeted homosexual relationship? Getting stuck with Tweedle Dee and Tweedle Dum every time we're in a vehicle heading away from the clubhouse ranks in at least the top five, top three if I thought long and hard about it.

We're at least a half hour behind everyone else getting to the Labor and Delivery wing of the hospital because they insisted on stopping by the gift shop. After fifteen minutes of arguing about what to get, I forced them to settle on flowers and balloons.

In a rush to leave the clubhouse, I left my phone. It's somewhere in the chaos left over after Snatch and I went at each other last night. I had to go back to his room after Kid left to get my boots, but I didn't think to grab my cell. Now, I have no way to text Snatch and see what Kid had told him. I'm standing against the wall beside Snake watching Snatch's leg bob up and down as nervous energy radiates off of him.

The entire room is filled with apprehension. Although Kid explained when we got here that the doctors aren't very concerned, saying twins don't usually make it to term, we're all worried that everything Kincaid and Em fought for the last year and a half will disappear in the blink of an eye.

I want to go to Snatch, place my hand on his leg to calm his nerves, and remind him how much of a fighter Em is, but I can't. Any form of public affection is a huge 'don't fucking think about it.'

Unable to hear what he and Dominic are talking about is beyond frustrating.

"Talk about a meat market," Snake mutters beside me.

"What?" I ask wholly confused at what he's talking about.

"Look around," he urges. "All these hot as fuck nurses."

"We're not here for you to pick up chicks, asshole," I chastise.

"I know." He pulls his head back a few inches, having the nerve to look affronted. "I love Em and Prez as much as anyone else here, but so long as we're waiting, there's no sense in wasting an opportunity to line up my night of celebrations."

"Jesus," I groan as I take a step away from him, needing to distance myself if he's going to start trolling the nurses for a quick fuck.

"Snake, Itchy, and Ace," Dom snaps from the chair beside Snatch. We all look over at him the second he speaks. "Back to the clubhouse."

The fuck.

"The babies will be here soon," I argue. I don't want to leave and I sure as fuck don't want to have to ride back with those two idiots.

"Look around, fucker," Dom hisses. "Doc's out of town. That leaves Rose and Makayla alone in the clubhouse."

I look around the room to verify his words even though I know as he says it, he's right.

Damn it. Before he even speaks again, I know we have to go back.

"Do we leave our women alone?" He asks. I answer him with a head shake, feeling like an asshole for jumping in the SUV in the first place. "Double time."

His words barely have time to leave his mouth before we're pushing out of the huge double doors leaving the L&D wing.

Our women?

I can't believe how fast Dominic got tangled up with Makayla. He's always been protective of women, but he's different with her. I can tell just from the outside looking in that he cares for her more than I've ever seen him care before. Prone to one night stands and no repeats, Dominic is acting out of character, but I can't blame him. When that one person you're meant to be with steps into your life, there's hardly any sense in fighting it.

I have my duties as an MC member, and I know that the other guys left at the hospital have closer relationships with Prez and Em, but that doesn't mean I have to be happy about missing out on the most amazing day the MC has had in a long time.

Snake and Ace grumble about being cock-blocked by Dominic the entire way home. What they failed to see was all of the nurses they were taking inventory of were looking at Dominic and Snatch. Not one of the nurses on that floor even considered either one of them. It's not that they aren't good looking guys because as a bi-sexual male I can see the appeal they both have, at least until they open their mouths and their stupidity is discovered. It's just when confronted with such a vast selection of hot, handsome men, Snake and Ace aren't at the top.

I head into the clubhouse, meeting up with Rose to make sure everything is okay.

The unofficial mother of the MC smiles at me when I walk to the fridge to grab a water. Beer is more tempting, and after a quick look at my watch, I decide any time after noon is perfectly acceptable to start drinking.

"Where is Doc anyways?" I ask as I toss the cap in the trash.

"He was headed down to Phoenix. Landed just over an hour ago," she explains.

"Landed? He flew down?"

She nods folding the dish towel she'd been drying her hands off on when I walked in. "Went down there to get that '63. He's getting the next flight back though."

I nod. Doc, in his retirement, has taken to collecting bikes. I know it drives Rose bat-shit crazy, but she never complains. I get the feeling she gets paid back in other ways.

"Any news from the hospital since we left?" I'm reminded immediately that I need to go search through blankets and discarded clothing to find my cell. I almost ask Rose to call it so I can hear it ring, but remember that it's in Snatch's room, and I'm not opening that can of worms today.

She checks her phone. "Nope."

"Have you seen Dom's woman?" I ask as I finish off my beer and head to the hallway.

"Her name is Makayla, and no. She came out made a sandwich and went back to her room."

"I've got to grab my phone from the bedroom, but then I'm heading out to the garage, text me if you hear anything."

"Will do," she says before turning back to the sink.

Ten minutes later and a ridiculous amount of crawling around on the floor, my phone is located under the damn bed. I look at the screen, feeling a little disheartened that it's devoid of any messages. Snatch and I, since Blade pretty much has access to everything we text each other, don't message about anything of importance, especially anything that would tip off the others.

I frown as I walk into the garage, finding both Snake and Ace in there already setting up shots. I may have just drank a beer in less than five minutes, but hard liquor should be saved until the sun starts to set at least. I decline Snake's offer when he holds out a shot glass to me. He doesn't give me a hard time, smiling instead because if I'm not drinking that gives them permission to get wasted. It's another one of the duties. There is always at least one sober person at the clubhouse per five people. We have to guarantee we can get out safely if we all have to pile into the SUVs to leave in an emergency.

"Twins," Ace says in celebration holding his shot glass up until Snake clinks his against the edge.

I smile at them just as my phone buzzes with a text.

Snatch: Babies are here! Both healthy. Em is doing wonderful, and Dom is back there with them now.

I relay the information to the guys in the garage, laughing as they toast again.

Me: That's awesome.
Snatch: Pretty fucking incredible.
Me: Let us know if you need anything. Give Em a kiss and tell her we said congrats.
Snatch: Will do.

My fingers hover over the keypad, wanting to ask him about his interaction with Kid. I've suspected for the last week or so, with just the looks he's been giving me that he's either figured out what's going on or Khloe spilled the damn beans. Kid's a pretty observant fuck, so I imagine he figured it out on his own. Even if Khloe said something to him, I can't get mad. They're in love and plan on spending the rest of their lives together. I don't think she'd just come out and tell him, but if he asked, she'd tell him the truth. Which I'd expect. I'd never ask anybody to lie for me.

"You guys are going to be too drunk to go to the hospital later," I tell Ace and Snake as they pour back yet another shot. I'd be concerned about alcohol poisoning if I didn't know for a fact that they can drink three times what they've consumed and still hit the bull's eye on a target from fifty yards.

I practically fall into one of the chairs, trying to tune out the idiots who've begun some made up drinking game that makes no sense. The longer I sit and think about the entire situation, the more frustrated I grow.

Shadow's married with an amazing wife and wonderful son. Kincaid is married with twin daughters. Hell, Kid and Khloe aren't far from walking down the aisle themselves. There's no way Dominic is walking away from Makayla anytime soon.

I'm in love with my best friend who has no intention anytime soon, if ever, to tell the people we love that we're together. He seems perfectly content to lurk in the shadows and go days without spending time with each other. It hits me then, that sinking feeling that has wound its way up my spine more than once over the last year and a half. Doubt that he'll ever come out. Doubt that he'd even consider it sits heavy in my gut, turning it sour even without the aid of tequila and whiskey.

I don't want to lose him, but I'm tired of hiding. Tired of restraining myself around him. Exhausted from worrying if my visceral responses when he's around is being noticed by others. I can't take it anymore. I decide at this moment, he can either give up the secrets, or he can say goodbye to what we have.

Tears burn like fire behind my eyelids because I know exactly what he's going to say. I sit, with the raucous laughter of Snake and Ace in the background, as my heart breaks at the imminent loss of the only person I could ever imagine spending the rest of my life with.

Chapter 30

Snatch

Hours.

We waited for hours to take turns to go in and see Gigi and Ivy. I had no idea how long it took for someone to feel like receiving visitors after giving birth.

Khloe, as Em's closest friend, got to go in right after Dominic left. Kid, being her shadow went in as well. I let everyone else go before me because Dom said he was heading back to the clubhouse so the other guys can come back to visit. I know it has more to do with Makayla being back there than visitation opportunities, but I don't say anything. I sent everyone in before me because I was waiting, hoping Itchy would show up. He never does, and not going into the room with him to see the babies for the first time, leaves me feeling a little downtrodden and miserable. Even though there's no room for it after such an amazing day, it casts a cloud over my mood, one I can't seem to shake even after Kincaid gives me a pointed stare.

I look into his eyes but turn them immediately back down to the tiny pink bundle in my arms.

I hear the click of a camera. I smile, turning my gaze to Em who has been taking photos with her cell phone since I walked in.

"It's amazing," she whispers. "Like the perfect combination of innocence and sin."

I frown, turning my attention to the tattooed arms encasing the soft pink of Ivy's blanket.

"I don't mean it in a bad way." Em sighs and I don't miss the growl from Kincaid at the notion that I may upset his wife. "I'm tired. That didn't come out right."

"I know what you mean," I tell her.

"You're a natural," Kincaid says even when his stiff stance remains rigid at my side.

He's waited so long for today to come to fruition. To say that he's cautious is an understatement.

"You, sweet angel," I coo down at her sleeping form. "You'll know the words to every Britney Spears' song by the time you make it to kindergarten."

Em chuckles as Kincaid mumbles, "Over my dead body."

"You guys are so blessed," I say with utmost sincerity.

"We are," Em says on a yawn. "You planning on children?"

I huff loud enough to make Ivy's tiny face crinkle up around her eyes, the beginning of a cry escapes her lips.

"Enough," Kincaid says reaching for his daughter. I know I'm watching the making of two soon to be spoiled rotten little girls.

"No children for me," I answer standing from the small rocking chair to make my excuses to leave.

Itchy doesn't have ovaries.

The thought makes me chuckle.

Reaching out, I clasp Kincaid's hand. "Let us know if you need anything," I tell him before leaning over and giving Em a swift kiss on the forehead. "You sure do make pretty babies."

She smiles but doesn't take her eyes from Gigi, who is sleeping peacefully in her arms.

* * *

I can't keep the frown from my face when I exit Em's room and find Kid the only person left in the waiting room. I was granted a reprieve back at the clubhouse because we had to get to the hospital, but being alone with him is going to give him the opportunity to speak freely. I'm dreading the interaction and was fully ready to call for an Uber.

"Where's Khloe?" I ask hoping she's in the restroom or down at the gift shop.

"I took her home. She stayed up all night studying, and needed a nap before studying more later this evening," he explains.

"She's going to wear herself out," I mumble, for the first time hating her diligence with her education.

"I said the exact same thing," he says as we make our way out to the SUV to head back home. "She just tells me it's only temporary, and she'll sleep after she graduates."

"She's not really leaving much time for anything else. It has to be exhausting," I add as I climb into the SUV, passenger side of course. Kid always drives unless Kincaid, Dominic, or Shadow insist on taking the wheel.

The smile on his face when he buckles his seat belt makes it very clear that she's making time for him, and that's all that matters.

On the drive home, I find myself hoping he brings up what he saw in my room this morning, yet at the same time, I pray he never mentions it again. I'm torn by the entire thing, so twisted up deep inside I don't even know where I stand anymore. I can admit it's my own cowardice that's keeping me from sharing with my closest friends the news of my relationship with Itchy. Once we open that door, it can never be closed, and that terrifies me more than facing an armed insurgent when all I have are my hands to defend myself.

How fucked up is it that society controls so many people by their preconceived notions and horrid opinions? Does it make me less of a man, less of a human because I'm worried about what everyone will think, how they would judge me by merely expressing my feelings for someone?

He hasn't said a word about it, not one single hint by the time we make it back to the clubhouse. I climb out of the SUV glad and disheartened at the same time.

I bid everyone good night without slowing my pace through the common areas and head straight to my room. It's been one long ass fucking day, starting with the interrupted argument with Itchy this morning and ending with the birth of two amazing little girls.

Even exhausted, I smile when I open my bedroom door to find Itchy sitting on the edge of my bed. It doesn't last but a second when I see the bend of his neck as he doesn't even look up at me, opting instead to keep his eyes trained on his wringing hands.

"Hey honey, I'm home," I jest, trying to lighten his mood. It falls flat, and my chest constricts.

I close the door, lock it for good measure, and kick off my boots. He still doesn't look up at me, and my mind races with worry that someone has discovered us.

"I can't do this anymore," he mutters, still refusing to look me in the eye.

"Excuse me?" He started this shit. He sucked my cock first, and now he just wants it to be over?

No take backs, motherfucker.

"Look at me," I demand.

He waivers for an endless moment, as if he looks me in the eye he won't be able to speak his mind. I'll take all the help I can get because him ending this is the last thing I want. The warring in my head, in my heart, that I didn't even know I was fighting for so long is quiet when I'm with him.

"Goddamn it, Rob. Now!"

His eyes finally jerk to mine at the use of his first name.

Sadness, pain, and even worse, resolve fill his eyes. The devastated look on his face cracks open my heart, and I almost spill my truths as they pour from the wound, but he interrupts me.

"I said," his voice is nearly a sneer, a way to mask his own heartbreak. "I can't do this anymore."

"Does your dick agree?" If he wants to be an asshole, I can give back in spades.

"My dick isn't the problem," he argues, the harshness increasing enough in his voice to make me almost back down. Almost.

"You tired of sucking dick? Tired of getting *your* cock sucked?"

He licks his lips, preparing to rip into me if the glint in his eye is any indication.

"Is it because I haven't let you fuck me yet?" In a bid of showmanship, I reach for my belt buckle, pulling the leather apart with determination. "We can remedy that shit right now."

His eyes, unsure for the first time, glance down at my cock, still concealed behind my navy boxer briefs.

"This isn't about the sex, *Jaxon*." The hiss of my name, so sweet on his lips the few times he's moaned it since we started this, is bursting with venom. I hate it immediately. "What is this?"

"This?" I ask confused because he hasn't stopped staring at me, his fingers gripping and clenching each other.

"Between us. What is it?" He drops his eyes again, and I know he's terrified of my answer, expecting me to say the opposite of what he needs me to say.

Fuck, *I'm* frightened of what I'll say.

"What's got you so upset?" I'm frozen like a statue in the middle of the room, and it's not lost on him that I didn't answer his question.

"I'm tired of hiding. I want to tell them."

Them being the entire collection of our friends, the entire MC, the only men we trust. The repercussions, if it isn't well received, have cataclysmic fallout.

Sincerity fills his eyes when he looks back up at me. "We don't have to hide."

"Itchy," I cajole. "I'm not ready."

"At the rate you're going, you'll never be ready. It's tell them, or this ends. So, I'll ask again, what is this between us? A good time? Love? You tell me because if it's up to me, I'm all in, with you... with us."

I shake my head on instinct, rejecting this entire conversation without a second thought. The idea of moving forward with what he wants terrifies me as much as losing him. It's lose-lose for me either way I decide. If I choose him, I run the risk of losing everyone else. If I don't choose him, I may have given up the most powerful thing I've ever had the luck to find.

It's quality over quantity, and I'm the asshole who can't legit decide.

"Please don't do this," I beg as I zip my jeans back up and lace the leather of my belt back through the loops.

"Do you love me?" Even behind his thick beard, I can see his jaw clench in frustration.

Put on the spot, I rub my hands over the stubble of my short Mohawk. "Dumbest question ever, man."

Once again I'm stalling. Fuck, where is the redo button on this fucking day? I should've headed to the garage instead of being excited to come in here and crawl into his bed.

"You've never said it," he counters. "I mean, unless I was reading too much into it, I could feel it in your hands when they reach for me in the middle of the night. I could taste it on your lips, but you've never said the words. The look on your face right now tells me no, but the vivid memories make me doubt what's before my eyes right now."

"You haven't said it either," I argue.

The tired corner of his right eye twitches, his lips unmoving for eternity before he chooses to respond. "I loved you for years as a friend, a brother in arms."

This is safe territory. The straining muscles in my entire body relax infinitesimally.

"I love you now as a lover, boyfriend or whatever we label what this is between us. I felt that way before I licked Darby's pussy off of your cock." My eyes widen. "It's the only thing that gave me the courage to take that fucking step."

Oh, fuck.

My pulse is pounding in my ears, leaving me reading his lips for the last part as his voice is drowned out by the thunder of my heart.

"I love you," he repeats as if needing to drive the three words home.

He stands from the edge of the bed, closing some of the distance between us, but I stop him with an upturned hand.

"But this is an ultimatum?" He frowns. "I just want to be clear. You love me, but you're willing to walk away from that unless I tell the guys."

The sparkle that shone in his eyes when he was making his declaration turns briefly to remorse but morphs quickly when his spine straightens with determination. He's legit willing to walk away.

"I'm not ready," I mutter, my lips speaking my truth before my brain can even analyze the situation as a whole.

He nods, solemn but not surprised. His boots eat up the distance between us until we're only a breath apart.

"I understand," he says before his lips brush mine in the faintest of touches.

My hands grip his shirt, needing to pull him to my chest, to feel the warmth of his body, the forgiveness of his love. I feel the harsh rush of his breath against my cheek as he battles with his decision.

Standing firm, he pulls my fingers free of the bunched fabric and walks away.

My heart crumbles at the finality of his lock clicking into place.

Chapter 31

Itchy

"You need to get laid," Snake grumbles when I fail to laugh at his ridiculous attempt at another joke.

"Don't worry about my cock, asshole," I mutter finishing my beer. "You probably have enough shit crawling around on yours for a lifetime of concern."

Ace's laugh bounces around the garage but stops immediately when Snake gives him a go-to-hell look.

"I'll have you know I got my shit checked last week, and I'm clean as a fucking whistle." I'd laugh if he didn't look so relieved at his own declaration.

"For now," I add. "Next month could be a whole other story."

I'm full of shit. I know he always wraps up, a Godsend considering his propensity for questionable women.

"You have crabs," he hisses, unable to let the insult die without an attempt at having the last word.

"Had, fuckface." I'll never live down the stupid fucking name I was given in boot camp, an impossibility considering it followed me out of the Marines. Sometimes I hate spending my days with so many guys from my first unit in the Corps. "Once, and it was years ago."

"Semantics," he mutters seeming to finally give up on the argument.

"Fact," I counter. He can tell by the look on my face that I'm not going to give up on this.

He rolls his eyes like a teenage girl and starts talking to Ace.

I know I'm being a jerk. I have been since I walked out of Snatch's room a week ago, and everyone around me seems to be taking the brunt of my attitude.

You need to get laid.

Fucking someone is the last thing on my mind at the moment. Even my go-to stress reliever is tainted by Snatch's rejection. I know any effort wasted on some woman would leave me unsated. My sexual encounters over the last year and a half have been soul deep, passionate, and all involved the man I love. Anything after that is a depletion of energy I can't be bothered with.

"I'm going in," I say tossing my empty bottle in the trash before walking to the door.

"Taking my advice, I see." Snake smiles at me, so sure of himself. "I suggest Gypsy. She's been extra fucking randy this week."

"To bed, idiot."

Ace and Snake reminiscing over the week's exploits turns from obnoxious chatter to silence as I make my way to the front door. Thank fuck they pull their weight on missions because if they didn't, their antics would surely get them booted from the MC.

I do my best to ignore Gypsy and Snapper who're making out on the couch without a man in sight.

I'm grumbling about double standards as I make my way to the hall entrance when out of the corner of my eye I see Snapper jump up from the couch and start toward me.

"Not tonight, Snap."

"Oh, believe me, Itchy you're going to want to talk to me." She leans in closer, whispering to Gypsy who is gawking at us like she believes Snapper is propositioning me. "Unless you want everyone to know about the romps you and your boy toy have been having for the last year and a half."

I almost laugh because if anyone would consider Snatch a boy toy in our scenario, they'd be stupid. Her words sober me, even as the endless supply of beer I'd consumed all day flows through my veins.

I grip her by her forearm, probably harder than I'd ever grabbed a woman before and drag her until we're locked inside of my room.

I don't think Snatch is even at the clubhouse. He's probably fucking my dick out his mind as we speak, but it doesn't keep my eyes from darting to his door. I swing her around to face me, and she smirks having caught the direction of my gaze. She knows. I can tell that by the indignant look in her eyes.

"The fuck are you talking about?" I'm steady enough on my feet to at least force her hand, make her play her cards before admitting to shit.

"This may explain things a little better," she says reaching into the back pocket of her jeans and pulling free her cell phone.

I wait impatiently as she unlocks the screen and opens up an app. Satisfied with what she's found on the screen she hands it to me. I frown at her but look down at the phone.

My breath hitches, heart skipping several beats when I press play.

"Where did you get this?" I ask but never pull my eyes from the screen.

"I took it myself." Her voice has an air of joy to it that makes my blood boil. "No one else knows about it."

I glare at the screen, only realizing after several long seconds that I haven't heard any audio.

"For now," she threatens just as my finger finds the volume control and I turn up the sound.

I ignore her, too focused on the video to handle both things at the same time.

I watch, both in horror at her catching such a private moment, but morosely happy to see Snatch and me together.

It isn't until I hear the argument that happened what seems like a lifetime ago registers that everything clicks in my brain. Her barely veiled threat, the evidence she wields, the ability to implode the very thing Snatch was against.

"Her emotional state is not my responsibility." Snatch's indifference still annoys the fuck out of me even after all of this time.

I hold my breath as I watch myself close the distance between us.

"Do you really think pissing her off while she's holding your secret in her hands is the smartest thing?"

"Your secret, too," he mutters.

I watch as his eyes dart in the direction of the camera. How he missed Snapper standing at the end of the hall holding a goddamned cell phone is beyond me.

"Would it be so bad?" I hear myself ask.

Fuck you Apple for being able to pick up every sound in a private conversation.

His laugh echoes around my room as if he's standing in here with us. Even the sinister sound from that day warms my blood. *"Bad? Would it be bad to be in some fucked up, labeled, relationship with a club girl?"*

"She's pretty awesome. I know you enjoy fucking her."

"I fuck her because that's what you want."

"I don't think giving it a try with her is such a bad thing."

"You can't be serious. She fucks everyone in the clubhouse, Itchy."

"Asshole," I mutter. Even watching this now I can see how much of a jerk he was.

"Really? When was the last time you fucked someone other than us? Other than the women we've tagged together?"

"I doubled with Darby and Snapper a while back, but only because I thought Snap was getting suspicious." I hear myself explain.

"That suspicion is what led me to try to get this video," she cuts in. I sneer at her, but she knows she's got me by the balls so it barely even registers on her face.

"I hate to state the obvious man, but there's no such thing as love or being in a relationship when the woman who's asking for it is fucking anyone she can get between her legs. You can't turn a club girl into a housewife, Itchy. There's no sense in even trying."

"I think it was that part that made Darby leave," she laments.

My eyes pull from her damning evidence, burning holes into her. "You fucking showed her this?"

"She's not going to tell anyone," she insists.

"I'm not worried about her telling anyone, Snapper. How fucked are you to hurt someone like that?"

"Seriously? I'm not the one who fucking said it." She shakes off my chastisement with the ease of a sociopath and continues. "She needed to know what you guys thought of her. She left the next day."

"You cold-hearted, evil bitch," I hiss.

"No, no, no," she says twitching her finger in my face. "Keep watching it gets better."

"The only person I've been inside of outside of these two rooms is when I was buried deep in you in that shower."

I nearly drop the phone at Snatch's confession, responding much the same way I did the day this video was recorded.

"That's the golden egg right there," she all but sing songs.

The video cuts off after a few more heated words between us. I clench the phone in my hand but gather myself enough to delete the mother fucker before handing it back to her. I don't bust it against the wall because the noise would draw unwanted attention.

Her cackle makes my skin crawl. "You think I don't have it backed up on the cloud? I'm not a fucking idiot."

I almost argue the point with her, but my mind is grinding trying to figure out a way to get Snatch and I out of this situation.

"What do you want?" I hiss. "That shit was shut down a long time ago."

Well, the last week has felt like a lifetime to me, so I'm not really lying.

"Marriage," she says without even blinking. "And babies."

I laugh like a patient in an insane asylum as she watches on with an unimpressed look on her face. When I finally gain marginal composure, I look up at her. "Tell the world, sweetheart. Marrying you is the last thing on Earth I'd do. Babies? You're off your rocker. I'd chop my dick off first."

I notice the slight fall of her face, but she schools it until her malicious intent is all that can be interpreted. There's no way I can give into her, trading one form of hell for a lifetime of misery instead. Not a fucking chance.

"You should've hit Snatch with your little blackmail plan. I couldn't care less if people knew. He's the one who refused to tell anyone."

Her anger turns to designed calculation, and immediately I know I'm fucked.

"Speaking of your boyfriend." She smiles.

I have never wanted to throat punch a woman so bad in my life, which is saying a lot because nine times out of ten when on missions there's a woman involved, sometimes running the sex trade houses we infiltrate.

"He's not," I argue, my last futile attempt to turn this around.

"When he's ready to kiss and make up from your little tiff last week, you shut him down. You'll tell him you moved on. You love me, and he was just an indiscretion you want to forget ever happened."

"He'll never believe it."

"You better make him believe. If this shit breaks open, it's his life that will be ruined. I know you don't give a shit about everyone knowing, but he does."

"Why the fuck are you doing this?"

I knew she was twisted and jealous, but fuck if this doesn't take the cake. Kincaid should've sent her ass packing years ago, before she made Em feel like shit, almost ruined things between Kid, and treated Misty like she was a pariah.

"I'm not going to be a club whore for the rest of my life. Twenty-five seems as good a time as any to get serious and settle down," she explains as if her reasoning is sound and bulletproof.

"And the fact that I'll never love you doesn't even factor in your little plan?" Surely she can see how insane this whole fucking thing is.

"Love will come later," she says as cool as ice. With a quick pat on my heaving chest, she makes her way to the door. "I'll give you forty-eight hours to decide. Check the time, baby. You won't get a second more."

I don't even make it to the toilet as my body rejects her words and every last drop of beer I consumed today while trying to forget about the man next door.

Chapter 32

Snatch

Makayla got justice tonight, her brother Scorpion, President of the Renegade MC, killing the man who's been violating her for years without so much as a second thought. Dom is all but twitching in the driver's seat as he drives toward the clubhouse. I can only imagine the level of anger he's feeling because Scorpion took his ability to avenge Makayla from him, but he has to know that the MC problem had to be dealt with by the MC President. Anything short of Scorpion pulling that fucking trigger tonight, sending Grinder to hell exactly where he belongs, would leave Mak vulnerable to retaliation and revenge.

Not a word is spoken on the way to the clubhouse. We sit in heavy silence, reflecting on the events of tonight. It all means something different to each of us. Dominic will struggle with Scorpion's actions. More than likely, Mak will feel relief at knowing her perpetrator is dead, but I know from experience from rescuing victimized women that it will take forever to heal. I'm grateful they have each other to lean on, and hopefully some good comes from all of this.

Me?

I stare out the window without seeing a damn thing, the sights so familiar it's as if I no longer pay attention to my surroundings anymore. My mind wanders back to the argument Itchy and I had a little over a week ago, which also happens to be the very last day he even looked in my direction. Keeping our distance from one another while under the watchful eye of everyone isn't anything new to us. It's catching his eye, finding that glint of hope and desire at the possibility of spending the night in each other's arms that's crushing me. He won't even look my way. He goes so far as to get up and leave the room when I enter, and the door between our rooms remains locked. Of course, I only test it when he's gone because catching me walking into his room would give him hope I wasn't ready to provide.

Until right now.

A split second delay on Scorpion's part tonight would've meant Dominic losing the love of his life, even if he's too stubborn to admit how head over heels he is with her. The thought of losing Itchy that way, in any way, nearly makes me want to ask Dominic to pull over so I can puke. Just the prospect crushes my heart and fills me with an animalistic desire to protect him at all costs.

Letting those emotions wash over me, allowing my mind to actually take in what my heart wants, what it needs, the decision to give him everything he could ever desire is the easiest one I've ever made. Regret fills my blood, making me wish I could turn back time and just agree with him from day one. We've lost so much time, and every second of pain and distance rests solely on my shoulders.

I climb out of the SUV with only a quick 'thanks' in Dom's direction. I'm a renewed man, one filled with determination and purpose as I walk into the clubhouse. The noise of an impromptu party vibrates through the door knob as I reach to turn it. The guys that were on bikes at the meeting made it back just a few minutes before us, but that didn't slow them from cranking on the stereo and passing beer and shots around. Itchy, Ace and Snake were instructed to stay back at the clubhouse since Em, Khloe, Misty, Rose, and Griffin and the twins were here.

I take in the room, surprised to see Shadow, Kid and even Kincaid in the living room. Even more shocking is their women sitting around with them. I know tonight was intense, but not to the point of throwing a party like this.

Khloe smiles over at Snake as he acts like the dumb ass that he is, but the air surrounding the other women is thick and filled with mild disdain even though they're too classy to be outright rude, they're unimpressed with whatever the fuck is going on.

"Beer?" Skid asks but shoves a bottle in my hand not waiting for my answer.

"What's going on?" My eyes scan the small crowd looking for answers.

They narrow when they land on Itchy, but more so from the sight of Snapper sitting on his lap running her overly long fingernail down the center of his chest. His eyes widen when he sees me as if he hates being caught in such an intimate position with the one club girl I have no love lost for.

Snapper notices the direction of his eyes, finding mine as I move farther into the room. I need to talk to him and wonder for the quickest of seconds if I shouldn't just blurt out my feelings for him. As far as grand gestures go, I think a proclamation of love with the intent to spend the rest of my life making up my asshole ways to him would rank pretty fucking close to the top.

"We're celebrating!" Skid says with a weird joy that makes my skin crawl.

I know before he even continues that my world is going to be rocked to the core.

"Itchy and I are getting married!" Snapper declares from my lover's lap.

I tilt my head, confused at first but then the chuckle at being played with escapes my lips. Only when Snapper frowns at my reaction, does my brain take the time to catch up on everything going on around me. Several members are holding up beers in salute, Em and Misty look like they're going to be sick at the prospect of Snapper having a tighter bond to the club.

She's not lying. I pushed him so far away from me he's considering being in a committed relationship, one with vows before God with one of the most heinous women the MC has ever seen. I swallow half my beer before looking at him again. His eyes avoid mine just as they have for the last week.

My lip twitches in barely controlled anger, but somehow I'm able to keep my wits about me. If he's choosing her, there's no way I'll embarrass myself by outing us in front of everyone. What I don't keep under control is my mouth when it comes to being the asshole everyone has recently assigned as my new everyday demeanor. They have expected me to act a certain way for a while now. Tonight, I have no intention of disappointing them.

Since Itchy refuses to talk and Snapper seems hell bent to maintain eye contact, I direct my question to her.

"He fucking knock you up or something?"

She grins, unfazed by the accusation, but I hear one of the other women hiss in surprise. No one steps in. Kid doesn't say a thing. Kincaid remains silent when he's normally the one who'd correct anyone for speaking to a woman the way I just did.

"I was wondering the same thing," Snake slurs from the other side of the room.

She ignores Snake, turning her attention back to Itchy.

"I'm not pregnant yet, but Robert and I plan to start our family very soon."

I see red at her using his first name. A certain level of ownership or blood given familial bond is needed for anyone calling an MC member by the name their mother gave them. She doesn't have that, does she? Em and Dominic can call Kincaid Diego all day long. I've heard Khloe say Dustin more than once, but his name coming from her over done lips is sacrilegious to the extreme.

I'm so pissed at her choice of moniker that it takes me a long moment to analyze the rest of her sentence.

Family?

He's going to have children with her. I'm a second away from pinching myself and trying to figure out how I landed in the fucking Twilight Zone when Snake says something that I actually need to hear the answer to.

"Does this mean we don't get to fuck no more?" He punctuates the question with a burp.

I wait for Itchy to look over at the slob everyone can't help but love, beg him with my mind to examine his decision long and hard, to take into account the women she's hurt in this club, the way she'd fuck anyone anytime. Then I remember that he didn't have a problem with Darby's over promiscuous antics. He was willing to be in a triad with her. My stomach roils at the thought he'd ask me to ever touch the nasty redheaded bitch.

"Nope," she says finally answering Snake but keeping her eyes glued to Itchy. "I can't risk the chance of ending up with one of your idiot babies."

I take a menacing step toward her, but Skid presses his hand to my chest.

"He was good enough for you to fuck for the last five years," I sneer. "But not good enough to fill your whore of a womb with a baby?"

I wait for the backlash from my President. It never comes. She glares at me and back down at Itchy, who for a man that has promised to spend the rest of his life with someone remains eerily silent. I hate the sight of the glistening diamond on her finger, hate the way she's resting possessively on the man not thirty minutes ago I was certain I'd spend my life with.

"Thanks, man," Snake says.

"Shut up," I tell him. "You are a fucking idiot, but this skank doesn't have the right to say it. As a matter of fact, I think such disrespectful words are enough to get her kicked out of the club."

She sobers quickly when I turn to look at Kincaid.

"You're treading on thin ice already, Snapper." He's failed me too. "Itchy, get her under control. I'd hate to lose you because she can't keep her talons out of everyone."

I revel in the look of disappointment on Snapper's face, but when her eyes meet mine again they turn devilish, an evil smirk playing on her lips.

"You seem more concerned than I figured you would Snatch. Something on your mind? Something you feel the urge to share with the club other than slinging insults my way?"

She knows, and she's challenging me. I feel betrayed that Itchy would go to her and tell her about us.

Kid scoots to the edge of his chair, and Khloe grips his hand with hers. They support me. I can feel it, but it's not enough to risk everything, especially when I look over at Itchy one last time only to find him studying the label on the neck of his beer bottle.

"I'm not going to offer my congratulations if that's what you're after because I know he'll be miserable for the rest of his life. I can't do anything about that."

He chooses this moment to look up at me. I can't tell if he's begging me for something, but it's too late. My heart's broken, and even knowing it's all my fault doesn't make it hurt any less. "I will offer some advice though."

I keep my eyes on hers, refusing to look at him just as he's done to me for days and days.

A million insults are on the tip of my tongue. The desire to tell him to get tested, even if she claims she's being monogamous. Give him my condolences for the overused pussy he'll be fucking for the foreseeable future. But I realize before the words spill out in hateful revenge that they won't help. If he chose this, that's on him. This club has put up with me being an asshole for over a year and a half in an attempt to protect our secret. I push it all down, the pain, the heartache, the love I have for him that has done nothing but bloom and thrive in the darkness. I'll let it die. It'll be as if my secrets and transgressions never happened.

"Never mind," I mutter before turning and leaving them all to follow the tension in my back as I leave the room.

Chapter 33

Itchy

I raise my beer in salute to Shadow and Misty's news. Baby number two is on the way, and although I'm so fucking happy to see one of my closest friends ecstatic over the prospect of being a father for the second time and being able to be with Misty the entire way through this time around, I can't seem to muster the emotions to give them justice.

We're in the back yard, around the fire pit, the place we always gather when we party and the weather's nice. This is a double celebration since Dominic finally got his shit together and confessed his feelings to Makayla. They got married last week. I'm surrounded by distracted, happy couples, miserable to my fucking center.

"Another beer?" Snapper coos in my ear.

I nod, thankful for even a minute's reprieve from her overpowering perfume and wandering hands. She knows exactly where we stand. We don't fuck or cuddle at night even though she insists on sleeping in my room every night. Hell, I'm not even civil to her when we're alone, but to protect Snatch's delicate fucking secret, I tolerate her in public.

I've hoped for the last couple of weeks she'd get tired of my indifference, but she clings to the hope that I'll eventually fall in love with her. I seriously think she needs to be evaluated by a licensed mental health professional because she's clearly lost her fucking mind.

Snatch has given me an even wider berth than we had before Snapper announced we were getting married. I had no warning, no time to prepare when the guys got back from the situation with the Renegades. She came out of her room, diamond ring glistening on her left hand, looped her arm through mine telling me to smile and remember the video. Then she proceeded to drag me out into the living room and announce our happy news.

I was surprised by several things that night. First, I didn't know the direct sales businesses she's been involved in could generate enough revenue to buy that fucking ring, and also that she announced our engagement before Snatch showed up.

I glance straight across the fire, finding Khloe watching me with sad eyes. Snatch is across the yard to the far right, so I know where not to look until Snapper has determined we've been here long enough. She'll start to paw at me, acting like we're getting hot and bothered and we'll make our excuses letting everyone think we can't get out of here fast enough to fuck in private. Fuck, I wish I could talk to Khloe, but she's distanced herself since the announcement.

Snake is pissed and avoiding me like the petulant child that he is, claiming and I quote: 'You took my hottest piece of pussy.'

I don't know who Snapper's been fucking the last couple of weeks, but to keep the ruse up, I'm sure it's not anyone in the clubhouse. I cringe every morning I wake up, and even an inch of skin is against mine.

"Hey, man." My eyes close, squeezing shut at the possibility that I'm dreaming. He hasn't directed any amount of attention my way, not one single sentence of conversation in over three weeks, not since I fucked up and gave him that stupid as hell ultimatum.

I don't feel him move, and my body hums with his proximity. When I open my eyes, I find him still beside me but focused on the bright orange and yellow flames from the massive fire pit.

I ache to touch him, to tell him the truth, beg him to tell everyone what we mean to each other. All he has to do is confess, and my life would be a million times better in the blink of an eye.

An insidious thought creeps in my head that the way we are now is what he's always wanted, that he may have enjoyed what we were doing together but he was never in it for the long run. If only I could forget the way we moved together, how his mouth felt on mine, how his body felt inside of mine.

"Fuck," I grumble and run my hand in frustration down my beard.

"Yeah," he mutters.

I open my mouth to force him to explain his response, but Snapper comes sauntering up, clearing her throat in agitation at Snatch sitting in the seat she'd vacated a few moments before.

She shrugs when he ignores her, and in a ridiculous show of possession, she climbs in my fucking lap, rolling her body against mine like a cat starved for attention. My hands grip my beer bottle, and the chair's arm rests respectively as I fight every instinct to push her off and not care that she's left in the dirt at my feet.

"Hey baby," she purrs.

I see Snatch's eye twitch at the corner, and she knows I'm paying more attention to him than her and she hates it. With her index finger, she chucks my chin up forcing me to look her in the eye. I hiss at the scrape of her overly long fingernail against my skin. Her wicked smile and the way she's making a show of grinding down on my flaccid cock may look like we can't get enough of each other to an outsider, but my blood is boiling in my veins.

When her lips hit mine, I feel like puking, clutching at her back in warning, my fingers digging into her flesh. I let her know as I press harder that if she sticks her tongue in my mouth, it's the last thing she'll do. Thankfully, she heeds the warning, keeping her assault to a closed mouth kiss.

"Yeah," Snatch says standing from the chair. "Good talk."

She only pulls away when the door leading back into the clubhouse off of the back porch slams shut.

I'm doing this for you! I want to scream at the top of my lungs.

"The fuck was that about?" I hiss as low as I can. With my hands on her upper arms, I grip her and pull her away from my chest.

"What were you guys talking about?" She has to be pissed if she's going to interrogate me in front of everyone.

"Wouldn't you like to know?" An immature response for such a serious situation, but it seems fitting with her blackmail.

"You want me to ruin him? Everyone is here," she seethes. "I'm sure they'd love to cap the night off with a video of you guys acting like faggots in the hallway. You seriously think Kincaid and Shadow are going to want you sick bastards around their children, tainting them. Shadow would kick you out of this club, worried that your gross little obsession with dick is going to overflow and you'll go after his son."

"Enough," I warn with no concern of who is overhearing us.

Does she seriously think being bisexual or even fully homosexual translates into pedophilia? Evil incarnate, that's exactly what this woman is. I'd rather eat my own fucking gun before I ever walk down the aisle and tie myself to her.

I stand not bothered in the slightest when she barely gets her feet under her, keeping her from falling. I look around the yard, finding nearly everyone staring at us. My eyes land on Khloe, and I can tell by the disappointed look on her face that she knows exactly what's going on. The girl is too damn bright for her own good. Without a word, I walk toward the clubhouse.

"Lover's quarrel," Snapper says excusing my outburst as I walk away.

"Someone's sleeping on the couch tonight," Snake says, hidden in the shadows. He's probably got his cock down Gypsy's throat yet still has to try to get the last word in on a conversation he wasn't even privy to.

Jackass.

I stop in the kitchen on the way back to my room, grabbing several beers and an unopened bottle of whiskey from the counter. A drunken stupor seems like the best thing in the world right now. I need to erase the pain that's burning a hole in my chest. Drown out the horrible things Snapper said. There's no way in the world anyone with children in this clubhouse would think for a second that either Snatch or I would go after their babies. I'd give my life for every one of them without hesitation, even that tiny one in Misty's flat stomach.

Just like it always happens, my retorts and hateful things I should've said to Snapper come to mind after the three long pulls I manage to swallow between the kitchen and my bedroom.

I'm pissed enough that I almost turn toward the back door, ready to blow this whole fucking thing out of the water, damn the consequences. I want to remind her that she's probably eaten more pussy than dicks. I want nothing more than to remind her that some of her kinks are more depraved in society's eyes than two men loving each other. I'd never judge her for the things that turn her on and get her off so long as I'm not involved, and it's legal.

Instead, I opt for locking myself in my room and daring her in my mind to knock on this fucking door tonight. I slide down the door, only two inches of wood and a door knob separating me from everything I ever wanted. I turn the bottle up again, the warmth running down my throat and radiating out as it hits my stomach.

I drink until my vision blurs. I drink until the pain is bearable. I drink until I pass out, the words: I still love you, a jumbled mess of slurred syllables.

Chapter 34

Snatch

"Not much different from Vegas if you think about it," I whisper to Kid even though we're a safe distance from the glorified whore house and there's not a soul in sight paying any attention to the rusted up truck parked across the street.

"Don't even say the word Vegas around me fucker," he mutters. Clearly, he's not over the mild case of amnesia and the aftermath of that from years ago.

Just another life Snapper nearly ruined.

It's been just over a month since the argument with Itchy, thirty-four days since I made the biggest mistake of my life. Which means it's been three weeks since he turned the tables on me and announced he was getting married to the redheaded skank of the MC. We've settled into a less strained acquaintanceship that resembles the rapport people who tolerate each other in the workplace would have. I guess I can appreciate it, even though just the sight of him hurts.

If this is love and heartbreak, it can kiss my tattooed ass. I pray for the day that I can walk into a room and see him without wanting to shake him, punch him in the nose and ask him just what the fuck he's thinking by letting Snapper sink her fake, acrylic nails into him.

I pull the neck of my t-shirt away from my throat feeling strangled by the humidity here in Brazil.

"Are you going to talk about it?" Kid asks but keeps his eyes on the building in front of us. It's not the neon lights and the bustling front entrance of the Luxury House that is our focus. The barely lit building a hundred yards away at the back is where we know the girl we're looking for is being held. Kid and I are here tonight making sure no one leaves without us having eyes on them. The other guys are back at the command center across town gearing up for the raid. We'll meet up with them within the hour to execute our infiltration.

"Nope," I answer him, pissed he's even bringing it up.

"You have to know he doesn't love her." He's only stating the obvious. It's clear he can barely stand Snapper even when he's around others in the clubhouse.

"Well, it's apparent he doesn't love me either." How the fuck did he manipulate me into talking about the very subject I have no desire to mention ever again?

"I'm not sure what exactly is going on, but there's no way he's going to marry her."

"The ring on her fucking finger says different," I grunt. "Can you just drop it? I just want to move past all of it."

"If you love him, that's the last fucking thing you should do."

I can't reject his reasoning totally. It's not like it isn't something I've thought a million times over in the last month.

"Tell me again who this girl is," I urge, ignoring the subject he seems so hell bent on rehashing. What's done is done, and I'm sick and fucking tired of living the heartache every damn day.

"White female, eleven-years-old. Daughter of a real estate mogul from Key Largo," he begins.

Just a fucking baby. I hate sick fuckers who hurt kids.

"Florida? Why the hell are we outside of San Paulo?"

"Retaliation. The guy who had her abducted from in the front of her private school is in battle with her dad over a high-end client list some other piece of shit is selling," he explains.

"So fucked up," I mutter. "Taking kids just to make more money when it's apparent from this place that he's not hurting for money."

"Greed and social status are strong motivators." He doesn't bother to hide the disdain in his voice.

"Blade check this Florida guy out? If he's going against this shady mother fucker, he can't be clean. Are we taking jobs from criminals now?"

I know Kincaid would never get involved in something like that, but I know he also has a soft spot for kids. Her father may not be winning Father of the Year awards, but letting her get hurt because he's a piece of shit isn't Kincaid's style either.

"Blade ran the dude out through every software he has. He makes a ton of legitimate cash. He told Prez that he's certain not every deal the guy does is above board, but he couldn't find anything in his background check that pointed to illegal dealings."

"But shady enough to piss someone off enough to have his eleven-year-old stolen?"

"You know better than that," Kid chastises. "Kids, women, hell, even men get taken all the time without having any criminal involvement. Sometimes being in the wrong place at the unluckiest fucking time in their life puts them in danger of being taken."

"This is purposeful," I argue just for the sake of arguing. "This isn't some sex trafficker working off a shopping list from their fucked up clients."

"Well regardless, we're here, and we have a job to do. This shit will be over soon enough, and we can go back home."

I want to tell him that home is just as stifling as the heavy air around us. At least this mission has served as a much-needed distraction from the train wreck that my life has become.

"We shutting this whole mother fucker down tonight?" I ask as I see another small group of American frat boys stumble out of the front doors.

"Can't," Kid mutters. "We've been doing recon on the Luxury House for the last three days, and haven't found a thing wrong. When Snake went in last night, he had a menu full of women to pick from, and they were adamant that he couldn't get an underage girl there. Even flashing a wad of cash didn't get him a hint that there might be anything other than legal prostitution inside."

"Why would anyone want to travel out of America to fuck a Brazilian hooker? Any club in Florida, LA, or the strip in..." I look over at him daring me to say the word. Wanting to keep my nose from bleeding I continue without finishing my sentence. "They can go all over America, skip customs and the damn airfare, and find some woman willing to put out for less than a steak dinner."

"Bragging rights? Fuck I don't know," he answers. "Snake said the inside is full of over the top amenities. There's a spa, restaurant, indoor pool. Fuck, he even mentioned a gym for the fuckers that come and stay a week while sampling the menu of girls."

"Maybe this place is part of their 'fuck a girl in every country' plan." I quirk an eyebrow at him.

"Asshole," he grunts at bringing up his lifelong goals before he met Khloe.

"'I've never paid for sex in my life," he corrects.

"We all end up paying for it one way or another," I counter.

"True," he concedes.

His cell phone buzzes on the seat beside him.

"Khloe?" I ask.

"Nope. Prez. Coms on. They're already in the tree line, eyes on the building. We have half an hour to get geared up and join them before we go in and pull that little girl out."

I crank the beater of a truck and pull away from the spot we've been parked in for the last two hours.

"Thank fuck," I mutter. "My ass was falling asleep just sitting here so long."

Less than two minutes later, Kid and I are out of the truck, tucked behind a dilapidated, deserted building in a lost and forgotten industrial part of town.

"Don't forget your night gear," Kid says as he pulls his goggles over his head and rests them against his forehead.

"Moon's bright," I tell him looking up at the near full circle in the sky. "I have a horrible headache, that shit is only going to make it worse."

In a record eight minutes, we're leaving the truck and hitting the trees for the mile trek back to the rendezvous point we decided on earlier in the day. It's the spot that gets us closest to the building without leaving the safety of the trees.

"Fuck," I grumble tripping over the exposed root of a tree. "Why didn't you tell me that shit was there?"

Kid chuckles but doesn't slow his pace.

"What are you children grumbling about?" Kincaid's voice blasts through my com.

"Sounds like old man has refused to wear his night gear again," Shadow taunts.

"Old? Dude, you're several years older than me," I counter.

"He's not the one with a birthday next week," Itchy interrupts.

"Oh that's right," Kincaid says with a soft chuckle. "How old will you be again? Thirty-five? Thirty-six?"

"Twenty-eight, jackasses." My voice is rough, but there's a smile on my face.

Itchy remembered my birthday, even with all the shit we've been through, it eases my heart just a fraction.

"Strippers again this year?" Kid looks back over his shoulder as he asks the question.

"No thanks," I say with honest disinterest.

My good mood falls flat at the memory of the strippers from last year. Itchy and I both left separately from that little party, keeping up the rouse of hating each other. We met up less than an hour later in a hotel a town over and fucked until we were dehydrated. Best fucking blowjob of my life is awarded to that night.

Itchy clears his throat, and it makes me wonder if he remembers the gift he gave me also.

"Thank fuck," Shadow mutters. Kincaid and Kid chime in the ascent.

Snake chuckles. The stripper party last year was hilarious. All three spoken for men in our club came along for camaraderie, but they were uncomfortable as fuck the entire time. Keeping their eyes on the beer bottles or talking with each other, eyes not wandering in the slightest.

I reminded them that night they could look and enjoy the show the girls were putting on, and it wasn't a form of cheating, but they shrugged me off and sighed with relief when Itchy left first, and I followed shortly after. I know it wasn't probably five minutes later those three pussy-whipped mother fuckers were out the door.

"I want strippers for your birthday," Snake counters.

"Shut up, Snake," Kid, Shadow and Kincaid all say at the same time.

We haven't joked like this while on a mission in a long time. It feels like things are finally getting back to normal.

Chapter 35

Itchy

Thankful for both the darkness and being positioned a little farther from the other guys, I adjust my cock in my utilities. How fucked up is it that the mere mention of Snatch's birthday last year is enough to make me swell in my damn pants.

I clear my throat, doing my best to ignore the friendly banter between all of the guys.

My eyes never leave our point of entry into the building in front of us, but my mind is a million miles away. When people think about their wildest fantasies, it focuses on more money than they can ever spend, frivolous vacations, and never having to work at a dead end job again. The future I'd give anything to have looks a lot like the one I'm living, only Snatch is by my side every night, and we're welcomed into society simply as two men who love each other, without all the opinions and hate speech, people would see us no differently than they would any other relationship.

"How close are you guys?" Kincaid asks into his mic.

"Two hundred yards," Kid replies. "I have to go slower with the blind man behind me."

"So maybe I made a mistake," Snatch grumbles, and I can hear him curse under his breath as he stumbles again.

"Maybe?" I taunt.

He huffs. "The moon is bright as fuck," he challenges.

"Yeah, how's that working out in the woods?" Shadow cuts in.

I feel his presence coming up on my left before I even look in his direction.

"Won't happen again," he says before crouching about twenty feet away. "Anyone leave or enter since we left?"

"We've seen a few shadows passing in front of the upstairs window, but the door hasn't opened," Kincaid says. "Let's move. I'm sweating my balls off in this fucking humidity."

"A couple of months of living the high life, and you've already forgotten what it's like in the trenches," Shadow snarks.

A collective chuckle echoes in my ears.

"Yeah, yeah fuckers. Laugh it up. I'll remember that when you take off for a while when your baby gets here," Kincaid says.

"That reminds me," Dominic says, speaking for the first time tonight. He doesn't say much, so we all quiet when he does. "I'm going to need some time off around the same time."

"What are you saying?" Kincaid says with hope in his voice.

My lips tilt up in a wide grin.

"That he's old as fuck and should retire?" Snake answers for him.

Kid laughs, something I'd never have the balls to do at Dom's expense. I wait for the growl to come through the mic, but Dominic isn't biting tonight.

"Mak's pregnant," Dominic answers.

"You tell us now," Kincaid hisses into his mic. "When we can't respond the way we should? Who the fuck does that?"

"Dominic," Kid says flatly.

"You're going to be a dad," Snake adds.

"I'm already a dad," Dominic hisses into his headset.

"Nothing against Jasmine," Snake counters.

"Shut up, Snake," several men say.

"Honest fucking mistake," Snake grumbles.

"I'm going to punch you in the damn jaw for telling us like this, asshole," Kincaid warns. "Let's get this shit over with."

An unfamiliar laugh rings out in my head, and I realize Dom is actually laughing at Kincaid.

"Focus fellas. There's a little girl's life at stake here. We can all sit around a bar in a couple of hours and give Dom shit about his timing, but it's time to work," Shadow says. He's always the one to bring us back down to level when we get out of line.

"Everyone ready?" Kincaid asks.

We all respond.

"Just like any other day, brothers," Shadow says as the click of taking our weapons off of safety can be heard through our mics. We arm ourselves as if we're heading into the battlefield yet praying no one has to discharge their rifles. "See you on the other side."

"Move out," Kincaid grunts.

Silently we move from the cover of the trees heading to the door at the back of the building. Approaching from the back guarantees that the people coming and going from the whore house closer to the street can't see us. It's also the point of entry closest to the safety of the trees, keeping us protected in the darkness for as long as possible.

Snake may be an idiot most days, but his size and brute force are needed in situations like this. His ability to kick in a door keeps us from having to drag a battering ram several miles. His oversized boot meets the wood and the sound of it splintering echoes around us.

We move fast and organized into the small building. Thankful for the floor plans and schematics Blade was able to track down, we all know exactly where we're heading, each one of us having different goals even though we breach as a single unit.

Just as we're all inside, the power goes out. I don't miss a beat, but I hear Snatch.

"I'm blind," he hisses into his mic.

I grin like an idiot on the wall opposite of him. Simple jobs like this always come with a level of danger, but we have no reason to believe that this mission will be any different from the others that we've had. I look over at him, lost in the way he stares blindly into the darkness, able to take him all in without him knowing. Fuck, I miss him and everything we had together. I shake my head, trying to rid it of the thoughts that have no business being in my head anymore.

"Fucking told you," I taunt. "Just stay against the wall, pretty boy. Let the men handle this sh—"

I grunt when my leg is knocked out from under me. The searing pain of being shot hits a couple seconds later. My vision swims, but I stay as quiet as possible. The last thing I need is to take on more fire when I'm not ready to fight back.

"Itchy's been hit," Kincaid says calmly into his mic.

I watch my best friend, crouched low to the ground, as his head turns in my direction.

"Right leg!" Shadow screams. "He's down, Snatch. Eight meters up and six to your left. I'll cover you, but you have to go now."

Snatch's concerned frown turns into pure terror, fear fills his eyes and twists his mouth. He begins to move toward me with no concern for his safety, ditching all training he's ever had. I love him even more at this moment, but hate him for not protecting himself.

He slips, face almost hitting the floor. I start to smile, but can't seem to find the strength. When he pulls his hand up, I notice the darkness standing out against his skin. Blood. A lot of fucking blood.

"Stay with me," he begs. "I got you."

The tone of his voice makes me tremble. He never gets flustered, and I don't know if it's because I'm the one that's hurt or if the situation is just that dire.

His hand wanders up my numb leg just as I open my mouth to speak. I yelp instead when he finds the bullet hole and a second later shoves his finger into the wound.

"Fuck," I hiss.

"Sorry, man," he apologizes as he begins to unbuckle his belt.

If it's bad enough for a tourniquet rather than just pressure applied to the wound, I know I'm fucked. The location of the pain radiating out from the wound tells me the femoral artery has been hit. I'm as good as fucking dead.

He reaches for my night vision goggles, needing them more than I do right now. Just before he pulls them from my head, his close proximity gives me an uninterrupted view of his face.

"You're crying," I whisper absently as I reach up and caress his cheek. My eyes close, half from exhaustion, half from needing to just be with him at this moment, but struggling at seeing his pain.

"Don't get all soft on me know," he teases.

Several curses leave his mouth, from what I assume is him finally able to assess the situation with clear vision.

"I'm cold," I tell him with a harsh shiver.

"Don't," he hisses. "Save your energy."

Energy? I have no energy. It's draining from me, pooling around us. I'm an analytical person. I know this is my end. There's no way I can survive. The distant sound of gunshots tells me the fight isn't even over. I'm mere minutes away from death in a fight that could go on for an hour. Nothing matters but him at this moment. I don't care who's around or what secrets I'm spilling. I know I can't leave this world with him thinking I'm marrying Snapper.

"I love you," I confess. "I'm so sorry I couldn't be what you needed."

I want to say so much more but the blackness working its way into my vision forces my eyes closed.

"Please, stay with me. You're all I'll ever need. I love you, too. Please open your eyes." Words that should've been spoken long ago, but would've had no bearing on how today ends. As much as I hate to leave him, this is my destiny. I can wish for more time, years and years if I'm being selfish, but it would be no use. I can revel in the fact that the last words I hear him speak is the very thing I've been longing to hear for some time.

I attempt to open my eyes, but a light flutter is all I can manage before the sincerity in his voice carries me into the depths of death.

Chapter 36

Snatch

"Calm down," Kincaid orders as I stand from the hospital bed and run my hands over the top of my head. "Maybe grab a shower or something."

"I'm not leaving him," I mutter. "We've been apart too long as it is. I won't waste another second."

"You want him to wake up and see you covered in blood?" Shadow, always the fucking voice of reason.

I look down at my clothes, saturated with Itchy's blood. I've at least washed my hands. The blood on them now is from the busted knuckles, the aftermath of what went down in that building when they carried him away on a stretcher. The sound of the portable defibrillator recharging over and over is still bouncing around my head, even hours later.

"Fine," I grumble heading into the bathroom. I'm only a couple of feet from him, but leave the door open just in case he begins to wake or something goes on.

"Really?" Kid asks leaning against the wall on the far side of the room but with a clear view of me stripping out of my clothes.

"You got a problem with it now?" I ask as I kick my boxer briefs off. I'm strung too tight for any comment he may have now that the guys know about Itchy and me.

"Not like you're thinking," he mumbles. "I've never wanted to see your junk. Close the door."

"The door stays open," I say giving him a pointed look, daring him to shut it when I climb in the shower.

"Get cleaned up, man," Shadow says from around the corner. I can't see him, but we've all stayed in the room since Itchy was brought back from surgery. Well, everyone except Snake and Ace. None of us are in the mood for their shit right now. "We'll call you if he needs you."

I climb in the shower, the sting of the hot water on my injured knuckles barely even registering. Not one of them has asked a question about what was said after Itchy was shot, and I haven't volunteered any additional information. They know what's going on. Every word we spoke was shared with each one of them via the coms we were wearing.

Less than five minutes later, I'm toweling off, unsure if I got all of the soap out of my hair.

"Your bag," Kincaid says dropping my duffel just inside of the door.

"Thanks, man."

"Anytime," he returns.

I take a minute, standing in front of the small mirror with my head hanging. The doctors repaired the gunshot in his leg, transfused several pints of blood to replenish what he'd lost, but they stopped short of telling us everything would be okay.

'Prognosis looks good,' the doctor said. 'First twenty-four hours are critical.'

"Way to fucking reassure us," I mutter looking up and staring into empty eyes.

"Hey," Shadow says sticking his head in the door. "He's starting to move around."

I'm out of the bathroom, by his side, and grasping his cool palm in my own hands.

"Itchy? Itchy?" I whisper softly.

His eyes flutter open, and he does the most amazing thing. When he sees me looking down at him, his lips twitch in a smile.

"Hey, baby," he says.

I swear my heart doubles in size at the moment.

"Hey, yourself."

"I thought I died." His voice is hoarse, a rough edge to it I've never heard before.

"I love you," I tell him, refusing to let another second pass without him knowing.

His smile, although weak, grows bigger. "I thought I dreamed that part."

I shake my head, unable to speak around the emotion clogged in my throat.

"Not a dream," I finally manage.

I lean in to press my lips to his, but he stiffens at the voice on the other side of the room.

"About fucking time," Kincaid mutters.

He's not strong enough to get away, but Itchy attempts to pull his hands from mine and turns his head.

"Don't," I warn.

"We'll be outside," Shadow says.

I turn my head and watch the three guys that have stood vigil with me leave the room, only turning back to Itchy when the door clicks closed.

"They know?" He asks, eyes darting between mine for clarification.

"Kinda hard to miss," I taunt. "With me professing my undying love if you'd just wake up and survive."

His eyes soften when my hand runs down his cheek. "Sorry I missed that."

I kiss his lips with only a fraction of the emotion I feel. I don't want to hurt him even though I want nothing more than to pull him to my chest and tell him everything I promised while he was in surgery.

"I can go back through it if you need."

"Tell me again," he prompts.

I wipe the tears that forms at the corners of his eyes before they disappear into his hairline.

"I love you." I peck his lips. "I want to spend the rest of my life showing you just how much."

"You actually said that without cringing," he whispers. I can tell he's losing strength again, even this short conversation proving to be too exhausting.

"I mean it."

"How bad is my leg?" he asks.

"It wasn't your leg," I tell him trying to keep a straight face. "Those bastards shot off your dick."

His eyes widen, and I continue. "But your ass is fine, so I still want you."

When I give him an over-exaggerated wink, he realizes I'm joking.

"Asshole," he mutters with a strangled laugh. "You may have to worry about your own ass after that."

"It's yours," I offer. "But your leg is going to be fine. You'll have a gnarly scar, but they were able to get the tourniquet off before there was any damage."

"How? The mission was still happening. I just knew I would die there."

"Blade, as always, was in on our coms. He dispatched emergency services before I crawled over to you. The team went up the stairs to get the girl, and I carried you out to the ambulance."

"My hero," he teases.

"You should get some sleep," I advise, even though the last thing I ever want to see is his closed eyes.

"I will," he promises, his grip on my hands tightening.

There is so much I want to tell him, so many questions I have. I'm struggling to not just dive in and lay them all at his feet. Ever aware of his surroundings, he notices.

"Just say it. Whatever has that beautiful face of yours all scrunched up," he urges.

"Snapper," I remind. "Tell me the only reason you were going to marry her is because of the fucking video she had."

His brow furrows. "How did you find out?"

"Answer me first," I hiss, unable to wait for a second longer.

"That's the only reason," he explains. "I knew you weren't ready, didn't think you would ever be ready, but I figured you'd hate me more than you already did if she told people. You made your choice very clear that night I was waiting for you in your room."

"The ultimatum you mean?" I can feel myself getting angry all over again. Not at him, but my own stupidity.

He nods. "I was willing to make that sacrifice with her, to keep our secrets buried where you wanted them."

I shake my head. "You fucking idiot."

"Me?" he groans and shifts his weight.

"On the way back from that shit that went down," I begin to explain. "I made the decision that night to come to you and tell everyone about us. I was in one hundred percent. I got to the clubhouse..."

"Snapper had just announced our engagement," he finishes.

"You should've told me," I say on a whisper because losing that time with him is awful but even worse considering how today could've ended.

"I was hurting at your rejection," he confides. "Even after everything you told me today, I'm still hurting."

"I needed time," I counter, my part of the argument I'm so used to saying.

"You had time. I didn't have a clue when or even if you would ever come to your senses."

He winces again.

"We can talk about this some other time," I say. "You're not in any condition to discuss this today."

"I suggest you get it all out in the open, fucker. Once I'm well I may beat your ass when we talk about it again."

I smile down at him and brush my lips against his. The sigh of his contented breath against mine a relief I thought I'd never feel again.

"How did you know about the video?"

"Khloe told Kid a couple of hours ago when he called her that she'd heard Snapper bragging to Gypsy." I refuse to speak the rest of the graphic information I had to pull from Kid because he didn't want to repeat it.

He narrows his eyes at me. "What aren't you telling me?"

"It's not important. I just need to know if you're still planning on going through with it."

He shakes his head almost violently. "Why the fuck would I do that?"

"Khloe said she heard Snapper bragging about how you guys have been fucking like animals. She told Gypsy she was pregnant." The words are like sandpaper in my mouth. "I'd never tell you to turn your back on a kid, so this whole situation is pretty fucking complicated. I just need to know if you're..."

"It's a fucking lie," he hisses. "I haven't fucking touched her since the day Misty showed up at the clubhouse. I'd never fuck a chick without a rubber, so if she's pregnant, it's not fucking mine."

"You fucked Darby without a rubber once," I remind him like the asshole I am.

"You did too, fucker. That night was chaos. I haven't done it since."

"So there's nothing there? With Snapper?"

He shakes his head. "Fuck no. She's been sleeping in my bed, but I don't even touch her. I was only pretending for you."

"That's a good thing," I mutter. "Kincaid told Rose to put her ass out. She won't even be at the clubhouse when we get back."

"He kicked her out thinking she was engaged to me and pregnant with my child. That's super fucked up."

I smile. "You know how Prez is. He has a sixth sense about this shit. He knew she was lying. Told as much to Shadow when we were discussing her leaving the club."

"Wow," he mutters.

"I will tell you that Kid didn't fucking care. He voted her out regardless if she was in a delicate condition."

"We could've avoided all of this," he adds.

"I know, and all of this is on my shoulders. I own it, and I'll do everything in my power to make it right." I peer into his eyes searching for the answers I truly need. "If you're beside me, I can conquer the world."

"You're getting soft on me," he says with a wide smile.

I shrug. "If you need me more manly right now, I have no problem shoving my cock down your throat."

"There he is," he whispers. "I'm so fucking tired."

"Get some sleep, Rob. I'll be here when you wake up." His grip loosens on my hand as he falls asleep. "From now on, I'll always be here."

Chapter 37

Itchy

"Still hurting?" Snatch whispers in my ear as I settle into the couch cushion.

"Physical therapy kicked my ass today," I answer. "It's still nowhere near as painful, I imagine, as that paper cut you had two years ago."

"Asshole," he mutters handing me a beer. "It was a cardboard cut."

"You don't find this weird?" I ask looking around the room full of happy couples.

We've been back from Brazil for several weeks, and no one has even brought up our relationship. I've talked about it a little more with Khloe, but that was more a litany of 'I told you so' and gratefulness that Snapper was finally gone. Gypsy left with her, so that's the end of the club girls. Snake, Ace, and Skid are the only single members left, but they've been having a good time hunting for their conquests.

"That no one even blinks an eye at us?" Snatch asks. I nod. "It just makes me feel even more like shit for not telling them two years ago."

"What's done is done," I tell him. The words have been on repeat since I woke up in the hospital.

Kid walks in, handing a cold bottle of water to Khloe. Bri is snuggled up to some guy on the other sofa. Dominic is playing rock, paper, scissors with Jasmine while Mak looks on, the glow from her pregnancy already pinking her cheeks. Griffin is trying to share his banana with Ivy who is in Kincaid's arms drinking a bottle. Em is beside him with Gigi sleeping on her lap. Shadow and Misty have their heads leaned in close, and from the fire in his eyes, I don't think they'll be out here much longer.

I make the mistake of looking over at Snake who's sitting on the floor in front of Ace. He catches my eye, and a devious smirk crosses his lips. It's a warning sign for what comes out of his mouth next.

"You guys don't act very gay," he says with skepticism.

"Act gay?" Khloe says, ready to go to our defense.

I hold my hand up. "Hold on, Khloe. Let him explain."

I fight the grin that is tugging at my lips because I know Snake doesn't have a mean bone in his body, his vocabulary is just limited.

"I mean, you guys just sit there. You hang out, drink beer, joke around with us exactly like you did before you turned gay."

I cock my head to the side.

"Before they *turned* gay?" Khloe argues.

Kid places a hand on her thigh and whispers. "Sweet Girl, what did I say?"

"Don't feed the animals," she mutters.

A collective laugh echoes around the room at her response.

"What are you trying to say?" Snatch asks leaning forward, so his elbows are resting on his knees. "You think we're joking just because he's not sitting in my lap or sucking..."

Dominic clearing his throat draws our eyes. His eyebrow rises in warning as Jasmine covers his rock with her paper hand.

"Sorry," Snatch apologizes.

"You should try it," I add. "Being intimate with your best friend is out of this world."

"Here, here," Kincaid cheers, pulling Ivy's bottle from her sleeping mouth and raising it in a toast. I swear Em melts into a puddle beside him.

Snake shakes his head, and I think he's outwardly rejecting the idea, but then he opens his mouth. "Tried. My gag reflex sucks and this one," he jerks his finger over his shoulder toward Ace. "He nearly puked before I got the tip in."

Silence washes over the entire room as we all stare at them.

"Dumb ass," Ace says breaking the silence and slapping Snake on the back of the head.

Dom clears his throat again. "You ready to go home, angel?"

Jasmine nods her head. "Matilda needs a bath."

"She got a bath this morning," Mak argues but stands from the couch. "The puppy is clean."

"We aren't trying to run you off," Snatch says, the apology clear in his voice. "We can keep it clean."

Snake snickers.

"Maybe not," I mutter.

"Oh you're not," Mak assures. "They said the tiredness is supposed to go away in the second trimester, but it just hasn't yet."

"Not in pregnancies with multiples," Em chimes in.

Mak's eyes widen as big as saucers, and Dom gets a glint in his eyes as if he's praying she's carrying more than one baby.

We all say our goodbyes as they leave and head to their house.

"Another beer?" Snatch says as he gets up from the couch.

"Bottle of water, but I can get it. I'm not an invalid."

He leans in close. "Save your energy. You're gonna need it in just a little bit."

My blood heats at his promise, which turns to boiling when he leans in all the way and kisses me as if no other soul in the room exists.

"That's so damn hot," Bri groans from the other side of the room.

"Yep, they're definitely gay," Snake adds.

Khloe chuckles, finally realizing Snake and Ace just lack filters and don't mean any ill-will toward us.

"Are you guys going to get married?" Khloe asks just as Snatch is walking back and handing over the bottle of water.

I hiss when his hand jolts and the bottle falls on my crotch.

"I'm not being a damn bridesmaid," Snake mutters.

My lip twitches, but I refuse to answer, not because I'm hiding anything, but because I honestly don't know. We've talked about forever several times, but wedding bells haven't been mentioned.

I turn the tables on her. "You and Kid ever getting married?"

Kid smiles, a knowing shine in his eyes. "I've told her no less than a hundred times this week alone that we're getting married."

"And I *told* you," she counter, "That just *telling* me it's going to happen doesn't make it a proposal."

They begin to whisper argue, but when I look up, I notice Griffin sitting beside Em and Shadow and Misty have disappeared.

"Wanna head to bed before they realize we never answered the question?" Snatch asks in my ear.

"Please," I say with a chuckle and get up off of the couch. I can't hide the wince when my muscles flex and strain against the repaired area in my thigh.

"Do you need a pain pill?" I love the concern in his voice. He's taken care of me every second since my accident.

"No." I give him an evil smile. "But I may need help getting my pants off."

"Can we watch?" Snake says from across the room.

I have to catch Snatch by the shirt before he flies across the room and Snake ends up with a boot to his face.

"Fuck is with you asking us that?" he hisses.

Snake shrugs.

"Would you ever ask me if you can watch while I make love to my wife?" Kincaid asks on a snarl.

"Fuck no, Prez. That shit's personal."

"Same fucking thing with them," Kincaid says with an exaggerated point in our direction.

I smile as the blood drains from Snake's face. Ace has the wherewithal to facepalm at his ridiculous best friend.

"I've put up with it long enough. Your mouth is bad enough when you're sober, but you stop drinking now."

"Forever?" Snake asks

"Until you can learn to control your mouth," Kincaid corrects.

We walk out while Kincaid continues to chastise Snake like the deviant child that he is.

"Why are you smiling?" Snatch asks as we turn down the hallway toward our room.

I chuckle. "I feel bad for him. It can't be easy being that stupid."

"He thinks he's funny. He's more than able to know what he should say and what he shouldn't," Snatch argues. "Don't feel sorry for him."

"It's more like pity. I think he's upset..." Snatch's fingers press against my lips, halting my words.

"I don't want to talk about anyone but us." He hits his knees in front of me the second the door is shut and locked.

"Are you proposing?" I whisper as he reaches under the bed and pulls out a box.

"Yes," he answers with a smirk that tells me he's not being serious.

He flips the top of the box off and holds it up so I can see.

"Will you marry me?" I laugh, nearly falling over when I see the black cock ring on the top of white tissue paper.

I grin down at him as he sets the box aside and works my basketball shorts off of my hips. I forget what we were even talking about when his mouth wraps around my dick.

He hums around my cock as if it's the best thing he's ever tasted. We haven't done much since the accident, and a couple of handjobs in the shower pales in comparison to what he's doing right now.

I bump against the back of his throat, and my vision swims.

"We have to take it to the bed," I groan. "I'm going to fall."

He works to get my tennis shoes and socks off, and I pull my t-shirt over my head. With our combined effort, I'm stark naked in under a minute. My hands find his muscled chest as his own t-shirt clears his head and is tossed to the floor.

"I can't wait for you to fuck me," I pant helping to push his jeans down his legs.

"I'm the one who's getting fucked tonight," he admits with a sly smile.

Chapter 38

Snatch

Itchy stares at me like I've spoken in Russian before his head starts to shake back and forth.

"I don't know about that," he says, doubt filling his voice.

I reach for and grip his cock. "Says the guy who's cock is hard as a steel pipe."

"You were just sucking it," he backpedals. "I don't expect that."

"But you want to," I counter.

"Of course, but not because you feel like you have to. I like getting fucked."

"You don't think I will?" I lean in and kiss his shocked mouth. "I want it. I've wanted it for a long time. I'm tired of being too scared to ask for what I need."

"You may not like it," he continues to argue.

"We won't know until we try, but I bet it's going to feel amazing."

"You got the cock ring because you knew I was going to come the second I got the head in."

He laughs, reminded of the sex toy he reaches down and grabs it from the box.

"It took every ounce of control I could muster not to blow the second I slid inside of you that day in the shower. I'm just being preemptive."

"You know me well," he murmurs against my mouth when I go in for another kiss. "Bed. Now. I need to get you ready to take my cock."

I lie on my side because I know his leg has to be screaming in pain. I don't want him to overdo it, but I can't wait any longer. He grabs a bottle of lube from the bedside table and positions himself opposite of me, the sight of his straining cock right in front of my face makes my nerves increase tenfold.

"Fuck," I moan when his talented mouth wraps around the head of my cock.

It's gentle, tentative suction at first, but soon turns to deliberate, long strokes. My hips buck of their own accord. Instead of gagging, he chuckles and takes me even deeper.

"Don't come," he commands popping off the top. "It'll be more intense if I'm in you."

My legs tremble when the sound of the lube top being opened reaches my ears. It's not the first time he's had his fingers inside of me, but it's what comes after that makes my nerves ratchet up.

"Ohhh," I hiss when his cold, probing fingers find their target. "Keep doing that while sucking, and I'll come too quick."

His mouth releases me, replaced by a soft stroking hand, the attention just enough to keep me teetering on the edge, but not enough to send me over the cliff.

Slowly, he works me, opening me, preparing me. My need to have him is growing by the second, and I fully understand what he's feeling when I tease him to the point that he's begging me to fuck him.

"Please," I beg, needing exactly that.

"Put the cock ring on me, Jaxon."

I'd forgotten about the damn thing even though I'm clutching it in my hand. My eyes flutter, and my hand grips the blanket under us as his fingers trace over that spot deep inside. Now I know why he jolts like he's being electrocuted when I do the same to him.

"Cock ring," he hisses.

His hand releases my cock, giving me back just enough focus to stretch the ring around the base of his cock and around his nuts. I lick them for good measure, loving the way they look all trussed up.

"Jesus. Stop that." His hips pull away the same time his hands release me.

I hit my hands and knees, past the point of needing him inside of me.

I feel him move on the bed, but never feel the tip of his cock against me or the warmth of his thighs against the back of mine. Looking over my shoulder, I see him laying with his back to the headboard stroking lube down his cock.

"I need you to ride me," he says.

I nod and turn back around, so I'm facing him.

"I'm an asshole and forgot about your leg."

"Not just that, this way," he says as I straddle his hips. "It gives you more control. I'll hurt you if I'm able to take over."

"I'm nervous," I admit as I position the head of his cock against my prepared entrance.

"We don't have to do this," he says but groans when I sink an inch down on his cock. "Never mind. We really need to do this."

I wince at the initial stretch.

"Go slow," he instructs. "That burn you feel will go away, just give it a second."

I lean forward and take his mouth with mine, tongue stroking his. It's aggressive almost like retaliation for the pinch of pain I'm feeling, but just as he promised the discomfort dissipates.

Flexing his hips, he sinks a little deeper. I clutch his shoulders, fingers digging in harder than I'd planned.

"So much for having control," I pant.

"You feel fucking amazing. Soft, hot, so fucking tight." His praise washes over me, and I settle farther on to him, nearly taking him to the base when he lifts me off with his hands under my thighs before urging me down again.

"Jesus." I close my eyes, squeezing them shut at the intrusion.

One hand leaves my thigh and immediately strokes down my cock. I continue the momentum, up and down, push and pull. This is the most intense thing I've felt before in my life.

"How does it feel?" he rasps.

"Amazing," I moan.

"Cock ring isn't gonna help this time," he admits. "I need you to come."

His hand works faster, but as wonderful as it feels, I know I can't come. The sensations are so overwhelming it's like my body can't focus on one single thing to cling to.

"I can't," I confess.

"You can," he urges. "Focus on my hand."

I do as he says, but my hips start working faster at the same time.

"Goddamn it," he groans. "That's going to end this."

My eyes find his, urging him on. The strain on his face almost comical as he tries to resist the orgasm that I can only imagine is trying to tie his nuts in knots.

"Let go. Come for me."

One hard, final drive of his hips and I can feel him pulsing inside of me.

"Fuuuck," he groans for the hundredth time tonight.

His eyes find mine once he regains focus. Hand still working my cock, he looks disappointed.

"You didn't come."

"Sorry," I mutter, climbing off of him.

"Don't fucking apologize. I'm the one who should be saying sorry." He shifts me, so I'm on my back. "Let me apologize."

My cock sinks into his talented mouth, and I'm lost. Nipping, sucking, paying close attention to the spot he knows I love on the underside, I'm on the edge in a matter of seconds.

"Your fucking mouth," I hiss. "Fuck, baby I'm coming."

Not much of a warning considering I was coming before the words left my mouth. Like the amazing man that he is, he never misses a beat, still sucking while swallowing my come.

* * *

"Do we have to fucking talk about it? Like living it wasn't bad enough," I mutter as we switch positions in the shower.

We'd laid in bed for a while after we made love, but a shower was necessary.

"I'm just saying that it's nothing to be ashamed of. I read an article, and it explained that a ton of bottoms don't come while being fucked."

I sigh. This makes the third time he's said that since we climbed in here. Seems like we have to hash it out or he won't drop it.

"You come like a fucking freight train when you're getting fucked," I remind him.

"I love being a bottom. I love it when you fuck me. I crave it." He frowns at me when I smile. "You needed to be sure before we did that. Now that you regret it, I feel like shit."

I take a menacing step toward him until our wet chests are flat against each other. "I enjoyed it, and I don't regret it. I feel like I let you down."

"You didn't," he whispers against my lips. "It was amazing. For you to give yourself to me like that. It was amazing."

"Good," I tell him before catching his mouth with mine, kissing him until both of our previously spent cocks are hard between us.

"I'll fall if you try to fuck me in this shower," he says with a smile against my lips.

"We better get rinsed off then."

I take a step back and hand him the shampoo. Grabbing the bar of soap, I spend exceedingly more time than needed washing his body, paying extra attention to his cock and balls.

"Is this how it's always going to be?" He tilts his head back, rinsing shampoo from his hair.

I huff a laugh. "Getting tired of me already?"

"No," he says wiping water from his face so he can open his eyes and look at me. "You made it very clear that you weren't gay. 'I'm bisexual.'" He says in a higher pitched voice, a horrible impression of mine.

"I'm not interested in a triad." I wipe at a patch of soap suds clinging to his cheek. "I meant it when I rejected Darby. That's not what I want."

"You don't ever want to fuck another woman?"

I search his face for answers, but he's managed to school it into impassivity.

"What do you want?" I ask when trying to read him fails.

He smiles. "I wouldn't mind sharing a woman every now and then. I think you could come with me in your ass if someone was sucking you off."

My laugh echoes off of the wall. "You think?"

"Only one way to find out," he whispers as he leans in to kiss my lips. "And I'm dying to find out."

"You just want to fuck me again." His lips smile against mine.

"I can't wait to fuck you again," he confesses.

I kiss him feverishly, keeping our mouths and hands busy for the rest of the night just so I don't admit that it's exactly what I want too.

Chapter 39

Itchy

Sitting in the garage with the guys, I smile when Snatch walks in with a couple of beers in his hands. Leaning in, he kisses me chastely before handing me one.

"That's one way to get around the 'No Women in the Garage' rule," Snake mutters.

Snatch kicks at his boot before sitting down in the empty chair beside me. Our knees touch, but that and an occasional kiss is usually the extent of our public affection. I'm sure it's because Snatch still isn't as comfortable with being 'out' as he wants me to believe. It's been months since my accident, yet he still maintains a respectable distance most of the time in front of everyone. It's a different story when he's been drinking.

"What's your damn problem anyway?" Snatch asks Snake who has continued to sit there grumbling.

"His girlfriend told him she needed space," Ace chirps.

Snake snarls at him, and my eyebrow raises since this is the first I've heard of Snake having anything serious with a woman.

"Her old man just got out of prison," he mutters, because he's Snake and he just can't help speaking what's in his mind.

Shadow leans forward in his chair. "Something we need to worry about?"

Snake shakes his head before tilting his beer up. He's discovered over months of research, that he's more tolerable when he lays off of the hard liquor.

"I don't think so. They got divorced shortly after he got sent up for dealing drugs. Been inside for a decade, but she said he wasn't the nicest fucker before he was locked up," he explains.

"From what I can see," Ace cuts in. "She doesn't have anything to worry about. She took their boy to visit the whole time he was in, and she says their relationship is amicable, but she was a little nervous about him getting out and seeing a biker hanging out at the house all the time."

So that's where he's been. He's been scarce for several months. I just figured he'd been mad that Kincaid ripped his ass a few months ago, but clearly, he's found a better way to occupy his time.

"Let us know if he becomes a problem," Kincaid says.

"I will," Snake grumbles. "I just hate being away from her."

Snatch looks over, catching my eye. The grin on his face matches the one on mine. Seems no one in our little club is immune to the love bug.

"How old is her son?" Dom asks from out of nowhere.

"Ten, I think." Ace answers for Snake. "Goes to Dolchester Elementary."

"That's where Jasmine goes," Dom says. "I wonder if they know each other."

"Couldn't tell you that," Snake says. "There are so many kids around I can't keep up with shit."

"More to come," Shadow says grinning around the mouth of his beer. "Three more months and my little boy will be here. A week or so after that Dom's son will be here."

"Like I said, so many kids." Snake tosses his empty beer bottle into the trash and grabs another from by his boot.

"You don't need to be involved in her life if you can't handle her kid," Dom chastises.

Look at Mr. Suddenly Talkative over here.

He's been an amazing father to Jasmine, and we all know he's going to spoil his son as much as he does her. I don't think he'll ever make her feel as if she's less just because she's not his blood relation.

"I just miss them. Haven't seen her all week, and phone sex really isn't my thing," Snake says with a sigh.

I chuckle. "So we get to the root of the problem."

"Could always hook up with the blonde from Jake's," Ace offers.

"No thanks," his best friend says.

Yep, he's definitely caught the love bug.

"What about you guys?" Snake says directing his attention to Snatch and me. "You ever plan on having kids? I mean adopting or some shit."

I look at Snatch who turns at the same time to look at me. We laugh as if the funniest joke has been told.

When we finally gain our composure Snatch speaks for the both of us. "No, man. No kids for us. Don't get us wrong, we love playing Uncle to all the wonderful kids around us, but we aren't the daddy type."

As if on cue, the baby monitor sitting beside Kincaid activates, and the small whimper of one of the girls can be heard through it.

"Nice chatting with you guys," Kincaid says as he stands. "But my sweet angel is awake."

"She doesn't sound very happy," Snatch adds when the whimpers turn into full on wails.

"The joys of parenthood. Ivy is teething, and it's as if Gigi feels her pain because she's fussy and upset too," he explains. "See you assholes in the morning."

We all say our goodnights as he leaves the garage to go take care of his girls.

"You guys looking forward to that stage?" Snatch directs his question to Dom and Shadow.

They both grin.

"I can't wait," Dom says just as Shadow says, "Not a chance."

Shadow looks over at Dominic. "You have no idea what you're asking for."

"I spent twenty years in the Marine Corps; I can handle an infant."

Shadow just shakes his head in disbelief. "Ok, then. When you realize how hard and exhausting it is, I won't even be an asshole and tell you I told you so."

"You staying over?" Ace asks Dom as he stands and grabs another beer from the fridge.

"Yeah. Jasmine said Ollie was missing Matilda, so we're here so they can visit." He smiles, knowing he's wrapped around that little girl's finger, and not giving one single fuck about it.

"You're going to end up with a litter of damn dogs at the house of yours, if you're not careful," Snatch warns.

He chuckles. "Yeah, I think we're past that. That dog's stomach is already swelling. But what can I say? Matilda and Ollie love each other. I can't keep them separated. Griff loves Ollie so I can't bring him home with us, besides Em would never let him leave the clubhouse overnight. So because my damn dog is head over heels for the dog here, I'm stuck with you assholes tonight."

"Not stuck with me," Shadow says as he stands from his chair. "Misty is waiting on a foot massage."

"Yeah, I'm sure Mak is ready for me to rub her back," Dom says getting up from his chair as well.

"Sweetheart," I say sarcastically as I stand and hold my hand out for Snatch. "Ready for me to massage your cock?"

"Jesus," Dom mutters with a laugh.

"What?" I ask with a wry smile. "His feet and back are fine."

Snatch swats my hand away playfully and stands up. "Only if you do that thing with your tongue."

Snake groans and begins mumbling about needing a cock massage and something about rubbing one out to Skype again.

We hold hands all the way back to our room, fingers twined and only break free when we cross over the threshold. His hands are in my hair, and I'm pushed against the wall almost immediately.

"You trying to make me blush in front of them?" he snarls against my mouth.

"You going to deny your cock being hard before we walked out of the garage?" I counter.

His lip twitches with a smile I can tell he's trying to hold back. "I always get hard when you mention wanting to do things with my cock."

"I'm going to take care of you for hours, but I wanted to show you something first."

He shakes his head, lips brushing against mine. "Play first then show me."

"Not this time, Romeo."

I push against his chest, and even though it's the last thing he wants, he backs up so I can slide past him.

I step into the closet and pull a cardboard tube from the back.

"You're done with them?" The giddiness is clear in his voice. "I thought it would take several more weeks."

"I had some motivation," I tell him.

"What would that be?" Snatch asks as he helps me spread the floor plans across our king-sized bed.

"I'm anxious for you to be able to fuck me in more than one room, of course." If his smile got any bigger, it wouldn't fit on his handsome face.

We both look down at the plans, and I begin pointing out different areas that we'd agreed on. We got together and decided as a club that as much as we love everyone here, it just isn't feasible with the kids multiplying for us all to stay here. Cerberus owns dozens of acres around the clubhouse, and we've all started working on plans to build our homes on the land behind our existing building. We'll be in shouting distance, and when we head out on missions, the wives and kids plan to stay in one house. Safety in numbers and all that.

"This is way too big for us," Snatch says noticing the second floor and additional bedrooms.

"It's not," I argue.

"This whole section up here," he says pointing to the second floor. "This wasn't what we discussed."

"I'll pay for it," I tease.

He glares at me. "It's not the cost, and you fucking well know it. Why so much extra space?"

I turn and cup his face in my palms. "Because, after you make me an honest man and propose with more than a cock ring, I know you're going to want kids. We have to have room for them."

His eyes glisten. "We've said we don't want kids."

"You said you didn't want kids, but I see how you play with Griff and the girls. Hell, last week you taught Jasmine how to fish. Dominic is still a little pissed about that."

"He should've taught her sooner," he mumbles when I hold his face tighter.

"He was on the way to the store to get her a fishing pole."

He grins.

"I know you're going to want children. I've said I don't want them because I figured that's what you really wanted until I started really paying attention to you when you're around kids."

"You just said in the garage you didn't want them," he argues.

"I didn't think the garage was the place to tell you that I want what you want." I kiss him softly. "It wasn't the place to get my cock sucked when it finally hit you that I'm saying yes to the family you've been too afraid to ask for."

His eyes dart between mine before he growls. "You better get those floor plans off the bed because I'm about to fuck you on them."

I don't get the chance to move the floor plans, but he's cognizant enough to fuck me on the floor instead.

Epilogue

Itchy

15 Years Later

"That's not the way to go about getting what you want, son." Snatch's voice is marked with irritation, but it's been the same thing over and over for the last couple of weeks.

"Dad," Samson whines again. "Everyone is going to be there. Jacob's dad is letting him go."

Snatch catches my eye, but I just tilt my head. He knows how I feel about letting our sixteen-year-old son go with friends from school on a trip to Mexico. He's against it, and I don't see the harm. Snatch cited all the missions we've gone on over the last two decades which have just recently begun to dwindle since Kincaid has hired a whole new outfit to work them so we can stay closer to home with our families.

"No, Sam. You're sixteen," Snatch points out.

"I'll be seventeen by the time the trip happens." This child will not give up. "It's the senior trip."

"Which is awesome, and when you're a *senior* next year, you can go on your *senior* trip." Snatch gives him the 'don't ask again' look, but Sam has never been one to listen when he's this worked up about something.

"Rachel will be there!" he yells.

I roll my lips between my teeth to keep from laughing.

"A little help here?" Snatch asks in my direction. I shake my head when Sam looks over his shoulder and pleads with me.

Snatch narrows his eyes at me and I know exactly what that look means, and I honestly can't fucking wait until we're alone later. Maybe he'll even schedule a visit to Alexa and Garrett's club in Denver. The sex club we've been to a handful of times over the last ten years has been amazing. We'd go more often if we could.

I pick up the tray of sandwiches from the counter in the kitchen and carry them out to the living room. We're all piled into the clubhouse which has transformed some to fit our needs. Half of the rooms, the ones that were on the left of the hallway have been cleared to open the space more.

"You aren't going to help him?" Khloe asks as she grabs a sandwich, places it on a small plate already on the table and hands it to her son.

"Nope," I answer. "He wouldn't want to hear what I have to say."

"You should fight for him. Sam really wants to go, Dad." I look over at my daughter, Samson's twin sister.

"Delilah," I sigh.

They were over a year old when we adopted them. Thankfully they were too young to have been greatly affected by the brainwashing that was going on in the religious cult their mother birthed them in. We still have concerns about their father, the leader of the sect, but he's been given life in prison for the atrocities he committed on the girls who were under his care.

"Do you want to go to Mexico?" I ask her.

"If I say yes, does that mean Sam gets to go?"

I shake my head, and she sighs in relief.

"Thank goodness," she mutters. "I have no desire. I plan to spend the summer filling out college applications for next year."

"Atta girl," I say with a quick kiss on her forehead.

"Suck up," Gigi whispers, which Delilah ignores.

"Enough," Kincaid says getting onto his daughter. "If you can't be nice, you can spend the day back at the house, alone."

Gigi crosses her arms over her chest and grumbles incoherently.

I ignore the teen girl drama. Delilah knows she can come to me if it gets to be too much. How Ivy and Gigi ended up so different, I'll never know. Ivy is a lot like Delilah, very brainy and bookish. I couldn't be more proud of my girl.

The doorbell rings, pulling me away from the group just as Shadow and Misty begin talking about Griffin's first deployment to Germany. He graduated last year and has already sailed through training.

I open the door, and my heart stops.

If it were twenty years earlier, I would've sworn my husband was standing right in front of me. His jet black hair ruffles in the breeze and ice blue eyes narrow when he sees me. It isn't until the slightly younger boy standing beside him shifts from one foot to the other, do I even realize he's got someone with him.

"Babe," I call out over my shoulder. "Can you come here?"

I feel Snatch walk up behind me, his hands sliding into the back pocket of my jeans before he looks past me to see the two young men standing on the front porch.

"You must be my dads," the older boy says.

A Very Cerberus Christmas

Copyright

Synopsis

As a child, I believed Christmas wishes were supposed to come true.
As an adult, I realized making those wishes were pointless.
As an original member of the Cerberus MC, I knew hard work and determination is what brought a good outcome so I stopped making wishes.
I didn't ask for Lucy or her son Harley, but when having them became a reality I knew I needed to hold on tight.
Her past makes her decisions for her, and letting them go will be the hardest thing I'll ever do.

A Very Cerberus Christmas is a 45,000-word novel featuring Micah "Snake" Cobreski.

Chapter 1

Lucy

I've ignored a lot over the years. It's a skill I mastered long before I got out of high school. Okay, maybe ignored isn't the right word. Maybe I've learned to not be affected by things is a better way to explain myself because I definitely see the stares each day when I pull up to the school in my ten-year-old car. I notice the cringes on the other parents' faces and the way they lean their heads in to gossip with moms on the PTA when they see me coming. My child is well behaved, gets good grades, and is very helpful. He's kind and courteous to other kids and always has a smile on his face. He's gracious and sweet. And he's still *that* kid. The child parents warn their kids to stay away from.

He's poor. His clothes aren't designer. Our car isn't shiny and new. He's carrying the same backpack in first grade that he carried last year in kindergarten. It's as if the parents are afraid if their children acknowledge him, his poverty is going to rub off on them and their investments will take a hit overnight. It doesn't matter how awesome my child is, he's never going to be accepted because of my income level.

If I could change it, I would, but short of winning the lottery, it's not going to happen. I can't even afford to play, and I'd never gamble away the little money we have on chance.

I give my little guy a huge genuine smile when my old clunker pulls up next in line. The teacher frowns when she sees me. She has to take extra caution to walk him around to the driver's side of my car to help him in because the rear passenger door doesn't open.

"Have a good day," she says with little sincerity before walking away, her head shaking as she looks at the other teachers helping with car pickup.

Harley smiles from the back seat, his cheeks pink from standing in the cold, waiting to be picked up.

"Hey, buddy. How was your day at school?"

"Amazing! Did you notice my new jacket?"

"I did," I say.

The jacket isn't exactly new, and I was waiting for him to mention it, wondering how he was going to react before speaking on it, but true to form, my child always finds the positive in everything.

"It has a pocket on the inside, but don't worry, I won't try to sneak a car to school in it."

He cuts his eyes out the window in a way that tells me I may have to check his pockets each morning.

The school-donated jacket is just another slap in the face, just another way for the school to tell me I'm a bad mother without actually coming out and saying those exact words. I've never sent my child to school hungry or cold. I'd go without before that ever happened, and I have, more than once, but sending him to school in layers to accomplish what he needs to stay warm must be just as bad a thing as nothing at all. I sent him this morning with a thermal t-shirt, a sweater and two hoodies. He was cozy. From the bulge of his backpack, I imagine he has traded most of those for the fleece-lined number he's now sporting.

I take a calming breath as I wait for traffic to die down enough for me to pull away from the school. It would be easy to point fingers and place the blame at someone else's feet, but I can own my own faults and choices in life. I was an active participant in my failures. Catching up is always harder than keeping pace, and although I don't regret a day I've had with Harley, I know parenting would be easier had I done it in the right order, namely, not falling in with a man who had no goals in life other than drugs, crime, and screwing over everyone he could before they caught on.

Robbie is different now, but there's not much the man can do behind the bars of prison. My relationship with Harley's father was off and on for years, and at any point, I could walk away, but I was as big of a mess and tangled up in the drugs as he was. If I were one to blame other people for my mistakes, I could point the finger at him for handing me that first joint, for prepping that first line of coke, but I was always looking for an escape. It was going to be him or someone else honestly, so there's no point in assigning blame. I thought it was love. Of course I did. I was young and looking for what I wasn't getting at home from my smothering parents. I was certain I found that in him.

I started to grow up; he never did. I said no to drugs after a couple of years because he was in and out of jail, and I didn't want that for myself, but I could never say no to him. I ended up pregnant; he landed in jail for five years with an additional eighteen months because he fancied himself a badass the first couple of months he was in and picked up more time.

I never kept Harley away from him. Once he started doing better, I started taking Harley to visit him. All our son has known is a dad behind bars, but that will end shortly because Robbie is scheduled to be released soon, and I have no idea how that's going to go. There's nothing between us any longer. Once both of us got fully sober, we both realized we have nothing in common, and neither of us is fool enough to think trying to work things out would be good for anyone, even for Harley's sake. But I won't keep our son from his dad.

"What did you learn today at school?"

"Nothing," he answers.

"We've talked about this," I say, my eyes on the road.

"Mom," he grumbles. "The other kids in class are working on high-frequency words, but I know them already."

"You didn't tell the teacher that, did you?"

I chance a glance at him in the rearview mirror.

"Of course not. I sat quietly and worked ahead in my math workbook."

This is something she could penalize him for later.

It's as if the teachers look for a way to cause problems for him out of spite. You'd think teachers would want to nurture his intelligence, but the ones at the school he's at seem to only want to keep him down, or at least at a lower level than kids with more money. Heaven forbid, the poor kid has a leg up somehow.

I pull into the gas station I know to have the cheapest gas.

"Can I trust you to stay in the car?" The cheapest gas also means the place isn't in the best neighborhood, and it's a gamble in whether it's safer to leave him in the car or walk him into the store. It also helps to stave off the guilt I'll feel from watching his eyes dart to the candy aisle, knowing he wants to ask for a piece. He never would. Somehow Harley knows we don't have the money. Maybe he's able to pick up on my stress from not having money even though I don't discuss such things with him. Maybe he hears other kids talking about our lack of it at school, but the child doesn't ask for things. He looks. I can see the want in his eyes. He's a kid after all, but he doesn't ask, and it kills me to not be able to give it to him. I do when I can, but it isn't often.

"Yes."

I lock the door, feeling confident in his answer because I lucked out with him. He's a very well-behaved child. It's like someone knew I needed calm and less challenging in my life.

The cashier sighs when she sees me coming, but I can't be the only person that comes in here and has to pay for gas with change. There are a lot of us in the neighborhood that have to do this very thing. Times are hard, and it's not just the economy right now. Life is freaking hard. The damn stock market could skyrocket and we wouldn't know. In the trenches, it's always going to be hard.

As I stand in line, I mentally calculate what we'll need between now and when I get paid on Friday, making sure we'll have enough so I can determine what I can put in the tank. I keep a few feet back from the person in front of me so I can keep my eye on my car. The line moves forward, and so do I. The cashier seems extra salty today, no smile on her face even though I've been coming here for years. The woman seems hell-bent on hating her job and everyone who steps foot in here. I decided long ago that she'll never build a rapport with anyone and gave up. She takes forever to count out my change as if I'm going to stiff her a dime on eight dollars in gas.

Having had my eyes off of him for longer than a minute, I'm in a hurry to get back out to the car, and my blood runs cold when I approach and don't see his form in the back seat.

"Harley!"

"It's an Indian, actually."

I jump at the masculine voice, and then startle further when I see the man the voice came from—dark beard down to his chest, bright blue eyes, bandana around the top of his head, full riding leathers, gloves on his hands.

Biker.

Bad news.

And he's standing beside my son.

Who is not in the car, but straddling a damn motorcycle. There are two others standing near, but neither speaks. Their presence feels like a warning. Bikers are known to travel in packs. I know this from experience. Where there's one, there's always a couple more lurking about.

"I told you to stay in the car," I snap.

I normally don't have to chastise my child. He's very well behaved, but right now I could twist his ear for not listening to me. I get that he's only six, and after this, I'll never leave him alone in the car again. I locked the door, worried about people getting in, not him climbing out, because he promised me he'd stay put. Leave it to the temptation of a motorcycle to draw him out. Where puppies may be the pull for others, damn bikes are his.

"Do you see this, Momma?" Harley leans forward, his arms too short to reach the handlebars, but he looks adorable as he tries. I don't think I've ever seen such a wide smile on his face.

I hate that I'm the one that's going to be the one to crush his good time, but the kid just doesn't understand the trouble he could be getting into. He doesn't know that his father got tangled up with bikers, and that's where all of Robbie's problems began.

"Harley, you—"

"Indian," the man says once again.

"His name is Harley," I hiss, not bothering to look over at the man.

"Really?"

I chance a glance at him. It's not really fair for a man with a wind-blown beard to have such an alarming smile. His leather vest is worn and well used— SNAKE—on a patch near his left shoulder. Charming. It seems like a warning, and one I'll heed.

"Get in the car," I tell Harley, reaching for him. I know how hot the parts of a motorcycle can get, and I don't want him burned. I just paid for gas with nickels and dimes. The last thing I can afford is a hospital bill.

"Listen to your momma, little man," the guy says when Harley looks up at me with pleading eyes, reluctant to end his fun so quickly.

I usher Harley into the backseat, nodding when he apologizes for getting out. I start to climb into the driver's seat, and nearly cuss out loud when I remember I stopped to get gas. For some people, driving off without getting their eight dollars in gas wouldn't be a big deal, but it would wreak havoc on our lives. I couldn't get to work or pick Harley up from school in the afternoons for the rest of the week.

"I can pump it for you," the man says, his smile still in place, despite how short I've been with him.

"I've got it," I tell him.

To his credit, the man doesn't reach for the gas nozzle, and he keeps his distance.

"He seems to really like motorcycles."

I start to pump my gas, keeping my back to him, but my eyes are on his reflection in the window. I don't know where his friends went, but I know they're around here somewhere.

"We're not bad guys, ma'am," he says. "We wouldn't hurt him."

I turn to face him at this declaration.

"So it's just normal for three bikers to talk to children when a parent isn't present?" I glare at him.

He smiles down at me, and I notice for the first time just how much bigger he is than me.

"I was swiping my card to get gas. I turned around, and he was sitting on my bike. Should I have picked him up and thrown him off? You showed up like fifteen seconds later. I can promise you, there wasn't anything creepy going on."

I swallow. It doesn't go unnoticed that he doesn't point out that I left my small child in the car alone. Many people would, and maybe it's natural to point the finger and blame others. I shove down the realization that these guys sound more like how Robbie is now—a changed man than the bikers he used to hang out with—and maybe that's just my own justification I'm trying to calm myself with for leaving my child and having him end up in a dangerous situation.

"Well, I'm sorry he bothered you."

"Didn't say he bothered me, ma'am."

The gas pump clicks off and despite the embarrassment it may cause, I hold the hose up just in case it helps. I don't know if it makes the gas left in the hose end up in my tank, but if it does, I'll take all that I can. I won't ever see this man again, and I refuse to let him derail my week.

"Thank you for not yelling at him. Have a good day."

I climb into my car and drive away.

Chapter 2

Snake

"You can't tell me you didn't see it coming," Skid says as he climbs off his bike, picking up the conversation right where it left off before we pulled away from the clubhouse.

Ace shakes his head. "Didn't have a clue."

"You haven't noticed the weirdness?" I ask.

"They were fighting. I figured it was because of Darby. Best guy friends fight over women all the time," Ace explains. "Hell, usually that's the only thing they'll fight over. That and if someone borrows money and never pays it back."

Skid nods in agreement.

"Who knew Itchy and Snatch were like falling in love and having a two-year lovers' quarrel?" Ace chuckles.

"Glad that shit is over," I mutter, but we all stand near our bikes for a long moment.

Itchy was shot on our last mission. We almost lost him, and that takes its toll on a team. It makes us realize, like a slap in the face, that despite how badass we are, we're also human.

"I think they're going to be happy together," Skid says, a twisted grin on his face.

"And y'alls budding relationship?" Skid asks, slapping me on the back.

I shake him off. "Shut the fuck up."

"What? Not going to be another happy Cerberus couple?"

"We were drunk," Ace grumbles. "Neither one of us were meant for sucking dick."

I shake my head. I always said I'd try anything once, and apparently I took that to heart. After a half a bottle of tequila that included trying a little man-on-man action with my best friend, we both learned very quickly that we weren't meant for the rainbow side of life.

Skid slaps me on the back with a chuckle.

"Hey, isn't that the chick's car from the gas station a few weeks back?" Ace asks as we walk toward the entrance of the diner.

Excitement fills my blood, and I walk a little quicker. Her fiery attitude hasn't been far from my thoughts, and after the shitstorm of Itchy getting hurt, I've been left wondering if I'd ever run into her again. People drive through town all the time. The station we stopped at to fuel up is on the highway, so there was a possibility that she was just passing through. Knowing she might be local makes my lips curl up into a smile as I tug open the door.

That smile immediately fades away as I enter and look around the dining room.

Harley, the cutest kid I've ever met, is standing up in a booth, his little chest puffed out as he faces two men. He doesn't look happy. His face is red, his little fists balled up like he's getting ready to punch them both in their noses.

The pretty woman has her hand on his shoulder, frustration drawing her brow in.

"She said she isn't interested. You need to leave," the little guy says, his voice a low growl, marked with his young age.

I know he's trying to sound intimidating, defending his mom, but he's all of forty pounds, tops.

Her eyes find mine, but the kid's back is to me as we approach.

The guys giving her a hard time spot us. The one in front has the wherewithal to widen his eyes just as Harley shifts his weight on the booth. I hitch my thumb to the right, telling the asshole to get lost. He sneers, but he must not be an idiot because he takes a hike. I watch as relief settles over Harley instantly. She pats his back, her eyes still on me, and I find that I like her looking at me. This time, she doesn't seem agitated with my presence like she did at the gas station.

But then there's a shift when I don't immediately walk away.

"See, Momma. I got this!"

The men didn't walk out of the diner. Maybe I'd leave her to her dinner if they did, but I wouldn't put it past two assholes like them to come right back once I stepped away.

"Hey there, little guy," I say to him once he settles down across from his mom. "Good looking out for your mom."

Harley turns in his seat to look up at me. His smile is wide when he spots me. Skid and Ace peel off, finding a table across the room. I may catch shit from them later, but they won't bother me while I'm trying to flirt with this woman.

"Hi, Snake," he says, reading the tag on my leather cut.

"Micah," I tell him, more for his mother's benefit as I hold out my hand for him to shake.

His hand is tiny in mine.

"Harley. This is Momma."

I chuckle as I release his hand and hold it out to his mother.

She looks down at it and I can see the battle in her eyes as she decides if she's going to stick with her anger from the gas station or give into courtesy.

"Lucy," she says after a long pause, but she never gives me her hand.

"Join us," the child says, and if it wouldn't be insanely inappropriate, I'd give the little guy a hug for the invite.

Lucy sighs, but she doesn't argue as I try to stuff my large frame into the booth. We always grab a table when we eat here, but I'm not going to argue that point right now.

"Why do they call you Snake?" Harley asks as he reaches for his glass of orange soda, his eyes wide with curiosity. I freaking love kids because I'll answer every single question he has with as many details as I can manage because I want Lucy to hear all of it. I could see in her eyes the moment we met that she had preconceived notions about bikers. Many people in town do. I want to prove her wrong about me and Cerberus as a whole.

"Well," I begin, "I was given that name in the Marine Corps. My last name is Cobreski, and the guys in my platoon weren't very original."

"That makes sense. I hate snakes, but I like you. How many motorcycles do you have?"

"Two, and one is a Harley."

"Really?"

The awe in his voice makes me smile. His joy makes his mother smile.

"Really."

"Will you let me ride on one?"

I look to her, knowing it would be a shitty thing to promise this kid something his mother would never allow to happen. Her head shakes only the slightest amount.

"That's not very safe, and I don't have a helmet small enough for you, little man. I'm sorry."

"Okay," he says with a tiny shrug.

Lucy clears her throat as if his quick agreement hurts her in some way. Most parents would feel relief at the lack of argument. I file it away, knowing there's more to this woman than what's on the surface. Although I normally wouldn't look twice at a woman that showed minimal interest in me, I find that I want to get to know more about her.

"So, you're in a motorcycle gang?"

I smile down at him.

"It's a club, not a gang." We often have to make the distinction, not that people really care what the differences are. "We do a lot of charity work and volunteering in the community. We help raise a lot of money. What school do you go to? We helped get some new playground equipment for Dolchester last summer."

"That's where I go! I love the new slide!"

The waitress swings by, dropping off a ton of food, and asking for my order. I look up at Lucy, once again making sure it's okay if I eat with them. She seems to have thawed a little because she doesn't scowl at me. I take it as a win and tell the waitress I want a burger and fries.

The conversation continues, Harley asking a million more questions around bites of grilled cheese and French fries. Lucy doesn't talk much other than reminders to Harley not to talk with his mouth full.

"I thought I heard you laugh from the kitchen!"

I stand when Edith approaches, my plate in her hand. She drops it on the table, her arms out a second before I wrap her in a hug. The elderly woman pats my back like she didn't just see me last week.

"How have you been, sweetheart?"

"Better now that I'm seeing you," she says as she steps out of my arms, her wrinkled hand cupping my bearded chin. "Where are your friends?"

I point across the restaurant to Skid and Ace, who each hold up a hand in a wave.

"Oh hi, dear. Are you two doing okay?" Edith asks, noticing Lucy and Harley.

"We're doing well," Lucy replies, a sweet smile on her face.

"I've got to get back to the kitchen before Luther burns it down. Tell that boss of yours and Emmalyn thank you for the Thanksgiving order." I take my seat as Edith scurries away, stopping by Ace and Skid's table for hugs before she heads into the kitchen to keep an eye on her husband.

"You know Edith and Luther?" Lucy asks, her first question of the afternoon.

"We've been coming here for years. Edith and Luther know everyone. Sweet people."

"They are," she confirms.

"They gave me a free slice of pie once when Momma didn't have enough money," Harley says.

"Harley," Lucy snaps, embarrassment pinking her cheeks.

"Really?" I say, looking over at the kid. "She didn't make you wash dishes? I left my wallet at home once too, and I had to scrub pots and pans all afternoon."

His eyes widen. "I didn't have to wash pots and pans. She must like me more!"

Lucy's eyes find mine, but they dart away quickly. I don't know if I helped the situation or hurt it more. I know she doesn't have a lot of money. Her car is proof of that, but she's gorgeous. She has a pretty awesome kid, and she's got an attitude that just draws me in for some reason.

The two guys that were harassing her give the waitress a hard time before getting up to leave, and I know Skid and Ace have eyes on them as they leave the diner. Hopefully, they're just a couple of assholes passing through.

The waitress stops by with the check, and I pull out my wallet.

"Together or separate."

"Together."

"Separate." Lucy glares at me.

"Together." I hand the waitress my card, and the girl just stands there confused until I nod at her to get moving.

"I can't let you do that."

"I interrupted your dinner. It's the least I can do."

"I'm capable of taking care of my child."

I lean against the back of the booth, my eyes on hers, and I pray she can see the sincerity in them. "I never said you couldn't. I appreciate the company and great conversation."

"With a six-year-old?" She scoffs.

"It was more mature than it would've been with those guys." I hitch my thumb toward Skid and Ace.

As if proving my point, those two idiots are having a competition on who can hold a spoon on their nose the longest.

"Looks like fun," Harley says as he notices what they're doing.

The waitress comes back with my card and take-home boxes for the food Lucy and Harley didn't eat. I sign the slip, leaving a generous tip. I should stand and leave, but when I look back at Ace, he shakes his head. The two guys that were giving her a hard time left the diner but they haven't left the parking lot.

I pull a couple of quarters from my pocket and hand them over to Harley.

"What are you doing?" Lucy snaps when I drop them into his hand.

"Hey, bud, why don't you go see what those machines have to offer," I tell him, pointing to the row of quarter machines on the far wall.

Harley looks to his mom, and she must see something in my eyes because she nods to him. He bounds over me, excited to have a fist full of quarters, and hauls ass toward the machines.

"I'm going to follow you home."

"The hell you are," she snaps, leaning over the table.

It's clear she wants to get her point across without others hearing her. I love that she doesn't feel any sort of obligation toward me, despite the fact that I just paid for her meal.

"Do you know the two men who were giving you a hard time when I walked in?"

Her eyes dart in the direction they were sitting. "I've never seen them before, but they're gone now."

"They're still outside," I tell her.

"How do you know?"

"I just do. My guys are going to stay here and make sure you aren't followed. I'm going to make sure you get home safely."

"And how do I know I'm safe with you knowing where I live?"

"I'm not a bad guy, Lucy, but I can promise those men can't say the same thing."

Her eyes search mine, and I bet she's going over every word that has come out of my mouth today, my interaction with her son, and the way Edith wrapped her arms around me.

"I won't even get off my bike, but I want to make sure the two of you get home safely."

"And if we have other plans?" she challenges.

"Do you?"

She shakes her head.

"I got tattoos! Do you have tattoos, Micah?"

"Quite a few, little man," I tell him, not pulling my eyes from Lucy.

Her gaze drops, eyes roaming over me, and I'm smiling when she discovers that I caught her looking.

"Okay, Harley. Let's go."

I block her before she can leave the diner, and somehow I manage without touching her. It's an easy thing to do since she seems so aware of me. Ace and Skid head out first, angling their bikes so the assholes would have to run over them to back their truck out. I wait patiently on my bike for her to pull out before following close behind her. I know the guys will give us several minutes to put some miles between us and the diner before they move. It may piss the guys who were bothering them off, but Ace and Skid know how to handle themselves.

Chapter 3

Lucy

I don't accept favors. I hate owing people, being indebted to them, especially men. Men want one thing because they're capable of doing everything else for themselves.

Micah "Snake" Cobreski, former Marine turned Cerberus biker, has now forced two favors down my throat. First was paying for dinner, and now because I was scared for my and Harley's safety, he's offered protection on our drive home. Other than coming out of the gas station a couple of weeks ago to Harley being on the stranger's bike, he hasn't done or said anything creepy, but still, trust doesn't come easily if it ever comes at all.

But as I drive home, trying to keep my eyes safely on the road ahead of me, I realize I'm not so much worried about him as a person and what his expectations are for those favors he's thrust upon me, I'm worried about what he thinks of me or what he's going to think of me once he sees where we live.

His bike is nice, and it's one of two he claims he owns. I bet he lives in a nice house. The one Harley and I rent is near shambles by any standards, but it's the best I can manage.

If I didn't get the feeling he's the type of guy to make sure I step inside safely before driving off, I'd pull up to a nicer neighborhood and flag him on. If those creeps hadn't had the nerve to say horrible things to me in front of my son, I would've put up more of a fight when he insisted on following me to safety while making sure those guys wouldn't find out where we live.

"Can we do these tattoos tonight, Momma?" Harley asks from the backseat.

"Sure," I tell him, my eyes going back to the rearview mirror.

We're at a red light, and just as he promised, Micah is right behind us. I pray my car doesn't stall out on us. Traffic is heavy, but it always is the day after Thanksgiving. Everyone is starting off their holiday shopping with a bang, spending money like crazy and going overboard. I didn't get paid until today, and it was our Thanksgiving celebration at the diner.

The interruptions from those two jerks ruined it, and I haven't decided yet if Micah's "rescue" was a positive or a negative.

I cringe as I pull into the driveway, trying to see what a newcomer would see as I look at our house. The yard is clean. The only thing on the front porch is Harley's neon green soccer ball. Even that we got used from Goodwill. Winter has killed the grass, and honestly, that's a blessing because I always have trouble keeping it cut. Gas money for the car is a big enough struggle without having to worry about sparing some for the neighbor's mower when he's feeling generous enough to let me borrow it.

I climb out, my eyes darting all over as Micah pulls his motorcycle up along the curb. As promised, he doesn't climb off his bike. He doesn't even power the thing off, and I take comfort in the low growl of the machine as Harley climbs out. At least I don't have to have any further conversation with the man. I make sure to lock my car because around here, anything will get stolen. Hell, even the locks sometimes aren't enough of a deterrent.

I give him a quick wave of gratitude, and Harley does the same before we climb the three steps onto the front porch. Before I can remind Harley about the screen door needing to be fixed, his excitement about getting inside and applying those tattoos make him forgetful, and he swings open the door and the wind catches it. The top hinge pops free, just like it did earlier today.

I know Micah watches it happen because the rumble of his motorcycle dies. With one hand on the screen so the thing doesn't completely fall away, I turn around to face him.

"I've got it."

"You sure?" he asks, one foot already on the ground and the other leg already swinging around. "I don't mind helping."

"I'm sure you don't," I mutter to myself, but I refuse to owe him another damn thing. "I'm sure. Thank you for the escort home."

He nods, cranks up his bike, gives me one last look, and then, thankfully, he rides away.

I'm near tears before I can manage to get the front door unlocked for Harley and the screen door back in place. I wouldn't be surprised if I come back out in a few hours to go to work and the thing is lying in the street. No doubt the landlord will blame me and I'll get billed for it. The guy is a complete asshole and constantly finds ways to shove his expenses off on me.

My chest threatens to cave in when I step inside and Harley is standing there with tears staining his little cheeks. "I'm sorry, Momma."

"Baby," I whisper, dropping my purse and the *Thank You* bag with our to-go containers in it. "What's wrong?"

"I forgot about the door, and now it's broken."

"Sweet boy." I draw him to my chest. "The door was already broken."

"I made it worse."

"The wind made it worse."

He sniffles some more, and I feel the burn of my own tears threaten. I promise myself five minutes to cry after I put him to bed. I feel his tiny shoulders shake with sobs, and it's only after the vow of ten minutes of crying that I get myself under control enough to hold him at arm's length and look down at him with a smile.

"I thought you were going to do tattoos? You can't do tattoos if you're crying."

"You'll still let me have them even though I broke the door?"

"You didn't break the door." I wipe away more tears. "The wind did. I can't wait to see how you look with tattoos, but no real ones until you're much older."

We spend twenty minutes applying tattoos to his stomach because I'll be damned if I will allow him to put them anywhere staff at the school would see them. The last thing we need is more conversation about how trashy we are despite other kids doing the very same things.

Since today was payday and I was able to get some grocery shopping done amongst the craziness of Black Friday, we settle on the sofa for a quick snack before his bedtime.

"You're not going to eat those?" I ask, noticing two of the four cookies still left on the coffee table.

"I'm saving them," Harley says, never pulling his eyes from the movie.

"For when?"

"Tomorrow."

"We have more cookies for tomorrow."

He shrugs, and I know what he's doing. We don't always have cookies or juice. Some days, we have meatless dinners. Many families do that. Some families do it to save money or to cut back on calories, and it's healthy and they're commended for it. The only difference is, when you do it because there aren't cookies, juice, or meat in the house and there won't be until payday, then it's pitiful, it's deprivation, it's abuse, it's bad parenting.

He wants to ration the things we don't always have so he can fill in the void on those days.

I open my mouth to tell him to eat the cookies, that I'll find a way to make sure we have more, but that may be a promise I won't be able to keep. I pride myself on not lying to him, or at least keeping my lies to a minimum.

"We have our park day tomorrow," I tell him instead. "Better eat them now so you have the energy to run and play."

I may actually have the ability to keep snacks in the house between paychecks this time since Micah paid for dinner today. The happiness that will bring Harley makes me dislike him a little less, and then I feel guilty for disliking a stranger for no reason.

He wasn't suggestive at all today or at the gas station when we first met. He was honestly a breath of fresh air after the disgusting things those other guys said, and I was grateful for the distraction he provided to Harley because I knew a hundred questions would come from my kid after he heard some new words today. He asked Micah those questions instead, but knowing my child, he'll get around to asking those things to me, eventually.

I smile when his tiny hand reaches out to take another cookie from the table.

"Can we watch another movie after this?"

"Aren't you tired?"

He yawns. "Nope, and I don't have school tomorrow."

"You can stay up until I have to go to work," I tell him. "Mind if I take a nap?"

He shakes his head. I set an alarm on my phone, but find it difficult to fall asleep. When I close my eyes, I see dark beards, piercing blue eyes, and quick, genuine smiles. I hear the rumble of motorcycles and husky laughter. I feel warm, work-worn hands on my skin, soft lips on my neck, promises whispered in my ear.

I wake with my alarm going off, the television dark, and Harley curled up in front of me on the sofa, asleep.

I shift out from behind him and get ready for work, waiting until the very last minute to wake him. I have to help him into his jacket and shoes before walking him next door to Mrs. Greene's house. The sweet old lady next door knows better than most what it's like to be a single mother. She raised six kids after her husband took off when her youngest was three. She watches Harley at night, refusing to take money from me because and I quote, "he just sleeps."

In turn, I take care of her yard, pick up her prescriptions, and do her grocery shopping. I'd do more if she'd let me, but she's as stubborn as I am if not more.

I unlock her front door with the key she gave me, kiss Harley on the forehead as he settles down on her sofa, and make sure to lock the door on my way out.

Working for an overnight cleaning service isn't going to make me rich, but it's honest work. There are a lot of people that can't find a job, so I make sure to be on time every day and work hard. At least being unemployed right now isn't something I'll have to worry about.

Chapter 4

Snake

Showing up at a woman's house when you don't know her last name probably isn't smart. Showing up at nine in the morning on a Saturday? Even less smart. Not realizing the woman could be married or have a live-in boyfriend until you arrive? Pure ignorance.

It doesn't stop me from getting out of the truck because let's face it, if she does have a man, he's not a very good one. That screen door nearly flew away last night, and that was over twelve hours ago. She did a good job of propping it up I noticed when I drove by again last night, but now it's just sort of hanging there. If she had a man, it should be fixed. The damn hardware store opened an hour and a half ago. That's plenty of time to go and get a new damn door and get it fixed. Hopefully, I'm getting pissed about a man that doesn't exist, because I want to be the man to fix her shit when it breaks.

I don't pull anything from the truck before I walk up her empty driveway. Her car isn't here, but that doesn't mean some deadbeat isn't inside. I knock on the door gently, but no one answers. I knock a little louder a second time, and it goes unanswered again.

So, I get to work.

I pull out my tools, first removing the frame of the old screen door. The thing is mostly rust anyway. I toss the thing in the back of the truck and pull out the new one.

I noticed the old woman standing on her porch when I first pulled up, but as I carry the new screen door up the driveway, it seems she's settled in for a show because she's got a cup of coffee in her hand and a warm jacket over her long nightgown. I give her a nod.

Hanging the new screen door isn't hard as much as it is bulky. I could've asked one of the other guys to come help me, but they went to *Jake's* last night and didn't get in until early this morning. Besides, I want to be the only one who gets credit for this. Not that I expect anything in return.

I can feel the neighbor's eyes boring into my back as I work, but I wait until I'm nearly finished before acknowledging her.

"Does it look straight?" I ask without looking at her.

"Seems so," she says, her voice sounding stronger than I would've given her credit for.

I turn, finding her right behind me on the stoop rather than across the yard on her own porch. She cocks an eyebrow at the shock on my face.

"That old one was nearly rusted through."

"What's Brinson paying to have this fixed?"

"Brinson?" I ask, wondering if that is Lucy's last name.

"The landlord," the old woman explains.

"I'm doing this for Lucy," I correct.

"I need some things done around my place," she hints, and I just love how forward elderly people are.

"Lucy is a friend." Well, I'd like Lucy to be a friend. "But I can give you the number of a guy in town. He does great work, honest prices, great turn around, and incredible work ethic."

"Is he as good looking as you are?"

I huff a laugh.

She sips her coffee, waiting for an answer.

"I'll make sure Lucy gets his information to you."

"You do that, dear," she says as she turns around and shuffles back to her porch.

I'm putting tools back in the truck when Lucy's car pulls into the driveway. Lucy is wary of me standing by the truck, but Harley bounds out of the backseat with a wide smile on his face.

"Micah! We went to the park!"

"Did you have fun?"

"I was the fastest on the slide!"

"I bet you were."

He runs up to me, stopping near my legs with only inches to spare.

"Are you here to see Momma?"

I look up at Lucy who is standing near her car.

"I had a spare screen door at the clubhouse, and I noticed you guys needed a new one."

Lucy looks from me to the new door on the front of her house. Her face falls.

"I broke the old one yesterday."

"The wind broke it," I tell him. "I saw the whole thing. It was pretty rusty."

Harley runs up on to the porch to check the new screen door out like it's a toy as I close some of the distance between his mother and me. She opens her purse.

"How much do I owe you?"

"Nothing," I tell her, shoving my hands into my pockets, making it clear I won't accept a penny from her.

"And I'm just supposed to believe you had one lying around that fit perfectly."

I shrug.

"Momma, can we have hot chocolate?"

"Yes," she says to him before turning back to me.

Her eyes search mine as if she expects me to say something. If I met her at the bar, I might make a suggestion. I might flirt and ask her to spend a little time with me. If I knew her expectations were to get my leather cut off my shoulders and my jeans around my ankles, I'd pounce on this woman in a heartbeat, but that's not where she's at. Lucy is nothing like the women I meet at *Jake's* or the women that used to come around the clubhouse looking for a good time.

She's exhausted, and it's clear in the shadows under her eyes and the slight droop in her shoulders.

"Do you like hot chocolate?"

"Love it," I tell her. "But you don't owe me anything, Lucy. You needed a screen door. I had one. I didn't do it to get something in return. That's not how I operate. Now, your neighbor. I think she wants me to do some work for her, and with the way she was talking, I wouldn't put it past her to ask me to do it in just my boxers."

Lucy chuckles, and the sound of it hits me in the gut.

"Mrs. Greene is harmless. Mostly." She looks at the front porch, smiling as Harley grabs his soccer ball from the porch and runs toward us. "Stay in the yard and I'll make hot chocolate."

She looks at me one last time before walking away, and I kind of like that she doesn't invite me in. She's cautious, and she should be, especially with having a young child. She's protecting her space.

"Do you play soccer?"

"I don't," I answer honestly. "Can you teach me?"

"I'm not very good, but we can kick the ball back and forth."

We stand about fifteen feet away from each other because her yard isn't very big and kick the ball back and forth.

"Did you guys not sleep very well last night?"

"Momma doesn't sleep at night."

"No?" I ask as I tap the ball with the tip of my boot back in his direction.

"Momma works nights. I sleep on Mrs. Greene's couch. We go to the park on Saturday morning. She has the weekends off."

"Nights? At that gas station out on the highway?"

There aren't many places in town that stay open all night long, but there are a few occupations in town that would keep a woman up at night. I don't want my mind going there, but some women have to do what they have to do to take care of their families.

"She cleans office buildings. She can't work during the day because the business-people are there," he says with a grunt as he kicks the ball with all his might.

"Ah, ok." Relief washes over me as I tell myself I won't look into her, but I know I will.

She seems like a decent woman, and I know most people wouldn't tell their kids what they really do for a living. It would flatten me to know she's selling herself to make ends meet.

"Yours is on the kitchen table," Lucy says as she walks out onto the small porch with a steaming mug in her hand.

Harley scoops up the ball, depositing it on the porch before heading inside.

"Thank you," I tell her when she offers me the mug.

I take a seat on the top step as she leans against one of the banisters.

"Harley says you work nights. That's got to be tough."

"I think Sure Clean has been one of the best things to happen for me," she says. "I can sleep while he's at school. We get the afternoons together. Mrs. Greene watches him at night while I work. I'm just happy to have a job. There are a lot of single moms that don't."

And she just answered my question about a spouse or boyfriend. I nod and take a sip of the hot chocolate.

"What do you do for a living?"

"I work for Cerberus."

"The motorcycle club?"

"Yeah. Heard of us?"

She shakes her head. "I've lived here for a couple of years, so I guess I probably should have. I've seen guys on bikes, but I haven't paid much attention. I keep to myself, don't ask questions. Do you guys own like a shop or something?"

I chuckle. "Watch a lot of TV?"

She shakes her head. "We watch a lot of cartoons, but you'd be surprised just how lacking kids' entertainment is on motorcycle diversity."

"Such a shame," I tell her with a smile. "We actually travel a lot. I can't really go into what we do, but it's all good stuff. We help people. We're the good guys."

"And you were in the Marine Corps?"

"Eight years. All of us were in the Corps, actually. It's a requirement for Cerberus."

"And that makes you how old?"

"Thirty-one."

"You seem older."

"Wow." I laugh.

"Sorry. I don't mean it in a bad way, just that you're mature. I knew bikers before, and they're—"

"Wild? Like they'll never grow up?"

She nods.

"We all have our moments. We see a lot of bad stuff, so we like to have fun when we can, but we know when to be serious."

"I'm sorry for the millions of questions. I know Harley asked you so many yesterday."

I look up at her, cup close to my mouth so she can't see just how wide my smile is. "I'm an open book, Lucy."

"I'm twenty-eight. Harley is six. He's in first grade."

"And his dad?"

She cringes, and I open my mouth to tell her never mind. I don't want the conversation to stop. I'll talk about myself all damn day if it keeps her from shutting down and asking me to leave.

"Prison."

Damn it. That can't be easy on either of them.

"He messed up when he was young. A lot, and often." She shakes her head as if looking back now, she can't believe that she ever got tangled up in that situation. "I wasn't an innocent angel in all of it. I made mistakes, too. He got caught. I didn't. I grew up quicker. We split before I got pregnant with Harley, but you know how exes go. Sometimes bad choices come crawling back, and more mistakes are made. Well, I wouldn't say mistakes because I wouldn't have Harley, and I love my son. But Robbie was a mistake. We both know that now."

"Does Harley ever see his dad?"

A small smile tugs at her mouth as she looks out across the yard. "I take him to Santa Fe once a month for visitation. It's as much a part of his life he can be other than letters in the mail. He was never a bad guy. He had a hard life growing up. I'm not making excuses for the man, but he's gotten better in prison. He's gotten his GED. He's staying out of trouble."

"You guys planning on making it work when he's released?"

She scoffs, her head shaking. "Not a chance. There was nothing there between Robbie and me. Once we were both clean and the highs wore off, neither of us could figure out how we connected in the first place. We aren't compatible at all. We'll always be in each other's lives because of Harley, but there are no romantic inclinations at all."

That's good news.

"And Robbie knows this?"

She looks down at me, and I make sure to meet her eyes. The woman has to know that I'm interested, but just in case, I don't want any trouble from the man. He could easily be biding his time, telling her what she wants to hear before he's released and gets out, ready to stake his claim once again.

"That ship sailed a long time ago."

"When is he due to get released?"

"Soon. Like in the next six months or so, but he has family in Las Cruces, so that's where he'll likely end up."

She mentioned being in Robbie's life because of Harley, but does that mean they're going to be near each other? Does that mean she goes where he goes or that Robbie stays around here? It may be a little soon to ask these questions.

"Do you date?"

She's silent a little too long, so I have to look back up at her.

She's staring down at me.

"Do you?"

She huffs a humorless laugh.

"No. I'm a mom."

"Moms date," I argue.

"I tried dating several years ago, but my responsibilities are to my child." She shakes her head as if she's trying to rid it of bad memories. "Men aren't interested in the real shit that comes along with dating a woman with a kid."

I hate that she's had bad experiences, but at the same time, I'm glad she hasn't met someone worth keeping.

I stand, handing her back the empty coffee mug. "You just haven't met a real man yet."

I wink at her before walking back to my truck.

Chapter 5

Lucy

"After this, I have to take a nap," I tell Harley as I pull the popcorn from the microwave.

"It's Sunday," he says, his little eyebrows dipping together from his frown.

"I picked up an extra shift."

I won't explain that it's getting closer to Christmas because I don't want to get his hopes up about extra presents. He could get sick, and I may have to use the extra money for a visit to the doctor's office, or I could have a flat tire and need to get one replaced. Any number of things could happen between now and then, but I never turn down an extra shift. They don't happen very often because all the ladies I work with need every hour they can manage.

"Don't pout," I tell him. "Get the movie started."

"Maybe we can play *Uno* instead."

I smile. "I'm not going to go easy on you."

He narrows his eyes. "You never do."

"Get the cards and get ready to get spanked."

He laughs, the best sound I could ever hear, as he scrambles to his room for the worn deck of cards. I pour the popcorn into a bowl and pour a cup of juice for him and a glass of water from the tap for me. By the time I'm setting everything on the kitchen table, he's there trying to shuffle the cards with his tiny hands. He can't quite manage it, but I don't step in. He hates it when he's made to feel as if he's not big enough to do something. I sit back, snacking on buttered popcorn and wait for him to either consider them shuffled enough or for him to ask for help.

"Are you going to go on a date with Micah?"

"What did I tell you about listening in on adult conversations?"

He shrugs. We had this conversation last year when he was being nosy during a conversation I had with Mrs. Greene after overhearing one of the other parents trash talking me at the end-of-the-year awards ceremony. I was ready to show the other mom just how trailer trash I was, and she was talking me off the ledge. Harley didn't take hearing it very well and shoved that parent's kid at the park that summer when he saw them a few weeks later.

"I like him," Harley says as he passes out the *Uno* cards.

"Because he has a motorcycle."

"Because he doesn't pretend like I don't exist, and he doesn't say nasty things in front of me."

Man, if he brings up what those men were saying Friday evening at the diner, I may track those guys down myself and set them on fire.

"Well, Micah didn't give me his number or ask me for mine, so I don't know if he'll go out on a date with me."

"I just want you to know you have my permission."

I try my best to hide my smile. "Oh, do I?"

He nods. "Is that seven? Count yours? I think I dealt too many."

"It's seven. How many do you have?"

"Seven."

"Okay, let's play."

We play hand after hand after hand until the popcorn is gone. I don't let the child win. I don't have to. He has a pretty decent strategy for a six-year-old. He wins more than he loses, and he's quite content to curl up on the sofa to watch a movie when it's time for me to get a couple of hours of sleep before my shift tonight.

I press a kiss to his forehead before turning toward my bedroom.

"Don't—"

"Open the door if anyone knocks. I got it, Momma. I'm not a baby. Don't turn on the oven or use the microwave."

"You're the best kid I've ever had."

"I'm the only kid you've ever had," he says with a huge smile.

I crawl in between my sheets, used to the scratchy fabric, and sink into the mattress. I'm exhausted, but it's nothing new. I'm always tired. Stress keeps me from sleeping. I worry about everything, and the problem is, I don't ever envision a future where I don't have to worry about tomorrow or next month's bills or living paycheck to paycheck. That kind of life just isn't in the plans for me.

The alarm on my phone goes off, and I catch it early, the vibration under my pillow waking me before the musical tone has the chance to get very loud, but then I stiffen because I hear voices. They aren't the familiar sounds of the movies Harley watches on repeat. We don't have cable or Netflix because we can't afford such luxuries. We're relegated to DVDs we're able to score at garage sales.

I rush into the living room to find Harley leaning into the open front window.

"What are you doing?" I hiss.

"You said don't open the door!" Harley says as he spins around to face me.

The boy is proud of his work around the rule, a wide grin on his face, cheeks rosy from the cool air.

And there's Micah, the man also has a wide smile on his face. His eyes dip before they meet mine again, making me realize I'm wearing a tank top, sleep shorts and socks. That's literally it.

"Shit! I mean, shit! I mean, crap! Shoot! Sorry!" I grab the lap blanket off the couch and toss it around my shoulders, wrapping it around myself. I don't know why I bother. It's not like the man didn't just see my peaked nipples.

"That's three quarters in the swear jar."

"It was my fault," Micah says with a wide grin as he leans to the side.

I swear I hear him whisper, "But so worth it."

"Go put this in the jar, little man."

Micah hands over change to my son who takes it with a smile before bounding away to the kitchen.

"Are you sitting on the front porch?"

I step closer, but his eyes don't inch higher. They're locked on my legs. Why do I like it so much? "Yeah. Umm. He said you were sleeping, and I didn't want to talk very loud."

"I picked up an extra shift tonight. I needed a nap."

I crouch down, so he has to meet my eyes.

"I told him you wanted his number, so I got it for you."

Harley shoves a slip of paper in front of my face, and Micah grins. "Heck of a wingman you have there."

"I didn't... that's not how the conversation went."

His teeth dig into his lower lip, his blue eyes sparkling as he watches me.

"There's a tree lighting in the park next Saturday. It's a community thing, so it doesn't have to really be a date since you don't do that sort of thing. We could ride together. You know to save gas."

I get the feeling he isn't trying to make fun of me at all, but he's wanting to take me out while still staying within the parameters I've set.

"I spend Saturdays with Harley."

"I wouldn't take you out without him, Lucy. I know you two are a package deal. It's gonna be cold, so make sure you dress warm." His eyes skate over me one more time. "If you wear that, I'll be tempted to warm you up myself."

That's probably the very first thing he's said to me that has had any form of innuendo to it, and it landed exactly where it was intended. I have to look over my shoulder to see where Harley is at in the room, and I breathe a sigh of relief to find him enthralled with something on the television.

I don't want to have to explain why Micah would even think I'd wear my pajamas out of the house or how he would warm me up, but I come up with several ways he could as I get dressed for work.

I realize just how good of a wingman my son is when I get a text thirty minutes later.

See you Saturday evening 7pm. Wear something warm.

I find myself smiling all night at work.

Chapter 6

Snake

"Texting again?" Ace asks as he settles in the chair beside me in the garage.

I nod, my face angled down at my phone.

"She only gets thirty minutes for lunch."

"Then shouldn't you let the woman eat?"

My nose scrunches up with his words because he has a point. I've been bothering her all damn week during her lunch break.

"Leave him alone," Skid interrupts. "The woman can text as she chews. She has a kid. I'm sure she's good at multitasking."

It only alleviates the guilt a little.

Me: Are you eating?

I watch the three little dots as they appear on the screen.

Lucy: Peanut butter and jelly today.

I smile down at my phone.

Me: Grape or strawberry?

Lucy: Strawberry of course. It's the best.

Me: Creamy or chunky?

Lucy: Creamy.

Me: You'd tell me if I'm bothering you, right?

Lucy: Yes. I like having an adult to talk to.

Me: You don't talk with the people you work with?

Lucy: They complain a lot. I don't like being in the middle of people's drama.

Me: Understandable.

"You really like this girl, huh?" Ace asks, kicking at my boot with his own.

I look up at my best friend.

"There's just something about her."

"She's hot," Skid says.

I nod in agreement. "That she is.

"There are always hot chicks," Ace adds. "What's different about her?"

I shrug. "Couldn't tell you."

"Is it the damsel in distress thing?"

I shake my head. "She's doing fine on her own. I mean, she struggles, but most single moms do. She's handling her business. She seems like a good mom. Harley is a great kid. He's respectful, well taken care of. She doesn't need a man. She was agitated when I bought their dinner the other day, not expectant at all. She wanted to pay for the screen door I replaced. Wouldn't even invite me inside. She's cautious."

"So now she's a challenge?" Skid asks, leaning forward in his chair like he feels the need to defend her in some way.

This is what I love about my friends. We've never had a problem getting women, and we're quick to accept an offer from a woman who's wanting to play but coercing a woman into bed isn't our thing. We don't play games or manipulate, and both of these guys would be on my ass if they thought that's what I was doing.

"She's not a challenge," I assure him. "She's different."

"Love different?" Skid raises an eyebrow, a small smile playing on his lips.

I grin a little too. "I don't know, man. It's early days, but she's special. I can just feel it."

"Dating a woman with a kid isn't the same as dating a single woman. Package deals have to be treated with a softer touch," Ace warns.

"I'm well aware," I grumble. "I'm not playing games with her. I'm taking both of them to the tree lighting on Saturday. I'm not alienating the kid to get to his mom."

"Good," Skid says as he leans back in his seat.

"So does this mean you aren't going to *Jake's* with us after the tree lighting?"

"Not a chance," I tell him.

"Pussy-whipped already," Skid says.

* * *

"Nice truck!" Harley says as he waits for Lucy to situate the booster seat from her car.

"Thanks, little man. I didn't think to grab one of those," I tell her.

"It's fine. I don't expect people without kids to have one. Honestly, it would be weird if you did. There you go. Seat belt," she says.

Harley, filled with energy, plops in the seat and reaches for the belt. His little body is thrumming with excitement.

"We went last year. It was so cold. My new jacket is going to keep me warm this year!"

Lucy's eyes dart away, and I have no idea what the look means, so I ignore it.

"Hopefully, there will be a vendor selling hot chocolate, but I doubt it'll be as good as your mom's."

"No one's hot chocolate is as good as mom's," Harley says as Lucy gets in the passenger seat.

I wait for her to buckle up before closing her door and walking around to the driver's side.

The drive to the main street in town is quiet, the roads already crowded by the time we arrive.

"I need you to stay close," Lucy says in warning as I try to find a place to park. "No running off."

"Okay, Momma." His nose is plastered to the window, his eyes wide as he takes everything in.

Before turning off the truck, I look to the back seat at Harley. I don't have kids, and I never dated a woman with one before, but I already feel protective of him.

"It's really crowded here tonight," I say to him. He turns to face me, nodding as I speak. "I don't want you to get hurt or lost, but I do want you to have fun. We're going to spend time doing all that you want to do, but we have to do it at old man speed, okay?"

He nods with a grin. "Okay."

I nod; he nods. We understand each other. Lucy chuckles.

"Wait for me," I tell her, turning off the truck and climbing out.

I circle the vehicle and offer my hand to help her down. Doing this is two-fold. One, I want to help her, and two, once I have her hand, I don't plan to let her go. She said she doesn't date, but that's exactly what this is. I keep my hand in hers as I open the door for Harley, offering my other to him.

He releases mine once his feet are on the ground, but I drop my fingers to his shoulder, stopping him before he can bound away.

"Mine or your momma's."

He takes Lucy's hand before we head toward the center of town.

Christmas music plays, and despite the lack of snow on the ground, the air is cold enough to put everyone in a festive mood. Kids run about, not being as disciplined as Harley. People smile and laugh as the scent of fried foods and coffee fill the air.

Lucy watches the delight in Harley's eyes, and I watch her. She is so damned beautiful, just absolutely gorgeous.

We walk around, and I follow her lead. If Harley wants something, I wait for her response. If she looks like she's going to reach for her purse, I buy it. If she shakes her head, I don't offer. I'm not going to go against her wishes. I want to make things easier for her, but at the same time, I'm not trying to buy either of their affection. It's a fine line because I want to give both of them the world. Dropping a couple hundred dollars tonight isn't a big deal, but it can be just what will make her tell me to stay away forever when I drop her off tonight.

Harley ends up with an elf hat, huge ears included, and a hot chocolate with too many marshmallows. I opt for a black coffee. Lucy sips on a peppermint tea while we wait for the lighting ceremony to begin, and in true Farmington fashion, the switch is flipped, and the entire town goes black.

I hold Lucy closer, making sure her arms are around Harley, and I wait, ears wide open and assessing the night for danger before the kinks are worked out and everything is relit.

Everyone gasps at the pretty lights, and it takes several long moments before my heart rate returns to normal. I'm not a stranger to adrenaline rushes. I get them every time we take on a new job, but I've never felt like I had so much to lose before.

"That was exciting and dramatic," Lucy says, a wide smile on her face.

"Very." I look down at her. She has no clue that the blackout wasn't intentional. All I can think is that there's a good chance bad people used it to their advantage, and I pray we don't wake up in the morning to reports of someone getting hurt or a child getting abducted during that two-minute period of blackness. Criminals use shit like that to their advantage, always looking for other people to slip up and make mistakes so they can benefit. "Do you want to walk around some more?"

Lucy looks from me down to Harley. He's rubbing his eyes, a tiny yawn escaping his lips.

"I think he's about ready to go. He was so excited all day, I think he wore himself out before you arrived."

Reluctant to back away and only touch her hand when so much of her is pulled against my body, I wait just a few seconds longer before nodding.

"How about a ride?" I ask Harley.

He looks up at me confused.

"Up here?" I ask, pointing to my shoulders.

His eyes widen as if he's never done it before, then I realize he probably hasn't. If his father has been in prison all of his life, and Lucy hasn't dated, then he's never had a male role model in his life. Lucy hasn't mentioned her parents, so there's a good chance he doesn't have a grandfather around much either.

"Is that okay?" I ask Lucy. "I should've asked before I offered."

She smiles before looking down at Harley. "Only if you're careful and don't bump your head on the moon."

Harley scoffs. "Mom, that's not possible. The moon is too far away."

He holds his arms up to me, and I don't waste a second lifting him to my shoulders. He grips my hair like he's terrified he's going to fall off. His squeals of happiness draw several eyes in our direction, but to those around us, we're just another happy family enjoying our evening. I'm not wearing my Cerberus cut because I didn't want her to feel uncomfortable. She already has this preconceived notion about bikers as it is. Ace and Skid are around here somewhere because according to them, the tree lighting ceremony is a better place to pick up women than the grocery store. If I needed them tonight, they would be around.

Lucy helps Harley into the back of the truck, and I resist the urge to help her into the passenger seat because she's perfectly capable. The little guy is asleep by the time we make it back to her house, but I don't offer to carry him inside. I do, however, unlock her door for her and hold the keys on her front porch until she gets him settled in his bed and returns.

"Thank you," she says as she rejoins me. "I had a lot of fun tonight."

"You're very welcome."

I'm mostly a gentleman, but holding this woman's hand all night, seeing the way she smiled up at me, I don't know that I can leave without pressing my lips to hers. She seems a little nervous, but not in a way that tells me she wants to escape.

She's not inching away or trying to put distance between us. She isn't holding onto the screen door. Hell, the thing is completely closed.

"I'm going to kiss you, Lucy."

She nibbles the corner of her lower lip, eyes blinking up at me as I lower my mouth. My fingers grip the coarse fabric of her jacket as I pull her closer to me. Her lips are warm, spiced with the mint of the tea she was drinking earlier, and I find myself starved for more.

She melts into me, her body angled as she trusts me with nearly the full weight of it.

My entire being is a live wire the second my tongue meets hers, and all those declarations of being a gentleman don't fade away. They disappear in a snap. Gone. Poof. Nonexistent.

Sharp breaths, what I would consider a gasp if they were made from her lips, not her nose, escape, and I know she's just as into it as I am. I pull back because if I don't, I won't have the power to stop.

I press my lips to hers, soft, gentle kisses three more times, loving that after just one kiss, her lips are cherry red and a little swollen. God, what will they look like after I've gone after her for hours?

"I want to see you again," I whisper, my mouth mere inches from hers.

"We don't have plans tomorrow, and Monday, Harley will be at school. I don't have work until that evening."

Jesus, I know exactly what she's saying.

"Want to see me both days?"

She nods.

"Pizza and movies tomorrow?"

"That sounds perfect."

"See you then, beautiful." I press my lips to hers once more before taking a step back.

God, I want to follow her inside the house and spend the rest of the night with her in my arms, but I know that's moving too fast. I'll get to see her tomorrow and then the day after. That's just going to have to be good enough.

Chapter 7

Lucy

I have great days with Harley. I've learned to count my blessings. Although I don't have a lot of money, we have fun when we can. We go to the park and play games. We spend time watching movies. We have cheap fun.

Micah showed up yesterday with a pile of pizzas and a stack of animated movies. I don't know if Harley told him we don't have cable, but the man came prepared.

We spent the day on the couch laughing so much I woke this morning with my stomach a little sore. It was an amazing day, and I can't seem to wipe the smile from my face. Micah paid a ton of attention to Harley while holding my hand the entire day. I didn't feel left out at all. I sort of loved that he focused on my son because I knew what I promised. I knew my day was today, and I didn't get much sleep last night after he left with that promise floating around in my head.

After sending Harley to school this morning on the bus, I flew around the house getting ready, his whispered promises in my ears.

He was appropriate yesterday, keeping a casual distance between us the whole day—a different man than the one that kissed me like he wanted to crawl inside of me the night before on the porch. He kissed me much the same yesterday evening before leaving, but while he was here and in Harley's presence, he was a complete gentleman. I love the dichotomy of it, that he knows who I need him to be and when.

It also sends a thrill up my spine as I wait for him to arrive today because I know who I'm going to get once he arrives.

I shake my hands out as I pace the floor, praying my deodorant does its job because I'm incredibly nervous. I'm also wondering if we're moving too fast. Micah is unlike any man I've ever met, and I'm second-guessing myself.

Am I attracted to him because he's simply saying the right things and acting the right way? He's the first man to come into our lives that's acted like a decent human being. The first person to acknowledge the importance of me being a mother first. I want to believe it isn't all an act, but I guess only time will tell.

I'm attracted to him as I suspect many women are. He's ridiculously handsome and kind. Not once have I caught him looking at Harley like he wishes he'd just disappear so he could get me alone, and believe me, I've been waiting to catch him do just that. Men say a lot of things and then get caught acting differently.

I catch sight of myself in the mirror hanging on the living room wall, and I see some of that guilt I can't manage to fully let go of. Maybe it's a mom thing. Harley likes him, and that makes me happy, but I don't want to be *too* happy. I don't want to lose sight of what's most important. I don't want to get lost in a man and make bad decisions. I did that with Robbie and my life went off the rails.

Maybe this is just a little fun. No one said it had to be serious, but if that's the case, then I've already made the mistake of letting Harley get close. He asked last night after his bath when Micah was coming back over. Of course, I didn't mention that he was coming to see me today. I wasn't about to explain why he'd visit me alone in the middle of the day. I find myself frowning at the thought of whatever this is with him not going anywhere because I really like this guy.

I don't have any more time to worry about it because the roar of his motorcycle filters in from the street, and that same anticipation that kept me from sleeping last night ramps back up to full force.

I resist the urge to open the door and meet him on the porch. I'm eager, but I don't want to come across as too anxious. I can't seem to get my trembling hands on the same page.

The motorcycle engine stops, and the silence is deafening. The pause between as I wait for the sound of his boots on my front porch as anticipatory as that three-minute wait after taking that first pregnancy test. Although I was expecting it, I still jolt when the knock comes.

"Hi," I whisper shyly when I open the door.

The man is huge, his leather-clad bearded body taking up nearly the entire doorway as he smiles down at me.

"Mornin', sweetheart."

He doesn't advance on me. His eyes skate up and down my body, and I wonder exactly how he sees my leggings and over-sized sweater. I'm not wearing shoes, only fuzzy socks. I didn't want to look like I was trying too hard, and I knew we weren't leaving the house.

"You going to stand out there all day?"

"You going to invite me in?" he challenges, his blue eyes sparkling with humor.

"What happens when you get in here?"

"Anything you want."

"Harley has *Uno*."

He grins.

"Or we could take a nap."

His smile grows. "I'm a great cuddler."

"Yeah?"

"Only one condition. I have to be the big spoon."

"Of course," I tell him.

"And I can't nap in jeans."

"I'd want you to be comfortable."

"I go commando."

I grin. "I do, too."

His eyes drop to the apex of my thighs.

"My jeans are really uncomfortable right now, sweetheart." His right hand comes down and adjusts the front of his jeans, and there's something seriously sexy with the sight of him doing that in riding leathers, that area framed by them as if keeping it on display.

"You should come inside and take them off." I step to the side and hold the door open wider.

He doesn't waste a second stepping inside my house. Nor does he miss a beat wrapping his arm around me and lowering his mouth to mine. The restrained man that was here last night isn't the same man that enters today. One hand is on my ass. The other shoves the doors closed and flips the lock into place.

I feel silly when he lifts me off my feet, but that doesn't stop me from wrapping my legs around his waist as he carries me to my room. He doesn't have to ask where it is. There are only three doors down the short hallway and since he used the restroom yesterday and Harley's door is always open, it's a simple deduction.

My room is plain, the sheets and comforter bought on clearance from the Dollar Store. Decorations are minimal, but I get the feeling this man isn't worried about any of it, and even if he were, he's not the type to worry about things like that.

"You're so overdressed," I mutter against his mouth, my fingers unable to reach the zipper on his freezing cold leather jacket.

"It's cold outside." His lips are on my neck, his beard abrading my skin in the best way. "Don't want to put you down."

"Just for a minute. Let me help."

I wiggle until he releases me, chuckling when he looks desolate at not having his hands on me.

"It's like opening an early Christmas present," I say as I reach for the zipper on his jacket. "Just stand there and let me unwrap you."

"It would be easier if you were already naked," he teased, and I take a step back and look up at him.

"Really? You'd be able to keep your hands off me?"

"Yes."

"Liar." I smack at his chest, but he's wearing so many layers, I doubt he felt it.

"What about a compromise? Just the leggings?"

"I'm not wearing anything under them," I remind him.

He groans, his head rolling back until he's looking up at the ceiling.

"Don't turn into a baby."

I push the jacket off his shoulders, but he catches it before it hits the ground.

"Never on the floor," he says. "Not when my cut is with it."

There's no anger in his tone, just an educational lesson. He steps to the side, laying it across the top of my dresser before stepping in front of me once again. My fingers trace the muscles of his chest on top of his thermal.

"You're supposed to be unwrapping me."

"I'm savoring."

"I have no patience. Keep that in mind when it's my turn, okay?"

I nod, but really my attention is on the hard plains under my hands as I lift the hem of his shirt.

"So much hair," I say in awe.

"I'm a man, sweetheart."

"Yes, you are," I whisper, swallowing hard. "Hold this."

He lifts his hand in time to clutch the shirt as my fingers wander over his abdomen. The muscles bunch and flex with my attention.

"You're killing me, Lucy. Can I take this off?"

I nod, my eyes still glued to his stomach, but I take a step back as he pulls the shirt over his head, getting a good look at his full torso as it's revealed. His smile is a little shy.

"Are you objectifying me?"

I nod. "Can't help it. You're perfect."

"My cock is big, too."

My eyes lift to his, but the humor is gone. The lighter blue tones have turned darker, needier.

"Do your boots have to be unlaced or can they be pulled or kicked off?"

"I can kick them off."

"Do that."

I stay back while he works his boots off, pulling my sweater over my head.

"You're cheating," he says when I drop it to the floor. "I'm supposed to unwrap you."

"I can put it back on." I bend to reach for the sweater.

"Don't you dare."

I give him a grin as he reaches for the belt of his riding leathers, working it open before he opens the button and zipper of his jeans. The head of his cock pops out of the top as if the thing has been trying for hours to seek relief. I can't seem to pull my eyes from it.

"Lucy? Eyes up here, sweetheart."

Guiltily, I snap my eyes back up to his, doing my best to keep them there even as he bends a little to kick the rest of his clothes off.

"I want to do everything under the sun to you today."

"I want that, too," I tell him.

"I want to taste your sweet pussy."

I nod because that sounds amazing. If the man does that as well as he kisses, then I'm in for a special treat.

"I want your mouth on my cock."

"Okay." I start to lower to my knees, but he shakes his head.

"But the first time either of us come, it's going to be with me buried to my balls inside of you."

I drop my eyes to his waist. "I don't know if that's going to be possible."

He laughs. "Oh, sweetheart. It's possible. You're so wet for me already."

"How would you—"

His eyes drop between my legs, and it's like the glance made me aware of my body. I know what I'm going to find before I even look, but that doesn't stop me.

Wearing white leggings was a bad idea. Like wearing a white bathing suit then getting in the pool, my arousal has left literally nothing to the imagination. I'm soaking through, my lower lips on full display.

"Don't," he whispers when I try to cover myself. "That's the sexiest thing I've ever seen. Peel them down slowly, Lucy. I want to see them stick to you. That's it. Damn it, woman. What a pretty pussy."

I bite my lips as I do what he says. I've never felt sexier before in my life. I've had two sexual partners since Robbie, but those were quick, unsatisfactory romps not worth mentioning. Today is already ten times better and we haven't even touched each other besides kissing.

"I'm so sorry," he says, and I snap my eyes up at him.

"Wh-What?"

His eyes find mine, and I see a little disappointment in them.

"You have to work tonight." His head shakes a little. "You're going to be sore, sweetheart. I hate that you're going to be sore, but I'm going to spend the entire day inside of you. I won't be able to help it."

"You're sorry for that?" He nods, genuine guilt in his eyes.

"I promise lots of orgasms. You'll probably beg me to stop, and if you really mean it, just say like spaghetti or something."

"Okay," I agree, knowing I never will. I mean, is there such a thing as too many orgasms?

"And this, too," he says as he steps closer, his hands going around my back to unsnap my bra with a skill level I don't want to think about right now, or ever if I can help it. "Fuck, sweetheart. Just one little taste. Don't touch my cock."

In an effort to keep from doing just that, I wrap my arms around his neck as his expert tongue goes to work on my nipples. Jesus, I've never felt anything like it.

"Micah," I moan, and then I lose all sense of myself when his fingers slip between my legs, teasing my clit before two slide inside of me with no resistance.

I'm so ready for him, so gone for this man that I don't notice him lifting me and producing a condom from thin air until he's spreading me out on the bed and rolling it down his very eager erection.

"It's... umm, been awhile," I whisper.

"I've got you," he says as he lines up.

Before he shoves inside, he leans down close, his eyes locked on mine.

He watches me as he slides inside, his hand on the back of my neck as it arches with his intrusion.

"Fuck, baby, take me. Jesus, Lucy, that's my girl." His hips flex back before he moves forward again.

I can't seem to close my mouth. My jaw refuses to work the way it's supposed to.

"Micah," I pant. "Please."

I don't know what I'm asking for or what I need, but he must read minds because he shifts a little, lifting my leg a little higher on his hip, and it opens me perfectly. A husky sound comes from deep inside of him as his lips meet mine, his tongue sweeping inside of my mouth, and then I realize he kept his promise. He's all the way inside of me, our bodies meeting fully in the middle. I'm so full, and it's never been like this before. It's a full-body experience, the penetration, the brush of his chest hair on my skin, the grip of his fingers on my neck, his lips on mine.

With Robbie, we were bumbling teens, and even after gaining a little experience, we were either too high to remember what we'd done or I was never really into it and only did it to get him off my back. It was never an enjoyable experience. I'm two minutes into this with Micah and I can already feel that fluttering deep inside I've only experienced late at night when I'm in my room alone.

"You okay?" he asks as he lifts up a few inches, his thumb sweeping down my cheek.

I nod because I know if I speak, I may cry. I refuse to be the woman that gets sappy because she's experiencing great sex for the first time in her life.

"Make me come," I manage.

He grins with a roll of his hips. "I like where your head is at. Spread your legs, Lucy. Hold them up under your knees. Let me do all the work."

And boy does he work.

Micah gets up on his palms, hips snapping, and it takes mere minutes for that fluttering low in my belly to turn into an inferno in my gut. My eyes go blurry. My legs tremble. A thin layer of sweat covers my entire body despite the chilliness in the air.

"I'm—"

I don't even have time to say it before I implode.

"Goddamn it," he grunts. "Fuck, baby. Milk my cock."

Micah freezes inside of me, giving my body something to clench around, and it's spectacular. Just as I'm coming down, he starts all over again, hips working. He leans back, repositioning his legs so he's bent at the knees and my body is angled up.

His thumb on my clit is like a bolt of lightning, and he doesn't stop working me over until I come again. Only then does he let himself fall over the edge.

The man is absolute perfection when he orgasms, his eyes glossy and unfocused, his muscles taut and flexed, a sheen of sweat covering his abdomen.

What an experience. If this is only fun, I have to say it's the most fun I've ever had in my life.

He gets off the bed to dispose of the condom and get a bottle of water. He gives me half an hour before he tastes me like he promised. Forty-five minutes before his cock is in my throat, but it isn't until two in the afternoon that I finally have to whisper the word spaghetti.

Chapter 8

Snake

Maybe it was a little sneaky, but it's too late now.

During the time I spent between Lucy's legs, she confessed that Harley had trouble at school with some of the kids and the staff because she doesn't make a lot of money. Dominic's daughter goes to the same school, and she doesn't have any problems. Of course, they live in a nice house on the lake, so no one looks down on her. Harley doesn't have it so easy.

When she was blissed out on orgasms, I offered to pick him up from school, on the motorcycle of course, because I was thoughtful enough to buy him a helmet. With the promise of driving very slowly and bringing back an early dinner, she finally relented.

I hate that he's having trouble, but I know that it'll never change. They could win the lottery tomorrow, and he'll still be the kid that was once poor. The only way to overcome something like that is to be the new kid in a new school that has money, and that's not something that's going to be different for him and his mother.

I wait patiently outside the school, waving to a couple of the mothers that I recognize from the events we've done in the community. I made sure that Lucy called the school to let them know that I'd be the one picking Harley up, so I didn't catch any grief. I provided my driver's license when I first arrived, and now I just have to wait for him to walk out. I don't have to wait long, and like little ducks in a row behind his teacher, I spot Harley before he spots me because he's looking for his mother's car. Several kids notice the motorcycle before he does. They point and get excited, and I give him a wave. He doesn't run to me like most kids would. He waits for the teacher to give him permission, and it makes me wonder why he has trouble with the staff if he's always this well behaved. I guess it just goes to show that adults never really grow up either. What an unbelievable world we live in when grown-ups don't act like adults.

His smile grows wider with each step he takes.

"Hey there, little man," I tell him when he's right up beside me.

His mouth is hanging open, but then it suddenly falls, and his little chin begins to quiver.

"What happened to momma?"

"Nothing. She's fine. I promise. She said I could pick you up. Look what I got for you." I hold up the child-sized helmet.

His little eyes search mine, and I know he's searching them for the truth. It makes me wonder how many people in his short life have lied to him.

"Look," I say as I place my hand on his shoulder. "We'll call her, okay?"

I step off my bike, uncaring if I'm blocking the car pickup line and stand on the sidewalk. Pulling out my phone, I dial Lucy's number.

"Hey, sweetheart," I say when she answers.

"He won't leave with you, will he?" she asks with a chuckle.

"He's worried that something is wrong. I'm going to put him on."

I hand the phone to him.

"Momma? Micah is at my school... Yes, ma'am... I can? Really!... Yes, ma'am. I will... Hold on tight. I will. I promise... Yes, ma'am. I won't... Yes, ma'am... I love you, too. Bye."

He hands me the phone back.

"You've raised a good one, sweetheart."

"Take good care of him."

"Yes, ma'am," I tell her. "How are you feeling?"

"The bath helped," she whispers.

"Good. We'll be back soon."

We say our goodbyes, and I end the call.

"A few rules," I tell Harley before I let him climb on.

"Yes, sir," he says, his full focus on me despite the loud kids all around.

"You have to sit in front of me. I'll have to wear your backpack."

"It's Mickey Mouse." He holds the pack up. "That doesn't embarrass you?"

"Coolest mouse ever," I say, holding out my hand and adjusting the straps as far as they go so I can get it over my arms. "When you get on, I need your hands here, but you can't touch any of the controls."

"Got it. Anything else?"

I look at my bike. "Nope. I think that's it."

He doesn't weigh enough to worry about having him lean with me on turns.

I hold my hand out, and we execute the complicated handshake we mastered yesterday while we were watching movies at his house. He's giggling when I lift him up and place him on the seat before climbing on behind him. I drop his helmet on his head, fastening it under his chin, and crank the bike. It roars to life, and squealing, excited kids wave at us as we slowly roll out of the pickup line. Not once does Harley pick up his hands from where I told him to keep them to wave back. I don't know if he's following the rules I set forth, or if he's realizing that he doesn't need friends who will now only like him because he rode off on a motorcycle when they couldn't be bothered before.

I promised Lucy slow, and that's exactly what Harley gets, but you'd think we were racing down the turnpike at a hundred miles an hour with the way he's squealing. I usually go from one stop light to the next at a faster speed, but the child is six, and I'm not taking any chances with such precious cargo.

Knowing Lucy needs a little time to herself when she's not either sleeping or working, I take the scenic route to the fast-food joints in town, grabbing Harley and I a couple of burgers and fries before heading to the park. We eat at a picnic table, and I tell him he can go play, but he seems just as content to sit beside me and watch a couple of squirrels chase each other through the grass. He's a chill kid, and I wonder how much of that is because Lucy has to work nights and is tired during the day. I know they do outings on Saturdays, and he gets plenty of recess time at school. I know she's doing the best she can. God, I just want to give her more. She has to be utterly exhausted, never getting a real break. I doubt the woman has ever had a vacation in her life.

"None of them," Harley says when I ask him what his favorite subject in school is.

"Are you struggling?"

He gives me that *are you serious* look. "It's too easy. I'm bored all day, and when I draw, I get in trouble."

I keep my mouth closed. I could say a lot on that subject but saying it to a six-year-old isn't where the energy needs to be directed. Also, I don't know that Lucy would appreciate me getting involved. I'm sure she's said something to the school in the past.

"What do you like to draw?"

He shrugs. "Cartoon characters. Monsters. Dogs. Do you draw?"

I chuckle. "I'm no good at drawing. I'm good at working on bikes. I was a good soldier."

"I want to be a soldier."

"Not an artist?"

He shrugs.

"There's a kid at school and his dad is a soldier. He said his dad makes a lot of money."

Not working for the government, he doesn't.

"They have a really good benefit package," I say instead.

"I just want to take care of my mom."

"That's noble."

"What are your intentions with my mom?"

I choke on a sip of my soda. "My intentions?"

He nods, his face a mask of seriousness as he rolls a French fry between his fingers.

"I really like your mom."

"I don't want her to get hurt."

"I don't plan on hurting her."

"I know my mom and dad won't get back together."

I nod because I was wondering if he had thoughts about this, but I wasn't in any position to ask. His mother said as much but little kids have different viewpoints.

"Dad is coming home soon."

This makes me wonder what idea of *home* Harley has for Robbie Farrow once he's released from prison. This is another thing I don't feel like I have the right to ask. I haven't been in their lives long enough to ask.

"Do you think your mom likes me back?"

His grin is wide, giving me hope. Harley nods. "She gets this silly look in her eyes every time we talk about you. It's that same look the girls at school get when someone mentions Ryder Jones."

"Good to know," I tell him before taking another sip of soda.

"Do you think you can take me to get a Christmas gift for my mom? I've been doing chores for Mrs. Greene to earn money."

"Of course I can. Today?" I look down at my watch.

"I won't get all of my money until closer to Christmas."

"You tell me when, and I'll make it happen."

"Thanks." He looks out over the grass again, his little eyes searching for the squirrels that disappeared while we were having our serious conversation.

"We better head back before she sends out a search party for us."

We gather our trash and head back to the bike. I go back over the rules once again because safety is important before we head out of the park.

At a red light, I lean closer and ask Harley what kind of food his mom likes the most. He says barbecue, but she doesn't get it very often, so we end up at the best place I know of in town. He isn't very helpful when we walk inside, saying meat when I try to get specifics. We end up with so much, I can barely fit it in my saddlebags, but we somehow manage.

He's just as happy on the ride back to his house as he was the first time.

Lucy is waiting on the porch when we pull up, but Harley waits for me to lift him off the bike, so he doesn't burn his little legs on the exhaust. He scrambles to her, talking a mile a minute about his exciting ride and about his early dinner and even the squirrels at the park.

I gather the food from the saddlebags and carry them up the driveway.

"Dinner as promised," I tell her, holding up the bags.

"Are you feeding the neighborhood?" She raises her eyebrow.

"I figured you could take some for your lunches this week. It's not peanut butter and strawberry jelly but brisket sandwiches are good, too."

Her teeth dig into her lower lip. "I love brisket."

"There's smoked chicken and sausage in there as well. Harley didn't know what you liked best."

She looks over her shoulder, checking for Harley's location before turning back around to press her mouth to mine for a quick but sweet kiss. "You're amazing, you know that?"

I grin against her mouth. "You make it easy, sweetheart."

Chapter 9

Lucy

"You know the drill," the guard says as she hands over the two visitor passes. "One hug upon hello, one upon leaving. No contact in between."

I nod in understanding, handing over my limited personal belongings. We don't bring much with us when we come to visit Robbie. I don't want to risk anything getting stolen out of the car, and we aren't allowed to carry anything on our person but change for the snack machine during visitation. That change is in case Harley wants a snack, but he seldomly asks. Robbie has never asked, and the one time I did try to put money on his commissary, he refused it. He never wanted my help. He feels guilty enough for using the money he makes working inside for his own personal needs, but I completely understand. He has to survive. He swears he'll help when he gets out, but I'm more nervous about him staying clean and out of trouble. He struggles with that a lot. I've never been to prison but having a lot of freedom in an unstructured environment never worked for him before. It's going to be the true test for him.

"Daddy!" Harley yells when he sees Robbie, but our son knows not to run through the room.

We walk slowly toward the table we've kind of claimed as ours.

Harley throws his arms around Robbie and they squeeze each other for a short period of time, releasing the other before the guards get involved and tell them to split up. There are visits where Robbie has had harder months, and he holds on a little too long to his son, and it draws more attention. He must have had a good month because this isn't one of those times. He gives my shoulder a quick squeeze as we sit.

Smiles are easy all around the table.

"How have you been?" he asks me.

"Good," I tell him honestly because I'm the happiest I've ever been.

I'm nervous. I know Harley is going to mention Micah, and although I thought about asking him not to mention him, I knew it wouldn't be fair to ask a child to keep secrets from his father. I don't know how Robbie is going to react.

"How have you been?"

"Living the dream," he says, but there's no animosity in his tone.

After the first year or so, Robbie accepted his fate and has tried to see his sentence as a time to grow and get better, to get clean and work on himself in a way that when he's released, he's a better person. He's honestly found himself, and I think he was looking for that man when he turned to drugs all those years ago. It took getting sentenced to prison and getting sober to actually get there. It could've gone either way. I know there are days he struggles. He's mentioned in his letters to me more than once how easy it is to get drugs, how there are temptations everywhere he turns.

It gives me hope that he can be successful on the outside, that it won't be such a culture shock for him.

"How are you doing in school, Harley?"

Our son scowls, crossing his arms over his chest.

"That good, huh?" Robbie says with a laugh.

He looks to me, and I shake my head, letting him know that he still isn't making friends.

"I got to ride a motorcycle!"

I honestly thought I'd have a little more time than five minutes into our visit.

Robbie's eyes dart to mine. It's been almost a week since Micah picked him up from school, and he hasn't stopped talking about it. He's been a little disappointed each day when he saw my car outside the school instead of that bike. Micah sends laugh emojis each time I text him about it, offering to pick him up, but I don't want to burden the man.

"It was a very slow ride," I assure Robbie.

"Was this like a carnival thing?"

Robbie keeps his eyes locked on mine as he shifts his weight on the metal bench across the table from me. He's getting agitated.

"It was Micah's bike."

"Who's Micah?" His eyes are still on me.

"Momma's boyfriend."

"He owns a motorcycle?"

"Two of them. He's a biker."

My son is so helpful and just full of details.

"A biker?" Robbie asks, knowing what it could mean.

All of his trouble started with bikers in Santa Fe. Bikers are the reason I moved away from the area when I found out I was pregnant with Harley. It's why I choose to drive several hours to come visit instead of living closer.

"I don't want my son around bikers," he says, his voice as calm as he's able to manage.

I take a deep breath. I know where he's coming from. I know what he's thinking. I just need a minute to get my thoughts in order. Robbie and I don't argue. We never really have. Even when he was on the outside, we didn't argue. He was always too high. If I told him to get out and leave, that I was tired of his shit, he just left. He had other places to be, other women he could be with. He was too laid back to worry about me. There was no reason to argue. He was nonconfrontational. Fights weren't worth the wasted energy.

Robbie is no longer high. He's invested in his son as much as he possibly can be.

He lowers his head, inching closer. "You promised to protect him from that life."

"Harley," I say, looking Robbie right in the eye, no sour inflection in my tone as I reach for some of the change in my pocket. "Can you go see if the snack machine has any candy you like?"

"I'm not—"

"I'd really love something chocolate," I interrupt.

He takes the change from my hand.

The second he scoots away, I give Robbie my full attention. "Micah is nothing like the men you got tangled up with. They're good men. They help the community. They do fundraisers and buy playground equipment for local schools. He served eight years in the military."

"My cellmate served twelve years in the military, and it didn't stop him from killing his wife, Lucy. Who do you have around my son?"

"The Cerberus MC is well respected in the community, Robbie Farrow. You do not get to dictate who I date. I'd never put Harley in danger."

"M&Ms, Momma," Harley says as he returns.

"Those are my favorites. Thanks, sweetie," I tell him with a smile as he sits back down beside me.

Robbie clears his throat, and I know it's his attempt to get his emotions back under control. The visit continues, and he doesn't say another word about Micah or motorcycles.

"I've got a release date," he says when they announce the five-minute warning.

Harley squeals in delight, gaining a glare from one of the guards. He settles when I place my hand on his arm.

"Really?"

"First week in January."

"That's really soon." My heart rate skyrockets.

"Less than a month," Harley whispers. "I can't wait."

"I'll be coming to Farmington."

"I figured Las Cruces," I say. "That's where your family is."

"My family is in Farmington." His eyes challenge me. "I've served my entire sentence so I won't have to worry about parole, so I can go where I want."

"You can meet Micah!" Harley adds helpfully.

"Can't wait," Robbie says, his eyes on mine.

Chapter 10

Snake

"Hey," Lucy says when she opens the door.

She looks tired as she steps to the side.

"Where's the little man at?"

"In his room getting his shoes on."

I don't waste a second pulling her to my chest and pressing my lips to hers. In seconds, I'm hard in my jeans, the heat of her body warming me up. I'm glad I drove the truck today instead of the bike. It means I'm not wearing leather, making it easier to feel more of her.

We've spent at least two hours together every weekday morning this last week after she got off work and sent Harley to school. I was worried about her being tired, but she assured me she slept better after spending time with me. Wednesday, she fell asleep before I left, so I just stripped right back down and crawled in bed with her. Staying up late to text her on her breaks has been wearing me down as well, so we both slept until her alarm went off to go pick Harley up from school.

She wasn't upset at all that she woke in my arms, so we did it again Thursday and Friday.

Yesterday, however, was her day to drive to Santa Fe so Harley could visit with his dad. When I offered to take them, she turned me down immediately. Now she's pulling back from the kiss way too soon.

"What's wrong?"

"Just tired," she says as she steps out of my arms.

I trace the shadows under her eyes, pressing my lips to each of them.

"Are you going to tell me what you two are up to today?"

I shake my head, leaning in to whisper, "Christmas surprises."

She grins. I step closer to kiss her again, but the sound of Harley's excited feet pounding down the hall makes me take a step back.

"To be continued," I whisper.

She doesn't smile.

"Ready to go?" he asks, his face bright and unaware of the weird mood his mother is in.

"I'm ready. Grab your coat."

I squeeze her hand, wishing I knew what she was struggling with so I could fix it.

"Listen to Micah and behave," Lucy says as we leave.

The ride to the shopping center is filled with little boy chatter, and I participate as much as I can, but the topics change so quickly it's hard for me to keep up.

Prepared, Harley knows exactly what store he needs to go into.

"I saw her looking at this set," he says, tugging on my hand, pointing at a pair of earrings and a necklace.

Once we arrive at the jewelry case, he digs into his pocket and pulls out a small wad of crumpled bills.

"I have enough to get them both."

We spend a couple of minutes straightening the money before he hands it over proudly to the cashier, explaining that he had to sweep a lot of floors and wash a lot of windows for Mrs. Greene to earn this money.

Next, I take him to the gift-wrapping station in the corner of the strip mall and pay to have the items wrapped.

"You got her such great gifts, now I don't know what to get her," I complain as we window shop along the strip of stores. "Any ideas for me?"

Like he's thinking incredibly hard, Harley taps his little finger against his lips. "She likes sandals. The strap on her purse broke last week."

"Okay. Both great ideas. I don't know if we'll be able to find sandals in the middle of winter, but we can check."

We head to a department store, and I was wrong. Apparently, sandals are always for sale in New Mexico. I find her a pair of the slip-on kind, praying she wears a medium and a purse that the salesclerk assures me matches because what the hell do I know about fashion? We head back to the wrapping store and have those wrapped in coordinating paper to the first two gifts.

Hoping she just needed a little time to herself, I try to waste as much time as possible in the shopping area, paying attention to what makes Harley's eyes sparkle. Not once does the little guy ask for anything or even hint that he'd like a certain gift. He's such a gracious kid. I know he said thank you a dozen times when I bought him a burger and fries the time I picked him up from school, and you'd think I handed him the world when I made those small purchases at the tree lighting ceremony.

I want to spoil his ass for Christmas, but I don't want to show up Lucy. I want to spoil her too, but I don't want him to feel like his gifts weren't good enough. What a hard fucking place to be in right now. He worked so hard for that money, so it wouldn't be right to give him more and tell him to buy her something more expensive.

Shit. I don't know what the right thing to do would be.

"My dad is coming home."

I trip over an invisible line in the concrete.

"What?"

"My dad. He's getting out of prison."

"Soon?"

"First week of January. We went to visit him yesterday."

I knew this was why I didn't get invited over. I don't think she was hiding it from me, but it never came up in conversation either. We've had the month off from missions with Cerberus going into the holidays, and I've been completely focused on her. I just assumed that I'd spend the day with her. She never texted. I figured she needed some space since we spent every day this week together.

Did something change? Did they have a conversation about what that looks like, his getting released? Is that why she's different this afternoon?

After making the circuit of the shopping center, we return to the truck, stopping to grab dinner before heading back to her house. I promise to keep the gifts safe and hidden in my truck until Christmas, and Harley seems satisfied with them in my care.

Her mood is no better when we get back, but Harley doesn't seem to notice as he settles in front of the television to watch cartoons.

"Hey," I tell her, pressing my hand to her back as she stands at the kitchen sink. "Can I stay the night with you?"

Her head shakes immediately. "I don't think that's something Harley needs to see."

"What about staying after Harley goes to bed? I just want to talk." She shakes her head again, her throat working on a swallow. "I can tell you're upset, sweetheart. If we don't talk later, just talk to me now. Whatever it is, I just want to fix it."

"I'm just tired. I did a lot of driving yesterday. Everything's fine."

The kiss of death.

Fine means nothing is fine. I know women enough to know that much.

She turns to face me, pressing a soft, emotionless kiss to my lips. "We're going to have an early night. I'll see you soon."

Dismissed.

I brush my finger over her cheek, wondering if this is the end of what we got started, and by the time I make it through the little house to tell Harley goodnight, I feel like I weigh a thousand pounds.

The drive back to the clubhouse is brutal, every cell in my body urging me to turn back around and demand that she tell me what's going on. I hate not knowing the problem. I hate leaving her when she's hurting.

I don't even enter the clubhouse when I pull onto the property. I head straight for the garage, knowing that's where I'm going to find Skid and Ace. I know going to them for relationship advice is like going to a buffet for a salad. I'm going to end up with a lot of junk, but I'm not going to bother any of the other guys. Kincaid and Shadow have babies to worry about. Dominic has Jasmine and another baby on the way. Itchy is recovering from being shot, and I don't want to catch Snatch giving him mouth-to-dick resuscitation. Kid and Khloe never leave their room when they're home. You'd think they were teenagers who have to sneak around to get naked.

Ace and Skid will have to do.

"You look miserable," Skid says the second I walk inside the garage.

Maybe this was a terrible idea.

I flip the switch for the overhead heater. "Why do you have it so fucking cold in here?"

"Makes the blue balls more bearable," Ace answers. "Are your balls blue, too? Is that why you have such a sour look on your face?"

"She's being distant," I mutter.

"Move on," Skid says after handing me a beer. "There are always more women."

"Especially ones you don't have to sneak around and fuck," Ace adds.

"I don't have to sneak around and fuck her."

"You have to make a schedule. Can only go to her house between certain hours when her kid is at school."

I glare at my best friend. "Dating a woman with children is different from dating a woman that doesn't have kids."

"I fuck women with kids all the time," Skid counters.

"Women who parent their kids and women who leave their children to party and be raised by others aren't the same," I remind him.

"Are you sure you aren't clinging to this one because of what happened a few months ago?"

I continue to glare at Ace. "Why are you bringing Roxy up?"

"Isn't it obvious?"

"No. Why don't you explain it?" I take a long pull from my beer.

"Roxy gets pregnant, has an abortion, but she doesn't tell you about it until after the procedure is done."

"I still think that's fucked up," Skid mutters.

I look away from Ace, a spot on the wall becoming very interesting all of a sudden. "That decision was Roxy's alone to make."

"For your kid," Ace argues.

"Her body," I spit.

"I think you're projecting. I think you're going after Lucy hard because she has that ready-made family you want. She has what Roxy took from you."

"I didn't want a kid," I mutter.

"Until you lost a kid," Ace says.

Fuck. Roxy telling me she was pregnant lit me up. I was terrified, then excited, so excited, that I didn't comprehend her use of the word in the past tense. I asked her why she didn't tell me, and she said I was a playboy. She cried, regret spilling from her face in salty rivulets down her cheeks. She confessed that had she known I would've been happy, she never would've made that choice. I never felt like a bigger piece of shit. That's when I took a step back and took a long hard look at how I was living my life. I never had a problem with how I was "dating" until that moment. What kind of man was I if women saw me as the type that got a woman pregnant, and their first instinct was to abort because they never thought I'd be the type of man to step up and take accountability for a baby we made together? It was a solid kick to the nuts.

"I really like both of them. I'm not projecting. I want to see how this plays out, but she may not even give me the chance."

"Invite her to the Christmas party," Skid says.

"Not like we're going to have extra women there anyway," Ace says, bitterness lacing his tone.

"That's gonna suck," Skid adds. "Honestly, I joined this club because of all the easy pussy."

"There's easy pussy at *Jake's*," I remind him.

"The easy pussy was in the clubhouse, man. I don't like having to work for my meals. I'm a veteran for fuck's sake."

Ace and I chuckle. Skid is one of the hardest working men we have in the field, but he's lost as hell when it comes to sex. He's more of the point to his dick and raise an eyebrow kind of guy. Drive to *Jake's* and flirt? He'd rather stroke off in his bed and pass out with jizz on his chest.

I pull out my phone, shooting off a text to Lucy asking if she and Harley would like to come to the clubhouse for the annual Christmas party. I expect her to ghost me, but her acceptance comes only a few short minutes later.

Maybe things will get better. Maybe she was just tired and needed to get some sleep.

Maybe everything is *fine*.

Chapter 11

Lucy

I have no reason to be upset or frustrated. I told Micah I was tired, and when I did it earlier today, I wasn't lying. I'm completely drained. It's more of a soul deep depletion than a physical one though. I have no idea what I'm going to do once Robbie is released from prison. I was just starting to get a life of my own, and after six years of being single, raising Harley alone, I could picture sharing myself with someone else.

The banging on the door doesn't surprise me. I haven't known Micah for long, but he doesn't really seem like the type of man to let me stew in a bad mood. We spent days in each other's arms talking and getting to know each other. The man has had his mouth on nearly every inch of my body. The intimacy we've shared in such a short period of time has left me wanting more, but I can't help but pull back from him because I don't know what my life is going to look like once my ex is released. I don't want trouble for any of us.

I sigh as I pull open the door, but it isn't Micah standing on the porch.

"Robbie?"

Confusion draws my brows together as I look at the man I've only seen sitting across from me at a metal table in a maximum security prison for the last six years.

His throat works on a swallow, and he has the wherewithal to look ashamed.

"I know I shouldn't have showed up here unannounced."

You think?

I look over his shoulder, for a second wondering if the police are going to storm the house looking for him. It wouldn't be the first time.

"You're out?"

"They upped my release date. I didn't have time to get a letter out."

"And the phones at the prison weren't working?" I don't bother to hide the irritation in my tone. We just saw him yesterday. He had to have known he was getting released today. I can't help but wonder if this is the old Robbie standing before me.

"I wanted to surprise Harley."

"He's sleeping." I know Robbie has very limited experience being a father, but I won't wake the child up just because he shows up on the front stoop at nearly midnight.

"Lucy, can I come in? It's fucking freezing out here."

Robbie wraps his arms around himself tighter. The man is wearing non-descript jeans and a thin flannel, and I pause for a long moment before stepping aside and giving him access to the house. I'm not physically scared of him, but there is a hint of worry coursing through my veins of what this man can do to our lives. Hell, he's already causing problems with the way I sent Micah home earlier without explanation. I just couldn't bring myself to talk about Robbie getting released from prison and what it could mean.

Robbie doesn't go far into the house. If anything, he seems a little shy to be alone in the entryway with me. At least he isn't taking liberties in my home. I'm grateful for that. His eyes look around the room. From here, he can see nearly the entire place—the living room to the right and the kitchen to the left.

"Is Micah here? I'd like to meet him."

"He doesn't stay overnight, Robbie."

He nods as if he approves. By the time we left our visit yesterday, he seemed resolved that there wasn't much he could do about me dating again while he was locked away. Now that he's released, I have no idea what kind of trouble he may cause.

"You didn't know you'd be released today?"

He faces me fully. "I swear I would've told you. They came to my cell today and told me to pack my shit. I didn't question it. You don't argue about something like that. Harley is sleeping?" His eyes dart down the hallway, and I inch myself in that direction.

"He has school tomorrow," I remind him. "I don't want to upset his schedule."

"Yeah. Okay."

"Where are you staying, Robbie?" I ask it in a way to let him know that there isn't space available here.

We've had this discussion before, and at the time he agreed, but when those conversations took place, he had a plan. That plan didn't include an unscheduled release like he faced today. My eyes dart to the couch, and I already feel myself caving a little. I hate myself for the lack of resolve.

It's freezing outside, and he is the father of my child, but we're toxic together. There's not even an ounce of sexual tension or chemistry between the two of us, and after what I've experienced with Micah, I can't believe I ever even thought there was something akin to that with Robbie. I don't want him in my house. I don't know where I'm headed with Micah, or if I can salvage what's going on between us after the way I shoved him out of the house earlier, but I'm not going to burn what we have down by letting Robbie stay in my house.

"The counselor I was working with, you remember the one I told you about?"

"I do."

"He set me up with a guy here in town. He has a place for me to stay and a job waiting for me."

"That's good," I say as relief washes over me. I didn't want to have to argue with the man.

"It'll only last about a month, and then I'll have to find something else, but I'll manage. I always do."

Those words should make me feel relief, but they don't. *Always managing* for Robbie meant bad news in the past. It meant stealing, dealing or some form of criminal activity.

"I was just excited to see him for the first time outside of those walls, you know?"

"I know. Maybe tomorrow after school? He gets out at—"

"Daddy?"

We both look to the mouth of the hallway. Harley is standing there, rubbing his eyes, a look of surprise on his face.

"Hey, buddy," Robbie says. "Did we wake you?"

"Why are you here?"

Robbie chuckles, but it seems pained. I don't doubt he's a little hurt that Harley didn't just race across the room and run into his arms, but his being here is completely out of the norm for the child and anything outside of his routine is suspicious to him. It's why he wouldn't get on the motorcycle with Micah without speaking to me first. The kid is naturally suspicious.

"They released me early. Aren't you happy to see me?" Robbie squats down, putting himself more on Harley's level instead of walking closer, and I appreciate him giving Harley the opportunity to come to him rather than forcing his proximity on our son.

"You're done in that place?"

"Finished."

Harley's eyes look up to mine, and tears start to form. "Can I stay up just a little while?"

I nod. "Just a few minutes."

Harley runs into Robbie's arms, his eyes squeezed tight as he hugs his father.

I know Robbie probably wants a little time alone with Harley, but I've been present for every single minute they've spent together. I'm not willing to step away from that level of supervision just yet, but I don't sit right on top of them as they chat. I busy myself in the kitchen, putting away the dishes I washed after dinner.

Harley talks a mile a minute, showing his dad the movies we've purchased recently from garage sales and the card games he's collected over the years. Robbie is the one to pull the plug on the visit after a half an hour, and I don't know if it's because he's trying to keep to the short time schedule I set or if it's because he's already growing weary of being here. He stands, gives Harley one more hug before sending him back down the hall to his room with a promise of seeing him again soon.

He turns toward me, a serious look in his eye once Harley is out of the room.

"I still want to meet this Micah guy."

I nod, in no mood to argue this late at night or list Micah's positive attributes. I did that yesterday during the prison visit. If there was something wrong with the man I'm dating, Robbie might have a leg to stand on or a position to tell me not to have him around Harley, but that's not the case. Micah is nothing like how Robbie used to be. He's a good man. I don't feel the need to justify him.

"School releases at three fifteen. I leave for work at ten fifteen, but Harley goes to bed at eight thirty. I wake him to go to Mrs. Greene's right before I leave for work."

"I can stay with him while you're at work."

"He goes to Mrs. Greene's. That's his routine. That's how it's going to stay."

He nods in agreement. "Okay."

"Do you have a phone? I think we need to communicate when you're coming over."

"Don't want me just randomly coming over?" He gives me a weak smile, and I know he's just teasing me.

"I have my own life, Robbie. You're going to have yours as well. There will be boundaries."

"I know. I'll see about getting a prepaid tomorrow. Sleep well, Lucy. See you tomorrow."

I press my forehead to the door after he leaves, but no matter how many slow breaths I take, the weight on my chest doesn't lift.

Chapter 12

Snake

Lucy: I just need a little time and space.

I've read that text message over and over for a week and a half.

We went from can't get enough of each other to a complete stall in our relationship, and I easily call it a relationship because I can't get the woman out of my head. Never in my life has a woman had me so damn tangled up. I mope around the clubhouse like a kicked dog. Ace and Skid make fun of me. The other guys avoid me because my attitude is awful. I'm a walking advertisement for the premedicated people on anti-depressant commercials.

I hate feeling this way. I hate that I've driven by her house on numerous occasions. I hate that I know Robbie Farrow is out of prison and is spending time at her house. I hate that I asked Shadow to do some research on the man. I hate that she won't talk to me and tell me what's going on herself.

More importantly, I hate that things may be over between us when we barely got started in the first place. I pictured myself starting a life with this woman. I know it was early days, but white picket fences and a yard full of kids? Yeah, I wanted that with her. I wanted the sink full of dishes and toys spread out around the family room. I wanted the dog getting into trouble for chewing the corner off the couch and baby giggles. I wanted soccer games, and hell, trying to get along with her ex because it was clear from watching Robbie play with Harley in the front yard that the man loves his son.

I want all of it.

I'm tired of slinking around in the shadows not knowing where I stand. She needed a little time and space, and I gave it. A week and a half is a little, at least by my standards, and enough is enough.

I thought about walking away, that maybe fighting for what I've imagined isn't worth it, but those thoughts make me sick to my stomach. I know what we have is special. I can feel it every time I look at her. Giving up on her isn't an option. If that's what she wants then I'll have to deal, but I need to hear it from her lips.

I watch as she walks Harley next door to Mrs. Greene's house, my restraint barely under control as she climbs into her car. I keep some distance between her car and my truck, thankful that she's a very punctual person, arriving fifteen minutes early to work each day. It will give us a few minutes to talk without me causing her to be late to work. I just want to know where we stand without making her late. I don't want to cause undue stress. I want to make things easier for her. I want her to know that I care, that I'm here for her.

I know she's too stuck in her head when I manage to get within a few feet of her as she climbs out of her car without her noticing me.

"Lucy?"

She gasps, turning in my direction, relief washing over her when she notices it's me. The company she works for seriously needs to replace the burned-out lights in the employee parking lot.

"Hey," I say stupidly as if we're running into each other on chance and I haven't been stalking her up to the exact moment she arrives at work. "Can we talk?"

Her eyes dart around the parking lot.

"I'm not going to hurt you."

Her face falls. "I... Micah, I wasn't even thinking that."

"Robbie is out of prison." I'm not going to waste time because she doesn't have much before her shift starts.

"He wasn't supposed to get out until January, and he just showed up the Sunday after our visit. He wants to meet you, but it's complicated."

"Complicated how? Are you two getting back together?"

She shakes her head, an instant reaction. "No, but he was around bikers before, and that's how he got into trouble."

"I'm not going to be best friends with your ex, sweetheart, and we're not criminals. He's not going to be in trouble with us. If he's got a record, he can't even come on Cerberus property."

She shakes her head. "That's not what I mean. He just has all these preconceived notions, and I don't know. It's just. Ugh." Her hands go to her face.

"I'll do whatever I need to do to prove that I'm not a bad influence on Harley," I tell her, hating the two feet of distance between us.

Just a few weeks ago, we were naked in her bed. There wasn't even a whisper of space between us and now the distance seems like a mile.

"You don't have to prove anything."

"I have to do something, sweetheart. I hate not seeing the two of you. I hate this time and space."

She sighs, and that's another thing I despise right now—her frustration with this whole situation. I came into her life wanting to make things easier, not cause her more stress.

"It's what I need right now."

"Baby."

I step close.

She inches further back.

I drop my hands, somehow knowing that she's not going to give in. I can't push her further away. She's already teetering on the edge of breaking this off completely.

I won't let her go. Doing so is impossible, but I can give her what she needs in the moment.

"I'm here when you're ready, Lucy."

It's difficult to walk away and not kiss her, not assure her with my lips on her skin that she has all of me.

I can't even look back at her when I climb in my truck because then I wouldn't be able to leave. I'd end up on my knees begging, and it wouldn't end well. She's a stubborn woman. She's done too much on her own to need me the way I've grown to need her. I feel her strength, and I hate that it's the one thing that's keeping me at arm's length right now. I don't want her weaker. I'd never wish that for her but being needed wouldn't be so bad either.

I'm bitter by the time I get back to the clubhouse.

The garage is empty when I sit down with a beer, but before long others start to filter in. Oddly, Itchy is one of them. He's well on his way to recovery now after being shot and nearly dying. I'm happy to see him closer to his normal self, but it's weird to watch Snatch walk in and kiss him right on the mouth.

"That's one way to get around the 'No Women in the Garage' rule," I mutter.

Snatch kicks my boot before sitting in the chair between Itchy and me.

"What's your damn problem, anyway?"

"His girlfriend told him she needed space," Ace pipes up.

I snarl in his direction. My best friend has no damn business spreading information about me.

"Her old man just got out of prison," I explain.

Shadow narrows his eyes as he leans forward in his chair. "Something we need to worry about?"

"I don't think so. They got divorced shortly after he got sent up for dealing drugs. Been inside for a decade, but she said he wasn't the nicest fucker before he was locked up," I explain. That's not the full story, but it's close enough. Lucy said he was in and out for the last ten years. She got pregnant in between those times, that's how Harley is only six, but the finer details don't really matter.

"From what I can see," Ace cuts in, "she doesn't have anything to worry about. She took their boy to visit the whole time he was in, and she says their relationship is amicable, but she was a little nervous about him getting out and seeing a biker hanging out at the house all the time."

It looks like I talk too much when I've been drinking, something I've done too much of since she declared her need for time and space. Ace, no matter how drunk he is, remembers every damn thing.

"Let us know if he becomes a problem," Kincaid says.

"I will," I grumble. "I just hate being away from her."

It's the truth, and with most of the guys here in serious relationships, I don't feel like a pussy for saying that out loud.

"How old is her son?" Dom asks.

"Ten, I think," Ace answers for me, getting it all wrong. The man doesn't know shit about kids. Harley doesn't even look close to ten. Hell, he's small for six. I don't correct him. "Goes to Dolchester Elementary."

"That's where Jasmine goes," Dom says. "I wonder if they know each other."

"Couldn't tell you that," I say. "There are so many kids around I can't keep up with shit."

"More to come," Shadow says, grinning around the mouth of his beer. "Three more months and my little boy will be here. A week or so after that, Dom's son will be here."

"Like I said, so many kids." I toss my empty beer bottle into the trash and grab another.

"You don't need to be involved in her life if you can't handle her kid," Dom chastises.

"I just miss them. Haven't seen her all week, and phone sex really isn't my thing," I lie, making it out like we've had more communication than we've had. I don't want to look like a complete wuss in front of them.

Itchy chuckles. "So we get to the root of the problem."

"Could always hook up with the blonde from *Jake's*," Ace offers.

"No thanks," I mutter. Do other women even exist any longer?

"What about you guys?" I ask Itchy and Snatch, trying to get the attention off of me. "You ever plan on having kids? I mean adopting or some shit."

"No, man. No kids for us. Don't get us wrong, we love playing uncle to all the wonderful kids around us, but we aren't the daddy type."

As if on cue, the baby monitor sitting beside Kincaid activates, and the small whimper of one of the girls can be heard through it.

"Nice chatting with you guys," Kincaid says as he stands. "But my sweet angel is awake."

"She doesn't sound very happy," Snatch says when the whimpers turn into full-on wails.

"The joys of parenthood. Ivy is teething, and it's as if Gigi feels her pain because she's fussy and upset too," Kincaid explains. "See you assholes in the morning."

We all say our goodnights as he leaves the garage to go take care of his girls.

"You guys looking forward to that stage?" Snatch directs his question to Dom and Shadow.

They both grin.

"I can't wait," Dom says just as Shadow says, "Not a chance."

Shadow looks over at Dominic. "You have no idea what you're asking for."

"I spent twenty years in the Marine Corps. I can handle an infant."

Shadow just shakes his head in disbelief. "Okay, then. When you realize how hard and exhausting it is, I won't even be an asshole and tell you I told you so."

"You staying over?" Ace asks Dom as he stands and grabs another beer from the fridge.

"Yeah. Jasmine said Ollie was missing Matilda, so we're here so they can visit." He smiles, knowing he's wrapped around that little girl's finger, and not giving one single fuck about it.

"You're going to end up with a litter of damn dogs at that house of yours, if you're not careful," Snatch warns.

He chuckles. "Yeah, I think we're past that. That dog's stomach is already swelling. But what can I say? Matilda and Ollie love each other. I can't keep them separated. Griff loves Ollie so I can't bring him home with us. Besides, Em would never let him leave the clubhouse overnight. So, because my damn dog is head over heels for the dog here, I'm stuck with you assholes tonight."

"Not stuck with me," Shadow says as he stands from his chair. "Misty is waiting on a foot massage."

"Yeah, I'm sure Mak is ready for me to rub her back," Dom says, getting up from his chair as well.

"Sweetheart," Itchy says in a sarcastic tone as he stands, holding his hand out for Snatch. "Ready for me to massage your cock?"

"Jesus," Dom mutters with a laugh.

"What?" Itchy asks with a wry smile. "His feet and back are fine."

Snatch swats his hand away playfully and stands up. "Only if you do that thing with your tongue."

I groan because a cock massage sounds pretty damn good right now.

All the married and taken men disappear, leaving just Ace, Skid, and me in the garage. Silence surrounds us for a long time as we drink beer. I'm thinking about Lucy and how much I miss her. Ace's mind is probably blank because the man has the uncanny ability to think about literally nothing. Skid is no doubt wondering if it's worth it to get up and go inside to sleep or if he can just pass out in the chair he's sitting in.

She agreed to attending the Christmas party, but with the way things are going, I doubt she's going to follow through with that. As the seconds tick away, I can feel her slipping away.

Chapter 13

Lucy

I hate breaking promises, but I must've known when I told Micah I'd go to the Christmas party that I wasn't going to attend because I never told Harley about it. I always do my best not to disappoint my son. I hate seeing his face fall and watching him try to hide his displeasure. Never mentioning it meant I knew deep down I didn't plan to go.

I feel more than a little guilty about that.

Micah: Okay.

That was the only response I got when I texted him, telling him that I wanted to keep to the Christmas Eve traditions Harley and I have always had. There have been too many changes this year already, and I didn't want him to have too many more.

I expected him to try to persuade me to still come. I sort of wanted him to, but he didn't. Is this him doing what I asked, giving me time and space, or is he giving up? Is that what I want? I'm so conflicted and torn, I don't even know.

I'm worried for Harley, but he seems to be taking everything in stride. He asks about Micah constantly, bringing him up in front of Robbie like it's no big deal to mention mom's boyfriend to his father. It stresses me out, making me wonder if I'm the one with the problem and not our child. Robbie has asked on several occasions to meet him, but I keep putting him off. I told him the last time he asked that we're taking a break. I don't know why I'm not seeing Micah. My reasoning felt solid at first, but now nothing makes sense.

Maybe I just don't want my two worlds to collide. I don't want Micah to see what I used to be. He's heard the words. He knows I used drugs in the past. He knows Robbie and I got married while we were high because it seemed like a great idea. He knows that Robbie was in and out of my life as much as he was in and out of jail. I made a lot of bad decisions. Robbie made even more.

But somehow, turning that from just conversation into something visual, something tangible, makes it real. It could ruin us.

Pushing him away could ruin you, too. If you're not careful, you could lose the best thing that's ever happened to you.

I shake my head, trying to get rid of that thought and smile at Harley as he opens the worn cardboard box we stored the Christmas tree in last year.

"Need any help?" Robbie asks.

Harley shakes his head. I grin at his independence. The tree we have isn't very big, but he's a little guy.

I'm trying not to be bitter about Robbie being here and inserting himself into our traditions. I knew it was going to be like this, but I got so used to it just being the two of us. I feel a little uneasy with the changes.

Robbie smiles as Harley struggles to push the box over to make it easier to remove the tree.

"If you make a mess—"

"I clean it. I know, Momma."

I laugh.

The Santa Clause plays on the television—another tradition we started two years ago—as Harley finally gets the tree out of the box. Robbie helps with the stand because that part is impossible for Harley to do on his own as I start unwrapping the ornaments we have.

One by one, I hand them to Harley as he decides where they need to go. I feel bitterness settle in my stomach when Robbie lifts our son to place the star on top. I'm not supposed to experience this on Christmas Eve. The holiday is about love and cherishing who you're with, but this isn't what I pictured going in to tonight. I want Micah here beside me, his hand in mine as Harley plugs in the lights for the first time on the little tree.

Instead, I have my amazing son staring at the tree and Robbie looking a little agitated because despite his best intentions, he struggles with being a dad for more than an hour at a time. He's honestly just not used to being around kids. He's responsible for his own structure and choices, and after years and years of being told what to do and when to do it, he doesn't know what to do with his freedom. He confessed that he's fine at work. He has tasks and within those confines he does well. It's the hours after the work bell rings that he struggles.

"Now it's time for hot chocolate," I say as I get off the sofa.

"What about gifts?" Robbie asks, his eyes searching mine.

He knows how hard we've had it all these years.

"I forgot mine back at the house, but I'll bring them over first thing in the morning."

I nod. There goes another tradition I have to make accommodations for.

"Santa comes at night, but I have to hide mine from Harley." I playfully glare at my son who has the decency to look guilty.

"Really?" Robbie asks, facing Harley.

"It was only once. I was curious. In my defense, I was four."

"Sneaky," Robbie says, ruffling his hair.

"Robbie, do you want hot chocolate?"

"I need to get back to the house," he answers.

"We have to do reindeer food first!" Harley disappears down the hallway, rushing back with his backpack.

"Reindeer food?"

"They make it at school," I explain.

"It's oatmeal for the reindeer and glitter so they can see our house from the sky. I don't want Santa to miss us!"

"You have to put shoes and your jacket on," I remind him as he rushes for the front door.

Robbie helps Harley into his jacket after he slips his shoes on without socks. Robbie tugs his jacket on last after handing mine to me.

"Thank you," I tell him, giving him a weak smile.

I wonder if he can sense my unhappiness. I know Micah was able to the second he saw me the day he took Harley on the super-secret trip the Sunday after our last visit to the prison, but Robbie hasn't said a word to me about it. Maybe he doesn't read me the way Micah does. Maybe he doesn't care that I've been feeling a little lost and broken. I mean, we aren't together, so maybe it's not his place to be worried.

"Let's go," I say to Harley as he waits patiently by the door.

"Look," Harley says with awe when the front door is opened.

To the right of the door is a stack of gifts, and the second I spot the motorcycle ornament sitting on the very top, I know who they're from. I look up and down the street, but I don't see his bike or the truck he drives. I hate that I missed him. These weren't here when Robbie arrived, and he's only been here for an hour and a half. I feel empty knowing he was so close so recently, and I didn't get to see him.

Harley and I should be with him tonight, but I texted that I wanted to stay home. I regret that now more than ever.

"These two are from me, Momma." Harley points to two perfectly wrapped gifts sitting on the top.

"I love them."

"You don't even know what they are." He giggles. "These two are from Micah."

He points to a couple more in similar paper. So, this is what they did on their little outing. What a sweet man to include my son on something like this.

"I don't know what these others are."

Robbie bends down, reading the tags on the other gifts. "Those are all for you, kiddo."

He's smiling as he says it, but I can see the strain around his eyes. I can imagine what he's feeling. He's not getting rich working for the man the counselor set him up with when he was released, and he's not getting a free ride either. A lot of his paychecks are eaten up with bills and rent. He had to buy clothes with his first check, and it didn't leave much left over.

"He's not trying to show you up," I whisper to Robbie. "He's a good man."

Robbie nods, his eyes darting away from me to watch Harley as he scouts out the front yard, looking up at the sky for the best angle to place the food.

"He seems like a good man from what you've said and from the way Harley talks about him. I wasn't able to get him much, Lucy."

"He never expects much. He's a grateful kid."

He shakes his head, and I know he's disappointed in himself, more now that he's on the outside and struggling. It makes me wonder if he's going to start pulling back, distancing himself from Harley because he doesn't feel like he can do right by his son. I wonder if Robbie feels like anyone can do better than he can.

"Robbie." I reach for him, but he steps off the porch.

"How about this reindeer food? Do we put it in a pile or is it more of a sprinkle?"

"We sprinkle it," Harley explains to his dad. "But wash your hands before you rub your eyes. Glitter hurts really bad if it gets in your eyes."

"Noted," Robbie says as Harley sprinkles some in his hands.

They spend thirty seconds spreading the "food" out for Santa's crew before Robbie waves goodbye. He's been walking back and forth from where he's been staying. I don't offer to drive him because money is tight for me as well and gas is expensive. He promised before he was released that he wouldn't be a burden on me, and he's been good about sticking to that. Financially, anyway. Emotionally, I feel like things couldn't get worse because I'm heartbroken. Robbie was here tonight instead of Micah.

I usher Harley back inside, urging him to wash the glitter from his tiny hands before getting ready to go to bed as I get the gifts from the front porch and situate them around the tree. We finish watching *The Santa Clause* and enjoy the hot chocolate.

"Will Micah be here in the morning when I wake up?"

"I don't think so, buddy."

He nods, his little face sad.

After getting Harley to bed, I pick up the phone and type out a text, thanking Micah for the gifts, letting him know that I'll get pictures of Harley opening them in the morning.

I get back a thumbs up.

It guts me.

I manage to get the hidden gifts out of the top of my closet, arrange them under the tree, and back to my room before I break down into sobs.

Chapter 14

Snake

Hangovers are the worst, especially after a night that's meant for happiness and fun. Fours kids were at the clubhouse last night. Shadow's son Griffin, Kincaid's twin daughters and Dominic's adopted daughter Jasmine. It should've been five. Harley should've been here with Lucy.

There was joy last night, even when Dom announced that the first sonogram they had last month was wrong and he wasn't having a son but a daughter. They're going to name her Sophia and are ecstatic that she's healthy.

Lucy didn't show. I knew she wouldn't. She texted earlier in the day saying she wanted some normalcy. I wasn't a part of that, but it didn't stop Robbie from being a part of their routine. The man they spent an hour with once a month for the last six years got to infiltrate that special night. I wasn't invited.

The day has been absolute shit, spent popping over-the-counter pain medicine and drinking bottled water to make up for the whiskey I drank last night like it would solve all of my problems. Even Ace and Skid left me to it after the party died down early. Everyone called it an early night because Christmas morning was fast approaching. Kid and Khloe disappeared because they couldn't keep their hands off each other. Snatch and Itchy had better things to do than watch me wallow in my heartache.

Jack Daniels was a shitty substitute for company and he did me wrong this morning. His companionship left me miserable and dehydrated. It'll be awhile before I meet up with that betraying bastard again.

The clubhouse is quiet, and I'm only half paying attention to the football game on the television. I'm watching the recording of it because I slept during the live version earlier. Lucy promised pictures last night of Harley opening his presents, but the images of him seeing his leather boots and various other riding gear never came. It's for the best I guess because he'll probably never get to use them, not with me at least.

If he was happy to receive them, I bet Robbie got to experience those smiles and that joy. I hate the man for it, but he's the kid's father. I wanted my dad around, remember longing for him on Christmas morning, hating the fake smiles my mom suffered through after his death. I don't begrudge the man for getting to be there with his son.

"We're heading to the bar," Ace says as he walks into the room, Skid close on his heels. "Wanna come?"

I roll my head on the back of the sofa. "No thanks."

I know exactly where I want to be, and it's not in a bar filled with lonely women.

I know she has to work tonight because there were still a few call centers open today despite it being Christmas day, and it wouldn't even be an option if she didn't have a shift. Harley is home, and I don't get to stay with her at night.

"Snake?" Ace asks from the front door.

"I'm staying here," I snap. "Get off my dick about it."

"You heard him, darlin'. He's not interested."

"I'm just—"

I pop up off the couch at her voice.

"Lucy?"

She gives me a weak smile, her cheeks rosy from the cold.

Ace winks at me as he steps around her on the front porch.

"Catch ya later!" My best friend gives me a quick wave, and he and Skid take off.

Tears are falling down her cheeks before I can get her inside.

"Did he hurt you? Where's Harley? I'll fucking kill him, Lucy."

She shakes her head, her eyes darting all around as if she expects someone else to be in the room.

"Come on," I tell her, my hand on her elbow as I usher her through the living room toward the hall. "We can talk in my room."

She comes easily, bypassing Snatch and Itchy who are in the kitchen getting something to eat without a word. Within seconds, we're closed inside my room. I flip the light on, my eyes raking over her person, checking for bruises or any sign that the motherfucker put his hands on her.

"I called in sick to work. Harley is with Mrs. Greene." Her eyes take in my room. "I expected the clubhouse to be more active."

"It was a couple of months ago." My head is a riot of questions and emotions, but if she and Harley are safe, we can get to why she's here at her own speed.

I swallow as her eyes search mine. If she's here to break things off for good, maybe it's best to just rip the bandage off and get it over with. I'm not one to shy away from pain, but I find myself scared to have my heart ripped from my chest right now.

She looks heartbroken as she drops to the edge of my bed, her focus now on her fingers as they tangle together.

"I didn't know I could feel the way I do, and then Robbie showed up."

"And you care for him."

Pain greater than I've ever felt before threatens to knock me right off my feet.

"There's no form of emotional connection to Robbie. I want him to succeed because he's Harley's dad, but when the high wore off, there was nothing left between us. I never lied to you about that. It ended years ago. We never should've gotten married."

I stay quiet because I'm confused. I don't want to speculate on where this is going.

"He's not going to stay in Farmington because there's no work for him here. After this job is done, he's going to have to move on." She draws in a shuddering breath, still refusing to look up at me. "He's a felon, and I'm not going to support him. Robbie would never ask me to do that, but I won't keep Harley from him either. He loves his dad."

I inch closer, knowing touching her right now probably isn't what she wants but I'm not able to stay away.

"I like what we started, but at the same time, it isn't fair to either of us."

"We don't have to make any decisions right now," I promise her. "Look at me, sweetheart."

She doesn't. Her head shakes, as if she's telling me it's just too painful to look at me.

I reach for her, lifting her chin with the crook of one finger.

"I don't give a damn about fair. I've wanted you since I first saw you at that damn gas station. You're gorgeous and strong, and you deserve this. We deserve this, Lucy. We deserve happiness."

She nods, and if it weren't for the tears on her cheeks, I'd almost be convinced that she truly believes what I'm saying.

"Can I hold you?"

She nods again, the only time she doesn't hesitate in her decision. She kicks off her shoes, and I do the same with my boots, and that's how we spend the next hour, her in my arms, her silent sobs shaking against my chest.

At some point, she turns in my arms, her breaths warm on my neck, her fingers tangled in my shirt, and when her lips meet my throat, I know she needs more.

I plan to give her exactly what she needs without making her ask.

Stripping her bare while lying down isn't the easiest thing, but I manage, first pulling off her jacket and shirt before moving to her jeans. I lick at her skin, tasting her, savoring her because I'm not a fool. I know there's a good chance this is goodbye. I heard her words. I listened even though I didn't want to understand what she was trying to say.

Her back arches when my teeth graze her nipple, her fingers working my own shirt up my torso. I take a break only long enough to pull it over my head and toss it to the floor, and then my mouth is on her once again.

"Get my cock out, sweetheart."

Her fingers immediately get to work, first on the button of my jeans and then my zipper.

"Missed you," she whispers, and it makes me want to growl in anger.

She didn't have to miss me. I've been here the entire time. This woman has me wrapped around her finger. All she'd have to do is text or call. Hell, send up a smoke signal, and I would've been on her doorstep in minutes. There was no need for either of us to have missed the other. We could be like this all the time. She's punishing us for no reason. Her guilt is misplaced. So, Robbie has to move for work. Big damn deal. Let the man work. It has no bearing on what we have.

"Missed you, too," I say instead, because telling her all that other stuff right now wouldn't go over well. "Need you, Lucy. Need you so bad."

And I don't just mean that I need to sink my cock deep inside of her. I need her with me, need her heart beating against mine. I need her smiles and her tears if that's the emotion she's struggling with. I need her to confide in me, to rely on me. I need *her*.

She tries her best to shove my jeans down, but her arms just aren't long enough. I have to leave her for a second to kick my jeans off and grab a rubber from the bedside table.

"Panties and bra off, sweetheart."

She disposes of them quickly as I roll the latex down my length. I plan to slide right inside of her, but shit, the sight of her center is honestly too good to bypass. I slide back on the bed, my intentions clear as I lick my lips.

She opens for me, legs spread wide, her fingers already reaching for my face, and I fucking love how her hands cup my jaw when I taste her like this.

I groan with the first lick, but then I get so lost in devouring her that sounds are no longer possible. She rolls her hips against me, the rhythm of the two of us the perfect choreography, something we mastered early on in her bed.

"Micah," she moans. "That. Do that again. Oh God."

Her body locks up, knees clamping around my ears, and I double my efforts until her core pulses against my mouth. I don't stop until it feels like she's going to rip my beard from my face. Her lazy smile and unfocused eyes are proof of a job well done when I look up at her. I don't waste a second slipping between her trim thighs.

My mouth covers hers as I slide home, my jaw tight with the sensation of her warmth swallowing me.

"Jesus, baby. Every time, it just gets better."

My hips move slowly. I'm going to savor every damn second I can get. I lick into her mouth, swallowing her whimpers and moans as she lifts her legs higher on my hips. Her nails scrape down my arms, and I don't care if she takes the ink of my tattoos with them. I love the bite of pain.

"Feel me, Lucy. Goddamn, feel me."

"Yes," she pants.

I want to demand that she tells me that she's mine. In this moment, I know that she will. She'd tell me whatever I want to hear. It's why I hold on to the words I really want to say because there's a chance she'd say them back. It would destroy me if this were goodbye. I don't want those words from her if they aren't a part of our forever.

For a split second, I wish I wasn't wearing a condom. I know she's not on birth control. That's another conversation we've had in the past. She didn't have a need for it because she wasn't sexually active. I want to fill her with my cum and pray that she's nothing like Roxy. I want her belly round with my baby. I want her tied to me like she's tied to Robbie, only I wouldn't end up in prison. The woman under me would have my ring on her finger. She'd be in my bed every night. The dream I had of babies and the dog chewing on the furniture would come true because I'd never let her go, but that's fucked up.

Trapping her into a life she may not want with me is next-level psycho.

It was just a flash, but the thought was there. I grind into her harder, deeper. I want her to feel me tomorrow. I want her to answer the door when Robbie knocks to visit his son and still be sore from where I've been.

"Micah," she moans. "Make me come."

Wrapping my arms around her back, I give her everything I have. In my mind, I say everything I can't utter out loud. In my head, she's mine. She clenches around me, her body fluttering down the length of me, and I try to hold off. I slow down, cherishing the way she feels as she orgasms, but it's just too good. She's just too perfect to resist following her over the edge.

I kiss her through my release, tasting her breathlessness on my lips as she comes down from her high.

Chapter 15

Lucy

I let myself get lost in him for a few minutes longer when I wake up in his arms. The strength and the warmth of them are almost enough to make me forget just how messed up everything else is, but reality won't stay in the darkness. Eventually, the sun will rise, and I'll have to face the real world.

He shifts slightly when I slide away, his face scrunching in displeasure when I manage to free my body from under his arm. Finding my clothes is easier than I anticipate because he tossed them all in the same direction. Other than our clothes, there's nothing else on the floor. His room is remarkably clean for a single man.

I can't look back at him as I pull my jeans on. I already don't want to leave. Seeing him one last time would be unbearable torture. Once fully dressed, I reach for the doorknob.

"If you're going to leave me, at least face me when you do it." His voice doesn't hold the hint of sleep like I expect it to. He's probably been awake since I climbed out of the bed.

The tears I thought I got control of last night are already falling by the time I turn around.

"Why are you crying? Don't cry if they're lies."

"They're not lies," I assure him, wiping angrily at them.

"Then don't make this goodbye."

"It has to be."

He shakes his head. "It doesn't."

"I want more."

"I'll give you the fucking world, Lucy. You have to know that."

"How is that fair? How can we keep doing this when I'm going to have to leave?"

"Leave? You don't have to leave."

"Robbie will have to leave."

"Then fucking let him."

He's not raising his voice, but I can tell that it's taking a lot not to.

"He's Harley's father."

"I'm not arguing that, but you're talking about what's fair. How is it fair for you to chase after him? To uproot your son? That's not fair to him."

Slapping me in the face would hurt less.

"It's not fair that you have to be unhappy just because Robbie Farrow made bad life choices."

"None of this is fair, but Harley needs his dad."

"And I need you. Fuck, Lucy. Don't you see that? And I need Harley, too."

"We barely know each other."

He nods, his face suddenly becoming an emotionless mask. "If that's what you truly think, then maybe you should go."

I watch him for a long moment, hesitant to walk out of here, but I really do need to leave. Had I gone to work, my shift would've ended fifteen minutes ago. I should already be at Mrs. Greene's house picking up Harley.

My son is and always will be my number one priority. Maybe one of these days, Micah Cobreski will understand that's why I have to walk away from him today. What I want, and what I need doesn't matter. My happiness comes second to Harley's. Even if my heart is breaking. If his heart is smiling, then it's worth it.

"Goodbye," I whisper as I turn to leave.

It's early enough that I make it out of the building without running into another soul.

I cry the whole way home, and there's no way to hide the destruction on my face when I pull into my driveway. I take a few minutes to myself, dabbing fast-food napkins from the glove box under my eyes, but they do nothing for the redness and swelling. I always try to hide my pain from Harley, but it'll be impossible today.

I have to clear my throat four times before I open my car door to make the tears stop, but at least my face isn't wet when I knock on Mrs. Greene's door.

"Momma?" Harley asks the second he opens the door. "What's wrong?"

I smile down at him. "Would you believe me if I said nothing?"

I clear my throat again, hating that I'm going to lie to him but telling him the truth isn't going to work either.

He shakes his head.

"It's really not a big deal, but they got a new cleaner at the office."

He sighs, a long deep exhale of air. "Let me guess, it has a lemon scent, and you forgot to wear one of those masks."

I shoot a finger gun at him and smile, hating that I've used this excuse so many times over the years with him. Being a single mother is hard, and sometimes the bad days outweigh the good.

He shakes his head. "One of these days, you're going to learn."

"One of these days," I echo.

I give Mrs. Greene a wave, nodding when she mouths, asking if I'm okay, and we head across the yard to our house.

"Do you need a nap?"

I shake my head. Despite the emotional rollercoaster I've already been on today, I slept very well in Micah's arms last night. I need to stay busy today to keep from calling him and telling him everything I said was a big mistake.

"Let me get a quick shower, and we can go grab breakfast, maybe go to the park or something."

I wash as quickly as I can, refusing to look at myself in the mirror. I can still feel him on my skin, and I don't doubt with the way he spent extra attention with his mouth on me that that was his intention all along. I dress in something warm, thinking I can use up some extra energy walking laps around the playground equipment while Harley plays, before heading back out to the living room.

I stop right at the end of the hallway, finding Robbie in the living room. I've always told Harley not to open the door, but I never told him not to let his own father in the house.

"No work today?" I ask casually.

"Job's done."

I frown. "Already? I thought you said it would last a month. It's barely been three weeks."

He shrugs. "Got it done quicker. Gotta look for something else now."

"We're getting ready to go for breakfast and then the park. Wanna come?"

Robbie's eyes roll up to me, but I turn before they can meet mine. I won't make the decision for him, but I hadn't planned on there being three of us today.

"Sounds like a fun time. We can kick the new soccer ball I got you for Christmas around the park," Robbie offers.

I've discovered that Robbie is a fan of doing things with Harley that don't require speaking. Harley asks a lot of questions, and Robbie doesn't always know how to answer them. Apparently, even keeping your nose clean in prison still comes with a lot of dishonest and sneaky behavior. He recognizes it as such and doesn't want Harley knowing those things so he's out of the loop on how to give sound fatherly advice.

"Is it in your room? Go get it," Robbie urges.

I head to the kitchen for a glass of water and something for the headache that started forming the second the tears began falling before I left Micah.

"Hey," Robbie says, following me into the kitchen. "Did you work last night?"

I turn to face him. Noticing his eyes on my neck, I know what he sees. I got a flash of the mark there on my way out of the bathroom.

"I want to meet him."

"It's over between us," I assure him.

"I don't have to go with you guys today."

"It's fine."

"My treat," he offers. "I insist."

I nod. I won't argue about the man paying for breakfast, and I don't see it as a favor. I've taken care of Harley his entire life without a penny from him. We're due a little something from the man. I refuse to feel guilty about that.

Harley joins us in the kitchen.

"I think I want pancakes."

"And bacon," Robbie adds. "Maybe sausage."

They talk about food all the way to the diner. I've found it's an easy subject for them, one that doesn't trip either of them up. I'm able to hide the tremble in my hands as I climb out of the car, but my eyes dart toward the two bikes parked on the far end of the lot.

"Maybe Micah is here!" Harley says excitedly. "You can meet him, Daddy. We haven't seen him in a long time."

Our son rushes for the front door of the diner, his eyes darting all around when Robbie holds the door open for the two of us.

I don't know if I'm relieved or saddened when I don't see any guys in familiar leather cuts with a three-headed dog on the back. The waitress seats us quickly in a corner booth, and Harley is a little more animated than he normally is. This is the very first time we've gone out to eat as a family. We haven't been back here since those two guys were jerks to me, and Micah stepped in.

I'm looking at the menu, wondering if I should be petty and order something expensive when the sound of male laughter makes my head draw up. The missing leather vests are drawing closer to me. The two guys that were with Micah that day are exiting the bathroom, both smiling and laughing at something one of them must've said before they walked out. They have to walk right past our table, and I realize they know exactly who I am when the laughter stops the second they notice me.

I don't dart my eyes away even though I want to. I left Micah in his bed less than two hours ago, and I already long to go back to him. I want to scoop Harley up and leave Robbie at this table. I want to tell him to figure his shit out, but I can't do that. Doing so would be selfish.

They both nod at me and keep walking.

"Those are Micah's friends," Harley supplies helpfully. "Momma, go ask them where he's at. Maybe he can join us for breakfast."

My eyes meet Robbie's for a quick second before I drop them to the menu again.

"Pancakes or waffles?" Robbie asks as if it will be enough to distract him.

It won't be.

"Momma? I need to tell him thank you for the gifts. I'm wearing my new boots."

"I'll text him after breakfast," I assure my son.

"Scrambled or fried?" Robbie continues, and I want to strangle him.

"Scrambled," Harley answers. "I don't like my food trying to run away from me."

I jump at the roar of the motorcycle engines despite them being outside, and I can't concentrate on the menu in my hands until they drive off and I can no longer hear them. Breakfast is a sad occurrence. I order oatmeal and juice because there's no point in wasting anyone's money when I can't taste it. Robbie doesn't try to carry on a conversation, and Harley seems content to color on the paper kid's menu.

The park is pretty active since so many kids are out playing with new Christmas toys. Harley, being the sweetheart he's always been, is just as excited for his new soccer ball as the other kids are with their new expensive drones and remote-controlled cars. Robbie is awful at soccer, and before long, Harley finds another kid willing to play with him and gives his dad a break.

"If I had half his energy," Robbie says as he falls to the bench beside me.

"Seriously," I mutter, keeping my eyes on Harley as he plays.

I had every intention of walking around the park, but I'm just not feeling it now.

"I'm sorry for you having to do this all by yourself all these years." I can feel his eyes on me, but I refuse to turn my eyes to him. "You've done really well with him."

I nod. It's the best he's going to get.

"I know he wouldn't be as well rounded as he is if I weren't locked up."

Now I turn myself to face him.

"That's where you're wrong." He frowns. "I will always put him first. Even if you were out and pulling all the stupid shit you pulled back then, he would've come first. He would be exactly who he is now despite who you ended up being."

He nods, swallowing as he looks away. "He's lucky he has you."

"I've made a lot of sacrifices for that child, and I'll continue to do so, but I swear, Robbie, if you start this poor me bullshit right now, I'll lose it."

"The fuck am I supposed to do, Luce?"

"Be better. Do better. Get a job. Be there for your son."

"That shit's hard."

"Life is fucking hard, Rob. Welcome to reality. I didn't quit. I never gave up. I'm not going to sit here and give you permission to. He won't understand if you do. He won't forgive you if you do."

He turns his face back in my direction. "Okay."

Simple.

I think it's the realest conversation we've ever had.

Chapter 16

Snake

Sleep after she left was impossible, but I didn't chance climbing out of bed. Sitting up meant putting clothes on. Getting dressed would only lead to me grabbing the keys to the truck. I wouldn't jump on my bike because it would be impossible to scoop both her and Harley up and drag them back here until she listened to reason. The truck would be the only way to accomplish that.

So, I just lay in bed, for hours, my eyes glued to the ceiling while I ran through scenario after scenario of how to make this work out in our favor. Ours, not just mine. She was hurting when she left, and not because she was hurting me. She wanted to stay. She wanted to be a part of what we were building, but she was afraid of what she would be taking away from Harley if she did. I'm a selfish fuck.

My first instinct was to tell her that he only saw Robbie's ass once a damn month for an hour. I could make that happen. I could keep that same damn routine up for the kid no matter where Robbie landed. He could live in China, and I could do better than that. I didn't understand the damn problem.

But Harley has been spending more time with his dad over the last couple of weeks. That schedule had already changed. Harley deserved every person in his life that loved him, even the man who messed up so badly that he couldn't be a functioning part of his life for the first six years.

I just want to be a part of his life as well, and fuck, I love the woman.

I love her. I'm *in* love with her.

I know that's crazy.

I know if I told her that last night, she wouldn't have stopped with her hand on the door like she did. She would've hauled ass out of here so fast, she would've set the carpet on fire.

It's too soon, too fast, but damn, if it isn't love that's eating its way through my chest, then what the hell is it?

I know I've never felt it before. I know I'd live the rest of my life in misery if it meant the woman never cried another tear. I'd lay down my life right now, no questions asked, if I could guarantee her happiness, if she never suffered ever again, if Harley was provided for the way he deserved.

And then it hits me. I know what I have to do. It'll kill me, but as they say, sometimes love hurts.

* * *

I've said a lot of things to Kincaid and the other men I work with in Cerberus over the years. Many things I regret, things I never should've let slip past my lips. A lot of those things I never thought twice about until someone else called me out on it.

Today, my hands won't stop trembling as I wait for them to enter the conference room. When they do, I think about bolting, calling the entire meeting off. I'm second-guessing myself, and as a man who has always trusted his gut, this goes against my nature.

Kincaid steps in first, clapping me on the back as he walks past.

"Did you have a good Christmas?"

"The bonus was nice. Thanks for that," I tell him.

"Of course. You guys work hard. You earned it." He sits in his usual spot at the head of the table, waiting for the others. "Did you hear about Dominic? A little girl. Can't believe they messed that up. Two daughters aren't the end of the world though."

I give him a weak smile. I know the man is just making casual conversation, but it's the last thing I can manage with what I'm facing right now.

Shadow is next to answer. He looks utterly exhausted, but that doesn't keep a smile from his face.

"Hey, man. Good Christmas?"

"Can't complain," I tell him.

Another lie. I can complain for days, but I'm a man of action. I'm not here to drag them down into my pity party. Shit needs to be done, and I need to make that happen.

Dominic is next. Not one for many words, he nods at me as he passes. Kid closes the door when he steps inside the room.

"Snatch and Itchy?" I ask.

"Itchy has a follow up doctor's appointment," Kincaid explains. "We can postpone until this afternoon if you need them here."

"No. It's fine," I tell them, waiting for Kid to take a seat.

Kincaid leans forward in his seat. "This seems serious. Are you quitting? I don't want to lose you. We have plans in the works to get more men on the team."

"I'm not here about me."

Kincaid frowns, and I know that he doesn't miss the fact that I haven't answered his question.

Shadow drops down in his seat in the corner of the room, and I give him time to fire up his computer. He's going to need it for the favor I'm going to ask.

"The other night we talked about Lucy Farrow." Kincaid nods, and I do my best to ignore the sound of Shadow's fingers working over his keyboard. "Robbie Farrow was recently released from prison. He's having trouble finding work in town."

"Not much around here, especially not for an ex-con," Kincaid confirms as he looks over his shoulder at Shadow.

"Robert Farrow, twenty-nine. Just released from the Santa Fe super-max after serving just over six years for drug charges."

"Super-max for drugs?" Dominic interrupts.

"Had some seriously violent behaviors in jail and prior offenses," Shadow explains.

It proves my initial reactions to her showing up crying last night as being on point, even though she was here to tell me goodbye not because he hurt her.

"He had some trouble once he got there, but then he seemed to have gotten his shit together. Worked as a machinist at the prison. No write-ups in five years. Monthly visits from Lucy and Harley Farrow," Shadow continues.

"That's their son," I add.

"Former drug addict," Shadow says as he lifts his eyes to mine. "Is he clean now?"

I shrug. "I don't know. I'd like to say yes. I don't think Lucy would let him around Harley if he were using. She seems to think he's a different guy than he was before he went down the last time."

"What do you need from us?" Kincaid asks.

"He needs work. Can you find him something?"

"He can't work for Cerberus, Snake. He's not even allowed on the property, changed man or not," Dominic says.

"I know," I say, looking up at him. "I know. From what I gather, he'll do anything."

"It won't be in Farmington," Kincaid adds. "Is she going to follow him?"

I nod. "She will."

"Out of state?"

I nod again. "Yeah, man. She's not going to keep Harley away from his dad. He doesn't fucking deserve her, man. She's one of the good ones."

"Sounds like it," Shadow says as his fingers continue to work.

"You're sure this is what you want?" Kincaid asks.

"I need him to be able to take care of his family. She's struggled long enough. I don't want him bouncing from place to place, and them trailing along after him. They need stability." My throat feels like it's going to close up on me.

Kincaid nods, as Dominic steps closer.

I stand before he can reach me.

I swear to God if he clamps a hand on my shoulder, I'll lose my shit. I'm barely holding it together right now as it is.

"I'll see what I can find for them," Shadow says. "I'll let you know."

"You're a good man, Micah Cobreski," Kincaid says.

I give them a quick nod before I leave the room and disappear down the hall. I have nothing in my stomach, but that doesn't keep me from bending over the toilet and heaving the second I get back to my room.

I think I just made the biggest mistake of my life.

Chapter 17

Lucy

My coffee has gone cold, but I'm still holding the cup in my hands, pretending that I'm drinking it. I'm hiding from my son because being in the same room with him means that he may ask questions. I hate myself for it. Normally, I'd be right there with him, giggling when one of the animated characters on the movie he's watching does or says something silly. I'm losing time with him because I can't get things right in my head.

The three days since I walked out of the Cerberus clubhouse have been miserable. I've spent them wondering if I've done the right thing, spent them telling myself that texting or calling him to come over is the worst idea in the world. If it weren't still Christmas break, I know I would've caved by now. My body aches to be close to him. My heart breaks a little more knowing he's right across town, and I'm the one putting the distance between the two of us.

He said he wanted both of us, not just me. He included Harley in that as well. He's nothing like any of the men I've met before.

"You're sad."

I look up at Harley, hating the frown on his young face as I lift my cup of coffee to my lips.

The cold liquid is bitter on my tongue, but I do my best to hide my distaste.

"We need to talk," I tell him, deciding right in this moment that I can no longer keep everything from him.

He can't be a part of the adult decisions I have to make, but I can at least keep him informed.

"Is this about Micah?" he asks as he pulls out the other chair at the small dining table.

"Some of it."

"He hasn't been around much."

"I'm not seeing Micah anymore."

"Did you guys have a fight?"

"We didn't, but some things are going to change, and it just isn't going to work out between us."

"I liked him." Harley hangs his head, pouting only the way a six-year-old can.

I hate seeing him sad, and it makes me regret bringing a man into his life only to have Micah leave so quickly. I wasn't thinking this would be the outcome. I make a mental note to do better next time, but the thought of there even being a next time makes my stomach turn.

"We're going to have to move."

This news gets no reaction out of him.

"Does that not concern you?"

He shrugs, his tiny shoulders hitching as if it doesn't even matter.

"The kids at school are mean to me. They probably won't even notice I'm gone."

As if my heart couldn't break any further.

"I guess Micah won't be coming with us?"

"No, Harley. Micah lives here. Your dad has to find work."

He finally looks up at us.

"And we have to go where he goes?" His little brows draw in, confused. "Why? Can't we just go visit him like we used to?"

I realize now who the child would choose if he had to pick between Micah and his own father. Micah plays soccer with him without getting tired after fifteen minutes. He holds conversations with him without having to look to me for help. He has two motorcycles. He took him shopping for Christmas gifts.

It's not that Robbie is a bad guy, but he's not very good at the dad thing. Robbie is almost scared to be a dad, and he gets flustered very easily. Harley loves his dad, but I think he's more comfortable and accustomed to spending time with him in a controlled setting.

"You don't want to move?"

"Can Micah come with us?"

I sigh, having already answered this question.

"No, Harley. He can't."

Harley nods as if he's trying to understand. He's trying to be strong because he doesn't like to upset me, but he's young and frustrated. He rarely asks for things, and I wonder if he's been building up all those asks for this moment right now, for the one thing that's impossible to give him.

I know following Robbie to wherever he finds work is selfless. It's helping my ex and giving Harley time with his dad, but I can't help but wonder if it's the wrong choice for all involved. Was the pep talk I gave Robbie the other day at the park the wrong way to go? I know it would hurt Harley if Robbie walked away, but would it be better in the long run? What if Robbie really messes up down the line? Is it better for him to give up and walk away now?

I've second-guessed a lot since Harley was born, and this is just another one of those things. Only this time, my gut is torn on what's the right decision because I can't tell if my choices are muddled because the decisions now involve things I want and things I feel Harley needs.

I wasn't going to ask Harley what he wants because it's unfair to put the weight of that on a child so young, but he's making it clear what his position is. As far as he's concerned, he can have the best of both worlds. He can stay and have Micah in his life, and he can keep with his routine of seeing his dad once a month. Nothing has to change.

I drop my head into my hands, the throbbing that has been a constant for nearly two weeks at the base of my skull threatening to get worse.

"I'm going to go watch TV," Harley mutters.

I can't even lift my head to acknowledge him, and that's another way I'm being unfair to him. He deserves better.

I'm zoned out, wishing for a miracle when a knock echoes through the small house. I no longer get excited that Micah may be on my front porch, and when I stand from the kitchen table, I notice that Harley doesn't even pull his eyes from the television.

We both know it's Robbie. He's the only one that's been coming over. I pull open the front door and step to the side, but he doesn't give me the soft smile he normally greets me with.

His face is animated this afternoon, and I immediately step in front of him. I recognize that look. It's one he's had numerous times when he was high as a kite.

"No," I tell him, blocking his entry into my house.

Emotions clog my throat. He hasn't even been out of prison for a month, and he's already back to his old ways. I should be livid, but a rush of relief washes over me. If he's going back to his old ways, then so can we. He can disappear, and we don't have to move.

"I'm not," he whisper-hisses, reading my mind, but his actions are jerky, his hands shaking as he bounces on the balls of his feet. "I have great news."

"Robbie," I warn. "I'm not doing this with you again."

I'm facing him fully, so Harley doesn't see what's going on, pleading with my eyes for this man to not ruin what innocence I can preserve for our son.

"I haven't been using, Luce. I swear. I got a call. I just got a really good job."

I take a long look at him, searching his eyes. His pupils are normal size. His skin is his normal color, cheeks a little pink from the cold. His lips are dry and cracked.

"I'm just really excited. I didn't think I could find work so quickly, and I didn't think I'd find something so good. The benefits are great. Medical, dental. Even a really good retirement plan. Lucy, it's going to be great. I'll be able to take care of you guys."

"I don't need you to take care of me."

"I can take care of Harley. Pay back child support. Whatever. It's going to be awesome."

"What kind of job?"

Deciding he isn't stoned, just thrilled to share his good news, I step aside because it's freezing outside.

If he found something so quickly, then it must be around here, and that gets me excited as well. I smile because things like this don't happen for me. Things don't work out for me. I'm always forced to make a sacrifice.

"Offshore oil rig," he states as he steps inside, raising his hands to his mouth and blowing on them to warm them up.

"Like in the ocean?"

He nods, his smile wide, eyes bright and beaming.

"We live in New Mexico."

"The job is in Texas. Well, offshore in Texas."

"Texas?"

He nods as if he's won the lottery, and he's still trying to wrap his head around it as well.

"What?" That screeched word comes from Harley, and we both turn to see our son standing to the side with tears rolling down his cheeks. "I don't want to move to Texas."

"It'll be fun, buddy. You can swim in the ocean."

Harley shakes his head violently before running up to Robbie. He pulls back his little leg and kicks Robbie right in the shin. Harley's eyes widen dramatically before he spins around and runs to his bedroom. His door slams, but the walls are so thin, we can both hear his little sobs.

I stare down the hallway in shock because Harley has never done anything even remotely violent in his life before. I don't know how to react. Do I punish him?

"I thought he'd be excited," Robbie mutters as he bends forward and rubs the spot on his shin. If he's not going to make a big deal about it, then neither am I.

"Change is hard for kids," I say because I refuse to lie and say that he'll get over it. I also won't tell him about the conversation I had with Harley earlier. "When do you start work?"

"In a week."

"A week?"

Robbie is still smiling. "I'll go ahead of you guys and make sure everything is lined up. I was told they provide room and board for families."

"We are not living together, Robbie."

"I'll be offshore nearly all the time, Lucy."

"Absolutely not."

His smile widens. "I figured you'd say that. It's a duplex. Any problem with living next door?"

I huff. "You're an asshole."

He chuckles, but then his face falls when he looks down the hallway. "Is he going to be alright?"

"I hope so. I'll have a chat with him."

Robbie leaves only a few minutes later because sticking around for a serious conversation with Harley would be just too much of a parent thing to do. I'm not winning any parenting awards either because it takes me twenty minutes before I go into his room to speak with him. He refuses to talk to me, so I just sit on the edge of his bed and rub his little back until he falls asleep.

Chapter 18

Snake

I'm a patient man. Three weeks ago, nothing bothered me. I was happy-go-lucky. I lived life in the moment. I went with the flow. Now? Every damn thing gets on my nerves.

I don't realize how bad I've gotten until I consider tilting over the fridge when the automatic ice machine in the freezer drops ice into the tray and then refills, the sound more annoying than ever today.

"You seem tense," Kincaid says as he enters the kitchen, heading for the coffee pot.

And not once since joining Cerberus have I wanted to punch my boss in the nose for just speaking.

He cocks an eyebrow at me as if he can read my mind when I turn to face him. I see the challenge on his face, but I only consider it for a second.

"I have news, but it doesn't look like you're in the mood for it." The slow stir of his spoon through his coffee makes me want to flip the fucking table.

"Will waiting change anything?"

He shakes his head.

"Might as well get it over with then," I mutter.

"We were able to lock down a job for Robbie Farrow."

I nod, knowing they'd be able to find something for him.

"It's in Texas, offshore oil rig."

I grind my teeth so hard I wonder how much more they can take before they crack.

"Shadow was able to find a duplex for them to live in, so they can live really close to each other." He watches my face as he takes another sip of coffee. "He'll be out on the rig a lot, but he'll be right next door and can see the kid easily when he's home. He'll be right there if Lucy needs anything."

My knuckles turn white as I grip the table. I manage a nod, but I'm not sure if it's because I'm acknowledging the information he's giving me or the decision I'm trying to maintain not to kill someone.

Robbie is going to live right next door. Whatever Lucy needs, he'll be able to give her.

I could burn this fucking world down right now. She doesn't fucking need him. She needs me. Fuck, I know I need her. Goddamn it. This is the worst fucking place to be in the world right now. I feel completely fucking impotent, and I'm the one that set this shit in motion.

"Shadow was also able to work out a transfer for Lucy. Galveston has a sister company of the one she works for here. The one there actually has promotional opportunities. I bet she'll be a supervisor in no time. The school system seems good. I'm sure they'll do well in Texas."

Kincaid takes another sip of his coffee, his eyes never leaving mine.

I can't get past the feeling that every word from his mouth is a fucking challenge, but at the end of the day, I respect the man too much to throat punch him. I stand from the table, walking slowly to the sink to wash my coffee cup.

"Anything else?" I ask.

"I think that's about it."

"Thanks, Prez," I tell him before walking slowly out of the kitchen.

My body is a fucking live wire by the time I make it back to my room, but I manage to close myself inside and count to thirty. Slow breaths in, slow breaths out. Eyes closed, my future flashing nothing but black images of sadness behind the lids.

When I open my eyes, I'm nothing but a ball of rage. I destroy the room, ripping the bed apart. The television, the dresser, the curtains, nothing is a match for the pain and anger I feel.

Robbie Farrow makes every damn wrong decision, ends up in prison off and on for the better part of ten years and he still gets the damn girl. He gets the family that I want, the family I can take care of. I've always known life wasn't fair, but fuck, a break every once in a while would be nice.

I'm sweaty and heaving by the time there isn't a single thing in the room left untouched.

I'm not surprised by the knock on the bedroom door, only surprised it didn't come sooner, but hell, whoever it is could've been knocking for the last five minutes and I wouldn't have heard them.

"Yeah," I huff, my breaths rushing past my lips.

The door opens, and I slowly turn to see Ace with his head through the open crack. He doesn't seem surprised by the mess I've made. He must've been standing in the hall waiting for it to end before interrupting me.

"What's up?" I ask, raking my hand over the top of my head.

"This probably isn't the best time to tell you that Robbie Farrow is in the parking lot asking for you."

My laughter is menacing, and I know he can see it in my eyes as well.

"I'll tell him to leave."

"No," I say, stopping him before he can turn away. "Just give me a few minutes. I'll be fine."

He takes another long look at the room. "It's going to take more than a couple of minutes."

"Have him wait."

He nods at me before backing away and closing the door.

Fifteen minutes later and several rounds of breathing exercises a military therapist taught me after my first combat kill later, I feel just sane enough to walk out of my room. I count my steps down the hall and through the living room, taking another deep breath before turning the doorknob on the front door. Skid and Ace are nearby. I can't see them, but I can sense them, and I know that's for Robbie's protection, not mine.

I appreciate them for it because I'm still feeling a little unhinged right now. I've made more than my fair share of bad decisions in life, but nothing that would land me in prison. Today could be the day though.

The sight of Robbie Farrow doesn't surprise me. I've seen pictures of him, but it's clear he's never seen me. I want to give him the same dangerous smile I gave Ace earlier as I approach him, but it's not even needed I realize when his throat works on a swallow.

"Micah?" Robbie asks as I step closer. "Robert Farrow."

I look down at his hand, but I don't reach for it. The man isn't exactly stealing my girl, but at the end of the day, she's still leaving because of him. I'm not exactly feeling very welcoming right now. He's lucky I don't grab him by the back of his scrawny fucking neck and drag him into the street. I'm already going to catch shit for destroying Cerberus property, and him being here is going to get me in even more trouble because he's a felon. The rules are clear.

"You need to be a man."

I growl at the motherfucker. "You have a lot of fucking nerve."

He holds his hands up, and he must not be as fucking stupid as I thought if he can predict how close I am to kicking his teeth in.

"You need to go to her and beg her to stay."

"Sounds like you're the fucking coward if you can't tell her you don't want her to go."

I can barely manage the words without yelling them, but calm is my go-to before losing my shit.

"She wouldn't listen to me if I did that."

Robbie bends at the waist, and I'm seconds from snapping his neck when he reaches for his pant leg, but he doesn't grab a weapon. He lifts the denim to show me a tiny bruise on his shin.

"Harley kicked me yesterday when he found out I got a job in Texas."

I don't bother to hide my grin. If I ever get the chance to see that kid again, I'll give him a high-five for the act of violence.

Robbie drops his pant leg, straightening to face me once again. His face is sad, but I don't have it in me to feel sorry for the sack of shit standing in front of me. He made his choices and living with the consequences are just part of the cards he's been dealt. As far as I'm concerned, he's getting off a little too damn easy.

"I want to get to know my son better, Micah, but I don't want to do it at the expense of him hating me in the end."

My jaw ticks, but I don't say a word to him.

"I know you had something to do with getting me that job. The guy I work with mentioned your club, so tell me. Did you do it to get rid of me, or were you trying to get rid of her?"

My knuckles crack when I squeeze my fists. "I love that woman, and I love your son. I don't want her to suffer because you can't get your fucking life together."

He nods as if he expected me to say those words.

"If you love them, you'll fight to keep them here."

"I love them enough to let them go." I watch his face, and I can see the disappointment already forming in his eyes.

But he's not disappointed in me. He's already disappointed in himself. He knows he's going to eventually let them down. He's already given up on himself. I don't know if it's because he's already starting back down that black hole Lucy was so sure he'd crawled all the way out of or what, but he's come to the realization that there's no escape for him. Sooner or later, he's going to end up exactly where he started, and he doesn't want either of them to bear witness to his inevitable downfall.

"She'll end up hating me if I come between you and Harley," I explain, even though he doesn't deserve that from me.

I'll give him the credit that's due. It takes a lot of balls to show up here and ask this of me, but it still makes him a coward for not sitting her down and explaining all of this to her.

He's less of a man than I gave him credit for. I didn't want the man to fail. Harley deserves the best everyone can give him, but it doesn't look like that's in the cards for him.

"She'll hate me if I come between the two of you," he counters.

I won't kick the man while he's down, but I could see that hatred for him already forming in her eyes when she walked away from me last week. That seed was planted long before she showed up on the clubhouse front steps with tears in her eyes. When he made her feel guilty for wanting a little something for herself, when she felt selfish for wanting a little slice of happiness, she started to despise him.

"I guess no one is going to win in this situation," he mutters before turning and walking away.

Robbie climbs into an old beat-up truck that I know belongs to the man he's been working for and leaves the property.

"Everyone fucking loses," I mutter before heading back inside to face the music on the condition I left my bedroom.

Chapter 19

Lucy

"It's like a picnic!" I tell Harley as he frowns at me for the millionth time.

I've gotten nothing but frowns for the last several days. I haven't seen a smile since Robbie came over and dropped the bomb about going to Texas. He watches television with a blank expression. Even the parts that would normally make his sweet little giggles bounce off the walls have been absent. He didn't get excited when I told him he'd get to ride on an airplane for the first time, or when I showed him pictures of the house we were going to be living in that Robbie forwarded.

I shouldn't have researched online about his behaviors because now I'm worried my young son is depressed.

"It's a cardboard box," he mutters as he carries his plate to the living room.

"But we now have twenty dollars we didn't have." I wave the two tens in my hand, hoping he'll be excited by the cash.

"But we no longer have a kitchen table or chairs."

I frown when he turns his back to me.

"The house in Texas is fully furnished. Do you want to see the kitchen table we'll have there? We'll have six chairs."

"No," he says, not in a disrespectful tone, but he really just doesn't care.

As each day passes, he's less interactive. He answers when I speak to him, but you'd think each day he wakes up that his vocabulary is cut in half.

"A lady is coming by this afternoon to pick up the couch," I tell him, so he doesn't throw a fit when the knock comes.

He shrugs.

We leave for Texas the day after tomorrow, and of course I have my last shift at work tonight. I didn't want to give up any shifts, and I didn't want our routine to change any more than it had to. Harley will stay with Mrs. Greene one last time, and although I could see it in her eyes when I told her our plans, she hasn't opened her mouth to tell me it's a bad idea.

"When you're done eating, I need you to finish packing."

"I don't have much left. You already shipped more than half of my things." I never knew a child could sound so bitter.

"They should be waiting for us when we get there," I remind him.

I've done as much as I can in the short time period Robbie gave us in the last week, shipping what I could. It's been easier only having to send personal things and clothes since the house is furnished, but the stress level is still through the roof. Things are easy to relocate. It's leaving people that kills me.

We won't know anyone but Robbie. I won't have a Mrs. Greene to rely on if I need help. I can't even think about Micah without my eyes burning.

"I'm going to pack a few things in my room," I tell Harley, leaving my own lunch plate on the counter.

Once I'm in my room, I close the door softly. Being strong for him is one of the hardest things I've ever done. Each time he gets upset, or I catch him with tears in his eyes, I want to draw him to my chest and cry with him. I want to tell him things will be okay, but I can't guarantee that they will.

Leaving feels so wrong. It feels like the biggest mistake I could ever make. Wrong for me. Wrong for him. Hell, it feels wrong for Robbie, too. As the days have passed, I've gotten the distinct feeling that Robbie doesn't want us to go to Texas. He hasn't said as much, but his initial speech about taking care of Harley and medical and dental and retirement started to shift, taking on more of a *this is a lot of responsibility* tone than *one of being ready to face the world* he started with.

Harley hasn't mentioned Micah again, but I didn't miss the way his ears perked up when he heard a motorcycle ride by yesterday or the way his eyes got wet when it drove by without stopping.

I press my forehead to the back of my closed door, taking long deep breaths, willing myself not to cry because I know if I start, I won't be able to stop. I've had to be strong for Harley for so long it's become second nature, but I'm starting to wonder if I've used all of that up and the supplies aren't replenishable.

I shouldn't text him. I know I shouldn't, but I just can't resist. We're leaving tomorrow. That train is set in motion, and nothing will stop it, but I can't leave town without seeing him one last time. I just want to touch his face, to press my lips to his one last time. I just want him to hold me in his arms, to feel what it's like to have been loved one more time.

I fire off the text I may end up regretting, asking if I can swing by the clubhouse before my shift. He doesn't respond, and I don't even know why I was expecting him to. I walked away from him. I told him there was no chance for us. I knew if Robbie were going to leave town, Harley and I would have to leave too. With my son so angry with me, it seems like a stupid choice now, but things have to get better because they really can't get much worse.

I stare down at my phone for long minutes, knowing he isn't going to text back, and that's all the answer I need. He was always so quick to respond when I texted before. Even when it got closer to the end, after I told him I needed time and space and he only sent emojis and a simple okay, he was pretty quick. His non-answer is my answer.

I drop my phone on my bed and go back out into the living room. If I give myself the chance to obsess over it, that's exactly what I'll do.

Harley's chuckle stops me in my tracks in the middle of the hallway. It makes a little sunshine come back into my life, but then he notices me, and his face goes blank again. He's punishing me. I'll take whatever he can dish out so long as he's not really living in his own little personal hell twenty-four seven.

I head to the kitchen, pretending that I didn't observe his quick change in attitude and wash his plate from lunch, then I spend ten minutes actually tasting my own food for the first time in days.

I manage to stay busy in the kitchen for several hours, packing dishes to take to Goodwill before heading back to the bedroom to check my phone. When I pick it up, I gasp, shocked to have a text waiting for me from Micah.

He doesn't shoot me down or tell me to go to hell, but the hotel name and room number is just as weird.

I don't message him back a million questions although they're running through my head the entire time I'm getting ready for work.

Harley doesn't inch away from me when I sit down on the sofa beside him. I'm counting it as a win. I miss his smiles and his quick hugs. I miss the way he crawls in my lap and invades my space. I miss the millions of questions he asks and the way he's always asking me trivia questions. I just miss him.

I know we'll get back to that eventually, but I'm sad that we aren't experiencing any of that right now while we have the chance.

"I read online that your new school has three slides on the playground."

"I don't want to talk about my new school," he mutters.

"Okay. Well, go get your pajamas on. I have to head to work."

I'm not going to mention that I'm going to see Micah before work. It would only break his heart, and he wouldn't understand why he can't come.

It only takes a few minutes before Harley is back out in the living room with his pillow and favorite blanket. My heart is in my throat when I kiss him on the forehead as he settles on Mrs. Greene's couch for the last time. I'm near a panic attack driving across town. My heart is racing when I lift my hand to knock on the hotel room door.

Chapter 20

Snake

I'll never get over that feeling I get the very first time I see her each time.

The most beautiful woman I've ever set my eyes on. I love it when she looks at me. I don't care if she's happy or sad, angry or scared. When her eyes are on me for a split second, everything in my world is absolutely perfect.

Tonight is no different.

Even with the nervousness tightening her shoulders, there's a blink of time where our worlds aren't crumbling around us.

"Lucy," I whisper, my hands aching to reach for her.

Her eyes dart up to mine, then they look past me almost as if she expects me to not be alone. I barely keep myself from huffing. She must not have much faith in me if she thinks I could ever spend another second of my life with any woman other than her.

I step aside, an invitation for her to come in but also proof that I'm here alone. She wavers on the threshold for a long moment before making her decision to enter.

She doesn't speak as she steps into the center of the room, turning to face me. I don't ruin the moment by speaking of regrets or begging her to stay like Robbie urged me to do days ago. Her mind is made up and so is mine. There's no turning back.

I watch her as she watches me, and I think we both make the decision at the same time. We know how this night ends.

Tears mark her pretty face, and I wish I could say that I'm able to keep mine dry, but that would be a lie. Our first kiss of the night is tainted with the salt of both of our tears as our lips meet, but it's not a hurried meeting of our mouths.

There's no rush. She's not making it to work tonight, and we both know it.

Clothes disappear a piece at a time, the fabric getting stripped away and fluttering to the floor at our feet.

My lips are soft on her skin, and I make damn sure to keep my teeth out of the equation this time because even nipping at her flesh would turn into biting. I want to punish her for the pain I've been feeling, for the torture we've both been suffering, but that wouldn't be fair. She's only doing what she feels is best for her child. I refuse to make her feel guilty for that.

Instead, I lick at her throat and suck on her nipples when she unclasps her bra. Working open her jeans, I drop to my knees and suck on her clit over the top of her panties. Her fingers tangle in my hair, the gasps and groans escaping her lips the sexiest sounds I've ever heard.

It's hard not praising her, begging her to come on my lips, but I don't want words to ruin the moment.

I tug off her shoes before I peel her panties down her legs, making sure to hold her up. I don't want her toppling over. She won't get on the bed until I put her there myself. Everything is spinning out of control, but this is one thing I can have power over, one place I can make decisions.

I lift one of her legs, placing the crook of her knee over my shoulder, opening her center up to me, and I spend a long minute just looking at her, memorizing the sight of her. Sweet, pink, and swollen with need. She glistens with arousal, the dim light in the hotel room doing nothing to diminish her appeal.

Her fingers flex against my scalp, a plea to stop torturing her, but it's the least I can do. I blow a stream of air on her naked flesh, but when she jolts in my arms, I can no longer resist. The first sweep of my tongue over her slit is all it takes to turn me ravenous.

I groan when the taste of her hits the back of my throat, and I know my grip on her ass is going to leave marks, but it doesn't make me loosen my hold on her. We may only have tonight, but I want her to remember me for the rest of her life. When she's in the shower, alone in bed, when her fingers roam down her stomach, I want this moment on her mind. When she sees a man noticing her, I want her to look at him knowing no one will do this as well as I can. I want her ruined, spoiled for all others. I want her knowing nothing else will compare.

She trembles, her knees buckling, but her leg over my shoulder won't allow her to topple. I've got her now, and I'd have her forever if she'd just let me.

The fingers of one hand slides between her ass cheeks, on a mission to find that soaked slit of hers, and it's an easy task. I'm going to have a bald spot, I realize when she tugs on my hair as I slip two fingers inside of her. The angle is awkward, but I'm good at improvising. I curl them the right way, and it sends her over the edge.

The rhythmic grip of her pussy on my fingers is a promise of what's coming later for my cock, but tonight, I need a little of everything from her.

As I stand, I drop her leg and add just the slightest amount of pressure to her shoulders. She obeys the wordless command just as I hoped she would, her hands going to the zipper of my jeans as she lowers herself to her knees. I'm shirtless, anticipating her arrival, and I'm not wearing my boots. I knew if she showed up tonight, I was going to end up inside of her, and I wasn't wasting time on pretenses.

Her lips are around the head of my cock the second the tip hits the air, and I groan at the warmth of her mouth. My jeans are tangled around my calves, but I'll worry about getting them completely off later. I do my best to use a gentle hand on the back of her head. The woman requires no fucking guidance when she's doing this. Even the periodic scrape of her teeth on the underside of me feels intentional.

I'll come too quickly if I'm not careful, and that isn't how I want things to end tonight. With one hand gripping the base of me, fingers tight and twisting, her other hand digs into my thigh. I tremble, legs shaking, muscles tight with pleasure and need. It's bliss, the feel of her suction and release.

I tilt my face up, the sight of her too much to watch. The swarm in my gut starts that low burn deep inside that can't be ignored, and I have to shift my hips back. I fall heavily from her mouth. Her lips are swollen, wet with a combination of her own saliva and my precum.

I kick my jeans the rest of the way off as I reach for her, my lips meeting hers the second she stands, and I want to get lost in her. I want to forget the rest of the world if only for an hour or so, but I refuse to compromise her future, to take away her choice and complicate her life any further.

I take a step back, loving the way she reaches for me in the distance I create as I reach for my jeans and produce a condom from the pocket. She watches, her teeth digging into her delicate lower lip as I roll the barrier down my length. She put the boundary between us when she chose going to Texas over staying and having a family with me. If she hadn't, I wouldn't worry with the damn thing.

I try not to be too rough with that reminder in my head when I lift her from the floor. By the time I press her back to the bed, I'm mostly under control once again.

I both want and need hard and fast. I want and need soft and slow. I'm at war with the two, a battle inside. I want to beg, but I also want to punish.

Her eyes beg me, and as well as I've gotten to know this woman, I don't know what she's asking for. Does she want the punishment, or is she needing forgiveness?

I give her soft and slow because I don't want our last memories together to leave a sour taste in her mouth. I press my lips to hers, lining my cock up at her entrance. That part of me has no doubts. It knows exactly what to do and pleasing her is its only mission. It's doesn't want to maim and hurt. It doesn't want to burn the world down and leave casualties lying around. It's only looking for pleasure. I obey him, drawing out her whimpers and gasps, smiling into her throat when her legs open further before she wraps her legs high on my hips.

My thrusts are slow and purposeful, the grind at the top for her gratification, the soft sound she makes because of it for mine. Sweat slicks our skin, sticking us to each other as we become a single entity in more ways than one.

I don't allow myself to picture us being more than that. Letting go tonight is already going to be too hard as it is. I live in the moment, the right now, and I seize what I can from here, breathing her in, memorizing every single second.

Her orgasm takes me by surprise, the slow roll of her hips the only warning I get before her body begins to tremble and that promise she made on my fingers becomes a reality as she pulses down the length of my cock. My hips slow as I fuck her through it, moaning in her ear because, fuck, she feels so damn good.

I follow shortly after. I couldn't hold back after that if I wanted to. Her body calls to mine like we were meant for—

No. I can't even think thoughts like that. They're not allowed.

The hope I had before she arrived, that idea I prayed for that she was going to tell me that she changed her mind, that she was going to choose me, died the second I opened the door and saw the look in her eyes.

She made her choice, and now I have to follow through with mine.

She clings to me a second longer when I try to pull away. I give it to her. I stay locked against her chest, kissing her tears away, not hiding the ones that fall from my own eyes.

Goodbyes fucking suck, and I know that this is going to be the last one. I'll never do it again.

As much as I wanted to ruin her for other men, she's done that very same fucking thing for me. No other woman would compare to her.

A chance meeting in a gas station parking lot, and Lucy Farrow changed my world forever.

Broken right to the center of me, I have to pull away.

She wastes no time climbing out of the bed, and I don't try to stop her.

We don't speak as she dresses, and I dispose of the condom.

Her tears are silent, much like the entire night has been other than me saying her name when she first arrived. She doesn't apologize for the pain or her choices, and I don't expect her to. Much like I won't apologize for the things I said back at the clubhouse. I meant them in the moment, and I still mean them now. Robbie doesn't deserve the blind following he's getting, and Harley deserves better, but the decisions she makes about her son are hers.

Fully dressed, she pauses at the door. I don't know if she's giving me the opportunity to try and stop her again or what, but I don't open my mouth.

She shocks me when she turns back around to face me with a gentle smile.

I smile back, my heart in pieces.

"It's going to be okay, sweetheart," I tell her, and as I say the words, I know it to be true with every part of me. "Tell Harley I said hello."

She nods, the tears falling more heavily now. She clears her throat, her head shaking like she wants to speak but she doesn't know if she'll be able to. "I can't stay, but I already don't want to leave."

I know she's talking about right now, but it feels like she means New Mexico, and I wish that made me feel just a little better.

It doesn't.

"I understand, sweetheart." It's the first and only time I'll lie to her.

She dips her head as a small sob escapes her lips, and then Lucy walks away from me.

Chapter 21

Lucy

Bad days happen.

For me, they happen often.

I don't really count them or consider them bad omens.

But when bad days happen on the day I'm starting a new life, it doesn't really lend me much faith that the move to Texas is the right choice.

Harley's first plane ride is also my first plane ride, and right now we're having to circle the airport in Houston because of some issue on the ground. I'm nervous, and he's irritable. We had to get up early and drive to Albuquerque to catch our flight, and we somehow still managed to nearly miss it because of airport security being slow.

Robbie is flying back to New Mexico in a couple weeks to sell my car, and he didn't give me a straight answer about how we're supposed to get around in the time being in Texas. It feels like my early twenties all over again, and we're flying by the seat of our pants. Only now, we have a kid we're responsible for.

I never thought I had a problem with other people's children, but it only took about thirty minutes into a two-hour flight with a crying toddler before I swore off ever having another child.

"How much longer?" Harley whines, his nose resting on the windowsill.

"I don't know, buddy. Hopefully not long."

As if someone is answering menial prayers today, the captain comes on the loudspeaker and tells us that we just got clearance to land. A cheer goes up through the plane, and it makes me feel a little better that I wasn't the only one annoyed with the delay. Honestly, I was more worried about running out of gas and falling from the sky.

Landing is just as uneventful as taking off, and I follow everyone else's lead on how we're supposed to file off the airplane. Harley and I follow the people through the airport, doing our best to watch for the signs directing us to where our luggage can be picked up at.

"Potty?" I ask Harley when he does that little dance.

He nods, heading for the restroom with the image of the guy.

"Fat chance," I say, holding his head and turning him toward the women's restroom.

He huffs, but there's not a chance I'm letting my six-year-old go into a men's restroom alone. I don't care how many looks I get from women who have an opinion on the matter. The child needs to pee. He's not going to be crawling on the nasty floor looking under the damn doors, and if women are in any form of undress in a public bathroom and don't mind being seen by other women, they sure as hell shouldn't worry about a child neither.

I feel mad and indignant as we enter the restroom, and that's just another hint that I've already had a full day and it's barely noon. No one gives us a second look other than a kind-looking grandmotherly person who grins at Harley as he rushes into a stall, a chuckle escaping her lips when he makes a noise of pure relief as he makes it in time.

"He's a little dramatic," I tell her.

"I must be too, because I did the exact same thing," she says as she dries her hands on a paper towel. "Have a good day, dear."

While I wait for Harley to finish and wash his hands, I turn my cell phone off of airplane mode, and it chimes immediately with texts messages.

Robbie: Don't freak out.

Robbie: My new boss just told me the duplex was accidentally given to someone else.

Robbie: But they found something else.

Robbie: This is the new address. 5609 Crescent Square.

Robbie: Don't get a cab. There will be a car waiting for you.

Robbie: Please message me back and tell me you aren't freaking out.

Robbie: You were supposed to land forty minutes ago.

Robbie: Lucy?

Robbie: Are you two, okay?

Robbie: LUCY?

Robbie: LUCY!

"Momma?"

I look down at Harley.

"What's wrong?"

I shake my head. "Nothing."

Chances are the house we're being sent to isn't furnished. Chances are all the things I had shipped here last week have either been stolen or sold. Chances are Robbie's choices have screwed me over again.

"Are you ready?"

Everything in me is telling me to use every penny I have to head to the ticket counter and buy us plane tickets back to New Mexico, but I know for a fact the landlord already has tenants lined up to move into the house we vacated. I doubt Micah will ever look at me again, and I'm not even sure the money I have is enough to get the both of us home.

I huff a humorless laugh as I grab the handle to my rolling carry-on and shove my phone in my back pocket. I'll think about messaging Robbie back when I calm down. I slip my other hand into Harley's.

"Ready?"

He shrugs. "Do I have a choice?"

"Not really?" I scrunch my nose at him, a little hint that I'm not as excited as I've tried to pretend recently. If anything, we'll still be on the same team. If we get to that new address and there's an issue, I'll just turn around and leave. I won't put Harley in a bad situation. If I can walk away from a good man because I feel like it's in his best interest, I can walk away from his father if it's in his best interest as well.

Our checked luggage is already circling the carousel when we approach, and a nice gentleman helps me pull it off when he notices me struggling. I thank him and walk outside, smiling at a man in a suit when Harley points, noticing him holding a sign with our last name on it.

"Harley and Lucy?" the man asks as we approach.

"That's us!" Harley says, sounding excited for the first time in weeks.

Weirdness settles in my bones. I wasn't looking forward to the expense of taking a cab for the hour-long ride from the airport to Galveston, but Robbie doesn't have a car. Being driven in a hired car must be even more expensive, and it makes me wonder if my ex is actually working for an offshore oil rig or he's gotten tangled up in something a little more sinister.

Did he get involved in something terrible while he was in prison? I'd like to believe he wouldn't let Harley get involved in something like that, but at the end of the day, do I really know the man? We were high when he was on the outside, and I only got to see what he wanted me to see while he was locked up.

The man places our bags in the trunk of the car and holds the back door open for us. Whoever hired the company was thoughtful enough to have a booster seat installed in the back, and Harley wastes no time settling in and pulling the seatbelt so I can lock it in place.

"Ready?" the driver asks when he takes a seat behind the wheel.

"Yes," Harley answers.

"Ma'am, your seatbelt?"

I rush to put it on, pulling my phone from my back pocket before snapping it into place.

"You have the new address?" I ask, pulling up the text thread with my ex.

"5609 Crescent Square," he confirms.

I nod.

"Yes, ma'am."

He pulls away. My mind is racing as we drive toward the ocean. Harley seems content to watch the traffic, and I'm grateful he didn't ask questions when I confirmed the address.

Me: You have a lot of explaining to do.

Robbie doesn't respond, and my mood is more than sour as Houston starts to fade behind us and things turn more industrial.

The air in the vehicle is thick, and I'm sure that's all my fault, but there's no conversation, and the radio isn't even on. I'm doing my best to determine if the man driving seems like a hired car or if he's the type of man to work full-time for a drug cartel. I don't notice any neck tattoos. His hands are free of ink, but then I feel like a jerk. Micah is covered in tattoos, and he's not a criminal. I don't think Robbie has any ink, at least he didn't before he went to prison, and he's got numerous offenses on his record, so judging books by those covers doesn't always pan out.

Robbie: I'm doing paperwork for human resources, but the key will be under the mat.

We cross a long bridge before taking an exit. Harley gasps at the ocean, but I know from doing research on my phone that it's not the real ocean. Galveston, on most days, isn't what he's probably imagining. It's not pristine beaches with sparkling blue water. It's the gulf and always a little dirty.

Several turns later, the car begins to slow before stopping completely.

"Ma'am?"

I look to the driver to see him nod out the passenger side.

The house he directs my attention to is adorable, painted a seafoam green with a little white fence around it. The entire house is trimmed in white. The porch is huge, and without even craning my neck, I can tell that the backyard is the beach, the ocean not very far from that.

"This isn't the right house," I mutter as Harley unsnaps his seatbelt and climbs into my lap. His breath fogs up the window.

"This is 5609 Crescent Square."

"I love this house, Momma."

I do too, I think, but I'd never say it out loud because this is a mistake.

"I'll get your luggage," the driver says as he opens his door.

"Can you just wait?" I ask, as I type out a text.

Me: This is a mistake. This can't be where I'm supposed to live. I can't afford this house, Robbie.

I climb out of the car because Harley is a ball of energy, but I manage to catch him by the arm before he races up the front porch.

"Please wait for me," I tell him.

The driver waits by the back of the car for further instruction.

"Momma," Harley groans in complaint. "You didn't tell me there was a swing set."

I can see it around the side of the house as well, but I won't let him go to go check it out.

Robbie hasn't texted me back. Of course he hasn't. Why would he actually be present while any of this was going on?

I reread the text thread, looking up and seeing the welcome mat near the front door.

Before checking the numbers on the house, I turn back to the driver.

"You're sure this is the right house?"

He nods.

"And there isn't a 5609 Crescent Drive or 5609 Crescent Road in a less expensive neighborhood?"

"I can check."

I wait on the front walk with a squirming little boy beside me as the driver pulls out his cell phone. The wait seems to take forever.

"There's not another Crescent anything in Galveston Texas, ma'am. This is the only one."

"Thank you." I look down at Harley. "Stay right beside me, understand?"

He nods. I walk slowly up the front porch steps, bending to look under the mat, and right where Robbie texted it would be is the key. It's like I'm living in the damn twilight zone. I pick it up, but I don't insert it into the lock.

I knock on the front door.

"You have a key. Why are you knocking?" Harley asks like I'm crazy.

I'm feeling a little crazy right now.

The front door is just as gorgeous as the rest of the property, more glass than wood, a beautiful, beveled floral design. I don't think I would've noticed the movement inside the house if I weren't looking at it so intently. I knock again, but no one comes to the door. Like a weirdo, I press my nose to the glass, hoping it will help me see better. It doesn't.

All I can make out is a huge shape standing right in the middle of the entryway.

"Use the key, Momma."

"Someone is in there," I say.

"Ask them if I can play on the swing set."

"Get back," I hiss when the shape moves.

Sensing my fear, Harley moves in front of me before I can shift to protect him.

I don't know when he deemed himself my protector, but the forty-pound little guy puffs out his chest as the door swings open.

"Micah!" Harley screams.

I'm speechless, tears burning my eyes at the sight of him.

Harley doesn't waste a second jumping into his arms, just like Micah doesn't waste a second crouching to catch him. I lose the sight of his magnificent blue eyes as they flutter closed when he hugs my son, his arms wrapped all the way around his tiny frame.

"Hey, sweetheart," he whispers, shifting Harley to one hip as he reaches for me with his free hand. "Welcome home."

Harley rests his head on Micah's shoulder as if it's the most natural thing in the world, and I get the sudden urge to pinch myself, terrified that I've fallen asleep on the plane, and I'm dreaming.

"What are you doing here?"

"I love you, woman. Do you really think I was going to let you move to Texas without me?"

I blink up at him. "Love?"

"Like a lot," he says with a wide grin.

"Micah, there's a swing set out back."

Micah looks from me to my son. "And an ocean. Wanna check it out?" Harley nods, wiggling to be set free.

"Through there." He points toward a door at the back of the house. "But just the swing set for right now."

"What is—"

He presses his fingers to my mouth, silencing me.

"We have a million things to talk about, and we'll get to them, but first—"

He covers my mouth with his, tongue sweeping inside. I groan, gripping his shirt as his hands grip my ass.

A cough pulls us apart.

"Sir?"

Micah chuckles against my mouth, but he presses one more kiss to my lips before pulling completely away.

The driver is standing there beside all our luggage. Micah pulls his wallet out and hands the man some cash. "Thanks, Brandon."

"Anytime, Mr. Cobreski."

The guy walks to the car and drives off.

"I know you didn't want me to stay the night at your house, but I'm inviting you two to stay the night at mine."

"I'm guessing Robbie wasn't lying about the duplex being rented?"

"Your half of the duplex was rented. Robbie still has the other half. He's about three miles away."

"And you two set this up together?"

"He was told what was going to happen." He gives me a small smile. "He didn't put up much of a fight. I'm not going to stir shit up with your ex, baby, but I can tell you that we're going to have to keep a close eye on him. I hope for Harley's sake that the man is on the right path, but I'm not so sure he is."

I nod my head because I've had my own doubts.

I walk toward him, my arms going around his waist. "I can't even begin to tell you how happy I am that you're here, but what about your life back in New Mexico?"

"I couldn't live without the two of you, Lucy. Once I realized that, the decision was easy."

"And Cerberus?"

"Kincaid would've kicked my ass if I let you walk away."

"Really?" I look up at him as he presses a kiss to my forehead.

"He literally used those very words. I have friends all over the world. I've got something lined up at a bike shop here in town."

"So my assumption about bikers in the beginning wasn't too far off, huh?"

His rumbled laughter against my chest makes me smile.

"We better get out back before that boy chooses today as the day he's going to start misbehaving."

I wrap my arm around his waist and let him guide me to the backyard. Harley is nothing but smiles and happiness as he pumps his legs, the swing he's sitting on going back and forth.

"Do you like it?" Micah asks.

"Love it," Harley says. "Is all of my stuff here?"

"It's at your dad's place," Micah answers.

I'm glad I don't have to repurchase everything.

The swing slows as Harley's face starts to fall.

"What's wrong? Tired already?"

"Hey, kiddo?" Micah prompts when he doesn't answer me. "Your momma asked a question."

He hasn't been around to see the shift in his attitude the last couple of weeks, and I hate that he's witnessing it now. It makes me feel even more like a failure. I've always been so proud of how well behaved he's been.

"We're not going to live here?" Harley kicks at the sand under his feet.

Micah puts me on the spot, turning to look at me, his head cocked a little to the side.

"I live here," Micah says, his words directed at Harley, but his eyes turned to me.

I narrow mine at him, noticing the smile he's trying to hide.

"There are only two bedrooms," the man adds.

"Okay," Harley says slowly.

I wait for the kid to offer to sleep on the couch, but then he surprises me completely.

"I'll take the smaller one, and you two can have the bigger one. Problem solved."

"Problem solved," Micah says, walking over to Harley and giving him a high-five.

When leaving the airport, I was sure that Harley and I were on a team. Looking at the two of them, I know a team has been formed, I just didn't know I was going to be on the outside of it.

"Is that right?" I ask, crossing my arms over my chest.

They look at each other, comic smiles on their faces before looking back at me and nodding.

"Well, maybe the boys need to share a room, and the girl gets her own room."

Harley's eyes go wide. Micah's narrow.

"We could get bunk beds," Harley whispers, like it's the best idea in the world.

"We need to discuss this," Micah tells my son. "You go back to swinging."

I feel like prey when he prowls toward me, but I hold my ground.

"How much is it going to break his heart when I tell him I'm sleeping in a bed with you?"

I shrug. "Not much. Just mention that you wouldn't be comfortable in a bunk bed because you're so big. He's a compassionate kid. He wouldn't want you to be in pain."

"I'm still going to spank your ass later for putting the idea in his head."

"Can't wait," I tell him with a wink.

"Micah!" Harley says, his swing soaring through the air. "Can I be a biker for Cerberus when I grow up?"

"Gotta be a Marine first, kiddo."

"Is that all?" he asks.

"That's it."

"Sounds like a plan," my son says.

Epilogue

Harley

25 years later

Growing up, my mom protected me from a lot of things.

I knew we didn't have a lot of money, but the important things were always readily available. I had hugs and food. She always smiled. I only caught her crying a couple of times.

I thought she was happy.

I didn't realize how truly unhappy she was in life until she met Micah "Snake" Cobreski.

Until then, a lot of her smiles were fake. At six years old and before, I didn't know a smile couldn't reach your eyes. I didn't know that laughter could be fake, and that she was never allergic to lemons. That her red, puffy eyes when she picked me up from Mrs. Greene's house with those excuses were the nights that were just too bad and she spent a lot of them crying.

She was willing to give up that man for me, and I think if things turned out that way in the end, I might have ended up hating her a little. Micah didn't let that happen. That man came into our lives like a battering ram, and I'm the man I am today because of it.

I wouldn't have served twelve years in the Marine Corps if it weren't for him.

I wouldn't trust my heart with Lana, my wife of six years.

I never would've found the courage to be a good father to Aria, my precious two-month-old daughter if it wasn't for the example he set for me.

I got nothing from my biological father.

Of course I remember the visits with him in prison, the man he tried to be, the advice he tripped over, the example he tried to set after uprooting us from New Mexico in the middle of first grade.

Thank God, Micah met us in Galveston because by that very summer, my father was on drugs and had been fired from the job that brought us to Texas in the first place. Micha was our rock, our touchstone, the example I learned to live by. I appreciate him in more ways than I'll ever be able to find the words to say.

It wasn't all butterflies and roses. I was stubborn growing up and used the words *you're not my father* more than once, but he stuck with me. He never told me he wished he'd made a different decision when my mother left him because she thought I needed more time with Robert Farrow. The man adopted me when Robert thought giving up his full rights when I was nine would be easier than being responsible for child support.

I owe Micah everything.

Guilt settles inside of me as the minister finishes his generic speech.

I don't bother to watch as the casket is lowered into the ground.

"Are you okay?" Lana asks as we walk back toward my truck.

"I'm fine," I answer honestly.

It's not the complete truth, but I know what she's referring to, and it isn't my guilt about being here. She wants to know where my head is at emotionally, and I'm fine with what I just sat through, if not a little annoyed to have had to arrange my day around the graveside service.

"Are you sure? Your dad just died."

I take a sleeping Aria from her arms and place her gently into the rear-facing infant seat in the back of the truck.

"My dad is with my mom somewhere in the Caribbean for the second time this winter. I barely knew that man."

I'm actually shocked it took Robert Farrow until the age of fifty-four to finally overdose. The greater shock is that he wasn't in prison when it happened. I haven't kept tabs on him at all, so to get the call from a hospital in San Antonio—only three hours away from where we live in Houston—five days ago was a surprise.

I called my dad—Micah. He's been that to me since the day he adopted me, and I asked for advice. I was planning to just let the state deal with him, but he said the right thing to do would be to take care of it, that if I regretted spending a little money, I could always make more money. If I turned my back on it, the regret later on couldn't be remedied. The man never steered me wrong in the past.

So I made the preparations—a graveside service, a basic headstone, a minister whose name I don't know that didn't know him. It's more than he ever did for me.

Lana's hand comes down on my arm, and like it always has, it has the power to calm everything inside of me.

"Tell me you're okay."

"Baby." I pull her to my chest and press my lips to her forehead. "I've got you and my little girl. Life is perfect."

"Almost perfect," she counters. "In a week, the last part of your dream comes true."

I grin against the top of her head because she's got a point.

I remember the declaration I made the first day Mom and I showed up in Galveston. I told Micah I wanted to be a biker with the Cerberus MC. At the time, I had no idea what that meant. At six, I thought it was riding motorcycles and having fun. As a man with a family he values over anything in the world, I know what they do, what their mission is, and I want it even more.

Next week, I sign my contract with that very club, and even though we aren't blood related, I'm still joining the Cerberus MC.

I get to carry on the legacy.

I'm Harley Cobreski.

I'm Cerberus.

LAWSON

Copyright

Synopsis

My plan was as simple as they come... in theory. Show up at the Cerberus clubhouse and give dear old Dad a piece of my mind. What I didn't expect was being welcomed into the open arms of a father who had no idea I existed.

More importantly, I didn't anticipate HER. Delilah Donovan was a breath of fresh air. She would soon become my reason for wanting to become a better man, my reason for getting out of bed with a smile on my normally sneering face. But no matter how much I changed, she'd always be too good for a man like me.

It was over before it could even begin.

Prologue

Lawson

"Please don't say that," I beg the only parent I've ever known.

Is that possible? Can you plead death away?

"You need to listen." She gives me a weak smile, the action barely tugging up the corners of her mouth. "You're so stubborn. Just like your father."

My ears perk. She hasn't mentioned the male DNA donor in years. The last time I caught her talking about him, she refused to give me details, citing she'd tell me everything when I was old enough to understand. All I knew was my father was dead, long before I was born.

Drew whimpers from the other side of her hospital bed, clinging to one hand while I hold on to the other.

"My time is up, beautiful boys."

I don't chastise her this time. I don't insist that I'm a man and beautiful is never a word I want describing me.

This time, I let the tear roll down my cheek unchecked.

"No, momma," Drew says through his sobs. "We're not ready."

"We'll never be ready," I murmur.

"Come here," she says to me. "I have so much to tell you."

We both position ourselves closer, fitting easily beside her cancer-ridden, frail body on the single bed.

"Promise me you'll listen to all I have to say." Drew vows, quick to agree even when he doesn't know what he's signing on for. I hesitate. Nothing good comes from that type of intro. "Promise me."

I nod my head in agreement. Ten minutes later, I'm broken, shattered. My mother is gone, my world is imploding, and the new information I've been given is enough to drive me mad.

Chapter 1

Lawson

"This is possibly the worst idea you've ever had," my younger brother Drew complains as we walk down an ill-maintained gravel road. "What do you expect? For him to just answer the door and welcome us with open arms?"

"That's the last fucking thing I want," I sneer. "I want some damn questions answered. We'll probably be out of there in an hour."

"Sure is a long ass trip for an hour of time," he grumbles.

"Watch your mouth," I warn.

"You cuss," he whines. "I should be able to cuss now, too."

I look over my shoulder at him, nearly tripping on yet another pothole in the road. How anyone on a bike navigates this road without ruining their suspension is beyond me. That realization makes me pull my phone from my pocket, checking the map for the hundredth time since we got off the Greyhound bus.

"I'm a man. When you're grown, then you can use whatever language you want."

He laughs at me, sputtering "a man?" in a way that makes my already simmering anger bubble to the top.

"I'm eighteen," I argue. "Legal in every way."

"Not drinking," he challenges.

"I have a fake ID for that," I mutter as my eyes catch the sight of a compound with numerous houses gathered behind it.

"I want one," he says excitedly.

"You wouldn't pass for twenty-one, idiot. I bet you don't even have hair on your nuts yet."

I smile, facing forward so he can't see me.

"I do, too." He mumbles something under his breath two steps behind me.

My fifteen-year-old brother has always tried to keep up with me despite our three year age difference.

"Wow," he hisses as our destination comes into view.

"Yeah," I agree. "The assholes in life always seem to have more than everyone else."

A half dozen houses are the backdrop for a more industrial type building. It pisses me off more, even as a part of me hopes this is the wrong place. Facing my past isn't something I ever thought I'd have to do.

I don't break stride as we head through the open gate and onto the porch. I press the doorbell as Drew, visibly uncomfortable, shifts from one foot to the other.

I look over my shoulder, making sure he's behind me and safe as the door swings open.

Unfamiliar brown eyes stare back at me. This man has auburn hair with gray sprinkled in at his temples.

"You'll know him when you see him," Mom says, using one of her final breaths.

As if he's seeing a ghost, he just stares at me. My eyes narrow at his scrutiny.

He breaks the eye contact first, turning his head to speak over his shoulder. "Babe, can you come here?"

I watch as the most tatted up motherfucker I've ever laid eyes on walks up to join us. His hand makes contact with the man who opened the door before his eyes even look toward me.

Recognition marks his face also. I stare back at him for a brief second. His ice blue eyes, the same color as mine, fight for understanding.

"You must be my dad," I sneer.

"What the fuck?" the blue-eyed fucker hisses, earning a slap to the chest from the other man.

"Please come in." The untatted man offers his hand. "I'm Robert."

I side saddle past him, finding more than a dozen pairs of eyes staring back at me while my younger brother apologizes for my rudeness and introduces himself. Regret swims in my gut at the sight of all of these spectators. The bravado I mustered on the walk here, dwindles away quickly as I take in the tough-looking grown men scattered around the room. I don't miss the handful of gorgeous girls in the room, either.

Just as I'd suspected, these old fucking bikers are still doing what bikers do; fucking young girls while throwing the used-up ones out like trash. Several older women, gorgeous in their own right, stare back wide-eyed and confused. They must be the ones training the new ones as their replacements.

"Time to clear out," a bald man with sleeves of tats peeking out from his t-shirt booms.

Groans and complaints echo around the room, but everyone begins to stand, gather their things, and disappear down the hallway at the back of the room.

The man barking orders must be Kincaid, the club president. The soft look he gives to the two assholes behind me isn't in character with what you'd expect from the leader of an MC. Information on the club was limited during my research over the last couple of weeks since Mom passed, but the internet had plenty of information on other clubs.

A pair of teenagers gawk at me. Clearly twins, or very close in age, they linger, eyes darting from the intruders in their world and back to the guys standing at my back.

"Go," one of them insists.

The boy moves quickly, but the ice blue eyes of the girl hold mine, the delicate column of her throat working on a rough swallow under my attention. It's clear she's attracted to me when her tongue swipes at her bottom lip. I'll fuck that mouth later, given a chance, but I have other shit to deal with right now.

"Dad?" she whispers.

"Go," the booming voice comes again.

She scurries away as disgust sends goosebumps down my arms.

Dad? I can't decipher which pisses me off more, that I may have just envisioned my sister on her knees deep throating me or that my father has other children he stuck around for when my mom, pregnant with me, was tossed to the curb.

I spin, my eyes first searching for Drew, something I've done my whole life until they land on the other two.

"How do you want to do this?" I ask the man who looks like an older version of the guy I see in the mirror each morning. He has tats on nearly every part of his body, stars on his pierced cheeks, and despite his age, it's still working for him. A look into my future doesn't seem so bleak, even if vanity is the only thing I honestly want to focus on right now. All of the other things that need to be said come with a pain in my chest that's difficult to get rid of.

"However you want," the brown-eyed man says. He motions to the vacated couch across the room. "We can sit."

Drew, always obedient, follows him while I stand locked in place staring at the man who ruined my mom's life. It isn't until I see the pleading in my brother's eyes as he looks at me after sweeping his attention around the room, that I cave and move to sit beside him. I didn't miss the pool table, arcade games, or the TV too big for any person to own when I first walked in. Those materialistic things don't mean shit to me, but Drew is easily impressed

"Nice place you have here." I avoid eye contact as I look around the open area of the room. "It begs me to wonder just how many pregnant women you forced out after they got used to such luxury."

Drew trembles beside me, and I hate having this conversation in front of him. I haven't given him the gory details of what Mom whispered in my ear on her last day in this world.

"None," Robert says.

I huff a laugh. "Funny, that's not what happened to my mother."

"And who is your mother?"

The gall of this motherfucker.

"What's wrong, Snatch?" I hiss. "Can't remember the last time you fucked a woman?"

He narrows his eyes at me but keeps his mouth shut.

"I'll give you a hint. I just turned eighteen."

Robert's eyes widen as my sperm donor hisses. "Darby."

I hear Drew sniffle at the sound of our mother's name and it pisses me off coming from his lips more than I ever thought it would.

"Don't speak her name, ever again," I growl.

The men across from us share a private look before turning their attention back to us, making my blood pump harder, thicker in my veins. It's taking everything I have to stay seated and not attack both of them.

"Are you sure?"

I glare at him. "Are you kidding me? I would tell you to take a long, hard look in the mirror," I point at my face, one I'd been proud of until seeing him. "But you're kind of looking in one, don't you think?"

Tattooed fingers sweep over his head as he soaks all of this in. Minutes drag by before he speaks again. "I'd like to speak with your mother. There seems to be a lot of things we need to discuss."

My eyes sting at the possibility of speaking to my mother again. "Like what? You want to bitch her out for telling me how to find you? Reject her one more time since I'm interfering in your life again?"

He shakes his head, but I continue.

"Tell me, Snatch, what was it about her or me for that matter that would make you reject us but have two more children with some other woman? Did we not fit into your life or was it her specifically that you couldn't stomach?"

"That's not what—" Snatch holds his hand up to stop Robert from speaking.

"One," he says with no anger or agitation in his voice. Cool, calm, collected, and more than a little infuriating. "You can call me Jaxon. I haven't gone by Snatch in over fifteen years. Your mother wouldn't know that because I haven't seen her in over eighteen years. She never knew my real name."

I bristle at the implication of my mother being the type of woman who would sleep with men before getting to know even their names. It's Drew's hand on my forearm that keeps me from knocking this asshole out.

"Two," he continues, not bothered by my restrained anger. "Your mother never told me she was pregnant. She disappeared one night, and we never heard from her again."

"Bull—" I get the same hand he held up at Robert. Even enraged, I silence my words, which pisses me off even more.

"Three, even though it doesn't make any difference, Samson and Delilah are adopted, so there was never another woman."

"Law," Drew whispers drawing my stunned eyes to him. "Just hear them out."

I shake my head, but words are impossible to form.

"Please," he begs, exhausted from traveling through numerous states to get here. He leans closer and whispers. "I'm tired and hungry."

Protecting Drew has been my focus since I was old enough to understand that my mother's continued bad decisions left him fending for himself many times. This time is no different.

I stand from my place on the couch. "We shouldn't have come here. Come on, Drew."

He hesitates at first, but I feel his presence at my back as I grab my duffel bag from where I dropped it on the floor when I'd first walked in.

"We'll find a hotel or something," I mutter to him as my hand encircles the doorknob.

"We don't have the money for that," he adds.

"I'll figure it out."

"Like last time," he whispers just as Jaxon calls out, "Don't go."

"Please stay," Robert says walking closer than Jaxon is willing to at this point. "We have plenty of room in the house."

I ignore him and look down into the pleading eyes of my baby brother.

"What will happen if you go to jail?"

"I won't," I promise and turn back to the front porch.

"You said that last time," he persists.

Guilt and a flood of memories hit me all at once. They're troublesome enough to make me turn in the direction of the two men I never wanted to see longer than to say my peace.

"I'm not calling either one of you dad."

Relief at my concession is clear on Robert's face. Jaxon looks like he could puke any minute.

Chapter 2

Delilah

"Who was that?" I ask my brother.

Nervous energy has me pacing my room as he sits on the bed, uninterested in the two boys that just showed up at the clubhouse. He's only able to focus on a way to convince Dad and Pop to let him go on the senior trip to Mexico when he's not even a senior until fall. I'm grateful for the lack of attention and the inspection my response would bring if he bothered to notice me.

"No clue," he says in a dismissive tone.

"Diego and Morrison seemed to recognize the older one," I add.

"Guys looking for work?" he offers even though it's a ridiculous notion.

"The dark-haired kid is younger than us, Sam. So I doubt that."

He doesn't even bother to pull his eyes from his cell phone as he types furiously on the screen.

"Does it matter?"

"Of course it matters," I hiss at him, the self-absorbed response has me stopping in my tracks. "He has Dad's eyes."

He huffs. "We have Dad's eyes."

"And we're blonde. How many guys do you know that have black hair and piercing blue eyes?"

His gaze pulls from his phone and meets mine. "Piercing? Really, Delilah?"

"What?" I shrug and continue walking across the room. With my back to him, I fiddle with things on my dresser.

"Maybe it's a long-lost son," he offers with no enthusiasm.

"Don't even say that," I squeal turning back to him. "That would be disgusting."

Dammit.

His phone drops to the turquoise duvet covering my bed, and I have his full attention now. The one thing I was hoping not to draw. I can handle a distracted Samson, but when his twin eyes stare into mine, all of my secrets spill out with minimal effort on his part.

"Disgusting? Tell me, Delilah, what would be so gross about Dad having a blood-related child with *piercing* blue eyes?"

"N-nothing," I mumble. "I misspoke."

"You're the smartest girl in our school, so I highly doubt that."

I turn away from him without a word. I can feel the heat of my embarrassment flushing my cheeks.

"They had duffel bags with them," he says as if I didn't notice them, too. "They're probably moving in with us."

I turn, fast enough to knock a few books off of my dresser, only to find his back at my door and his laughter echoing down the hall as he heads to his room.

Moving in?

There's no way the beautiful stranger will end up here.

I let it sink in as I pick up the things I knocked down. Neither one of my dads would turn away a kid in need, and even though the older one looked one hundred percent grown, the younger one isn't.

Sticking my head out of my room, I listen for my brother. I'm met with silence and knowing him, he's locked away in his room on his phone or he's masturbating.

I shudder at the memory of forgetting to knock before entering his room last week. As I try to force bile back down, I head to the spare bedroom. It's clean, but I'm not sure who slept in the bunk beds last, so I strip them and grab fresh, clean sheets to remake them. Sometimes Dustin and Khloe's little boy stays in here and sometimes it's friends from school or others from next door.

Satisfied that the beds are ready to go, I scoop up the dirty linens and run them down to the laundry room. From the small window, I see Gigi sitting on her front porch painting her nails. Her body is angled so she can keep an eye on the back door of the clubhouse. Seems the handsome, blue-eyed stranger caught her attention too. There's no other reason for her to be battling the late May heat, and I know for a fact she hates to sweat.

Disgusted with myself at finding him so handsome and the possibility that he could be my brother, I head back upstairs and keep the door cracked so I can hear them if they come home with my dads.

I don't wait long before the sound of the front door opening and closing makes it up the stairs. Sticking my ear to the crack in the door, I listen for movement and conversation from below. Unable to decipher the voices, I step out on the landing just as my dad, Jaxon, is coming toward me. Both boys, the younger one with excited anticipation in his eyes, the other with more anger on his face than any guy his age should suffer, follow behind him.

"I changed the sheets on the bunk beds," I inform him.

"Thanks, sweetheart," Jaxon says with a quick kiss on my temple as he walks past to the spare room.

"Perfect little ass kisser aren't you?" the older boy sneers as he walks past.

I recoil at his rudeness but follow them into the room.

"You guys have free run of the house except for the bedrooms. Stick to your own so personal boundaries aren't broken," my dad explains as Drew bounds up the bunk bed stairs and plops down on the mattress. "Hopefully you'll be comfortable."

"Are you kidding?" Drew yips. "This is better than anything we've ever had."

My heart clenches. A bunk bed is better than anything? That's both sad and pitiful.

"Drew," the tall guy beside me chastises with a frown.

I see my dad's eyes soften as he looks up at Drew who's crossed his legs at his ankles and positioned his hands behind his head. The kid is truly in hog heaven right now.

"Which room is yours?" The gruff whisper from beside me has more effect than it ever should.

I take a step back and to the side, creating some distance between us. Bumping into the door and causing it to knock against the bump stop garners my dad's attention and he turns to face us. First, his eyes assess the boy, and then they turn to me.

"Lawson, this is my daughter, Delilah. Delilah, this is—"

"His bastard son," Lawson interrupts holding his hand out to me as my eyes flash to my dad.

His lips flatten, but the slight nod of his head tells me to shake his hand, and that he's handling a difficult situation the best he can.

When he wraps his hand around my smaller one, there's no burst of electricity, no zing up my arm predicting my future obsession with this man. The only thing I feel is the cold sweat on his palm betraying his anxiety over this whole situation. It's almost worse than that burst of adrenaline I've read about so many times in books. His somatic reaction to this situation makes me feel sorry for him, pity the life he may have had up until this point. It pushes away the anger I felt with his snide comment in the hall and makes me want to pull him against my chest and tell him everything will be fine.

"Nice to meet you," I manage after an awkwardly long handshake.

"I can't wait to get to know you better," he says as I jerk my hand away.

In a rude gesture, I rub my hand against the fabric of my cut-off shorts, a way to let him know I feel his discomfort. It's mean and something out of character for me, but he needs to know I can read him like a book. Let him act macho and pissed off with everyone else, but his secrets were revealed in a simple handshake.

"This is Drew," my dad says interrupting the stare off Lawson and I are having.

I divert my eyes to the younger boy, closing the space between us with an outstretched hand. "Nice to meet you, Drew."

He shakes my hand over the rail of the top bunk and due to my height, or lack thereof, I have to stretch to reach it.

I pop back down on the heels of my bare feet when an appreciative grunt echoes around the room. Embarrassed, I pull down the hem of my tank top that had shifted up on my back.

Turning and not making eye contact with anyone but my dad, I direct my words at him. "I'll be in my room until supper."

He nods as I reach up on my tiptoes and kiss his cheek. "Maybe change your clothes."

A suggestion I plan on following the second I get back to my room. "Yes, sir."

Lawson is chuckling as I scurry past him and make it to the safety of my bedroom. Closing the door, I twist the lock for good measure.

With no time to ask my dad questions, my mind races with what putting Lawson and Drew up in the spare room means. Are they living here? Is it only for a few nights?

Bastard son?

Samson was right. The worst possible explanation of this situation has just been laid at my feet. I feel sorry for them. Just the small glimpse into their lives with a few spoken words from Drew's lips paints a dreary picture.

The ding of my cell phone pulls me from my selfish thoughts of wondering how them being here is going to affect my life. I'm no better than Samson.

Gigi: What's going on? I saw them go inside your house.

"Of course you did," I mutter to the text message.

Ignoring her text, I toss my phone back down on my bed and change my clothes.

Avoiding him without seeming rude will probably be my best bet. He's a grown man, or at least he looks like one so he won't be here long. The rules in the house aren't what I'd call strict, but there are limitations to our choices. Lawson doesn't seem like the guy who's going to stick around after the 'my house-my rules' speech is given to him.

Chapter 3

Lawson

"Dinner is in forty-five minutes," Jaxon says as he steps away from the bunk bed where my brother is acting like Oliver Twist who's climbed into a real bed for the first time.

Way to keep things close to your chest there, Drew.

"Not hungry," I mutter before he reaches the door. I pray my stomach doesn't growl in protest to my lie.

"Kitchen's always open if you get hungry later tonight," he offers, unlike the asshole I made him out to be. Leaning in close and focusing on me after checking to see if Drew's attention is on us. He gets closer than he ever has before. "I'll give you anything you need, money, opportunities, a real chance at life, but don't hurt my family."

My jaw clenches to the point of pain, but I keep my focus across the room.

"That includes my daughter."

Now he has my attention. He read me like an open book, or he saw my cock thicken in my jeans when she reached up and shook Drew's hand. I nearly groan for the second time at the memory.

The door snaps shut before I realize he left.

"They don't want us here," I tell my ecstatic brother as he reaches his hands up to see if he can touch the ceiling while lying flat on his back.

"They seem shocked, but I never got that vibe from them," he counters.

"You wouldn't," I mutter sliding the strap of my duffel off of my shoulder. "You were too busy jizzing in your pants over a goddamned bunk bed."

He chuckles, used to my brashness. "Wait until you lay down, asshole. These mattresses are perfect."

"Language," I warn.

He huffs but doesn't respond. My mother's stubbornness runs through my blood like a living thing. It's the exact reason I choose to sit in the rolling chair in front of the desk on the far side of the room.

Movement outside of the window catches my eye, and the sight of long, golden legs peeking out from the steps leading up to the house next door makes me smile and reminds me of the slew of hot chicks who were in the main building when we'd first arrived.

Maybe living here surrounded by hot chicks won't be so bad.

I shake my head, clearing that thought. I have no desire to spend more than the minimal time needed on this property. I have to get Drew settled, make sure that he'll be safe and they won't just shove him off into the system, and then I'm out of here. The fact that these two men adopted twins helps settle my nerves somehow. Anyone taking the step to welcome non-biological children into their home is an act of compassion many people wouldn't consider.

Drew's slow and steady breathing tells me just how exhausted the kid is. We've been traveling for several days. Add in the emotional stress of losing our mother less than a month ago, and it's no wonder he can fall asleep only minutes after invading some stranger's home.

Dark hair and dark eyes clear the front edge of the porch's roof. The girl sitting there meets my gaze as if she either feels me watching her or she knew exactly where we'd be in this house. I don't turn my head after getting caught. Instead, I smirk at her. Her head dips back, out of view, but less than a minute later, she's wiping lotion or tanning oil down her legs. The motion isn't economical in the least. Her attempt at a sensual rub down makes my eyebrow quirk and my dick jump more from underuse than attraction.

Note to self: avoid the brunette.

Aggressive women aren't my style at all. The last thing I need is a girl trying to take control of any situation we're tossed into together. It's the thrill of the chase that gets my blood pumping, the prospect that I'm convincing an otherwise uninterested party to act a certain way.

I have a feeling that the toy I want to play with most is somewhere in this house. The girl on the porch, performing for some guy she doesn't even know, doesn't hold a candle to the fun I'll have with Delilah.

***

"Hey."

I spent several long minutes looking at Drew sleeping peacefully before waking him. He's the picture of innocence, long dark lashes resting against his cheeks and a slight pucker to his lips. I know different though. This kid has seen more, been forced to endure more heartache than anyone ever should. My only goal in life is to protect him.

He draws in a long breath, stretching his muscles out on the bed. "I told you this bed was awesome."

"You need to go down and eat," I tell him.

"Awesome," he says climbing off of the bed. "I'm fucking starving."

"Seriously, Drew?" I narrow my eyes at him. "You need to watch your mouth. These don't seem like the type of people who are going to tolerate that language from a fifteen-year-old."

He nods, both in understanding and not wanting anything to ruin his chance to sleep in a soft bed rather than a worn out mattress on the floor. The last month has been tough on both of us. Hitchhiking across several states before some sad fucker felt bad enough to give us the money for bus tickets took a lot out of us.

He pauses at the door, looking over his shoulder at me sitting back in the desk chair. "Aren't you coming?"

I shake my head. "Not hungry."

I can tell by the look on his face that he doesn't believe the lie, but he just nods and closes the door behind him when he leaves.

"Drew," I call out a second later.

I spring up from the chair and pull the door open. Both my brother and Delilah are in the hall walking toward the stairs.

"Drew," I say again.

"What's up?" he asks as he turns back to me.

Delilah stops, turning her nosey ass attention to us. "Can I help you with something, Princess?"

Her nose shrivels as she looks at me with disgust, but she takes the hint and disappears down the hall.

"What, Law? I'm hungry."

"Don't tell them anything," I instruct. "Don't give them details about our life. Hell, tell them we came from Utah or something. Feed them anything but the truth."

He frowns. "You want me to lie to your dad?"

"He's not my fucking dad. He's merely a sperm donor who treated Mom like shit."

"Fine," he mutters and walks away again without a backward glance.

I wait, annoyed by the laughter that's flowing up the stairs, for Drew to return to the room. Boredom sets in, and the girl next door is no longer on her porch, but the pull isn't strong enough to get me to leave this room to join the happy little family.

Fifteen minutes after I give up looking at random shit on the internet with my phone, Drew comes back up to the room with a grin on his face. I hate that it falls when he steps through the door.

"What's up?" he asks looking at my phone with apprehension. "Are we leaving?"

We haven't stayed anywhere very long for a while.

"Not just yet," I answer. "Happen to get the Wi-Fi password?"

He shuffles on his feet. "I did, but Samson keyed it into my phone, so I don't know what it is."

I slide my phone back into my pocket.

"I can go back down and get it for you," he offers.

"No thanks," I grumble and sit further back in the desk chair with my arms crossed over my chest. "Sounds like you were having a good time down there."

"I won't next time if you don't want me to."

I'm an asshole.

"It's fine." I want to ask him what they were doing, but I just can't bring myself to, and now that I mentioned it, Drew will avoid telling me anything.

A yawn escapes his mouth before he has time to react and cover his mouth. "I'm so tired."

"You should go to bed," I say without inflection. "I'll keep first watch."

He shakes his head but climbs the stairs on the bunk bed anyway. "I think we can both sleep at the same time, dude. I don't think they're going to bother us."

"What have I always told you?"

"Safety is an illusion, and it's not worth the risk," he mutters before kicking his sneakers over the side of the bed.

Rolling my eyes, I scoop them up and place them under the edge of the bed, all the way to the left just like always. It's just part of the routine, in case we have to get out fast.

"I don't mind staying up with you," he says, sleepiness already clouding his voice.

"I got it." I turn off the bedroom light and sit back down in the chair. "Get some rest."

Soft snores fill the room mere minutes later. I force away the possibility of making a life in New Mexico. The last thing I need is to be in the shadow of a couple of washed-up bikers.

From the darkness of the room, it's easy to look out over the perfect stone-faced homes. Four homes make a semi-circle behind the building we first came into earlier today. Perfect, but not cookie cutter, each one having its own personality to fit the occupants. They're bigger, nicer, more substantial than any home I've ever been inside of before.

I shudder thinking about the last time I was in a house this nice. I wasn't in it long before streaks of red and blue lights filtered through expensive, sheer curtains. I feel as unwanted in this house as I did in that one.

Chapter 4

Delilah

Sighing, I snuggle deeper into the sofa. My happy place. The perfect time of day where everyone heads to their rooms and I can sit and read without being distracted.

There may be no one around, but my focus isn't on the eReader in my lap, but rather the guy upstairs who refused to come down for dinner. Drew showed his face, and pleasantly, although extremely guarded, interacted with the family. I couldn't keep my eyes from the base of the stairs, every second of dinner spent waiting for him to show up.

Noise at my back startles me, but when I look over my shoulder, I find myself alone.

I turn from having my back against the arm of the couch to facing the direction the noise came from. It doesn't take long before an unfamiliar figure clears the bottom of the stairs.

Lawson.

Of course, he would show his face after everyone disappeared for the night.

Sitting in the shadows, I watch in silence as he stops and looks around. I can't tell if he's familiarizing himself with the layout of the downstairs or if he's casing the place.

"Can I help you find something?"

He doesn't jump like I expect, or even turn his head in my direction. He knew I was here the entire time. Under the dim light at the base of the stairs, I watch his hands clench, closing and opening twice before he finally acknowledges me.

"What do you have in mind?" His throaty voice is more seductive than I'd like.

I swallow, the growing lump in my throat. "I-I can make you a sandwich. You must be hungry."

"You don't know a fucking thing about me," he sneers, his anger an overreaction to my simple offer.

"I know you didn't come down for dinner. I know Drew ate three plates of lasagna before he was full enough to stop shoveling it in."

The sadness I felt earlier creeps back up at the defensiveness he feels he has to exert at me.

"I just figured you'd be hungry, too." I set my eReader on the low coffee table. "If you don't want to eat, that's fine, but if you're planning on sneaking out, you can't use the doors. My dad has already set the alarm."

"Which one?" he asks.

"Huh? Which door? All of them," I inform him.

He chuckles, the sarcastic tone grating over my sensibilities.

"Which dad?" he corrects in a way that makes my eyes narrow.

I can get behind him having a crappy attitude because of the life he's had up until now, but having a problem with my dads because of their sexuality isn't going to fly.

"Does it matter?" He stays silent, staring in my direction as if he has night vision. "Do you have a problem with gay men?"

He shakes his head, but I can't tell which question he's answering.

"They aren't the first gay couple I've encountered, Princess. Which one has you on lockdown?"

My lip twitches in agitation. "We aren't on lockdown. It's for our own protection."

"Protection?" He huffs and turns his head away from my direction. I sag, finally relaxing a little from being under his hard eyes. "Sounds like something Jaxon would do. He seems like a control freak."

I stand from the sofa, angry at this jerk coming into our home and questioning the way we live. He doesn't have a damn clue the trouble that could find us from the years my dads spent battling bad guys all over the world. If he could find us so can others. It's not like we advertise where the Cerberus' hub of operation is, but it only takes a simple web search to find it.

"Listen, asshole," I growl closing the distance between us but not getting close enough that he can reach out and touch me. "If you don't want me to question your life, where you came from, why your brother ate dinner like he hadn't eaten in days and was terrified he wouldn't eat again for a week, then you need to stop making hasty judgments where my family is concerned."

"I think I like you feisty," he teases with a smirk.

I hate that damn smirk.

"How about you stay away from me and I'll stay away from you."

He shakes his head again. "That's the last thing I want."

Crossing my arms over my chest, I gawk at him, hating the confusion this entire conversation is causing. "Well, you're rude, and the last thing I want is some boy with a chip the size of Texas on his shoulder ruining my summer."

He steps a foot closer, and warning bells go off in my head. Immediately, I question my safety in my own home.

"I promise you, I'm all man. There's not one part of me that's still a boy."

I tense, unsure of how to take his blatantly sexual comment. I stand my ground but remain quiet.

"Besides, how will you suck my cock if we're avoiding each other?" He draws another foot closer, so close I can feel the energy flowing off of his body. "Maybe I can sneak in your room at night? I won't mind coming to you as long as you stay quiet."

With wide eyes, I stare up at him, but he's not finished speaking. For the life of me, I don't know why I want to hear everything he has to say.

"But don't worry, Princess. When I'm pressing against the back of your throat, you won't even be able to whimper."

"I'd never," I hiss, taking a step back and finally coming to my senses. "That's never going to happen between us."

He shrugs, nonchalant as if he hasn't just said the filthiest thing I've heard directed at me.

"Does that usually work for women? Or is it just another defense mechanism?"

"Women?" He snorts. "You're far from a woman."

I want to argue with him, but proclaiming adulthood right now doesn't seem like the best course of action.

"I normally don't go after *girls*, but you'll do in a pinch."

"I can assure you, you're wasting your time."

"You'll suck me off eventually," he predicts.

"I'd rather drink bleach," I hiss, giving him a wide berth as I walk past him toward the stairs.

"Bleach won't pull your hair and make your pussy wet," he calls after me.

Taking the stairs two at a time, I get away from him as quickly as I can. When I realize my eReader is still on the table, I debate going back down to get it. I shake my head at the idea.

"Not even worth it," I mutter. "I can read on my laptop."

I click the door lock in place, hoping he can hear it echo in the quiet house. Hopefully, he'll take a hint and won't even try to get in here tonight. I war with myself as I climb into bed and grab my phone from my nightstand, wondering if I should tell my dad about what he said.

I decide that he's just an asshole, all talk and no follow through. He wouldn't hurt me, especially not in my own home. I know my dads to be teddy bears, but they're more than a little intimidating. Rob is muscled and fit similar to a college linebacker, and Jaxon is covered with so much ink and piercings only an idiot would challenge him.

The vibration of my cell phone is just the distraction I need. Gigi's name flashes on the screen, full-on duck lips and a peace sign. She demanded I use the picture.

"Hello," I answer.

"So?" she hisses.

I don't answer. I know what she wants, but making Gigi wait for answers is always fun since most everyone in her life gives her what she wants, be it attention from the boys at school, the teachers who think she's perfect, or her mom and dad who have no clue just how wild their daughter is.

"I saw your light come on, Delilah. I know you're alone so spill." I smile at her insistence. "Tell me about the hottie."

"He's a jerk."

"Hmm. He looked like a bad boy." I hear rustling in the background as if she's settling in for some serious gossip. "Tell me more."

"Not much to tell. He's rude, crude, and egotistical."

She laughs. "So you hit on him, and he turned you down?"

I roll my eyes at her assumptions.

"That's gross. He's Jaxon's biological son."

"And?" she says. "I know that part. I heard Mom and Dad whispering about it in the kitchen earlier."

"That makes him like my brother. So no I didn't hit on him."

More like he offered or expected me to do devilish things to him.

"Not even close," she responds.

"What?" Shaking my head, I try to focus on the conversation rather than wondering where in the house Lawson is.

"He's not your brother, not by a long shot. You're adopted, he's blood. You've been there your whole life. From the looks on everyone's faces at the clubhouse earlier, they'd never seen those boys before in their life. It's different, but it isn't gross," she explains.

"No thanks," I mutter.

"Give him my phone number," she urges.

"What? No, I'm not doing that."

"If you're not staking a claim, then I should have a shot."

"He's not some uncharted territory you can claim, Gigi."

"Why are you arguing about it?" I shift on my bed, uncomfortable with her questions.

"I'm not," I finally answer. "He's all yours."

"Good." I can hear her grin through the phone. "Now just let him know."

"Sure," I tell her and hang up the phone.

Like I'll ever have an intentional conversation with Lawson again. Avoiding him at all costs seems to be the best way to survive his and Drew's intrusion into our lives.

Chapter 5

Lawson

A genuine smile, the first in a very long time, is on my face as I watch Delilah scurry up the stairs. Toying with her is going to be more fun than I ever thought possible. I'd judged her wrong, thinking she'd cower or cry, run to daddy when faced with my teasing. She challenged me. Stood her ground like she was invincible. It's stupid on her part, but more than a little entertaining for me.

I hear the lock turn on her bedroom door, and my smile grows bigger. If she thinks a simple door lock will keep me out of her room, she's got another think coming.

Standing still, I listen for the sounds every house makes as it begins to calm from the day's events. I familiarize myself with each one, the low rumble of the AC, the quiet murmurs coming from the master suite, and the New Mexico wind rustling the trees outside of the dining room window. Feeling sure that no one other than Delilah knows I'm down here, I slink into the kitchen.

The mention of lasagna from my earlier conversation with the blonde bombshell has my mouth watering and the hunger pains from my stomach setting into my bones. As silent as possible, I pull open the door to the fridge, and I'm met with the most organized shelves I've ever faced before. This has to be Delilah's doing. She seems like the OCD, anal-retentive type.

I almost want to cry when I see that even though Drew ate his weight in the meal, there is still lasagna left over on the shelf. Not bothering with the microwave or a plate, I grab a fork and begin shoveling the food into my mouth. The flavors explode on my tongue, but I can't be bothered to savor the best meal I've had in weeks. My only goal, satisfying the hunger in my gut, doesn't allow me to even pause in between bites much less appreciate the effort that had to have gone into preparing it.

After getting my fill, I replace the lid and place it back on the shelf. It's only then that I consider the fact that this meal was prepared, time was taken, from the looks of it, to be made from scratch. No store-bought Stouffers for this family. Even as happy as my stomach is, it angers me even further.

Contemplating just leaving the dirty fork in the otherwise spotless sink, I hold it in my hand and look around the kitchen. Sleek stainless steel appliances with every cooking gadget known to man, down to the canisters labeled with flour and sugar take up space on the counter. Perfect little kitchen for a perfect little family.

I shake my head, thinking of ways to knock them down a notch or two and wash the damn fork. After drying it, I place it back in the silverware drawer, upside down and backward of course. This asshole act is the only thing that comes to mind at the moment.

My hand shakes as I push the drawer closed, the urge to destroy this entire house a physical being in my body. I won't. I can't bring any more trouble down on me. I won't do anything to compromise Drew's future. Jaxon seems like a big enough asshole to get rid of him the second the cops would slap cuffs on my wrists.

No. Fucking with Delilah and making Samson's life a living hell seem like a much more fitting task. Every day, they live the life I should've had. Every day, they wake up in a perfect home not having to worry about their safety, where their next meal is coming from. Those two have no idea just how good they have it, how lucky they are. It's my job to make them realize what an imperfect world is really like.

With my belly full and a sinister smile on my face, I push off of the counter and make my way back to the stairs. My plans can start first thing in the morning. Right now, I need to catch a few hours of sleep and rejuvenate my body.

The low murmurs I'd heard after Delilah shook her ass all the way up the stairs are louder than before. I creep along, getting closer to the door to what I can only assume is the master bedroom. Keeping my feet over a foot away, I angle my head so I can hear better.

"I can't fucking believe her," Jaxon hisses. "She just leaves, pregnant with my son, and doesn't bother to tell anyone?"

"It's pretty fucked up," Rob responds.

"Eighteen years!" Jaxon hisses. "Eighteen fucking years and not so much as a letter? A phone call?"

"She was mad you rejected her," Rob interjects.

My fists clench, the words my mother whispered in my ear on her deathbed showing up, unwanted, at this moment.

Your father isn't dead. Find the Cerberus MC when I'm gone. He didn't want us. You'll recognize him when you see him.

This asshole has the nerve to pretend he didn't know about me?

Maybe he knew and never told Rob?

"She was a club girl for Christ's sake," Jaxon bellows.

"Keep your voice down."

I hear him huff but his next words, although coming out on a hiss of breath are quieter. "She was fucking everyone in the club, Itchy."

Itchy?

"Not just you and me," he continues. "Ace. Snake. Snapper. She knew where you and I were heading. She pushed us together. She had to have known she didn't factor into the equation."

"Feelings are messy," Rob cajoles. "You know neither one of us had a damn clue this is where we'd end up when we started the whole group sex scene."

"And Drew? Do you think she told that poor kid's dad?" Jaxon has no damn clue about Drew's asshole father. "She probably lied about him also. Hell, knowing Darby she doesn't have a clue who his father is. She probably didn't know Lawson was mine until he got older."

I'm seething, angry enough at the shitty way he's talking about my mom to reach for the door handle.

I don't consider that he's right. I don't let the memories of all of the men that filtered in and out of our lives figure into the equation of my anger. I won't concede to his way of thinking, even if it is so fucking close to the truth that it's eerie.

I pull up short when he starts speaking again.

"He spent his entire life, living God knows what way, no father when he had two perfectly good men here willing to give him everything he could ever want. Who does that to a child? Who is so damned prideful that they stew in their stubbornness and let their son suffer for almost two decades?"

"I'm sure she did what she thought was best at the time," Jaxon growls, but Rob keeps going. "We told her we didn't want children. Do you remember the numerous conversations we had, lying in bed after Misty showed up with Griffin? She was only reacting to what we had said."

I wasn't the only product of some quick fuck by a biker? This club is more fucked up than I thought.

"What the hell are we going to do now?" Defeat fills Jaxon's voice.

"He needs us now," Rob says softly.

"He doesn't want a fucking thing to do with us," Jaxon counters.

Damn right I don't.

"He doesn't have many other choices. We give them a place to land, provide both boys with what they need." Rustling of bed covers can be heard before Rob continues. "It's all we can do. Provide that and hope they're smart enough to take it."

"That's doubtful," Jaxon interrupts. "Did you see the look in Lawson's eyes? I had that same look in mine. Coming from a shitty home, living the way I had to, the things I had to do just to survive. I was pissed at the world, ready to take any motherfucker on that challenged me. Hell, I was willing to destroy my own life for just the smallest taste of revenge."

"I remember the angry fucker you were when you showed up at boot camp," Rob recalls. "I don't think you spoke a word to anyone until at least Swim Week."

"Exactly," Jaxon mutters. "It took the Marine Corps for me to realize that I could have a different life than the one I'd thought I was destined to all my life."

"Maybe that's exactly what he needs, too."

My hands shake, the trembling damn near bone-deep, as I step away from the door.

Marine Corps?

Fuck those two if they think even for a second that I'm going to sign up or participate in that shit. Taking the stairs two at a time, I head to the bedroom they were pitied into giving us. I keep in mind that Drew is sleeping, oblivious to the pain he's going to feel tomorrow when he wakes up to find me gone. Leaving is the only option. If they ship me off, I won't be able to help Drew at all.

Silently, the door opens, and I lock us both inside. His soft breathing fills the room, and I envy the peace he's found in sleep. Sitting down on the desk chair, I give myself a few moments for my nerves to settle.

"The doors have alarms on them."

Delilah didn't mention the windows, but is it a risk I should take? This house is out in the middle of nowhere. I don't have a clue about the terrain, and navigating it in the dark will be almost impossible. I flex my neck, leaning my head over the back of the chair, trying to think of the best course of action.

I'm eighteen. They can't force me to go into the military, but they can use Drew as a bargaining chip.

I can't allow that to happen, but leaving right now seems impossible. I close my eyes as the exhaustion from the day, fuck, the last several years, begins to weigh me down. Stomach full of lasagna, I don't stand a chance. My eyes flutter closed before I have the ability to realize I'm falling asleep.

Chapter 6

Delilah

A thump outside of my room wedges its way between sleep and conscious thought. Rolling over, I ignore the intrusion. I tossed and turned all night, and Sunday mornings are made for sleeping late.

"I don't want to leave." The unfamiliar whining filters through my door, and I sit up in bed.

"We can't fucking stay," Lawson snaps at his younger brother. "Hurry before you wake everyone in the house."

I didn't figure that they would stay long. Lawson isn't the type to abide by rules, and my dad isn't one to cave or bend his rules for anyone, much less an angry boy who's mad at the world.

I find nothing but their retreating backs when I pull open my door. Each with the duffel bag they arrived with, they slowly make their way down the stairs.

That's when all hell breaks loose.

"And where do you think you two are going?" The anger and irritation in Jaxon's voice are palpable.

I creep down the stairs, finding the boys in a standoff with my dad in the living room.

"Leaving," Lawson hisses. "And you can't fucking stop us."

I believe him, and the surety in his tone tells me he believes it too. The only problem is when my dads, Jaxon specifically, make their minds up about something, it's as good as written in stone. He's not one to be pushed around, but I fear digging in will only make Lawson push back more.

"Not going to happen," Rob says with quiet authority.

"Try and keep us from leaving," Lawson challenges.

Jaxon takes a step closer, and the tension in Lawson's back is visible.

"You're eighteen, Lawson. I can't keep you from leaving this house. I won't even attempt to, but Drew is not leaving with you."

"He's my brother," Lawson sneers.

Chill bumps race over my arms at the menace in his voice.

"What's going on?" I jump, startled when Samson speaks over my shoulder.

I turn back to the cluster of people ten feet away, praying they don't notice our intrusion. Of course, my dads know we're here, but the other two seem oblivious to our eavesdropping.

"Lawson is trying to leave," I explain not taking my eyes from the altercation that seems to be seconds away from turning physically violent.

"Let 'em leave," he whispers. "I have no idea why they showed up in the first place."

It appears my brother's goal of distraction for my dads isn't going to work the way he wants. I can tell by the tone of his voice that he anticipates Dad being too angry to change his mind on the senior trip.

"He's a minor," Jaxon interjects. "You're not leaving here with him to end up God knows where."

"The world is a scary place, Lawson." Rob is doing his best to de-escalate the situation.

Lawson's maniacal laugh makes my skin crawl.

"Scary? You have no fucking idea what we've been through. We'll be fine."

"That's the fucking point," Jaxon rages. "You shouldn't have to face the awful things you've been challenged with for as long as you have."

"Don't start caring now, *Daddy*."

Uncomfortable with the direction everything is heading, Drew shifts from one foot to the other before deciding to take a step back from his brother.

"Who do you think will win?" I roll my eyes at my brother even though he can't see me do it.

"Let's hope it doesn't come to that," I whisper.

"Dad's pretty strong, but Lawson seems like a psycho. It'd be an awesome fight to watch, but I think he'd win because dad's old."

"Dad's not old. Now shut up so I can listen."

I must speak too loudly because Jaxon's eyes lift to meet mine. I can tell he wants us to leave, to let this be just between the four below, but I can't turn away.

Noticing the direction of his eyes, Lawson turns his head enough so he can look over his shoulder at us. Anger, animosity, and hostility fill his bright blue eyes, but I also don't miss the twinge of fear in them either. I beg him with my eyes to calm down. There may even be a hint of pleading, asking him to stay, but his lip turns up in a sneer, either unable to read my expression or not caring how I feel.

"Looks like the whole family is here," he spits before turning back to Jaxon.

"Would you like to go into the office and speak privately?" Rob offers.

"Talking is the last thing I want," Lawson says. "We're leaving."

He goes to walk around Jaxon but surprisingly stops when Dad holds his hand up. "Feel free to leave, but Drew stays here. You can ruin your life all you want, but I won't stand by and watch you ruin his."

"Fuck you," Lawson barks. "Let's go, Drew."

Lawson grabs his younger brother by the arm. The wince on Drew's face makes it clear that the grip Lawson has on his arm is painful.

"You're hurting him," I say, unable to watch the tear rolling down Drew's cheek.

"Mind your own fucking business, Princess. This doesn't concern you."

Lawson's command doesn't surprise me. He's pissed and practically cornered. I would expect nothing less.

"No," Drew yells, yanking his arm out of his brother's grasp. "I'm not going anywhere."

Confusion swarms Lawson's face. It's apparent he's never gone against his brother's orders before.

"Now," Lawson commands.

"I'm staying," Drew says in refusal, crossing his arms in defiance.

Lawson remains silent, mulling over his options as he glares at his younger brother.

"What would Mom say right now? What would she tell you about choosing these people over family?"

Another tear rolls down Drew's cheek, and his throat works on a hard swallow before he speaks. "She would tell you to stop being stubborn. She would tell you that Rob and Jaxon are offering a chance at a real life. She would tell us to be grateful and take every opportunity we were handed."

Lawson shakes his head. "You'll regret being here with them."

Jaxon steps out of his way this time when Lawson heads to the front door. "You're always welcome here, son."

"Don't fucking call me that," Lawson mutters before disappearing out the front door and into the cool, morning air.

Drew all but collapses. Thankfully Rob anticipated it and catches him on his way. Drew shies away from Pop but doesn't make a move to get off his knees.

"Go get dressed," Jaxon instructs as Rob consoles Drew.

Looking down, I realize I'm only in my sleep shorts and a thin tank.

"Yes, sir."

After changing in my room, I head back downstairs, finding Samson, both of my dads, and Drew around the kitchen table. Sunday morning breakfast is going on like the blow up didn't just happen ten minutes ago.

Jaxon is at the stove making an array of different pancakes just like he's done for as long as I can remember.

"Samson?" he asks as he flips a pancake over with the spatula.

"Simple is fine," he responds without looking up from his phone.

"Delilah?"

"I think banana and blueberry would be perfect."

"Drew?"

I look over at the young man. His face is still red, but the tear streaks have been wiped away. He looks uncomfortable and out of place.

"Apple cinnamon is the absolute best," I tell him with a gentle smile.

"I'm allergic to cinnamon," he answers weakly.

"Noted," Jaxon says from across the kitchen as he throws the bottle of cinnamon in the trash. I have a peanut allergy, and no form of them are allowed in the house. Watching what my dad just did makes my heart swell. He'll make sure Drew is safe here as well.

"The mint chip is excellent," Samson offers, and my eyes sting at his generosity.

Drew's eyes light up. "I love mint chip ice cream."

Jaxon chuckles from the stove. "These pancakes will be so much better. I promise."

"Babe?" Jaxon prompts.

"Simple works for me today," Rob answers.

I grab the seat next to Drew, so he's not left alone on this side of the table. He moves his phone closer, and I don't miss the protective edge to the action, but I understand it.

"Has he called? Texted?"

Drew shakes his head. "He'll be back." He tries to sound hopeful, but the skepticism in his voice betrays the front he's putting on.

"Of course he will," I agree.

"He gets mad sometimes. He comes back after he walks it off."

"Our door is always open to him," Jaxon says as he slides pancakes onto Samson's plate. "If he texts or calls, remind him of that."

Drew meets Dad's eyes, seeming to analyze if he's being genuine.

"He said some pretty awful things," Drew reminds my father.

Jaxon shrugs, as if having arguments in the living room at nine in the morning is nothing to worry about. "It's an adjustment, Drew. We're allowed to get angry. Could he have handled it better? Of course. But, I get the feeling your brother has been fighting and clawing to keep you guys safe for a long time. He'll come around once he realizes we're not out to hurt you or him."

Drew nods. "He'll be back."

Only this time there's more confidence in his words.

Chapter 7

Lawson

"Stupid motherfuckers," I mutter as I jump off of the front porch and leave all five of those assholes in my dust.

If Drew wants to live in some swanky ass house that's fine. So much for fucking loyalty. All he gives a shit about is his damn stomach.

Mine growls at the thought of more of that lasagna from last night.

Voices draw me to the front of the metal building we entered for the first time yesterday. Moving my duffel to my other shoulder, I peek around the house. Paranoia is vital in every situation. I can't believe Jaxon and Rob just let me leave. I was so sure after last night there would be a Marine recruiter standing in the living room first thing this morning. It wouldn't surprise me if the voices were coming from a group of guys heading my way to get me to step in line.

Instead of a mob coming after me, I find a group of guys, mostly in their twenties it seems, hovering over a motorcycle.

One guy, with his back to me, is struggling with the rear tire.

"He'll never get it," a tall guy mutters.

"This is fucking hard, you asshole," the guy working on the bike hisses. "Harley's are completely different from dirt bikes."

"Rocker can do it in a couple minutes, and he started with dirt bikes," a blond guy taunts.

"He's been doing this shit for years," the crouched guy complains.

"You don't get to wear the cut until you can change a fucking tire," the tall guy responds.

With my head down but still peeking over at them, I step away from the corner of the building. The crunch of my boots on the gravel draws the attention of several of the guys.

"Hey kid," one calls out.

I bristle but keep walking with a firmer grip on the strap of my duffel bag.

"He may look like his daddy, but he sure as hell doesn't have his personality," someone taunts with a southern drawl.

I spin around, facing them but not knowing which asshole is bringing Jaxon up right now.

"Kid acts like he's got the weight of the world on his shoulders," a dark headed guy working on the bike adds.

"You got a fucking problem?" I ask the group in general.

"Enough," a booming voice commands from the front porch of the metal building. The bald tatted-up guy, thick with muscles, looks ominous as he looms above us. "Scooter, you got that damn tire on yet?"

"No, Prez," he mutters.

I chuckle, and several of the guys look at me.

"Think you can do better, Lawson?" Why in the hell does the Cerberus MC President even know my name?

"I wouldn't be bitching and complaining. It's a simple fucking tire, not a goddamned flat."

Kincaid steps down from the front porch and gets closer to me. I don't miss the fact that he keeps several feet of distance between us, and I appreciate the space.

He angles his head to Scooter who's now standing, glaring at me. "Give it a try."

I look at the curious group of guys. They watch our interaction with interest.

I take a step back, holding my hands up. "No thanks. He's got that so fucked up, the next person riding it will end up as road kill."

Scooter growls at me, but Kincaid stops his advancement with a hand on his chest. "That one then."

I follow his finger to a magnificent bike, albeit a little dirty.

"Prez," one guy mutters. "Surely you're not going to let some punk work on your bike."

"Shadow's gonna be pissed if he has to fix something that kid breaks," another adds.

All it takes is a quick look from Kincaid to make the heckling stop.

"Go ahead," he urges when he sees the hesitation in my eyes.

Challenges like this I can take. The cockiness that has been forming all my life may be half false bravado, but my skills around anything mechanical are nothing but pure talent.

With a grumble, Scooter rolls over another jack, and I situate it under the bike. Once it's suspended, I take a step back, envying not only the money a bike like this costs, but also the care that has been taken to maintain it. I shouldn't expect anything less from bike lovers though.

All the tools I need are readily available which makes this even easier.

Less than ten minutes later, I stand, having taken Kincaid's rear tire off and put it back.

"I'd suggest a power wrench for those bolts on the exhaust before you ride." I swipe at the sweat trailing down my face with the bottom of my shirt. "The roads around here are complete shit. That tire's liable to roll out from underneath you."

"They are," Kincaid agrees with a smile.

"He didn't even take the caliper off," Scooter mutters.

I cough, clearing my throat to keep from laughing at the awe in his voice. Growing uncomfortable with everyone shifting their attention between the bike, Kincaid, and me, I grab my duffel and start to walk away.

"A word, Lawson?" I stop but don't turn around. He may have expressed it as a question, but the command in his voice is still there.

I hear his boots crunch on the gravel, but when I turn my head to look back at him, he's walking toward the door he came out of a bit ago, not walking toward me.

"Can someone teach Scooter how to change a tire?" Kincaid says as he walks past the group. "It's dangerous for him not to know how."

"Lawson seems to be the perfect teacher," the tall biker answers.

"Fuck that," I mutter, as I follow behind Kincaid. "He's unteachable."

I chuckle when Scooter growls as I walk past.

A fellow biker claps him on the shoulder. "You can't get pissed that the kid schooled you today."

"This is the clubhouse," Kincaid explains when we walk into the wide open front room of the building we arrived at last night. "Looks a lot different now than it did when your mom was around."

I remain silent, not wanting to know if, as club president, he took advantage of what my mom was offering while she was here.

"Knocked that wall out." He points to the area to the left. "Still have rooms down the hall to the right. That's where the guys outside stay."

"Where was my mom's room?"

His steps falter, but he turns and faces me like I'm a man and not a child. I can tell by the clouded look in his eyes that I'm not going to like what he has to say, so I steel my spine. "Darby didn't exactly have a room. She, umm... she stayed in different rooms while she was here. Same as all of the other women. Khloe was the only female who had her own room for a while, and that was only because she was underage when she arrived."

I nod, trying to act like the man he's expecting me to be. "I understand."

And I do. My mother was always a giving person, be it the shirt off of her back, the last piece of bread in the cabinet, *her body* to any man that smiled her way. Realization is painful, but it's no less the truth because of the pain in my chest.

"It's the same now?"

Kincaid chuckles, but I can tell he's not laughing at me. I suspect he thinks I'm wondering about the women for personal use.

"There aren't any women around much these days. Original members have gotten married and built their houses out back, like your d-, like Snatch... I mean like Jaxon and Rob have."

I follow him as he heads into the surprisingly clean kitchen off to the right and accept a bottle of water from the fridge.

"Thanks."

"Anytime," he says with another smile.

"Back to your question. It's not unheard of for one of the guys to bring a chick home, but they entertain in their rooms. We gather here sometimes. It's the only place on the property big enough to house us all and summertime in New Mexico is brutal. We were having a Saturday lunch yesterday when you and your brother showed up."

I appreciate the explanation, even more so since I don't have to ask for information. I know he can tell I need it but would rather die than ask Jaxon.

"My girls Gigi and Ivy rarely come over here unless I'm here. Delilah keeps to herself mostly. The guys come over. Sam mostly. The younger kids tend to stick around the pool, especially this time of year."

"There's a pool?" I hadn't seen one since showing up.

"Two actually. We have an indoor one. It's in the building to the far right. That's the one the kids use." He points in the opposite direction as if I can see through walls. "The other one has a fence around it, but it's for Cerberus members only."

"Don't want the dirty bikers around your kids?" I clarify.

He laughs. "Spot on, kid." I frown even though I don't think he's using it in a derogatory way. "I have two teenage daughters, Lawson. Ivy, I don't have to worry about so much. I'm sure she'll find the love of her life at the library. Gigi?" He shakes his head. "She's a handful. The more I can keep her away from the guys the less chance of me having to kill one of them."

He narrows his eyes at me, and I don't miss his warning. Gigi has to be the one that put on the show with her tanning oil yesterday.

"Hands off," I say with a grin. "Got it."

After a long chug from his own bottle of water, Kincaid speaks again. "Where were you headed just now?"

"I don't have a fucking clue," I confide.

"Strong language," he chides.

"I'm a man," I say standing from my leaning position against the counter.

"Men don't run from their problems," he counters. "Where were you running off to?"

"I—" I shake my head and clear my throat. "I was trying to cool off."

"In the summer heat with a heavy duffel bag? You were sure to fail just because you were attempting the impossible."

"I manage just fine," I hiss.

He holds his hand up. "Calm down. Life is about preparation. You have to be prepared for everything."

"I've managed this far," I mutter. "I'm prepared for anything life can throw at me."

"You're wrong." The soft tone of his voice makes me uncomfortable. "You're prepared for the bad, the ugly. You're prepared to survive things no man your age should be faced with."

"Damn straight," I agree.

"But." He holds a finger up, pointing it to the ceiling for emphasis. "You're nowhere near prepared to accept help from Jaxon and Rob. You're not prepared to understand that even though none of us knew you existed until sixteen hours ago, every one of us is here for you."

"I don't—"

"You do," he interrupts. "You do need us. Drew needs us. There's no reason for you to fight every day, to scrape for food, to get arrested for just trying to survive."

Silence falls over the room as his words sink in.

"Did Jaxon tell you about his own youth?" I narrow my eyes at him. "Of course not. With that chip on your shoulder, you wouldn't have given him the time of day."

I shake my head. Why? I'm not sure. I don't want to listen to him, no matter how much sense he's making.

"No shame in just going back over there." He hitches his thumb over his shoulder in the direction of the house I never wanted to enter in the first place.

I knew less than a minute after slamming the door that I wouldn't be able to walk away from my brother. I was afraid that they would use him as a bargaining chip to control me, but it seems Drew has found his own voice. It makes me both irritated as hell, as well as proud he's finally growing into his own person.

"Jaxon makes like twenty different pancakes. You don't want to miss it." He begins to walk away. Stopping at the threshold, he turns back. "Your father is one of the most loyal men I know. If he seems agitated, frustrated, or unhappy it's because of the years he's missed with you in his life. His anger is with your mother, where it belongs. Not one bit of it is because of you."

My heart pounds a rhythm matching his boots as he heads back out the front door of the clubhouse, no doubt to do whatever it was he'd planned before finding me facing off with his members.

I don't want to stay, but I'm terrified to leave. Cupping my head in my hands, I crouch on the floor, trying to clear my mind enough to make the right choice.

Chapter 8

Delilah

"This is so freaking awesome," Drew says as his hands manipulate the controller in his hands.

"You ever play this one before?" Samson asks, not taking his eyes from the racing cars on the screen.

"Not this version. The one before this I played a little at a friend's house last year." He smiles wide. "But it wasn't on a TV this damn big."

"Makes all the difference," I chime in even though I don't play video games or have a clue about what's better and what isn't.

I want Drew to feel welcome in our home, and if I'm being honest with myself, I want the same for Lawson.

"So," Drew begins, but pauses as if he's thought better of what he was going to say.

"What's up?" I go for nonchalant, but I wonder if he can hear the curiosity in my voice.

"Jaxon and Rob make Sunday breakfast every week?"

"Awesome, right?" Sam says before grumbling when his car spins out and crashes down a steep embankment on the screen. "Taco Tuesday is even more epic."

"I wouldn't call it Taco Tuesday," I say.

Drew's eyes turn over to mine. "No?"

Samson chuckles when I smile. "The kitchen pretty much turns into a Mexican restaurant. Tacos, fajitas, enchiladas, you name it, and we will probably have it."

The look on Drew's face is almost euphoric. "You like Mexican food, dude?"

Drew looks over at Sam and nods. "Love it, but if you guys are feasting every day how do you keep from getting fat."

"Swimming," I answer when Sam blurts, "Sex."

I kick at him with my foot when Drew's cheeks heat and turn pink in embarrassment.

"Don't let him fool you, Drew." I stick my tongue out at my sneering brother. "There's not a girl in Farmington who will give him the time of day."

Drew laughs as Sam's scowl deepens. "Bullshit. Rachel is going to come around. You'll see."

"Of course she will," I assure Samson when I realize I may have taken it too far. I'm not one to hurt people's feelings just to get a laugh. "I think a serious love connection will happen at our birthday party."

"When is your birth—?"

The front door opens, and we all fall silent as Lawson walks inside. He's been gone for over an hour, but just as Drew predicted, he's back. The blank look on his face and the fierceness in his eyes are still present, but I no longer feel the vibrations of anger rolling off his shoulders.

First, his eyes find his brother, and I commend him for his loyalty. When his eyes sweep to me, I feel his hot gaze like a physical thing. His blue stare rolls slowly over my bare feet, up my calves, and to the hem of my cutoff shorts. By the time they scroll over my stomach, I'm panting.

You'll suck me off eventually.

Lips parting to accommodate my harsh breathing, I find that I can't look away from him.

"Dude," I register Samson saying from the other side of the room. "Quit eye-fucking my sister."

Lawson's eyes narrow, but he doesn't say anything as he leaves the room, heading toward the stairs. I sag deeper into the couch as if him walking away was the relief I needed to have control over my own body again.

I look down at my eReader, but my fingers are trembling too much to type in the PIN to open the screen. Calming breaths help some, but each time I close my eyes to regain composure, I feel his hot eyes on my body again.

Clearing my throat, I turn and place my feet on the floor. The motion sends a ripple of awareness up my spine.

"Wanna go again?" I look over at Sam and find him pointing his controller at the screen.

"Umm." Hesitation is in Drew's voice as he swipes his eyes from Sam to the direction his brother disappeared. "I need to go talk to him."

His voice cracks and I sit up straighter.

"Are you afraid of him? Will he hurt you?"

Drew gives his head a vehement shake. "Never. Lawson wouldn't lay a hand on me in that way."

He shudders and stands from his spot on the floor. Placing his controller on the low coffee table, he looks back at both of us. "My brother is an asshole on his best day, but he loves me. He'd never hurt me."

"I didn't," I begin, but he cuts me off.

"He's the only family I have. He'd protect me with his life."

Before I can respond, he's flying up the stairs.

"What was that about?" Samson mutters tossing his controller on the table with a clatter.

"Loyalty," I whisper with my eyes on the empty staircase. "Family."

"Well, I can tell you Drew is pretty cool until that asshole is around. He's just dragging him down if you ask me." Samson shifts and sits beside me on the couch.

"They're a package deal," I tell him.

"Too bad." He scoops his phone up and activates the screen, sighing loudly when he doesn't have any notifications. "Life would be much better if it were only Drew here."

"How can you even say that?" I turn my eyes to his. "They're brothers. Would life be better around here if I wasn't in the picture?"

He shakes his head, frustrated. "This isn't about you. Lawson is a grown man."

"And? Next year when you hit eighteen, you just want to be thrown out?"

He rolls his eyes. "That's not what I'm saying. My point is he doesn't have to be here if he doesn't want to be. I just get the feeling he's going to make everyone's life miserable on purpose."

I remain silent because I'm pretty sure those are Lawson's exact intentions.

"Have you talked to Dad?" I raise an eyebrow at him. "About the senior trip?"

"One, when have I had time in the last twenty-hours? Two, he's already made up his mind."

"If you get Pop on board, I don't think it will take much to get him to agree."

I shake my head. "Why do you keep worrying about it? You'll get to go next year."

"You can't be serious." He's snarky. "Next year? That's like a lifetime from now. Rachel could fall in love with someone else. This may be the only chance I get."

He has to know that he doesn't have a chance with Rachel right? Every guy she's dated is a dark-haired, all-around bad boy. The girl loves danger, and she definitely has a type. Samson comes nowhere near it. After inserting herself into our lives at a few parties over the years, I realized that she comes in hopes of catching the eye of one of the Cerberus guys. High school boys are the last thing she'll consider.

"Isn't she dating Tristen?"

"For now," he insists.

"And isn't Tristen going on the senior trip?"

"That's the rumor." He frowns when I raise my eyebrow at him again. "The relationships never last very long."

"Exactly." He stares at me, clearly not connecting the dots. "What makes you think you will last longer?"

"I just," he stares down at his hands, and I hate the vulnerability he's showing while talking about a girl who wouldn't even consider him a friend. "Things feel different with her."

"I'm sorry." I sympathize with him. I really do, but he needs to manage his expectations.

Wanting to hook up or date Rachel is a lofty goal. The equivalent would be me driving to Ireland with mapped-out plans to catch Jamie Dornan's eye.

"If you agree to go, they will let me go." A smile spreads across his face and makes his dimples pop out.

"You don't know that. Dad is pretty set on you staying home this summer."

"Only because they've cooked up all these dangers. Mexico isn't all that bad."

I glare at him. "Cooked them up? You've heard their stories. You're well aware of the things Cerberus has done, the missions they still get called out on."

"Girls get abducted. I'm in no danger," he counters.

"Guys have been taken as well." I sigh. "But you want me to come along and risk that chance?"

"You're ridiculous," he huffs. "I'll be there. You'd have nothing to worry about."

"You'll be following Rachel around like a lost puppy."

"And?" He's getting angrier which has happened all the times we've had this conversation over the last couple of weeks. "You'll be in the hotel room, reading a damn book. You'll be safe."

"Right," I say. "Your loser sister has no life."

"You're so fucking selfish."

"Enough," Dad says walking into the living room. I wonder how much of our conversation he's heard.

I look up at him, smiling and relieved for the intervention.

Samson looks up at Dad with resolve in his eyes.

"You don't have the money to go on the senior trip, so there's no point in even arguing about it."

"We have plenty of money," Sam counters.

"I have money," Dad corrects. "You've done nothing but sit on your ass all summer."

I do my best to hide the smile I feel tugging at my lips.

"But if I come up with the money, I can go?" Hope fills my brother's voice. We both know Dad is changing his mind, and he's elated.

"And how do you plan to do that?" Dad looks at him, waiting for a response.

"I'll do anything. Pick up cans, work in the shop. I'll sell plasma if it means I can go."

I shove his shoulder. "You're not old enough to sell plasma."

Dad laughs at Samson's eagerness. "Well? No time like the present."

Samson is on his feet and out of the room so fast he doesn't even realize he's left his cell phone on the cushion where he was sitting.

We both laugh as he hightails it out of the room.

"How are you, baby girl?" Dad brushes his lips across my forehead. "I hope the drama that unfolded this morning hasn't upset you."

"I'm good, Dad. Worried about them." I see nothing but compassion in his eyes. Why can't Lawson see that he's a good man and only wants to help? "They seem to have had a rough start."

"I imagine they have," he agrees. "We'll do anything we can to help them, but you may want to stay away from Lawson. He seems the type to self-destruct. I don't want you in the middle of that."

"Yes, sir," I say as his phone starts to ring.

He pulls it from his jeans pocket and looks down at the screen. "I have to take this."

I nod, watching his back as he walks out of the room.

"Blade, tell me how bad it is."

I figure the conversation is about the boys upstairs, but he walks out the back door, and I'm unable to get the full scoop.

Chapter 9

Lawson

"So you decided to stay?" Drew asks as he closes the door to the bedroom. I brood, knowing it's not his fault, but feeling pissed off regardless.

"I couldn't leave you, could I?"

He gives me a small smile.

"I wasn't choosing them over you," he says softly. "I was choosing me over the unknown. If there's a chance for me to have a different life than the one we've had, I feel like I need to jump at that opportunity."

I bristle, knowing I've done the best I fucking can for the both of us.

"Sorry for providing such a shitty life, man."

I turn my back to him. The view outside, although empty, is better than seeing the disappointment he has for me in his eyes.

He huffs, agitated with my response. "You didn't give me a shitty life. We had shitty circumstances."

"So it's Mom's fault?" I round on him and sneer. "She did the best she could, also."

I ignore the clenching of his fists. He hasn't tried to punch me in over a year, but I know he has as much anger in him as I do. I blame his abusive father for both of us responding with fists rather than words. We learned from the best after all.

"Really? Her best?" I hate the indignant tone in his voice. My own knuckles pop when I roll my fingers into my palms. "You seem to have forgotten the parties, booze, drugs, and a revolving door of men."

"I haven't forgotten," I hiss, hating that I couldn't protect him from all of it. "She wasn't perfect, but she's our mother."

"Was," he spits.

"I'm well aware that she's gone." My words are pushed past closed teeth, my jaw clenched so hard it hurts.

"What you seem to forget is it was her choices, her lifestyle that put her in that hospital bed."

I shake my head, even though I know he's telling the truth. You don't live the life we have and not think of all of the things that could've made it better.

"She chose cancer?"

He swallows before speaking, and I already know his voice is going to tremble. No matter how upset he is or who he blames, he loved our mom as much as I did, maybe more than me since I had to endure that life longer than he did.

"She chose to drink and party. She chose a lifestyle that would make her body prone to disease."

My anger falls away as the tears roll down my brother's cheeks.

"Listen," I rush out.

My hands scrape over the top of my head. I want to reach out to him, pull him against my chest and vow to protect him from the world, but I know I can't protect him from the pain of losing our mother and the disappointment he feels toward her. I'm unable to placate him because deep down, I feel exactly the same way.

"We'll stay here. Things will get better."

"Y-you don't want to leave?" Longing fills his eyes as he waits for me to answer.

"I'll stay," I assure him.

The knock at the door has me instantly wanting to take my words back. I knew I couldn't just waltz back into this house without at least having a conversation with Jaxon, but I'd hoped for a longer reprieve.

Drew turns and opens the door.

"Hey, Jaxon," he says as he hastily wipes the back of his hands over his damp cheeks.

"Drew," he says looking over my brother's shoulder. "May I have a minute alone with Lawson?"

Drew looks over his shoulder at me. He's both asking if it's okay and begging me not to fuck things up at the same time. I give a slight nod and watch as he steps past Jaxon and closes the door behind him.

He stands near the door, not stiff but not inviting either. I can't get a clear read on how this is going to go down. That alone makes me want to puff my chest and act like a bulldog. Defensiveness has always been my go-to response for most situations.

Silence fills the room, and I can sense his eyes on me. Although my phone is lit in my hands, I'm not seeing a damn thing on the screen. Yet, I refuse to give into the pressure to speak. It feels like an interrogation tactic.

When I look up, I don't find anger on his face, but the pity is full-blown, and it enrages me. Remembering the begging in Drew's face, I do my best to keep my calm.

"If you're here for an apology about earlier, you're wasting your time."

He clears his throat as he tries to fight a smile. Maybe staying calm is the last thing this asshole fucking needs.

I make to stand from the chair.

"Don't," he says. He's not loud, but the warning is clear in his voice.

"I don't like being mocked," I hiss, but my ass stays in the desk chair.

"I'm not mocking you." His eyes light up. "The resemblance, the reaction, the anger and draw to a violent response is very familiar to me."

"I'm nothing like you." He raises an eyebrow. "We may look similar, but that's it."

"You want me to prove that you're wrong?" I shake my head. I don't need some long life story from my sperm donor, but fuck if I don't want to know everything about him. "I don't mind. I'll answer any question you have."

"Father/son bonding?" I chuckle at the absurdity of the concept.

"You're a man, Lawson. You don't need some guy acting like your father, but you can't deny that you need help."

"I don't do fucking handouts. I'm not some charity case."

A smile spreads across his face, and my lip twitches in anger.

He holds his hand up and walks across the room. My blood simmers from boiling when he takes a seat on the last step of the bunk bed stairs.

"I don't know if you're aware of what Cerberus actually does," he says.

"Drugs, guns, and women," I say filling in the rest.

His eyes widen. "The only thing in this house that can be considered a drug is Delilah's EpiPen because she's allergic to peanuts. She's only a *girl*, so no women."

He emphasizes the word as if I haven't noticed how fucking sexy she is, and I don't miss the warning either.

"There are plenty of guns, but those are locked up and safely put away."

"And?" What kind of MC did my mom get involved in?

"We're getting off course," he says but doesn't seem irritated with the diversion. "Cerberus is hired out for missions. We specialize in recovery and extraction. Rescuing people who have been abducted, mostly women who've been sold into the sex trade."

It's time for my eyes to widen in shock.

"With that responsibility comes the need to know everything we can about a situation. Most everything is digital these days and tracking information is child's play."

The hairs on my arms stand on end because I'm beginning to understand where he's going.

"You researched me?" That spot above my eye begins to twitch in annoyance.

"Blade did. He's our main intel guy." He watches my face for a reaction. "So I know all about what happened in Texas. I know you still have time to serve and there's an active directive to apprehend you."

Unconsciously, my eyes dart to my duffel bag near the door.

"Don't even think about it," Jaxon says already anticipating my response. "Running will only make everything worse."

"I won't go back to detention." He nods as if he knew I'd say that.

"I'll do everything in my power to make sure you don't even have to step foot back in Texas to resolve this issue."

"You have dirty cops in your pocket? I mean my PO was pretty cool, but his boss is something else."

"We're the good guys, Lawson. I don't have anyone in my pocket, but we're well known and have a lot of connections."

There isn't a hint of malice or threat in his voice. He's going to what? Take care of my situation the legal way? That never works, but when I look at him and see the confidence in his eyes, I can't help but wonder if it's a possibility. I knew Texas would come after me eventually, I'd just hoped I could run long enough for Drew to be grown before my past caught up with me.

"Tell me what happened," Jaxon urges.

"Don't you already know?" I can't help the anger that rushes out. I may take his offer to help me get out of this, but I don't have to spill my guts about what went down.

"I've been given the summarized version, but I want the truth from you. I'm well aware the police reports are swayed by opinions and personal bias."

I fold my arms over my chest, keeping my lips tight.

"Okay," he says with a nod. "Some other time."

"What do you want me to do?" I ask, hating that I even have to.

"What do you mean?"

"To stay here? What do I need to do to earn my keep?"

"You work, go to school, and finish whatever obligation you have to probation. After that, we can go from there."

"I'm not going to school. It's a waste of time."

He smirks, but not in a way I feel like he's going to give me pushback.

"GED?" he offers.

"I can do that," I compromise and don't feel as angry about giving in part way as I should be. "And Drew?"

"What about him?" Jaxon stands from the bunk bed and walks across the room toward the door.

"I do that, and he's safe?"

Jaxon shakes his head. "He's safe whether you hold up your end of the bargain or not."

"No strings?"

"None," he says twisting the doorknob. His back is to me, but he doesn't make to leave. "I'm glad you're here, Lawson."

His words take some of the sting out, but it doesn't fix a damn thing. Drew may be able to blame our mom for everything, but I can't help but place some of that on Jaxon's shoulders as well. He didn't love my mother the way she deserved. He used her and tossed her away. It's something I'll never be able to forgive him for.

Chapter 10

Delilah

"What's he like?" Gigi asks as she looks down at her bikini top. Finding that it's revealing enough, she turns her eyes to me.

I shrug. "I don't really know. We haven't talked much."

Other than grunts and thigh clenching growling when I walk by, Lawson hasn't said a word to me in the last week. It's like we coexist without any actual interaction.

"Really?" She looks across the pool at him. Sitting with Drew on the edge, Lawson swishes his feet through the water. "He seems like he has a lot to say."

"Not to me," I mutter.

I'd imagined how my life was going to be after the first twenty-four hours, and how it actually ended up is nothing like I thought. I'd prepared myself for sexual harassment, and sickly find myself disappointed that he hasn't continued what he'd started the first night he was here. If he didn't watch me, lick his lips when I walk by, and groan when I reach for stuff in the top cabinet, I'd question if he even knew I existed.

"Does he talk to Sam?"

I shake my head. "Drew is pretty personable, but Lawson has kept to himself. I'm surprised he's actually out here this afternoon."

"I'm not complaining," Gigi says with a small wave of her fingers in his direction when he looks over at us. "He's got a body most boys would die for."

Ivy snorts. "There is nothing *boy* about him."

I laugh, remembering that he told me the same thing not long ago.

"They seem to be settling in fine," I say to change the subject from his muscular arms and ridged stomach.

Why can't he and Drew look alike? I can handle his younger brother's gangly frame, but knowing now what's under his clothes is its own type of torture.

"Is he a senior this year also?" Ivy asks as she adjusts her eReader on her lap.

"No clue. I was serious when I said we haven't talked." I steal a glance in his direction finding his eyes burning in my direction. His hands run up and down his thighs, and I can feel the echo of his touch on my own skin. I should've opted for a one piece.

"I'm sure your dad would know." She stares, unabashedly in his direction. "All you have to do is ask."

"I'm not that interested," I say, making Gigi laugh.

"Yeah, okay." The corner of her mouth tugs up. "Hot guy living in your house and you're not interested. Lie to someone who doesn't know any better."

"Not everyone is a walking sex fiend," Ivy says in my defense.

"Yes," she says pulling her eyes from Lawson. "They are."

Ivy shakes her head in disbelief.

"Seriously, everyone between the ages of thirteen and thirty thinks about sex constantly. It's a statistical fact."

Ivy and I both laugh before Ivy mumbles, "Like you know anything about statistics."

"Hey, Lawson."

My eyes dart to the entrance leading into the pool. My dad is standing there looking at the guys.

"We have an hour before we have to take off."

Lawson nods, but the look on his face isn't as tight as it was days ago. It seems my dad and he have settled into some sort of truce.

"Why is your dad dressed up?" Ivy whispers as he turns around and leaves the pool.

"I wouldn't consider a polo shirt and nice jeans dressed up," Gigi says. "But he's fine as hell."

"Gross," I grumble. "That's my Dad."

"Who's a total DILF," Gigi continues. "My dream guy looks exactly like him."

I watch as her eyes track Lawson as he stands from the edge of the pool. Leaning over, he whispers something in his brother's ear. I try to swallow past the lump in my throat at the sight of the sun reflecting on his glistening skin.

"I wish you wouldn't say stuff like that about my father," I say ducking my head as Lawson rounds the pool.

"He can't seem to get enough," Gigi says absently, but she must not be able to tell that even though she's on full display in a bikini her dad would never approve of, Lawson isn't looking at her.

His admiring eyes run the length of my body, hand adjusting his package as he walks past.

"Bye," Gigi says with a tone she seems to catch tons of boys with. "Always great seeing you."

As hard as it is, I pull my eyes from his body, refusing to watch him walk away. When I look across the pool, I find Drew looking over at us with a wide smile on his lips. He shakes his head and slides off of the edge of the pool into the cool water. The look Drew just gave us makes me wonder what Lawson told him before his epic exit.

"Where are they going?" Ivy asks as Lawson closes the door to the indoor pool.

"No clue," I answer.

"I think I need to stay the night tonight," Gigi says almost absently. "I don't mind digging deeper as far as Lawson is concerned."

I roll my eyes. Gigi never wants to stay unless it's because she thinks she can sneak out of my house easier than her own.

"Speaking of staying the night, Rachel texted yesterday and asked if the party was going to be a sleepover this year."

Ivy snorts and Gigi looks put out. Rachel Grant is the only girl in school she sees as competition. They both like the boys that will undoubtedly break their hearts. They go in with eyes wide open but act surprised when they put out and then are told to get out, each one thinking they'll be able to tame the bad boys they manage to cage for the night.

"Why would she ask you that?" Gigi practically spits. "You're not friends with her are you?"

"Not really," I answer.

"Then why?" Ivy is confused as well.

"Samson?" Gigi asks.

I shake my head. Samson's obsession with the blonde bombshell isn't even close to being secret. "I doubt it. Much to his disbelief, I don't think the girl really knows he exists."

Gigi narrows her eyes. "Has she seen Lawson? Does she know he's living here?"

"Ohhh," Ivy responds dragging the word out.

"I know Sam came home the other day excited like a little Chihuahua. He ran into her at the store, invited her, and she said yes."

"Was Lawson with them?"

I shrug again. "No clue. Maybe?"

"It's the only reason."

"That's not true. She came last year," I argue.

"That's because she found out it was in the clubhouse. She was here for Cerberus, not Samson," Ivy says.

"Exactly," Gigi says pointing at her twin.

"Cerberus wasn't even in town that night," I counter.

"She didn't know that, but didn't she leave after like twenty minutes?" Gigi searches my face for the answer.

"Come to think of it, she did. Samson was devastated." Pissed was more like it. I think he punched a hole in the wall that my dads made him patch the next day.

"She's going to go after Lawson. I just know it." Gigi sits back with a huff and crosses her arms over her chest. "That bitch."

The realization makes my skin crawl. I've never been attracted to anyone Rachel would consider hooking up with, but the thought of her coming onto Lawson makes me territorial.

"RBF much?" Gigi asks with a stupid grin.

"Huh?" I turn my head toward her.

"Just the mention of Rachel and Lawson and your claws are ready to come out."

"No." I do my best to relax. My resting bitch face is usually enough to deter anyone, but Gigi calls me out on it every time it shows up.

"You know I hate to agree with Gigi," Ivy says. "But I could feel the tension rolling off of you, and I'm two feet away."

"I just don't want Samson to be hurt. We all know he likes her, yet he's invisible to her." I hope they buy what I'm selling, but it doesn't sound convincing even to my own ears.

"Samson deserves better," Ivy agrees.

"You can't tell him that though." I frown in Sam's direction as he tries to teach Drew how to do a backflip off the diving board without belly-flopping into the water.

"Kids," Gigi says with a soft voice like she's older than my brother. "They have to get burned a couple times before they learn."

Ivy and I shake our heads as Gigi slides her sunglasses down over her eyes and lies back on the lounger.

"You about ready to go?" My dad stands in front of us, blocking the sun.

"Hey, Pop," I say looking up at my dad. "Where are we going?"

He shakes his head, his beard full enough to almost hide his soft smile. "I thought you wanted to do the shopping for the party."

I sit up on my lounger. "Of course I do."

"Might as well knock it out today." I nod, excited to get away from the house. "You gals won't be able to decorate the clubhouse until the morning of. I don't want the guys to have to live in a teenage hell, or worse, ruin what you decorate."

"You want to go?" I look over at Ivy.

She smiles, always willing to help with stuff like this. "Of course. Have you decided on a theme?"

"Not really," I say and look over at Gigi. "You coming?"

She waves me off as Ivy, and I stand to go get changed. "Not interested."

We begin to walk away when Gigi calls my name. "Just not weird stuff this year."

"Ignore her," Ivy says as we exit. "I loved the hippie theme last year."

"She acts like it's her party," I mutter as we part ways at the branch in the sidewalk. "See you in a few."

I straighten my spine and put a smile on my face. I won't let the thought of Rachel going after Lawson, or Gigi implying I'm a baby, ruin my party planning.

Chapter 11

Lawson

"It's less than twenty miles away, but traffic can be difficult to get through this time of day," Jaxon explains as we stop at yet another red light.

I fucking hate small talk, so I look out the window without engaging.

"The kids are having a party a week from Saturday," he continues, either ignoring my silence or refusing to tolerate it.

I grunt. That's all he's getting.

I don't give a shit about some teenage party. It'll be nothing like the ones I've attended before, so I'm not interested. Well, I try to be uninterested, but the prospect of getting my dick sucked interests me a little. I don't pay attention to him until the unbidden thought of Delilah in that damn simple bikini hits me like a weight in my chest. Black and covering more than some one-piece bathing suits do, it made my cock hard the second her flip-flop clad feet hit the concrete inside the pool room.

"Their birthday is actually on the Monday after," he says hitting the accelerator only to tap the brakes as the next light turns red. "Same as yours."

That gets my attention, and I turn my head toward him. "You know my birthday?"

He chuckles like it's a ridiculous notion that he wouldn't. "Of course."

"More online stalking?" I grumble.

"I had to get copies of everything from Texas, for both you and Drew. We can't register him for school or get you signed up for a GED test without it."

"And you what? Studied and memorized it?"

"No, Lawson," he says turning his head toward me and meeting my eyes. "I've been celebrating that day for the last fifteen years. I noticed it, that's all."

I turn and look out the windshield.

"I was a lot like you not too long ago," he says as we make it through what appears to be the last red light before hitting the open road.

"Can we not take a trip down memory lane?" I don't know why I say it. I want to know everything there is to know about him, but doing that while trapped in his SUV on the way to the probation department is the last place I want to find out about dear old Dad.

"I'm in a shit mood," I explain after a long silence. "All I can think is that they're going to cuff me and drag me away."

I steal a glance in his direction. "Promise me you'll take care of Drew if they ship me back to Texas."

"That's not going to happen, son." The sincerity in his eyes eases the anger that normally rises when he calls me that.

"Promise me."

"Promise," he says with enough surety that I almost believe him.

* * *

"You're going to shake yourself right out of your seat," Jaxon says as we wait to be called back by the San Juan County Juvenile Probation Officer.

I try to stop the up and down hitch of my leg, but give up after a minute of sitting still.

The door to the back opens and an angry mother, along with her crying daughter exit. I pray that whoever made that chick cry isn't the one to call me back.

We wait a few minutes longer before the door opens again.

"Jaxon Donovan?" A lady says after stepping through the door. "Margie Gleason."

She holds her hand out to shake, and Jaxon reaches for it.

"My son, Lawson O'Neil." I shake her hand, refusing to apologize for the sweat that's coating it.

"Follow me," she says turning and typing in a code to reopen the door.

My throat dries as we follow her down a short hallway to her office. The space isn't very big, but it's decorated with a menagerie of random shit she's obviously collected over the years.

We take the seats offered in front of her desk, and my knee begins to bounce again.

"Navajo County wasn't very shocked when I called and told them you were in New Mexico," she says as she settles into her chair.

I don't say anything. She didn't ask a question, and less is always more in these types of situations.

"There's an active directive to apprehend you, Mr. O'Neil."

I want to look over my shoulder, to prepare myself for the cops coming in to put me in cuffs, but I don't want to show weakness.

"Yes, ma'am," I say, but don't explain why I haven't reported to my PO in several months.

"It says here." She drops her eyes to the thin file on her desk. "That your mother passed about a month ago."

"Yes, ma'am," I grit out. I know how to be respectful, and I always try my best when someone holds my freedom in their hands, but talking about my mother isn't going to happen.

"I've spoken with Mr. Garrett in Texas, and he assures me that we only have a few things that need to be done to take care of all of this."

She looks up at Jaxon, eyes narrowing suspiciously. It makes me question his power and the connections he spoke of last week.

"There are procedures we have to follow, Mr. Donovan." She closes the folder and clasps her hands together on top of it. "I'm already suspicious of how quickly we were contacted by the New Mexico Interstate Compact officer."

"He's nineteen on Monday," Jaxon says.

"I understand that's the oldest a youth can be on probation in Texas, but New Mexico allows juvenile probation to extend until a youth's twenty-first birthday in some instances."

Twenty-one? There's no damn way.

"It's my understanding that Navajo County has no desire to file a violation and extend his probation. His adjudication is in that state. They have no plans to transfer a new disposition to New Mexico."

She clears her throat. "Texas has no business speaking with you directly. Interstate Compact dictates that their department works with their state who then works with our state. We then receive information from Santa Fe and proceed accordingly."

"As I've said," Jaxon leans in closer, but not in a threatening way. "Time is limited. I, as well as Navajo County, see no need to drag this out any longer. Lawson is regretful for what he's done, and we're all trying to move past it."

He has no damn clue how I feel about the situation. We haven't talked about it, but now is not the time to argue.

"He broke into a house. The babysitter watching over the two kids was so terrified she ended up in counseling," Ms. Gleason clarifies.

"The house was supposed to be empty," I hiss.

She raises an eyebrow as if she'd been waiting this whole time to prove her idea of me right. "The report says she was terrified you were going to rape her."

I bristle. It's not the first time I've heard the babysitter's side of the story. "I was going after the jewelry," I hiss. "Little girls do nothing for me. I would've hit the house next door had I known anyone was in the house."

"Regretful you say?" Ms. Gleason says with a twisted smile on her face.

Jaxon glares at me until I fall back in my seat.

"Are we able to get Mr. Garrett on the phone? I'm certain he'll be able to clear all of this up."

She shakes her head. "That's not how the process works."

Jaxon leans forward again, but this time pulls his cell phone from his back pocket. Swiping to activate the screen he looks back up to her. "There is no process, Ms. Gleason. Navajo County isn't going through Interstate Compact, as I'm sure you've been told. I'm certain that's the reason you're wound so tight. The phone call your department got from Texas was a courtesy."

The phone begins to ring on speaker and Jaxon places it on her desk.

"Hey, Mr. Donovan." My old PO's voice can be heard clearly on the phone. "How's that kiddo doing?"

Kiddo... It's the one thing I hated about the guy.

"He's great Alan. Listen, I'm at San Juan County with Ms. Gleason, and you're on speaker phone."

"Ms. Gleason," Mr. Garrett says in acknowledgment. I can tell by the tone of his voice that he's spoken with her before and isn't impressed. I get the feeling she isn't well received very often.

"Mr. Garrett," she mutters.

"I told you, Jaxon has no responsibility to San Juan County."

I smile at the PO sitting in front of me, but Jaxon smacks the side of my leg with the back of his hand. I clear my throat and sit up straighter in my seat, relief a tangible thing in my blood.

"What exactly is required for us to put this past us?" Jaxon asks, speaking to Mr. Garrett but keeping his eyes on the woman in front of us. She looks like she could spit nails.

"He has forty hours of community service to satisfy, five hundred and eighty dollars in fees to pay, and there's also the requirement that he be actively enrolled in school." I nod because all of that sounds about right.

"Would your county consider a GED rather than public school enrollment?" I watch as a smile spreads across Ms. Gleason's face and her head begins to shake back and forth.

"He would have to complete the actual GED. Enrollment in GED classes won't satisfy the judge."

"He turns nineteen on Monday," Jaxon shares as if Mr. Garrett hasn't been counting down the days until I age out of the system.

"I'm aware," he says. "We can give him a month. The paperwork for his violation has already been filed with the court."

I freeze as Mr. Garrett continues to speak.

"If he's able to knock out the community service, fees, and get that test passed, we'll just dismiss the modified petition."

Jaxon looks over at me, his eyes analyzing whether he believes I can get it all done. The community service and test are not a problem, but five hundred and eighty dollars is a lot of money. If I had that kind of money, I never would've broken into that house to begin with.

"Consider it done," Jaxon says.

"Thanks for calling, Mr. Donovan. Keep in touch."

Jaxon's phone lights up showing that Mr. Garrett has ended the call. When he stands from the chair and holds out his hand to Ms. Gleason, I stand right along beside him.

"Thank you for your time, Ms. Gleason. I think we'll be dealing with Navajo County directly from now on."

I turn my back on her, needing to get out of there as quick as possible. I'm shaking by the time we make it back to the SUV.

"That could've gone better," Jaxon mutters as we climb inside.

"How am I going to come up with that money?" I mutter to myself.

"You work for it," Jaxon says, and I realize I said it out loud. "You can knock out your community service with Delilah. She volunteers at the animal shelter three days a week."

"Perfect." I can't even hide the bitterness in my voice.

Like it hasn't been hard enough staying away from that girl? As much as this summer is going to suck, I can't deny that resisting Delilah is the lesser of the two evils. Juvenile detention is no joke, and the last thing I want is to end up behind bars again in Texas.

Chapter 12

Delilah

"Wait up," I hear from behind me.

I stop, turn around, and face Gigi who's jogging toward her sister and me.

"No," Ivy grumbles as her twin bounces up with a smile on her face.

"What's up?" I ask even though I know why she's standing here.

"I'm going with you," she beams. "Samson insisted that I come and make sure you don't end up with some stupid birthday theme."

I bite the tip of my tongue until a faint coppery taste fills my mouth.

"We're not going to pick anything stupid," Ivy defends with her arms crossed over her chest.

"Of course not, especially with me tagging along."

Gigi slides past us and climbs into the front seat of the SUV. Pop raises his eyebrow at me as he walks up with the keys swirling around his finger.

"Leave it alone," I mutter to him and climb into the back with Ivy.

The trip to the store is filled with Gigi chattering about what supplies we'll need as she plans *my* birthday party. My anger increases, my mood teetering on not even wanting to have a party anymore.

"You have to stand up to her," Ivy mutters as we watch Gigi's animated arms twirl around.

"Yeah?" I turn my gaze toward her. "You first."

She frowns but doesn't say another word.

"Exactly," I mutter.

I keep my eyes straight ahead, calming breaths passing through my lips as we pull into the parking lot at the party store. Pop meets my eyes in the rearview mirror before he opens his door. Giving him a slight nod, I let him once again take the reins, and I hate myself for it.

"We'll need everything that glitters, but nothing too girly." Gigi takes a breath then continues. "But nothing pink or purple. If you want turquoise, show it to me first before you put it in the cart."

"Gigi," Pop begins, looking over at her. "Feel free to dictate how your party will be in a couple of months, but you're not running this show."

Gigi huffs, disappointment clear on her face. "But Samson—"

Pop holds his hand up. "If Samson cared about decorations he should've come with us."

She turns around, the pink on her cheeks betraying her embarrassment. She isn't reeled in very often, but when she is things get better for a while.

Gigi isn't a mean person on purpose. She just has tunnel vision and is so self-involved that she doesn't pay much attention to others' feelings. Inconsiderate would be the perfect word to describe her.

"Thanks, Pop," I whisper as I walk past my rescuer.

"We'll talk about this later," he says with a smacking kiss on my forehead.

It's a warning of sorts. He tells me all the time to stand up for myself, to not let her take control over the things that are mine. He's reiterated more than once, that doing it now will give me the courage and strength to do the same when I'm on my own in the world and faced with the same type of people.

I hate confrontation, but I know Gigi's lack of consideration for others is coming to a head, and I won't be able to avoid the altercation that's been building for years for much longer.

"What are you thinking," Ivy asks as she loops her arm through mine.

She ignores her sister as Gigi grabs a shopping cart. There's less pep in her step, and her shoulders are hunched noticeably. Ivy, used to being treated poorly by her twin, gets almost jubilant when Gigi is chastened. I, on the other hand, hate seeing anyone upset, even if her own actions brought on the castigation in the first place.

"Dark," I tell Ivy, pulling my eyes away from her sister. "Black lights and neon."

A smile spreads across Ivy's pretty face. "I think that's a perfect idea."

Pop trails along behind us as we make our way around the store. He points out several things that would go great with the theme we're working on, and I'm grateful for his input. Unlike Dad, he loves to shop and get involved in things like this.

"Glow sticks?" he asks holding up a huge package of multicolored sticks.

"Of course," Ivy says and takes it from his hands. She grabs a second package and adds it to the pile growing in the cart. "Did you see any necklaces or bracelets?"

"Down the other aisle," he answers and leaves to go find them.

"What the hell is he staring at?" Gigi mutters, speaking for the first time since we arrived.

I look in the direction of her eyes and see Clay, a guy I shared homeroom with last year. He grins when we make eye contact, and I feel my lips turning up in a smile in return. Gigi sighs when he begins to make his way over to us.

"Such a creeper," Gigi says under her breath.

"Be nice," I tell her. I may allow her to be a certain way with me, but I won't sit idle while she's mean to others.

"Hey," Clay says as he gets within a few feet of us. "How's your summer been?"

"Good," I answer. "Yours?"

"Hot, boring," he responds as his eyes dart to the shopping cart. "Getting ready for your birthday party?"

"Of course. Did you get your invite?" Summer birthdays are tough, but Samson uses social media to let everyone know the details of it each year.

"I did." The smile never leaves his lips.

The silence between us grows awkward as I fully take him in. He's no longer the skinny boy from class. His shoulders have gotten wider. His once thin, wiry arms have filled out, stretching the fabric of his t-shirt. It's almost as if he's gone from boy to man in a matter of months.

Gigi must have noticed his transition as well because she takes a step closer, admiration of his body clear in her eyes.

"Hey, Clay," she all but purrs.

"Hey," he says with quick acknowledgment before his eyes find mine again. "Wanna trade?"

"I'm sorry," I say, confused.

"I go to your party, you come to mine?"

I clear my throat, unsure of what to say. I've always found Clay handsome, but chasing boys or even having the nerve to speak to one I find attractive has never been my strong suit. Now that he looks different, more like the type of guy I'd never engage with in fear of rejection and less like the nerdy boy who would've been a perfect match to my equally awkward personality, I'm not sure how to act.

"When's your party?" Gigi asks, sliding even closer to Clay's elbow. "I think one last awesome party is just what I need."

His eyes dart to her, and as if realizing for the first time that Gigi is flirting with him, a slow, seductive smile slides across his face. All of his attention is directed at her. I hear Ivy huff as we watch her sister trail her finger over Clay's muscled arm.

"Good to see you, Clay." He doesn't even acknowledge me as Ivy and I turn away to continue our shopping.

"Well that didn't take her long," Ivy hisses when we're two aisles over.

"Never does." I grab a package of green, glow-in-the-dark mustaches. "What do you think about a photo booth with all kinds of props?"

I turn to find Ivy grinning and holding a package of lime green and hot pink face masks. "It's like you're in my brain."

"Here are the bracelets and necklaces," Pop says emptying his arms into the cart. "I also grabbed plates, cups, straws, and these little bags for party favors."

I frown and Ivy giggles at Pop's cluelessness. "I think we're past party bags."

"What?" He looks at the package pinched between his fingers. "You're never too old for party favors."

"Never," Gigi says bounding up, back to her old self after having been doted on by a boy. "We can put the jello shots in them."

"Like hell," Pop says looking at the package of small, lidded containers she's waving in her hand. He tosses the neon colored package back on the shelf. "Okay. No party favors."

Gigi frowns when he snatches the package out of her hand and tosses it next to his discarded item on the shelf.

"Food shopping next?" Ivy asks as we make our way to the front of the store to check out.

"Catered," Pop answers. "Delilah didn't want to have to worry about cooking."

"Awesome," Ivy says with genuine happiness.

"Can we start the car?" Gigi holds her hands out for the keys.

Pop's eyes go from Gigi to Ivy. Unspoken conversation flows between them. With a small nod of her head, Pop hands over the keys. Ivy follows her twin out of the store, knowing he would never let Gigi go alone. It's not only a safety measure, but we can never guarantee Gigi won't get a wild hair and take off. Impulsive isn't a strong enough word to describe her.

"D," Pop begins as we wait for the lady in front of us to load her luau items on the counter.

"Please," I beg, holding my hand up to stop him. "I know what you're going to say, but you don't see her like I do."

"Enlighten me," he says, a smirk playing at the corner of his mouth.

"It's all a front for her. I honestly think Gigi is more insecure than any of us."

"I can agree with that," he says pushing the cart to the counter as the luau lady rolls her cart away. "But you shouldn't allow her to treat you poorly."

I hand him several more items from the cart so the cashier can ring them up. "I seriously don't even think she realizes she's being rude."

"Even still," he says. "You have to stand up for yourself, especially with the people you're closest to. Feeling taken advantage of and disrespected by the ones we love does more damage than when it happens with strangers."

I nod, knowing he's right but also unsure of how to proceed from here.

Half an hour later, we're pulling up to the front of the clubhouse. There's no sense in carting our purchases to the house, so we opt to just store them in the front entry closet until Saturday morning. Ivy is carrying an armload, and surprisingly Gigi has offered to help as well, when Dad and Lawson pull in, parking beside us.

Lawson, never making eye contact or offering to help with our bags storms past, taking the sidewalk toward our house rather than cutting through the clubhouse.

"What's his deal?" I mutter, startled to the point of jumping when Dad's hand lands on my shoulder.

"He's had a rough life," Dad whispers in my ear. "Just treat him with kindness."

I watch his back as he disappears around the corner, but my thoughts stay with him as we get all of the purchases stowed away in the closet.

Chapter 13

Lawson

"Community service," I grumble as I run a soft towel over my wet body. "Fucking probation."

Working for my money has never been a problem. The burglary was out of necessity when the work around the small town we lived in dried up. Jaxon's offer to let me pay off my probation fees in the shop working on the motorcycles is like a dream come true. I'd do that shit for free just to fill my time.

After wrapping the towel around my hips, I swipe my hand over the condensation on the mirror. Empty, ice-blue eyes stare back at me. It's strange finding their familiarity in those of my long lost father. The compassion he's shown since mine and Drew's arrival has never faltered. That type of humanity is a foreign concept to me. I can see, feel even, the love he has for me. It's been there since realization struck him in the chest the day we showed up at the clubhouse.

Pissed about the things I've missed, the opportunities that have been lost by not knowing this family, it takes all the strength I have to not punch a hole in the wall. My anger isn't dissipating by any means, but the blame is beginning to shift, and it makes me sick to my stomach that I'm starting to have ill feelings toward my deceased mother.

"So fucked up," I say to myself, stepping out into the hallway.

A squeak and a hiss register in my ears, but it's the hands on my bare stomach that have my undivided attention. Warmth, flowing from the lime green tipped fingers against my skin, spreads from the point of contact all over my body, my cock getting the message first. Twitching against the softness of the towel brings a smirk to my face, as I watch Delilah jump back a step.

"I'm so sorry," she apologizes quickly and bends at the waist to grab a stack of laundry I'm just noticing must have fallen to the floor.

The top of her head grazes my already straining cock when she stands upright.

"Oh, God." Her cheeks flush the most amazing shade of pink when she realizes what she's done. "Did I just head-butt your... your... penis?"

Rolling my bottom lip between my teeth to keep from laughing at her, I remain silent, letting the awkwardness seep a little further in. I love the color on her face. It means she's not unaffected by me even though she's avoided me for the better part of a week.

"Gives a whole new meaning to giving head," I whisper, noticing the huskiness in my own voice.

Her eyes dart from mine to below my waist, pausing long enough to understand exactly how I feel about the situation.

"Oh." I don't even know if she realizes that she's staring at my towel-covered cock, but he's received the memo loud and clear.

Betting on a shy reaction, I flex, making it jump behind the towel. She only gawks harder. Her perusal only serves to make me harder, the tip growing wet with desire.

"It's yours if you want," I tell her palming my length.

She may see it as taunting her, but relief from the pressure exerted by my hand is immediate. A groan rumbles in my chest as she continues to stand, staring as if she anticipates it revealing itself to her.

God, I wish.

"Is your mouth watering to taste my cock, Princess?" Her eyes snap up to mine, the trance she was in broken by my filthy words. "I'll return the favor. I bet your pussy will be the best-tasting thing I've ever put my mouth on."

Heat overrules the agitation in her eyes when she looks up at me, but she remains silent. My cock screams in protest when I release it from my grip. A second later, the same hand is reaching for her, running my thumb over the fullness of her bottom lip.

"I don't fuck very often," I whisper taking another step closer to her. "But I'll make an exception for that tight virgin pussy of yours."

She blinks up at me. Once, twice. Then searing pain radiates from my foot and up my calf. She's already down the hall and inside her room before realization hits. She just stomped on my fucking foot with her sneakers on.

"Goddammit," I hiss, hopping on my uninjured foot while I try to soothe the pain she's just inflicted.

"What happened?" Jaxon is the last person I want to interact with tonight.

"Stubbed my toe," I lie and place the throbbing foot back down on the carpet.

His eyes narrow, dart down the hall toward Delilah's room, and back at me, but he doesn't say anything about his suspicions.

"I was coming up to give you this." He offers a piece of paper, and I take it.

"You already paid my fees?" I ask looking down at the printed receipt.

He shrugs. "I was just waiting for the receipt. I paid them as soon as I found out about them. Navajo County is a little old school, so I had to wait for snail mail for the receipt."

"Thanks." The word tastes like shit in my mouth, but the man did me a favor, and I refuse to just brush that off.

"No big deal," he responds, but to me, five hundred and eighty dollars is a fuck ton of money. "You'll work it off."

"Yes, sir."

"Delilah leaves at nine in the morning to head to the animal shelter. Knock out the community service first then you can worry about working the money off."

"I'll be ready," I tell him and turn toward the bedroom.

"Lawson?" I face him again. "There's a lady in the house. Please don't roam around in only a towel."

I nod, acknowledging him and leave him standing in the hallway.

I can't shake the image of Delilah's chest rising and falling with her harsh breaths when she was touching me. My skin still burns from the contact, even though it's been several long minutes since she pulled away from me.

"What's up?" Drew asks from the top bunk of the bed.

His eyes never leave his cell phone to look over at me as I drop my towel, of which I'm thankful because just the thought of Delilah's soft lips is making me thicken again.

I tug on the tightest pair of boxer briefs I own in an effort to constrict my cock and then a pair of athletic pants. "Not much," I finally answer. "Just that I'm now at the mercy of this fucking family because Jaxon paid my fucking probation fees without even bothering to consult me on it."

He laughs before speaking. "You're the most ungrateful asshole I've met."

"Don't cuss," I mutter as I sling myself on to the bottom bunk. "And it isn't about gratitude. He shouldn't just do shit without speaking to me. I could handle the money without his fucking help."

"Now you're just lying to yourself."

I glare at him through the bottom of his mattress.

"You wouldn't be able to get that much money without breaking the law, and you know it."

"Whatever." I roll over and face the wall.

Silence fills the room, and just as I'm sure he's fallen asleep, he speaks again. "Gigi was eating you alive this morning at the pool."

"Who?" I ask refusing to play into whatever game he's trying to start.

"The twin with the dark hair?" I don't answer. "The wild one in the barely-there bikini?"

I grunt a noncommittal sound. Of course, I noticed her. With her tits on full display and a devious smile, she's kind of hard to miss. Man-eaters aren't my style at all though. Now, the gorgeous blonde in the navy suit beside her? That's a whole other story.

"You planning on going to the party next weekend?"

"Probably not," I lie, knowing even though I shouldn't, I want to be wherever Delilah is. Even if that means some lame ass teenager party.

"I'm going to go," he says, and I can hear the smile in his voice. "There are going to be tons of fine ass girls there. I bet I can convince one of them to get on their knees for me."

I laugh, so deep in my gut, I get a cramp.

"Dude, seriously?" I hear him huff in agitation.

"Asshole," he mutters as I feel him turn over above me.

He doesn't say another word. I hate that he feels like he has to act like a badass all the time. I've done it for years for self-preservation, but he should be able to live worry-free.

"You have plenty of time to worry about shit like that," I say to him. "Don't try to grow up any faster than you have to. Being grown fucking sucks."

Especially when you're not grown at all and have to depend on your absentee father to foot the bills for crimes you committed because your mother lied to you about his existence.

I sprawl out on my back and relegate myself to another sleepless night of thinking about Delilah until my balls ache so bad I want to scream.

Chapter 14

Delilah

"Perfect," I whisper with a quick pop of my lips.

I could lie to myself, claim dry lips as the reason I've slicked on tinted gloss rather than my normal chapstick, but it would do no good. Lawson hasn't left my brain since the minute he showed up. Last night, after feeling his hot skin against my fingers, I tossed and turned, the interaction on repeat in my brain. There's nothing I can do about the redness in my eyes from lack of sleep, but he doesn't really pay me any attention, so maybe I'll get lucky, and he'll not even notice.

But, I want him to notice me.

Shaking my head at the ridiculousness of it all, I grab my keys and cell phone from my desk. I don't get boy crazy. Yeah, I've found guys at school good-looking, but getting to the point I want to doodle their names on my notebook never entered my mind.

Making sure I pulled my door closed behind me, I make my way down the stairs with a grin on my face. I know most teens spend their summers vacationing in the sun, going to parties, and sleeping late, but I've enjoyed going to the animal shelter four to five days a week. Even though summer is coming to a close, and I've been busy with the animals, I still get excited about my volunteer work. There's nothing greater than the smiles on the dogs' faces when I show up.

In the kitchen, I find Dad, Pop, and Drew at the breakfast nook, each eating breakfast. Over the last week, Drew has stopped shoveling food into his mouth like someone is going to take it away from him. He's growing comfortable in his skin here, acclimating better than I thought he would, after witnessing his first meal with us.

"Hey, Delilah," Drew says with a quick smile before taking another bite of chocolate cereal.

"Morning," I respond and head to the coffee pot.

"Coffee?" Pop asks noticing my change in routine.

"Yeah," I mutter pulling two cups from the cabinet. Being nice, I decide to make a cup for Lawson. He hasn't gotten out of bed before noon since his first night here, so I know these early days are going to be brutal for him. "I didn't sleep very well last night."

"Too excited about the party to sleep, huh?" Dad smiles over his own steaming cup of java.

"Something like that," I answer. "Where's Lawson? You told him nine, right?"

"He's still sleeping," Drew answers before Dad can respond to my question.

"I'm sure he's awake," Dad says. "Run up and grab him. You don't have a set time to be there, but I know you hate being late, even if the schedule you're keeping is your own."

I grumble to myself as I finish fixing my cup and refuse to be nice any longer. His cup sits empty when I turn and head back up the stairs. It's rude to keep people waiting, and rudeness is a pet peeve of mine.

Knocking on his bedroom door goes unanswered. I look over my shoulder, noticing the bathroom door is open, and the light is off. Last night's scene runs through my head again, and I do my best to ignore the full body shiver that runs up my spine and out of my fingertips.

Agitated, I turn the doorknob and swing open the door. The bang as it swings wide and hits the wall startles the sleeping boy on the bottom bunk. He jerks, his large hand shooting straight to his dick as if protecting it at all costs is priority number one. The sheets are tangled around his legs as if he got too warm in the night and kicked them off.

Unbidden, a small sigh escapes my lips at the sight of his straining penis, large and thick, behind his sweats. I swallow around the lump that is forming in my throat until his husky chuckle makes the lean muscles on his stomach jump.

Unable to pull my eyes away from his body quickly, my eyes take long seconds to meet his. White teeth clamp onto his bottom lip, and his eyes hold mine in challenge.

"Wanna help me take care of my little problem?" If I thought he had a sexy voice before, I can vouch that his early morning, throaty words nearly make me breathless.

"Little?" I squeak before catching myself.

Now is not the time to get all weird and awkward, spouting the words that have no place out in the open.

"I'll be gentle," he assures me, the playful smile never leaving his lips. "Unless you like being gagged until tears run down your beautiful cheeks? I'm more than willing to give you what you need to have those rosy lips wrapped around my cock."

Cock.

Such a dirty word, but for some reason, it has that shiver reigniting over my skin.

"You look terrified," he husks out, shifting, so his body is angled more in my direction. "Sweet really. The little virgin girl scared of me. The thought of you choking on my cock makes my nuts ache. Take care of it for me, Princess."

My eyes are once again pulled to his hand gripping his length.

"No thanks," I finally manage to say. "You disgust me."

He really doesn't, but the blatant sexual innuendo is being taken too far. I hate him for calling me Princess. I hate him for thinking he can say such awful things to me. But more so, I hate myself for wanting to open my mouth to a boy for the first time in my life.

"You'll have me in your mouth eventually," he promises.

I shake my head and turn back to the door. "You have five minutes to be downstairs, or I'm leaving without you."

I turn right, heading to my room and into my en-suite rather than left to join the rest of the family in the kitchen. My cheeks are burning and much to my dismay, my mouth is watering.

"Vulgar, disgusting asshole," I hiss as I splash water on my face. Next up is the wad of tissue paper that swipes the color from my lips. "This is never going to work."

I contemplate telling Dad that he's going to have to find something else for Lawson to do, but I know that means explaining why I have an issue driving him to the animal shelter. Even though he acts like a total jerk every time we speak, I don't want him to get into trouble. The last thing I want is to put my dad in a position where he feels like he has to choose between the two of us.

"I'm doing it for Drew," I remind myself in the bathroom mirror.

I don't know the specifics, but I've overheard enough to know that Lawson is on probation for something that happened a while back in Texas. He has community service hours, and if he doesn't complete them, he'll be in more trouble. If he is arrested, Drew will suffer, and I'm not petty enough to do something to compromise that. Drew's nice to me, respectful and actually a pleasure to be around.

"For Drew," I say with more conviction before turning around and making my way to the front door.

"Been waiting for you, Princess," Lawson says as I descend the stairs. He glances at the screen of the phone to check the time.

"Have fun you guys," Pop calls from the kitchen. "See you at dinner time."

We walk outside, heading around the clubhouse to my car.

"Did you have to change your panties?" Lawson whispers, leaning in so close I can feel the warmth of his breath on my bare shoulder.

"Stop," I warn.

"Personally," he says with an audible smile in his voice. "I've never gotten off so fast."

I glare at him. "You can't be serious?"

I climb inside of my gently used Corolla and hit the unlock button for him. Cranking it, I blast the AC immediately. Even at nine in the morning, New Mexico is hot as hell.

"I can't wait to get to New England," I mutter and crack the windows to allow some of the heat to pour out.

"What's that, Princess?"

"One," I turn to glare at him. "Stop calling me Princess. Two, quit making sexual advances toward me."

"You like it," he counters as I put the car in gear.

"I don't."

"I bet if I slide my hand in your panties, you'll be wet for me."

I snap my head in his direction, pissed, less about his words and more so because he'd be right. "Try it, and I'll break your fucking hand."

In mock surrender, he holds his hands up by his ears. "Damn, Delilah. Chill the fuck out."

"Please, just stop."

"I'm just joking with you, giving you a hard time."

I crinkle my nose oddly annoyed that maybe he doesn't find me attractive enough to want to do dirty things with. It makes no sense, but I have no control over the emotions.

The trip to the animal shelter remains silent until I speak as we pull in and park in the employee lot. "You'll be meeting with Dana. She's the day supervisor. I know Dad spoke with her, but I'm certain he didn't give her details of why you're here."

He nods, the only clue I have that he's even heard what I said. With anxious energy, his fingers drum on his jean-clad legs. For reasons I don't even understand, I reach over and calm his left hand by placing mine over it, the contact no less heated than it was last night in the hallway.

"Don't be nervous," I say when his eyes meet mine. I pull my hand away when his lip twitches.

"I'm not," he assures me. "Just ready to pet some dogs."

I laugh and climb out of the car. When he meets me at the front, I just smile over at him.

"What?" he asks, voice tinted with the agitation I've come to associate with him.

"There won't be much petting for you today."

"The hell does that mean?"

"You'll see," I tell him, the bounce in my step growing with the knowledge that he's about to have an eye-opening experience.

*　*　*

The grumbling meets my ears before I round the corner to the kennels. We've been here for four hours already, and I haven't seen Lawson since I dropped him off with Dana in reception. I went about my day walking the dogs and sitting on the floor while the cats surrounded me to get their ears scratched.

"How does something so little and cute make so much shit?"

I can't help the grin that spreads across my face. Lawson thought he'd be doing what I come here to do every day, but the community service hours given by the shelter are a little more interactive than the ones of the volunteers. Dana's take on the situation is that if probationers have to get down and dirty with the less shiny part of the job, then maybe they won't re-offend. I've done my fair share of kennel cleaning when there wasn't someone else here to do it, so I don't feel sorry for him at all.

Rounding the corner, I find Lawson crouched low to the ground, coveralls doing nothing to make him any less appealing. He's scratching at the head of a mid-sized dog of questionable breeding. The dog revels in the attention it's getting, flopping to his back for a tummy rub when he's had enough attention paid to his head.

"You didn't deserve to be left to fend for yourself, did you, Buddy?" The dog yips in excitement. "I know exactly how you feel. Life sucks sometimes."

My heart begins to thunder in my chest. The pain and understanding in Lawson's voice are enough to make me take a faltering step back.

"He's had a rough life. Treat him with kindness," Dad's voice rings in my ears.

He stands abruptly, the classic Lawson sneer marring his gorgeous face. He can't even be real with himself. The thought saddens me.

"You gonna help me tomorrow?" The dog yips and turns in a quick circle. "You can't spray a hose so maybe just shit a little less?"

He grins when the dog yips again and tries to bite at the spray coming from the end of the hose as he begins to clean the kennel.

I back away, giving him the time he needs, but knowing just how much it sucks to be stuck in your own head. He needs a friend, someone he can speak to without judgment, but his mouth ruins everything. His defenses are up so high he'll destroy any form of friendship I try to offer.

Chapter 15

Lawson

"Another day, another pile of shit to clean."

At the stoplight we have managed to get caught at the last three days we've been going to the shelter together, she looks over at me. I grin at her, and she returns it. I haven't said anything off-color since that first drive in. It makes her uncomfortable, and for some fucked up reason, I find myself giving her what she wants. As much as I love the color of her tongue and the way she licks her lips when I talk dirty, I hate the distance it puts between us. She avoids me, either in repulsion or because she's tempted, so I've refrained the last two days.

We've chatted about our futures. She has everything planned out as much as possible. Rhode Island for college, where she'll major in Sociology. She explained her need to understand how her mother was drawn into a cult, giving up her entire life for an eccentric megalomaniac. I can relate, even though I'd never admit it to her. My mom may have never been in a cult, but drugs and the party life were just as detrimental to her family and her health.

Personally, I have no long-term goals. Getting off of probation and finding a job is my only immediate concern. I can work off the money that Jaxon fronted me, but that doesn't mean I have a paid job once it's repaid.

"Those dogs love you," she tells me as she hits the gas when the light turns green.

"I don't know how you manage not to bring them all home." I grin at her again. "Buddy is seriously hard to leave every day."

Buddy, the name I gave the dog I connected with on the first day, greets me with a smile every morning.

"I tried," she confesses. "Pop put the brakes on it the first day he came to pick me up."

I laugh, imagining her standing there pouting when he rejected the idea. "You mean those pretty blue eyes of yours didn't work that time?"

Her fingers grip the steering wheel tighter. "I don't get everything I want."

"You will." My voice sobers when she turns to look at me. "The entire world will open up for you. I'm certain of it."

"The world?" She huffs. "I'm terrified to leave the little bubble my dads have created. Moving clear across the country to go to school? I must be crazy."

"What are you running from then?" Why I'm so interested in the trajectory of her life, I have no idea. Maybe it keeps me from thinking about my own, a simple distraction to my own limited options.

"I'm not running," she assures me with a frown. "Gigi? She'll end up being the runner. I doubt she'll make it through senior year before she hits the road. The grass is always greener and all that."

"She's the wild twin?" Her eyes follow me wherever I go. If Delilah thinks I'm suggestive, she should hear the shit that comes out of that chick's mouth.

She nods. "Like you haven't noticed her."

"Oh, I've noticed her." I scrub my hand over the stubble growing on my jawline. "She's kind of hard to miss."

Delilah's lips form a flat line as she studiously looks ahead, suddenly distracted by the traffic around us.

"Everyone wants her. The boys fall at her feet. The *world*," she says with disdainful agitation, "is at her feet, not mine."

"Not everyone," I whisper barely loud enough for her to hear.

* * *

One thing I didn't inherit from my mother is my work ethic. Day three cleaning kennels and I've managed to cut my time from the first day by almost half. Granted, I spent most of the first day bitching and bemoaning my position on the animal shelter ladder.

"Jesus, your breath stinks," I tell Buddy as he puts his wet paws on the coveralls covering my legs and tries to lick my face. "What do they feed you?"

He yips in my face and I recoil at the disgusting smell.

"I'm going to bring you some gum or something, dude. You have a serious problem."

"We have dental sticks in the back closet."

I look up, hands still rubbing at Buddy's ears to see Dana smiling on the other side of the kennel.

"Perfect," I say looking back down at my furry companion.

"You should get him a treat and then take him for a walk."

"Really? I have three more kennels to clean, and that Doberman takes bigger shits than a horse."

She shakes her head, but her smile never falters. My first day here, Delilah noticed how nervous I was. I'm sure she thought it was because it was a new place, but it had more to do with getting treated like shit at the place in Texas I was supposed to work my hours at. Being in trouble for breaking into a house to steal so you and your brother could eat for the month was a low point in my life, but being made to feel like the scum of the earth for being hungry only pissed me off. That attempt at community service lasted fifteen minutes and ended with the supervisor clutching his bloody nose.

"Okay. Clean the last couple of stalls then head out and help Delilah. She's taken it upon herself to walk five dogs at the same time, and I know they're only going to end up dragging her through the pasture."

I clean the stalls in record time, grab Buddy a treat for his god-awful breath, and head out to find the girl I can't get out of my head no matter how hard I try.

"You're going to break my leg," she screeches.

My smile turns into wide eyes as I sprint toward her. On the ground, with several leashes wrapped around her legs, she bats one dog away. The opportunistic motherfucker has jumped on her back. I manage to push him away before he starts hip thrusting at her.

The laugh spills out and is met with glaring blue eyes. "Really? You find this fucking funny?"

I shake my head no, but the laugh still rolls through me. "Upsetting more than anything. You were just batting him away. If I tried to mount you, you'd probably break my dick off."

I grin down at her as she bites her lip trying to hide a smile. "A little help, please?"

"Yeah. Shit, sorry."

I detangle the leashes from around her ankles, my heart thudding when I realize I dropped Buddy's leash and he's probably halfway to Colorado by now. I look over my shoulder, relieved to find him bouncing playfully near a terrier. Bored, the smaller dog lies in the grass with his head on his paws, waiting for us to get back to his walk. Being ignored doesn't stop Buddy from entertaining the idea.

She takes my outstretched hand and lets me pull her back to her feet.

"Thanks," she mutters. "They normally aren't such jerks. That new one has them all riled up."

I look over at the solid white dog. "She's probably in heat. Would explain Blackie over there trying to take a ride on your back."

"Gross," she laughs and smacks my chest with the back of her hand. "Help me?"

Regretfully, I pull my eyes from her face and look down at the tangle of leashes in her hands. We spend the next ten minutes getting them back in order.

When she looks up smiling as the last one is pulled free, I notice the smear of dirt. God, I hope it's dirt smeared on her cheek.

I take a step closer, my hand instinctively reaching for her face.

"Dirt," I whisper as my thumb brushes the softness of her face.

Her eyes find mine, innocent and filled with a need I'm certain she doesn't understand.

"You're gorgeous," I pant. "Your mouth—"

Her face shifts, leaning into my hand.

Buddy barks just as I'm leaning in, refusing to let this moment pass us by. She jumps, startled by the intrusion into our moment. With lips parted, I read her face. Trust, desire, and compassion fill her soft blue eyes. An unfamiliar rush washes over me, heating my skin and making me uncomfortable. In true form, I ruin the moment the only way I know how.

"Your mouth would feel amazing wrapped around my cock."

She blinks, unsure if she heard me right. I can see the anger flash across her face before she just turns and walks off. I'm left, standing in a field holding leashes to six rambunctious as fuck dogs, watching her walk away because intimacy, even on the simplest level, isn't something I can tolerate.

When the walk is over, my arms are killing me. Fighting half a dozen dogs is better than any day I've spent at the gym.

"After you get them kenneled can you come out and help me?" Dana says as I pass by the rolled up door outside of the large animal shelter. It's empty now, but I've heard that they sometimes have farm animals and horses that have been recovered by animal control. "I need your muscles."

"Sure," I say with a smile and a wink.

"One big flirt just like your daddy," she mutters with a quick laugh.

For some reason, the comparison doesn't even bother me this time. I want to go find Delilah, but I figure keeping my distance is best. I don't have a damn thing to offer her. I ruin everything I touch, and the last thing she needs is some horny fucker like me taking everything she has with nothing to offer in return.

"What's up?" I ask Dana as I make it back to reception after caging the now tired dogs.

"This is Rachel Grant," Dana says pointing to the wet dream of a teen standing near the desk. "She brought a truckload of dog food. Can you unload it for her?"

I smile at her, and she doesn't even notice that it doesn't reach my eyes. Who in the world delivers dog food in a bikini top and shorts so short the bottom curve of her ass hangs out?

Man-eaters that's who. No thanks.

I follow her out, ignoring the blatant shake of her ass.

"Truckload?" I ask opening the tailgate of a newer Chevy pickup. "It's four bags."

"Big bags," she counters.

"Your muscles," she says as her fire engine red fingernail drags down my arm from shoulder to wrist, "are so big, you shouldn't have any problem."

My eyes narrow, but her smile only grows bigger. "Maybe next time spend less on your truck and buy more dog food. We can use more donations."

"Oh," she says with a flip of her hair as I reach for the first bag. "My family can afford loads more dog food. If I bring more will you unload it?"

"Of course," I answer and toss the dog food to the ground and reach in for another. The sooner I get them off her truck the sooner she can get the fuck out of here.

"I may bring so much you'd have to take your shirt off to keep cool."

I smile and grab the last bag, refusing to explain that the blazing ass sun would do more damage than sweating with a shirt on.

"You about ready to go home?" A genuine smile crosses my lips at the sound of Delilah's voice. Fuck, at least she's talking to me even though the derision can't be ignored in her voice.

"Yep," I say over my shoulder. "Anything else you need Ms. Grant."

The blonde in front of me smiles while the blonde at my back huffs. Jealousy. I love it. It means I still may have a chance even though Delilah Donovan is probably the only thing that can complicate my life even more than it already is.

"Nothing today." She rolls her bottom lip through her teeth. The sight is more off-putting than the sexiness she's clearly trying to exude. "What else do you need, Lawson?"

"Really?" Delilah mutters loud enough for me to hear.

"Leashes and dental sticks." Rachel recoils. "Seriously, those dogs have some of the nastiest fucking breath."

I turn my back to her to scoop two of the four bags of food.

"See you at the party on Saturday!" Rachel says either to my turned back or Delilah. "I'll bring my overnight bag."

"Can't fucking wait," Delilah mutters as I walk past her to the storage room.

I feel her presence behind me. After dropping the bags on the empty pallet in the corner, I turn to her.

"What I said earlier—" I sigh and run my hand over the top of my head.

"Is it that difficult?" Her words sting, but at least there's a smile on her face and no sharp tools in her hands.

I quirk an eyebrow at her.

"Apologizing? Is it that difficult?"

I grin, my eyes lingering on her lips before meeting her gaze.

"I don't do it very often. Will you forgive me?"

"For what?" she prods, insisting I actually say it.

"For saying those awful things. I'm sorry." Well, that wasn't as painful as I imagined it would be.

"You didn't mean them?" Her throat works on a swallow, the action drawing me closer to her.

It's my turn to bite my lip, trying not to lie to her because fuck if I didn't mean every word out in that field. I release it immediately, wondering if I look as stupid as the chick from earlier.

"The truth?" I whisper mere inches from her mouth. She nods, eyes focused on my lips. "You sucking my cock, me licking the length of your pussy, the way you're going to feel sliding down my cock when I take you the first time is all I think about. I meant every word."

She swallows again and nods. "Good to know."

My eyes flutter as my mouth reaches out to hers. She deserves more than being Frenched in a storage room that smells like dog food and mothballs, but not everything in life is as glorious as we watch in movies.

My lips meet air, and when I open them, I see her back as she walks away from me. My cock aches at her rejection, but a smile is on my face all the way to her car.

Chapter 16

Delilah

"Can you be any more obvious?" Ivy sneers at her sister's question, but she pulls her eyes from Griffin anyway.

"You can't tell me you didn't miss him while he was away," Ivy says looking down at her clasped hands.

I hate to tell her that while she's had her eyes on Griffin; his eyes have been on her sister. She either doesn't see the way he watches her or she ignores it.

"He's been gone a couple of weeks," Gigi says with a shrug.

"Months," Ivy corrects. "He's been gone for months, and he's fixing to deploy to Germany."

"Okay?" Gigi says but doesn't pull her eyes from whatever guy she's honed in on tonight.

"There's no telling when he'll be back home," Ivy whines. I rub a hand over her shoulders. "Or *if* he'll ever make it home."

"None of that. We're supposed to be having fun." I tell her. I look over at Gigi. "Quit being a bitch."

She turns her head, shock in her eyes and just stares at me as if I've grown three heads in the last five minutes. "Sorry."

It's a half-assed apology, but it's the best she ever has to offer. When she looks across the room, I follow her line of sight. Lawson. I should've guessed.

He's not looking at her, however, his eyes are locked with mine. Drew calls his name from the other side of the room, but he winks at me before turning his attention to his younger brother.

"He seriously likes you," Ivy whispers and I can feel my cheeks flush.

"He likes embarrassing me," I counter.

"You either go after him or I will," Gigi spits before she stands in a huff and walks away.

"She's disgusting," Ivy says. "You don't have to worry though. I don't think he'd touch her. I heard her on the phone with someone bitching because she came on to him and he shot her down. She thinks something's wrong with him."

"Because he didn't accept when she threw herself at him?" Ivy nods. "She's nuts."

"Mom and Dad have been talking about sending her to boarding school."

My eyes widen. "They wouldn't."

I look across the room finding Griffin, Shadow, and Diego huddled together. I wince when Gigi bounces up to them and commands all of Griffin's attention without so much as a glance in his direction. Diego frowns and shakes his head. Gigi walks away, pouting like a reprimanded child. Griffin's eyes follow her until she disappears into the small crowd on the make-shift dance floor. He doesn't stop looking until he takes a punch to the shoulder by Diego. I grin when Shadow tries to hide his laugh behind his beer bottle. Griffin straightens, nearly standing at attention as the MC President rips into him for checking out his underage daughter.

"He doesn't even know I exist."

I turn to find a tear glistening on Ivy's bottom lash.

"Maybe I should be a slut like my sister. He'd have no choice but to notice me then."

God, I feel terrible for her, but I have no experience with guys, so I don't have anything to offer.

"I doubt that's the best course of action. Acting that way just makes them want to use you and toss you away."

"Really?" Ivy asks, her eyes darting to the bare skin of my thighs not covered by my shorter than usual skirt. "Are you wearing half a skirt for Lawson?"

I clear my throat, knowing she's exactly right. I have no defense.

"He gets his jollies by torturing me. I'm sure if I actually challenged him, accepted one of his grotesque offers, he'd back away in a flash."

"I doubt that," she mutters.

"He's an asshole," I assure her.

"Yet you say it with a smile." She returns my grin. "Delilah has a crush on the bad boy. Never thought I'd see the day."

I look at her but refuse to say anything else. It isn't until the light from the neon pink disco ball is blocked that I look away.

"Hey, ladies." I smile up at Griffin, but then wince when Ivy's fingernails dig into my thighs.

Without pulling my eyes from his, I grab her hand and bend a finger back until she releases her death grip on my leg.

"How long do we get the pleasure of your company?" I ask sweetly.

"I have to be back in San Diego tomorrow," he says as he takes the empty spot on the sofa next to Ivy.

She's stiff as a board, but she deflates when he wraps his arm around her shoulder and pulls her to his chest for a hug. "How are you, kiddo?"

I wince. Kiddo? Damn, that's got to hurt.

"Fine," she grumbles but doesn't pull from his embrace.

"Looked like you and Diego were having a heated conversation. What was that all about?"

At least he has the decency to blush, but Ivy glares at me when he pulls his arm away to run his hand over the top of his crop-top. I don't imagine she'll ever wash her shirt again.

"He was.... Ah... giving me some advice that could save my life. Pointers about survival and shit."

"For your deployment? Or the enemy combatants in the clubhouse?"

His eyes dart back to Diego, and the glare in his President's eyes has him putting a little distance between himself and Ivy.

"Stop," she mutters.

"Cut me some slack, D. She's less than two years younger than me."

I tilt my head, taking in his discomfort. He defends his sexual attraction to Gigi, but calls Ivy kiddo?

"Did you tell him that?"

He shakes his head back and forth almost violently. "Fuck no. He'd kill me."

"Hey," Samson says as he walks up. "You said we could use your playlist."

"Yeah, sorry." Griffin stands and walks away with my brother.

"And I thought Gigi was a bitch."

I sigh, hating that teasing Griffin was at her expense.

I slap my hands on my knees, the uncomfortable sting from the impact lighting my nerve endings on fire. "You just need to take your mind off of him."

"Impossible."

"Let's try anyway."

I hate to dance, mainly because I suck at it, but if she needs the distraction, I'll throw myself on the proverbial altar for sacrifice.

"I hate this song," she mutters as Dawin's Dessert begins to fade out.

She perks up the second it transitions into Nelly's The Fix. We both look up to find Griffin grinning at us. Thumb up in the air, he winks at Ivy. She may think she's invisible, but playing her favorite song reveals that it's so far from the truth.

Before the song is over, we're both glistening with sweat, and there's a smile on her face I haven't seen in a very long time.

"And this one!" Ivy squeals when Anaconda by Nicki Minaj blares through the speakers.

I shake my head, fanning my overheated face with my hand. "I have to sit this one out. You want a water?"

She nods and bounces around in a circle with her arms in the air. I can hear her singing the lyrics as I walk away.

"Jesus," Dad mutters when I step up to the refreshment table. "It's like watching mating on Animal Planet."

I grab a water and turn back to the dance floor.

"I hope nobody gets pregnant out there," he grumbles.

I laugh, head thrown back at his complaint. He's smiling when I turn back toward him. "That's not how it happens, Dad."

An eyebrow shoots into his hairline, the star tattoo on his cheek twitching. "And just what do you know about it?"

I smile wider. We've had the birds and bees talk a couple of years ago. It left me broken and disgusted, and it's not a subject we've revisited since.

"Just what I've watched on PornMD." Both eyebrows disappear into his dark hair.

"I'm canceling the data on your phone." I roll my teeth through my lips. "And turning off the Wi-Fi in the house."

"I'm seventeen, Dad. I can't stay a little girl forever."

His eyes narrow in challenge. "Seventeen on Monday," he corrects.

"Old enough to consent," I tease.

"I'll kill any bastard with the balls big enough to touch you."

"So violent," I say as I tilt my water up to my lips.

"We'll talk about it tomorrow," he hisses and storms off.

I watch as he joins Pop on the other side of the room. Pop looks over at me as Dad flails his arms and animatedly tells him about our conversation. He smiles and rubs dad's back to try to calm him, but the look in his eyes tells me to stop torturing the man. I give them both a little wave and head back to the dance floor.

I bite my lip when I pass Lawson stretched out on the sofa. Rachel is practically in his lap. If I thought my skirt was short, it has nothing on Rachel's. I know I'm not the only one who can see her lime green panties glowing between her legs.

"So fucking skanky," I whisper to myself as I walk past them.

Samson is still standing near the stereo system with Griffin, but he's throwing daggers at Lawson. My night just went from playful and fun to disappointing in an instant.

I can't wait for everyone to leave so I can go to bed and just forget about the whole damn thing.

Chapter 17

Lawson

"Where are you going?" Drew asks with a yawn from the top bunk.

I reach for the doorknob. "I need to find Delilah and explain that what she saw earlier with Rachel wasn't what it looked like."

He chuckles. "You're screwed."

"I hope not," I tell him as I pull the door open.

"Why in the world didn't you go find her then?" He shakes his head and looks back at his phone.

"I tried to find her. She just disappeared," I explain.

"If Jaxon finds you in her room at two in the morning he'll rip you to shreds."

"You let me worry about Jaxon," I mutter stepping out into the hallway.

"Famous last words," he says with another laugh as I pull the door closed. I still hear him through the door. "Your funeral."

I tiptoe down the hallway, grateful for the plush carpet under my bare feet. Her door isn't pulled all of the way closed, so I stick my head in. The bed is made, and she's nowhere to be seen.

I turn back and make my way down the stairs. If I'm caught in the common areas by Jaxon or Rob, the fallout will be less intense.

The sight of Delilah, bent over in her short skirt, is worth anything the men of the house can throw at me. I'd gladly spend time in jail so long as they have no way to pull these images from my mind.

Backlit by the light inside the fridge, her golden hair seems to glow in a curtain around her. Resisting the pull her body has on mine would only be in vain, so rather than announcing myself, I close the distance between us and wrap my arms around her middle. She stiffens, frightened at first, but soon settles into my embrace.

"I couldn't keep my eyes off of you tonight," I whisper in her ear, nuzzling into her soft neck.

She whimpers when I pull her closer. I never imagined the warmth of her skin against mine would be life-altering, but here I stand in the dark kitchen of my newly discovered father's house a new man.

"Jesus," I pant into the web of her tangled blonde hair. "I can die a happy man."

"Well isn't this cozy." The kitchen light flips on bathing us in light that leaves nothing to the imagination.

Releasing Delilah, I turn to face a pissed off Samson, only to find the shimmering eyes of—

"Delilah?"

My stunned eyes flash from the devastation on her face to the blonde now standing directly against my side. I recoil, taking a few steps away from Rachel. She bats her eyelashes at me, and I move further away until my hip collides with the counter.

"What the fuck is going on?" Samson seethes through gritted teeth.

"Isn't it obvious?" Rachel's breathy voice makes my skin crawl. The look in her eyes dares me to tell him I've made a mistake.

"We were..." I sigh and drop my hands to my sides. I've got nothing. I can't explain to Samson that I thought Rachel was his sister. The look in his eyes says he's ready to snap me in half, and a week ago I would've welcomed the chance to beat his ass, but things have shifted for me since working with Delilah at the animal shelter.

"We were just getting to the good stuff when you so rudely interrupted," she sneers at Samson. "You need to get over your little obsession with me. It's never going to happen. I'm only interested in real men."

I bite my tongue but stand stock still when her fingernail scrapes down the front of my bare chest.

I can't even look at Samson. His anger is secondary to the pain that's crushing me under Delilah's devastated stare. She just nods, gives me a weak, sad smile, and turns and walks away.

"Don't," Rachel warns catching my arm when I take a step to go after her. "She's upset that her twin is upset. She'll be fine."

I squeeze my eyes shut, only able to hear the soft retreat of her footfalls on the stairs. Even as upset as she is, I don't even hear her door close with a thud.

"Was this your plan all along?" Samson says with fists balled at his sides.

I shake my head.

"You knew I liked her." He jabs his finger in Rachel's direction. She merely rolls her eyes, looking bored.

"Doesn't matter, Sam. There's no mutual attraction. We're only friends." She says it sweetly, but the twinge on his face tells me it doesn't make things any better.

"You're a whore!" Samson yells.

I take a step forward. Rachel may not be an innocent angel, but I wrapped myself around her, and he's out of line. "Enough," I hiss.

"Enough? You've got to be fucking kidding me. You show up out the fucking blue, with some devious agenda and you have the nuts to stand there and tell me enough?"

"What the hell is going on?" Jaxon's booming voice circles around us.

Only now does Rachel step away from me, having closed the distance between us when Sam started ranting.

A menacing grin spreads across Samson's face, and I just know the fallout from this is going to be awful.

"Lawson here is pushing up on my girl. Pretty sure they were about to fuck on the kitchen table."

"She's not your girlfriend."

"I'd never touch you. Gross."

Jaxon and Rachel speak at the same time.

Jaxon holds his hand up when Samson begins his rebuttal. "And watch your mouth."

Samson's eyes narrow as he looks at his dad, but he doesn't make a sound. Jaxon commands respect, and I find myself standing a little straighter, even though what I'm about to face could end up with me on the street.

"Rachel, go get your things. Rob will give you a ride home."

"But I drove?" she argues, stopping short when Jaxon's glare lands on her.

"You can come get your truck in the morning. I'm not sending you out on the road this late at night."

"Yes, sir," she mutters and walks away.

Silence fills the room around us when she leaves. I'm not going to be the first person to speak, but I also haven't been given permission to speak. Why I'm resorting to the things I learned in the probation boot camp last year, I have no idea. Yet, here I stand, waiting to be addressed like I'm still in that hell hole with a drill instructor in my face.

"Calmly," Jaxon says with a warning in his voice. "Tell me what's going on."

He looks at Samson first, who crosses his arms over his chest and pouts for a quick second before he begins to speak.

"D and I came down to cut into our birthday cake early." Sam looks at his father, who smiles at him? The hell? "We—"

"Didn't want to wait for the family." Jaxon grins wider before schooling his face back to impassive seriousness. "Just like every year."

"Right." Even pissed Samson gives his dad a quick smile.

Seems my impromptu need for Delilah has ruined a family tradition. And my night just keeps getting better.

"When we stepped into the kitchen, Lawson and Rachel were all hugged up on each other in front of the fridge."

Jaxon looks toward me. All I can do is shrug in response and pray Jaxon doesn't figure out that it was his gorgeous daughter I'd wanted in my arms instead. I have a feeling though, that if Samson saw my arms wrapped around his twin, he'd lose his shit even more than he is now.

"And they were naked?" Jaxon asks.

"No," Samson cringes at the idea.

"Your yelling woke me up because your brother was hugging some girl in the kitchen?"

"We're not brothers," Samson insists while I say. "Not related at all."

The only thing we can agree on.

"Semantics," Jaxon says as he pinches the bridge of his nose in frustration.

"No," Samson insists. "Not related."

I nod in agreement. Adding, "like at all."

Being related to Samson in any way would be more of a slippery slope with Delilah, and I have enough problems with that situation. More along the lines of needing her more than I should ever feel about any other human other than Drew.

"Fine," Jaxon concedes albeit reluctantly. "Not related, but this is how we're going to settle this mess."

He turns to me. "No messing around with chicks in the house."

I agree even though there's the little issue of Delilah. "No problem."

"Also, I think it's best that you stay away from Rachel Grant," Jaxon adds.

"That's not a problem either."

He turns to Samson. "You don't just get to claim a girl because you think she's pretty."

"But—"

Jaxon holds his hand up, and Sam silences immediately. "It's not right to stake a claim on another person. Besides, it's creepy as hell. You have to let go of the idea of her if she isn't attracted to you."

"This sucks," Samson mutters.

"She told you how she feels, son. Just let it go."

"I've liked her for as long as I can remember, Dad. There's no way I can just walk away from that."

"You are blinded by her." I shift from one foot to the other, not wanting to be anywhere near this little father/son moment. "So much so that you didn't see the way that Kennedy followed your every move tonight."

His eyes widen, a small smile playing at the corner of his mouth. "The girl with pink hair and huge tits?"

Wow, this boy is driven by his hormones. He even cups his hands out in front of him for exaggeration.

"Really?" Jaxon frowns. "Don't talk about women like that. I've taught you better."

"Double D's dad." Samson is full on smiling now.

"Is this over?" Jaxon asks looking back and forth between us.

I nod, the first one to extend my hand to Samson. I don't miss the pride in Jaxon's eyes, but it doesn't exactly give me warm fuzzies.

"Sure," Samson says, his smile faltering as he reaches out to shake my hand. I let him squeeze harder than necessary. He's the one with the bruised ego, so I'll give him the small victory. I have a girl I need to speak to, to explain what actually happened in the dark tonight.

"Kennedy fucking Farmer," Samson sing songs as he leaves us and makes his way to his room.

"Rachel Grant? Really Lawson?" Jaxon's full attention is on me, and I wonder if this is when the calm, cool, collected guy disappears and he slams my head into the cabinet for hurting his son.

I shrug. "What?"

"Nothing," he says with disappointment in his eyes as he turns and walks toward his bedroom. "I just thought your interests were somewhere else."

Rob walks into the room with Rachel right behind him, gives Jaxon a quick kiss, and heads out to take her home. She waggles her fingers and does that unattractive lip and teeth roll again before she disappears out of the door.

When I hear Jaxon's bedroom door, I bound up the stairs, meeting Gigi and her twin on the upper landing.

"I thought you were staying the night?" *Please be going home.*

"She wants to be alone," the bookish twin says. Gigi doesn't even look in my direction. I appreciate the reprieve from her attention.

When Gigi is a few steps ahead of her on the way down the stairs, the other twin turns to look at me. The seriousness in her eyes makes me wish I could remember her name.

"You really hurt her," she whispers before she follows her sister out of the house.

"Hey, Kennedy. It's Samson Donovan." I'm not surprised he ran up the stairs to call her, but it's really putting a damper on the plans I have.

I groan, knowing I can't go to her right now. Leaving her alone, letting her stew in her anger isn't going to happen, but Rob will be back before too long, and there's the possibility that he'll check in on his little girl before calling it a night. Either he or Jaxon has opened our door and peered into our room at least once a night since we arrived. I figure they're either making sure we haven't snuck out, or it's one of those parental safety things I'll never understand.

I close myself into my room. Drew is snoring softly as I settle into the desk chair and hope that it doesn't take the house long to fall into slumber. I have a girl to win back.

Chapter 18

Delilah

"I'm fine, Daddy. Just can't sleep. Too much excitement today," I lie not even bothering to look up from my phone. He or Pop checks on us every night before they turn in. They have for as long as I can remember.

The door clicks closed. No 'night, sweetheart' or 'see ya in the morning.'

I look up to see the dark figure still standing in my room.

"Daddy?" The husky voice sounds pleased. "We can play it like that if you want, Princess, but that's not really my thing."

I sigh, closing out of the casino slots game I'm playing on my cell phone. The last thing Lawson needs as ammunition against me is knowing I can't stop playing those stupid apps.

"What do you want?"

"To talk." His response is quick.

"Find out just how intellectual Rachel isn't?" I pull my eyes from him and stare off into a dark corner of my room. "I don't have the time or patience to deal with you right now."

He chuckles. "I never would've even confused her with someone with brains." He takes a step in my direction, ignoring the second part of my statement.

"Go to bed Lawson. I've had enough of your shit tonight." I grab my headphones from my bedside table. "I'm sure you'll find another way to hurt me tomorrow."

"I didn't know you cared." I can hear the playfulness in his voice, and it does nothing but make me angrier.

"I don't," I argue. "It pissed me off that you pulled that shit with the one girl that Samson will never get over."

He laughs and takes another step forward. He's hesitant and calculating, and I wonder if he's afraid I'm going to attack him. He's got another thing coming if he thinks I'll waste that type of energy on his sorry ass.

"Samson is on the phone with Kennedy Farmer, probably jacking off to her voice while they talk about Pokémon Go or something."

I tilt my head, confused. "The pink-haired girl with the umm..."

"Big tits?" He takes another step closer so his face is now bathed in the light of the moon coming through the window. "Yeah, her."

"He just handed Rachel over to you?"

"Not exactly." He runs his hand over his head. "I need to talk to you about what you saw. I have to explain myself."

"No need," I tell him. "Your silence downstairs said a thousand words."

"What did you want me to say?" He sits on the side of my bed, on top of the blankets so I can hardly move my legs. "Was I supposed to tell your twin brother that I went into that kitchen and wrapped my arms around the girl I've been obsessing over for weeks?"

I huff. "You met her like two days ago."

"You sure are dense for a smart girl."

I could pop him in the eye right now.

"Short skirt, gorgeous blonde hair, legs that go on for days."

"Seriously, Lawson? Do you just enjoy torturing me?"

"I have a mind to tie you to this bed and gag you. Force you to shut the fuck up until I'm finished speaking."

"I don't want to hear a fucking word you have to say." My voice quivers and I hate that he has enough power over me to make me cry. "You could've stayed in your room tonight, but instead you want to rub it in my face? That's cruel, but probably a great decision on your part. I'm sure she's great at giving head. She's sucked off practically every popular guy at school."

His hand covers my mouth. When I try to turn my head to get away from him, his other hand fists the hair on my nape, tilting my head back and forcing me to look in his eyes. They practically sparkle in the dim light, and I feel hypnotized by them.

"Be quiet." Fear and something very similar to heat settles low in my stomach. He notices my reaction and smiles like the devil that he is. "Naughty girl. You like it rough?"

I draw in a hissing breath through my nose.

"I. Thought. She. Was. You."

I try to shake my head, rejecting his words, but my movement is impeded by his grip in my hair.

"If I pull my hand away will you scream?"

"No," I mumble against his palm.

"Promise?"

I nod as best as I can.

I lick my lips the second he pulls his hand away, the tip of my tongue running over his finger. Accidental? Deliberate? At this moment I can't tell.

"Fuck," he mutters. "The things you do to me."

"I'm not her," I finally manage to say. "I will never be like her, throwing myself at your feet, flirting with you until you cave."

"There's nothing about her that appeals to me, Princess." He presses his index finger against my lips, but I turn my head forcing him to pull it away. "Everything about you makes my blood boil, makes me want things I've never wanted before."

"Like my lips around your..." I swallow. "Cock?"

"Damn, Delilah. I love your filthy mouth." I expect a grin to hit his mouth, but it stays in a flat line. "I'd sell my already dark soul to the devil for that, and all in good time, but you're more to me than a blowjob."

I let the sound of my heavy breathing fill the room, grateful that my covers are pulled up so he can't see the quick puckering of my nipples.

"And you'd never have to throw yourself at my feet. Although I get the feeling I may end up doing just that to you."

I search his eyes for deception, finding nothing but wide-open honesty.

"Why now?" My voice is thick with arousal and temptation.

He shakes his head as if he doesn't have an answer, but he finally speaks. "I'm tired of fighting it. Tired of jacking off to thoughts of you, dreaming of you every night knowing you're in here all alone."

"That's... descriptive." His hand finds mine, and I suddenly feel too warm, too open and exposed. "I'm not just going to jump into sex with you. I'm not the type. Rachel maybe—"

His fingers brush against my lips again. They part on a harsh breath at the contact.

"Let's agree to never mention her name again." I agree with a quick jerk of my head. "Tell me you want this too."

"I don't know what you want," I confess.

"I want to spend time together, talk, and get to know each other."

"You don't talk. You grunt and give one-word answers. You're a vault, Law."

He smiles brightly. "I love when you call me that." His finger sweeps over my lips again. Talk about obsessive behavior. "I'll open up."

I frown.

"I'll make an effort to open up to you. I want to."

"What made you change your mind?"

He sighs. "Honestly?"

"No, Lawson," I snip. "Lie to me some more."

"There was this sense of calm that washed over me when I wrapped my arms around Rachel earlier." I jerk my hand from his. He grabs it back immediately. "Don't. I thought she was you. Every spark, every raised hair on my body was yours. It all belonged to you."

"I was jealous of her," I admit.

"And I love that about you." His hand cups my cheek. "Can I replace the warmth of her body with yours?"

I laugh. "Do you know how fucked up that sounds?"

He gives me a sad smile. "I do, but it doesn't make me want to do it any less."

"Over the covers?"

"I'll take anything you're willing to give me."

I stretch out, sliding down to rest my head on my pillow rather than my back against the headboard.

"When did you turn into this softy?"

He chuckles as his body lines up behind mine. "I can try to cop a feel if that makes things more suitable for you."

I laugh but pull the blankets down to my waist. The heat of his bare chest against my thin tank top is absolute bliss. His arm wraps around my stomach, but rather than reaching high or low he settles it palm down on the sheet. Needing just a little more, I intertwine my fingers in his.

"You're so warm," I whisper.

He grumbles incoherently just as my mouth stretches in a yawn.

"Okay, Romeo. You have to go. If we fall asleep, Dad and Pop will kill us both."

"Worth it," he mumbles against my neck.

"Go," I tell him and hitch my shoulder to jolt him.

I roll to my back as he climbs off of the bed.

"Goodnight," he whispers as his lips brush my forehead.

"Nope," I tell him with a hand tugging at the back of his neck.

I press my lips to his, giving his tongue the access it demands when it presses forward.

His strong hands cup my face as he controls the kiss I instigated. Fire shoots all over my body, this kiss nothing remotely similar to Brandon's lips last year at the homecoming game.

Lawson worships me with his tongue, taking the time and care to explore my mouth and allowing me to do the same. When he pulls away, I'm hungry for more. My neck flexes up, lips seeking his. He pecks them like an elderly relative and pulls away.

"Sleep, Princess. I'll see you in the morning."

I'm still smiling, still have fingers pressed to my lips as I drift off to sleep. This year may be the best birthday I'll ever have.

Chapter 19

Lawson

"What are you thinking about?"

I turn to find Delilah watching me as we wait at the red light.

"Your mouth," I answer truthfully.

She grins wider and shakes her head. "And exactly why does that make you smile like a fool?"

"I was thinking about the way the syrup from your waffles yesterday morning clung to your bottom lip." I take her right hand from the steering wheel and close my fingers around it. "The way your tongue peeked out to lick it away."

Fuck, I'm getting hard.

"You're obsessed with my mouth." I nod knowing I'm obsessed with every single thing about her.

She's still staring at me when a horn blares behind us. Her eyes dart to the rearview mirror before she pulls her hand from mine and places it back on the steering wheel as she accelerates. I leave my hand on her thigh, the innocuous touch shooting fire into my blood.

Her throat clears. "How did your test go last week?"

I'd already forgotten that I went in for my GED exam on Thursday.

"Good," I answer. "I passed."

She beams with pride, and it makes me a little uneasy. Did she think I wouldn't?

"What's that look for?"

"What look?" she says but doesn't take her eyes off the road.

"Did you doubt my ability to pass it?" She shakes her head. "I'm a criminal deviant, not an idiot."

I can't even hide the agitation in my voice as I pull my hand from her thigh.

"Really?" she asks looking down at her leg as if the sensation of moving my hand is all that she can focus on. "I can't be proud that you passed your test without you getting upset that I'm happy?"

"Whatever," I mumble and look out the window.

"Don't whatever me," she snaps. "I don't think of you in a negative light at all. What you're struggling with is self-deprecation and shit from your past. Don't deflect that mess on me. I don't deserve it."

I bite the inside of my cheek until the taste of blood fills my mouth. She's right, but admitting that out loud is another character flaw.

Without a word, I put my hand back on her thigh. She doesn't swat it away, but a tension fills her muscles where there was nothing but welcoming calm a few minutes before.

***

My day has gone from bad to worse, I realize as I stand in front of Buddy's empty kennel.

"What happened?" I ask Dana when she walks up.

"He was adopted on Saturday." She's beaming, pride filling her eyes.

"By who?"

"A family with two excited little boys," she answers. "They'll take great care of him."

"How the hell do you know that? They could be budding psychopaths and only adopted a dog so they can torture him."

Far-fetched, but with my luck lately, I can see how it may have rubbed off on Buddy just by association.

A calm hand clasps my shoulder, and even though I want to pull away from her, I remain stock still.

"The preacher at the Baptist church, his wife, and their two very excited little boys will treat Buddy like the king that he is. I guarantee it."

"Did you vet them? Run a background check?"

She only chuckles as she walks away.

"Be careful," I hear Dana say on the other side of the door. "He's crabby today."

My brows are drawn together by the time Delilah comes into view.

"Crabby?" She tilts her head a little to the left. "You're not supposed to be crabby."

I shrug. "Buddy's gone."

I point to the empty kennel.

"Buddy is with a loving family. He's not gone. Now you can direct your attention to another sweet puppy."

She grabs my hand and drags me behind her to the supply closet.

"We're going to clean the kennels, then we'll walk the dogs and pet the kitties."

"You're going to help me clean kennels?" I raise a skeptical eyebrow at her as she pulls down two sets of coveralls.

A smile plays at the corner of her mouth. "Don't make assumptions about me. It's rude."

"Touché," I mutter.

We dress in the coveralls in companionable silence and then get to work on cleaning.

"I passed my test," I confide as we strip out of the soiled coveralls. "All I have left now is wrapping up my community service this week."

"I bet that's a huge relief."

"The biggest," I agree. "I feel lighter. Like I can get on with my life. Make plans for the future."

I hand her a bundle of three leashes and grab the same amount for me.

"What kind of plans?"

I follow her to the kennels all the way at the end. We'll start there and work our way back.

I chuckle. "Couldn't honestly tell you. I'll start in the garage today. Jaxon made me wait until the test was over. He wanted me to study for the test, but it's one of those things that if you don't know it, spending a couple hours a day for a week isn't going to do much good."

"You spent those hours in your room," she says as she clips a leash to the collar of a black dog.

"Yep," I say with a pop of my lips.

"But not studying? Were you hiding out from everyone?"

"At first, but then after a while, I would just lie in bed and think about where I'm heading." She smiles waiting for me to expand. "Don't give me that look. I haven't figured shit out."

"College?"

I shake my head. "I'm not really a classroom kind of guy."

We make our way to the second set of kennels so I can leash my three dogs. She remains silent, but I can tell from the mood surrounding her that she has plenty to say.

"Out with it," I say nudging her shoulder with mine as we begin to make our way across the field.

"It's just..." She looks off into the distance. "I don't want to sound naggy, but you need goals or something to work toward."

"I know." Her telling me this doesn't cause the same agitation as it would if it was Jaxon or Rob. "I think a mechanic would suit me well. Bikes, cars, that sort of thing."

"To be a legit mechanic, you'll have to go to school."

"Yeah," I shrug. "But it's mainly hands-on experience. I can deal with that. I just have no interest in taking government and history."

"The History of the Harley?" she offers.

"Now that I can get behind."

The dogs bounce around, not having been walked by Delilah since Friday. I'd be anxious and full of energy if I had to go two full days without her, so I understand their eagerness.

When we finally have the last of the animals back in their kennels, fed and watered, we make our way to the supply closet to rehang the leashes.

With her back to me, I wrap my arms all the way around her, enjoying the way she relaxes into me.

"I hate that things were so hectic yesterday." My breath whispers past the hairs that have escaped her ponytail. "It's been over twenty-four hours since I've tasted your lips."

"There you go with my mouth again," she says with a sigh, but I can tell she's not agitated by it. If anything, her breathless words reflect the same need I feel.

Turning her in my arms, I look down at her.

"Not just your mouth," I vow against the soft spot below her ear.

Her head tilts, giving my mouth unfettered access to the delicate column of her neck.

"Every inch of you." My hands find the break in the fabric between her tank top and the top band of her jeans. The coolness of her sweat-misted skin is almost more than I can bear.

My mouth seeks hers. When she whimpers at the kiss, I press against her more.

"Dana is going to catch us," she pants against my swollen lips.

I grin and close my mouth over hers again. The world could implode around us, and it still wouldn't be enough to pull me away from her.

As much as I hate it, the soft push against my chest by her small hands is enough to make me back away. I want this girl more than anything on this earth, but she's calling the shots. If things are too heavy for her, if she's pumping the brakes, all I can do is wait until she's ready for everything I want to give her.

And I want to give Delilah Donovan the world.

"It's time to go home." Her breathless warning skates across my mouth, drawing my eyes to the pink of her lips.

I take a step back, my hand reaching up to cup her at the nape.

"Would you throw me out if I snuck into your room tonight?"

I see the war in her eyes as if she wants me there but being able to resist her temptations isn't something she can handle. Her gaze drops to my chin and I miss the gorgeous beauty of her eyes the second they fall away.

"I'll never push you, never pressure you. I'll never expect more than you're willing to give me."

She takes a step back, her back meeting with the rough wood of the outdoor supply building. "My head doesn't work like normal when I'm around you."

"Likewise, Princess." I clasp her hand in mine, uncaring of who sees us walking together to her car.

She's not some dirty secret, some fling I don't want to be questioned about in case things don't work out. She doesn't seem to mind either and only releases my hand long enough to climb behind the driver's seat. Our hands are joined once more after we settle inside and get our seatbelts in place.

"Are you excited about working in the shop this afternoon?"

"More than I probably should be."

"I heard Scooter and Rocker talking about you the other day."

"Really?" I frown. Showing Scooter up with the bike tire my first day here probably didn't make me a friend in his eyes. "I bet they hate me."

She shakes her head and uses our joined hands to put the car in drive. "They were impressed. I know Diego is impressed with your skill level. He wouldn't allow you in the shop if he didn't think you could handle it."

"The vote of confidence is a huge ego boost. I still have lots to learn," I add.

"Make sure you talk to Dad about mechanic school. He knows people all over, and I know he'd love to get you hooked up with someone to make your dreams come true."

"We'll see," I tell her with non-committal wariness.

If only for being the catalyst to meet Delilah, I feel like I owe him everything. I don't know how much more I can give the man without handing over my soul.

Chapter 20

Delilah

"You're hiding," my brother says after the quick knock on my door and enters without me answering.

"You could wait for me to invite you in," I scold as he walks up and sits on the end of my bed.

I shouldn't be snippy with him, but it's the only way to get out my agitation that it's Samson and not Lawson coming in here.

"I feel like we haven't talked in forever." Falling to his back on my bed, he stares up at the ceiling.

I put my novel on my bedside table, shift my body, and lie down beside him.

"We won't ever see each other in a week after football practice starts," I tell him.

He sighs. "I don't even know if I'm going to play this year."

I shake my head, confused. "You've played every year since you were five, Samson. Of course, you're going to play your senior year."

"Kennedy thinks it's dumb."

"Kennedy is dumb for thinking that." I pause when he stiffens beside me. "Okay, maybe she isn't dumb for thinking it, but she sure as hell shouldn't try to change you."

He grunts but doesn't reply.

"So," I begin. "About Rachel."

"What about her?" He doesn't pull his eyes from the ceiling, staring as if it holds the answers to the universe.

"You've switched your focus." Not a question. It's obvious now with his attention on Kennedy. "Does that mean you're not upset with Lawson anymore?"

He grunts again, and I wait in silence, knowing he'll respond if I fill the room with awkward silence. The wait isn't long, and I hate that because it means he's still fired up about Lawson's mistake in the kitchen last week.

"It's like he's purposely trying to destroy us."

"I don't see things that way," I defend.

"Well, you're obsessed with him, so I wouldn't expect you to be on my side."

I recoil at his view of the situation. "I'm not obsessed with him." I totally am, but not for the reasons he thinks. "He made a mistake."

I'm hesitant to explain to him the man I know, the man that Lawson is around me when no one else is around, but with the attitude my brother is tossing my way I know the outcome won't be him understanding but using my feelings for Lawson against me. Samson has such strong opinions about the situation, there's no way to change his mind.

"He's a calculating asshole," he mutters. "And you're all cozy with him."

"He has community service to finish," I explain. "Dad set that up, not me."

"You didn't object."

"Do I ever object to anything Dad tells me to do?"

Another grunt.

"He's not a bad guy. He's done what Dad told him to do and is staying away from Rachel."

His eyes close, the corners crinkling with agitation.

"Only because the damage has been done."

No, because he never wanted her and his fixation is on a different blonde-haired girl.

"What's he got planned next?" he asks. "Is he going to start sneaking in here, trying to fuck you, too?"

I stiffen beside him, my body responding to his words before I can stop it.

"What?" He turns his head in my direction. "Has he already started?"

"No," I answer with incredulity. "Don't be ridiculous."

My voice breaks, causing his eyes to narrow. He can always tell when I'm lying.

"What aren't you telling me?"

"There's nothing to tell," I lie. "We don't even talk. We go separate ways at the animal shelter. He cleans up shit, and I walk dogs and play with the cats. Besides, his last day was today."

I'm going to miss our time together, but he'd mentioned still going to the animal shelter to help a few days a week. Dana likes having some muscle around for the heavy lifting. I love watching his muscles bunch under his t-shirt, and I lose my breath when he gets so hot he pulls it off to wipe sweat from his face. My cheeks flush, but I refuse to look away from Samson.

He studies my face, and his scrutiny makes tears burn the backs of my eyes. I'm upset that he would hate me if he knew about the private moments Lawson and I shared. I'm hurt that the feelings I have for him have to be kept secret. I hate that I can't profess how I feel and have everyone around me be happy.

"You'd tell me if he tried anything, right?"

"Of course." Another lie. "He won't though. He seems pretty focused on getting done with probation and maybe going to school to be a mechanic."

I realize my mistake the second the words are out of my mouth.

"Don't talk, huh?"

I shrug. "I mean. Sometimes we chat to and from the shelter, but nothing like what you're thinking."

He turns his eyes back toward the ceiling. I know he knows I'm lying, but it's still not enough to lay it all out and confess the things I so desperately want him to hear and be okay with hearing.

"I texted Rachel," he says after several long minutes.

"Since the party?"

"Yeah. She told me she doesn't date boys." I watch him as his left eye twitches. "She implied that Lawson was a man and she didn't have time to waste on me."

"That's Rachel's hang-up. I don't think it's an honest reflection of who you are."

"He's only two years older than us," he spits. "And he's a fucking criminal."

"Hey," I chide. "That's not fair. He did what he thought was best while taking care of Drew while his mom partied all the time. She didn't care that she was supposed to be raising two boys. He had to be the man of the house, and that led to some decisions he now regrets. He didn't see any other way out."

Samson's huff as he gets off of the bed makes my skin crawl.

"Sure do know a lot from just chatting."

I flinch when the door slams shut behind him. Calming breaths don't help to ease the tremble in my fingers. I wish I had a Magic 8 Ball. Looking into my future, knowing how Dad and Pop would respond to the news of what Lawson and I are building, would be amazing. Living in fear that Samson will say something, and they hate me for it is my worst nightmare.

I need someone to talk to, but confiding in Ivy is tricky when Gigi seems to find out everything we say. I know being honest is best, but the fallout could be monumental, disastrous even. Dad and Pop could insist we stop, which would be impossible. They'd know how hard it would be and could make him leave. Distance from him is the last thing I want. Being separated from Drew isn't an option, and I could never put myself between Lawson and his brother.

"It's just a stupid crush," I mumble to myself.

The tears rolling down my cheeks tell a different story.

He's forbidden, so that makes him more appealing.

I can stop what we've been doing. Lie.

I can go back to ignoring him, wanting him in private without him even knowing I'm hurting to touch him. Lie.

I can get over him as quickly as I became attracted to him. Lie

Destroying my family is worth my temporary happiness. I waver on this one. I'm not a martyr, but the pain I could potentially cause those I care for isn't something I can handle as easily as suffering in silence.

Determined, mind made up, I head downstairs.

"Hey, sweetheart," Dad says with a quick kiss on my forehead.

I fall unceremoniously into a chair at the breakfast table.

"What's wrong?" he asks as he pulls the lid from the saucepan and stirs its contents.

"Not feeling so well."

Seeing Lawson today while my decision is so fresh will only have me doubting it. I have to create distance between us, even if it means pretending to be sick and missing supper. My stomach growls at the thought, and the amazing aroma of alfredo sauce only makes it worse.

"Hungry?"

"No. I can't even think about eating."

"About to start? You always get like this around that time."

I groan. "Seriously, Dad? I'm not talking to you about my cycle."

He shrugs.

I want to tell him. The words are right on the tip of my tongue, but a cheer from Drew as he plays Xbox makes my mouth snap shut.

"I think I'm going to skip dinner and go to bed early."

He replaces the lid and drops the spatula on the spoon rest. He walks across the room, his warm lips meeting my forehead. I nearly cave again.

"You don't feel warm."

He pulls back, studying my face with hands cupped on both cheeks.

"I think I got too hot at the shelter today. New Mexico summers suck."

He releases me, believing my lies and takes a step back.

"Well you only have one more, then you have the choice of whether you want to stay in Rhode Island or come home to visit."

The reminder about college helps. It keeps me focused, and forces me to focus on the light at the end of the tunnel. A couple of kisses and a few kind words isn't enough to take the chance of ruining a family.

I don't feel like what Lawson and I are feeling for each other is wrong, but my opinions aren't the only ones to consider.

"Get some rest, sweetheart." He heads back to the cabinet to pull out pasta. "Maybe consider missing tomorrow at the shelter."

"Night, Dad."

I head up the stairs, thankful I have a few snacks up there. Maybe once everyone is asleep, I'll sneak down and grab some leftovers.

Avoiding Lawson may be easier than I thought. I lock my bedroom door behind me and settle in for a long, boring night alone.

Chapter 21

Lawson

"Damn, you're quick."

I find myself at ease with Jaxon's fatherly clap on my shoulder.

"Quick?" Diego snorts from the other side of the garage. "The boy's a natural around these machines."

"He sure as hell didn't leave much work for tomorrow," Shadow adds.

I frown. Knowing I need more work to pay Jaxon back, but going slow just for the sake of wasting time isn't something I'll do either.

"There's plenty more where that came from," Diego says with a nod before walking out of the garage.

"Not easy to impress Prez," Shadow says with a quick nod before heading out of the garage.

"Not easy to impress Shadow either," Jaxon says in a low voice. "Finished up community service this morning. GED test is taken and passed. Fees are paid. You're finished."

"Not yet," I mutter, sure there are still hoops to jump through.

"Sign this," he says pulling a small stack of rolled paper from his back pocket.

I look down, recognizing the probation discharge from Navajo County. The PO back in Texas had shown it to me when I was first placed at the boot camp.

"Your light at the end of the tunnel," he'd told me. "Something to work toward."

I take the pen he offers. "I'll FedEx it to them, and they'll send official copies signed by the judge no later than two weeks from now."

I sign and hand it back to him. He signs it and puts it back in his pocket.

"Relieved?" He slaps me on the back again.

"More than you could ever know," I confess.

He shakes his head. "I know exactly how it feels to cut those kinds of chains off."

I tilt my head, but he just smiles and walks away. Juvenile probation? Maybe we're more alike than I want to admit.

"Oh, I forgot," he says sticking his head back around the door. "Dinner is in an hour. Be quiet when you head up, Delilah isn't feeling well, so she's napping."

I nod but rush to the house. She didn't mention feeling unwell earlier. I couldn't keep my mouth off of her today at the animal shelter, and I feel fine.

Jaxon is already back in the house talking to Rob in the kitchen. Bolting up the stairs, I find her door locked. My light tap goes unanswered, so I decide to take a shower. If she's sick, I want to hold her, but ruining her sheets with grease stains won't go over very well.

By the time I get out of the shower, I'm met with glares from Samson in the hallway. He may be messing around with Kennedy now, but the sting of rejection from Rachel will hurt for a while.

"You need to stay the fuck away from my sister," he seethes but doesn't push himself away from the wall and into my path.

I huff, annoyed, but not wanting to engage with him. I have other plans for my evening, and it doesn't include beating his ass. That would put a damper on my life here.

"I don't need some boy telling me what to do." I walk past him toward my bedroom. The former softness of my towel becomes a harsh scrape on my head as I do my best to calm down. Backing down from confrontation isn't easy for me.

"I'm a fucking man." I snort and continue to my room, but think better of walking away without saying my piece.

"If you're a man then that makes Delilah a woman."

He shakes his head.

"So that means," I continue. "That she can make her own decisions."

I hear his fist slam against the wall as I close myself in my bedroom. A sense of calming relief washes over me from all but admitting that there's something building between Samson's twin and me. I want everyone to know, but she hasn't mentioned bringing our feelings to light. I have to defer to her in this situation because she knows her family better than I do. I'm ready when she's ready.

Samson is gone from the hall when I step out. Delilah's door is still locked, but the sun is just now going down. Even a locked bedroom door isn't going to keep me from comforting her while she's ill.

I head downstairs, just in time to see everyone sitting down at the table for dinner. Jaxon may be a hardened biker covered from head to toe in tattoos, but he's the best fucking cook I've ever encountered.

"Chicken alfredo," Drew says with a lopsided grin. "Your favorite."

I smile wide, ignoring the glare from Samson on the other side of the table. "Looks great."

Jaxon nods, the delight of my praise is barely hidden behind his eyes.

"Where's D?" Rob asks with a smacking kiss on Jaxon's forehead before he sits down.

"Not feeling well," Jaxon answers, handing the salad bowl to Drew.

"That time of the month? She always gets like this." Rob looks at his husband for verification.

Drew and Samson groan at the female issue conversation. "Really, Pop? At the dinner table?"

"It's a fact of life, Sam. Pass the chicken?"

I hand Rob the platter of juicy chicken breasts, doing my best to keep my eyes from the stairs leading up to the girl I'm obsessed over. Girl problems are something I have no issue with. Mom always needed painkillers and the heating pad, so this is definitely something in my wheelhouse.

I rush through dinner, drawing glances from both Jaxon and Rob. The food is delicious, but my concentration is elsewhere.

I mention being tired from a full day at the shelter and in the shop, and Rob excuses me from the table without an issue.

Longingly, I eye Delilah's door before closing myself in my own empty bedroom. I hate that I have to wait what will end up being hours for everyone to be asleep. Drew may suspect that Delilah and I have been sneaking around, but I won't confirm his suspicions by blatantly going to her while the sun is still up.

I shoot off numerous texts, but they go unread. She's more than likely asleep, resting like her dads said she was.

Head hung low, Drew walks into the room, phone in hand.

"What's wrong?" I sit up from my nap on my bottom bunk.

He shakes his head, clearing his throat but doesn't speak. He strips out of his jeans and t-shirt and crawls up into his bed.

I wait him out, but the time ticks slowly. My mind races with things that can cause his normally carefree personality to act like he's just watched his puppy get run over on the highway.

"I fucked up," he finally admits.

"You're fifteen. How bad can it be?"

"I sent a message to Aunt Kathy."

"Your dad's sister on the East Coast?" My brows draw together. He never has wanted anything to do with them.

"Yeah." His voice is shaky, and I can tell he's on the verge of tears.

I want to get out of bed and reach for him, but he's just as stubborn as I am. Doing that will make him lockdown, and we'll never get to the source of his pain.

"I just wanted to let her know about Mom. I know they hate her—"

"They never hated her," I cajole. "They were angry about Carl and how she allowed him to treat her."

He clears his throat again, but this time I can tell he's crying.

"Just get it out," I urge.

"She wants me to move in with her and Uncle Pete."

I shake my head. "No way," I hiss. "You don't have to go if you don't want to."

"They're my family." I despise the resigned tone of his voice.

"I'm your family," I spit.

"I'm a minor. I don't want to go. I love it here."

The girl I'm falling in love with is here.

"But they're blood, and Jaxon and Rob aren't related to me."

"Did they threaten you?"

"No," he defends. "I want to be near my family. You have yours now, and I w-want that, too."

Deep breath in, slow breath out.

"I don't want to keep you from your family," I admit. "I'll just have to come with you."

"You will?" I hear the relief in his voice.

"I go where you go."

Can a heart actually break, tear apart and die inside of your chest? With a rough palm, I rub my hand over the aching part in my soul. It does nothing to alleviate the burn that's starting to build.

"Your dad is here."

"My brother will be there. You're my responsibility no matter the sacrifice for me."

The quiet crying begins anew. Squeezing my eyes shut, I let him cry for both of us.

My fists clench at hearing his anguish, but at the same time I'm pissed that the second my life begins to look up, it's turning completely upside down again.

"When will they be here?"

There has to be time. Time for Delilah and I to plan; time for me to assure her that things will be okay between us.

"School starts next week in Fall River."

No.

"They'll be here tomorrow."

Shattered. Broken. Left for purgatory.

It's not enough time to assure her that things will work out.

Long distance relationships aren't that bad my mind says in an attempt to convince me. We can make it work. She'll wait for me if I ask.

How the fuck can I ask her that? How can I demand she put her life on hold for me?

The answer is simple.

I can't.

Chapter 22

Delilah

Five seconds is all I give the heat of his body to soak into mine.

"You shouldn't be in here," I warn.

"Jaxon said you weren't feeling well."

"I'm fine," I lie. Well, I'm not sick in the traditional sense.

"I wanted to hold you," he confesses with a desperation that sends chills over my skin. "Make you feel better."

"I'm fine," I repeat. Maybe saying it over and over will convince my own mind.

"So you said," he mutters with a quick kiss on my shoulder before he pulls at my shoulder until I'm flat on my back.

"You shouldn't be in here."

"You said that, too."

His lips hover over mine, an endless pause before he presses his mouth to mine. It's then that I feel the tremble in his body. Anger? Need? I'm not experienced enough to differentiate.

My groan of resistance transforms into a moan of arousal as his lips continue their coaxing and his hard length presses against my hip. My neck flexes, reaching for him when he pulls back.

"You're the best thing that's ever happened to me," he whispers before taking my mouth again.

Soft pecks turn into aggressive licks of his tongue. Floating above it all, I somehow feel overwhelmed with sensation and completely separate from it at the same time.

He ignores the tremor in my hands as they find the over-heated skin of his chest. Fingers flexing against his pecs, I dig in to keep my hands from roaming lower, which my brain is telling me is the right thing to do. Never in this position before in my life, and instinct is trying to drive me to the next step.

Will my heart survive taking what we have one step further, only to slam on the brakes the second that it's done?

I fear that it won't, but living my life without sharing this with him seems like an even more unmanageable burden.

"Touch me," I beg.

"Delilah," he pants pulling his mouth from the delicate skin on my neck. "That's too much."

"It's not," I promise.

"I can't," he hisses and backs off of the bed.

For a long moment, I stare up at him, his chest heaving as if he is running from demons I can't see.

I slink out of bed. One thing he may never learn about me is that rejection hurts more than a physical blow.

Growing bold even though I know it's a risk, I reach for him, my hand hovering over the elastic band of his sweats.

With eyes clenched as tight as his hands, he turns his head up to the ceiling, as if he's warring with his restraint.

With the slightest movement, the palm of my hand brushes against his erection. It increases in size as if it senses me and is seeking out my embrace.

"Law," I whisper against the column of his neck. "Touch me."

His eyes find mine, his throat working on a thick swallow.

Resolve and something sinister fills his icy-blue eyes. I don't even try to fight the heat it causes low in my belly. No matter the will he was trying to keep alive, the resistance he was holding on to, my need, my own form of manipulation has worked.

"You need me, Princess?"

"Touch me," I repeat for the third time, embarrassment marking my cheeks at my inability to tell him everything I want from him.

"Turn around," he commands.

The soft fabric of my pajama shorts abrades my skin as I shift on my feet. It's too heavy, too thick, and restrictive to what my body is demanding.

I reach for the waist of my shorts as his feverish skin presses to my back.

"Stop," he pants in my ear.

My body obeys before my mind has the chance to catch up.

"Where do you want to be touched?" I hate the calmness in his hands as they both grip my waist.

"Everywhere," I moan with a quick shift on my feet.

"Here?" he asks as one rough thumb sweeps over the tightened bud on my left breast. "Or here?"

My knees nearly give out when his right hand finds my center with a skilled precision I choose not to consider in fear it would ruin this moment.

"Oh God," I breathe. "Yes."

"Filthy slut."

I stiffen in his arms, but it only lasts a second as both hands toy with areas only I've ever touched before.

I'm dizzy from lack of oxygen by the time his right hand runs up my hip and then lowers inside of my shorts and panties this time.

"So wet for me, dirty girl."

Dirty girl is better than slut, I guess.

Before the unease can settle, his fingers spread me, thumb searching for the spot that has never needed something as much as it does right now.

He presses harder against me, hissing in my ear at the friction against his own body. I squirm, unsure of what to do, but blissfully aware of the contact on my clit.

"I bet it'll only take one finger to get this perfect little pussy off."

"Oh God." I quiver, shake, and become putty in his hands.

The slow, teasing circles of his thumb is the best torture, the thing my body recognizes as essential for survival.

"Jesus," he mutters against my hand. "Come for me."

"For you," I pant as my body shudders in a release that nearly destroys me.

He pulls his hand away long before the tiny quivering comes to a full stop. "Turn around." I obey. "Knees."

With the hand that was on my breast, he pushes his sweats down. His other hand, glistening with my arousal strokes the length of his erection.

"Lick it clean."

I want to refuse, insist that he not speak to me the way he is, but my mouth waters at the prospect of tasting him, of tasting me.

He takes a step forward, resting the blunt head of his penis against my lips. I swipe at the pre-cum on the tip with my tongue, my senses flaming to life at our combined tastes.

I lick again, hungry for more. My hands find his powerful thighs as his free hand fists my hair. The small bite of pain, the same as the night we first kissed in here, stokes the fire that was already burning from my orgasm.

"Open wide," he commands, his voice growing unsteady. "Take it all."

He presses in, and my throat constricts immediately at the foreign intrusion. Gagging, I pull my head back. Surprisingly, he allows me to take a deep breath before he pushes in slower.

I look up, hoping to find pleasure in his eyes, but they stare back at me, empty and shuttered. He's not even here right now. He's lost in his thoughts, somewhere other than in this monumental moment with me. The tingle of awareness that I'd pushed down earlier at his horrible words begins to travel to my brain, pushing away the desire to please him.

"I told you you'd have those pretty pink lips wrapped around my cock."

I rip away, the haze of need doused as if I'd been thrown into the Antarctic.

"What is wrong with you?" I sputter wiping the back of my hand over my mouth.

"Don't stop now, Princess. We were just getting started."

"Was this your plan all along? Get me to fall for you just so you can get me on my knees."

Doubt tugs at the corner of his eyes before he shelters it and sneers at me.

"I can fuck your mouth while you lie on the bed if it's easier."

I shake my head, the slickness between my legs growing cold and becoming too much to ignore. I feel dirty and wrong and used. None of the things I'd anticipated feeling after getting to know him these last couple of weeks.

"You need to leave." The resilience I feel in my bones doesn't translate as strength in my voice.

With arms wrapped around my waist, I step back until my thighs hit the mattress. My body is near convulsing as I watch him swallow. His fingers twitch as if they're going to reach out for me, but I stiffen, and he backs down. I'm confused and my heart, which I'd planned on breaking myself soon, has now been ripped out by a guy that only paid attention to me to manipulate me into this exact situation.

He turns to leave, and I expect him to open and slam the door behind him. When he turns and the light of the moon catches on a single tear on his cheek, I've never felt more confusion before in my life.

"Have a nice life," he says with a trembling voice. "Hating me has always been what's best for you."

My door closes with a soft click, the tiny noise echoing in my skull.

The shaking continues even as I bury myself under the covers on my bed. The house alarm goes off, ringing loudly for all to hear, and then the front door slams.

Chapter 23

Lawson

The alarm blaring at my back has nothing on the sirens ringing in my head. The warmth of the New Mexico night only serves to irritate my already over-heated skin.

Fighting the insistent demands to go back to her, to apologize and find some way to make us work with me all the way across the country causes a stutter in my steps. I fight the urge, knowing that walking away right now is best for both of us.

The shop, the mechanics of machines with their structured uses, pulls me away from the house. I need the consistency, the perfect way they fit together, and if done right, work in sync with each other. Motorcycles and cars make sense. Loving a girl I could never ask to sacrifice a damn thing for my unworthy ass is a complication I can't focus on right now.

Laughter meets my ears, but my feet keep on moving. Being under the scrutiny of the Cerberus MC guys is the last thing I want, but the draw to get my hands dirty, to work on something I can fix is stronger.

Scooter, Rocker, and Kid all sit around a small table, beers and cards in their hands as they joke about their stupid perfect lives.

"Hey, Lawson," Rocker says angling his beer at me in salute.

A nod is all I'm able to manage as Kid looks at me, reading me like a book.

"Guys." The rough voice at my back causes the same tension in my muscles as it did the first time I showed up on the clubhouse steps.

They look behind me and move to leave the garage without one word of rebuttal. Kid slaps my shoulder, but I stand my ground, not shying away from the sympathy in his eyes.

I know how they see me. I'm just some fucked up kid with a chip on my shoulder, getting pissed off over the simplest things. I don't acknowledge the fact that my heart is being torn in two to the point that breathing is difficult.

"Sorry about the alarm," I mutter as I pull out some tools and sit on the ground beside an old project bike Shadow and I have been working on.

"No big deal," Jaxon says as he pulls up a chair and sits down beside me. "Want to tell me why you stormed out of the house?"

I treated your perfect daughter like shit while she had my cock in her mouth.

I resist the urge to draw my hand to my nose before losing her delicate scent to oil and dirt on the bike.

"Drew contacted his family."

He remains silent, and I'd give anything to be in his head right now. Does he know what's coming? Is he glad we'll be out of his hair tomorrow?

As much as I want to hate him, I let hope flicker that he'll be upset to watch me leave.

"They're coming tomorrow to get him."

He clears his throat.

"I'm going with him."

He shuffles his feet.

"How do you feel about that?"

I sigh feeling as if I need a couch to stretch out on while he plays one of the many therapists probation tried to get me to connect with.

"I can't let him go on his own," I reason.

"Are they bad people? I can put an end to it."

I shake my head. "That's his family. They're good people. His dad was a piece of shit, but luckily he was the black sheep of the family."

"But you don't want to go?"

I shake my head. "I'd gotten it in my head that I was going to be here for a while."

"You can stay as long as you like, but I understand needing to make sure your brother is okay." He shifts again, the chair legs scraping across the concrete floor. "He's been your responsibility for a long time."

"You don't give up on family." I stare down at my hands agitated from the night's events but relieved to be getting all this shit off of my chest.

"And that's why I'll never give up on you." His words hit home.

Looking up into eyes that are the perfect reflection of mine if only with a little more creasing at the edges, I see the truth in his words.

"Delilah hates me," I confess without going into any detail.

"Delilah isn't the type of girl that hates anyone."

I shake my head trying to erase the pain I saw in her eyes when I walked away from her.

"She may be angry," he continues. "She may think she hates you now, but she'll be fine."

The sad downward turn of his lips are reflective of him knowing more information than what I've spilled tonight, but I don't elaborate.

"Where is Drew's family from?"

"Massachusetts."

His lip twitches, eyes growing brighter as if I've said something that pleases him.

He stands and claps me on the shoulder. "I get a feeling that things are going to work out just fine."

I clear my throat as he walks toward the door.

"T-thanks," I stammer, the words unfamiliar in my mouth. "Thanks for everything you've done for me."

He turns, a full smile on his tattooed face. "You're more than welcome, son."

He leaves, the sound of his boots on gravel a comforting sound I know I'll miss.

"Well?" he says returning and startling me to the point I drop the wrench I was holding.

"What?"

"Come to the house with me. I have some things to show you."

***

"Hey."

I come awake in the desk chair with a rough shove to my shoulder.

"What's up?" I ask Drew as he looks down at me. "Are they here already?"

He shakes his head. "Not yet. Jaxon and Rob wanted us to have breakfast with them before we leave."

I rub tired eyes, only having gotten a couple of hours of sleep last night.

"I'm up," I tell him and stand from the chair. "You head down, and I'll be there in a few minutes."

"I went ahead and packed for you." He points to the duffel bag that is bulging compared to when I first brought it up to this room.

"Thanks, man. Give me a few minutes."

All I can think about is getting to Delilah. I have to apologize. I have to make her understand that last night wasn't even close to a true reflection of my feelings.

I wait, antsy and trembling, for Drew to make his way downstairs before heading to Delilah's room. If I know her like I think I do, she'll be holed up in her room, avoiding the sight of me.

My gentle knock goes unanswered, but there's no way I'm leaving today without her understanding what she means to me.

I push open her door, surprised I don't have to pick the lock like I did last night to get to her. The room is empty, bed made and no sounds coming from the bathroom. The dock where she charges her cell is empty, but I check the bathroom anyway.

My shoulders sag as I close her door behind me, hating that I'm going to have to sit across from her glaring eyes at breakfast without explaining.

Only, when I make my way into the dining room, she's not there either. A quick look into the kitchen remains unfruitful as well.

I look at Jaxon, at the head of the table as he passes a tray of bacon and sausage to Drew.

"Delilah went in early to the animal shelter," he explains.

A knot forms in my gut, but the satisfied look on Samson's face has me taking my seat rather than insisting on keys to a car to go to her. I want to blame him, blame anyone for this change of events.

Jaxon doesn't mention the lengthy conversation we had after returning to the house last night, so neither do I. The dining room fills with laughter and talk of Drew's plans when we get to Massachusetts. Drew has always been one to roll with the punches, and I hope he remains happy and unaffected by the bad shit we've dealt with in our lives. I've protected him from almost everything in my power that could harm him, and I'll continue to do it even though I'm shattered myself.

It's not long after breakfast that the doorbell echoes through the house. A quiet, sad calm washes over the household as Jaxon opens the front door. Drew's Aunt Kathy searches the room, her eyes landing on me first with a quiet nod before coming to life at the sight of Drew on the couch.

He shoots up, and they embrace. It's not until that very moment that I realize just how much Drew has needed more than just me. Tears are on his face as Kathy pulls back to cup his cheeks in her hands. The pain at losing our mother is clear in his wet eyes as he nods softly at something she whispers to him.

"Don't forget what we talked about last night." Jaxon is only a few inches from me, talking low enough that only I can hear him.

"I won't." I turn to face him, both loving and hating the anguish in his eyes.

"I'm always here. Anything you need, even if it's just to talk."

"Del—"

"She'll be fine," he assures me. "Become the type of man she could never hate."

I don't even stiffen when his tattooed arms draw me in for a hug. The embrace lasts longer than one I've ever had, and I let his pride in me seep into my bones. I'm going to need every ounce of strength I can muster to walk away from her and leave the ball in her court.

Chapter 24

Delilah

"Where's Lawson?"

I tense at Dana's question as I get the last two dogs back in their kennels from our walk.

"Probably working in the shop."

I have no idea where he is. A million miles away would be best.

"Something on your mind?"

I've always spoken to Dana, told her about the things bothering me. I've used her more than once as a shoulder to cry on when something upset me at school. I've confided in her my frustration of not having a mother. I love my dads, but there are just some things, as men, they'll never understand.

As her question sinks in, I know this isn't a door I'm opening between us. Lawson said he still plans to work here, but that may be off the table now since his true colors shined through bright and blinding last night.

"Nope." I lock the kennel and begin to coil the leashes as I make my way to the supply closet. "Anything else you need before I leave?"

When I face her, she tilts her head to the side. She's not an idiot, so I know she can tell something is bothering me. What she isn't is a nag, so she won't hound me to tell her what's bothering me.

"Not a thing," she says with a quick smile. "You've put in ten hours today."

I nod and walk past her.

"See you on Monday."

"Drive safe," she says to my back as I make my way out to the parking lot.

The smell of Lawson's lingering cologne assaults me when I climb in the car, so I crank the AC to full blast and roll down the windows. All the way home, I pray that the car is aired out enough that I never have to smell him near me again. It also reminds me to wash my sheets. I fell prey to the beautiful scent last night as I cried into my pillow, but today is a new day.

He only acted that way as a defense mechanism. He's done it almost every day since he showed up.

To get the voices trying to convince me to forgive him out of my head, I crank the radio up and tap my fingers on the steering wheel. I ignore the fact that people are staring at me at the red light. I can't be the first person to ride around with the windows down and radio blaring as a distraction.

I turn the music off as I pull through the front gate in front of the clubhouse, parking in the main lot rather than driving around to the back. If I need to leave quickly, it's faster to go from here than navigating the narrow driveway on the back of the house.

No talking or laughing is coming from the shop. Not one person is in sight when I make my way around the clubhouse and toward my front door.

"Hey."

Ivy. As much as I love her, being alone is the only thing on my mind right now.

"Hey," I say turning toward her front porch where she sits with a book in her lap.

"Only a week before school starts. Are you ready?" Her eyes are wide and bright even though there's a light sheen of sweat on her forehead. The fan above the porch swing is working overtime to no avail.

"As ready as I'll ever be." I sit beside her, realizing this conversation will postpone the inevitable argument with Lawson once I get to my house.

"The birthday party was pretty epic. I'm sure your popularity will be at an all-time high."

I raise an eyebrow at her. "You sound more like Gigi than the girl I know."

She shrugs. "It's just our senior year, you know? I love my life and my small group of friends, but at the same time I'm a little jealous of the attention Gigi gets from all the guys."

"You want the attention Gigi gets from *Griffin*, you mean."

"Exactly like you beam anytime Lawson looks at you."

"Nope," I say without delay. "There's nothing between Lawson and me. I doubt we'll ever speak again."

"What happened?" she asks on a whisper.

I look away, begging the tears burning the backs of my eyes to stay put.

"His true colors coming to light is what happened." I sniffle, the action pissing me off because I swore to myself after last night I'd never shed another tear at thoughts of him.

"As in?"

I ignore her question for as long as I can, but she's relentless.

"I'm your best friend, D. You can tell me anything."

So I do. I lay out the last couple of weeks right at her feet. By the time I'm finished, and the sun is setting, shooting pinks and oranges across the sky, Ivy hates Lawson O'Neil as much as I do.

The air is thick, filled with unease, as I open my door and close it behind me. The familiar sound of Drew and Samson playing video games is oddly absent.

"Hey, sweetheart," Pop says walking out of the kitchen drying his hands on a dish towel.

"Where is everyone?"

His face softens as his eyes fill with a sadness that's peculiar on his generally happy face.

"Sam, Gigi, Sophia, and Jasmine are down at the pool." The hesitation in his voice is clear as day.

"And Drew?"

He shakes his head and clears his throat.

"Drew's family from the east coast showed up to get him today."

Confused, I just stare at him.

"Lawson went with them."

The second it seeps in that he's gone, all of the anger I'd had for him disappears.

"W-where?"

"Massachusetts."

"That's all the way on the other side of the country." I shake my head. "They didn't have a family. Darby died, and Drew's father's in prison."

"It's his dad's sister that showed up."

I swallow past the dryness in my throat and pull my eyes from his.

"Okay." What else could I possibly say?

"I know you'll miss them, but you'll still be able to see them."

I shake my head again, the almost violent action causing my temples to throb. "No, this is for the best."

He reaches for me, but I back away.

"I'm filthy. I'm going to go grab a quick shower before dinner."

Without another word, I hit the stairs, making sure to keep my eyes focused on my door rather than looking into their empty room as I walk past.

I strip my bed, strip out of my clothes, and climb into the shower long before the water warms. I blame the frigid water rolling down my spine as the cause of my shivering. I convince myself that I don't need him, that I have my whole life ahead of me and he'll do nothing but drag me down.

What I don't realize while I tremble in that shower is that I'll spend two years building up walls against my feelings for Lawson, only for him to come crashing back into my life as if he never even left.

Chapter 25

Delilah

2 YEARS LATER

"Are you going to call him?" Ivy looks hopeful sitting across from me at the restaurant.

I shrug. "Of course not."

"Really?" She looks confused, but she should know how I am by now. "He was crazy hot. Popular. Muscles for days."

"They all are." I wink at her, and she only sinks lower in her seat.

"Don't do that," she mutters.

Refusing to look at her, knowing what's coming, I give all my attention to the straw between my fingers. Stirring my already flat soda is better than facing the best friend that knows me too well.

"You can act flippant right now all you want. You can put on this carefree brave face for everyone else, but keep in mind I hear you crying through the walls when they drop you off."

"It's my life," I argue. "I can do what and who I want."

"Until it involves someone else who loves you." She pauses, letting that sink in. "Until you get pregnant or end up with an STD."

I glare at her. "I'm on birth control, and I use protection every time."

"And you go to parties without a friend."

"You won't go with me." She hasn't changed much since high school, opting to stay closer to home than get involved in any outrageous campus activities.

"You risk the chance of getting drugged," she says without acknowledging my statement. "Getting raped."

"You sound like Dad." I hang my head even lower. I can't hide my true feelings, not even the hatred I have for who I've become.

"He sounds like a very intelligent man."

I chuckle. Leave it to her to throw out some hard truths and still make me laugh. I didn't start Brown University last year as a freshman with the intention of hooking up with guys that lead to nothing but one-night stands. I've had a few encounters but nothing like some of the girls around campus. What I'd wanted was to be different, to be free from the stereotype that I left behind in New Mexico. It took me the better part of a year to build up the courage to accept an invite to a college party, and after a few drinks, nearly everything sounds like a good idea.

"No more random guys," I vow.

"No more risky behaviors," she counters.

"One hundred percent studious and no life," I mutter. "Got it."

"Poor D. has to actually go to class so she doesn't lose her scholarship."

I grin at her. "You know as well as I do that my grades are great and my scholarship is in no danger."

She shakes her head. "What I know is that you started all of this wild behavior in May and it's only gotten worse as summer progressed. There's no telling what the semester will look like in two weeks if you don't shut it down now."

"True." I smile. "So stop the partying in two weeks when school starts?"

Her head twists back and forth in disbelief. Her finger stabs the table to emphasize her point. "I think you need to practice. Starting now."

"Buzz-kill."

"You have to be responsible." She pushes the ticket across the table. "Now's as good a time to start as any."

"Only because you paid yesterday," I concede as she excuses herself to the restroom.

The waitress takes the ticket along with my card on her next pass by the table. I spend the time looking around the restaurant. Dark, mysterious eyes across the room catch my attention. As if trained around good looking guys, my mouth tilts up in a seductive grin, and he looks away.

Total turn off.

Men who know what they want, who are insistent in their attraction to me is what gets my blood running. Shyness and men that need to be chased don't appeal to me in the slightest. After the waitress returns my card, I make a second sweep around the room. He makes eye contact again, only to duck away.

Nope done.

"Leave that poor boy alone," Ivy says walking back up to the table.

"He's not my type anyway," I tell her and stand from the booth.

I follow her through the front door toward my car.

"Wanna go do some shopping?"

"Not particularly," she murmurs.

"It's Saturday, two weeks before we start our sophomore year at college. Surely there's something you need," I urge.

"I need shampoo and a few more notebooks." She shrugs. Ivy is the easiest chick to please. Her obsession with spirals, pens, and stationery should be sad, but somehow it works for her.

"I'm not spending my Saturday at Wal-Mart," I insist.

I grin, and she grins back.

"Target," we say at the same time.

"Starbucks first," I say as I climb behind the wheel.

"You just drank an entire carafe inside," she reminds me. "You're going to end up with holes in your stomach lining."

"Judgmental much?" I say with a grin. "I didn't get home until early this morning. I need more caffeine."

I smile and focus on starting the car. It's the best I can do to try to get the hazy memories of last night's party out of my head.

Turning the key, absolutely nothing happens. The radio nor the AC kicks on, and there's no clicking.

"I told you," Ivy says looking out the window.

"Yeah, yeah," I mutter. "I'll call Dad."

I pull out my phone and unlock the screen.

"Call a tow truck. Jaxon is in New Mexico. There's not much he can do for us in Rhode Island."

"Hush," I hiss playfully as the phone begins to ring in my ear.

"Sweetheart," Dad answers in lieu of a hello.

"Hey, Dad. I have a problem."

"Don't tell me you spent all the money I sent last week."

I shake my head. "No. I've barely touched it. My car won't start."

"Did you check the battery? Is it out of gas?"

"It has gas, but check the battery? Seriously? I don't know crap about cars."

"I told you to trade it in last year."

I sigh. "'I told you so' doesn't exactly get me out of this parking lot."

He laughs. "Fair enough. I'll call a towing company, but you seriously need to get a new car."

"Tell her I'll send her some links later," Pop chimes in from the background. "There are a few dealerships in town that are running some great end of summer deals."

I narrow my eyes. "Don't you need to know where I am?"

I hear both of them laugh. "Sweetheart," Dad says. "I always know where you are."

"Creeper." I look over at Ivy who isn't surprised that my dads know our location even from thousands of miles away. "I bet you have a satellite on me."

"That's ridiculous. The White House turned down that request, but I do track your phone." He hangs up, and my mouth just drops open.

"Dad does the same with me," Ivy mutters. "Gigi got a new phone when she left last year. So he has no idea where she is. Drives him nuts."

I cringe at the idea that something could happen to me and they couldn't find me. Having grown up with the stories of horrors going on around the world, there's no way I'll insist on them pulling their "surveillance." Safety first, as I always heard growing up.

"Control freaks," I whisper but loud enough for Ivy to hear me. I push open my door to let some cooler air in. "I hope it doesn't take forever."

"I don't think they're control freaks."

I snort. "I wouldn't be surprised if they had microchips planted in Sam and me when we were adopted."

"Oh." Her eyes scrunch together. "I thought you knew about the chips."

I grin when she runs her hand behind her left ear, implying hers is planted there.

"I hope it's something simple. I'd rather not spend my day looking for a place to rent a car."

"You should just junk it and get something else."

I run my hand over the recently cracking dash. "I've had this car since I turned sixteen."

"And it was ten years old then. It's time for something newer."

Sighing, I look around the parking lot. I've heard it all before from everyone in my family. Many were surprised the old clunker actually made it across the country last summer.

"That was fast," Ivy says angling her head so she can see out of the side mirror better.

The side of a massive towing truck blocks my car at the rear bumper.

"What does that say?" I squint, but the reflection off the shiny metal door makes it impossible to read.

"Camel Towing?"

I laugh. "Yeah. Dad would definitely send something like that my way."

The height of the truck combined with my low to the ground car makes me unable to see the driver through his window. I don't have to wait long, as his door swings open.

"Nice," I say with genuine appreciation when the driver opens the door and his muscular legs and firm, jean-covered ass steps down from the truck.

I'm nearly drooling as I watch him face the truck again and reach in to grab a yellow reflective vest. The sliver of revealed skin on his back makes my mouth water.

"I think the 'no boys' rule is going to have to wait until Monday. This guy is just too sexy to pass up."

I step out of my car and turn in his direction. Seductive smile playing on my lips, I give it all I've got.

Shielding my eyes from the sun in an attempt to actually see his face I say, "You're my hero for coming to my rescue."

I hear him chuckle, throaty and low, and echoing low in my belly. "So does that make me your prince, Princess?"

Chapter 26

Lawson

There is not enough saliva in my mouth to keep my lips wet at the sight of Delilah Donovan. Two years have transformed the quiet, demure angel of my dreams into a sex kitten with a low riding top and lace shorts that make my mind wander immediately to lingerie that would look best on my bedroom floor.

"Oh shit," Ivy mutters as she climbs out of the passenger seat and notices me, but I can't even manage a glance in her direction.

The long tan legs that I remember vividly from her time around the pool seem to have lengthened. She's gorgeous, my memories not serving her justice at all.

"What the fuck are you doing here?" she spits, and the only thing I can do is grin.

She ignores the wind whipping her blonde hair around her face and glares at me. If I didn't know any better, I'd believe she truly hates me.

"If you ladies wait, I can pull the wrecker around the front and get the car loaded up."

She shakes her head and with stubborn defiance crosses her arms over her chest.

"I want someone different."

"I am someone different." Her eyes narrow at my declaration.

"Another wrecking service," she specifies, ignoring the implication of my words.

"Not gonna happen, Princess. Now go stand over on the sidewalk and let me work."

Ivy, having come around the trunk of the car to join her friend, tugs on her arm. She's reluctant at first, but eventually lets her friend guide her out of the way.

I make quick work of the disabled vehicle, and before long, I'm standing in front of her once again. This moment, being a long time coming, is one I savor. Ivy has a weird, yet happy, look on her face. Delilah? Well, if looks could kill, I'd be a pile of ash on the ground with the fiery daggers she's shooting my way.

"Your chariot awaits, Princess." I sweep my arm toward the open driver's door on the wrecker.

Ivy moves first, climbing in and scooting across the bench seat so she's against the passenger door. It puts Delilah where she belongs, right next to me where our thighs will be touching the entire way back to the shop. Man, am I thankful it's a twenty-five-minute drive.

"Not gonna happen, Lawson." She takes a step back rather than one closer to the truck. "I'll call an Uber."

"You're beautiful," I whisper and reach out to push some of her wild hair behind her ear. It only serves to anger her more.

When she slaps my hand away before I can make contact, I know it was the wrong move.

"Don't touch me, and keep your meaningless comments to yourself."

I shrug, the smile never leaving my face. She's going to be a tough one to get on my side. "Just telling the truth."

She takes another step back. "I experienced your true character two years ago. I want nothing to do with you."

For a split second, my mind races, wondering if this approach is the best way to go about trying to win her back.

"Oh, Princess, don't be like that."

"Don't 'Princess' me."

"Your dad told me to make sure you get home safely. I promised him I would. I don't break my promises. So." I scrub my hand over the light stubble on my chin. "You can get in the truck on your own, or I can carry you there."

Her eyes dart from me to the open door of the cab and back to me. It's as if she's evaluating if I'm serious and can't make up her mind.

"Personally, I hope you refuse. I've thought about getting my hands back on you for the last two years."

She huffs. "And my mouth around your cock, right?"

I stiffen as my past and bad decisions are tossed back in my face.

"We can talk about that right now if you like. I can explain my fucked up reasoning, the reasoning of a boy."

"You always said you were a man," she mocks in a lower voice.

"I said a lot of things while trying to protect myself." I take a step toward her, arms out, my intention to lift her over my shoulder clear. "I'm an open book now. You can ask anything you like, and I'll tell you anything you want to know, but I'd rather have that conversation in private and not on the damn sidewalk. Now make up your mind, Delilah."

She glares at me, tension in her cheeks and stubbornness in her jaw.

"Walk on your own or be carried?"

"Asshole," she mutters as she walks past me and climbs inside.

My hands clench as the need to help her up with a gentle push on her ass hits me in the chest. I think my greasy handprints on her amazing ass would be the best thing ever, but I have a feeling she wouldn't be receptive.

"No fucking way," she hisses and tries to climb back out.

Her body meets my chest as I climb in behind her and give her no room to escape.

"What's wrong? The seat's clean. You won't get anything on your clothes."

"Let me down. I'm not straddling your damn gear shift."

I press against her, a challenge. She can either sit down, or she can continue to grind against me. I'm fine either way.

"I think I like this even more," I whisper in her ear, my voice going hoarse when the scent of her lavender skin hits my nose.

She elbows me in the gut but sits down. At first, she tries to position both of her legs to Ivy's side of the seat, but then she splits them apart when she realizes it won't work. I notice Ivy trying to take up more room than necessary for her slight frame. I wink at her when my spitfire isn't looking. It's great to have someone on my side, because I know I have a very long damn road ahead of me, and I'll take all the help I can get.

I settle into my seat and shut the door. The intensity of her scent grows in the enclosed space. I do my best not to look like an idiot when I draw her into my lungs.

"Seatbelt, baby."

She bites her lip so hard I wait for the blood to run from her mouth, but she just looks ahead and uses her fingers to find the belt and click it in place. Safety first has always been her family's motto, and right now it works for me. No matter how upset she is with the pet names, she wouldn't purposely put herself in danger just to spite me.

The truck, idling the entire time I loaded her car up, responds immediately when I put it into first and pull away from the parking lot. Not pressing my luck, I keep my hand fisted around the top knob of the shifter. What I don't do is pull my hand away when I'm at cruising speed with no need to shift anytime soon. The heat of her thigh against my forearm is enough to make me thicken in my pants.

I sense some form of nonverbal communication going on between the girls and watch them out of the corner of my eye.

"So," Ivy begins, and Delilah freezes beside me. "You live out here?"

"More like lying in wait like some weirdo fucking stalker," Delilah mutters.

I ignore her. If she only knew that I've purposely stayed away from her until a situation presented itself maybe her opinions would be different. I've known she's been close for the last year, but I didn't press my luck by going to her.

"I've been in Providence since shortly after I left New Mexico," I inform her.

"And Drew?" Delilah shoulders Ivy for continuing to talk.

"He's not far. Starting his senior year in Fall River." I keep my eyes on the road but can feel my beauty relax a little next to me. She may act angry that I showed up out of the blue today, but I know she has no ill will toward my brother, and she's curious about him. "His Aunt Kathy is an amazing woman. He's adjusted well. Makes good grades. Stays out of trouble, mostly."

"You're not here because of me?" Delilah asks softly, confused as if she really had it in her mind that I'm stalking her. The sadness in her voice hurts me, but it also makes my heart smile because no matter how much she wants to pretend she hates me, I know she doesn't.

"I'm here for you as much as I am for Drew. Never doubt that."

"Whatever," she mumbles.

When I look past her at Ivy, she's the one to wink at me this time. I pull my lip between my teeth to keep from smiling as I drive up to the front of the shop.

"You work here?" Ivy asks as she leans forward to get a better look at the building through the windshield.

"Yep," I answer. "Almost as long as I've been on the East Coast."

I put the truck in park and open my door. "Need help getting down, Prin—"

I frown when I see that she's already climbing down behind Ivy.

I have a long ass way to go, but luckily she's going to be worth every ounce of pushback she gives me.

Chapter 27

Delilah

"I won't ever forget which side you chose," I warn Ivy.

She grins at me as I jump down from the cab of the wrecker. Getting away from the warmth of his thigh and the amazing scent of his spicy cologne is all I could concentrate on since leaving the parking lot.

"I don't know what you're talking about." She feigns interest in her surroundings.

"Like hell you don't," I hiss at her back as she walks around the back of the wrecker.

"If you ladies hold tight and let me get this off the flatbed, I'll take you home."

Even in a bright yellow vest, grease stains on his jeans, and a smudge on his left cheek, he's still the hottest guy I've ever seen. Acknowledging that, even in my head, pisses me off. The least he could've done is to turn gray or grow warts on his face. The thought of him having salt and pepper locks makes me tingle, and my anger grows.

I've learned a lot in the two years since he treated me like shit and disappeared into thin air. Well, it wasn't exactly thin air, but I avoided any talk of him in the house and made no effort to reach out to him. He made his feelings more than clear that night in my bedroom.

"It would've taken less time for you to drop us off before we drove all the way across town."

I cross my arms over my chest again, an action I've done more than once since he showed up. His eyes dart to the swell of my breasts as the action pushes them a little higher in my tank top. His eyes piercing into me does more to my libido than the boy from the restaurant could ever hope.

"Yet you didn't say anything when I drove right past your street on the way here," he challenges.

Busted.

He winks as Ivy laughs behind me.

We stand off to the side as an older man comes out of the huge roll-up door on the front of the shop. He stops short and just watches us. I stare, unabashedly at Lawson, as he strips out of the vest and begins to work on getting my car off of the wrecker. I know my mouth is hanging open by the time he's done. I'm also well aware of the show he's putting on. It's not very hot out here so when he lifts the bottom of his shirt to wipe at his face, I know it's not because he's sweating and overexerted.

I sneer even though my face is as deep as my irritation goes. Ivy laughs again when a grunt slips out at the sight of the dark trail of hair snaking from his belly button and disappearing into his low-slung jeans.

"Jesus," I say before I can stop myself.

"Do you need a minute alone," Ivy jokes with a quick shoulder bump.

I shake my head. "A minute wouldn't even do him justice. A month would probably barely scratch the surface."

"He's always been very handsome."

"I hate him."

I stand straighter, my back stiffening in defiance, but I never pull my eyes from him. My brain warns that I may have limited time with him, and is insisting I get my fill while I can. It makes no sense. I've spent two years doing my best to not think of him. Two years of wasting time with other men who just don't seem to measure up. Two years of silently comparing him to everyone I encounter only to find them lacking. The problem is, he's an asshole, a jerk who treated me like a whore when he had me believing there was something building between us.

"You're still mad?"

I'm not surprised by Ivy's reaction. I haven't spoken out loud to anyone about Lawson O'Neil since I explained what had happened between us on her front porch before I even knew he was gone.

"He treated me like shit," I tell her, angling my head to see him when he steps around the wrecker and I lose track of him.

"People change," she says.

"Not really," I argue. "But that doesn't mean I can't have some fun once or twice."

She grabs my upper arm, turning me and forcing me to look in her eyes.

"What exactly do you have planned?"

I shrug, but even the thought of what I could do to Lawson O'Neil heats my blood. "Fuck him and forget him of course."

"Delilah," she chides. "I don't think that's a good idea."

"It's the best one I can come up with."

"You need to reconsider that plan," she urges. "You'll only get—"

She stops abruptly when Lawson, smile on his handsome face, comes walking back up.

"Ready to go?" He points to a silver truck parked directly in front of the building. "Four doors so you don't have to straddle my stick."

The innuendo is plain as day, the words frighteningly similar to something he would've said two years ago. My faith in my 'love him and leave him' plan begins to slip. I know exactly what Ivy is getting at. She's well aware that there's no way I can play with his fire and not get burned. I reason with the voice in my head telling me to run far and fast. I figure if I can be the one to turn the tables on him this time, I can walk away with my pride intact.

I walk away from him and toward the truck without a word.

"Icy, Princess," he mutters walking close enough to my back that I feel the heat coming off of his skin. "Good thing I like it."

I shake my head, but a grin he can't see lights up my face.

"You don't stand a chance. Might as well get over it and move on."

"Nice truck," Ivy praises as she climbs into the back passenger side.

"Selling drugs?" I ask and immediately hate the inference to some of the things he admitted to being forced to do when he was younger to help support his family.

"Nope," he answers, schooling his face back to the gorgeous smile that's been there since he got out of the wrecker in the parking lot. "I just work a lot."

"An honest living?" I continue despite the bile rising in my throat at the mean words. "What a change of pace."

Ivy hisses in the background, and I cringe, ashamed, as my behavior reminds me of Gigi.

"Sorry," I mutter, turning my eyes to look at him as he drives down the road.

"Lots of things have changed," he says softly but refuses to look at me.

Ivy reaches between my seat and the window, pinching my arm in chastisement. Jerking my arm out of her reach, I don't bother to say anything to her. I deserve worse for what I just said.

"Turn right up here," Ivy instructs.

"I know where your apartment is," he tells her with a quick wink in the rearview mirror.

"You've been this close to me for two years, and I'm just now running into you?"

Now he looks at me. The red light we're waiting at giving him the opportunity.

"If you wanted to see me sooner, you could've asked your dad where I was," he challenges.

"I didn't care to know where you were." Even as I say the words, I know, deep down, that it's a lie.

"And that's exactly why we haven't seen each other before today."

"I'm glad you're close," my traitorous best friend adds from the backseat. "I feel safer knowing family is nearby."

"We're not family," Lawson and I say at the same time.

At least we can agree on something.

"Not yet," he says with so much conviction, I almost believe him.

"What do you do at the shop?" Ivy just won't give it a rest.

Tension still thick in the cab of the truck, Lawson grins at her over his shoulder.

"Mostly motorcycles, but we get the occasional car. I'm apprenticing with Joel, the old man you saw back at the shop."

"And when you're fully trained?" Ivy speaks for me. I both love her and hate her for it. I'm hungry for the knowledge, but we all know I'll never ask the questions myself. Vocal curiosity about what his life has been like the last two years gives him power I'm not willing to relinquish.

"Joel is retiring. The shop will be mine by the time I turn twenty-five."

Unwanted pride swells in my chest.

"That's amazing," Ivy says, once again speaking my words out loud.

"Jaxon has helped me a ton. I couldn't have done anything without him and Rob."

Dad and Pop never mentioned anything of the sort. Why would they? Dad tried to talk to me about Lawson and Drew when I got home two years ago, but I shut him down and asked him to never mention them again. He respected my wishes, but it doesn't surprise me that they would've stayed involved in Lawson's life. Moving across the country doesn't mean giving up on your son. I respect them immensely for any help they may have provided.

"You planning to keep everything the same when Joel retires?"

"Ivy," I chide. "What is this twenty questions?"

"I don't mind," Lawson says with a quick chuckle. "I plan to re-image. Joel isn't exactly happy with his life work changing, but I have to do something to bring the business into this century."

They continue on, talking and asking each other questions all the way to the apartment. He's spoken more, revealed more in the twenty minutes it takes to get home than he did in the weeks that he was in New Mexico.

"Oh look, there's Cindy." Ivy pushes open her door the second the truck is in park. "Thanks for the ride, Lawson. Hope to see you again soon."

I scowl at her back as she darts across the parking lot to talk to her friend, effectively leaving me alone in the truck surrounded by Lawson's cologne and soft leather.

"I've missed you," he confesses, turning slightly, so his upper body is angled in my direction. "I can't take back how I treated you, but I want you to know that I'm sor—"

I'm out of the truck and walking toward my apartment before he can even finish his apology. I don't regret leaving him sitting in his truck, but him driving off without coming and trying to talk to me stings more than it should've.

Chapter 28

Lawson

Watching her walk away was harder than I could've ever imagined, but she's not ready to hear what I have to say. Hell, I've been practicing it all in my head since I moved here. Leave it to the gorgeous Delilah Donovan to throw a wrench into my perfectly constructed plans with her snarky attitude.

I imagined her running into my arms the second she saw me, telling me how much she missed me, and how she's happy we can finally be together. I knew it would never happen, but daydreams and fantasies aren't ever rational.

At the first red light I catch, I use the truck's Bluetooth to call Jaxon.

"Hey, son," he answers after the second ring.

"Dad," I return.

"How's our girl?"

I love that he extends the possession to include us both, but even more, I love that he no longer sighs happily when I call him Dad rather than Jaxon. I can still remember the day it changed. He and Rob came to my house after getting Delilah settled into her freshman dorm. It wasn't the first time they'd flown across the country to visit, but something shifted. He gave me partial responsibility for his daughter, grateful I was here in case she needed me, so I gave him something in return.

"She's safe. Just dropped her off at her apartment."

"That's great. Did she give you any trouble?" Laughter is barely masked in his tone, but I'm still flying high from seeing her after so long, I don't complain about him sending me into the lion's den today. Rather, I'm indebted to him once again for the opportunity.

"She hasn't changed a bit."

"Are you purposely lying to yourself, or just saying shit so I feel better about my daughter on the other side of the country?"

"I'm not sure. Do you want to fill me in on what you're talking about? Would make it easier for me to make informed observations."

She's a spitfire, just like always, but she acted that way when we were alone back in New Mexico. She behaved differently in front of Jaxon and Rob.

A sad chuckle echoes in my ears. "I'm not spilling any secrets, but just let me say, I'm glad I was able to send you her way. Maybe things will calm down now."

I wait for him to elaborate, but he never does, so I change the subject. "I'll make sure she gets a rental car first thing in the morning. I think she tolerated me as long as she could today."

"Use the credit card I gave you for emergencies," he instructs.

"Find her a new car," Rob says in the background.

"I'll take care of it."

"Use the card, Law."

"I will."

"Liar. You never do."

"A rental car isn't an emergency," I mutter, having pulled up in front of the mechanic shop. Three cars I don't recognize are now parked there. Joel is speaking with one man about a mid-sized SUV. The driver of a black BMW is nowhere to be seen, but a woman stands, leaning against the driver's door of her red Camaro. I already know she's trouble by the smirk she gives me as I pull my truck in and put it in park.

"Dad, I have to go. Got three customers waiting at the shop."

"Sure thing. Let me know how tomorrow goes."

"Will do."

"Love you, son."

"Have a good day."

I hang up. I may call him Dad, but the 'I love yous' haven't happened yet. I have no time to feel like an asshole this time as I climb out of my truck. My focus is on the driver I can see when a paunchy bald man walks out of the front office. I frown in his direction, irritated that no matter how many times I've told Joel we need to keep that door locked when we're not in there, he still just leaves it open for everyone. He can't get it through his head that we aren't living in the damn fifties anymore, and the trust you had in people back then can't be given to assholes of this day and age.

"About fucking time someone else showed up," he hisses as he closes the distance between us.

I just stare at him.

"There's some sort of rattling noise," he says pointing to his car.

"Give me just a minute," I tell the woman standing outside of her car.

"I'll wait all day for you," she purrs.

I chuckle. She has to be in her late fifties, but it's clear she's taken very good care of herself.

"Quit fucking flirting," the bald guy hisses when I finally make it over to him. "I've been waiting twenty minutes, and that geezer over there doesn't seem to be in any hurry."

"We don't do imports." I cross my arms over my chest, legs spread shoulder-width apart.

"Bullshit," he sneers. "You got a fucking Toyota up on the rack."

I don't bother looking over my shoulder. I'm well aware that Delilah's car is in the first bay of the shop.

"Family car," I appease. "My insurance wouldn't cover me if I fuck up your pretty little car. It's newer and should still be under warranty, take it back to the dealership."

He's cursing me and muttering about it getting repoed since he hasn't made the last three months payments, but I ignore him. If I had to guess, I'd bet he got fired from his job because of that nasty ass attitude he's sporting. Tires squeal when he pulls out, but I just continue my trek across the lot to the last waiting customer. I swear I'm going to lose my shit if she asks for blinker fluid, which, oddly enough, we get on average twice a week. Always from women dressed to the nines with a coo in their voices like either Joel or I would be interested.

"How can I help you?" I ask, keeping a respectful distance between us.

"I need a full body inspection." I cock an eyebrow at her. "I mean the emissions thing or whatever."

"I hate to turn you away, but we ran out of stickers two days ago."

We do more inspections than anything else. Mostly on cars that pass with flying colors, by owners who wear tons of makeup and jewelry. It's serious craziness, especially for a shop that specializes in motorcycles and ATVs.

"Surely you can help me out."

I grin when her pink lip juts out in a pout.

"I can't do anything for you without a sticker, ma'am."

A devious smirk lights her face. "Oh, I'm sure there's plenty you can do for me."

Ignoring her, I point down the street. "I'm pretty sure Mack's just down the block still has some."

"But," she begins, but I turn away from her.

"Have a great day," I say over my shoulder and walk toward Joel and the customer he's been chatting with.

When I round the corner, I take in the scene. The man stands, not stiff, but also not relaxed in this environment. His MC cut stands out like a waving flag.

"Hey, Law," Joel says when I walk up. "This is Eric Quintal. President of the Ravens Ruin MC."

I offer my hand while he eyes me up and down, until his scarred-knuckled hand clasps mine.

"The old man here tells me you're the best in town at keeping bikes running." I nod because it's the truth. "How are you with modifications?"

"Get better with each one I do."

I take in the grime on his cut, 'Lynch' in bold print just above his 'President' patch, the old scar running down his left bicep. I'd wager that he didn't earn the damage to his body doing recon and rescue like Cerberus.

I'm not sure I want business from this man, so I don't elaborate.

"He's great at paint, exhaust mods, bodywork. You name it, this kid can do it."

I can hear the pride in his voice, but now is not the time for it. His emphatic trust in all people isn't helping in this situation.

"I'm more interested in the body mods," Lynch says with narrowed eyes.

"We're booked up," I lie.

Thankfully Joel keeps his mouth shut. We never turn business away without scheduling them on the books to ensure a greater chance of them returning.

"Check back in a couple weeks, and we may be able to get something lined up."

"I'll be back." Simple words that still feel like a threat.

I don't turn to face Joel until he's on his bike and halfway down the block. Three other bikes pull out further down the block. Assuming they're the vice president, sergeant at arms, and possibly the road captain, they get into formation and drive away.

"How long has he been harassing you?" I ask Joel once the sounds fade out in the distance.

"Since about ten minutes after you left." I follow him to the stool on the far wall of the building, surprised he's been able to stand as long as he has.

Apprenticing is what I called it when speaking with Delilah and Ivy earlier, but it's more like point and yell. He sits on the stool and tells me shit like he's right beside me. His knowledge is unparalleled, and his instruction is the same if he's sitting beside me or fifteen feet across the room.

I wait for him to get settled in before speaking. "Any clue what he wanted?"

"Of course, child. I'm not an idiot."

"So you're well aware it's probably illegal?"

He shakes his head as if I'm an idiot, but I can see the smile playing on his wrinkled lips.

"If you consider built-in hidden compartments for their wallets and jewelry store purchases illegal."

He eyes me, toying with me, waiting for me to respond.

"Jewelry, right."

He's chuckling as I walk away. I close the door between the garage and the office and settle down in the chair. My phone is out a second later. What does any young man do when faced with potential danger? I call my dad.

Chapter 29

Delilah

A headache, more from the banging on the door than the over imbibed wine from last night, taps away in my skull.

"Ivy," I yell from in front of my bathroom mirror. "Can you get the door?"

She doesn't respond, and the banging continues.

"Dammit," I mutter and toss my eyeliner on the vanity.

Passing by Ivy's room, I notice that she's gone, bed made just like she does every morning.

"I don't eat cookies," I mumble loud enough for the visitor to hear as I turn the deadbolt on the door. "And I already found Jesus."

"Tell me, Princess. Just how many times do you cry 'Oh, God!' each week?"

Lawson.

"More times than I can count," I lie. "Depends on how good he is with his mouth."

I watch his throat fight down an angry swallow. Not the response he thought he'd get apparently.

"Don't give me that kicked puppy look." I turn away from him, leaving him standing in the doorway and walk to the kitchen.

The front door clicks closed, but I know he isn't gone. He has a force that surrounds him. It literally affects the hair on my arms whether I can see him or not.

"I'm sure you have tons of stories to tell, a line of women fighting over the opportunity to choke on your cock," I continue.

"Not even touching that one." He pulls a chair out from the table and sits down, uninvited yet undeterred by my glare.

I rise up on my toes to get a cup out of the very top cabinet even though there are clean mugs in the dishwasher. I love torturing him, and I know how well it's working when I look over my shoulder and find his eyes on the backs of my legs. The short skirt wasn't something I did on purpose for him, but the everyday wardrobe choice is helping me right now.

"Like what you see?" I taunt as I make a cup of coffee, rudely not offering any to him.

"More than I could ever describe," he whispers.

Keeping my back to him does nothing to abate the shiver running over my body.

"Why are you here?"

I lean my hip against the counter, refusing to join him at the tiny table. There are only two chairs, and he's larger than life, so there's no way I could sit without part of my body brushing against part of his. My fingers already tremble against my warm coffee cup. I'm certain if we just barely brush against each other, I'll pounce on him.

"I'm here for you." In my mind, it sounds like a seductive whisper, but from the look on his face, he said it like any normal person would.

"How very Denny and Izzie of you."

"Huh?"

Seriously? Can you trust a man who doesn't watch Grey's Anatomy?

"The rental car?" he says with a tilt of his head like it's supposed to remind me of something.

"Okay?" I give him the same head tilt. "I'm getting one later."

"Right after you finish that coffee. I don't allow liquids in my truck. Don't want anything spilled on my seats."

"One, I'm not going any damn where with you, and two, I'm not a child. I can drink in a vehicle without spilling shit."

"I would tell you to hurry up; that I don't have all damn day, but it would be a lie. I cleared my schedule for you." His grin is almost contagious, but I catch myself before my lips part to mirror his.

"Nope." I drink the last sip of my coffee and rinse the cup before placing it on the counter.

"Your dad told me to make sure you got one so let's go." He sweeps his arm out toward the door.

I stay exactly where I've been standing and give him a pointed look.

"You keep mentioning him. How often do you talk to him?"

"If you want my life story, Princess, you're going to have to get into my truck."

I need a rental car, and I also need answers, but I don't know if I need them enough to be alone with him. I remind myself that I'm alone with him right now, in the apartment, where there are beds and a very comfortable couch.

"I'll grab my purse," I say and run out of the room.

He waits, somehow a little too close yet still too far away while I use my key to lock the apartment door, and his hand finds the small of my back as we descend the stairs. Once we're buckled in, he cranks the truck and puts it in gear.

"Every day," he says out of nowhere.

"Huh?"

His smile is blinding. "You asked how often I speak to Jaxon. We talk every day."

"No way," I hiss. "I don't even talk to him every day."

"And he misses you when you go days without checking in."

Well, if that isn't a kick in the gut.

"I'm trying to be independent," I mutter, already guilty over my sporadic contact with my dads before he even mentioned it.

"I get it."

"He doesn't talk to me about you." The meanness I hate so much rears its ugly head once again.

"You told him long ago that you didn't want to know anything about me."

I stiffen. "You talk about me? Did you tell him why I didn't want to hear about you?"

He laughs at my ridiculous question. Of course he didn't. He wouldn't live to tell the tale if he did.

"We talk about you all the time."

I let that sink in and stare out the window. We drive, five minutes longer than it would take to get to the rental place.

"Where are we going?"

"Figured we could find someplace quiet to talk." He looks over at me, and I instantly want to shut him down. If not for the sincerity and pleading in his eyes I would've. For some reason, today, being this close to him for the first time in years, I just don't have the strength to push him away.

We ride in silence for another fifteen minutes, until he turns off of the highway, pulling into the State Park. Slowly, he drives along until he finds a deserted parking area near the water. He surprises me when he parks with the nose of his truck against the trees and the tailgate facing the water that's on the other side of the lot. I anticipate him climbing out so we can sit and watch over the water, but he puts it in park and makes no move to get out.

"Tell me about your relationship with my dad," I plead.

"Tell me about school," he counters.

The fire in his eyes makes me think he's asking more about the nightlife and parties than the core classes I took last year and have already registered for this year. I realize now why he parked the way he did. This way there's nothing to look at but trees, so he's forcing my hand. There are, however, worse things to look at than his sexy lips and clear blue eyes.

"Don't," he murmurs.

"Don't what?"

"Lick your lips and stare at my mouth."

The corners of my mouth twitch before turning up with a wide smile.

"Tell me about my dad," I insist.

"Tell me about the boys you've met at college," he counters.

"Men," I correct. "And I thought you said you haven't been stalking me."

"So there have been others?" I stare, stunned at how quick he is to ask about my romantic life. "Are you seeing anyone?"

"That's none of your business."

"It's my business now," he says with quiet authority.

The domination in his voice is exactly what was missing in the darting gaze of the boy from yesterday.

"You want details?" I ask, unclicking my seatbelt and shifting my weight. I bite my lip as he stares, fingers tightening on the steering wheel. "You want the truth?"

"Always the truth," he says, voice cracking at the end.

"You want to know that your voice does more to my body than their mouths, their fingers, their," I lean over the console close to his ear, "cocks?"

"Stop," he commands, loud enough that I back away into my seat.

I told myself that my choices were just that, mine. I reminded myself each time I cried after a boy dropped me off at the end of the night that I was getting exactly what I'd wanted. I wasn't being used; I was the one doing the using. No regrets, I'd told myself each and every time.

I lived by that rule over the last three months. I was having fun, partying, and living life to the fullest.

Right now? This very second? I hate the woman I've become. I despise each of the three guys I used. More so, I hate the look of disappointment in Lawson's eyes as he realizes I gave something away that should've belonged to him. I hate him even more, blame him, for who I've become.

"What?" I ask defensively, another mask to my pain. "No dirty talk from you? No declarations of how much better you'd be?"

"I'm not that angry kid that moved away from New Mexico, Delilah." The intensity of his stare holds my eyes. "Now, I'm simply a man who knows what he wants."

"What do you want?"

I swear if he says anything about my mouth on his cock, the police will never find his body.

"You," he answers. One simple, three-letter word. How in the hell is it enough to tilt my world off of its axis?

Chapter 30

Lawson

Her lips are on mine before I can consider that honesty is the best aphrodisiac for women.

My first thought is to push her away, but at the end of the day I'm not a saint, so I kiss her back. I let the warmth of her tongue sweep over mine, and I offer her mine in exchange. In amazing contradiction, a sheen of sweat and goosebumps trail down my spine and branch out all over my body.

My cock, pressing against the denim of my jeans, having been hard since she agreed to talk, throbs in need of attention. The sound of coins clanging echoes around the cab of the truck as she flips up the console and tugs me closer to her.

We're in dangerous territory. I'd wanted to be alone with her. Wanted the chance to talk without interruption, but the way her lips are gliding over mine will only lead to one thing, and talking isn't it.

She's not quite straddling me, but her chest is pressed against mine, and the contact is beyond amazing. "Delilah."

I pull my head back but don't loosen my arms. They managed to find their way around her back, one hand resting dangerously low near her ass.

"Missed you, too," she whispers.

For the first time since I saw her yesterday, I see sincerity in her eyes. It's brief, only lasting a couple of seconds, but my heart soars at the possibility of what it could mean.

"Princess."

Her mouth hits mine again, and rather than push her away, my fingers dig in harder and pull her closer.

The heat between her thighs burns my cock as she shifts her weight to straddle me.

"Fuck," I groan.

Her hips rotate as she grinds down on me. Jesus, the tell-tale tingle is already present in my underused balls.

"Slow down," I urge.

With a mischievous grin, she swivels her hips in the slowest, most delicious circle. I grip her hips, but I'm no fool. My hands may be on her body, but I haven't made any real effort to make her stop. I'm powerless against her, against the situation I've envisioned while I stroked myself off in the shower, her name on my lips for the last two years.

If I concentrate hard enough, I can still feel the warmth of her pussy as it constricts around my finger. Can still feel the swipe of her tongue over the tip of my cock.

I squeeze my eyes shut, doing my best to stave off the orgasm that's churning with hurricane strength force in my nuts.

When I open them, Delilah has her shirt pulled up and both cups of her bra tugged down. Her perfectly round, pink-tipped breasts are mere inches from my mouth. Saliva pools as if I'm a hungry dog tempted with a T-bone steak.

Tilting my head back, I look in her eyes. Having dreamed of this moment, I don't want to give in, but I only have so much strength.

Lips parted, her breath ghosts out in uneven pants. She leans in, placing the puckered tip of her breast on my bottom lip, in similar fashion to the way I rested my cock on hers back in New Mexico. I want to shake my head to clear out thoughts of how epically I fucked that up, but doing so would break the contact with her perfect skin. That sacrifice isn't one I'm strong enough to make.

I don't waste time. I don't give her breast a gentle swipe of my tongue. I wrap my lips around it and suck like I'll never be offered it again. She whimpers, squirming once again as I draw her puckered flesh deeper. When her fingers get lost in my hair, I'm lost in her. I disappear into her scent, into the glorious taste of her warm skin. I'm entranced by the irregular breaths leaving her lungs. I'm adrift in the sound of her erratic heartbeat, or is it mine that's reverberating around us?

The pressure surrounding my cock is relieved. So much so, that I have to look down to see if I've just busted a nut in my jeans. It nearly comes to fruition when I look down and see her small hands gloriously wrapped around my cock.

"Oh fuck," I hiss as her black skirt clears her thighs and her bright pink panties are revealed.

"Feel good?" she asks, swiping the tip of my cock at the wet line on the pink fabric.

"Too good," I hiss.

"What about this?"

My mouth, once flooded, now runs dry as I watch her pull her panties to the side and use my cock to stroke that perfect bundle of nerves. I've felt that sensitive flesh on the tips of my fingers, but fuck me sideways if it does any justice to what she's doing right now.

I'm concentrating so hard on the sight of her skin against mine, that I don't even notice that she's produced a condom until she caps the end of my dick with it.

"Delilah," I groan but don't make a move to stop her.

"Lawson," she mimics.

"I can't tell you no."

My mind is screaming for me to put an end to this, but my grip holds tight to her hips, even helping her as she situates me at her entrance.

"Then don't," she pants against my lips as she slides down my cock.

We moan in unison when she seats herself fully and begins to rise.

"Help me," she begs.

Holding her against my chest with one hand, I use my other to push my jeans down to the floorboard. I gain the leverage I need with my thighs no longer being restricted and press into her as she sinks down.

I hold her up, easing into her and retreating in the most delicious way. I opt for slow, hoping to have the lasting power to take her over the edge with me, but she wants nothing to do with slow. I want romance, to make love to her. The look in her eyes tells me she needs to be fucked. She needs to be taken in the filthiest way possible. Being in the truck and not a bed covered in rose petals dictates that she gets what she's searching for.

We move in sync with each other, her forcing herself down as I pound up. The brutality of it is also beautiful in its own right.

"Fuck me like a filthy slut," she hisses when I pull her down, thrusting deeper. "I'm your dirty girl."

God help me, I wish I could stop the train that's barreling down my spine ninety to nothing as she throws the words that ruined us years ago in my face. I squeeze my eyes shut, a feeble attempt to gain some control, but lose the battle. Her words, even as bitter as they sound, send me straight over the edge and fuck if that first pulse of my cock isn't the heaven I've always imagined it would be.

"Fuck, fuck," I hiss. "Too soon."

Somehow still cognizant, I lick my thumb and swipe it repeatedly over her clit as I fuck her through my orgasm.

"Yes," she moans before she clenches around me.

The rhythmic clenching of her core around me is enough to keep me thick inside of her. When I can focus on something other than her flushed cheeks, I notice the condensation from our breaths covering the windows. If people weren't able to determine what we've been up to by the rocking of the truck, the windows would be a dead giveaway.

"I've never," she says, the look on her face almost worshipping. Shaking her head, she just stares down at me. "It's never been like that before."

I smile up at her, reaching up to brush my lips against hers. "You deserve more than this fucking truck."

"I figured it would've lasted longer with your sexual prowess and all." I'm unable to tell if she's joking or not.

"I haven't come with a girl present since before my mother passed away," I confess.

An emotion I can't distinguish marks her face as her brows draw together. The brief tremble in her lower lip makes my heart clench. It's gone as quickly as it showed up.

She looks down as she slides off my still semi-engorged cock.

"Looks like I still managed to get your seat wet, even without bringing a cup of coffee in here."

I don't bother to look down. I can feel the evidence of her orgasm pooling below me on the seat. My truck is going to smell like her for a long time to come, and I'd be lying if I said I wasn't looking forward to climbing inside and letting the scent settle in my lungs every day.

"Let me help you," I say and grip her hips before she can move away fully. Leaning over, I flip open the glove compartment and pull out a few napkins stashed there from random fast food places.

When she trembles against my hand at the contact, I swear I'm ready to take her again. My eyes meet hers, and I immediately know whatever moment we just shared has come to an abrupt end.

"Thanks." Her tone is flat as she repositions her panties and once again conceals her perfect little pussy. Next, she's back on her side of the truck and covering her breasts. I mourn the loss as I tug the condom free and wrap the napkin I used on her around it.

"Well, that was awesome." I look around my truck for some place to stash the evidence as she uses the visor mirror to put more lip gloss on.

"It was okay," she says absently, smacking her lips and refusing to look my way.

Anger at her unwillingness to acknowledge how great we were together when only moments ago she was quivering around me during her release pisses me off. I jam the trash in the cup holder in the driver's door and turn to glare at her.

"Excuse me?"

I clench the steering wheel as I fight the urge to grab her chin and force her to look at me.

"I mean," she begins, still looking down at her clothes. "Most guys don't fuck me in a truck. I at least get a bed."

My eyes nearly bulge out of my head at her words.

"You jumped me. You took my cock out. You rolled that rubber down my dick and sat on it like it was yours." I put the truck in reverse and back out without even checking my surroundings. When I pull out far enough, grateful to not have run over some kid or hit a guy unloading on the boat ramp, I put it in drive and peel out heading toward the main road. "Don't regret your actions now, Princess."

Chapter 31

Delilah

The echo of him inside of me is almost unbearable as we bump along the road, heading back out to the highway and eventually back into town to get my rental car. Clenching my thighs together does nothing but make me yearn for more.

I've been lying to myself. I can tell myself repeatedly that I was using the guys I slept with, but after what Lawson and I just did, there's no denying that those men were using me.

I didn't mean for my confession to slip past my lips, but I was delirious with pleasure, my orgasm the first by another's touch since the last one he gave me in my childhood bedroom.

If I were using them like I've proclaimed more times than I can count, they would've made me come, would've been invested in my gratification. Having been focused solely on their own release, makes the truth sit heavy in my stomach, souring the coffee there from this morning.

I find the courage to look over at him. He doesn't acknowledge me, but I know he's aware of my gaze because his hands tighten on the steering wheel.

How do I tell him the truth? How do I explain to him that his confession rocked me to my core?

"I haven't come with a girl present since before my mother passed away."

I can't presume he was waiting for me, but while he was living a life of self-imposed celibacy, I was getting drunk and letting vodka make major decisions for me. Blame wasn't one hundred percent on the alcohol. I made my choices, and I'll live with the fallout.

"Are we just going to ride in silence with you over there bristling like a wet cat?"

He stretches his neck, first to the right, then to the left before he speaks. The tension doesn't ease up in the truck as he figures out what he's going to say. My eyes narrow, hating that he just doesn't speak his truth without worrying how I'll respond. It feels calculating and manipulative and pisses me off.

"Talk to me," I demand. "Tell me what you're thinking."

He shakes his head. "It's not that simple. My feelings are... confusing."

"Confusing? Just use your words, Lawson. It's not that difficult."

He chuckles, his hands easing up slightly on the steering wheel. "We're going to my house."

My eyes widen. "No, we're going to go get a rental car."

"You implied that I took advantage of you, or treated you less than you deserve because we fucked in the truck. I'm going to take you home, lay you out on my bed and make it better than anything you've ever had before. Make you forget every other encounter you've had before me."

I wince at his words, wishing that he would be able to make me forget. Praying the amnesia took the guilt and self-recrimination right along with it.

"No."

He looks over at me. "What do you mean, no?"

"Take me to get a rental," I insist. "I have no desire to go back to your house."

It wasn't part of the plan, and resisting him after today is only going to be a million times harder.

"I waited two years for you."

I do my best to ignore the pain and pleading in his voice. Walls up and defenses on high alert is the only way I know how to maintain imaginary control over this situation.

"Well," I look out the window, hating myself. "I didn't wait for you."

And, God how I wish I had.

"I have a past, too," he says with more understanding in his voice than I deserve.

"It was a one-time thing." My body trembles in disapproval at my words.

"So you're just going to fuck me then walk away?"

I don't respond immediately, and my anger grows as I think about how offended he sounds.

Lowering my voice to sound more masculine I say, "I told you you'd suck my cock."

He nods. As he swallows, I watch his Adam's apple work under the pressure.

"So it comes back to that?"

"The last two years, all of my decisions have centered around the moment you made me feel like a whore," I confess.

"I was hurting." He holds his hand up when I try to respond. My jaw snaps shut, and I wait for him to continue. "Drew had just told me about his Aunt. I knew he was leaving, and I knew that meant I was going to leave with him."

I huff. "So you just figured you'd get me on my knees before you took off?"

The truck jerks and rocks back as he puts it into park. Looking around, I realize we've made it to the car rental place. I'd been so lost in my own head, I hadn't even noticed we'd traveled so far.

"You begged me to touch you," he hisses as he shifts his weight to look at me.

I pull my eyes from his, the scrutiny of his gaze more than I can handle. "So I was a whore then, too."

"You're not a whore!" He rages. "I've never seen you that way. Not once since I met you have I let that thought cross my mind."

"You manipulated me. You told me exactly what I needed to hear to get me to sink to my knees in that bedroom."

"I figured you hating me would've been easier on you."

"Hate." I bite my lip to keep the sob from slipping out. "More like hating that I loved you."

"Delilah." He reaches for me, but I pull my hand away before he can make contact.

"Don't worry, Lawson. I crushed that shit a long time ago."

"I couldn't ask you to put your life on hold for me," he barters a few years too late.

Tears spill down my cheeks. "I would've," I whisper.

"What?"

I look at him, not hiding my pain. I need him to see it, to feel it. "I would've waited for you."

"I'm here now." His eyes plead with mine, but there's no use.

"It's not even an option now. Too much time, too many bad decisions."

I push open the door to the truck and climb down. When I reach back in to grab my purse, he once again reaches for me.

"Talk to me."

"There's nothing to talk about. Let me know when my car is fixed."

I make it to the front door of the rental office before I feel his heat at my back. I'm torn between wanting him there and wanting him to leave me the hell alone.

"I'm perfectly capable of taking care of this myself," I mutter as he reaches past me to open the door.

I walk through, and he follows behind me.

No one is at the front counter, so I tap the top of the small bell and wait. His warm breath is in my ear, and there isn't a sliver of possibility that I can hide the tremble that takes over my body.

"I get that you're hurt. I've felt the pain from that night just as much as you have. We've both made bad decisions, the wrong choices, but if you think you making some declaration and getting all growly and mad will make me walk away from you again, you'd be wrong."

I try to turn, but he clasps my hips, pressing against my back until my front is flush against the tall counter.

"Listen," I say softly as if I'm a negotiator talking him down off the ledge of a building. "We had sex. It was decent."

He's the one growling now.

"But it will never happen again," I continue. "I've always wondered what it would be like with you. That opportunity presented itself today, and I jumped at the chance."

"I'm going to be making love to you for the rest of my life." There's so much surety in his voice, I almost believe him. "There's no getting rid of me this time, Princess. You're stuck with me."

Before I can respond, a tall man with a wiry beard comes to the counter.

"How can I help you?"

"Lawson O'Neil," he says reaching over my shoulder to hand the guy a credit card. "We're here to pick up a car."

I glare at the red and black logo on the front of his card. The familiarity of the three-headed Cerberus dog on the front makes my heart skip a beat.

Lawson, feeling the tension in my shoulders moves to my side and looks down at me.

"That card," I begin but don't say another word.

He smiles and shrugs. "It has a great interest rate."

The man at the counter takes the card and sweeps his eyes over me. "And will you, your girlfriend, or both of you be driving the car?"

"Not his girlfriend," I spit at the same time Lawson says, "Only my girlfriend."

The guy, Jerry if you believe his name tag, smiles at me and my explanation.

"Do you have a death wish?" Lawson watches Jerry, his tone no different than if he was asking the guy for a pen.

Jerry shakes his head, asks for my driver's license and gets to work. I should be angry or mad, but the possessiveness, even when I'm confused, turns me on like nothing else.

Chapter 32

Lawson

My cards have been played, my hand dealt sooner than I'd wanted, but letting her drive away in that rental car without her knowing my intentions wasn't a possibility.

My cock throbs as I inhale and pull her scent into my lungs. It's the best kind of torture and nearly has me turning right instead of left. Heading to the shop rather than her apartment is an exercise in restraint that's ten times harder now that I've had her.

Trying to ignore the insistence in my nuts, I do what I always do when I'm driving.

Dad answers on the second ring, his voice echoing around the cab of the truck through the hands-free.

"I forgot to tell you about my visitor when we spoke last night," I say after we both deliver our hellos. "Are you familiar with the Ravens Ruin MC?"

"The name's familiar, but I haven't had any dealings with them personally. I can have Blade look into them." I hear him mention the name to Rob. "Did they threaten you? Who did they send?"

"I had the pleasure of meeting Eric "Lynch" Quintal, the president. He didn't threaten me, didn't even tell me what he specifically wanted other than body mods for bikes."

"Body mods can mean a lot of things, son."

"I know. I told him I was booked out and to get with me in a couple of weeks."

"That was smart." I smile at the nonchalant praise. "He didn't give you any grief?"

"No, which surprises me. Joel told me after he left that he'd mentioned compartments for their wallets and jewelry."

My dad's laugh rings in my ears. "So they're either running guns or drugs."

"That's my guess. Rhode Island has concealed carry, so there's no reason for them to need to hide a weapon inside their bike."

The weight of the pistol in my boot increases at my statement.

"I'll have Blade look into them. Hopefully they're just fishing to see if they get any bites around town, but let me know immediately if you see any of them hovering around."

"I will," I agree.

"And how's Delilah?"

More gorgeous every day. The best thing that's ever slid down my cock.

That's the last thing I can tell him, but the reminder doesn't keep the low groan from escaping my lips.

"Something you want to tell me?"

I clear my throat.

"Man to man?" I ask testing the waters.

"That's always a good policy."

No guts; no glory, right?

"I'm going to marry that girl someday."

I'm met with silence, which I guess is better than him threatening to kill me from over two thousand miles away.

"Dad?"

"She's not very fond of you," he finally says amusement tinting his voice.

"I won't give up." I put my truck in park outside of the shop and run my hands over my hair. "She's the one who made me want to be a better man."

"She's an amazing woman."

"I don't know where my life would've ended up had I not met her. Had I not met you and Rob."

It's his turn to clear his throat, but he doesn't speak. I'm met with dead air so long I have to check the dash to make sure the call is still connected.

"Good luck, son."

His voice, sounding much like his blessing, eventually sounds through the speakers.

I turn my gaze to look at her car, still in the first bay on the rack. "Thanks. I'm going to need it."

"Before you go," he begins. "Rob had Blade run an initial check on the Ravens Ruin MC. They're not anyone you want sniffing around you. Feds are all over their asses."

"Got it," I say thankful he transitions so easily from my declaration and future plans.

"Take this seriously, son. These fuckers are sick, deadly, and nothing but trouble. Lynch got his name because his alleged calling card is hanging people from fucking trees in their family's yards. You don't need that kind of heat."

"Jesus," I mutter.

"Call immediately if you see anything suspicious. You're not going to like this, but I need you to distance yourself from her. I don't need them connecting the two of you. If you even get a Spidey tingle that something is off, you get her to the safe house."

"Yes, sir."

"Keep her away from the shop until I get the all clear." I hear him speak away from the phone, more than likely to Rob. "And, as much as I love him, don't tell Joel a damn thing. He runs his mouth too much. That poor bastard is living in the fifties. You and I both know times are much different now."

I let the heavy silence and weight of his words wash over me. Stay away from her. Don't tell the only person I've longed to see over the last two years a damn thing about what's going on. My life just went to shit over a visit from some psycho, asshole biker.

"Did you hear what I said?" His voice isn't exactly frustrated, but there's a hint of uncertainty in his voice that wasn't there ten minutes ago.

"Yes, sir." I swallow around the thick lump that's formed in my throat. "If I'm being honest, it scares the shit out of me."

Just the command to stay away from her for now, right after getting her back in my life, is like a sledgehammer blow to my chest.

"You're a man. You can handle yourself. I have no doubt. But you would be a fool to not have a little fear in the back of your skull."

"Delilah," I whisper.

"She's safest where she's at right now, Lawson. It's not for forever. A couple weeks tops." His tone is sure and full of faith I don't think should be placed on my shoulders. "Besides we'll have something in place soon."

Weeks? Damnit. I press the heel of my hand into my chest as the restriction grows tighter.

"Care to expand?" We're talking about the safety of my girl. She may be reluctant to that idea, but it doesn't make it any less true.

"I'll let you know more when I know more."

"Okay." I can't hide the defeat in my voice.

"Keep your head down, work, and I'll call you when I know something."

"Got it." Overwhelmed with the news I just got, coupled with the fantastic sex, and weighed down with the oath I made to Delilah earlier, I end the call without even telling him goodbye.

I'm diligent in my duties the rest of the day, but I keep one eye on the door and my ears open for the rumble of motorcycles. My pulse quickened no less than three times. Twice when customers drove up on Harleys for scheduled work, and once when a lone rider cruised in front of the shop. He wasn't wearing a cut, and I know for a fact that an MC member, especially one in a one-percenter club wouldn't be caught dead on a bike without letting everyone know where his loyalties lie.

As much as it pained me, I went home after shutting down the shop and making sure the doors were secure.

"This shit has got to stop," I mumble looking at the mess on the living room floor.

I reach down and pick up the pile of fuzz at my feet, then take a few feet and scoop up the carcass of the monkey that was in pristine condition when I left the house.

"What did he ever do to you?"

I hold the destruction in my hands. Per his usual, Raider has his forehead against the wall, the only sound he makes coming from the occasional thwap of his tail on the hardwood floor.

"You won't chew on a rawhide or a tennis ball, but you maim every stuffed toy I bring in the house."

I grin when he looks away from me, eyes down, thoroughly chastised. I drop the wreckage in the trash and walk over to him. His tail thumps harder on the floor.

"Did your mom drop you on your head when you were a pup?"

More tail thumping, only this time he actually puts some energy into it.

"I thought service animals were supposed to be regal and well behaved."

His jowls flutter, popping against his teeth as if he knows I should know better than to expect more from him.

"Come here," I call and slap my leg. He turns, jovial, all signs of remorse gone from his smiling face as he bounds the couple of feet across the room and nearly knocks me on my ass.

He licks my face, and I rub him all over as he squirms under my hands. When I snap my fingers twice, he's all business again.

"Good thing," I say reaching into the bottom drawer of the cabinet I have the living room TV on and pull out another monkey, "that I have a spare."

His eyes dart from me to the monkey and back again. He's begging, but after I've given him a command, he won't break until I relieve him. Smiling, I pat my leg and toss him the monkey whose fate is sealed the second he catches it in midair and trots off with it between his teeth.

I click the TV on, turning to some random channel I can't concentrate on. I need to shower. I'm filthy as hell, a deep, hard scrubbing the only thing that will get my hands clean, but fuck if I want to clean Delilah's scent off of my body. Hell, I stood over the toilet at the shop earlier to take a piss and nearly sprayed the damn wall. When the delicate scent of her pussy made it to my nose, the good Lord couldn't have even stopped the erection.

Jaxon Donovan better get his shit together and quick because staying away from Delilah is going to be next to impossible, and waiting isn't my strongest trait.

Chapter 33

Delilah

"Why are you frowning this time?"

I pull my eyes from my phone and look up at Ivy. The scowl on her face rivals the one that has marked mine for the last week.

"There's a party near campus," I mutter and slap my phone on the coffee table.

Tucking my legs up and resting my head on my knees, I watch her as she stuffs her purse full of lord knows what.

"And you didn't get invited?"

I huff. "I'm always invited. It looks like it's going to be a blast and yet I'll be here, seeing as I promised to stop partying."

"Such a travesty," she mocks. "Now tell me the truth."

My head lifts from my knees, and I look out the window.

"No clue what you're talking about."

"Don't give me that crap." Sitting down on my left she forces herself into my line of sight. "You've been grumpy for days."

"I haven't," I argue.

Her eyebrow cocks up, and she gives me the look, the one that says she knows I'm full of shit and I just need to spill it.

"I'm pretty sure it has everything to do with Lawson. You told me he took you to get the rental, but something else happened didn't it?"

"I'm going to be making love to you for the rest of my life," says the man who then never calls or stops by.

I close my eyes, but the heat of her gaze burns hot on my face. She's relentless, and I know she won't give up.

I squeeze them tighter, the sting of the tears I allowed on the drive back from the rental place renewed with thoughts of him.

"We had," I begin, but stop short. "We fucked in his truck."

"He had sex with you in a truck?" I can hear the disdain in her voice, and for some reason, it rubs me the wrong way.

"I fucked *him* in his truck." I don't question the defense of his honor. I can hate him all day long. I can regret the things we did, a week ago as well as back home, but I won't put the blame on him for something of my own doing. I won't let anyone else do that either.

I hear her sigh. Opening my eyes, I find sadness in hers.

"Well, you said you were going to." A comforting hand reaches out and rests on my shoulder. "So it was awful? You built him up all this time, and then he sucked at the banging?"

"*Banging*?" I chuff a laugh. "I wish he sucked at it."

A wide grin spreads across her face. "You liked it too much, and now you're having trouble with the one and done."

Not a question. She reads me like a book.

"Not like I have much of a choice. He hasn't called or come by all week. Seems he doesn't have a problem with one and done."

"He will. I'm certain of that. He's not like the shitheads you meet at those stupid parties. The way he looked at you." She looks away, a dreamy light shining in her eyes. "I'd give anything for someone to look at me like that."

"You mean Griffin."

She snaps her head back in my direction. "What?"

"You want *Griffin* to look at you that way."

Her lips tilt up in the corners, but she catches herself before it turns into a full smile.

"I'm no longer waiting for him," she says with confidence.

It's my turn to reach out to her. "If you love him, you need to wait. He's worth waiting for, Ivy. Believe me, you don't want to live with the regret if you get a chance with him."

I should know, my own regret nearly levels me every day.

"He's supposed to be home for Thanksgiving," she adds changing the subject.

I may have silently pined after Lawson for two years, but Ivy has been infatuated with Griffin since she realized boys existed. He was the first boy she ever saw, and she's been watching him ever since.

"I say corner him and kiss him senseless."

"I wish," she mutters.

Before I can offer any more sound advice, my cell phone rings.

Although the number is unfamiliar, I can see that it's local. I shrug at Ivy and answer.

"Hello?"

"Ms. Donovan?"

"Speaking. How can I help you?" I eye Ivy as she gets off of the couch, grabs her gym bag and waves her goodbye.

"This is Joel from Camel Towing. Your car is ready to be picked up."

I let out a relieved sigh. "Awesome. Give me about an hour? I have to drop the rental off."

"Sure thing," he replies. "We're open until six."

***

"Ready my ass," I hiss as I climb out of the Uber and see my car still up on that damn rack inside of the shop.

On a mission to rip Lawson's ass, I stomp across the parking lot to the big garage door, stopping short when the man of the damn hour appears wiping his greasy hands on a shop towel.

He looks over my head, darting his eyes back and forth.

"What the hell are you doing here, Delilah?"

I take a step back, caught off guard by his irritation.

"Joel called and said my car was ready," I explain when all I want to do is find the heaviest thing in my reach and knock him upside the head with it. Violent idealizations are new to me, and the realization only makes me madder.

"Obviously he's mistaken," he says looking over his shoulder, first at my car and then at Joel.

The wide grin on the old man's face doesn't match what I would expect from someone sorry for making a mistake.

"What did you do?" Lawson asks his business partner.

"Wrong car," Joel murmurs and disappears back inside, but pops his head back out. "You've been bristly for a damn week. I was getting tired of it."

"This isn't your business," Lawson hisses.

Joel, I'm sure used to his attitude, just waves a shop towel at him and disappears again. I bite the inside of my cheek to keep from smiling. Just the thought of Lawson being as miserable as I have over the last week brings a certain joy.

"Ma'am," he says as he sweeps his arm toward the front door of the shop. His official tone enrages me.

Fuck me in the truck then pretend I'm some random customer? Not today, Satan. Not today.

"If you'll follow me, I'll be able to provide more info on your vehicle."

I follow him, only because I'm losing my shit, and crying this close to the street isn't something I'll ever do. I want to turn and walk away, but my rental car has been safely returned, and it would take ten to fifteen minutes for another Uber to show up.

He closes the blinds on the door the second I step inside. Next thing I know, I'm plastered against the wall, and his body is hovering over mine.

"The fuck are you doing?" I push at his chest, but I'm not strong enough to create even an inch of distance between us.

"Why are you fighting me?" The low purr of his voice combined with the desire visible in his eyes is more than I can handle.

"Get off," I spit.

I straighten my clothes when he backs away a few inches.

"Why?" he asks again.

"Seriously? You treated me like shit two years ago, you talk to me that way outside?" I point behind me for emphasis. "Then you want to jump on me the first fucking second no one is around?"

"You don't understand," he mutters, his large hand running over his face.

"I sure as hell don't. I also don't trust you. It's like you're two different damn people and I never know which asshole is going to come out and play when I'm around."

"I've got a lot of shit going on right now," he says taking another step back. "It's not safe for you to be here right now."

My blood runs cold. "Afraid your girlfriend will find out we fucked last week?"

I slide past him and sit down in the old chair in front of the desk. After pulling my phone out of my pocket, I use the app to schedule another driver to pick me up.

I realize too late that sitting in the chair only gives him more power over me.

With hands resting on the armrests, he leans in close enough that each of his exhales are breathed into my own lungs. "My girlfriend was there when we fucked, and she's sitting right here looking amazing, gorgeous, and totally fuckable."

I tilt my head to the side, the only way to get a couple of inches between our mouths. "You need your head checked."

"We've been apart for too long, and you're crazy if you think I'm walking away from you again."

"Two years," I lament more to myself than him before turning my eyes up to meet his. "Things would've been different if you'd only waited eighteen months."

He looks confused.

"I could've given you all of me then."

Why am I even vocalizing this to him?

"You gave me all of you last week," he counters.

The tears that only seem to make an appearance when he's around pool on my bottom lashes. He kisses each one, the moisture glistening on his lips when he pulls away.

"Quit fighting this," he begs.

"I'm not that same girl from New Mexico."

"You're better," he whispers.

I shake my head. "I hate that you waited. I hate that we've been so close for so long and you came to work every day and couldn't be bothered to reach out to me."

He backs away, his full face coming into view. "I was working on myself, becoming a man you could be proud of."

"I was proud of the man you were then." I frown. "Well, I thought I was, but your actions proved who you really were."

"I can apologize for that night a hundred times a day for the rest of our lives if you need me to, but eventually you need to forgive me so we can move past it."

"I don't know if I can."

A loud bang snaps both of our heads in the direction of the shop.

"Shit," Joel grumbles.

When Lawson looks back at me, all of the care and comfort that I love so much is there, but there's a tinge of agitation in his eyes that's making his brow furrow.

"Let me take you home," he offers.

"No need," I say and stand from the chair. "I called an Uber."

"Princess," he chides. "Just go get in the damn truck."

I smile as he escorts me with a hand to my back, but regain a look of impassivity before he can see it. I hate the alarm bells and constant arguments going on between my head and my heart.

Chapter 34

Lawson

My lips part, a puff of air leaving my lungs when I watch Delilah climb in my truck and breathe deep. I know she does not smell what I longed for every day when I got inside. To my despair, the scent of our love-making didn't last as long as I'd hoped.

"You like the smell in here?" She nods, pink creeping up her neck to her cheeks at being called out. "The leather of the seats?"

It's all I can smell now.

She shakes her head. "Your cologne. You've always smelled so good."

"I can say the same thing about you." I crank the truck and pull out of the parking lot, praying I hit every single red light between here and her apartment. "It smelled like both of us until Tuesday. Made me hard as steel every time I got inside."

Her teeth scrape over her bottom lip as chill bumps race up her arms and disappear under the short sleeves of her t-shirt.

"I was sore for two days," she confesses as her head tilts a few inches to the right. My mouth waters with the need to lick the delicate column of her throat.

She's right about not being the same girl from years ago. That young, innocent girl wouldn't have had a clue on seduction. The minx sitting in my truck right now doesn't have an ounce of cluelessness in her body. The realization of her words hits me in the gut and steals my breath.

"Things would've been different if you'd only waited eighteen months."

I look away from her, hating the patience I somehow managed even knowing she was only a few miles away.

"I could've given you all of me then."

White-knuckling the steering wheel and trying to focus on anything but her is an exercise in futility. Her movement catches my eye as we slow at a red light.

"Jesus," I mutter when her finger traces over her collarbone.

The tip of her pink tongue is trapped between her teeth, and her eyes never waver from mine.

"Want to go back to the park?" Raspy words filled with promise.

"I'm not making love to you in this truck again." If I don't get her home and put more than three feet of distance between us, my cock is going to revolt.

"Okay." A provocative word only because it releases on a breathy moan. "You can just fuck me then."

My eyes narrow, but they stay on the traffic in front of me. She's purposefully trying to piss me off by separating the act from the emotion it includes.

I'm fuming by the time we pull up to the parking lot of her apartment complex.

"What are you doing?" she asks, eyes darting from me to the front of the building.

"Walking you up." I close my door and walk around to get hers.

Regardless of her words and attempt at enticement in the truck, she's a lady and waits for me to open her door for her. She's also agitated that I didn't just drop her off and refuses to take my hand so I can help her down.

I steady her when she bounces out of the seat and wobbles from the impact.

"You know what they say about men who drive big trucks." She shoves off my aid and tries to walk past me.

Closing her door with more restraint than I actually feel, I urge her back against the door, crowding her and forcing her chest against mine. "I think you know I'm not compensating for shit, Princess."

"Meh," she mumbles.

I chuckle at her feigned apathy. "Sore for two days. You said so yourself."

I want to nip at her throat as it swallows roughly, but I keep my eyes on hers, my face mere inches away. She's not unaffected, but for some reason, she's fighting me every step of the way. If she wants proof that I'm not the same man, that I'm not walking away from her, I have no problem proving it to her in any way she needs.

"I was sore because you didn't bother to make me wet w-when..." She swallows again and the pink I love so very much creeps back into her embarrassed cheeks. "When we fucked."

I press against her harder, the thickness of my cock pushing against her stomach. I've never hated clothes as much as I do right now.

"One," I say nipping at her throat and smiling when she gasps, and her body shudders. "We made love. No matter where, no matter how hard I pound into that sweet pussy of yours, it's still making love. I don't care if I have you bent over my motorcycle on a deserted gravel road in broad daylight with you begging me to slip inside of your ass, it's still making love."

Her lips part, breath quickening.

"Two." I lick at her lips, but pull back as she opens her mouth further. Her small hands cling to my shirt as I lean in close to her ear. "You were wet at just the thought of me slipping inside of you. You creamed so much on my cock, your pussy juice coated my balls."

My pulse is pounding in my ears. My mouth dry from taking ragged breaths, and I'm seconds away from embarrassing myself by coming in my jeans.

"Gross," she hisses and pushes against my chest.

I take the reprieve she offers and move back a few steps.

"Seems you haven't changed a bit." She turns to walk in the direction of her apartment, but I don't miss the wobble in her first couple of steps. She's just as affected as I am.

I adjust myself in my jeans and follow behind her.

"I'm capable of getting myself inside," she mumbles as she begins to climb the stairs.

"I wouldn't turn down the opportunity to follow your gorgeous ass, ever."

She huffs as she presses her key into the lock on her door. The second it opens a terrified scream echoes around us. On instinct, I press Delilah's back against the outside wall and reach into my boot.

"Stay here, baby."

She nods, tears already welling in her gorgeous blue eyes.

"Ivy," she whimpers.

"Oh, God," Ivy screeches again.

I follow her voice down the small, narrow hall. I'm man enough to admit that I'm scared, my nerves causing a slight tremble in my hands.

Peeking around the corner to the small bathroom, I do my best to evaluate what's going on in the split second I give myself to look.

What the?

I lower my gun and take a step into the bathroom.

"Are you fucking kidding me?"

Ivy turns and screams again, this time pointing her can of hairspray and toilet brush at me, her new perpetrator.

Her eyes widen and sweep over me before going back to the spider clinging to the wall of the shower.

"Ivy," I nod and turn away.

She hisses, the hairspray and toilet brush clattering to the floor as she realizes that her robe was open. I can admit that Ivy has a great body, but I'm also so fucking thankful she still has on a bra and panties because this situation is already going to be awkward as fuck.

"Delilah," I call and watch as her tear-stained face comes into view around the door frame. I hold out my hand. "It's fine, baby. Come here."

She walks toward me, but her steps falter when she sees the pistol down by my side. Clearing my throat, I bend and place the weapon back into the holster in my boot.

Ivy slides past me, the width of the door barely enough to keep us from touching, but she manages.

"Spider," she tells her friend with a shiver that tells of a room full of black widows, not one little guy probably more terrified of her.

"Wuss," Delilah mutters walking past her into the room.

She picks the daddy long legs spider up and carries it out the front door.

"You should've killed it!" Ivy shouts as Delilah walks back in and closes the front door.

"Get in the shower," Delilah says and plops down on the couch.

I join her in the living room just as she's wiping the tears from her eyes.

She laughs when I reach for her but pulls her head away before I can make contact.

"I think that's enough excitement for one day," she says with a laugh.

"Scared me, too," I confess and sit down beside her.

"Why do you have a gun?"

She was apprehensive when she noticed the gun in my hand. I imagine being around her dad, and the other Cerberus guys have given her a ton of respect for weapons, but the way she eyed me is confusing.

"I have a permit."

"You have a criminal record," she counters as if I'm lying to her.

"Not anymore." More confusion draws in her brow. "It was expunged."

"Dad," she mutters.

"He's been very helpful in many ways."

We sit in silence. I want to talk to her about what was said outside. I want to assure her that she doesn't have to fight me at every turn, but she stares off, looking at nothing, and not saying a word.

For the first five minutes, I watch her, reorienting myself with every dip and delicate curve of her face. After that, I take in her apartment, waiting for her to speak. She doesn't tell me to leave, so I see that as progress and mentally put a tick in the win column for myself.

"Well, that was exciting," Ivy says breaking into the quietness of the room.

Ivy smiles at me when I look up at her. Her hair is still wet, but thankfully she's now fully dressed.

"I hope you're hungry, Lawson. I ordered pizza for lunch."

"He's not staying," Delilah huffs.

"I'm starved," I tell her friend and sink deeper on the sofa.

Chapter 35

Delilah

"Really?" I frown as I walk up to the couch and notice the new seating arrangement. "I leave to get napkins, and you pull this shit."

Ivy chuckles as Lawson spreads his legs further apart, taking up the center of the sofa. He was down on one end, Ivy was in the middle, and I was on her right, but thirty seconds later and they've both moved.

"You're as transparent as air," I mutter to Ivy.

"You can sit on my lap," Lawson whispers when I give in and claim the end of the couch.

My heart thumps behind my rib cage at his offer, one I'd love to take him up on, but keeping my distance is more important.

"Don't you have work?" I hand each one of them a napkin and pick my paper plate up off of the coffee table.

"Joel can handle things for the afternoon." He looks at me with seductive promise in his eyes. "I'm yours for the rest of the day."

I roll my eyes but grin behind my slice of pizza as I raise it to my mouth.

"If you had a little better work ethic, my car would be done already."

"I'm not wasting time or money fixing that heap of junk, Delilah." My eyes widen.

"What the hell have you been doing for the last week and a half?"

He shrugs as if it's no big deal that I've been in a rental car. I shouldn't complain because the car I've had is ten times better than the Corolla, but it's the principle.

"Fixing bikes. Working on cars that are worth fixing."

"Unbelievable," I hiss.

"Who's up for a movie?" Ivy interrupts, feeling the tension that's growing by the second in the room.

"I've got nowhere to be." The smug smile on Lawson's face makes me want to slap him and kiss him at the same time.

After wiping his mouth with his napkin, he stands and takes both of our plates to the trash and even slides the uneaten pizza into the fridge before excusing himself to the bathroom.

"You need to quit whatever it is you think you're doing," I tell Ivy with a pointed look. "It's not helping."

She just smiles at me. "I'm a virgin, but the sexual tension bouncing between you two is making me tingly."

"Stop," I hiss when I hear the toilet flush. "Sex isn't everything."

"Sex *wasn't* everything," she corrects. "That man loves you, and you'd be a fool to let him go."

She snaps her head back in the direction of the TV and scans through the channels as Lawson opens the bathroom door and sits even closer to me on the sofa.

"Game of Thrones marathon?" Ivy asks, already knowing how hot I get for Jon Snow. I refuse to acknowledge his dark hair and blue eyes because it means confessing my attraction to him over the years has more to do with him resembling Lawson than Kit Harrington.

"Love this show," Lawson says scooting even closer to me.

His warmth, his scent wash over me. God, this man will be my undoing.

"Come here, baby." His breath heats my neck, and my body responds with goosebumps. "I'll keep you warm."

Like the bipolar sadist I am, I allow him to wrap his arms around my back as I snuggle into his chest. I sigh my contentment, and it seems to calm him.

But true to Lawson form he ruins the moment of surrender with his damn mouth. "Try not to think about my cock while we watch Khal Drogo take command of his queen."

I try to pull away, slapping him the only thing I can concentrate on.

"Wrong," I whisper when I realize exactly which scene we're watching. "Daenerys owns his cock."

Lawson shifts uncomfortably as we both watch the scene playing out on the TV screen in front of us. It looks very similar to the way I straddled him in the truck and rode him until we both came.

He groans and shifts again when my fingers curl against his thigh.

"You own my cock," he pants, uncaring that my best friend is a few feet away.

I dart my eyes in her direction, but by the way she's nibbling on her thumb, I don't think she heard him.

"Hush," I tell him.

His chest rumbles against the side of my face, but he doesn't argue. Before long even the battles playing out on the TV can't keep me awake. The hand roaming from the top of my head and down my back in slow, rhythmic strokes is my downfall.

It isn't until I feel my body being lifted from the couch that I realize I fell asleep.

I cling to his shirt when he pulls away after placing me on the bed and covering me up. I'm begging without words as I look into his eyes. Normally, I would feel too prideful, but in the quiet of the room, with nothing but care and concern in his eyes, I feel a sense of freedom I've never felt before.

"Princess," he whispers against my cheek.

He could crawl in behind me, spread my legs, and sink deep inside and I wouldn't object. By the tension pulling at the corners of his eyes, I know he's well aware of that fact.

His hand cups my cheek just before his lips sweep over mine.

"I don't hate you," I tell him. "But my heart can't trust you yet."

He smiles against my lips, a reaction I wasn't expecting. I wait, looking into the blue depths of his soul, once again preparing myself for some remark that's only going to serve to burn another bridge so precariously built between us.

"That's the most honest thing you've said since we reconnected." He kisses me again. Soft, sweet, with love, not the fiery passion that seems to overflow between us. "Take all the time you need, baby. I'm not going anywhere.

***

I smile into my pillow, the scent of his skin all over mine from our snuggling on the couch. What I don't have is the warmth of his skin against my back any longer.

Maybe his promise of not going anywhere was meant in a not-quite-so literal sense, but that doesn't ease my anger very much.

I stagger to the coffee pot, only to find Ivy already at the small kitchen table.

"Sleep well?"

The playfulness of her voice tells me she suspects more happened last night with Lawson than actually occurred.

"Yes," I answer honestly. I didn't realize until he climbed behind me, insisting on staying on top of the covers even after I'd tried to persuade him differently, just how exhausted I've been. I haven't slept well since he showed up in the parking lot when my car broke down, but last night was different. I'm wide awake, though annoyed he's not here, and ready to take on the day.

"What's that?" I snap out of it and look over at her.

"What's what?"

I smile behind my coffee cup.

"That silly grin on your face." She smiles too. "Did you catch feelings for Lawson?"

"Catch feelings?" I mull over her words while my mind races for an excuse. "I didn't catch anything."

"True," she says with a quick tilt of her head. "I guess since they were always there, you can't really catch them again."

"That's not what's happening."

"Tell that to Lawson. He's head over heels for you." She points to a set of keys on the counter. "He left his truck. Said he had to get to work."

"He needs to stop doing shit like that." I hate the words the second they're out of my mouth. It's clear I'm not one hundred percent over my anger. I lock down the vulnerability I showed last night in the soft light of the moon.

"Don't do this to yourself." I turn my back to her, adding unnecessary sugar to my already sweet coffee. "You going to punish him for words he said so long ago?"

"He spoke to me like I was some filthy whore," I rebut.

"He said some pretty dirty things to you on the couch last night while watching TV."

"Exactly. See he'll never change."

She shakes her head in disbelief. "Did you squeeze your thighs together like you did last night when he said that stuff to you two years ago?"

I hiss, jolted by her words enough that I spill my coffee down the front of my shirt. I stare in disbelief, and if I'm being honest a little proud of Ivy as she leaves me reeling in the kitchen.

I've thought, probably more often than I should've, about that night in my room with Lawson. My mind was overwhelmed then, wondering if Samson was going to tell Dad and Pop about things he'd only suspected. I worried over whether they would kick him and Drew out. I know deep in my heart that had Lawson not done something to push me away that I would've done the exact same thing to him.

I can be indignant all damn day, but the outcome would've been the same, only he would hate me instead of me pretending to hate him.

Pretending.

It's the first time I've allowed myself to admit the truth.

I've never hated Lawson. If anything, seeing him again, feeling his lips on mine, takes me right back to where we were when I was just an immature, inexperienced girl who wanted nothing more than the love of a boy she shouldn't have wanted in the first place.

"Fuck," I grumble as I place my half-consumed coffee in the sink and make my way to the bathroom.

I turn the radio up almost loud enough to drown out the thoughts and images of Lawson that bombard me as I strip out of my clothes.

While I scrub his scent from my body and wash my hair, I steel my spine once more. Even with my feelings, there are a million reasons why Lawson and I shouldn't be together. The only problem is as I rinse the suds from my hair, I can't think of a single one.

Chapter 36

Lawson

"You sound frustrated."

I huff into my phone, ready to knock the head off of the Uber driver if he so much as looks over his shoulder while I'm in the back seat of his car thinking of ways to kill my dad.

"Explain it to me one more time," I hiss into the phone.

"Blade sent a few guys to Purgatory Chasm. Ravens Ruin has found a shop in Worcester that will do their bidding."

"And Cerberus is just going to let that happen?"

"Calm down, Rambo." His chuckle is like nails on a chalkboard right now. "They're under surveillance, and you don't need to worry about it. You didn't want the club."

"And you won't talk about it. I wasn't spending four years in the Corps to join." We've been through this a hundred times. The time in the service is a requirement for official acceptance in Cerberus MC, one I wasn't willing to commit to.

"I *can't* talk about it," he clarifies. "Why the attitude?"

I take deep breaths before I continue. "You said you found out two days ago."

"Correct." His voice lowers, calming and sedate. "Why are you upset?"

"Are you sure she's safe?"

"She was never in danger, Law. We were just keeping it that way."

"I spent a week away from her." I scrub my hand over my face doing my best to keep from telling the driver to take me back to her.

"I haven't seen her since May," Jaxon informs me. "So I know what it's like to miss her."

"Exactly," I agree too soon.

"You didn't miss her last night." There's mirth in his voice, but only having known him for two years, I still worry about when the conversation will change from support and morph into disgust.

"I swear nothing happened."

He laughs. The chuckles from farther away tell me I'm on speaker phone and Rob is nearby.

"You're both grown," he clarifies.

"I don't feel very grown with you tracking our phones," I murmur.

"When you have children, you'll understand."

I nod even though he can't see me. The thought of having kids doesn't scare me one damn bit because I know Delilah will be an incredible mother.

"In years," Dad says in a long breath. "When you have children years down the road. *Years*, right Law?"

I laugh.

"Law." Rob's voice this time. "His head's about to explode."

"Years," I concede as a smile spreads on my face. "We'll still be having children years from now."

I hear him yelling when I hang up on them. That's what he gets for not telling me forty–eight hours ago that Ravens Ruin MC wasn't a threat to her. I may have spent time with her yesterday, but we could've already had another day of connection under our belts. I need every second to build what Delilah is trying to reject.

***

"Put your shirt on."

I smile as the voice of my angel echoes through the shop. I was hoping she would stop by today, but as time dragged on, I let doubt creep in.

I turn in her direction, using the shop towel to swipe at the sweat running down my abs.

"You seem to be enjoying the view."

Her lips smack together as if she's getting ready to say something, but no sound comes out. Her eyes don't pull from my stomach either. If it's a weapon in my arsenal, I'll use it. Leaning back against the truck I was just bent over, I kick my legs out, crossed at the ankles. The position allows me to contract my stomach for optimal viewing.

"You look..."

"You're pretty fucking spectacular yourself." She's wearing the same lacy shorts she had on the day her car broke down, but her top is different. This one slides off of her shoulder, revealing a thin strap and hinting at the lace covering her perfect breasts.

Her eyes snap to mine. "Grungy and dirty. That's what I was going to say."

I hold my tongue as I watch her fight the urge to take another look.

"Where's my car?"

"Round back. Waiting for a tow to the junkyard."

I expect a fight, an argument at a minimum, so when her breath shudders, it catches me by surprise.

"Was it really that bad?"

"Sorry, Princess."

"I've had that car since I learned to drive."

I never thought I'd see her so emotional over a damn car, especially since I know she knows how much I care about her and she's all too eager to push me away.

"You've only been driving what three? Four years tops? You'll get another one."

"Is it that easy for you to just replace things that were once important to you when you get tired of them? When they're no longer pristine and perfect?"

I recoil at her words. "It's just an old car, Delilah."

She turns her back to me and mutters. I stop cold.

"What did you just say?"

She shakes her head and walks out of the front of the garage.

"What did you say?" I repeat.

She spins, wiping at fresh tears on her cheeks. "I said I loved that car."

I shake my head. "It sounded a lot like 'I fell in love in that car.'"

She shrugs, and I clench my fists so tight my knuckles pop. "His name was Danny. We spent a couple weeks together in the summer."

I growl at her but keep my distance. It's the only thing keeping me from shaking some damn sense into her.

A mischievous glint hits her blue eyes, the corner of her mouth twitching. I can already tell, true to Delilah form that she's going to mask her emotions with some damn joke as a distraction. "We laughed and sang together. Frolicked in the surf of the ocean."

I tilt my head, confused as fuck. "What?"

She nods towards the shop. "He loved cars, too. Seems I have a type."

Frolicked in the surf? Loved cars?

"Wait." I take a step toward her. "Did you just describe fucking *Grease* to me?"

She rolls her teeth to stop her laugh, but it's not enough as it bubbles up her throat. God, I love her smile.

"You realize every one of those songs is filled with tons of sexual innuendo. If you pay attention, you'd realize they have filthier mouths than I could ever dream of."

Her eyes dart to my mouth and down my glistening chest.

My phone buzzes in my pocket, and I make sure my stomach flexes in all the right places when I reach to get it. I look down at the text and frown.

"What's wrong?" I love the concern in her voice.

"An emergency," I lie. Well, not a total lie, but my neighbor may try to kill me in my sleep if I don't get home quickly. I pull my t-shirt over my head and sweep my hand toward my truck. She offers me the keys. "Your pussy wagon, my lady."

She snorts but walks in that direction. "Travolta drove a Ford."

"I'll trade the Chevy in tomorrow, baby. Hurry. I have to get home."

She hustles inside, still letting me open and close her door for her.

"You going to tell me what's going on?" she asks as we make our way around the block toward my house.

I smile at her but shake my head. "You'll see."

We drive, with the radio playing softly. She hums along to the lyrics of a song I've never heard before but has somehow managed to become my favorite.

"Why did you leave so early this morning?" I grin even wider at the insecurity in her voice which makes me an asshole.

"Miss me, Princess?"

"No," she insists, but I see the smile on her face before she turns it from view.

"I had to make sure Joel didn't burn my shop down yesterday. Had a few things to check off my list before the weekend, and then I planned to come right back to you."

"I don't want you—" She stops right before shutting me down once again. "Is this your house?"

I frown because I know she's just putting off the inevitable.

"It is." I turn the truck off and point. "And that is my very pissed off neighbor."

I open her door for her, and it surprises me when she places her hand in mine to climb down and doesn't pull it free when we start to walk across the yard.

I whistle and wait for the clinking of Raider's dog tags. The sound never comes, but a bark can be heard from inside the house.

"Mrs. Houston?"

She hitches her thumb over her shoulder. "I'm calling the Homeowner's Association if that satanic dog isn't locked up immediately."

Delilah stiffens beside me.

I smile when the dark headed woman appears behind Mrs. Houston.

"Hey, Lawson," Cynthia says as she wraps her arms around her grandmother's shoulders. "Raider's been agitated more than usual. I normally wouldn't bother you while you're at work."

"I'll take care of him. Thanks for letting me know."

I tug on Delilah's hand as I pull her toward my house and Cynthia turns her grandmother around and guides her back to her house.

"She's pretty," Delilah says with a huff as I unlock my front door. Jealousy coming from Delilah Donovan has to be the best thing to happen since Harley came out with its Softail. "And she has your cell phone number. That's lovely."

I remain quiet as she enters my home for the very first time, but I can tell she's working herself from mild envy of Cynthia to full-blown agitation.

"Does she come to visit when the old lady goes to sleep?"

I grab her by her shoulders and spin her around. "She has my number because sometimes her grandmother can't hear when the phone rings and she gets worried about her. She's never been inside of my home. Hell, I don't know that she's even stepped foot on my grass. And yes, Delilah, Cynthia is very pretty. A trait I'm absolutely certain her husband loves about her."

A banging noise bounces off of the walls down the hallway. I give her a quick kiss on her stunned lips and head to my dog.

I whistle and the banging stops.

When I open the door to the nearly empty guest bedroom, Raider doesn't even bother to act ashamed of the mess he's created. He lunges for me.

"You," I tell him scratching at his face as he licks my neck. "Are defective. I'm going to take you back if you keep this shit up. How does such a smart dog close himself inside of a bedroom?"

He yips, keeping to his inside voice and licks me more.

"You would never take a dog back to an animal shelter." Delilah sounds thoroughly offended behind me.

Standing on his back legs, Raider is almost as tall as I am which makes it very easy for him to peer over my shoulder. I've never seen his tail wag so hard in the time we've been together.

"Shelter?" I laugh. "A shelter animal would be smarter than this dummy."

Raider withdraws his legs and makes it to Delilah in less than a handful of steps. She's knocked on her gorgeous ass before she can prepare herself for the dog's attention

I snap my fingers, and he backs away immediately, a low whimper his only sign of discomfort.

"That's impressive," She says wiping dog spit from her face. Her smile is the biggest I've seen since before I left New Mexico.

"He's not a shelter dog?" Sad eyes look up at me. "Please tell me you didn't get him from a breeder. Tons of places breed animals in horrid conditions. Unless you visit there yourself, you never know how they're treated."

"He's a therapy dog," I confess waiting for the shame to hit me in the chest, but it never comes.

She grins back at Raider and pats her lap. The longing look he gives me over his shoulder is almost enough to make me let him go, but he knocked her down and could've hurt her. I don't care how excited he is that another human being is in my home, that's entirely unacceptable.

"He seems fine," she says but frowns when the dog stays. "Does he have a brain condition?"

She pats her lap again and the dog whimpers.

"Raider." His ears perk up, tail giving the slightest twitch. "Be gentle."

He eases toward her, almost crawling on his stomach until his head is on her lap, tongue lapping at her hand for attention.

I sit beside them on the floor in the hall.

"He's *my* therapy dog," I clarify. "I was struggling about a year after I got here. Drew was living his life, doing better than anyone expected. He was busy with his friends, and even though I was working crazy hours at the shop, I was lonely. Da-Jaxon suggested a counselor, but I shut that shit down the second the word was out of his mouth."

I expect her to laugh with me, but her face softens when she looks into my eyes.

"A week later he and Rob showed up with this asshole." I rub the scruff on the back of Raider's neck. "They told me he was super smart, knew every trick in the book, but as you can tell from his behavior just a minute ago they were fooled."

Indignant eyes look from me and back to Raider. "How would you act if your person left you locked in a bedroom with no way to use the restroom, eat, or drink?"

I reach for her arm and guide her to the kitchen and point to his food and water bowl, both nearly full. She looks dumbfounded as I guide her to the back of the house and show her the dog door that gives Raider access to the backyard. "Do you really think I'm the kind of guy who locks his dog in a damn room?"

Her head angles in the direction of a soft click. "What was that?"

"Perfect timing," I mutter and tug her arm once again until we're standing in the hallway.

The door to the spare bedroom rattles and Raider whimpers from the other side.

"He shuts the door," I tell her as I push it back open.

"You need to put a stopper under it," she suggests.

"I've done that. He pulls it out and chews it up." I stare down at the deviant who looks up at me as if he understands exactly what I'm saying. "I don't know what else to do."

"Put a dog door in," she says and walks back toward the living room. She looks back over her shoulder. "Aren't you glad you have me?"

I close the distance between us, wrapping my arms around her stomach and pulling her against me.

"So glad I have you," I whisper in her ear before nipping at the spot on her shoulder that drives me wild. "How have I survived without you?"

A low moan escapes her lips as her arm reaches over her head and her fingers run through my hair.

"If it's for my safety, then I think it's best if you just move in tonight."

Chapter 37

Delilah

I stiffen in his arms.

"Stop," I demand as my fingers leave the silk of his jet black hair and claw at the forearms trapping me. "Why do you say shit like that?"

"Like what?"

He doesn't release me but rather turns me in his arms so I'm facing him.

I lower my voice to sound manlier. "Move in. I'll be making love to you for the rest of my life. Take your time, Princess. I'm not going anywhere." I swallow around the lump forming in my throat. "Is this all a damn joke to you?"

"I mean every word I've said to you." His brows draw together, and I resist the urge to run my thumb over the crinkles.

"You can't ask me to move in fifteen minutes after I step inside of your house for the first time."

"I just did." His eyebrow raises in challenge.

"You claim you'll be making love to me forever, but you denied me last night."

"Princess." He cups my cheek and brushes his lips over mine. They part of their own volition as my breathing grows shallow. "You were exhausted. So bone weary, you were asleep seconds after you suggested…"

I love the rush of heat that turns his cheeks pink as he clears his throat.

"After you mentioned us making love."

I shake my head, a smile marking my face as my frustration slowly begins to fade away. "That's not even close to what I said." He grins back at me, hips grinding against mine. "Do you not like it when I talk dirty to you? You can dish it out but can't take it?"

He leans in, mouth less than an inch from mine before he begins again. "You were asleep seconds after you suggested you hug my cock with your tight. Little. Cunt."

My insides quiver. I knew I'd propositioned him and that he turned me down, but I didn't know exactly what I'd said. I just knew it didn't sound anything like 'make love.'

"You said you weren't going anywhere, yet I woke up alone this morning." My voice cracks and he holds me tighter.

"If I woke you to tell you goodbye, and you looked up at me exactly like you're looking at me right now, I never would've gotten out of your bed."

His lips devour mine in a heated kiss that sets every inch of my skin on fire. I'm panting yet reaching for him again when he pulls away.

"And if my tight. Little. Cunt," I punctuate each word just as he had with a smack of my lips against his, "wanted to give you a hug right now?"

"That word on your lips makes me as hard now as it did last night." His tongue snakes across my lips tracing the upper curve.

"I'm a dirty girl."

"*My* dirty girl."

My heart pounds in my ears as his fingers curl against my ass.

"Can I hug you?" I beg as his tongue teases the dips and curves of my neck. "With my pussy."

"Filthy mouth," he praises against my skin.

I stiffen and push his head back until his eyes meet mine. "Make one suggestion about my lips wrapping around your cock, and you'll never see me again."

"Delilah."

"No," I tell him taking a step back but not fully escaping his arms. "Hard limit."

He nods, understanding why I can't bear to hear that coming from his mouth again. Greasy hands run over the top of his head, and he looks harder, noticing the smear of dirt on his forearm.

"Shit," he grumbles. "I bet I ruined your clothes."

He spins me, eyes lowering to my ass.

"Jesus, D. Those shorts will have to be trashed." His eyes look up into mine as I peer over my shoulder at him. He's more upset about stains on my clothes than I am. "I'm so sorry."

"They're just clothes."

"Let me get you something to change into, and I'll grab a quick shower."

"Okay," I agree quickly.

His eyes search mine. "You'll be here when I get out?"

I smile at his insecurity, and the longer I look, the easier it is to tell just how genuine this man is.

"I don't plan to walk home, and I don't want to be arrested for taking your truck."

He laughs as he clasps my hand and pulls me toward his bedroom at the back of the house. Raider, the most amazing dog in the world, tracks us with his eyes and lumbers behind us once we've cleared the threshold to his room and he loses sight of us.

Having forgotten about the possibility of his mouth comment just as fast as I'd imagined it, I shake my head when he offers me a shirt to change into.

"Don't need it."

I watch his mouth go slack as I tug the loose shirt and camisole over my head in one movement. My lacy shorts hit the ground next, revealing that I didn't bother with panties before leaving the house today.

I stand in front of him completely naked for the first time ever.

"Ten minutes," he mumbles. "I'd say seven, but I want to make sure I'm clean."

"Ten minutes," I repeat as he backs out of the room and smacks his head on the open door.

I can't help the laugh that escapes when he turns and sprints down the hall. His boots tumble to the floor in the hallway, and a sock flies past his bedroom door, a pair of jeans comes a split second later.

"Ten minutes is going to seem like forever," I tell Raider as I climb under Lawson's comforter and get lost in his scent.

I'm tracing the stitching on the side of the pillow when I feel his mouth trail kisses along my spine.

"Sorry I took so long," he whispers against the curve of my ass. "I didn't want to embarrass myself again."

I turn over to face him, not realizing until it was too late that my new position put his mouth hovering right over the apex of my thighs.

"You pre-gamed in the shower?"

He nods, the stubble on his chin scraping in the most delicious way on my inner thigh.

"You said I came too fast in the truck." His tongue parts my most sensitive flesh, but his eyes never leave mine. "I didn't want to disappoint you again."

I shake my head, the overwhelming sensation coming from his mouth's contact with my body making the movements jerky and violent.

"I came, too. You didn't disappoint me."

"I don't want to rush tonight." Another swipe of his addictive tongue. "I want to savor you."

My back arches, the glorious licks of his tongue too much and not enough all at the same time.

His eyes close on a soft blink as he teases my entrance. His warm breath, although hot on release doesn't compare to the burn, the need in my clit. My flesh cools with the gusts then heats again on his inhale.

"You're torturing me," I hiss and grab his hair. My hips grind against his mouth.

My legs are spread even further as he devours me. My vision narrows as all the sensation in my body shrinks down to the tiniest pinpoint before exploding over every nerve in my body. I whimper, begging him to stop all the while pushing harder against his face.

"Fuck you're beautiful when you come."

A weak smile is all I'm able to offer him as he kisses up my body. He didn't bother to dress when he finished his shower, and I'm grateful he doesn't have to waste a second taking off clothes.

His fingers trace the lips of my pussy before diving in an inch and dragging back out.

"Just fuck me already."

He shakes his head, but a lascivious smile spreads across his beautiful face. "I have to make sure you're wet."

"I'm so fucking wet," I pant and wiggle my hips.

"I thought you were last time, too, but when you feel me for the next two days, I want it to be from overuse not because I dry fucked you."

I groan and cover my eyes with my forearm. Why I teased him about that is beyond me.

I hiss, my neck lifting off of the bed when his fingers are replaced with his thick cock.

"Damnit." His breath ghosts over my lips. "I don't think pre-gaming is going to even matter."

I start to laugh, but it comes out as a moan when he circles his hips and pulls my thigh higher on his. The soft thatch of dark hair at the base of his cock works wonders on my bare, waxed skin. The contact is absolute as he mumbles and pleads with his cock not to fuck this up.

"Hey," I manage between pleasure filled sighs as I look into his eyes. His hips slow, but that is the last thing I need. "Make love with your mouth, but fuck me hard with your cock."

He swallows my cries as his hips piston me through another earth-shattering orgasm, and he's still thrusting after he crashes over the edge himself.

"Jesus," he pants as he pulls his cock free and sits back on his heels.

I mewl like a kitten when his finger sweeps across the overly sensitive bundle of nerves.

"I never thought your pussy could look more amazing, but my cum dripping out of it tops all I've ever seen."

"What?" I look down, and sure enough, there's a puddle between my legs. "You didn't use a condom? Why didn't you use one?"

I'm frantic, pushing at him with my feet so I can climb out of his bed.

"Why are you freaking out? I'm clean, D. I swear it. I'd never put you at risk."

He clasps my shoulder before I can get away.

"And if I get pregnant?" I ask turning on him like a rabid dog.

His eyes waver between mine and my stomach, with a longing look in his eyes that heats my blood and somehow makes it run cold at the same time.

"My baby growing in your stomach would be the best thing that could happen to me." I glare at him.

"You can't be serious. So that's your plan? Get me knocked up so I can't walk away from you?"

"I felt your IUD jab the head of my cock on the first thrust, Delilah."

"So what," I say shrugging off his arms. "You think that gives you the right to creampie me?"

His eyes light up, and a chuckle falls from his lips.

"And now you laugh at me. Perfect," I mutter and reach for my clothes on the floor.

"Don't," he says with humor still in his voice. His arms wrap around me from behind. "I'm not laughing at you, but the words *creampie* coming from your pouty lips is funny."

"Let me go." I twist and try to escape him even knowing I won't be released from his strong arms until he wants me to leave them.

"Where do you think you're going?"

"We fucked," I say stating the obvious. "It's time for me to leave."

"Stop," he says turning me to face him. There's more anger in that one word than I've ever heard from his mouth before. "Quit running from me."

"You got what you wanted." I lower my eyes. "Just let me leave."

"Got what I wanted?" He catches my left hand and holds it against his chest. "I won't get what I *want* until there's a ring on your finger and our vows have been spoken before our friends and family."

"It was just sex," I insist even though I know the words are a lie.

"It's not just sex with you, and you know it."

I shake my head, rejecting his words before they can sink into my heart and make me want things I don't deserve.

"If you keep running from me, I'll never be able to prove to you how much I care."

When he pulls me against his chest this time, I don't push him away. I let myself give in to the fantasy.

"Stay with me," he pleads as he inches us closer to the bed.

I don't say yes, but I don't stop him from lowering his mouth to mine and spreading me out on his tangled sheets.

Chapter 38

Lawson

As if I can sense the empty bed in my sleep, I wake with a sheen of cold sweat covering my body.

"This is not happening," I mutter as I climb out and pull on a pair of jeans.

The house is empty, my truck keys left abandoned on the counter in the kitchen, right where I dropped them off last night.

We'd made love a second time before falling asleep tangled in each other's arms. I'd cleaned her after releasing on her flat stomach, not willing to take the chance of another outburst.

"Where did she go?" I ask Raider as if he'll be able to tell me. His head cocks to the side, and I know he's calling me an idiot. "How did she get home?"

The clock on the oven says it's after three in the morning.

"Fuck it," I hiss and head to the bathroom.

Less than ten minutes later, I've dressed, brushed my teeth, and I'm out the door, refusing to let another sunrise happen without getting it through her thick skull that we're going to happen whether she likes it or not.

I bang on her door and pray someone doesn't call the cops.

"Really?" Ivy says when she pulls the door open. "Get your shit together. It's starting to interfere with my life now."

I follow her, going down a door farther when she goes back into her room. I'm in the room and on top of Delilah before she even knows I'm there.

"What are you doing?" She presses ineffectual hands against my chest, so I seize the opportunity to pin them over her head.

Dammit, she smells like sin and everything I need.

"I was a complete asshole to you two years ago. From the day I showed up, I told you all the dirty things I wanted to do to you."

I run my nose up her neck and let her sensual moan wash over me.

I squeeze her wrists harder, and she squirms under me.

"Do I need to treat you like shit again to get you to see me?"

She shakes her head but her lips part on a soft pant.

"I hate being this way to you."

"Liar," she challenges. "You're hard."

I press into her harder, hating the covers and clothes separating us.

"It's biology. I can't help it. You breathe near me, and I get hard. You look at me, and I'm hard. I think about your lips, and I'm hard."

"So fuck me then."

"No."

"You know you want me." Her hips rotate against mine, grinding the zipper of my jeans against my cock.

"Always," I swear. "Every minute of the day I want to be inside of your body."

"You can have me," she offers.

"I won't deny I want to be here." I punctuate my words by pressing my straining dick against the center of her thighs. "But I want to be here more."

I press my mouth over her heart, my lips warming against her heated skin.

"That's not part of the deal," she whispers and turns her head as her eyes close.

I rest more of my weight on her. "That's what you're not getting, Delilah. You can fight this between us as much as you want and it will only serve to make me fight more."

"Don't." The plea from her lips is sad and full of despair as if she can't accept the things I'm saying to her.

"I'm going to fight for you," I promise. "For your time, your heart, and most importantly, your love."

"Loving you has never been the problem."

My heart soars...

"Trusting you not to walk away when things get hard is what I can't allow."

...And crashes to the earth, shattering into a hundred pieces.

"I'll do anything for a chance to prove that we belong together." I softly kiss her lips. "Tell me what you need, baby, and it's yours."

"I need time."

I shake my head. "You'll only use it to push me away."

"You're smothering me."

I lean back some, taking most of my weight back and putting it on my knees.

"Not in the literal sense." She reaches for me when I release her hands and pull away. "I love the press of your body against mine."

"That's contradictory, Princess. I don't know if I'm coming or going with you."

"You could be coming soon." She swivels her hips again, and I back away entirely and sit on the edge of the bed.

My head hits my hands as I press my elbows into my thighs.

"You make me wonder if you're only using me for sex."

The tinkle of her laugh meets my ears and makes my throat burn. Now I know how she felt when I laughed at her earlier in my room.

"That's funny to you?" I ask and angle my head so I can look in her eyes.

"You're an amazing lay. The best I've ever had."

The words sting like a thousand pinpricks on my skin, but I don't know if it's her callous delivery or the knowledge that she's been with other men.

"You've probably ruined me for other men."

"Enough," I roar and pin her back down to the mattress. "You won't have to worry about comparing me to other men, Princess. My cock is the last one that will ever have the pleasure of bringing you to orgasm."

"Your cock is the only one that's managed it to begin with."

"You gave yourself to men who didn't deserve you, baby. Now I'm tasked with making up for my mistake for the rest of your life." I lean in close, our mouths a mere inch apart. "Challenge accepted."

"*My* mistake," she says, her voice breaking on the last word.

"I own it a million times over, baby. I should've shown up and banged on your dorm room door the minute you arrived. Fuck that," I correct. "I never should've left New Mexico without telling you how I feel."

"How do you feel?" There's a softness in her eyes I haven't seen since I kissed her the very first time.

"I love you with every molecule of my soul." She gasps. "Don't act surprised. I've told you as often as I can."

"You never used those words." Her eyes squeeze shut.

"Don't block me out when I've laid my heart in your hands. If you can't see yourself feeling the same way, I have the patience of a saint. I'll spend every second of my life making you realize that you're safe." I press my lips to her forehead. "Your *heart* is safe with me."

I back away from her.

"Where are you going?" she asks when I climb off the bed.

"Home," I answer, still unable to face her.

I don't know what I was expecting from her when I finally had the courage to say those words to her, but the sting of her not saying them back burns more than I'd like to admit.

"Stay," she pleads, but I shake my head.

"I can't."

"You can."

"If I climb under those covers and feel the warmth of your body, I'll end up sinking inside of you."

"Sounds like an incredible plan to me." The playfulness after such a serious conversation gives me hope and makes my already hard dick twitch in my jeans.

"That's not what either of us needs." I lean in and kiss her one more time, lingering on her lips for a long moment before standing up again.

"Who's walking away now?" She asks my back as I reach for the doorknob. I know she's teasing but now is not the time.

"This isn't a game, Delilah."

"I never said it was." The hint of anger in her voice comes from nowhere.

"Then quit playing. Your words have consequences."

Her bottom lip quivers in the darkness. "I asked you to stay, and you say you have to go. I can't beg you, Lawson. I don't have it in me."

My shoulders slump forward at the thought of causing her pain, but I need to back away, go home, and lick my wounds. Only then can I regroup and figure out how I need to approach this situation.

She turns over, giving me her back before she speaks again. "I just wanted you to hold me."

"Damn it," I grumble and kick off my boots. My jeans and t-shirt hit the floor next.

She moves forward, giving me more room behind her when I pull the covers back.

"You left my bed," I remind her as my arms wrap around her. "We were lying just like this when I fell asleep. Tell me why you left."

"I don't feel like I deserve you."

I hold her tighter. "You deserve the world, baby, and I plan to give it to you."

Chapter 39

Delilah

"Do you think he even noticed?"

I smile at the guy from my Ethics in Psychology class as he follows me out of the building.

"I don't know how he couldn't. He wasn't wearing any underwear," I tell him with a quick laugh.

"Exactly! If my fly was down while going commando, I know I'd feel the cold air on my dick."

"What would you feel on your dick?"

I stop cold at Lawson's words, but my heart warms at the sight of him standing in front of us, hard scowl and everything.

The guy I was walking with, whose name I don't even know, takes a step back.

"What about your dick?" Lawson asks again with more fire in his voice than the first time.

"Stop," I tell him with a gentle hand on his chest and a quick kiss on his lips.

"Not my dick, dude." He holds his hands up in mock surrender, but Lawson's face still doesn't settle.

"Umm..." I look at the guy from class.

"John," he says eventually.

"John and I were discussing whether our professor knew his fly was down."

"He was commando. I was telling Delilah that he had to have felt the cold air on his dick." He clears his throat. "His dick, nothing about my dick."

"Which class?" Lawson asks without pulling his glaring scrutiny from John.

"Ethics in Psychology," I answer when it seems John has suddenly become mute.

Only then does Lawson look over at me, his eyes softening immediately. "He was testing you. I wouldn't be surprised if he failed all of you for staring *unethically* at his junk all through class without telling him."

I grin at Lawson, knowing full well he's full of shit. I had the same professor last semester, and he's a hot mess on his best day.

"Fuck my life," John mutters. "I already failed that damn class last year. My parents will kill me if I don't pass it this time around."

Lawson's arm curls around my hip, and he turns me away. "Nice meeting you, Jim."

We walk away, John refusing to correct the man at my side.

"Stop," I tell him with a playful slap to his hard stomach. "You'll give that poor boy a heart attack."

"You need a bodyguard," he mutters as we near his truck.

"Where are we going? And you need to stop worrying about the boys in my class."

"Lunch," he tells me offering his hand so I can climb inside. "And that *boy* wanted to fuck you."

I wait to roll my eyes until he's behind the wheel of the truck. "He's awkward at best, besides you have nothing to worry about."

"Yeah?" He cranks the truck but doesn't make a move to put it in gear to leave the parking lot. "And why is that?"

"Lawson O'Neil, are you fishing for compliments?"

He shrugs. "I'll take what I can get."

"Waking up in your arms again this morning was amazing." I flip up the console separating us and crawl closer to him. "But my body misses you. It's hard being so close to you and not feeling you between my legs."

His hands clench the steering wheel until his knuckles turn white, but he doesn't touch me.

I lean in and swipe my nose up the stubble on his chin, relishing his sharp inhale.

"We've slept in the same bed the last three nights." I lick at his ear. "I miss you."

"I'm right here, Princess."

I cup him through the denim of his jeans.

"And ready for me," I whisper in his ear.

"I'm not fucking you in the truck again."

"Then make love to me on the hood," I tease.

He finally turns his face so I can kiss his lips. "You have the ability to test the virtue of a saint. I'd bet my life on it."

"Yet, you're the only one I want to sin with."

"No." He pulls my hand away from his cock, but the strain on his face tells me it pains him to do so. "You're on a new diet."

I raise an eyebrow at him.

"Cock light."

I chuckle at the ridiculousness, but it doesn't thwart my efforts like I'm sure he hoped it would. I turn his palm in mine and press it between my legs. I've never been so glad to be wearing a skirt than I am today.

"Cock light?" He nods and a grumble roars in his chest at finding me wet. "So just the tip then?"

"Sorry, Princess." He pulls his hand away, and I whimper at the loss.

"What's your end game?" I say giving up and flopping back in my seat.

"Your heart." Two simple words that leave me speechless as he puts the truck in drive and leaves my college in the distance.

"This is all your fault to begin with," I accuse with my arms crossed over my chest. "I wasn't even worried about sex until I straddled the damn gear shift in the wrecker."

"I could smell you then," he whispers. "I had a wet spot on my jeans from my cock leaking the rest of the afternoon."

"Gross." I cross my legs but resist the urge to roll the window down. "No, you couldn't."

"I swear it, baby." He licks the tip of his finger that he just had against my panties. "Smells even better now that you've gotten past the hating me stage."

"That's disgusting." Those are my words, but my body responds differently by softening, quickening, and begging for him to take me.

He inhales deep into his lungs when we pull up to a red light.

"Stop," I say with a laugh and slap his chest. "You're crazy."

He grabs my hand that I left lingering against the muscled wall of his chest and brings it to his lips. I pull it back when my phone chimes a text. I pull it out and frown at the screen.

"What's that look for?" It's the same question Ivy asked last week when a similar text came through.

"Party," I mumble. "I left all the groups on social media, and now people are texting me about them."

"I'm not going to stop you from having a good time."

I roll my eyes. "I've never had a good time at a single party I've gone to. Well, it no longer seemed fun the day after."

I look out the window and pray he asks me about them. I have a ton of things that need to be out in the open, for us to talk them through before I ever have a hope of getting past them.

"Really? I thought you couldn't go wrong at a college party, but hangovers suck."

"And vodka makes everything seem like a good idea."

He chuckles, not catching on to the serious tone of my voice.

"The three guys I slept with this summer, I met at college parties."

He stiffens, squeezing my hand a little too tight at my admission.

"Sorry," I mutter. "I shouldn't have brought it up. I know you don't want to hear about it, but I swear I didn't bring it up to make you mad."

I try to pull my hand back, but he maintains his grasp.

"I hate hearing about it, but I understand that you need to get it off of your chest." He kisses the soft skin on my wrist. "Put it out there, baby so we can work through it."

I wait until we're moving again, his focus on driving making it easier for the words to come.

"The first party I went to was after a long conversation with Samson. I was feeling brave and admitted my feelings for you. Put some of the blame on you hurting me right at his feet."

We stop at another red light, and I wait, keeping my eyes focused outside even though I can feel his eyes on the side of my face.

He inches forward, turning right which leads to a more rural area with fewer red lights. He's already caught on and wants me to keep talking.

When the open road stretches out in front of us, I continue.

"We'd had a similar fight the night you snuck in my room. I had every intention of pushing you away that night. He'd threatened to talk to Dad and tell him what was going on between us. He only had suspicions but he can read me like an open book, and I was scared for what that info in Dad's lap would mean for you and Drew."

I trace the window seam with my finger searching for the words.

"That night three months ago, he was an asshole all over again. He told me that I just needed to get over it, get over you. I went to that party and took every drink that was offered to me. When a guy I didn't even know suggested we go somewhere private, I thought it was the best idea in the world. I mean I went there on a mission, but that didn't mean I wanted to do all of that with an audience."

I swipe at the tears rolling down my cheeks and ignore Lawson's ragged breathing.

"When it was over, I felt vindicated. Free from whatever ties I had to you, but then I woke up the next day realizing what I'd done. I cried for a week. I cried until the next party. Then I did the same thing again, praying it would be different. Hoping that I'd feel something, anything with him, but I only felt empty and used."

I look over at Lawson as he pulls the truck over to the side of the road. The tears staining his cheeks makes the bile crawl up my throat, but I'm not done.

"I did it a third time." His eyes search mine, and I have no clue what he's looking for. At this point, I imagine he's going to call me a whore and kick me out of the truck. "The day before my car broke down I was with someone else."

Shame weighs heavy on my shoulders. "I don't even know their names. I was drunk every time. Not that I'm using that as an excuse, but I had to have the alcohol to go through with it."

"Baby."

I shake my head when he tugs my hand, an indication for me to get closer to him. "I cried each time. Even Ivy heard my sobs through the bedroom wall. I cried after we made love in this very truck."

Another squeeze of my hand.

"Not because I was ashamed of you, but because I ruined what could've been between us. I understand if you hate me, but please don't make me walk home from here."

He releases a pitiful laugh. "I could never hate you."

"You should've been my first," I tell him. "It was always meant to be you."

"And you should've been mine," he adds quietly. "But it didn't work out that way."

"You're being too nice."

"Do you hate me for the women that came before you?"

"I hate that there were others," I confess.

"But do you hate *me*?"

I look into his red-rimmed blue eyes and shake my head. "I never hated you."

"Then understand that I feel exactly the same way."

I finally allow him to pull me into his lap. His lips rest against my temple as he cradles me to his chest.

"Even now with all of this sitting heavy in the air around us, my body hums for you," I confess against his t-shirt.

"Is it only your body that wants me?"

I know exactly what he's asking, and I know that if he can forgive me for what I did while hurting, then it's damn time I forgive myself.

Chapter 40

Lawson

"Where are we going?" There's a smile, a lightness in her voice that hasn't been there in a long time.

"You'll see." I wink at her and take the next road to the left.

"You mentioned lunch back on campus. Are you planning some romantic picnic?"

I frown. "I wish I'd thought of that, Princess, but honestly I'd just planned to eat a meal with you while staring at your mouth."

"Oh." She doesn't sound disappointed, but there's an edge to the word that I don't like.

"The conversation got super serious really quick, and that wasn't planned either." I make another right and come up to the fast food place. "I don't have a picnic planned, but we can grab something quick and then go someplace where it's just you and me."

"That sounds perfect." She leans her head on my shoulder as we wait in line at the drive-thru. I'm thankful for the adjustable console in the truck. She'll never sit apart from me again.

The speaker crackles with a generic menu suggestion when we make it to the ordering sign. "No onions," she whispers.

No onions mean kissing, and I'm totally down for that. I place our order and wait to move up to the window.

"How was class today?"

"Are you asking about school or the boys in my classes?"

"Both," I say telling the truth.

"Was Jim one of the guys you umm... met at the parties?"

"His name is John," she corrects. I know that, but don't want to give her the satisfaction. "And no. I haven't seen any of them since their respective parties. There's a chance they aren't even college students."

She leans away long enough for me to pull cash out of my wallet, but then her tight little body is back against mine.

"Why are you asking?"

I shrug and hand the cashier the money.

"You planning on tracking them down and beating them up."

"Fuck, I wish," I mumble.

Her lips form a smile against my skin.

"Does it turn you on that I want to beat up the men that hurt you?"

"*I* hurt me," she corrects. "They were just the catalyst that allowed it."

I take my change and pull up to the second window.

"I love how possessive you are."

My heart clenches at the word *love* coming from her lips. She may not be saying it in the context I want, but I'll take what I can get.

"I love how you fight for me, knowing exactly what you want and not taking no for an answer." She nips at my neck and as sweet as her words are, it doesn't stop my cock from jerking in my jeans. "How you knew what I wanted, what I *needed*, even when I didn't."

"It's my job, Princess."

"I let less than a dozen words spoken in one sentence two years ago ruin me. I let them have power over me."

She pauses as our food is passed through the window. I hand her the bags so she can place them beside her on the seat and reach to place the drinks in the backseat console. I'll be damned if I'm separating us while this conversation is still going.

With my mind, I beg her to continue, but she remains silent as we head out of town. It isn't until the city scene transitions into empty fields that she begins again.

"I wasted two years of my life pretending to hate you. I let my anger fuel my bad decisions while I was self-destructing."

I pull over at a deserted rest stop, no longer able to concentrate on driving, and when I turn her face up to mine, I no longer see the pain that's been on her beautiful face all afternoon. I find acceptance and a small smile that tells me everything is going to be okay.

"I'm tired of wasting time."

"What are you saying, baby?"

Her eyes drag down to my lips before focusing back on mine.

"I'm not fighting you anymore. I'm not running from you. I'm not pulling away when all I want is to be near you."

I kiss her lips, soft and sweet, full of promises of forever rather than instant sexual gratification.

"That's the second best thing I've heard from your lips."

I kiss her again.

"And the best thing?"

Smiling I turn her chin and run my tongue down the soft slope of her neck, and nip at her earlobe before whispering, "That tiny whimper you make when I sink inside of you."

She makes that sound now, and my balls tighten as if programmed to respond. I groan and flex my hips up when her hand strokes down my length.

"You sure are a dirty talker." She squeezes with just the right amount of pressure. "Are you sure about my new diet?"

Her lips find mine, tongue seeking entry which I allow without hesitation.

"I think you can splurge." My hand wraps around the back of her head, and I angle her mouth to the perfect position. "A cheat meal so to speak."

She stiffens in my arms, and that's when I know that although she may want to forget about her anger and her pain from two years ago, it's still something she's going to have to work through.

"Seeing as I know how hungry your pussy is." She relaxes. "I might be persuaded to feed it my cock."

"Right here?" she pants, pulling back and reaching for the hem of her short skirt.

"No." Damn, that was difficult to say. I ease the rejection with a swipe of my finger over the wet lace between her thighs.

"You know I thought it was hot fuc... making love in this truck the first time." Her hips swivel against my fingers, and my resolve begins to slip. "Don't you want to smell my pussy in here for the next couple of days?"

"Jesus, Princess." I conjure the willpower that seems to be non-existent around her. "I won't be able to smell your pussy, taste your pussy, or thrust every inch of my cock inside of it if I'm sitting in jail pending addition to the sex offender list."

Her eyes narrow until I point down the road. The Rhode Island State Police car rolls by, the officer taking in the scene. Delilah shoves her skirt down and repositions herself in her seat as the patrol car turns into the rest area and parks behind us. I pull out my license, insurance, and gun permit placing them on the dash.

A couple of years ago, my first instinct when watching a cop walk up to the back of my truck would've been to run. Today? I simply roll the window down and place my hands on the steering wheel, smiling when he introduces himself.

"Hello, Officer." The purr of Delilah's voice pisses me off because it's not directed at me, but my cock doesn't mind and remains thick in my jeans.

Officer Hamill leans in further, looking around and I don't miss the deep inhale of his breath.

"You folks eating lunch?" His knowing smile tells me he can smell more than just the fast food.

"Yes, sir," I answer.

He takes the documents from the dash and tells me he'll be right back after making sure everything checks out.

"We weren't doing anything wrong," Delilah mutters as she looks over her shoulder at the officer as he slides back into his car.

"We were only minutes from getting arrested." My eyes trail up her golden thighs.

"He had no clue what was happening before he pulled up."

I shake my head. "See the way he leaned in." I check the rearview mirror and run my finger up her thigh, the fabric of her skirt lifting the higher I go. "He knew exactly what we were up to."

She slaps my hand away. "You're giving me a complex. I feel like I need to shower."

"You have the sweetest pussy in the world, Delilah and you smell positively intoxicating." I pin her with my eyes. "I wouldn't be surprised if he has to wait in his car for his erection to dissipate, or worse yet, trump up some fake charges and arrest me, so he can have a chance at you."

"I'm yours," she whispers.

"I know, baby, but you can't blame the man for being desperate."

She catches movement out of the corner of her eye and straightens again just before the officer reaches the window.

"Everything looks good, Mr. O'Neil." He hands me the documents back. "Have a nice day. Drive safe."

I chuckle when I hear him mutter 'lucky fucking bastard' as I situate my license back in my wallet.

"You're incorrigible," she mutters and puts her seatbelt back on. "Let's get out of here. I'm hungry."

The look in her eye tells me that our meal has been forgotten. I can't get out of that rest area and back to my house fast enough.

Chapter 41

Delilah

"Does he always do that?" I ask around a bite of burger.

"I told you he was useless," Lawson says with a chuckle, but he tosses Raider a French fry anyway.

"I love that you have a dog," I tell him after a quick sip of my drink.

Raider catches another fry with a quick snap of his jaw. "I always liked dogs, but I began to love them when I helped you at the animal shelter."

For the first time, I don't stiffen when he references our time then.

I pat Raider's head and give in when all he wants to do is lick my fingers. "I wanted a dog when I moved here, but I knew I didn't have enough time for one. It wouldn't be fair."

"You can visit him anytime," he tells me with a smile on his face. "If you moved in..."

"Too soon," I mutter, but there's no venom in my voice.

"Never," he whispers, which is just barely audible over the sound of him crushing the take-out trash in his big hands and walking to throw it away.

"What now?" I ask when he returns from the kitchen.

"Stay the night with me?"

I grin.

"Please? I sleep better with you in my arms."

I melt into a puddle on his damn couch.

"And you think you'll get any sleep if I stay?"

His teeth scrape over his bottom lip, and I long for that on my nipples, my clit.

"Eventually," he says as he prowls closer.

"I thought I was on a cock light diet."

His hand cups my cheek as he leans down and brushes his lips across mine. "I thought I mentioned a cheat day."

"So I go back on a diet tomorrow?"

He shakes his head. "Three nights is my limit."

Smiling against his lips, I twine my arms over his shoulders and around his neck. "We had sex here before you went all caveman and showed up at my apartment. So it's only been two nights."

"I'm a weak man."

My fingers flex on the corded muscle at his nape.

"You feel incredibly strong to me."

"You flatter me, baby." With this, he lifts me from the sofa. My legs, instinctively, wrap around his waist as he carries me down the hall.

"So strong." I nip at his chin and slide my hand down until I'm gripping his length. I moan at the brush of my own hand against my panties. "Every long, thick inch of you."

"I love it when you touch me," he hisses into my neck when I squeeze him harder. "Love it when I wake in the morning, and your scent is all over my skin."

"I love *you*," I confess.

"Baby." His voice cracks as he's unable to hide his emotion over my words.

I move my body with him as we strip each other naked before falling onto his bed. When he nibbles at my breast and presses inside of me, I finally feel complete. I'm whole after having been shattered and broken for such a long time

"Every day," he vows against my throat when he pushes to the hilt. "Every single day for the rest of my life, I need this with you."

I clench around him, my body agreeing before I can find the words. His back arches when my short nails scrape down his spine, and it drives him even deeper.

"You're close," he predicts with the truth. "You get hotter, tighter."

I moan my response.

"Fuck, baby. I'm going to come inside of you."

"Please," I beg.

The bite of his teeth on my neck beckons me to the edge, and I crash over not even a second later. The trembling of my body is matched by his as we both struggle for breath.

"Tell me again," he urges after pulling from me and holding me against his chest.

I trace the ridges of his stomach with the tip of my finger. His muscles are rock solid and standing out, the exertion of our love-making acting as an incredible ab workout.

"I love you."

He holds me even tighter, and as I fall asleep, sated and completely in love, I pray that he never lets me go.

***

"This is lovely," I say looking around at the small café. "Seems like we're the wrong clientele though."

"What do you mean?" Lawson asks as he blows over the top of his steaming hot coffee.

"We're the oldest ones here, and that's saying a lot since I'm only nineteen."

"Just a baby."

I give him my best, salacious grin and lean in closer. "You didn't treat me like a baby this morning."

He clears his throat. "Was I too rough?"

I lick my lips, drawing his attention to them. "I don't think that's a possibility, but I still feel you deep inside."

"Princess," he warns. "I don't care if I have to shove a dozen teenage boys out of the bathroom, I'll fuck you in there if you don't stop."

I slip off my flip-flop and run my toe up his leg until my foot is nestled against his hardening cock.

"Make love," I correct.

"No, baby." He leans closer, and I mirror his action. "I will stuff your panties in your mouth, hike that too short fucking skirt up, and bend you over the sink. I'll twist that blonde ponytail around my fist until your back bows to the perfect angle and pound into you until you beg me to stop."

"There's your problem," I coo while stroking his length with my foot under the table. "I'd never beg you to stop."

"Bathroom, now," he hisses, but before he can stand fully, a shadow looms over the table.

I look up into the familiar eyes of a boy I never thought I'd see again.

I nearly knock everything over on the table in my rush to get out of the booth and my arms around his neck.

"Drew!"

He squeezes me, holding me against his hard chest. I push back a few inches, my hands placed over muscles he didn't have a few years ago. His hands slide lower on my back to give me the room I need.

"Nice," I tell him. I'm beaming, probably looking like an idiot in this café full of adolescents, but I don't have a care in the world.

"I swear, little brother," Lawson sneers. "If your hands go any lower you won't be able to hold your lacrosse stick."

"He seems as sunshiny as ever," Drew mutters before giving me another quick hug. As his brother commands, his hands stay where they are.

"He's very possessive," I whisper as Drew reaches out and shakes his brother's hand. Lawson scoots over on his side of the booth, but Drew, being the shit stirrer that he is, sits beside me and wraps his arm around my shoulders. Unconcerned with the mirth and feigned anger on Lawson's face, I allow Drew to cradle me against his chest.

"Fuck you smell good."

Lawson chuckles at Drew's comment, and I kick him under the table. He winks at me, and I pull away from Drew immediately.

"What is that," Drew asks not giving up.

When his nose sweeps up my neck, inhaling like a maniac, even the smack on his chest doesn't stop Lawson from growling at his brother.

"Quit," I tell Drew and scoot a few more inches closer to the wall.

He looks down at me. "Fuck, I've missed you."

He shifts in his seat and swipes a lock of blonde hair behind my ear. A second later he's being hauled out of the booth and repositioned on the opposite side of the table.

"Get your own," Lawson says sitting down beside me and practically pulling me into his lap.

A wide grin spreads across Drew's face, one so similar to the first one Lawson gave me in the dark back home on his first night with us, my breath catches in my throat. Oh, this boy is going to be a lady killer.

"Believe me, big brother, I get plenty." He winks at me, and all I can do is shake my head and laugh at how even years later he's riling his brother up. "None as pretty as Delilah though."

"Stop," I tell him on a laugh. "Lawson is the most protective man I know."

"Not even blood will keep me from breaking your hand." Drew smiles even wider, his eyes never pulling from mine. "Or poking your eyes out if you keep staring at my girl like you want to eat her."

Lawson slaps the table, making the condiment basket jump an inch when Drew over-exaggerates licking his lips at the suggestion.

His eyes sober when they find his brother's, and his throat works on a hard swallow. He's not afraid of Lawson so I know that's not the cause of his change in emotion. They share a look, Lawson nodding at his brother as he holds me tighter.

"I'm so fucking happy for you."

Tears clog my throat at witnessing the relief in Drew's face at finally seeing his brother happy.

Chapter 42

Lawson

"Quit fidgeting," Ivy whisper-hisses to her best friend as we near the front of the clubhouse.

I tried to hold her hand in the back of the SUV after all of the hugs Dad and Rob showered us both with, but she jerks her hand away from mine.

Sitting between Ivy and myself, she doesn't have anywhere to go.

"Stop." Her eyes dart to the front of the vehicle before turning her fiery blue gaze back to me. "We haven't told them yet."

Rob twists the knob on the radio and turns the volume down. "What was that, sweetheart?"

I chuckle finding Dad's eyes in the rearview mirror.

"N-nothing, Pop."

Rob insists on taking our suitcases upstairs the second we make it through the front door, and my fingers itch to guide Delilah to the dining room with my hand on the small of her back. Knowing she'll freak out is the only reason why I don't.

The last three months have been the most blissful time of my life. Sure we fight and argue, but I can always pull her back before she storms off. We don't say things in anger or bring up our past. We left all of that on the floor of my bedroom the night she told me she loved me the first time.

"Smells great in here," I say to the room, but my words ghost over Delilah's back and I revel in the sight of goosebumps crawling up her back.

She steps away as if I swatted her on the ass.

"I've missed you," she tells Samson as she wraps her arms around his neck.

He gives me a quick nod before spinning her around. It's not the evil eye, so it seems like progress. When he releases her, he shakes my hand and pulls me into a back-slapping hug, I wonder what Dad used to bribe him with. Samson has never been my biggest fan, so the olive branch is a little weird.

"How was the trip?" he asks when we separate.

"Good," Delilah answers giving us a wide berth. I hate the distance between us right now, but I know how seriously freaked out she is about informing them of our relationship.

I spend the next couple of hours talking with the guys while Delilah, Rob, and Dad take turns baking, mixing, and preparing things for Thanksgiving dinner tomorrow.

I love spending time with them, but exhaustion hits me hard in the chest and my night isn't even close to being over. I tell everyone good night while Delilah is in the pantry searching for a lost can of sweet potatoes. She's made a plan, one we discussed ad nauseam about how we will go about the next four days.

One of us is to go upstairs while the other waits an acceptable amount of time, then the other can go up. At first, she insisted we just sleep separate, but after a three-hour session where I toyed with her but didn't let her come, she agreed to let me join her after she was sure everyone else was asleep. That's not happening either.

The wait is miserable, thirty minutes of lying in her bed waiting for her to join me.

"You can't be in here," she hisses but closes her door quietly. "Damnit."

She cusses when she damn near trips over my suitcase.

"Why did you bring your luggage in here?"

She's still standing in the middle of the room, petulant fists on her slim hips.

"I didn't bring them in here." Her arms fall. "Rob did."

She hisses, but remembers herself. After looking over her shoulder, she closes the distance between us.

"They know?"

"Do you think we could hide it from them if they didn't?"

"I'm an open book."

"You are, baby."

Her bright white teeth scrape over her bottom lip as she reaches for me, and the rule she'd made me swear to chooses this moment to infiltrate my brain.

"You can hold me at night, but we can't have sex."

"Keep looking at me like that, Princess and I'm going to break my promise."

"The last time we were in here together," she begins, and my blood runs cold.

I have no idea what being back here is making her feel, but I pray we've made enough progress that we can work through her feelings quickly.

I groan when her hand runs over my cock. He's been behaving but gets her message loud and clear as he thickens for her on contact.

"The last time we were together here, I started something I didn't finish."

I'm breathless by the time she drops to her knees and molten lava when she unzips my jeans and pulls my cock free.

It's my turn for my teeth to sink into my lower lip, and when I look down at her, I see a different expression on her face than I did back then. Tonight, the softness of her features are combined with more love than anyone has ever offered me.

"Baby, you don't have to." In fact, she never has before, and I'm not asshole enough to even raise the subject around her.

"I want to." I wobble as her tongue snakes out and swipes the dew from the tip.

"Fuck," I moan as she widens her jaw, cheeks hollowing as she sucks rhythmically on the tip.

She smiles, lips pulling away revealing the slight contrast of my deeper pink tinted cock on her perfectly pink tongue.

"Say it," she urges me.

"I love you." My hand trembles as it cups the delicate curve of her jaw.

"Not that."

"No." With resolute surety, I shake my head and try to take a step back. She clings to my thighs with both of her hands preventing my retreat.

"Say it," she repeats.

"Baby, I can't. I *won't*."

"Please?" Begging isn't something she often does, so I'm well aware of how serious this situation is. "Say it."

She must see the resolve to please her in my eyes because her mouth goes to work on my cock, sucking, stroking, and teasing her fingers over my tight sac.

"I told you, you'd have those pretty pink lips wrapped around my cock."

Brightness fills her eyes at the same moment I fill her mouth.

"Goddammit," I groan when she sucks me through my release. "Stop."

The sensation of her tongue licking the tip sends bolts of electricity up my spine.

She smacks her lips, grin never faltering as she stands. I accept her mouth against mine and hiss when her tongue, heady with the taste of me, slides against my own.

"I bet I can still make you come with one finger."

Her pants become my own as she pushes against my chest until I'm flat on my back on her childhood bed.

"Add in that talented tongue of yours, and you have a deal."

"Be quiet, baby," I warn when I grip her hips and position her over my face.

A minute is all it takes with my tongue, my finger, and the grinding of her hips. She, in fact, doesn't stay quiet as she comes down my throat with a roar.

"Do you think they heard us?" Even in the soft light of the moon, I can see the pink tint to her cheeks, there, I'm certain, from both her orgasm and the embarrassment of being heard by her family.

I chuckle as I slide off the bed and dig in my suitcase.

"Answer my question, and I'll answer yours."

She rolls over to her side, unconcerned about the exposure of her breasts and the shadow at the apex of her thighs that is hiding the luxury between her legs.

"And what is your question?"

I hit my knees on the edge of her bed. With the odds in my favor, the moon hits the diamond in the ring at just the right moment.

"Lawson?"

"Put me out of my misery and marry me?"

"But Dad—"

I press my fingers against her lips.

"Your Dad accepted my love for you long before you did, baby."

"You asked?" I can hear the wobble in her voice, but I know what she's going to say because there's only one viable answer to the question.

"Three months ago."

"Three?" I smile at the edge of shock in her voice.

"The night you told me you loved me."

"I love you so much."

"Baby, you still haven't answered my question."

A tear streaks down her face as she looks from the ring and back up to me. "Ask me again?"

I swallow, emotion clogging my throat in the best way. "Delilah Donovan, will you marry me?"

"Yes!"

Her arms wrap around my neck, the warmth of her happy tears on my chest. I slip the ring on her finger at the exact moment I slip my cock inside of her. Bliss.

Chapter 43

Delilah

"Jesus, everyone is here already." The sounds of multiple conversations wash over us as we enter the clubhouse from the back door.

"That's perfect." Lawson pecks me on the lips. "Stop shaking. Why are you nervous?"

He stops near the door to the laundry room and pulls me to his chest.

"Are you happy?" I nod against his soft t-shirt. "Then they'll be happy for you."

I take a deep breath, kiss his perfect lips, and let him lead me to the family room.

"She said yes!" he yells the second we cross over the threshold.

"Real fucking subtle," I mutter as applause and yells of joy fill my ears.

Dad and Pop are the first to reach me.

"I couldn't be happier for you," Dad says in my ear before releasing me to wrap his arms around Lawson.

"Sweetheart," Pop says before engulfing me in his big arms. I edge away from the tickle of his beard on my neck, laughing as he squeezes me again.

"Congrats, brother." I freeze at the sound of Samson's voice and nearly faint when I look over to see him hugging my fiancé.

Hell has officially frozen over.

"Thanks," Lawson says just as shocked as I am.

"I couldn't imagine a better man for my sister."

Lawson only nods, the same emotional look on his face when Drew gave his approval three months ago. I know if he talks right now, his voice will crack, so I do the only thing I can; I cry for him.

The endless line of congratulations and hugs seem to take forever but stops eventually. It isn't until I see Gigi across the room that I realize she's the only one who didn't walk up to us during the procession of well-wishers. She gives me a small smile, and there's more heartbreak in that one action than I've ever experienced for myself.

I go to walk in her direction, but Lawson pulls me against his chest.

"I told you everything would go just fine."

I'm lost when I look up into his eyes, forgetting all about the pain in Gigi's eyes.

"I've never been happier."

"Let's go have a seat until dinner," he suggests, but I pull away from the warmth of his chest.

"Can't." I step away from him. "I have to make the rolls."

I expect him to head over to the guys and talk about manly shit, but he follows me into the kitchen, helping me butter the tops before slipping them into the oven.

Wrapped around my back with his hands low on my belly, he kisses my neck. "I can't wait to put my baby here."

I smile but shake my head. "Not for some time. I want you all to myself for a while. Plus, I need to get through school."

A throat clears behind us, and Lawson turns both of us without releasing me. Dad is standing there, and I freeze. I know he knows we're together. I know he said he was happy for us, but it doesn't make facing him all wrapped up in Lawson any easier.

"Do I need to spray you two with the hose?" His voice is serious, but the smile on his face makes me think he's joking, mostly anyways.

"No," I say and try to pull away. Lawson only holds me tighter.

"What were you talking about?"

"Babies," Lawson answers immediately.

Dad's hand stills mere inches from the handle on the refrigerator. When he turns and shoots lasers at Lawson, I freeze.

"You promised me at least two years, Law." He holds up two fingers for emphasis. "Two."

"About that." My eyes widen when Lawson runs his hand low on my belly. "Will Pop still go by Pop when he's a granddad? What do you want them to call you?"

I swear my dad stops breathing.

"Them?" I've never heard my dad's voice squeak before.

"Quit." I step out of Lawson's arms and reach for my dad, laughing at how wide his eyes are as they focus on my stomach. "I'm not pregnant, Dad. He's messing with you."

Dad's eyes narrow as he looks at Lawson. "You're sleeping on the couch."

"The bunk bed would be more comfortable," Lawson counters.

"Like hell," Dad mutters. "You snuck in her room two years ago, and I know you'll do it again. The couch is all yours."

"Yes, sir."

Not the response I was expecting, but I also don't expect the wink Dad gives me before he walks out to repair his damaged nerves.

"That was fun," Lawson says with a wide smile on his face.

"You're awful," I tell him with a soft laugh and turn back to the oven to pull out the first batch of rolls.

***

"How are you liking that *cream pie*?"

I nearly choke on the bite in my mouth when Lawson whispers those dirty words in my ear.

When the wheezing stops, I turn and glare at him and shrug. "I've had better."

"It's a shame that so many people think Boston makes the best ones, but I know mine is better."

"I'd ask for proof, but that would be rather difficult from the couch."

He chuckles, but when he focuses on something across the room his brow furrows.

"What's going on with those two?"

I follow his line of sight and see Griffin talking to a very straight-backed Ivy.

"Don't you know," I tell him in a low whisper. "Ivy is so in love with that boy she doesn't see anyone else when he's around."

"Really?" He sounds surprised. "I thought he was into Gigi."

"And thus lies the problem," I mutter.

The mention of Gigi's name causes me to look around the room and search for her. She was abnormally quiet during dinner and excused herself before she'd eaten half the food on her plate. Something's going on, and everyone at the table could feel the tension between her and her parents.

When I find her, she's across the room and Diego is in her face. I can't hear what they're talking about, but if the tears on her cheeks are any indication she's not happy one bit.

"Gigi doesn't have a clue, and I'm pretty sure Griffin is clueless about Ivy," I respond to him without pulling my eyes from the parental confrontation.

"Shit. That's kind of sad."

"Incredibly," I agree.

"Ready for bed?" The suggestion in his tone has my thighs squeezing together.

"That's not even a possibility. It's barely seven. There's not one person in this house that would believe we're going back to the room to sleep."

Lawson, facing the challenge raises his arms over his head and yawns. In a voice loud enough for everyone near to hear, he says, "Man, that turkey is making me sleepy."

I swat at him even though he gets several agreements from the room.

"Worked like a charm," he says with a quick grin. "Let's go."

"Not so fast." I tilt my head in the direction of my Dad and Pop.

"Dammit," he mutters when Dad glares at him and shakes his head.

"You should've kept your damn mouth closed." I lean my head on his shoulder. Just the mention of being sleepy in relation to the big meal I just ate makes me truly sleepy. "Too bad because now I have to sleep alone."

"We'll get a hotel ro—"

"I forbid it!" Diego roars across the room.

"Yeah, well. I'm fucking grown so what you say doesn't even matter," Gigi hisses before turning and walking out the front door of the clubhouse.

I make to stand, but Lawson puts a hand on my shoulder. "Stay out of it, baby."

"She's upset."

"She'll be fine," he assures me.

Little does anyone in this room know we won't see her for a very long time, and when we do, we won't even recognize the woman she's become.

Hound

Copyright

Hound: Cerberus 7
Copyright © 2018 Marie James
Editing by Marie James Betas & JA Essen

Chapter 1

Hound

"Best job ever," I mutter to myself as the topless waitress brings me another glass of whiskey.

Leaning in close, she runs her hand down my arm. "I don't normally offer private lap dances, but for you, I'll make an exception."

Acknowledging her with only a quick wave of my hand, I keep my focus on the stage. In front of me are the best pair of tits and abs tighter than I've ever seen on a woman before. I'm mesmerized by the red-headed seductress as she twirls around the pole in the center of the stage.

I toss back half of the whiskey in my glass but never take my eyes from the woman I plan to have before the sun comes up.

The girl I came here to find is nowhere to be seen. I did my job for the night, looking for the whiny kid who's giving her dad fits by not staying under his command. I search the front of the house as well as the back of the house where the girls are getting ready before taking it all off on the center stage. The brunette with bright blue eyes that I'm tasked with finding and removing is nowhere in the building. Determining that she must be off tonight, I let loose. Having a few drinks and watching the topless entertainment is only a perk of the mission. Of course, it's not reconnaissance, infiltration, and extraction, but there are benefits to this type of work as well.

The girls flitting around with bare tits and asses exposed by glittery thongs are nice to look at, but they each pale in comparison to the siren on the stage.

Hips rolling and long red hair following her like a smoky shadow dancing at her command, she's got the attention of every single man in the room, and I'm not immune to her charm. Hell, if all of my money wasn't tied up in savings accounts I'd write her a check for the entire sum just for the taste of her skin and the tight embrace of her cunt.

My mouth grows dry as I breathe heavily, short panting breaths taken in an attempt to keep my cock from busting through the seam of my suddenly too tight jeans.

Strippers are nothing new. Seventeen years in the Marine Corps traveling the world has led to more adventures with loose women than I can count, but there's something about this beauty that has me chomping at the bit to get her beneath me. The great thing about underpaid whores is that for the right amount, they'll let you do just about anything to them. I imagine this one will be no different.

Paying for sex used to make my skin crawl, but bedding a professional woman, who will have no expectations when the sun rises gained appeal as I got older. Leaving broken hearts in my wake is never my intention, and lying to a woman just to fuck her, I've decided, is more messed up than paying for a hole to plow for the night.

She hits her stride, the deep bass of the song ricocheting off the walls, the hoots and hollers becoming almost unbearable. Enthralled by the sway of her hips, just like every other man in here, I don't notice when the song ends, and she bends to gather the bills tossed at her feet.

Moving my eyes from the sway of her firm tits to look into her eyes, I'm met with a soulless, dead stare. She's definitely not one of the dancers who get off on dozens of men fawning over her naked body. I wish I could say I feel sorry for her, that seeing her misery so clear but ignored by every other guy in front of her will make me change my mind, but it doesn't. We all have demons we have to fight, and she's no different. Since I have my own shit to deal with and things to prepare for in the near future, I can't be bothered to concern myself with her issues. What I can do is make her come like a freight train and give her enough cash to make it easier to leave this life...if that's what she chooses.

When her eyes lock with mine, a tingle of anticipation rushes down my spine and straight to my cock. The swipe of her tongue over her full lips as she takes me in is enough to make the tip of my cock thicken and weep for her. I wink, pretending to be as unaffected as I can and mouth 'soon' to her. She's flushed from the exertion of her dance, but it doesn't stop her cheeks from pinking even more. She gives me a slight nod, acknowledging that our plans for the evening include each other before she stands and exits the stage with enough swing to her hips to keep every man in the building pining for her.

The DJ announces that "Orphan Annie" will be back at the top of the hour, forcing me to look down at my watch. Contemplating if I should find and fuck her now or wait for another show on the stage, I think about her odd choice of stage name. The little, redheaded girl with no family, as the story goes is, adopted by a mean woman who is never short of voicing her dislikes even after her husband, Daddy Warbucks comes into the picture.

I huff a small laugh, thinking about the storyline in today's age and why a woman no older than twenty-five would pick it. It makes me wonder if she was abused. Did *her* Daddy Warbucks take advantage and that was the real reason for the discord with the wife? Is she into older men?

That thought makes me smile considering I'm probably ten years her senior. Attraction to older men would benefit me in the persuasion part of the night. I shake my head. Honestly, it wouldn't matter. The wad of cash in my pocket ensures I'll be inside of her regardless.

Draining my whiskey, I wait for her next performance. Once again, as she makes her way on stage, I can't pull my eyes from the glistening skin of her body. The sweat dripping between her tits, rolling down the tight muscles of her stomach makes my mouth dry no matter how much amber liquid I pour down my throat. "Bad Girlfriend" by Theory of a Deadman blares from the surround sound as she keeps perfect tempo to the beat.

Her eyes find mine, holding them captive. Her emerald eyes bewitch me as I consider an attempt to access those savings accounts I thought about earlier in the night. Paid whore or not, I know one night with this temptress will never be enough.

She seems to be the headliner, the one woman who draws the men in, which means, from my past experience, her night is over. She's closing out the stage with one final dance as the waitress who's been serving me all night tells me it's last call.

Declining the offer for a final drink, I head to the door before she walks off of the stage. I wait in the shadows near the rear exit listening to the men grumble as they're escorted out the front and wait for my redheaded beauty to make an appearance.

The wait is so long that I question the interaction between us, question the sincerity I saw in her wide green eyes. She's the perfect tease, making me think she wants me just as I'm sure she does with every man who walks through the dingy front doors of The Minge Palace.

I'm near giving up, realizing that Orphan Annie is more trouble than she's worth when the back door opens and a flash of red exits the building before laughing at something someone inside says before it closes again. I step out of the shadows when she's less than a handful of feet in front of me. I expect her to startle, to clutch at her chest in an attempt to ease her pounding heart. Instead, she shocks me by staring directly at me as if I'm her puppet and waiting in the filthy alley is exactly what she expects. I clench my fists at the idea that she thinks she can have the upper hand.

"I've been waiting," I growl, loving the pink that returns to her cheeks.

"I searched for you out front," she whispers closing the distance between the two of us and running her small hands over my heaving chest.

"I figure you'd want the cloak of darkness even though your screams of orgasm will echo down the alleyway."

"So confident in your ability to please."

Her hands leave my chest and run across my back as she circles me. I'm her prey tonight, even more confident in her power than she displayed on the stage earlier. No matter how much I want to fight it, how much I want to prove to her that she'll be taking my cock as I see fit, I know without a doubt that Orphan Annie is going to use me and have me begging for more.

"Care to make a bet?" I offer as she stands in front of me once again.

Petite yet solid, she looks up at me as I imagine all the ways I can easily take her.

"No," she pants, her pupils so big in the moonlight I question the small halo of blue circling them.

Didn't she have green eyes on the stage?

I don't give it a second thought when her tiny hand covers but a fraction of my cock over my jeans.

"You want to stand out here making bets?" She gives me a squeeze tight enough to make me groan. "Or do you want to fuck?"

"Brazen little thing aren't you?"

I drop my hands to my sides as she fumbles with my belt and the zipper on my jeans. The relief is immediate as she pulls the denim back and my cock springs free.

"Mmm." The tiny noise from her mouth not only makes me jump in her hands but forces me to wonder what that noise will feel like if I push my cock down her throat.

"Another time," I hiss.

"What?" she asks confused just as I lift her and turn her with her back against the cold brick wall.

"Enough talk." The insistent ache in my cock doesn't leave much room for anything else.

Urging her legs around my hips, I can see the pain the stretch is causing as she tries to get them all the way around me. She doesn't have a hope of doing it though. I'm twice her size and ready to handle her, to position her any way I see fit.

Her skirt rides high exposing the glistening slit of her pink cunt.

"Dirty whore," I hiss as my fingers move the wetness up to lubricate the friction of my fingers on her clit. "You came out here prepared to fuck me?"

Her eyes slam shut, a tiny whimper escaping her lips as she rolls her hips against my hand trying to find her pleasure. Without warning, I slip two thick fingers inside of her, watching her face for the response I know she'll give. Eyes dashing open, hers find mine.

"So fucking tight," I praise. "If two fingers are all you can take, there's no hope my cock will fit inside of you."

Lips parting, she tilts her head to the side. "Give me more," she begs.

I withdraw and delve back in with three fingers, working them in and out, preparing her as best I can.

"Please," she whimpers, near the edge I refuse to let her fall over.

"I'm going to hurt you," I warn as I pull free from her tight pussy.

"Please," she repeats.

Against better judgment, I replace my fingers with the head of my cock and slam home.

She screams, half in pain, the other half in pleasure.

"Oh God."

"Fuck, Annie," I grunt as I pull back only to slam forward again.

"It's too much," she complains but relents when my thumb begins to strum over the tight bundle of nerves at the apex of her thighs.

"That's it," I urge.

I'm certain her back is going to have abrasions from shoulders to tailbone, but the consideration isn't something I have to give as she clamps on my cock, the tightest thing I've felt since I fucked a virgin in high school. The quick thought of that night, so many years ago, makes me realize my mistake, the same one I made then. However fucked-up and consequences be damned, I can't stop the ache of release already teasing my balls. My head flexes back, my orgasm becoming a living thing under my skin as I pulse inside of her. Bare. No condom.

When I'm done, I release my hold on her and stumble backward. I can't even look at her. I'm so disappointed in myself for the whiskey I drank that allowed the haze of my senses to make such a monumental mistake. I fumble with my jeans until I finally get them up and zipped, not even concerning myself with my belt.

"You said you'd make me come," she coos in front of me. "But you came too quickly for me to get mine. Want to go back to your place to finish what you started?"

"No," I hiss, keeping my eyes down as I shove my hand into my pocket and pull out a wad of cash.

She crosses her arms over her chest when I offer it to her.

"I'm not a whore," she growls, and it's then that I find her eyes.

"You just fucked me in a filthy alley after dancing for dozens of men on a stripper pole." I shove the money into her hands. "Believe me, Annie; you're as close to a whore as it comes."

"You motherfucker!"

"That," I say pointing at the cash she reluctantly holds in her hand, "is for the abortion if my stupid ass put that shit into motion, or for your bus ticket out of this fucking town, because so help me God if I caught something antibiotics won't get rid of from that filthy snatch of yours, I'll come back and kill you."

Her eyes narrow in challenge, and it gives me hope that a VD isn't going to be in my future.

Not giving her a second glance, I make my way out of the alley and stumble back to my shitty hotel room. I try to push her from my mind as I fall on the bed and pass out.

When morning comes, and the incessant chirping of text messages on my phone is frequent enough to drive me mad, she's still on my mind. I almost feel guilty about the blood on my cock, knowing I was too rough with her. I check each one of my piercings, knowing that one of the barbells must have cut her, but they're all intact.

The regret doesn't set in, however, until I check my messages and see the first one from Blade which was sent a mere two hours after I left Annie in that disgusting alley without concern as to whether or not she'd make it home safely.

Blade: I told you to find Georgia Anderson. Not fuck her like a whore in the alley.

So much for my new life. That redheaded woman from last night just fucked me harder than I fucked her last night.

Chapter 2

Gigi

"Shit," I hiss when I roll over in bed. My whole body aches, but the scratches on my back and the thrumming between my legs are my greatest concern.

The time on my cell phone may say ten after noon, indicating I've been in bed for no less than seven hours, but I feel like I haven't slept at all. I scrub at my eyes with the backs of my hands and twist my neck in both directions until the satisfying crack echoes around my shitty, one-room apartment.

Feeling dehydrated, as I always do after a night of dancing and cocaine, I reach for the half-empty water bottle on the coffee table in front of the crappy couch that doubles as my bed. I down it, wincing once again as I climb off of the couch and head to the sink to refill it.

Once the bottle is filled, I turn with my hips against the counter. The wad of cash that asshole gave me last night mocks me from the opposite counter. I could've tossed it back at him or thrown it to the damp, trash-riddled ground, but only a fool would do something as ridiculous as that.

Instead, I came home, feeling like the whore he suspects and counted it. Twice.

It's been a long time since I had access to that much money, and I couldn't help letting my mind wander to the next place I could go. I'm always moving, always planning for the next city, praying it's better than the last, but knowing better.

It doesn't have to be this way.

This thought makes my eyes shift from my ill-gotten gains to the empty cocaine baggie sitting beside it.

I'm a social user. That's the lie I tell myself right before I inhale the poison and take the stage at the club. I allow myself to believe it most days because I don't use on my nights off. Those are spent curled in a ball, feeling like total shit, while thinking of nothing but the better life I walked away from. It's in those moments that home doesn't seem so bad. It's those moments that the controlling hand of my father and his expectations don't seem like a reason to run at all.

I squeeze my eyes shut, letting the water soothe my sore throat and try not to once again feel bitter for turning into the twin that no one can love. I envy Ivy and her perfect grades. She's always been the one they can be proud of, while I remain the constant thorn in their side and the disappointment of all of the Cerberus kids.

The alarm on my phone chimes, telling me whether I want to or not, I have to get to work. At least tonight I'll get off at a decent hour since I'm covering another girl's shift. Working my off days as often as possible ensures I can move on quicker. Although not my intention when I walked up to the stranger in the alley, the money he gave me gets me a lot closer to my next city than I could get working at The Minge Palace in two weeks. I cringe at the name and head to the shower.

After my shower, I towel off and dress. With the red wig in place, I leave my apartment and walk down the street to the club so filthy even the low lights can't disguise how disgusting it is.

My throat, still dry from the cocaine and cigarette smoke from last night, only grows even more irritated as I make my way to the small corner I share with ten other women. The owner's office is ten times this big, but he expects us to walk on top of each other to get ready for the stage, going so far as to bitch and yell when we're late because we're waiting for others to get ready. I've been dancing here for two months. In two weeks I should have enough to leave. Dallas isn't my ideal geographical location, but I hope to make it to Austin soon. Sixth Street, or somewhere near there would at least bring younger, hotter guys; not the geriatric fucks that have made The Minge Palace their home away from home.

I hate the way the dull lights on the vanity make my skin look almost green. I hate the amount of makeup the owner requires us to wear so our faces stand out against the stage lights. As if the men are looking at our faces. They may glance at our mouths and wonder what it would be like to have our lips on their cocks, but our full faces aren't important to them.

I hate that I'm getting damned near naked on stage for money. But most of all I hate that I was running behind today and wasn't able to swing by Javi's place to grab another baggie of coke. Dancing sober is up there with a root canal or surgery without anesthesia. It's brutal and almost impossible to suffer through.

I look over at Dolly. The stage name was given to her in reference to her incredibly huge, albeit natural, breasts. The sneer she gives me tells me that asking for a bump would be fruitless, so I don't even bother.

I steel my spine and wait in the cluttered wing just off the stage. After shaking my hands out, a futile attempt to stop them from shaking, I tighten the knot on the front of my shirt. I mean, if you can call a sequined bikini top with Velcro at the neck and back a shirt.

I don't bother to lotion myself up at this club. The owner keeps it so damn hot in here it's a wonder I can control my movements on the pole. His reasoning is that if the men are warm, they're also thirsty. He makes money on the liquor and cover charge. He reminds us constantly just how gracious he is to let us keep our tips.

I roll my neck, but the soreness from my lack of sleep prevails. I hate myself for taking this extra shift even if it's nice to go to work while the sun is still out.

Peaches makes her way off stage, giving me the same sneer Dolly did just moments ago. Every one of the other dancers hates me. I usually find at least one woman at the club I'm working in that's friendly. The only person who pays me any attention in this shit hole is the owner, who talks to my tits more than he talks to my face and Gerardo who's creepy and makes me think he's picturing himself peeling my skin layer by layer when he looks at me.

The intro to Pour Some Sugar on Me is my cue to hit my knees and crawl out on the stage toward the pole. Mom and Dad always played this kind of music while we were growing up. As much as I love this song, I know I strip to it as a silent slap in the face to them.

Look at me now, Dad. And you thought you could dictate my life.

The men in the audience sit straighter, and I realize that this is the exact reason the other girls hate me. These guys here pay attention to me. They want the attention, the salivating mouths, catcalls, and horrendous suggestions of what I could be doing to them. I despise it. Dancing, stripper pole or not, is a means to an end. The only problem is, I'm so far from the end, considering I have no idea what my long-term goals are, that there's no conclusion to the degradation in the near future.

I tried waitressing. The money is shit, and even with clothes on, the men in the seedy diners I was able to gain employment and be paid under the table are just as vulgar as the men here.

When Def Leppard sings "loosen up" my top comes off. "Squeeze a little more" has my hands fondling my own breasts. I get way more tips when I touch myself. I trail my fingers from my lips, trying not to cringe when an awful taste fills my mouth, between my breasts and over the soreness left by the stranger last night. I revel in the discomfort, turning myself on for the first time since I first wrapped my legs around a stripper pole.

By the time I'm two-thirds of the way through the song and swinging around the pole, I'm turned on to the point the heat in the room actually cools my damp skin. When the final hard beats of the song ring out through the room, I'm on my knees barely able to catch my breath. I shouldn't be concerned about my breathing because it stops completely when I meet the dark, angry as hell eyes of the stranger from last night.

Before I can push myself up to stand and collect the wads of cash on the stage, he reaches in and jerks me off of my feet.

"The fuck are you doing, psycho?" Tossed over his shoulder, the ineffectual hits of my small fists against his muscled back don't even faze him.

"The hell, man?"

Gerardo. Thank goodness, I think but remember just how creepy he is. I'm torn, leaning more toward going with the stranger than owing the creepy ass bartender any favors.

"Move, dick face." My captor's words echo against my own body.

"Chad left me in charge tonight," Gerardo says as if it means anything to this big bastard.

Gerardo is shoved to the side, and I push against my stranger's ass with my hands to look up at him as we walk away.

"He's going to be pissed, Annie."

"Tell him I had a stomach ache. I'll be back tomorrow night."

"Like fuck you will," my jailer says with a swift, sharp slap to my bare ass.

I should be scared when a man I don't know, a man who treated me like shit last night, carries me out of The Minge Palace. I should be terrified when he slides me off of his shoulder and into a darkly tinted car smelling faintly of his cologne and stale cigarettes.

I may have made horrible grades in school, but my instincts have always been spot on. I knew the second I looked in this man's eyes last night, even with the clear intent that he wanted to fuck me written all over his face, that he isn't the type of man to hurt a woman.

Questioning my gut, I try to unbuckle the seat belt he pulls around me and snaps into place. The low growl in his throat is warning enough, and for some fucked-up reason, it turns me on. It's the same sound he made last night when he shoved me against the wall and slammed balls deep inside of me.

"Put this on," he hisses as he climbs into the driver's seat and tosses me a button-up shirt.

I unsnap the seatbelt as he pulls out of the parking lot, raising an eyebrow as I shrug it on. The fire in his eyes says he'd love for me to challenge him.

I question him. Ask him where we're going, just who the fuck does he think he is, and what his plans are, but I'm met with utter silence until we pull up outside of a hotel that isn't but a few degrees better than my apartment.

"Am I going to have to carry you inside?"

I narrow my eyes at him, trying to gauge exactly what the fuck is going on and spending more time than I should actually considering doing it without argument.

"Are you going to hurt me?"

A sinister smile turns his plush lips up until the corners disappear in his well-groomed beard.

"Only if you beg."

The arousal I'd thought had abated during the short drive once again flares to life. I anticipate another suggestive innuendo from him, but instead, he tosses my small clutch that I'd left locked in the back room into my lap.

"You look nothing like your driver's license photo, Georgia Leigh Anderson. Want to tell me what you're doing so far from home?"

I glare at him, pissed that he went through my things, but at the same time terrified for what it means for my family back in New Mexico. I want to get away from them, not rain down hell on them. I start to shake, wondering if this is the first step in sex trade abductions.

"You said you won't hurt me."

He frowns as if the notation is absurd.

"That means my family, too?"

He recoils, head snapping back.

"Surprised my head would go that way? You threatened to kill me last night."

He shakes his head, jaw flexing to the point I hear his back teeth grind together.

"Not one of my finer moments. Last night was more about fucking up than fucking you. What is a twenty-year-old girl from New Mexico doing stripping *illegally* in Dallas, Texas?"

How the fuck does he know where I'm from?

"What is some former Marine doing in Dallas fucking young girls in the alleyway," I challenge.

It's his turn to narrow his eyes.

"You see more than you let on."

I ignore his words. "Why am I here?"

"Do I have to carry you in or can you walk on your own?"

Call me curious, but the appeal to join him inside, to figure him out is too strong to do anything but climb out and wait for him to lead me to the door of his outside entry room.

Chapter 3

Hound

"Why am I here?" she asks, not for the first time.

I tilt up the bottle of whiskey I left on the particle board dresser earlier to my lips. I don't even notice the burn as it travels its way down my throat. She sits on my bed like she owns that place the second we step into the room.

"Why do you think you're here?"

It's crazy how quickly your maturity drops in the face of young people. I huff, and she gives me a questioning look.

"I imagine you enjoyed yourself so much last night that one time inside of me wasn't enough." She tilts her head, red hair flowing over her shoulder and touching her bare thigh. My shirt swamps her, but she knows exactly what she's doing showing that hint of bare flesh.

I tilt the bottle up again as a means to fortify myself when I know it will do nothing but lower my inhibitions.

She. Is. Work.

No matter how many times I repeat that fact over and over in my head, my body still craves her. My memories from last night drive me to touch her, to taste her.

I shake my head. That along with the whiskey have no effect on the need I have for her skin against mine.

"You need to stop being a little fucking tease. I don't have time for that shit."

She smirks, and I want to do nothing more than kiss that look off her damn face.

I shake my head again. No, not kiss. Kissing is the last thing I need to do. I have to convince her to head back to New Mexico with me and find a way to do that without her telling her father I fucked her in a filthy alleyway.

I was diverted from my very first day with the Cerberus MC in New Mexico to Dallas. Blade, the IT man behind the MC gave me specific orders to get Georgia "Gigi" Anderson out of the strip club she was dancing in and get her home safely. I fucked myself out of a job by literally fucking an MC princess. I've heard the stories of Kincaid, Dominic, and the others in New Mexico. They're fair, but nothing short of murder is headed my way unless Gigi and Blade both get onboard to not breathe a word of this to Kincaid.

"It's not teasing," she says pulling me from my frantic thoughts, "if it's what I want."

She spreads her legs, the thin sliver of glittery fabric the only thing between me and the tightest cunt I've ever slid inside of.

"I fucked you raw last night. A second round of my cock is the last thing you can handle right now." I mean it as a warning, but it comes across as a challenge instead.

"My pussy is sore but far from raw."

Those filthy words coming from her mouth may be the sexiest thing I've ever heard.

"I woke up this morning with my cock covered in blood. Don't tell me it isn't raw."

She grins, the light reflecting in her green eyes. Green? Blue last night? She has to be wearing contacts.

She rolls her lip between teeth too straight and perfect to belong to your everyday stripper. Girls like that are dancing in much better establishments than the one I pulled her out of tonight. It's a fact I should've realized last night before I let the sway of her hips and the tightness of her stomach distract me.

"That's what happens the first time," she reveals causing my blood to run cold and the bottle of whiskey to fall from my hand.

It hits the dingy carpet with a soft thud, and I watch her, frozen in place as she unfolds from my bed and reaches down to get it. The luscious curves of her breasts are visible as the shirt gapes open at the neck.

"You're twenty," I argue.

"You're forty," she counters.

"Thirty-four," I hiss letting her sassy ass attitude get the better of me.

If I thought I was screwed by fucking the Prez's daughter, add taking her virginity in a depraved way, and I know the police will never find my damned body.

She places the whiskey bottle on the dresser at my back, making sure to lean her lithe body against mine in the process.

"I promise I'm not too sore."

She trails her finger over me exactly the way she did last night. I imagine her doing exactly this to the men who spend the cash to get private dances, and it pisses me off more than it should. I try to convince myself that I'm angry for her father. Angry that she's someone's little girl who's dancing half-naked on stage, and not because I loathe anyone she's touched before.

You fucked her first. That's something she can never give to another man.

I shake my head again. Thoughts like that will get me killed, but I can't help but consider keeping her happy until I can convince her to go along with the lies I have to tell Cerberus.

I grip her wrist, remembering from last night that she liked it rough, liked it when I commanded her body.

"I owe you one," I remind her.

"True," she coos.

I shove her on the bed, and her eyes widen when her back hits the hard mattress. Her wet pink tongue swipes across her lower lip when I shift the erection in my jeans to a better position.

"Better make it two," she whispers when my knees hit the bed, and my lips begin to trail up the soft skin of her calf. "Call it interest."

I nip at the delicate skin behind her knee, fully expecting her to pull away or slam her thighs together. She surprises me when they open further on a moan.

I fucked her bare last night. Came inside of her like she was mine to do so. Tonight, under her spell again, I don't even question lowering my mouth to her heated flesh, pulling the thin strip of fabric to the side, and sucking her clit into my mouth.

She whimpers, unable to form words I assume, as I give her over eighteen years of pussy licking experience. I don't hold back. I want her liquid, pliable, willing to do what I say when the time comes to face her father.

She writhes under my attention, gripping the sheets and coming as her hands tug at the fabric in her grasp. By the time she's ruining the bed with her second orgasm, I've almost convinced myself that licking her into submission is not only the best course of action; it's absolute bliss for me as well.

Why I push her through a third release until she's begging me to stop is beyond me. I'm just as confused by my reluctance as she looks, lying on the bed satiated with a flushed glow on her skin.

Before I question myself, I'm pulling a condom from my wallet, the same one that was in there last night and releasing the buckle on my belt. I'm rolling the latex down my shaft when my phone buzzes on the dresser at my back.

Like a bucket of ice water being tossed on me, my hands still, pausing mid-stroke of my aching cock.

There are only two people in the world who have that number: one I've devoted my life to, and the other, a man I have to convince not to betray a lifelong friend.

Blade I can possibly get to understand the sin of giving into temptation; Isabella, on the other hand, would hold it against me forever. I've fucked up enough in the last twenty-four hours for a lifetime.

"Where are you going?" Gigi asks when I slide off the bed.

"Shower," I grunt as I pull my t-shirt off and lock myself in the bathroom.

With rough hands, I rip the unused rubber off my dick and toss it in the trash. The cold water does nothing to cool my heated skin. I grip my cock, stroking it from base to tip, knowing if I go back out there without coming I'm only asking for trouble.

I have no damn clue what my next step is. I don't know much about her, but I know a couple of orgasms aren't enough to convince her to go home and lie for me.

"Motherfucker," I hiss as my strokes grow harder.

Resting my forearm against the shower wall, I hunch over, giving into the sensation in my nuts as my orgasm begins to build. I'm disgusted with myself as I paint the wall in cum to the thoughts of the young girl in my shitty hotel bed.

I take my time drying off before pulling a clean pair of boxers from the small suitcase in the corner. I can't focus with her in the other room. I can't think of ways to make this work. Every idea ends exactly the same. My new job is gone, and my only other option puts me even further from Isabella, doing work I know I'll hate.

"Listen," I say when I pull the bathroom door open.

I don't say another thing, my words caught in my throat at the sight of her half-naked body asleep on the bed.

Relief washes over me at not having to deal with this shit tonight. Exhausted, I drop down on the other side of the bed and pray that I find some clarity, in the form of a solution, comes to me in my dreams.

Chapter 4

Gigi

Waking up to the sun streaming through the threadbare curtains without a cocaine headache almost makes me want to never use again. Dancing on stage last night sober to the thoughts of my dark stranger seems to have awakened something in me, something that makes me believe that there's a future for me after all.

Thoughts of last night encourage me to turn my head, looking at the sleeping man on the other side of the bed. I have no hopes of a relationship with him, but I'll be forever grateful for whatever fire he has sparked back into my life.

As quietly as I can manage, I climb out of bed in an attempt to not wake him. As much as I enjoyed our evening together, he's too much like my father to continue what has started between us.

I slide my heels on, unsure of when he even took them off, and tug my bikini top back on. The walk of shame in such little clothing is going to suck, but I get naked for money and became shameless long ago. With one last look at his sleeping form, I leave him sleeping in a bed rumpled by my orgasms, and not his.

Despair always hits me in the chest when I open the front door to my crappy apartment, and today is no different. I look at my clean but dismal surroundings. The worn sofa and scarred coffee table are the only furnishings. Only a handful of dishes fill the cabinets in the kitchen, and limited food takes up space in the small fridge. Looking at my life from a bird's eye view, going home almost seems better, but in doing so, I allow my parents to make decisions about my life. It's a sacrifice I'm not willing to make anymore now than I was several years ago.

My options were the military or college, neither of which interested me then, and they sure as hell aren't on my radar now. If I live at home, those are my choices. I asked my father last year at Thanksgiving to let me work at Jake's Bar. I'd be happy there. I know I would. My mother worked there when she and my dad got together, so I know he doesn't have an issue with Jake. It's the thought of his daughter working as a barmaid that leaves him less than thrilled. He forbade me, dismissed the idea in a second flat. That same night I walked away from the Cerberus MC knowing it would be my last time to walk away from it.

"Pity party, table for one," I mumble as I close my apartment door and kick off my heels.

Checking the calendar for tonight's schedule, I determine that I can nap for a couple of hours before I have to head to work. Unfortunately, I only toss and turn for what seems like an endless amount of time before my cell chirps an alert to get ready.

I'm shocked when I arrive at work and my stranger isn't waiting for me. Seems he got me out of his system even after his machismo act last night. Realizing I lost my virginity to a man whose name I still don't know sends a chill down my spine. It's reminiscent of the discomfort I felt after my first line of coke.

"I figured Chad would've fired your ass," Peaches huffs as she all but shoves me out of the way to get in front of the dimly lit vanity.

"I guess he's not ready to get rid of his top earner just yet," I snip with a quick shoulder jab to regain my space in front of the mirror.

"You'll be back at the bottom soon enough," Dolly says interrupting our conversation. "I've been here eight years. Featured more times than I can even count."

I huff a humorless laugh. "Seems like your good years are behind you."

"Hardly," she counters.

I cock an eyebrow at her. "Really? Your tits are nearly to your bellybutton, and you can't even swing yourself a foot off the floor on the pole."

Her eyes narrow, filling with a fire I hope I have in eight years after having to do God knows what in the future to survive.

"I have tendinitis in both elbows, you little bitch," she sneers.

"Get over yourself," Peaches says in a bored tone. "You know you'll have to hang it up sooner or later."

No one at this damn club has alliances. We're all each woman for ourselves.

Peaches fluffs her hair in the mirror, taking over the space that Dolly vacated.

"We all will eventually," she mutters taking stock of her own dim future.

I sigh and step back, guilty of my own self-doubt. It's still on my mind after I change out of my t-shirt and yoga pants and put on another gaudy, barely-there bikini. My nerves, as I stand just off the stage, are nothing like they were the first time, but they're still there.

I consider Vegas and the possibility of performing in some manner on Fremont Street. I have several months before I'm twenty-one and Vegas, other than the seediest parts, is known for being sticklers on the rules.

A new girl I've never seen before exits the stage and I can tell by the fresh look on her face that Chad has once again hired a teenager. She's years away from twenty-one, but that doesn't stop him from paying her under the table until she's of age. He does the exact same thing for me.

The intro to Thunderstruck by AC/DC pulls me from worrying about *her* future and forces me out onto the stage. I have three dances on the stage tonight and then private dances if there are paying customers, which there always are. The lights seem brighter this evening, but I do my best not to squint and cover my eyes with my forearm.

I make it through more than half of my shift, and I hate that I'm disappointed that the guy from the last two days hasn't shown. He heard me tell Gerardo last night that I'd be at work today.

"You make me so hot," I lie as I grind down on a younger looking guy in the shadowed back booth of the club.

His hands clench on the cheap leather, unlike most guys who pay for private dances he keeps his hands to himself through the entire dance.

"I have lots of money," he pants against my ear as my back and ass rub against his front. "Name your price beautiful, and I'll gladly pay it."

I get no less than half a dozen offers just like this a night, but tonight it stings more than usual. Forty-eight hours ago, I'd just blow it off and tell the truth that I don't do that sort of thing. I'd give him the names of the girls that are always willing to go the extra mile for cash. Tonight, two days after I accepted cash for a quick fuck in the alley, I feel dirty. Not enough to give in, but shame hits me for the first time in over a year.

The song ends, and I pull away from him.

"Use it to buy your wife something nice," I tell him with a quick look down at his left hand.

The sparkle from his gold wedding band caught my eye more than once during the two dances he's paid for.

He clutches his left hand to his chest, coveting it and covering it with his right.

Shaking his head, I'm confused to see pain in his eyes, as if I'm going to search her out and tell her about his indiscretions.

"I'm not." He shakes his head again, more violently than the first time. "She's gone."

And I'm a huge asshole.

I give him a sympathetic smile. "There are several girls here who work after hours."

"No," he rushes out. "It has to be you. You look like her."

This poor sad bastard.

"Sorry," I tell him shrugging back into my top. "I don't do that sort of thing."

I try not to think about the pitiful man who's looking for nothing more than a connection to his wife after she's gone. It's difficult to comprehend that type of love for myself. My parents have it. I don't know that either one of them would survive the loss of the other, but I'm beyond certain that type of love isn't something I'll find in this lifetime.

Chapter 5

Hound

"That slippery bitch." I punch the empty spot beside me on the bed.

I never sleep through someone moving around in a room. I never let my guard down. Doing so is a disaster in the making in my line of work. It rankles that a tiny, twenty-year-old girl was able to sneak out of this shitty hotel room without me knowing it.

I can't let it bother me for long. Getting out of this room is all I can focus on. I've ignored Blade's texts and calls for two solid days, and I know the damn cavalry is coming, and there's no way to prepare for it other than having Gigi accessible when her father arrives.

I spend my day walking around the shitty town on the off chance that I catch her going to work, but give up after several hours and go back to the room. I'm ready to leave, whether it be to New Mexico or California. The security job in Cali is what I know I'll end up with. There's no way the Cerberus Prez is going to forgive a failed mission, especially one as simple as extracting his daughter from a strip club. Especially not after I fucked her.

I shower and head to the club just as night is falling over Dallas. Even the bright outline of the Bank of America Plaza in the distance doesn't improve my disposition. I want nothing more than to bend her over and whip her ass for the trouble she caused me, but I gave up blaming others for my actions many years ago.

I order a whiskey the minute my ass hits the sticky chair near the back. I watch, waiting for my moment and nearly come out of my seat when I see a flash of her hair as she provides private dance services to some sad schmuck in the back. She gives the dance one hundred percent, but I can tell her heart isn't in it. The only thing that keeps my fist from meeting that fucker's face is the fact that he keeps his hands to himself and never attempts to touch her. Even that asshole has better control over himself than I do.

Downing the whiskey, I wave the waitress over for another. With her here tonight, I know she'll be the one to close down the club, the final dance on the stage. So I wait, keeping an eye on her. A glance at my watch lets me know she'll be up there soon.

With only a look, I'm able to force a man from his front row seat. It's as close as I can get without being up there with her. Another whiskey. Another half-hearted dance by a girl too young to be a high school graduate. I'm disgusted at her presence on the stage, so I keep my eyes down, staring into my glass of whiskey like it's the most interesting thing ever.

One song fades to the next and I know, just by the musical selection that my red-headed temptress is ready to perform.

The hard-hitting bass of Thunderstruck pounds in my ears, and it makes me wonder about her song choices. AC/DC and Def Leppard are barely within my musical range.

I'm struck stupid when Gigi appears, once again in the smallest scraps of clothing known to man. She might as well be naked, the fabric only covering the areolas of her nipples and that tiny, glorious seam of her pussy. I instantly hate every man in this room, contemplating killing each one of them and ripping their eyes out.

She doesn't bother looking into the crowd. She concentrates on her moves as she rolls with incredible ease up and down the pole. Every muscle in her body is utilized during her routine. They jump, flex, and respond to her actions. So much control. So much power. My cock, just as it always does when she's around, thickens and lengthens uncomfortably in my jeans.

When she does finally look out over the crowd, and her eyes meet mine, all I get from her is a sweet knowing smile. I wink, hold my nearly empty glass up to her in salute, and continue to watch her performance. Her back bows deeper, her moves become even more sensuous, and her breathing more labored, which I know from watching her prior to tonight that it has everything to do with me and not exhaustion from dancing. She could dance for days without growing tired. Her body was made for it.

I'm damn near bereft when the song ends, and she begins to gather the money on the stage, triple the amount the other girls before her earned.

Enthralled by the delicate sway of her tits, I come out of my seat when one of the patrons reaches up and squeezes her to the point that she cries out in pain. I get two hits right in the man's nose before he's cognizant enough to stumble away.

Exactly like last night, I sling her nearly naked body over my shoulder and head to the front door.

A different man than yesterday, this one somehow managing to look even sleazier, steps in front of me and blocks my path.

"Gerardo told me what happened last night, Annie."

I feel her tense across my back.

"You know that if your boyfriends can't handle you stripping, they're not allowed in my club," he continues, talking to her even though he can't see her face.

I don't even attempt to stop the growl that begins low in my stomach only gaining strength as it makes its way up my chest and out of my mouth.

"You don't see a problem with these disgusting fuckers grabbing your dancers?"

The asshole's sinister laugh bubbles up, angering me even more.

"She knows better than to step out of the green zone. She took that risk when she got greedy for the cash on the other side of the line."

"You're a piece of shit," I hiss.

"True," he agrees. "But I'm the piece of shit that owns this place. You're fired, Annie. Don't ever darken my door again."

"Like I would," she mutters to the backs of my thighs.

I carry her out, only allowing her to slide down my body once we reach my car. I buckle her in the second her ass hits the seat.

With my nose nearly touching hers, I speak to her for the first time since last night. "Didn't you learn your lesson last night when I pulled your naked ass from that filthy stage?"

I expect her to cringe, to shy away from the acrimony in my voice, but she just gives me that same sweet smile she gave me from the stage.

"I'm a whore and a stripper. I don't even know your name, and you think you can dictate my life? You've lost your fucking mind."

I pinch my bottom lip between my teeth so hard I expect to taste the coppery tinge of blood any second. I made her feel like a whore. That mindset is on me, and it makes my stomach turn.

"You bled on my pierced cock which proves you're not a whore," I remind her. "And your stripping days are over."

She cocks an eyebrow, challenging me.

I hang my head and sigh. How can I expect her to trust me, to lie for me if I give her nothing in return? "My name is Jameson Rawley."

She smiles wider and whispers, "Jamie."

"Jameson," I correct. "Never fucking Jamie."

The nickname is salt in old wounds created by my father when I was a small child that apparently have never healed.

She rolls her eyes at my insistence, but her gorgeous face still holds the smile that will live in infamy in my dreams for years to come.

"Where are you taking me?" she asks when I climb behind the wheel.

"Back to my hotel," I advise as I pull out of the parking lot. "Unless you'll be more comfortable back at your place. We have a lot to discuss."

Finding out where she lives would be ideal. She's not going to like what I have to ask of her, and I know she'll want to run again.

"Yours is ten times better than mine," she mutters.

So she's left a nice home in New Mexico to live in squalor and dance naked for money? It makes me wonder if her father and the Cerberus MC are as upstanding as they're rumored to be. I can't imagine a young girl wanting to leave the comfort of her childhood home without there being a reason.

"Are you hungry?" I ask before we get on the road to my hotel.

She nods, looking nervous.

"What?"

"I left all my money at home. I was in a rush this morning and even left my clutch." She pauses. "And I dropped everything from the stage when you tossed me over your damn shoulder."

My brow wrinkles in confusion.

"I can't buy anything," she says. "I don't want to owe you more than I already do."

"One," I begin without even looking in her direction. "You've been around the wrong fucking boys if you've been paying for your own meals. Two, it's a cheeseburger and fries, not dinner with dessert at Reunion Tower."

She sighs, and from the corner of my eye, I watch her turn her face toward the window.

"And you don't owe me a damn thing."

We order at a drive-thru, but other than giving me her selection she doesn't speak until we pull up outside of my hotel room.

"I need to give you back the cash. That's your money," she says sullenly. "Keeping it only makes me a paid whore."

I lick my lips and let my eyes close as I try to calm down. Without another word I grab the food and head inside, knowing she'll follow me.

I unlock the door and set the food on the small table just inside. When she closes it behind her, I move and press my body against hers.

"That's the second time you've called yourself a whore in front of me."

"You called me a whore more than once the other night."

My blood runs cold in my veins. I'm guilty of that. Guilty of letting the night get away with me and taking it out on her. I do the only thing I can. I ignore her comments and continue.

"A third time will guarantee I stripe your ass with my belt."

Her chest heaves up and down as she lets my words sink in.

"Do you understand me?"

Her green eyes find mine, and I'm once again lost to her.

"Yes, Sir." It comes out sarcastic and petulant, just like she intends, but it doesn't stop the chill that races over my skin and the blood from rushing to my cock.

"That money is yours, for no other reason than I want you to have it. Do you understand?"

I press harder against her, knowing she can feel my thickening cock against her bare stomach.

"Yes, Sir."

I groan at the words slipping from her mouth in a breathless whisper, this time with no hint of the contempt it carried before.

"We should eat," I tell her and take a step back.

She sags against the door at the loss of my body. "I recall you being very good at eating last night."

"Not happening again, Georgia. Don't even think about it."

"Gigi," she says. "No one but my mother, when she's angry, calls me Georgia."

"Gigi then." I smile at her over my shoulder as I begin to pull the food from the paper bags.

We're silent for a few short minutes as we begin to eat, but I can't let this night end without talking to her about her dad, Cerberus, and the consequences of what I've done.

"Tell me why you left New Mexico." I shoot for nonchalance, but this girl can read me like a damn book.

Seventeen years in the Marine Corps, expert training in infiltration and interrogation, and I forget it all in the face of a gorgeous twenty-year-old who has only recently become a woman.

Chapter 6

Gigi

"Tell me why you want to know," I counter.

"Just curious," he lies.

I can see it in the erratic change in his pupils, but the tapping of his foot and barely noticeable tremble in his hands are enough to give him away.

"You want to know all about me?"

"Just making conversation." Another lie.

"How about," I begin but throw my last fry in my mouth before standing, "I give you all the sordid details of my life back in New Mexico after."

I reach for his hand.

"After?"

I nod and scoop his free hand up. The last couple of bites of his burger hit the paper wrapper, but he stands when I tug on him.

"After we're basking in the afterglow of fucking, of course."

He stops suddenly and our hands separate. "Not gonna happen, Gigi."

The nervousness in his voice confuses me. Less than twenty minutes ago, he got hard instantly when I responded to him with 'yes, Sir.' Now he's shying away from a romp between the sheets? I question his mental health as I turn to look at him.

"You want information?" He nods so fast it makes me grin. "You have to work for it."

A devilish glint appears in his eye, and I know that I have him. He's so turned on around me, I knew the battle would be a short one.

There is something different about him. Has been since he ripped me off the stage yesterday. It's almost as if he's a changed man from the aggressive one who fucked me against the rough brick outside of the club two nights ago.

"Strip," he commands before I can sit on the bed.

I'm only in a bikini top and thong, but I love that he wants me completely naked.

"You don't have any dollar bills," I tease.

"Strip because you want to, Gigi. Not because you're getting paid."

"There's no music," I pout.

"You don't have to make a show of it, woman. Just get naked. I have plenty of thoughts of you dancing and taking your clothes off burned into my brain."

My top comes off first. I toss it to him, hoping it lands on top of his head, but he snatches it out of the air and drops it to the ground. I go slower with the thong, ignoring the wetness that cools when the air of the room rushes over my exposed skin.

"Your turn," I suggest. "I'd love you to do it to music."

He growls when I wink at him. Why does that sound so hot?

"Not gonna happen. Not today or ever."

"Too bad," I whisper. Another smart-assed remark is on my tongue, but I'm rendered mute when he pulls his shirt off. I saw his back last night when he went to take a shower and saw most of his front this morning as he slept in bed, but those memories provide no justice for the sight in front of me right now.

"Wow." My lips smack together as if he's a gourmet feast. "You must work out a lot."

"Occasionally," he mutters as his fingers work open his belt and then lowers his zipper

I stare in awe, waiting for the reveal. I only got a quick glance at him last night before he chickened out and left the room.

"Oh," I pant when his dick flexes up, and not only a single piercing but a row of barbells is revealed. "That had to have hurt."

He kicks off his cowboy boots and shakes his jeans free of his legs. No underwear, exactly what I'd expect from a guy like him. A grunt fills the room when his hand reaches and strokes down his erection.

"It wasn't the most comfortable situation. Every one after the first sucks because you know what you're facing then."

I can't take my eyes off of his working hand, and swallowing doesn't dislodge the lump in my throat.

"So why get so many?" I'm stalling, and when he chuckles, I know that he knows it too.

How in all things holy did that fit inside of me the other night? It's very possible that the blood from our union was from damage rather than just losing my virginity.

"Getting shot hurts more." He says it with a nonchalance that makes my eyes snap up to his.

It's something my dad or one of his men would say, as if getting shot or stabbed is just another day on the job.

He gives me a small grin before walking toward me. His hand never stops handling his shaft. "Get out of your head, Gigi. This is supposed to be fun."

"It's bigger than I remember." I take a step further away from him.

"And when I bend you over the bed and fuck you from behind those barbells are going to feel incredible." He leans in and licks at my ear before speaking again. "And that ring at the top is going to send you over the edge more times than you can count."

Harsh breaths rush past my lips, and I'll be damned if his promises don't ease my nerves and make me want to just turn around for him.

I reach for him, but with practiced ease, he takes a step back so I can't touch him. Please tell me he's not one of those weirdos that doesn't want a woman's hands on him.

"Condom," he mutters with an agitation that doesn't fit the current mood.

I almost call him out on it, but he's bending at the waist and reaching into the back pocket of his jeans.

Holy. Glorious. Ass.

"Your ass is amazing," I observe.

He's smiling when he turns back around, the wrapper to the condom already at his mouth and tearing open.

"That makes two of us I guess."

I smile. He clearly works out. My body is from pole workouts and practice. I burn so much energy at work that other than perfecting a routine, I hardly ever go to the gym.

"It doesn't look any older than twenty-five, twenty-seven tops."

His eyes narrow but there's a playfulness to the glare he's giving me right now.

"Definitely doesn't look like a forty-year-old ass."

He charges, all aggressive and asserting his power, but I don't miss the arm around my back or the other catching our combined weight as we hit the mattress.

Mouth close to mine, he looks down at me. His eyes jump between mine, taking me in as if he's trying to read social clues I'm not even trying to hide. God, I love the weight of his body on mine. The heat of his dick on my inner thigh. The clean, masculine scent of his skin. I'm consumed by him.

"Thirty. Four," he hisses.

"Thirty-four," I repeat.

"My cock is thirty-four also," he says with a roll of his hips.

I moan and grind against him.

"Do you have a problem with me fucking you with my old cock?"

"No." I whimper when, with expert precision, he presses the head of his cock against my throbbing clit.

"Good. Now, I'd love nothing more than slam inside of your tight cunt and ride you hard all night, but that wouldn't be very good for you."

"Fuck me hard," I beg. "I can handle it."

"I'm going to fuck you all night long, Gigi. We can do hard some other time."

I nod. All of it sounds amazing. Hard. Soft. In the bed. Against the wall. Missionary. Twisted into a pretzel. Sign me up for everything and summer school to boot.

"Are you ready for me?"

How do I tell him I've been wet since I spotted him in the crowd back at the club?

"So ready," I say instead.

With an expert shift of his hips, his cock and the attached barbells leave my clit and rest right against my entrance. Without conscious thought, I tense.

"You have to relax, or I'm going to hurt you more than I want to."

The thought of a little pain with my pleasure brings a riot of emotions to my head, but he begins short strokes. Only a tiny dip inside before he backs away and moves in just a hair deeper each time.

"You're so good at this," I praise as he teases me open.

"Lots of practice," he grunts with an even deeper jab.

"Nice," I mutter.

Here he is thirty-four and fucking a girl who's only done this once before. I should be proud that he's being gentle and taking my inexperience into consideration. I know a man my own age wouldn't be bothered with easing in and making sure I'm comfortable, but the thought of him with other women makes my skin crawl.

It's the pheromones.

"What?" His hips stop assisting his intrusion, and he stares down at me.

I shake my head, realizing I said that out loud. "Nothing."

I moan so loudly I wonder if the neighbors hear when he shifts again.

"Are you jealous?" He continues to move in and out of me, and the sensation is making me lose my mind. Holding any train of thought is impossible at this point.

"No."

"I was jealous. More like pissed each time I saw you dancing for another man earlier. It has to be the pheromones because there's no other explanation."

He drives forward, deeper than he ever got in the alleyway.

"Fuck you feel good."

His praise washes over me leaving goosebumps behind.

"Am I hurting you?"

Speech is not a skill I'm capable of right now, so I shake my head. At least, I think I shake my head because in the next second my back is arching up and I'm speaking in Tongues.

"That's it. Fuck, take it all." He repositions, and when I realize he's looking down where we're joined, I swear I nearly come. "You like that reverse prince? Best piercing of them all."

He's got so much metal in his dick I have no idea which one he's talking about, but they feel amazing.

He rolls and grinds, and I have no idea how sex with him can hurt and feel like the best thing in the world at the same time. He's an expert. Sex is a skill he's mastered beyond anything I could've imagined.

"Don't tighten up, Gigi, or you'll end this too soon."

"I-I ca-can't help it," I stutter as my core clamps down on him. The orgasm catches us both by surprise. Hissing, he pulls out, and before the haze can clear, I feel his hot breath on my pussy. His hot tongue hits me next. The sensations are too much, more than I'm capable of handling. With hands flat on the mattress I try to push away from him, but he doesn't allow it.

"It's too much."

He chuckles. "As it should be."

"Why are you down there? Did you come?"

"I just need a minute."

Now, it's my turn to laugh. "Who's the inexperienced one here?"

"It's your tight-as-fuck pussy that's the problem." He nips at my inner thigh, and just like that, I'm ready for more.

"It's been a minute," I complain rolling my hips, pussy right in his face. "Make me come again."

"Jesus, you're perfect." He crawls up my body, nipping and sucking at my exposed flesh. I imagine it's only to give him more time to settle, but eventually, he makes it back up. We're once again face to face, and when he enters me this time, he doesn't take the same care he did earlier.

He thrusts in one long drive. I whimper, loving both the pain and the pleasure. When he makes me come the second time, he follows me right over the edge, using the growl that makes me tingle all over.

I don't realize I've fallen asleep until I open my eyes. I'm turned on my side, and he's sliding into me from behind.

I clutch his forearm that's resting against my stomach and lift my leg allowing him to plunge deeper.

"So good," I pant.

"It's the barbells this time," he reminds me.

I shake my head as he pulls out to the tip and shoves back inside. "Your cock would feel amazing without all the metal."

"I can't wait for you to suck it," he hisses growing close to release.

"I can't wait," I promise just as his fingers reach down and work my clit.

We come together, and it doesn't go unnoticed that he's still inside of me, arm still wrapped around me when I fall asleep again.

Chapter 7

Hound

"Hey," I whisper in Gigi's ear and push gently on her shoulder.

She grumbles incoherently and rolls further away from me.

"Gigi," I say louder this time.

The only response I get is a soft rotation of her hips as she tries to wiggle even deeper into the bed. How she can sleep comfortably on this shitty bed is beyond me.

Pulling back the blankets in an attempt to wake her with the cool air over her skin serves to be fruitless as well, but the pull of her bare ass can't be ignored. I reach my hand back, readying to slap the supple cheek, but think better of it. Instead, I slide further down the bed and plant my mouth at the apex of her thighs. I lift her hips to achieve a better angle, but it isn't until I tongue inside of her that she responds.

"Who knew such a little thing could have such a dirty mouth," I tease after she screams expletives even a sailor would cringe hearing. "Are you awake now?"

Whimpering, she rolls her sweet cunt against my face. It isn't until she's coming that I pull away.

"Hop on," I say with a sharp slap to her ass and fall back on the mattress.

"What?" she asks finally pulling her face out of the pillow.

I give my condom covered dick a quick glance. "Ride me."

She rolls her lips between her teeth, and I notice the sleep lines on her face. She's young, gorgeous and wise beyond her years. More mature than she should be. A couple of years of hard life experiences will do that to a person. I had to grow up fast as well, so I recognize all of this in her.

I grip her hips, helping her get settled. I'd love to act like I'm in control, even from the bottom, but when she clasps her little hand around my cock and lines it up with that perfect slit between her legs, I'm a goner.

We both hiss when she slowly slides down my shaft. Her eyes flutter closed when she pulls up, abs flexing, so I let mine do the same. Every sensation is multiplied without sight. The skin of her hips is softer. The smell of sex and her faint perfume is stronger, like a blanket surrounding us. The taste of her pussy is sweeter on my tongue. The tiny moans that transition to grunts and screams of pleasure are the icing on the cake.

She's insisting on slow with her movements, but slow isn't something my cock can take. I'll come too quick feeling each and every one of her tiny internal muscles gripping at me.

"Faster," I urge holding her hip and flexing to ram inside of her. "God, that's not any better."

My eyes snap open when I feel the sting of her slap on my face.

"The fuck?"

"Why are you fucking me if you don't like it?"

As if by some miracle, my cock thickens even more at her insecurity.

Grabbing her and pulling her to my chest, I flip her over and ram inside of her harder.

"Slow was going to make me shoot my load too soon." I punctuate my statement with a deliberately slow rotation of my hips before speeding up and pounding into her. "Fast, I thought would be better. I'd last longer."

She moans, head thrown back, the soft skin of her neck exposed.

"I was wrong. The clench of your pussy is too much, no matter the tempo."

I bite and suck at her neck, ramming, sawing in and out of her like I'll never be inside of her again.

When the door crashes open at the first clasp of her orgasm, the first pulse of mine, I see it as a sign, an omen of things to come.

I couldn't stop coming if someone was holding a knife to my throat. I just signed my death warrant anyway, because when I look up, I'm staring right into the eyes of Diego "Kincaid" Anderson.

"Daddy!" Gigi yells, trying to wrap the tangled sheet at her side over her chest.

I tug it free and help cover her body, ready to fight all the men standing at Kincaid's side for seeing what they have. True to their reputation, the men turn, giving us their backs and Gigi the privacy she deserves.

"You could've knocked," she mumbles.

"Georgia Leigh Anderson," Kincaid hisses. "Get your ass dressed right now!"

I can feel the tremble in her body, and I want nothing more than to protect her, but four against one with these motherfuckers are horrible odds.

I tuck the sheet closer to Gigi before pulling out of her. If he wanted to hurt me before, Kincaid is likely imagining my dismembered body when I groan as I leave her body.

"Not helping," Gigi whispers as she crawls out from underneath me.

"I'll kill you," he sneers before turning his attention back to his sheet-wrapped daughter. "Go get dressed."

I expect her to defy him, to argue that all she has to wear is a thong and bikini top, but she scurries into the bathroom without a backward glance.

I see the fist coming. I have time to react, time to deflect the punch, but I let the hit land on my left cheek, right where Kincaid intends. I deserve every punch he lets fly at my face. I deserve the gruesome crack of my nose as it shatters under his angry fists.

"Enough," one of the other MC members says as he drags Kincaid off of my chest.

Wiping the blood from my face onto the sheet, I can't even look him in the eye. What argument would I have? There's nothing I can say to make what I did right. There's no way to explain away the reason I ended up in bed with the boss' daughter. Again. And again. Hell, I'd do what he did and more if I walked in on my daughter getting plowed by a man that was sent to protect her.

"This?" Kincaid hisses. I finally meet his eyes as he points at me. "This is who you recommend for my club. I can't trust him not to sleep with my daughter. How in the ever-loving fuck can I trust him with my men when things go to shit on a mission?"

The man that pulled him off of me, the one Kincaid is challenging, is his older brother Dominic.

"Dammit," I mumble looking over at the grey-haired man. He's massive, the silver color of his hair and small smile lines at the corners of his eyes are the only things that hints at his age.

"He comes highly recommended," Dominic says with doubt in his eyes.

And I do. My time in the Marine Corps and my FORECON training and experience, on paper, practically over-qualifies me to be a Cerberus member. But, Kincaid is right. Trust is more valuable than experience. Faith that I'll have the men's backs is paramount to success. I've lost it before I could even prove to them how valuable I can be by fucking a girl I never should've touched.

I can't blame her. I can't burden her with my choices. I had every intention of speaking with her last night, convincing her to see my side of things, but the temptation of her body was too much, irresistible by her mere nearness. It would've been all for nothing seeing as we were just busted in on in flagrante delicto.

Kincaid doesn't say another word. He merely glares at me, chest heaving and paying no attention to my blood marking his knuckles.

The bathroom door opens, and Gigi steps out. The gorgeous red hair that trailed behind her when she scurried in there earlier is now clasped in her hands in the form of a wig. My attraction to her had everything to do with that red hair, but I can easily admit, with long dark hair flowing over her shoulders, she's even more gorgeous. The sight of her timidly standing on the threshold, swallowed up by my t-shirt, a pair of my boxers peeking out at the bottom cause more problems for me. She's beautiful, and even with five angry bastards in the room, my cock doesn't seem to mind.

I grunt, twisting to the side of the bed, feet planted on the floor and cover my thickening cock with the thin blanket at my feet.

One of the men chuckles, and I look to see another guy, bearded like myself and maybe only a few years older. I'm not as inconspicuous as I thought. The laugh is odd though. Meeting his eyes, all I get is a smirk and a slight shake of his head before he walks over and reaches out a hand for her.

"Come on, Gigi. Let's head to your apartment and get you packed."

"I don't need an escort, Kid," she grumbles drawing my eyes back to her. "What are you going to do to him?"

I look over at her father when he begins to speak. "Hound is my problem now."

Her eyes widen, confusion drawing her brows together.

"Hound?" She shakes her head as she glares at me. "You know my dad?"

"Let's go," Kid says making me almost come off of the bed when he places his hand on the small of her back to guide her out of the room.

A man covered in tats and piercings follows them out, leaving myself, Kincaid, Dominic, and another bearded man alone in the room.

"You had the simplest job." Kincaid begins to pace back and forth on the worn carpet, the other two men giving him a wide berth. "Blade tried to hide the fact that she was dancing from me. Gave you the opportunity to extract her and bring her home. I can tell you, Hound, coming in here and watching you come inside of my daughter is ten times worse than coming to Dallas myself and pulling her naked from the stage."

"Topless," I correct. "They sell liquor, so they have to keep their pussies covered."

"Jesus. What's wrong with you?" the bearded man I don't know asks, speaking for the first time.

"He seems like an idiot, Shadow," Kincaid says. "Like a man who can't keep his mouth shut or his cock in his jeans."

I shake my head. "I didn't say it out of disrespect. I just don't want you to imagine her on stage completely naked."

"Like it makes any difference with the memory of seeing you fuck her!" He roars loud enough to make my head snap back.

The tattoos on his arms dance and ripple as he continues to pace, his hands clenching open and closed repeatedly.

"I won't touch her again," I vow. "It was a mistake. A lapse in judgment on my part."

"Biggest mistake of your life," Kincaid adds.

I look him straight in the eye. "Not even close."

Kincaid holds my gaze for a long silent moment, and I feel the relief of reprieve when he turns and walks out of the room. Shadow follows him, but Dominic stays behind. I wonder if it's his turn to throw a couple of punches. Gigi is his niece after all.

"Don't go anywhere," he instructs. "We haven't decided what we're going to do with you."

"Yes, Sir," I answer giving him the respect he deserves. From what I know of the Cerberus MC, Dominic is the only one who served longer than I did. He's the one with the most experience of the group. A man I'd hoped would mentor me while working for Cerberus. It's another thing I'll lose when they leave me behind because I couldn't keep my dick out of the Prez's daughter.

Chapter 8

Gigi

"They know each other?" I ask as Kid shuffles me into a dark-tinted SUV in the parking lot.

"It's club business, Gigi," Jaxon mutters before closing the door in his face.

When he opens the front passenger door and takes a seat, I've had enough of the unanswered questions. Enough of the dismissals I've been getting my whole life. They may think they protect us from danger, but they leave us open to manipulations and betrayal.

"I don't give a shit if it's club business, *Snatch*." He turns his head toward me, mirth on his face. His son Lawson, my childhood friend's fiancé, looks so much like him it's almost startling. Using his club name, the one we were never allowed to use as kids gets his attention. "How does he know my dad?"

"He *was* going to work for Cerberus," Kid answers as he snaps on his seatbelt.

"Was?" I shake my head. "It's not an option for him now?"

Why does the thought of Jameson, or Hound, whoever the hell he is, being back in New Mexico make me want to go back to my childhood home?

I find Kid's eyes in the rearview mirror. "What do you think, Gigi?"

"I think I'm a grown ass woman who can make her own decisions. Who I have sex with is none of his damn business. It's only another way for him to try to control me."

"It isn't about who *you* sleep with that concerns your father. Hound sleeping with you was a betrayal your dad probably won't be able to get past," Jaxon chimes in. "Where are we heading?"

I give Kid the address without a second thought. I have no job since I was fired last night. Staying in Dallas isn't an option now, and Farmington is closer to Vegas where I plan to head in a couple of months after my birthday. I'd be a fool to refuse a free plane ticket and a nice place to sleep for a while, but it doesn't mean I can't play the only card I have.

"Make sure you tell my dad that if he holds what Hound and I did against him, if he doesn't allow him to work for Cerberus because of me, I won't return to New Mexico."

"You're going home," Jaxon assures me.

I shake my head. "I may get on a plane and step foot on the property, but I'll be gone in days. If he wants me to stay for any period of time, Hound will be there, too."

Jaxon huffs, and I feel like a little girl all over again. It doesn't matter that I'm a grown woman; to these men, I'll always be a child.

"He'll never allow a relationship between you and one of his men," Kid says from the driver's seat.

"You're too young for him," Jaxon adds.

"I'm what? Three years older than Khloe when you first brought her to the clubhouse." I watch the pink coat Kid's cheeks.

I laugh when Kid chokes a little. "Yeah," he agrees.

"The age difference is too much," Jaxon amends.

"There's a fourteen year age difference between Uncle Dom and Aunt Mak."

Jaxon once again narrows his eyes at me. "You deserve more than being the fuck buddy of a biker."

I raise an eyebrow at him. "Didn't Aunt Misty get pregnant with Griffin when she was Shadow's fuck buddy?"

Jaxon doesn't have a leg to stand on or a rebuttal. Kid laughs from the front as I sit back further on the bench seat in the back and cross my arms over my chest.

"That's what I thought," I mutter. "If Hound doesn't go back, neither do I."

I try to ignore the tension in the SUV by looking out the window, but a red Dr. Pepper sign painted on the side of an old brick building reminds me of the blood staining Jameson's face. So I opt to stare at my hands instead. If I concentrate hard enough, I can still feel the flex of his muscles under them from last night and this morning.

Is his lie of omission a betrayal?

Is this exact situation what he wanted to talk to me about before I persuaded him to fuck me instead?

Was my father the reason he seemed nervous?

"And you definitely deserve better than this," Jaxon mutters as we pull up outside of the shitty apartment complex I've called home for the last two months.

I don't justify my living arrangements with a comment. Honestly, there's nothing I can say that can make this place look any better.

"I don't have much," I tell them as I open the door. "Give me twenty minutes."

Kid and Jaxon both push open their doors.

"We have a plane to catch in two hours," Kid says coming around to the front of the SUV. "We'll help, so it only takes five."

"You didn't bring the Cerberus jet?"

They rarely travel commercial.

"We did. But your dad, Uncle Dom, and Shadow will be sticking behind for a few days. They have business to take care of," Jaxon clarifies.

It turns out I only needed the five minutes on my own to pack my meager belongings. Taking stock of what little I do have is depressing each time I move on from one city to the next.

The trip to the airport is spent in silence just like the entire plane ride back to New Mexico. People stare and move out of our way wherever we go. Mainly because Jaxon looks like the scariest man that's walked the face of the Earth, but Kid has bulked up in recent years, becoming a force of his own. I feel safe, protected around them, even though I'm not one hundred percent here of my own free will.

***

When I step out of the SUV in front of the Cerberus clubhouse, my first instinct, just like every time I return home, is to run. Judgment, pity, and looks of disappointment mark the faces of the new generation of Cerberus members. I barely know any of them, so any of them thinking they can judge me only pisses me off.

"Boys," I say and wink at the small group gathered around a motorcycle.

Every one of them nods in acknowledgment but cringe away from the flirtatious greeting.

"Leave them alone," Jaxon mutters under his breath as he walks by. "You've caused enough problems for the club."

I huff an incredulous laugh. "Didn't realize I had to get club approval on the guys I decide to fuck."

"None of these Cerberus members will touch you, Gigi. Leave them be." Kid has now joined ranks with Jaxon and my dad.

The Cerberus guys have always been off-limits. It was easy for them when I was a teenager. Their standards were too high to mess around with a young girl. After adding in my father being their president and boss, we were untouchable.

"None of the ones here at least," I challenge as I walk past both of them and around the clubhouse to my parents' house.

I left my scant belongings in the SUV. They wouldn't let me carry them even if I offered, so I don't bother to waste my breath.

My mother, the amazing, beautiful woman that she is, waits for me to approach on the porch.

"I've missed you," she says with pain in her voice. I walk into her open arms. "I'm so glad you're home, Georgia."

I let her warmth wrap around me, let it seep into my bones, let it strengthen me because I know I'll need it when my dad gets home.

"I missed you, too, Mom."

She sniffles, and unlike the last time I was home and her tears pissed me off, today after the way I've lived my life the last couple of months, they almost make me cry along with her. Tears after coming home show weakness. I know I'm leaving again soon, and they would only be used as ammunition against me when it's time to go again.

"Are you hungry?" she asks not letting go of me.

I shake my head against her chest. "No, I ate at the airport."

When she releases me, she doesn't bother to wipe her tears away. She's the strong one, the one who holds the family together, the one who is often on my side, even when I'm fucking up.

"Ivy, Delilah, and Lawson are home for the next two weeks before they head back to Brown for their senior year."

"Mom," I groan and pull completely out of her grasp. "Please don't start in on the college thing before I even step inside of the house."

"I'm not," she vows with her hands held up in surrender. "I just wanted you to know that you have people to hang out with if you wanted."

"Thank you," I tell her, but I'm still suspicious of the information she's given me.

Maybe she thinks I'll take off within days, like last year. I was home for three days before my dad shut down my idea of sticking close to home and working at Jake's.

I follow her in the house, loving how it smells exactly like my childhood and hating it at the same time.

"I put fresh sheets on your bed and dusted. The windows are open to air it out some, so make sure you close them before you go to bed." She turns and smiles at me again. "Are you sure I can't fix you something to eat?"

"No, thank you."

Unsure of what to do next, I just stand there swinging my arms at my side, much the same way I did as a kid.

"Maybe a shower will perk you up?" A gentle suggestion, but I know she doesn't leave any room for an argument.

My parents aren't harsh. They don't often yell. They've never lain a disciplinary hand on us. I assume because mom was abused by her first husband. They weren't mean, but Ivy and I were raised in a very strict household. My dad runs his home the same way he runs his club, with military precision and no room for argument.

Chapter 9

Hound

"I'm like a fucking caged dog," I bitch to the empty room.

It's been nearly a solid day since Kincaid and his crew busted down the door. Three days since I made a mistake, that after thinking it through, seems less like a lapse in judgment and more like the only outcome.

I'm certain the draw I have to Georgia Anderson would still be there if I saw her on her dad's property in New Mexico. I know without a doubt that even if I'd known it was her that very first night, there's a massive chance the night would've ended the same way. The only positive is that I wasn't entrenched in the club when I saw her for the first time.

I'm sitting at the small table when the banging comes on the door. I debate whether I should answer it, but I know if I don't they'll just kick it open again. I only left once yesterday to grab food and Breathe Right strips because my nose is so swollen from Kincaid's fist I could hardly breathe.

When I open the door, the man I identified as Shadow is standing there.

"Nice sticker," he says with a chuckle, indicating the strip still on my nose.

His attitude suddenly pisses me off. Sitting in a room not sure of what's going to happen, but having enough respect for the club to face the consequences, has made my normally expansive patience a little thin.

"Want one to match," I growl.

He laughs again.

"Come on. We got shit to do."

When he turns and walks away, I just stare at his back for a second before grabbing my wallet and keys to the room.

"Where are we going?" I ask after hustling to catch up with him near an SUV with completely blacked-out windows.

"For a ride," he mutters. Pointing his finger, he all but commands me to get in on the back driver's side.

"Lovely," I say to myself and open the door.

Dominic is driving, and Kincaid is glaring at me from the passenger seat.

"Sir," I say to him with a nod. It doesn't thaw him in the slightest.

I don't ask where we're going again. I ride in silence, and they do the same.

Ten minutes later, we're pulling into the nearly empty parking lot of the strip club.

"The Minge Palace?" Shadow mumbles in disgust as he looks out the dark window.

Kincaid shakes his head, fists clenching against his thighs. Not for the first time, I imagine how I would act if a daughter of mine was involved in the things Gigi has been up to. I'd burn this place to the ground.

"The owner has girls younger than Gigi working here. Saw another girl that couldn't be over seventeen."

Dominic looks at me in the rearview mirror and Kincaid and Shadow turn their glares in my direction.

"Information Cerberus or Blade at a minimum could've used days ago," Dominic growls.

"You made me a promise," Kincaid says in an even voice that doesn't fit the mood inside of the SUV.

"Yes, Sir."

"If you go back with us to New Mexico, are you going to be able to keep it?"

I nod, praying I can, but knowing I just told my first lie to my new boss.

"Yes, Sir." I swallow roughly and hate the sweat that is popping up on my forehead.

The parking lot is suddenly filled with activity. Police cars, unmarked SUVs, and even one patrolman on a motorcycle circle our SUV.

"You get the security tapes," Dominic says to me. "We don't have time to cut Georgia out of them. Destroy every one but the one from last night. She won't be on that one."

I nod and climb out of the SUV the same time they do.

We fall in an arrow pattern with Kincaid leading the charge until a man in a Texas Alcoholic Beverage Commission jacket steps in his path. I wait for the guy to shut us down, but he reaches out his hand.

"Kincaid," the man says in greeting.

"Agent Mooreland," Kincaid returns.

"Thanks for the heads up on this. How did you hear about it?" Mooreland releases Kincaid's hand and turns to face the front of the building as the other men get ready to enter.

"My man Hound came in for a little peep show and noticed how young the girls were. Said half of them weren't only underage, but the owner was supplying them with alcohol and drugs."

I realize with the lie that he has no intention of letting any other person outside of Cerberus know that his daughter was one of the underage girls dancing here just a few nights ago.

"Good catch," Mooreland says.

The praise makes my stomach turn.

"We ready?" Kincaid asks to move things along. I know he doesn't want to spend a second longer here than absolutely necessary.

Entry is simple enough. The patrons are grouped together in one corner, girls in the other as the local agencies move in further looking for the owner. When Kincaid nods at me, I take it as my cue to head to the security office. The lock is easy enough to pick, and I make entry in less than twenty seconds.

For privacy for the felony I'm about to commit, I shut the door behind me. I ignore the cocaine, marijuana, and various bongs. They aren't the reason I'm here.

Surprisingly, the security cameras are top notch. Not surprising is the owner is so narcissistic he wouldn't think that anyone would get past that simple damn lock because he didn't even have the program password protected. Quickly I download the entire database to the jump drive I always carry on my keys.

I imagine being able to keep my promise to Kincaid will be much easier if I have Gigi on video, for those nights I'm alone and can't keep my mind off of her. It's sick and disgusting, but even knowing that doesn't keep me from doing it. I wipe the video feeds from the system, plant a virus in the computer, and pray the techs that run through it will be able to find the video from last night. I imagine the owner has enough trouble coming, but a little child pornography is always a good thing when a piece of shit is going down.

I scoop up the brick of pot and a bag of coke and leave the room.

"Whatcha got there?" Mooreland asks as I turn the corner from the hallway.

"Party favors," I tell him and toss them his direction. "Found them in the security office."

"Perfect," he says and begins talking into a handheld radio to, I assume, the DEA. "Got something you'll be interested in."

He nods and walks away.

"Let's bounce," Shadow says coming from out of nowhere.

I follow him, meeting Kincaid and Dominic near the front door.

"Find what you needed?" Kincaid asks when we close ourselves into the SUV.

"Yes, Sir," I answer. "Added a little photo gallery and fake web searches as well."

The small twitch at the corner of Kincaid's mouth gives me hope.

"Of what?" Shadow asks from beside me as Dominic pulls away from the shitty club.

"Kiddie porn and a little bestiality for good measure."

Shadow begins to laugh, and Dominic's and Kincaid's chuckles follow.

"Yeah," Dominic says. "You'll do just fine, Hound."

At least the tension is lifted some before we reach my hotel.

"How much time do you need?" Kincaid asks.

"Just have to run in and grab my go bag and suitcase."

He nods as I climb out. I lied to him again because I spend at least a full minute with Gigi's pillow to my nose, breathing her in and trying to memorize her scent.

If she's in New Mexico, I know staying away from her is going to be the hardest mission I've ever faced in my life. Even knowing that if I touch her again, Kincaid will make me wish I was dead may not be enough to keep my hands off of her when she's standing in front of me.

I toss the pillow down, clutch my keys in the pocket of my jeans to remind myself that at least I have something of her, and grab my bags and head back to the SUV.

Silence fills the inside of the SUV when I climb in, and the tension hanging in the air means they were discussing me. They don't tell me to get my ass out, so I settle in for whatever comes next.

"I'm going to keep you very busy," Kincaid says five minutes into our drive to God knows where.

"Yes, Sir," I respond.

"I can tell you to stay away from Georgia, and for your safety, I pray you can. But understand that stubborn girl doesn't listen to a word I say. In fact, she does exactly opposite of what I instruct. So even though I'll forbid her to speak to you, know in advance, she's going to do it anyway."

"Yes, Sir."

It's then that he turns to look at me.

"You can just give her up that easily?" I swallow the lump in my throat. "Pretend like nothing happened? Don't feel an urge to fight for her?"

I shake my head. "I don't know what you want me to say, Sir."

He continues to glare at me.

"I made a promise to you. I'll do my best not to break it."

"You'll try?" It's the calm in his eyes that makes my skin crawl.

"Yes, Sir." Another swallow.

"Yeah, Hound," he sneers. "I think you'll be very busy."

I feel like a million pounds have been lifted off my back when he turns to face the front. Just the scrutiny of his glare was weighing me down.

"You're fucked," Shadow whispers before turning his focus outside the window.

Chapter 10

Gigi

"I still don't understand," I tell my sister.

"What's not to understand?" Ivy says with her brows drawn tight. "After our senior year, Delilah, Lawson, and I are moving back to New Mexico. We want to be close to family."

Even though we're twins, Ivy and I couldn't be any more different from each other.

"Doesn't Lawson have that repair shop in Providence?" I thought I heard some mention of it at Thanksgiving last year.

"He's going to open another one here," Delilah says with a light squeeze to Lawson's thigh.

"But you left years ago to be near Drew," I remind Lawson.

He shrugs. "Drew graduated in May, and he plans to attend a year of college on the east coast and a year here in New Mexico before going through the police academy in Albuquerque."

"A cop?" I ask.

A wide, proud smile spreads on Lawson's face. "It's what he wants to do."

Even a kid as young as Drew has a plan for his life. I look around the empty clubhouse living room when Delilah and Ivy start talking about friends from college. My dad is expected back at any time, but most of the other members left on some mission to South Africa this morning. They aren't expected to be back for over a week. A few members are around, but they always hightail it out of the clubhouse when we show up, either to get away from us or preferring to be in the garage during daylight drinking hours.

"What do you think?" Delilah's question pulls me from my wandering thoughts.

"What? I'm sorry. I spaced."

All three of them placate me with smiles. Ivy has already said something about my loose t-shirt and sweats, and I have no idea if they know what my life has been like since the last time I saw them, but no one has asked.

"Do you want to go to Jake's this evening?" Delilah asks again.

"What's the point? He won't serve us." I shake my head, a second away from turning the offer down, but I know anything is better than being stuck here. "Sure."

I can always sneak a flask like I used to do in high school.

"What about that blue dress you brought?" Ivy asks.

I'm only catching bits and pieces of their conversation, but that's no different than it's always been.

When the front door opens and my dad, Shadow, and Uncle Dominic walk through, I wish we were already at the bar. I may have to pregame with that flask long before the sun sets if my afternoon goes the way I suspect it will.

I haven't said a word to my father since he busted in on Jameson and me back at the hotel in Dallas.

"Hey, Daddy." Ivy beams as Dad walks in our direction.

The front door closing with more force than necessary draws all of our attention. My blood heats at the sight of Jameson looking back at the door in confusion.

"Sorry," he murmurs, refusing to make eye contact with me.

"He's trouble," Lawson whispers to Delilah.

"Everyone," Uncle Dom says walking a few feet closer. "This is Jameson 'Hound' Rawley, the newest Cerberus member."

"I'll show you to your room," Shadow says and turns toward the long hallway off of the kitchen.

I watch his muscled back until he disappears, and then I meet my father's eyes. Per usual, I can't read his face. He's a master at calm and cool passivity, but I'll take this over the anger and violence I saw in Dallas.

"Hey, sweetheart," Dad says accepting Ivy's hug.

Dad shakes Lawson's hand, and they do that weird manly back slap thing as if he and Law are old friends. It's weird, especially when I consider how little time they've had to get to know each other.

"Georgia," Dad says after he's done with greeting Delilah. "I'd like to speak with you in my office. Give me an hour to greet your mother, and I expect you to be there."

I nod my compliance, glad to have an hour reprieve.

"Gross," I mutter after he walks away and I take a moment to consider why he needs an hour to say hello to my mom.

Lawson chuckles at my discomfort.

My eyes stay glued to the door leading to the hallway, hoping, praying, and wondering if Jameson will come back through it before I have to go face the firing squad.

"Want to tell us what's going on?" My sister didn't allow even two minutes before the questioning began.

"Seems Dad doesn't approve of my choice in men," I tell them without pulling my eyes away.

"He's never approved of your choice in men. Well, not since Jordy. He liked that boy."

Looking away from the hall, I turn my attention to Delilah. "Jordy was the last guy Dad should've ever liked."

Good 'ol Jordy. He was my boyfriend my sophomore year. We dated for eight months, a lifetime in high school years. We messed around after his junior prom. A dreadful attempt at a blowjob somehow transformed into rumors of me sleeping with half the baseball team. My reputation in Farmington never recovered, and neither did my attitude.

"We all have regrets," Ivy says reaching for my hand.

I jerk it away before she can touch me.

"What's done is done," I tell her before standing up and walking away.

At first, I think of running out the front and hitchhiking into town, taking off and leaving New Mexico before Dad can yell at me, but the pull in Jameson's direction is stronger.

Ignoring the whispers at my back, I take the hallway that leads to the guys' rooms. We aren't allowed back here, so I'm not surprised Ivy and Delilah are having a mild freak out in the living area. I realize my mistake when I get to the middle of the long narrow hallway. I have no idea which room is his. Short of banging on every door, I have no other way to determine where he is. I have a million questions. Why is he even here? How did Dad go from hating him to hiring him in a matter of days?

"Jameson," I hiss. No answer, so I say it even louder, but it still doesn't pull him from his room. "Hound!"

"What are you doing?" Shadow's voice snaps my eyes to him just as a door down at the end of the hall opens.

I weaken at the sight of Jameson's gorgeous face, but my world is crushed when I realize he's looking past me at Shadow.

"You're not allowed back here," Shadow reminds me in a gruff tone.

"I want to talk to you," I tell Jameson just as his door closes.

"You need to leave him alone."

"We're both adults," I remind Shadow.

"It's a conflict of interest and not allowed, Gigi. It's been that way since day one, and nothing has changed." Shadow sweeps his hand toward the doorway. "After you."

Without a glance into the living room, I head out the back door of the clubhouse. Going inside my parents' house right now isn't an option. I'll wait until I hear my mother tinkering around in the kitchen, in order to prevent hearing my dad tinkering inside of her by going inside too soon.

Sitting on the front porch, I notice the always empty field past Jaxon and Rob's house is breaking ground, preparing for another home to be built. It has to be Lawson and Delilah's. There's no one else that would be allowed to build out here.

Homeownership and marriage, which are their plans, seem like an anchor, and would only serve to drown me in obligation I never want to be burdened with.

I have no idea how long I sit on the front porch, but my back has rivulets of sweat running down it when my mother opens the door and lets me know my dad is waiting.

I notice the flush in her cheeks and grin for the first time thinking about my parents getting down and dirty. Maybe their romping will help Dad's demeanor toward me.

"Take a seat," he snaps the second I walk through the door of his office.

"Should I shut the door?"

He shakes his head. "No, your mother will be joining us."

"Why?" I question. "This is a club matter, not a family matter."

I don't want to face my actions in front of my mother even though I know my dad will hold nothing back when he speaks to her about it. They have no secrets. They kept tons of stuff from Ivy and me growing up, but they don't keep things from each other.

"It's both," he corrects just as my mother walks into the room and takes a seat in one of the chairs in front of Dad's desk.

I take the other seat, just wanting to get this over and done with.

"You will stay away from Hound," he commands.

"Why is he even here? How do you know him?"

"It's club business, Georgia, which means it's not yours."

I draw air into my lungs, preparing to let him have it, but my mother speaks up first.

"Maybe explaining Hound will make a difference," she appeases.

Dad makes eye contact with her before steepling his fingers under his chin. He squints when he looks back at me, considering his options.

Decision made, he sighs and leans in, elbows and forearms on the top of his massive desk.

"Hound was heading to work for me when Blade sent him on the fool's errand to collect you from your," he clears his throat, "latest place of employment."

"The strip club," I state, trying to rile him up for no other reason than knowing I'm going to agree to his demands, and this is the only power I have.

"He's off-limits," Dad says reiterating his point.

"He knew who I was then?" His eyes shoot to my Mom's before looking back at me.

"Not the night he met you. I don't think he recognized you with the contacts and wig."

He never would've touched me if he'd known the girl who met him in the alley was Kincaid Anderson's daughter.

It makes my heart deflate, but then I realize that Hound wanted me for me, not the appeal of fucking the boss' kid.

I smile at Dad. "You don't have to worry about Hound and me. It was just one of those things. A couple of wild days. It's over."

"Good," Dad says as Mom releases a long whoosh of air.

"I'm going to Jake's this evening with Ivy and the others."

He nods. I don't need permission to go, but his 'my house-my rules' still sticks even now at twenty. He wants to know where we are. It's the least I can do with the plans I have for later tonight.

Chapter 11

Hound

"Hey, man. I'm Hound." My proffered hand hangs in the air as the younger Cerberus member looks at it in disgust. "Okay."

I draw out the last word as I turn to grab a cold beer from the fridge.

"Nothing personal," he mutters. "But you won't be around long enough for us to spend time getting to know you."

"That so?" I lean my ass against the counter and tilt my beer to my lips.

"Yeah." He grabs his own beer out of the fridge. "Plus, there's no one here that's going to risk pissing Kincaid off by hanging out with you."

I know he's joining all the other guys outside in the garage. They all seem to gravitate in that area.

Word of my fuck up with Gigi has clearly spread from Dallas to New Mexico, and the cold shoulder I've gotten from all of the three members who aren't out on a job is just the way it's going to be for a while. What they don't understand is I have staying power and no plans to go anywhere anytime soon. I hope they change their tune when they realize that Kincaid has enough faith in my skills that even after what I've done, he's allowing me to work for him.

Emptying my first beer in one long swallow, I grab another from the fridge and head to my room. The Cerberus clubhouse isn't super fancy, but it's efficient. My room has a bed, dresser, and a full bathroom. I couldn't ask for much more.

I'm in the middle of stripping out of my jeans and t-shirt when my phone chimes. I smile without even thinking about it. Isabella is the one thing that can always bring me out of any funk.

Izzy: What are you doing?

I fold back the covers and climb between the sheets before responding.

Me: Getting ready for bed.

Izzy: You're such an old man!!

Me: But you love me anyway.

Izzy: With my whole heart.

Me: What are you doing?

I wait and wait for her to respond. A picture precedes her next text. I immediately save the shot of her smiling to my phone. Big green eyes and silky, black hair. She's the most beautiful girl I've ever laid my eyes on.

Izzy: Heading out with some friends.

I clench my fists knowing the kind of trouble she can get into.

Me: Be safe and have fun.

Izzy: ALWAYS!

I almost tell her how much I miss her. I almost tell her I wish we could be together sooner than I know we can be, but doing that will only drag her current good mood down. I'm a big enough person to shoulder the weight of our separation all on my own.

Instead, I go through my phone, looking at each and every picture she's texted me and the handful I've stolen from her social media profiles. The joy of seeing her pretty smiling face in all the pictures is almost enough to forget about the pain caused by the distance and time that separates us.

***

The safety is off on my Glock before the intruder can even get the bedroom door closed. I presumed this would happen. After being ignored so rudely by the MC members that are here, I've waited for their retribution. It wouldn't come in the form of murder, but I figured a late-night roughing up was in my near future.

What I don't expect is the hiccup and feminine giggle.

I stash the handgun back under my pillow and watch as Gigi tries to be quiet as she walks across the room. I should tell her to leave, not let her get any closer, but that's something I don't have the strength to do. I can't let anything progress, but that doesn't mean that I can't let her get close enough to smell her perfume.

She giggles again when her knees hit the end of the bed. Two soft thumps, presumably her shoes falling off, echo around the sparse room.

The scent of liquor on her breath makes it to my nose long before the soft floral scent of her perfume. That doesn't hit until a few seconds later, and rather than it being off-putting, the combination is intoxicating. My cock thickens, even further from the realization that she's brave enough to sneak into my room.

Even though there's limited light in the room, I can see her bright smile and the dark smudges of her makeup under her eyes. I want nothing more than to fuck her so hard she cries, making it run in streaks down her cheeks.

I wait until she's halfway up my body before speaking.

"What the fuck do you think you're doing?"

Startled, her eyes widen as far as the alcohol will allow, and she gazes around the room as if the voice could've come from anywhere else but under her.

She pats around, her eyes clearly not adjusted to the darkness. Her hand slides over my cock, and I growl.

"I'm going to see how far I can take that huge dick of yours down my throat."

Jesus, that sounds like the best thing in the world right now.

A glutton for punishment, I let her stroke me over the thin sheet. Up and down, with soft grips near the base and the tip, I let her continue until I'm half a second away from making another bad choice.

"Stop," I hiss and still her hand on my cock. "You know damn well I'd snap that pretty jaw of yours before you even made it halfway down."

"What a way to go," she coos. "If you're worried about hurting me, you can always just hold it straight up so I can bounce up and down on it."

"You need to go."

Please don't go.

"I'm so wet for you," she says ignoring my orders. "I've been thinking about the way you fucked me in that alley."

What a coincidence, I've been thinking of the exact same thing since I turned off the light this evening.

"It'll still be a tight fit, but I bet I just slide right down."

I keep my grip on her hand, right over my cock, even when she wiggles her fingers to try to get free. I know she has no intention of leaving, so letting her go is only a ploy so she can touch me somewhere else. God, do I want to let her do just that.

"You need to go," I repeat.

"I need *you*."

"Not gonna happen, Gigi. Now get the fuck out."

I hate the sound of her swift intake of air, but I release her hand instead of pulling her against my chest, exactly the opposite of what every single instinct in my body is telling me to do.

"You're an asshole," she whispers, but she doesn't say it in a hateful tone. She purrs it like the sultry sex kitten that she is.

Instead of moving further away, she inches closer. Rum, her choice of liquor tonight washes over me. I love the smell, knowing it probably makes her pliable, even more open to anything I'd like to do to her. I hate the smell for the exact same reasons.

"Seriously, Gigi." I roll out from under her and climb off the bed. "The last fucking thing I need is Kincaid finding out you've been in here."

I flip the light on. Big fucking mistake. Sprawled out on my bed in a tight green dress, Gigi fucking Anderson has her knees bent with her legs open. No. Fucking. Panties. I'm staring at the direct proof of that tight, slick seam she mentioned earlier.

I grip my dick.

She licks her lips.

It's sloppy, not as sexy as I'm sure she thinks, but her wet mouth has more appeal than this damn job does.

"So," she slurs. "You think he'll be mad if he finds out I'm here?"

I narrow my eyes at her, already knowing where she's going to take this. I remain silent, waiting for the drunken blackmail.

"You can fuck me, and he can never find out, or you can deny me, and I'll tell everyone I run into what a great fucking lay you were tonight."

"Not a chance."

I grip her by her upper arm and pull her off of my bed. On the way to the door, I scoop up her shoes and press them to her chest until her free hand reaches up to hold them.

"Blackmail doesn't work for me, beautiful." I swing open the door, praying someone is there, someone to serve as a witness to me throwing her out. The hall remains empty. "You'll only be wasting your time if you try to pull this shit again."

I shove her out of my room and close the door, locking it this time for good measure.

"I hate you," she seethes from the hallway.

"I hate me, too," I mutter.

Stripping out of my boxers, I hit the shower. To prove how much I despise what I've just done, I clamp my balls in my fist to the point of pain as I say her name and shoot my load down the drain.

Chapter 12

Gigi

Rejected. Again.

Always. Rejected.

I sniffle and straighten my back as I walk out the back door of the clubhouse and into the front door of my parents' home. I waited until everyone was asleep before sneaking down the sidewalk to Jameson's room. I couldn't care less if I wake the three people sleeping in this house now. Indirectly, my father is once again controlling my life. I can't even choose Jameson if I wanted to. Dad made sure of that.

My tears have dried, and a sense of calm resolve has settled in that gaping hole in my heart that never seems to be filled with anything else but the need to get away. So that's exactly what I plan to do.

I didn't unpack my bags when Jaxon brought them up the first day I got back, so too much of the room inside is filled with trinkets and shit I have no use for on the road. It takes a mere fifteen minutes to get them emptied and refilled with necessities.

"You're leaving already?"

I'm not surprised to find Ivy standing in the hall when I leave my room. Even the tears on her cheeks and the heartbreak in her voice isn't new.

"I wish I could be more like you," I confess. I blame the rum still in my system for that slip-up of honesty.

She shakes her head. "You're fine just the way you are."

I try to swallow the lump forming in my throat. Saying goodbye to her is always the hardest. You can't really share a womb with someone and not have a connection so deep it's unexplainable.

"I wish Mom and Dad felt the same way."

I put my bags down and wrap her in a hug, holding on just a little longer than the last time I walked away from New Mexico. Something in my gut tells me this time is going to be much different. This time feels like forever.

"You're not running from Dad this time." The truth burns my ear, but I ignore it just the same.

"I'll miss you the most," I tell her as I pull away and reach for the straps of my two bags.

"You can call and text," she offers.

"I will," I lie and walk away.

The cab I called for earlier is idling out front when I make my way around the clubhouse.

The lone Cerberus member standing on the front porch having one last smoke before calling it a night doesn't even faze me. I know he won't try to stop me. There's only one living Cerberus member who ever physically touched me without my father's permission, and he made sure to make me burn.

"Prez won't stop looking for you," he says on a thick puff of smoke.

I ignore him and climb inside of the cab. Just like always, I keep my eyes closed until the bump in the road three miles away. I never look back. I never second guess my decision to leave this place. Well, I never did until tonight.

***

"Hey, sweetie?"

I startle awake, looking right into the soft, tired eyes of the elderly woman that sat beside me on the bus out of Farmington.

"You said you were heading to Phoenix, right?"

I nod, draw in a lung full of air, and stretch my back out.

"We're only a few miles away," she informs me and points an arthritic finger toward the window.

"Thank you."

"Anytime, dear." She begins humming again with her eyes closed. It's what lulled me to sleep to begin with a couple of hours ago when she got on at the Tucson stop.

Even though I don't use my cell phone very often, traveling from Farmington after having tossed it in the trash hasn't been the most pleasurable. At least with a burner and a pair of headphones, I can ignore the world around me. Traveling and circling back, going out of the way has always been how I traveled.

It's how I found myself in an all-but-deserted bus station at three in the morning. Unable to buy a phone then, I knew in daylight hours I'd be able to grab one in Phoenix.

When the hiss of the bus's brakes make their final gasp, I wait for the elderly woman to stand. She manages on her third attempt, and I find myself uncharacteristically worried about her. I help her traverse the steep stairs at the front of the bus and wait for her while the attendants pull her suitcases off.

When she tells me that her son will be there to pick her up in an hour, I forgo my seat on my original bus to catch the one later in the evening.

"Thank you," she says in the sweetest voice I imagine a grandmother would have, as I pull out her chair and hand her a small ice cream cup.

I've always wondered what it would be like to have an elderly family. My dad's mom met an awful fate at the hands of my grandfather when he was only a teen. My mom doesn't have any family to speak of. Ivy and I have had some interaction with grandparent-type figures. Shadow's parents came around often enough, and her obsession with Griffin always ensured we'd be where he was. Doc and Rose have been very active in our lives as well.

"You didn't have to miss your bus for me."

"I have a little shopping to do," I tell her before filling my mouth with a huge bite of chocolate frozen yogurt.

"Where are you heading again?"

I know she's just curious, but cautious no matter who we are around is something that Dad drilled into our heads.

If you're not with family, you're not entirely safe.

"San Diego," I lie, a little weirded out and cautious since I never mentioned where I was heading before, just that I needed to grab some things in Phoenix.

"That's right," she says with a sugary sweet smile before diving back into her ice cream.

My nerves relax a little when she starts re-telling me the story about her travels and the three grandchildren she's visiting. It's the same story she told me when she got on the bus. She speaks of how busy her son is. My heart hurts for this woman. She's closer to eighty than seventy and shouldn't be traveling alone, and yet her family couldn't be bothered to drive two hours to get her.

"The world is heavy," she says in her soft, weak voice.

"I'm sorry?" I put my ice cream down and look over at her. "I was lost in my own head."

"You have the weight of the world all around you," she repeats. "It's too heavy of a burden to carry yourself."

I placate her with a smile but keep my mouth shut. In thirty minutes, I won't have to worry about her rambling. I'll make sure she's safe with her family, and I'll head North-West to Vegas just like I'd planned.

"You'll carry it on your back until you stop running and give someone the chance to love you."

"I'll keep that in mind," I cajole and stir my spoon through my melting ice cream.

"Mother?"

We both look up to see a middle-aged man walking toward us.

"Oh, Dave," she says in a near giddy tone. "Meet my new friend Annie. She's traveling to San Diego."

"Nice to meet you," he placates his mother without as much as a nod in my direction.

Asshole.

He helps her stand, taking no care to allow her to straighten and be firm in her stance before he releases her and reaches down for the handles on her suitcases. I stand, hand near her back, just in case she's not as sure-footed as he presumes she is.

"The next time he finds you," she whispers in my ear. "Stick around long enough that he can prove how much you deserve to be loved."

I watch, stunned and a little confused at her words, as her son shuffles her away almost faster than she can walk.

It's minutes after they've disappeared through the crowd of people buying tickets that I find myself wanting to yell, to chase her down and inform her that *he*, if she's referring to Hound, rejected me just like every guy I got close to did. I wasn't enough for him to go against my father's wishes. I can't imagine him changing his mind.

He's thirty-four years old, and I'm sure has had more women than he can count. There's no way he'd ever be interested in me for more than what he already got.

Chapter 13

Hound

"Where the fuck is she?" Kincaid says after opening my door with what I presume is the master key to the building.

"What?" I sit up in bed, trying to scrub the sleep from my eyes. I did nothing but toss and turn all night after I escorted Gigi out of here. How I can feel both regret over it and proud I did the right thing is beyond me.

"Where is Georgia?" he asks again.

"She's not here."

"She *was* here." He holds up the shoes I handed Gigi before throwing her out of my room. "I found these outside of your door in the hallway."

"I gave my word to you, Prez. She showed up. She'd been drinking." I swallow and refuse to tell him that she offered herself to me. I squeeze my eyes closed, a futile attempt to block out the memory of the tightest, pinkest slit I've ever had the pleasure of sinking inside of. "I made her leave."

"What time?" he asks, defeat clear in his tone.

"Two-thirty? Maybe three." I stand and pull on a pair of jeans. "Think she took off again?"

"She packed her bags," Shadow says as he steps into my room behind Kincaid. "Misty checked her room."

"Did she tell you where she was going?" Kincaid's eyes are back on mine. He's pleading, grasping at straws, trying to control a daughter who has no interest in such a thing. I want to tell him to lay off of her and maybe she'll stick around, but he's only being a protective father.

I shake my head. "It wasn't...last night wasn't pretty."

"The fuck does that mean?" Kincaid growls, dropping the shoes and taking a menacing step in my direction.

"She made...advances. I didn't reciprocate." He growls, and I know he's torn between her being rejected and his command that I stay away from her. "I kept my promise."

"Are you saying you forced a drunken girl out of your room last night?"
Seems the rejection is winning out right now.

I can't win for fucking trying at this point.

"I kept my promise," I repeat. "But, yes. I had to physically remove her. I didn't hurt her, but she wasn't happy when I closed my door on her."

"She ran," Kincaid says with disappointment. "Again. Shadow."

"On it," Shadow says and leaves us in the room.

"Did she ever mention going somewhere? A city? A certain job? Friends?"

I shake my head. "We never really talked about life goals and futures."

I'm disgusted, standing in front of this man and practically telling him I treated his daughter like a whore. Even after knowing who she was, I took her to bed, and if I'm honest, I can admit that the thrill of fucking her, the pleasure I gained from sleeping with the boss' daughter was part of the appeal.

"Pack your shit," he hisses.

I should've seen this coming. Fuck her or don't fuck her. The end result was always going to be the same.

"You, Scooter, and Rocker are heading to Tijuana. Simple extraction. Three days max."

He leaves without another word. My head is spinning from everything that just happened. Gigi is gone, more than likely left because I pissed her off, and I still have a job? Either Kincaid has something planned for me of devious proportions, or he actually is a decent man, and isn't holding a grudge even where his daughter is concerned.

"Fuck," I mutter scraping my hands over the top of my head. "I don't even know if I'm coming or going in this fucking place."

* * *

"This," Scooter says handing over a flash drive, "has all of the forms you have to complete before we can leave Mexico. Send them to Blade so he can finish the mission remotely."

I look at the sleek black device in my hand and then to Scooter's and Rocker's back as they turn to leave the hotel suite.

"And where are you guys going?"

Rocker grins over his shoulder. "Tijuana nightlife is the best thing ever. Sexy-ass girls all half-naked and ready to fuck."

"We're heading to the club," Scooter adds.

"And I'm staying here to do the paperwork?"

They both grin. "Being the boss sucks sometimes."

I look at Rocker, and he just shrugs.

"You can come with us," Scooter offers. "We can show you how Cerberus celebrates a successful recovery, but you'll still have to have that shit submitted before we leave."

My eyes cut to Rocker, who sobers a little, his smile falling to a flat line. He knows as well as I do that this mission wasn't as simple as we all thought.

One of the guys guarding the young girl that was abducted got the jump on him. He also got a bullet to the head, but Rocker was mere seconds from having his throat slit in the basement of a makeshift whorehouse that caters to men who have singular tastes, their sexual proclivities leaning toward pre-pubescent girls and toddlers. He was distracted by the depravity, and it almost cost him his life.

"It's no big deal," I offer. "I'll knock this out and grab some sleep. I haven't slept well in a couple of weeks. I'm sure I'll crash like the dead tonight."

"Your loss," Scooter says and turns back to the door. He turns back when he realizes that Rocker isn't with him. "You coming?"

"Naw," Rocker answers before grabbing a laptop out of his bag and sitting down on the bed. "I'm gonna help Hound fill out this paperwork."

"I appreciate it, man," I tell him. "But you don't have to do that. I can handle it."

"Shut the fuck up. The sooner we knock this shit out, the sooner we can slip inside of some sweet Mexican pussy." I can hear the playfulness in Rocker's voice, and for the very first time since joining Cerberus, I feel like part of the team.

"Dammit," Scooter mutters, but he grabs another laptop from his bag and opens it.

Rocker and I work in silence, but Scooter feels the need to hum stupid ass songs as he works. What would've taken me several hours to complete alone is finished in just under one with all three of us working.

"This is what Kincaid and Shadow spend all of their time on after missions?" I ask as I close my laptop.

I verified all of their forms and made sure they were sent to Blade.

"I guess," Rocker answers. "I only went out with them a few times when I first started. Grinch usually heads up the missions, but since he's in South Africa with the rest of the guys, Prez picked you."

"And if I wasn't an option?"

"More than likely we wouldn't be here," Scooter says as he puts his laptop away. "They only allow the guys with ten or more years in the Corps to head up the missions."

"So the girl we extracted tonight would've just been left?"

"Not necessarily," Rocker begins. "There are other companies. The family would've just gone down the list until they found someone available."

"Cerberus needs a bigger team," I mutter.

"Kincaid is expanding as fast as he can. I know you saw them breaking ground across the street. They have to have somewhere to house the new members. The new clubhouse will look more like a two-story hotel. We'll be able to have three times the amount of men, but until then we have to wait. You took the last available room." Rocker slaps me on the back and heads to the door. "You coming?"

I waffle between building a relationship with these men or just staying the hell inside. Getting laid, for the first time in my life, doesn't appeal to me.

"We can always bunk up together," I offer as a solution to the lack of space back at the clubhouse.

"Never," Scooter objects. "That's Kincaid's view. When we're in New Mexico, we're home, and having to share space with others is something he wouldn't force on us. We live that way when we're working. He doesn't want it to be that way all the time."

I nod my head in understanding but knowing more men means more chances for us to help those in need.

"Besides," Rocker says with a quick laugh. "You'd change your mind the first time you saw Scooter rutting around in some chick too stupid to turn him down."

I laugh. Scooter shoots Rocker a double middle finger.

"You coming?" Rocker asks again. He stares at me when I don't respond. "She always runs."

As if he's reading my mind, Rocker responds to thoughts I'd never verbalize to these men.

"Every once in a while, she'll show up like a lost dog, but she never stays long," Scooter adds.

"Who?" I ask playing dumb.

They both laugh and shake their heads.

"Come on," Scooter urges. "Tijuana is the best place to fuck her off of your mind."

I stand and join them. Not doing so would raise more questions, more suspicion than I'm willing to answer for.

Chapter 14

Gigi

"Order up," Benny says for at least the hundredth time tonight. He slaps the bell in the window beside the steaming plate of chicken fried steak as if I'm not standing right in front of him.

"Thanks," I mumble and drop off another ticket.

I carry the plate of food to the trucker who ordered it. I drop it the last couple of inches unintentionally.

"Sorry. Be careful, that plate is damn hot."

The trucker, unfazed by the hot splash of gravy on the back of his hand smiles up at me. Lifting his hand, he licks the food from it.

"That's alright, darlin." The quick flip of his tongue, I know, is supposed to be seductive, but half of it gets stuck in his ratty beard, and my stomach turns. "You can make it up to me later."

I just nod, used to the sexual solicitations from the clientele this crappy diner pulls in. Three more weeks until I turn twenty-one and I won't have to work for less than waitressing wages under the table. Benny hires all of the women who work here that way, so he doesn't have to pay payroll taxes. If an accountant took a long hard look at this place, they'd question how it operates without staff.

"I still need ketchup," a woman barks when I walk by.

"Coming right up," I tell her with a smile.

"They know your smile is fake," Farrah sneers when I reach behind the counter for ketchup.

"And?" I hiss. "What does it matter if I fake smile?"

"You get better tips if you're genuine."

"The fake smile is the best I can do," I murmur before dropping the sauce off to the female trucker who's looking at me the same way the gravy guy did.

"Thanks, baby," she purrs in a rough smoker's voice. "When do you get off?"

"I work all night," I lie. My shift ends in a couple of hours, and all I can think about is falling into my bed and passing out. Sleep and work. It's all I can manage these days.

"Too bad. I pull out at midnight. Have to make it to Salt Lake City by ten." She winks at me, and I offer my fake smile. "I could possibly be a little late."

I take a step back when she reaches for my hip. "Have a safe trip. Maybe next time you're coming through."

"You bet your tiny, sweet ass, baby," she says as I walk away.

I know I shouldn't give them any hope. I know it's a dangerous line I'm walking, but tips generally suck, or they go to the girls like Farrah, who will either jump from sleeper to sleeper or bring these men and women up to our tiny two-room apartment over the diner.

I have to scrape for every dollar I earn because whoring myself out for twenty bucks isn't something I'm willing to do.

"She would've paid at least fifty," Farrah says looking back over at the lady trucker. "I bet she'd be more interested in getting you off than the other way around."

"No thanks," I say standing near the window and waiting for my next order to come out.

Farrah has been trying to get me to see the brighter side of prostitution since she arrived over a month ago. I started working here less than a week before that, but she isn't the first girl to pick the diner for the extra earning ability. The girl that I shared the apartment with for four days before she took off with a trucker that promised her the world also earned extra cash in the parking lots.

"Not my thing," I mutter when Farrah just stands there staring at me.

"Women?" she questions. "I'd choose the women over the men any day, and one like that one where I'll probably just have to lay back and get licked? Those are the best."

"She's all yours," I offer.

"Sweet," she says turning her back to the patrons eating and waiting for food. She doesn't turn back until she's lifted her already exposed tits up an inch higher.

Shaking my head, I do my best not to judge her. I know some women are forced into this kind of life. They do things they never thought they would because they have no other choice. I also know the probability that Farrah will either end up on drugs or with a pimp that controls her every move is high. I also know the likelihood that she may end up in the sex trafficking trade is even higher. The difference in her and the women Dad has spent his life rescuing is that there's no one out there for Farrah. There's no one looking for her, worried about her, or willing to pay a ridiculous amount of money to keep her safe. She's one of the truly lost ones.

Just like me.

Shaking my head again, I try to dislodge those thoughts. I know all of the risks Farrah is taking with her life, other than the prostitution, are the same ones I take with mine.

The difference is, she's looking for someone to love her whether she admits it or not. I'm running from parents who, in their own weird way, only want what's best for me. I'm running from people who love me and want me around. Tears sting my eyes when I look over and watch Farrah shove her tits in the female trucker's face.

I've managed to keep the money I whored myself out to Hound for, but I know that if something doesn't change soon, there's a real chance I'll be doing exactly what my roommate is doing to earn a couple extra bucks. Farrah truly seems to enjoy the extra attention she gets from the truckers. She's not crying into her pillow when they leave. She's not using drugs to get through the act of selling herself.

I'm the one teary-eyed and questioning every choice I've ever made. I'm the one standing here and ignoring the ding of Benny's bell. I'm the one who's considering that maybe community college and the comfort of my parents' home isn't such a bad thing.

* * *

The sounds of familiar grunts and a shitty bed frame squeaking wake me up. It's the third time it's happened since I got off work early this morning.

I cover my head with my pillow and wait for it to stop. It never takes Farrah long to escort her Johns from the apartment, so I wait, bladder ready to explode until she's done. I never look up, never wonder what's going on. I've never had any desire to see first-hand what it takes to earn a little extra cash, but today the yelling makes my head pop up.

"Let go," Farrah says clawing at the man's hands around her throat.

"I'm not leaving until I come," he hisses but loosens his grip.

She takes as deep a breath as she can manage, and despite this man, twice her size and menacing as the devil himself, who is in front of her with the ability to kill her in a flash, Farrah never looks scared.

"I'm done," she hisses. "If you'd stay off of the dope, I'd have more to work with than a half-hard dick."

My eyes shoot straight to his crotch. If that's half-hard, I can't imagine what he looks like fully erect.

His grip tightens again, but even with breaths being pulled in on harsh wheezes, she never loses the fire in her eyes or drops the sneer from her lips.

The click, that tell-tale sound of a hammer being pulled back, draws both of their attention.

"Let her go," I command.

Farrah frowns, but the guy immediately releases her and pulls up his pants.

"I didn't sign up for this shit, Farrah," he mutters before shrugging on his jacket.

Farrah glares at me before turning back to him. "We can finish in your truck."

The fuck is going on?

"Next time." He angles his head in my direction. "Make sure that crazy bitch doesn't pull this again."

I watch as the man digs out a few bills from his wallet before handing them to my psycho roommate and kissing her lips. He doesn't kiss her like a man who just had his massive hand cutting off her air supply, but someone he genuinely cares for.

"Unless you want to take this next trip with me?" Hope fills his voice, but Farrah takes a step back and shakes her head.

"Maybe next time." She pecks him one last time before he leaves the room.

I release the hammer on the small gun I got a week ago and shove it back under the edge of my shitty mattress.

"What the hell is that all about, Homeless Barbie?"

"He was hurting you," I hiss. "Well, I thought he was hurting you."

"It's his kink," she offers folding the money and shoving it into a tin cookie can.

"I know that now."

"Did it turn you on?"

I huff a humorless laugh. "Turn me on? Not a fucking chance. I was seconds away from shooting him."

"You'd kill for me?" Confusion draws her brows together.

"No," I lie. "I'd probably shoot him in the leg. I won't sit around and watch any man hurting a woman like that."

Another lie. Yes, I'd kill him. Dad trained us to shoot center mass, and that's exactly where my weapon was pointed.

"You need to go home," Farrah says as she tugs on a t-shirt. "You don't belong out here with girls like me."

"Girls like you?" She better not start in on trying to convince me to be a prostitute again. I've heard all I can take.

"Girls like me would've looked at the reversal of this situation. If I saw you dangling from the fist of some deadly trucker, I would've wondered if I could work my shift at the diner before reporting your dead body up here. Girls like me would've covered my head with my pillow while you died, not out of fear, but because if you die, then I get to keep the money you have stashed under that broken tile in the bathroom."

My stomach turns.

"You'll never be a girl like me, and that makes you more dangerous than the men that choke me when they're not role-playing. I'll take those creeps over some girl running from problems any of us would trade our shitty lives for any day."

I fall back on my mattress, wondering if she's stealing my money when she walks away and closes herself into the bathroom.

Chapter 15

Hound

"Jesus," I hiss when Scooter slams the door to the SUV at least ten times harder than required.

"The day after always sucks," Rocker says with a quick slap to my back.

I cringe harder, the movement jostling my brain that's been swimming in Russian vodka for the last three days.

"It was a three-day bender," I correct him.

"You can't tell me you didn't do this shit in the Corps," Grinch says no worse for the wear even though he put back more alcohol this last week than all of us combined.

"I worked. All the time. I didn't risk getting drunk in foreign countries."

"We worked, too," Catfish says with a little irritation in his voice.

I shake my head. "You spent four years in the Corps. I was there seventeen. You really want to compare our work ethic?"

He flips me off. When I first got here two months ago, I wouldn't have bothered to joke around with them or call them out on their shit. After several missions and a couple of close calls, these guys have finally accepted me into their inner circles.

I can't say the same for Kincaid. He talks at me, barks orders, listens with professionalism when there's a problem, but for the most part, he sends Shadow with information or Blade with intel. I stopped taking it personal weeks ago when I realized he's not really treating me any differently than he does the other guys.

His inner circle: Shadow, Dom, Kid, Jaxon, and Rob are different, but he's been with those guys going on twenty years. I understand that type of brotherhood. I can also accept that I'll never be a part of it.

"You wanna grab a beer?" I glare at Rocker as I walk past him into the clubhouse. "Don't be a pussy."

I growl, no menace in the act. A long hard look at him and I can tell he's fucking with me. He looks tired as fuck, and I bet we all lay down and sleep for the next two days.

The mission to Russia was beyond fucked. The three girls we were sent to recover were dead before the wheels of our plane left New Mexico soil two weeks ago. We didn't find that out, though, until four days ago. All the guys took it hard, but I took it harder.

The trio of seventeen-year-olds were all abducted after softball practice. Same graduating class, same small town. Two were cousins, so that family took a double hit. They just never showed up for dinner that night. Hell, I found out the small-town Baptist church they all attended offered to pay for the recovery. Grinch, the other Cerberus member who leads missions when we split up, informed me that Kincaid wouldn't take a dime from them. He said we have funds and accounts to help people like this. Kincaid isn't the type of man to bankrupt a small community just because they wanted their children back.

So the three-day Cerberus bender was about healing, regret, and the stolen lives of three young women who didn't deserve the fate they ended up with. We were waiting for Kincaid to work some things out, giving us the ability to carry home the decomposing bodies so their families will have some closure.

"It never gets easier."

I look up and see Kincaid standing in the kitchen of the clubhouse. He offers me a beer, and even though the thought of turning it up to my lips makes me want to vomit, I take it from him.

"Thanks." I tilt it his direction in salute before turning it up to my lips.

We stand in silence for a long moment, me just letting the weight of the mission hang heavy in the air. He, being the true leader he is, gives me this moment of reprieve.

"It's not my first loss. It's not even my first civilian loss, but it just fucked me up more than I thought possible."

My phone buzzes in my jeans pocket, but I ignore it.

"I was affected when I was younger." His calm voice is like a balm to the wounds our trip opened. "But when I became a father to two precious, helpless little girls it was always more difficult."

"It's why you'll never stop looking for Gigi even when she's adamant that she doesn't want to be found."

It's not a question. I know I'd do exactly the same thing he is. I'd do everything in my power to keep my child safe, even if she fought me every step of the way.

"You'll understand when you're a dad." With a quick nod of his head, he leaves me standing alone in the kitchen.

"Right," I mutter and pour the rest of my beer down the drain.

My phone buzzes again, the second notification from the text I got a moment ago, but I don't pull my phone out of my pocket until my bags are thrown in the corner, and I'm stripped down to my boxers.

My stomach turns, and I nearly vomit for a whole other reason when I finally look down at the message.

Blade: Georgia has an appointment at the abortion clinic in two days. Sending info.

It buzzes again in my hand with the address of a women's clinic on Sahara in Las Vegas.

A cold sweat chills my skin.

My first instinct is to grab the keys to one of the SUVs and make the sub-nine hour trip across the desert.

My second instinct is to allow her to make her own decisions.

Her body, her choice.

I made the same argument once before, and that didn't work out the way I'd expected it to either.

Without a second thought, I unlock my darkened phone and make a call.

"Hey, you."

My eyes close at the sweet sound of her voice.

"Hey, you," I mimic.

"I have a ton stuff to take care of tonight."

I can hear the TV going in the background and other voices close by.

"I just wanted to call and hear your voice, baby."

"My day is pretty busy tomorrow, too."

I nod. "Maybe the day after?"

"Who are you talking to?" The male voice I despise echoes through her phone, and I clutch mine even tighter.

"Nicky from work," she lies.

"Tell her I said 'hi.'"

"Jim says hi," she says into the phone.

"Tell Jim to jump off of a cliff."

I clamp the bridge of my nose with my fingers.

"Saturday will be best," she assures me, ignoring my jab. The noise level lowers, and I can tell that she's walking away from whatever group she was with. "He'll be gone Friday night and won't be back until late on Sunday. I can talk more then, but I'll text you later."

"I love you, Izzy," I tell her.

"Love you, too," she whispers before ending the call.

I haven't told Izzy about my fuck up with the Prez's daughter. I haven't even mentioned her once. She's asked more than once about my job here. I give her the basics, protecting her from my mistakes, but she'll know eventually. If Gigi is pregnant, if I do exactly what my instinct is telling me to do, then I risk losing Izzy altogether. For the first time in my life, I'm honestly torn between two decisions. For the first time in my life, I second guess whether choosing Izzy over all others is what's best. I'm torn between breaking the heart of a girl I swore to love and protect seventeen years ago or a twenty-year-old wild child who spends her life running away from her family just because they want her to grow the fuck up.

My hands clench until they hurt as I lie in bed trying to make a decision, a decision I knew wasn't a fucking decision the second that fucking text came through.

"Fuck," I roar as I climb out of bed and get dressed.

Hoping to find Grinch in the living room where chatter is coming from, I stop dead when I see Kincaid and Shadow having a couple of beers with some of the guys that just returned from Russia.

"Beer?" Scooter asks, pointing to the cooler near his feet.

"No thanks." I turn to Kincaid. "Can I borrow one of the SUVs, and take a couple of days off?"

He watches me for a long moment, analyzing the look on my face and trying to figure out exactly what's going on.

"Can I ask what's up?"

I clear my throat.

"You can."

This isn't going to be pretty.

"And you'll tell me the truth."

"Yes, Sir."

His face softens. "But you don't want to tell me."

"I'd rather not."

"Do you need backup?"

I shake my head. "No, sir. This is mostly personal."

His eyes widen, but only a little. He nods, and I can see a pleading on his face. I've seen that look once before, so I know he knows the nature of my business.

"Be safe." I turn to leave. "Keep your promise."

I walk out without responding. I did make him a promise, but I won't repeat it, especially when I know I may not be able to keep it.

Chapter 16

Gigi

"Seriously?"

I roll my eyes at my new roommate.

"Calm the fuck down," she hisses. "I worked a double yesterday."

I swipe at the angry tears running down my cheeks as I toss another small pile of clothes out of my way.

"You worked a double *two* days ago. Then you got fucked up on pills." I kick the small table between our beds just to make noise. "*I* worked your double yesterday. On my one and only day off I had scheduled for the next two weeks."

"I'll work your shift tonight," she offers.

My eyes narrow at her kindness.

"I'll work my own shifts, thank you very much."

I'm normally nice to my roommates, but this one has a different guy in her bed sometimes twice a day, and the fucked-up part is she isn't a prostitute. At least with Farrah, I knew she was working to build up a nest egg. Kori just sleeps with guys to sleep with guys, and she's not even courteous about it.

"But today's your *thing*, right?"

Nosy bitch.

"Right?" She sits up in bed. "You won't be able to work after."

"I'll be fine," I hiss, hating that she overheard me on the phone when I made the appointment last week. I even gave them my real name, knowing Blade would probably track me down in whatever IT magical way he finds me.

"I'm not saying you're a weak person, Annie. I'm saying, from experience, working a ten-hour shift on your feet after an abortion isn't going to be possible."

I collapse on my bed.

"I need the money," I mumble.

She laughs. "For what? It's not like you're saving up to take care of a baby."

I stare at her back when she goes to the restroom, but turn my eyes when she doesn't even bother to close the door before she sits on the commode.

"How are you getting there?" The toilet flushes and the water in the shower starts. "I can get Simon to take you."

"I'm taking the bus. I don't want to be anywhere near Simon."

I shudder at the thought of her boyfriend taking me to do something so personal. Technically, he's not her boyfriend, just a guy she keeps around and uses for things like money and transportation. He's head over heels in love with her, has been since they ran away from home together a couple of years ago, but Kori is too wild to see what's in front of her eyes.

"He's not a bad guy," she yells over the sound of the shower.

I know he's not, but today is going to be emotionally exhausting. Simon always wants to talk about Kori and what I think he should do to make her love him. The last time he asked and I was in a shitty mood, I told him to walk away from her. Let her live her life like she wants. Even if she's fucking up, it's her choice.

He wasn't very happy about that. So unhappy in fact, he told her what I said. She was livid with me, which I normally wouldn't have an opinion one way or the other about, but I have to trust this girl enough to at least not slit my throat while I'm sleeping. Praying she wouldn't rob me blind was even asking too much of her.

"Like I said." Kori comes in buck ass naked and drying her unhealthy hair with a sheet-thin towel. "The first one is always the hardest. I'll cover your shift tonight."

"It's the last one," I mutter to myself.

"Huh?" She turns her head in my direction.

"I said thanks. I won't ask you to cover another. I appreciate it."

"Don't worry," she says with a wide grin. "You'll owe me."

I only nod, not willing to argue the point of covering her double shift yesterday while she slept off the effects of the handful of pills she took that should've killed her.

After I find the jeans I was looking for earlier, I scoop up my clothes and toiletries and head to the bathroom, making sure to lock the door. I miss Farrah more than I ever thought I would when she came home three weeks ago and said she was getting married to the choking trucker. She promised to stop by when they drive through, but I haven't seen her yet. Probably never will again.

I shower and dress before opening the door. Steam follows me out of the room, and my clothes stick to my body. There is not one window in this small apartment. If it weren't for both of us having keys to the deadbolt, It'd almost be like a prison cell with only one way in and one way out. It goes against everything my father instilled in us as kids.

"You sure you don't want Simon to take you?" She looks back down at her hands and types away on her phone.

"I'm good, thanks though."

"It's free if Simon takes you." She looks up again.

Why is she hounding me about this?

"It's free for me, not him. I'm not going to owe Simon a damn thing."

"You won't owe him anything. I will."

And she'll never repay him. She uses people. She always has an ulterior motive. Always thinking of deception two steps ahead. I won't owe her by proxy either.

"The bus is fine."

I flip my hair over and gather it in a loose ponytail before twisting it into a bun. I'm in desperate need of a haircut, but I've been so tired. I add keeping my long hair to my mental pro/con list I've been building since the second line showed up on the dollar store piss test. I get too hot with it down against my neck, but I have a raging headache within an hour of pinning it up.

"Suit yourself," Kori says as she tosses her phone on her mattress and tugs a Benny's Diner t-shirt over her head. She doesn't bother with a bra. Hell, I don't know if the woman even owns one. She probably left it back home with her modesty.

"Where did you get the money?"

"Huh?" I look up at her after putting my real ID in my purse.

"For the abortion. You said you're going to the clinic down on Sahara? That's not some back-alley procedure. That's like a legit fucking place. Expensive. Where did you get the money?"

Holy hell. What has this girl been through?

For a second I wonder if she's going to shake me down for the cash, and that's the reason she was pressing so hard for me to ride with her friend.

"The father is paying for it."

"He just handed over six hundred dollars in cash?"

Her head pulls back a few inches as if she's shocked, but then she licks her lips, literally salivating at the thought of having access to that much cash. No doubt she's imagining all of the drugs she could buy with it.

"Fuck no." I release a heartless laugh. "He's meeting me there. Said he didn't trust a whore with that kind of money."

My stomach turns, part with the morning sickness I haven't been able to kick but also at the thought of how Jameson would actually act if he found out that he knocked me up during our little tryst.

Her face falls, filled with disappointment, and I immediately begin to think of moving on soon. She doesn't seem to be going anywhere soon, and there's no way I can stay feeling so unsafe. As soon as I heal from this procedure, I'm on to bigger and better things.

I wait until Kori heads downstairs to work my shift before going back into the bathroom and pulling away the broken tile behind the toilet. Thankfully, the wad of cash I've managed to hang onto for months is still there. I take all of it, even though it's more than today will cost. I have to find a different place to keep it, and I'm thinking outside of this apartment is going to be best.

The trip on public transportation isn't as bad as it could be. At least it's daytime, and no one tries to sit on my lap like the last time I made a trek across town.

I do like always, keep my head down, headphones in with no music. It's a deterrent for people who want to bother me, but still gives me the ability to be cognizant of what's going on around me. I'm closed off, angry look on my face, as unapproachable as possible.

Forty-five minutes and one bus switch later I'm standing near the parking lot of the clinic. I take a deep breath, having already made my decision before today. Keeping a baby while running from town to town isn't possible, so there's only one solution.

I pat my pocket, making sure I didn't get rolled by the teenager who bumped into me on my way off of the bus. Relieved, but for some reason also saddened by it still being there, I walk toward the front door.

For the third time in my life, I'm hauled off of my feet and tossed over a shoulder. Even as embarrassing as this is, when the scent of his cologne fills my nose, I smile against his back, and I don't even argue when he roughly shoves me into the front seat of an SUV I recognize as my dad's. I remain silent as he clips my belt and walks around to the driver's seat.

Chapter 17

Hound

"You look like shit," I spit when I settle in behind the steering wheel.

Fun fact, she actually looks gorgeous. Her long brown hair is more radiant than I remember, and her blue eyes, although not as bright as before, shine.

"Nice talk," she says and reaches for the door handle.

I growl before I even realize I want to. My hand clamps on her thigh, squeezing until she yelps from the unintentional pain.

"Why are you here?"

I angle my head toward the women's clinic.

"You know exactly why I'm here."

She huffs a humorless laugh. "This is a Cerberus SUV."

Small talk isn't her style, and since neither is keeping her thoughts bottled up, I wait for her to get to the point she wants to make.

"I have to say," she begins looking away from me and out the window. "I'm surprised you're still working for him. Figured you would've tried to fuck my mom by now."

"I'm sure my employment will end today," I say not taking her bait and getting riled up at the mother comment.

"Why are you here?" she asks again. "To stop me?"

I look out the window, the battle in my heart and head telling me to beg her to walk away from this place raging like a literal fire.

"I'm here to hold your hand or—"

"You're here to make sure I follow through with what you said in the alley."

"I don't rem—"

She lowers her voice, trying, and failing, to sound more masculine.

"That money is for the abortion if my stupid ass put that shit into motion..."

Chills race over my skin, leaving behind the sting of regret.

She pats her pocket. "I still have the money, so thanks for that."

I bite my bottom lip until I taste tangy copper on my tongue.

"You don't have to go in with me." Her lack of bravery is betrayed by the crack of her voice. She's trying so hard to make me think she's strong, all I want to do is wrap my arms around her and promise her the world. "I'll make sure it's taken care of."

I reach out and clamp her thigh again when she tries to open the door.

"Georgia."

Her tear-streaked face turns, telling me she's listening, but she's looking past me, not directly in my eye.

"You didn't let me finish. I'm here to hold your hand in that clinic if that's what you want."

She nods.

"Or to hold that baby when it's born and help you raise him." Her eyes finally meet mine. "I'm not here to convince you one way or the other, but I'm here for you—whichever direction you go."

"You're not here to stop me?"

I shake my head, but her eyes trail to my throat where I work on the dry lump that has formed there.

"You're lying," she whispers. "You do have an opinion about what I should do."

I follow her eyes when they look down at the hand gripping her thigh, the hand that's keeping her from getting out of the SUV.

"It's your body. It's your choice." I shake my head, fingers flexing against her jeans as I resist the urge to cup her cheek.

She looks out the window, staring at the entrance to the clinic, and I sit in silence with my heart pounding in my chest.

"You want to marry me and raise this baby together?"

I can't stop the laughter that bubbles up my throat. "Fat fucking chance."

I can see mirth in her eyes when she looks back at me. The reaction on my part was natural, but the smile on her face tells me it's exactly what she wanted to hear.

"No happily ever after for us?" She gives me a weak smile. "No handful of kids and white picket fence in our future?"

"That's not what you want either," I add.

"You said you're unemployed after today. Why would you think that?"

Shaking my head with a quick chuckle, I look back over at her. "Fucking you is one thing. I don't imagine your dad is going to be happy that I knocked you up."

It's her turn to laugh. "I'm a grown woman, Jameson."

God, I love the sound of my given name on her lips, the breathy way it falls off of her tongue.

"You are," I agree.

"We can just not tell him," she suggests.

"A baby is kind of hard to hide," I reason with her, but the fact that she's considering keeping the child makes my heart soar.

When she looks up at me, a small smile playing on her lips, the brightness she lacked in her eyes is there once again. She's breathtakingly beautiful.

"We don't have to go back." She shifts in her seat, anxious for the future she's imagining. "We can stay here in Vegas. Get a three-bedroom house or apartment."

My brow furrows.

"One for me, one for you, and a nursery."

I told her there's no happily ever after for us, and I meant it, but for some reason, the thought of us living together sounds perfect until she specifies that it'll be in separate rooms. As if I would have the ability to stay out of her bed. Out of *her*.

I can't live in Vegas. It's too far from Izzy. I've spent years too far from her. When I discharged from the Corps, I told myself, I promised her, I'd never be more than a few hours away.

"I'm not living in Vegas," I mutter. "And I'm sure as fuck not getting a three-bedroom apartment and hiding a grandchild from your dad."

Her mood changes the second the words are out of my mouth.

"Why do you keep running? What's so bad about New Mexico?"

She clears her throat past the emotion that's playing in her tear-filled eyes. "I hate it there."

"Not good enough." I cup her cheek like I wanted to earlier.

"They want me to be Ivy."

The twin. The one that looks so much like the woman sitting in this SUV, but amazingly different at the same time.

"You're nothing like your sister."

"Much to my parents' disappointment," she mutters.

"You're not a disappointment."

She gives me an incredulous look before turning her eyes back to the clinic. "My appointment is in five minutes."

"Okay."

What else could I possibly say to her?

Silence fills the inside of the SUV, thick and full of unsaid things.

Five minutes tick by, then another ten.

"Are you going in?"

Her head shakes, and relief fills my heart.

"Not today," she whispers.

I put the SUV in drive and pull away before she can change her mind.

"We have to tell your dad."

"And he's the deciding factor?" I can't ignore the bitterness in her voice.

"It's your choice. I won't force you to make a decision one way or the other, and I sure as fuck won't let anyone else either."

"You'd go against my dad?"

"For you?" I ask. "For that baby? For your right to choose what happens to your body? How you want to live your life? Any day. Every day for the rest of my life."

"Careful, Jameson. You're making me want things I know I can never have."

She refuses something to eat, so we head back to the hotel I checked into late last night. It's better than the one back in Dallas, and I know I got the upgrade hoping she'd come back here with me at some point. I wanted her in comfort if she followed through with the procedure, all the time praying she'd be here under different circumstances.

"You seem way more okay with knocking me up than I ever expected," she says as I open the door for her and let her walk in first.

"I feel guilty," I confess as I toss the keys on the table in the corner. "I should've taken the time to wrap up that night."

She winces and turns so I can't see her face.

"You regret hooking up with me."

I don't even try to stop the laugh that bubbles from my throat.

"Regret? Not a fucking chance." Her shoulders tense, but she doesn't turn around. "I don't know that I'd change a damn thing, even considering exactly where we are right now."

That's the fucked-up truth to this entire situation. Even risking losing my job, even the different scenarios of how Dallas could've ended, I wouldn't change a damn thing.

"I'm tired," she says in a soft voice. "Can I take a nap?"

"Of course. Bed is yours."

I watch, my mouth going dry when she pulls off her t-shirt and jeans. Crawling between sheets I tossed and turned in last night, she sighs heavily before settling into the comfort I know she isn't afforded in whatever shithole she's been staying in.

I don't ignore the text I get from Shadow. I don't pretend like we're living on borrowed time in some bubble like I did before. I don't know how much Cerberus knows, but it won't be long before the cavalry shows up and tries to sweep her away. I imagine they've done it so many times; it's just become part of their routine.

I send Shadow the name of the hotel and room number, then I spend hours trying to figure out a way to make this entire fucked-up situation work for all involved.

Chapter 18

Gigi

I stiffen in the bed, even though it's the best night of sleep I've gotten in months. The last, of course, is the night I slept in the bed with Jameson in Dallas. It's surprising, considering he spent the night on the small sofa in the room. He woke me after the sun had set and convinced me to eat something which I did, but fell asleep again shortly after.

"She's sleeping," Jameson says from the hallway.

"It's noon, Hound. Is she sick?"

Shadow.

I should've known that they would arrive shortly after my knight in biker boots scooped me off of the sidewalk yesterday.

"Kinda," Jameson responds.

I have no clue why they haven't busted down the door and insisted I go pack my shitty apartment. Dad wouldn't let Jameson block the door, so I know he must've bowed out of my latest 'rescue.'

"The fuck does kinda mean, Hound?" Shadow's voice is filled with irritation and only tinted with anger.

You'd think they'd get tired of chasing me all over the damn place.

"You need to get her up so she can go home."

Kid.

Those two always travel together.

"She has a choice to make." I stiffen as worry settles into my bones.

Is Jameson just going to put my business out there with these two?

"Kincaid expects her to come back to New Mexico."

"I'll let her know."

I smile, the concern I was feeling that Jameson was here to drag me back fading away.

I flip the covers back, stretching my back, arms high over my head. The ding of a cell phone notification draws my attention. I don't have a phone right now. Paying for the minutes after I left a couple of months ago seemed like a waste of time, so I didn't buy new minutes when the original ones ran out.

The voices go quiet in the hallway, and I wonder if Shadow and Kid have dragged Jameson away to beat his ass behind the hotel. I can't concentrate on that for very long because I know when my stomach grumbles that the nausea is only a few moments behind. I consider the crackers and room temp ginger ale Jameson went out and grabbed last night.

Even though I know it's a waste because I'll just get sick again, I sit, legs tucked under me on the bed and nibble the crackers, washing it down with the smallest sips of ginger ale I can handle.

When twenty minutes go by without Jameson returning to the room, I turn on the TV and flip through not finding anything I'm interested in. I never watch TV, especially since getting pregnant. There's one in the backroom of the diner, but when I'm not working, I've been sleeping.

I stare at an episode explaining how baseballs are made, but I'm not really watching it. I nap on the couch and eventually crawl back into the bed. Benny is going to be pissed. Kori took over my shift yesterday, but I was supposed to be at work over an hour ago. I'm certain my stuff will be in the dumpster, and another girl will already be living in my space by the end of the day. Too tired, I can't manage to even care. These shitty waitressing jobs are a dime a dozen, and honestly, Kori is so fucked-up, moving on soon was in my plans anyway.

The ringing of Jameson's phone wakes me just after two. I have no intention of getting in his business, but when it silences and rings again, I pick it up.

IZZY CALLING flashes on the screen.

"Hello?" I say after the call connects.

"Who is this?" the caller asks.

"I could be asking you the same damn thing," I mutter.

I didn't have grandiose plans about a charmed life lived in bliss with Jameson, but I also didn't consider another woman being in his life.

The call disconnects without the woman saying another word.

I move to put the phone back on the bedside table, telling myself, pregnant or not, I have no say in anything he does. He didn't insist we be together. Hell, he was adamant that there was no happily ever after where I'm concerned.

Anger builds, and irritation grows exponentially as I stare at his phone.

"Not your business," I say out loud trying to convince myself.

Curiosity and the need for full disclosure win out just like I knew it would.

I swipe the front of the screen, surprised that a man like Jameson doesn't have a lock code on his phone. Then I'm hit with the insidious thought that he left me here alone with the phone so I can discover things he doesn't have the balls to just come out and say.

First, I see the text to Shadow giving him the address to this hotel and the room number. It may not say 'come get her' or anything like that, but the text is bad enough. I realize he's on my dad's side, loyal to the end even though he knows when we disclose the pregnancy that he may be fired, if not strangled.

The next text thread is with the woman who just called. Without remorse, I tap and pull up the thread. Picture after picture of a young girl, duck lips and all assault me.

I stare, disgusted at what I see. I'm young, but there is no way this girl is even out of high school. With majestic green eyes, surrounded by lush lashes, and so much dark hair it's almost a curtain over one in many of the pictures, I can't deny that she's gorgeous. Even in tank tops with puckered lips, there's an innocence about her that I can't see Jameson being attracted to, but the proof is in the evidence. He's saved every one of the pictures she's sent in a folder title MY HEART.

That stings.

The texts are cryptic, not really saying anything specific about meeting or hooking up, but the I LOVE YOU staring at me right in my face is hard to stomach. It's not only said once but comes at the conclusion of every texted conversation that they've had.

Jealousy, other than directed at my perfect twin, isn't an emotion I'm very familiar with, but it rumbles in my stomach until nausea hits me in the chest. Unable to ignore it, I'm off the bed and over the toilet a second later. The small meal of crackers and ginger ale rebel in my body and I get sick.

Trying to convince myself that it's the morning sickness I've had for the last couple of weeks, I rinse my mouth out and stare at my face in the mirror. Rosy cheeks and that dull look in my eyes I hate so much stare back at me.

For the first time since Jameson practically abducted me in front of the clinic yesterday, I doubt my decision to let him drive me away from that place. Walking away from him right now would be so much easier if the deal was done, and I only had myself to worry about.

Sure that I'm not going to get sick again, I crawl back in bed and ignore his cell phone on the floor.

I don't know how long it's been since I laid down, but it feels like hours I've been trying to fight the tears that want to fall.

"Still sleeping?" he says with a chuckle as he closes us in the room.

The walls feel like they're closing in all around me. I sit up, needing to run, but knowing I have to face him.

His brow crinkles when he reaches down and picks up his phone.

"Izzy called," I say with a nonchalance I don't feel.

"I'll call her back later," he replies and places the phone back on the nightstand.

"She didn't seem very happy that another woman was answering the phone."

I stare into his green eyes, challenging him and waiting for a reaction of some sort.

The cocked eyebrow isn't exactly what I expect.

"You answered my phone?"

I shrug. "It was ringing. Ringing phones get answered."

"I see."

I have no idea why he's so aloof and cryptic but he sure as fuck isn't giving anything away. The red-hot anger I felt earlier bubbles from just under my skin. It was as far as I could push it down while waiting for him to return so he could give me the answers I need before I leave him and this fucking city far behind.

"She seems a little young." I shoot for an easy, conversational tone, but my bitterness is hard to hide. "What is she fifteen? Sixteen?"

"Seventeen," he corrects with his stance just a hair wider and arms crossed over his chest.

"She let you fuck her hard?" He sneers. "Up against the wall? Does she enjoy your cock? Your piercings?"

"Georgia," he warns.

"You think I would keep this fucking baby around you worrying what you'd do to her since you like them so fucking young? You've lost your mind."

I expect his anger, but what I don't expect is his hand around my throat.

Chapter 19

Hound

"That's my daughter you're talking about you filthy-mouthed bitch!"

Her eyes widen, but she doesn't try to pull away.

The anger and jealousy fade away, and when she whimpers, I can see the arousal in her eyes. She gets off on the brute force, the power I have over her. My cock thickens, going from half-mast at her jealousy to full-on steel in my jeans.

"Jesus, you make me insane," I hiss, letting her go to fall back on the mattress.

"Daughter?" she asks as her hand comes up to the base of her throat. She doesn't touch it in inspection from injury but caresses it almost like she's missing the clamp of my fingers. "You're only thirty-four."

"Yeah," I say and sit down on the couch. "I didn't like condoms at sixteen any more than I like those fuckers now."

I don't miss the way her hands flow over her lower belly.

Her eyes fire with need, and I shake my head at her.

"No, Gigi." It's what my mouth says, but my eyes stay pinned to her when she shoves down the satin covering her pussy. A second later her tank top hits the plush carpet at her feet.

"No?"

She prowls, graceful like a panther across the room with the same elegance and sure moves I've watched her use on stage. This woman knows exactly what she's doing, exactly how she needs to move to entice a man. It's early, and the pregnancy isn't showing at all, but there's a fullness in her perky tits that wasn't there months ago.

I swallow, eyes sweeping from her toes all the way up to her messy hair.

Her shift in mood, going from disgusting insults about Izzy, saying things I'd kill any man who even considers doing to my daughter, to the sex kitten now standing directly in front of me, is concerning.

"No," I repeat, this time with my hands on her slender hips.

When she tries to move closer, I tighten my hands, but the grip of my fingers into the plush flesh of her ass stirs a need in me I never feel unless she's around. It's then that I start to question my own mental health. I should tell her to get dressed, tell her we're going back to face her father, but I've already sent Shadow and Kid away, assuring them I'd do my best to get her back to New Mexico. Even speaking with them, I know it's a long shot. I won't force this woman to do anything she doesn't want to do.

I'm struck with the thought of shoving her head so far down on my cock that she chokes, but from the gleam in her eyes, I don't think it would be unwelcome. Punishing her for making me want her so fucking bad only entices her to seek more punishment.

Her teeth scrape over her bottom lip, and her hands find the top of my head.

"Fuck," I grumble when her nails dig into my scalp with just the right amount of pain and pleasure. I roll my head on my shoulders until her nails are scraping over my beard and onto the sensitive skin of my neck.

Her arousal is thick in the air, filling my lungs, drowning me in a heady need I can barely keep control over.

I know I'm going to cave long moments before I actually do it. The anticipation is nearly unbearable, but I know the prize is going to be a bliss I can only find with her.

My skin is itchy, tingling with need and desire, but I wait. I just watch, looking at her lithe body until her breathing grows heavy and her eyelids droop with a sexiness I know I'll dream about for nights to come.

She's trembling by the time I spread my legs and allow her to stand in between them. She's gasping for much-needed air by the time I press my lips to the flatness of her lower belly. And she's barely able to stand by the time I snake my tongue out and lick her from her slit all the way to the top of her throbbing clit.

"Ja-Jameson," she stutters, and the sound of my name on her lips ignites a fire in my gut that can only be extinguished with her taste, her scent filling my body until I've wrung her dry and she's trembling beneath me.

"Fight it," I command with another harsh lick to her most sensitive flesh.

"I can't," she objects. "It feels too good."

She's shaking, near convulsing in my grip, so I hold her tighter, so tight that my fingers will be imprinted on her skin for days to come. My cock thickens painfully, leaking at the tip with the knowledge.

"I'll spank your ass if you come before I give you permission."

Her moan filters through the room as her body begins to quiver in earnest. She's fighting the one thing her brain is telling her to take, and it pleases me like nothing else ever has.

I toy, tease, and tangle my tongue around the epicenter of her desire. I'm relentless, challenging her to obey my command, but hoping she's unable. The idea of pinking her ass warms my palm against the fleshy part of her thigh with anticipation.

"Please, please, please," she begs.

The beseeching inflection of her voice is enough to make me cave. This is Gigi I'm drinking down my throat. It won't be long before she presents another situation where I can take my frustrations out on her beautiful ass.

"Now," I hiss, my breath hitting her marvelous cunt and forcing goosebumps to race down her legs. "Come for me."

"Only for you," she whispers and splinters apart.

I honor her submission by extending her pleasure with quick, pulsing swipes of my tongue.

Unable to wait, unable to care about what happens tomorrow, my hand is releasing its punishing grip on her thigh and working open the zipper of my jeans. The next second, the denim is pushed down past my balls, and I'm stroking, with a brutal fist, the length of my metal-studded cock.

"Oh God." The awe in her voice draws the pre-cum from my shaft until it's glistening at the tip. The lick of her tongue over her lips is enough to make me forget every woman before her, a victory no one else can claim.

"It's yours," I offer with my grip at the base.

"No," I tell her when she makes to straddle my thighs on the couch. "Take my boots and jeans fully off."

I know how hard I want to fuck her, how hard I need to fuck her. She's athletic, but she's not going to have the stamina I'll demand from her taut, little body. I plan to punish her, to assault her, to push inside of her so deep and so hard that she'll feel me tomorrow and the day after. When I watch her squirm, I'll know it's the echo of my cock that's pushing the blush up her chest and on to her cheeks.

Eager hands unlace my combat boots and tug my jeans down. The only help I give her is the slight lift of my hips so she can get my jeans down my thighs and eventually off my legs.

She stands, impatiently waiting for my next command, and fuck if that doesn't stir something deep inside my chest. My cock jerks in my hand, reminding me that it's not the time or place for introspection. The sight of her swollen clit peaking past the delicate lips of her slit is glorious. I'm an undeserving asshole, but I'm going to take what never should've been given to me in the first place.

"Come here," I shift my gaze down, indicating the throbbing cock I'm holding straight up. "Have a seat."

A coy smile plays on her lips but her feet move quickly, and her knees hit the couch cushions at my thighs with a speed that rivals Olympic sprinters.

"Condom?" She blinks up at me.

A harsh breath leaves my lips. Not at the thought of wrapping up, but with the memory of why we won't.

"I'm already so deep inside of you." The thumb of my free hand rubs the soft skin below her navel. I lift her hips, kissing her sensitive flesh with the tip of my cock. "I'm already a part of you."

I ease her down, the gravity of the situation and unanswered questions, decisions that have yet to be made and verbalized is the weight that forces her to sink to the base.

The need to fuck her wild, fuck her until she's nothing but liquid in my hands fades away. She whimpers at the fullness, shifting her hips, rocking with small sweeps side to side to help her body accommodate the thickness of mine.

I rock up, enjoying every centimeter of her gripping cunt as it flexes, tightens, and pleads for more. The ache in my balls is bearable. The tension gnawing at the base of my spine just as willing as I am to take my time.

Her eyes flutter, but she's able to keep them open. The shine, the glisten of wetness near the corners of her eyes draw me in. I revel in the keen ability to pull such emotion from her, but when one lone tear crests and rolls down her face, the demon in me wants a hundred more. I want to see them gushing down her face, while she begs me to stop, while she's choking on my cock, while she loves every aspect of every deranged thing I want to do to her.

But, it isn't until her forehead rests against mine, and she looks down at the carnal union of our bodies that my restraint begins to crack. The tension at my spine, the ache in my balls is no longer bearable.

The slow and steady, the feathery ripple of her pussy along my erection has become a tease. The soft huffs of her breath abrade my skin rather than flush it with satisfaction. The delicate noises she makes are contradictory and insufferable to what my body is demanding I take.

Then, it's the puncture of her teeth in the hard flesh of my pectoral that makes my head snap up.

"You feisty bitch," I hiss and stand from the couch.

I bite my tongue as her fingernails seer a hole into my back. She knows I have her, knows I'd never drop her so the aggression, although welcome, will be punished.

"Yes," she moans when I walk her to the bed and lay her on her back.

I chuckle at her greediness when her hips flex, and she's fucking herself on my dick the instant her back hits the mattress.

"No." I pull out, the whimper she emits landing in my gut.

After flipping her over, I'm almost tempted by the arch of her back, so much so that I don't resist the temptation to run my hand down the ridges of her spine and trace the heart shape of her ass. Fucking her from behind becomes my only mission, but the disappointment in not seeing her face isn't something I'm going to tolerate. She squeals, a gleeful, silly sound in this moment when I lift her, back to my chest and stand. Her giggle turns to a brutal moan when I impale her down my shaft and position our bodies, so we're standing in front of the full-length dressing mirror.

"Jesus," she hisses as I hold her aloft, the bends of her knees cradled in the bend of my elbows.

She's spread open, the pink of her pussy a sharp contrast to the angry, purple hue of my brutally hard cock. The glint of the light in the room radiating off of the barbells along my cock adds to the depravity we're both so wrapped up in that nothing else in the world matters.

Her head rocks back on my shoulder, eyes mere slits as she continues to watch me fuck up into her like a man possessed.

"You need to fucking come," I demand as her hands find the furled tips of her nipples. Her face scrunches, and I love that she's causing the bite of pain to get her off. "Now."

Like a genie rubbing a golden lamp, my words, my insistence to put an end to both of our misery is obeyed the second the words push past my lips.

I hold her closer as her small body curls in on itself. I groan my own release at the sight of her stomach ridging and flexing with the force of her climax.

"God damn," I cry when I explode inside of her, the force of her pulsing leaving no room for my own release.

Warm, thick liquid, a combination of both her and I, slicks her thighs and the length of my shaft and balls. I need to get us into the shower before we ruin the carpet any more than we already have, but it's not even an option.

As carefully as I can manage, I walk us the few feet to the bed, setting her down before climbing in behind her.

"I just need a few minutes," I explain when she looks back over her shoulder at me.

She laughs at the weakness in my voice, the words nearly slurred like I'd been drinking whiskey all night rather than feeding at the offerings of her body.

The stroking of her fingers up and down the arm wrapped around her stomach calms my pounding heart, if only for a second because true to form, she opens her mouth, and the world spins again.

"Tell me about your daughter."

Chapter 20

Gigi

I expect him to release me, to climb off of the bed and refuse to talk, and as the silence drags on, I imagine him telling me to mind my fucking business and never ask him about her again. Then, to my surprise he sighs, his body settling in closer to mine, heavier into the mattress, his fingers twisting until our hands are joined, and he begins.

"Isabella Roze, with a Z, not an S," he explains, "Montoya is everything I never knew I wanted."

Did he rub our combined hands over my lower belly on purpose? It's not the first time tonight he's touched me there in a way so loving it's almost out of character for the man I hardly know.

I shiver at the soft press of his lips on my bare shoulder.

"Gabriela Montoya showed up in the middle of my sophomore year. There was only one high school in Kaufman, Texas at the time. All of the rich kids, all of the poor kids, and every kid in between were thrown together. Her dad was some executive for a nearby refinery, so if there was an opportunity for her to go somewhere else, I'm certain her upper-class parents would've made sure she did."

I let my eyes close, loving the soothing tone of his voice, but I hang onto every word, hurting as he begins to speak of another woman, but too curious to tell him to stop.

"She showed up in clothes that cost more than my rusty old pickup truck with a gleam in her eye that drew in every boy, made every teenage cock rock solid at first glance. I wasn't immune. I fantasized about her for days before I built up the courage to approach her."

"What did she look like?" I need to compare her to me, to see if he's attracted to traits we may share.

"Long, rich brown hair." He kisses the back of my head, and I stiffen. He either doesn't notice my unease, or he ignores it. "The thickest, most luscious ass I'd ever lain eyes on. Eyes so dark, you couldn't tell the iris from the pupil."

"She sounds lovely," I mutter.

He releases my hand and grips my thigh.

"Be careful, Georgia, your jealousy turns me on."

I huff as he continues.

"She was new and exotic. Colombian. She came from San Antonio, the big city compared to our quiet little town. I wanted her the second I saw her. Needed her the second I smelled the sun on her skin."

"Did you love her?" Sounds a lot like fucking love to me.

"At sixteen? I sure as hell thought I did but looking back I realize there were things I loved *about* her. I loved her body, the way she moved with sensual grace whether she was dancing to David Allan Coe or Shakira. I loved the way my hands would tangle into her thick hair as if once I touched her, she refused to let me go. I loved the way she welcomed a terrified virgin boy into her body and taught me things no seventeen-year-old girl should've ever known in the first place."

I whimper, his words and the sensual way he described his young lust turning me on.

"You got her pregnant."

"Almost immediately," he says with a quick chuckle, his hand grazing low on my stomach again. "I didn't ask if she was on the pill."

"Seems to be a problem for you."

He pinches the lips of my pussy until I moan with need. "Can I finish my story?"

I nod, unable to speak while he has my clit clamped between his thumb and forefinger.

"All the girls at school talked about birth control. The first time I slid inside of her, a latex barrier was the last thing on my mind. Every time after, I couldn't imagine anything dulling the sensation, so I didn't bother. Figured she'd tell me if there was a problem. That problem," he sighs and releases my clit. I hiss when the blood flow returns in the form of a throbbing pulse. "Came a couple months after we started dating. I was ready to quit school, go to work, do anything and everything for her and our child."

"What did you do?"

"I made plans. We made plans. When she started to show and her parents got suspicious enough to ask, we sat down and told them. She'd hidden it too long for an abortion. We'd talked about it in passing, but it wasn't something either of us wanted. We were a family. We were going to raise our child in a happy home and give it everything that it could ever want."

He swallows, I'm certain remembering the time when life was easier. When he faced things with pride and determination without being bogged down with the reality that only maturity and age can bring, or in my case growing up too fast.

"Her dad was livid. Her mother cried the whole time, upset that her Catholic soul may never recover. I offered everything I had, which amounted to less than a complete sophomore education and a shitty truck that didn't crank more days than it actually did. I should've been a junior, but I have a late birthday, and my parents made me repeat kindergarten. I couldn't offer her that extra year of education.

"Her dad pointed all of that out of course. Convinced Gabby that a life with me would be lived in poverty because he sure as hell wasn't being financially responsible for some poor ass white boy. He gave her an ultimatum, and I've never seen a girl who claims to be in love make a decision so fast."

I don't miss the tremble in his now unsteady hand or the deep breaths he pulls in to calm his anger.

"She chose the money, the life I now know I never would've been able to give her. She chose the support of her family even to the detriment of our relationship. I knew she'd love that baby, that her parents wouldn't fault a child for the sins her teenage parents committed. I was told to take a step back, to leave her alone."

His laugh is bitter, filled with years of something akin to remorse or regret.

"I couldn't though. I convinced my parents to let me drop out of high school. I was a year behind on paper, but I was smart enough to pass my GED. They let me join the Marine Corps at seventeen. I was in Miramar, California when my parents called to tell me that the letters I'd been sending to Gabby had all been returned to their house, unopened. They'd promised me a relationship with my child. I never would've walked away, joined the Corps if I knew they were going to pull some shit like they did. When they drove by, the place was deserted by the Montoya's and another family was already moving in."

"That's so fucking shitty," I whisper even though he knows it and doesn't need it spoken out loud.

"Yeah," he agrees.

"How did you locate her?"

He tugs the sheet over us when I shiver, half burning up from his heat at my back, but frigid where the air conditioner is drifting over my shoulders and chest.

"Her dad was easy enough to track. They didn't live a secret life, just a nomadic one because of his line of work. I saw Izzy for the first time when she was four. She was doing her best to kick around a soccer ball on a field. Her long brown hair flowed behind her, and when her eyes turned in my direction, they were *my* eyes, and I never knew love like I found on a children's soccer field that day. She's everything wonderful about Gabby and me. None of the bad, none of the struggle. She's pure and beautiful, and now she's nearly a woman, and that scares the fuck out of me."

I clasp his hand again in mine.

"So Gabby let you have a relationship with her?"

"Hardly," he spits. "She'd gotten married to some pompous asshole. She made threats. I made threats. Hers were backed up by a team of attorneys. There's not much you can do with a military salary, and her family, her new husband, knew that. The only faith I had in life that day was the saddened look on the nanny's face when she carried my daughter away."

"You just let her walk away with Izzy?" I can't help the disdain in my voice. What parent just lets someone steal their child?

"That day? Yes. I let Gabby think she won. I let her new husband keep the smug smile on his face as he walked out, hand gripping the curve of Gabby's ass tight, the same ass I used to obsess over every night before her parents ripped my life apart. The crazy thing is, all I felt was anger. I wasn't bitter he got the girl. I was upset she'd so easily tossed me away. My only concern was the brown-haired, green-eyed girl who was just strapped into a car seat in the back of a nanny's minivan.

"I sought out that nanny, having a buddy run the license plate. I explained that I needed a relationship with my child, and she agreed. It started with pictures at first. The letters, written in the heavy hand of a child, came next. On her fourteenth birthday, Gabby got her a cell phone for her birthday. She'd written and given me her number. We texted at first. Her stepdad isn't as bad as I made him out to be. She's happy, but I'm one thing he would never budge on. She learned early on that my name, the subject of her actual paternity isn't on the table in any shape or form."

"You've only seen her in person once?"

"We video chat, and we've met a few times. She's on a protective leash and isn't allowed much leeway, but we find time to see each other."

"That sucks," I say honestly.

"She wants to move in with me when she graduates, and God, do I want that. The ability to actually get to know my daughter has been all I can think about since she mentioned it about a year ago. It's why I served seventeen years rather than staying in for twenty. It's why I was so fucking excited about the job offer in Farmington. She's currently living in Flagstaff but wants to attend college in Albuquerque. It seemed like the best fit."

"Sounds like you have it all figured out." I don't even know how I should feel right now. His separation from his daughter is shitty, but at the same time, I wonder if all of his energy is going to be used to the point he wouldn't have any for the baby I'm carrying. It's selfish and greedy, but I can't lie and pretend it's not part of the deciding factor in the direction my own life is going.

"I did. It's all fucked now."

I tense, anger so close to boiling over my vision starts to blur.

"Shadow and Kid instructed me that I'm to head back to Farmington and pack my shit. Cerberus can't trust a man who can't be honest with their President."

"My dad is an asshole."

"He's really not, Gigi. He's trustworthy, protective, and he's doing what he thinks is best to protect his daughter. I promised him I'd never touch you again, and here I lay with my cock between my stomach and your back, my fingers drifting over this perfect little cunt." He drives his words home by slicking his thumb over my clit. "He can't trust me because I can't trust myself when it comes to you."

"What will you d-do?" I stammer, moaning my displeasure when he stops.

"Pack my shit. I have other job offers. They aren't Cerberus, more private security, boring shit. Mainly in the LA and San Fran area. It's almost twice as far away from Izzy and even further when she goes to college. But," he says as he turns me in his arms until my sore breasts are pushing against the t-shirt he never bothered to take off. "My next step depends on yours."

Chapter 21

Hound

I shake my head when she buries her pretty face into my t-shirt.

"That came out like pressure, and I promise you I'm not pressuring you. I won't lie to you either." I tilt her chin until her tear-stained eyes are looking directly into mine. "I can't make a move until you make yours."

I release her chin, my hand falling naturally to the place her body holds my precious child, the tiny bundle of cells I may never get to meet.

My heart constricts at the thought.

"You'd want to raise this baby?" I hate the uncertainty in her voice.

"I told you it's your choice." I've said it more than once, and it gets harder each and every damn time.

"And I'm asking about your stance."

"You know where I stand. I told you yesterday in the truck."

"Dammit," she says as she pushes away from my chest until she's sitting crossed-legged on the bed. "You told me I have options, but I need to know that if I keep this baby, you'll want to be involved. I don't want to force you into anything."

"Force me?" I can't help but laugh at the ridiculousness. "Are you sitting there and telling me that I'm the deciding factor."

My lip curls in rage at her stoic posture and the way she refuses to answer my question.

"It's your fucking choice!" I yell and climb off of the bed.

"I can't do this alone," she screams, just as angry as I am.

I tilt my head and swallow the words I want to say, the ones that won't be received well and speak slowly. "You. Don't. Have. To."

"You'll help raise this baby?" She's asked that now several times, each one like a jackhammer to my heart.

"I want to raise this baby." Tears streak her face. "More than anything, I want the chance to be a dad. From start to finish. From day one until the day I die, I want it."

She nods but doesn't say a word. She doesn't calm my fears or attempt to appease me with even a small smile.

"I'm tired."

Two simple words.

Seven letters that do nothing to hint at where her mind is at.

I want to rush to the bed, shake her, and force her to make the right decision. I want to beg her to keep our baby. I want to redden her ass for even contemplating an alternative to bringing that precious child into the world. I want to tease her, suck her clit, and keep her orgasm just out of reach until she agrees that there is but one choice in the matter.

I do none of those things.

I watch the sway of her naked ass and the swish of her gorgeous brown hair as she lies down on the bed, back pointed in my direction. I run my hands harshly over my head as she tugs up the sheets and covers the silkiness of her back, hiding herself from me.

Her breathing is still ragged as I tug on my jeans, boots, and t-shirt.

"I'm going to grab something to eat." She doesn't move. Doesn't look over her shoulder. Doesn't offer one word. "Can I get you anything?"

A simple shake of her head. "I can't keep anything down."

I turn and leave the room because the alternative of climbing in behind her, wrapping her in my arms, and soothing her until she falls asleep isn't an option.

The small store in the hotel has nothing to offer other than shitty Vegas memorabilia and antacids. A quick internet search on my phone is so uninformative, I'm wondering how women have managed to have healthy babies at all. The information provided is always contradicted by another post. Do this. Do that. NEVER do this. It's overwhelming. The only thing that seems to have the least objections is that ginger ale and crackers seem to be a lifesaver. She had that last night, so I set out to grab myself a burger and supplies to settle her stomach.

While at the burger joint, I go ahead and grab one for her as well, hoping she'll be up for something more than carbs and soda.

Just like when you're buying a new car and narrow it down to one or two, and you start to notice that car everywhere, for the first time in as long as I can remember, I notice every child. I focus on their laughter, their crying, the innocent questions they ask their parents while standing in line at the pharmacy.

Back at the hotel, trying to wake Gigi is pointless. She's out like a light and isn't interested in ginger ale and crackers, so I sit on the couch and eat, never taking my eyes off of the soft rise and fall of her back. I can't help but wonder if my child in her stomach is the reason I'm so drawn to her.

I shake my head, clearing it of the ridiculous thought. She was a sleek piece of metal and I a magnet, feverishly attracted to her long before I knew about the baby, long before I put that child inside of her. The memories of seeing her on that stage for the first time flood my brain and all of my other senses. The slide of her athletic thighs on the pole. The roll of her abdominals. The perfect sway of her hips.

I run a rough hand over the erection tenting my jeans. It's pure physical attraction, unadulterated need from knowing just what it feels like to slide inside of her. It's carnal, instinctual biology to be attracted to, to crave the person who's continuing your bloodline.

After eating, I lie back on the sofa, arms behind my head, feet propped on the end because it's way too fucking small for my body. How I fall asleep with the distance between us, I have no clue, but my slumber is short lived.

I snap awake, unsure of what pulled me from a dreamless sleep until I hear a small whimper fill the silence in the room.

The once soft up and down of Gigi's back as she slept has been replaced with jagged jerks with her sobs.

I don't consider the ramifications. I don't worry if she wants me to touch her or not. I climb off the couch, hitting the lights and enveloping the room in darkness before climbing on the bed behind her.

"Shhh," I purr in her ear. "I'm here."

My comfort only makes her cry harder, so I don't say another word. I don't ask her what's wrong. I don't offer advice. I don't tell her what she should do or remind her of her options. I hold her, as close to my chest as I can manage without suffocating her. I lean my head in and breathe in her scent, nose pressed deep into her hair. At first, she's a stiff board in my arms, but as the sobbing ebbs away her body relaxes and she settles into my hold. She allows herself the comfort of my embrace until her breathing begins to match mine.

Not a word is spoken. Not a promise is made, but I reassure her with the light sweep of my fingers on her arm. I touch her hip, pushing her legs until she's curled in a ball, I mirror her position and nestle her even closer.

Just when I think she's asleep, she speaks with a hint of devastation and sadness in her voice.

"I'd be a horrible mother."

I squeeze her. I can't object to her assessment. I don't know hardly anything about her, and lying isn't really my thing.

"My mom is the greatest," she continues. "There's no way I could ever even come close to being like her. Bake sales, PTO, and fucking classroom chaperoning?"

She gives a humorless chuckle and shakes her head a little.

"That's not me. I can't even picture myself doing those things."

I open my mouth to tell her I'd do all of those things in her place. The idea of taking a handful of rowdy kids to the zoo and experience everyday sights through the brand-new eyes of a child sounds like a great time to me. I close my mouth again, only opening my lips slightly to brush them over the soft skin of her naked shoulder.

She begins crying again, torn with her decision.

"I don't want to abort this baby." I smile against her skin, my heart filling with eagerness. "But I can't see myself as a mother either. I thought it was instinctual. I thought once my suspicions were confirmed with the positive test I would transition from who I am into someone different."

All she gets is silence from me, and since she hasn't called me out on it, I imagine it's just what she needs.

"But I'm not different." She shakes her head slightly to punctuate her point. "Other than the sickness I don't even feel different. I still want to run. I want to take off and put it behind me, but no matter where I go this baby will be right there. I can't run from this."

She clasps my hand and lowers it to the flatness of her stomach. She doesn't say another word. She merely takes one last shuddering breath and falls asleep.

My eyes stay on her until the pink hue of the dawn stabs across the room. It's only then that I take my eyes off of her, that I stop counting her breaths and allow myself to get a little rest. Later today, no matter which way she decides, she's going to make a life-altering decision. One that's going to change the course of my previously decided future.

Chapter 22

Gigi

Oppressive heat surrounds me, blanketing me to the point my stomach rolls, urging me to get out of bed. In the split second I have before my body revolts against the emptiness in my belly, I look back over my shoulder at Jameson. He reaches for me, hand skimming over the warmth my body left behind on the bed. My smile turns into a grimace as I run, as quietly as I can to the bathroom.

Dry heaving is the devil's work I'm certain by the time I lift my head and rinse my mouth. Rinsing the smell of his skin from mine is the last thing I want to do. His scent, the combined smell of our wild sex last night coats me like a living being. I revel in it, running my nose over the soft skin of my shoulder before giving in and turning the dials of the shower.

The warm blast on my now cool skin sends pinpricks over every inch of my skin. It's not altogether different from the way my body responded watching Jameson fuck me in front of the mirror. I sigh a breath of remembrance and wash him off of me.

My cries. The pleas. The whispered confessions in the dark last night.

I laid my heart bare to him, and unlike all the others so quick to give me advice, he held me. He didn't try to bring me to his side. He didn't give his opinion. He embraced me and let me draw my own conclusions. As much as it pained him, he gave me exactly what I needed.

After the suds from the hotel soap disappear down the drain, I turn the water off and steel my spine. I know exactly what I have to do. I've known it all along. It's just that being an adult, actually making those decisions on my own, the ones others have been so quick to make for me all my life, is much harder than I had ever anticipated they would be.

I dress, right back into the clothes I wore to the clinic what seems like a lifetime ago, and take one last look at Jameson asleep in the bed. His hand is still stretched out, searching for me even in his sleep. The crinkle of his brow is calming as I imagine he's missing me even in his sleep.

Instead of brushing my lips against his to wake him up like I want to, I jerk the floor to ceiling curtains open, bathing the room in the blinding sunlight.

He jerks in the bed, almost violently, as he's ripped from his dreams.

"The fuck," he grumbles, sitting up on the bed and swiping harsh hands over his tired green eyes.

Why I didn't see it last night, why I didn't recognize his eyes in Izzy's pictures on his phone is beyond me. It's clear as day right now as those amazing green orbs are turned on me in almost angry agitation.

"Get your boots on," I instruct, hating that he's fully clothed.

I resist the urge to once again strip naked in front of him and taunt him with my body. There will be plenty of time for that later.

He sighs, leaning his back against the wooden headboard. "What's the damn rush?"

I smile at him. "What's the delay?"

He growls. "I got you more crackers and ginger ale last night."

His large hand motions toward the mini fridge against the wall.

"That's very sweet of you."

"I got crackers with peanut butter. That way you're eating more than just shitty carbs and soda."

I cock an eyebrow at him. "A little controlling, don't you think?"

My question is playful, not annoyed like it would normally be.

A passive look fills his eyes as he glances my way. How he can look so apathetic and dominating at the same time I have no idea. The single look makes my skin itch. The same way it did last night when he challenged me not to come on his tongue until he gave me permission to do so.

"You're growing my baby," he says, voice flat.

"Our baby," I correct.

"Until you make your decision, you need to take care of it. The protein in the peanut butter is good for him."

"Him?" I question. "So sure we're having a son."

I don't miss the hopeful swallow of his throat as mine clogs with some of the same emotions I was unable to shove down last night.

"You still haven't made a decision." I hate the break in his voice, the opinion he was terrified to give power to last night.

"But I have," I correct. "It's why you need to get dressed."

I turn my gaze down to the boots on the floor.

His hands tremble as he shoves back the sheets that cocooned us last night.

"Back to the clinic?" Pain washes over his face even as I can tell he's doing his best to fight it.

"Nope," I say, both hating and loving that I'm keeping him on edge with such an important choice.

"To your apartment?"

Just the thought of that shitty place and my deviant roommate makes me shiver.

"There's nothing there for me. There's nothing from this life that I want to remember."

"Where are we heading?"

I turn to the mirror, the one that finds me swiping my fingers through my sleep-messy hair and not splayed open for both of our pleasure like I was last night.

"I'm going home," I whisper.

"Home?" His voice cracks with hopefulness, a smile spreading his cheeks in the reflection of the glass.

I woke up this morning a new woman if that's even possible. I woke up with renewed faith in not only life but also my ability to be the best mother I can be. It may not look exactly like my mother's did, but it'll be me and Jameson and our child. We'll make the best of it. I won't have to do it alone, and that was my one and only true fear because I knew motherhood in the form of single parenting isn't something I could ever manage.

"Someone has to tell my dad that you knocked me up."

I turn back to him expecting to see the smile still in place and hope in his eyes. Instead, I find him nearly green, resembling my face every morning before I get sick. I can't help but laugh as he turns white at the mention of telling my dad, even though he's the one who pressed the point yesterday.

***

The normally eight-hour trip back to Farmington takes closer to eleven with the multiple stops we're forced to take because my stomach doesn't agree with the miniscule rocking of the SUV over the interstate. When I wasn't dozing, I was getting sick.

"I'm going to go pack my room," he says as we pull into the gravel lot in front of the Cerberus clubhouse.

"I think that's a little premature," I object.

"I have my orders," he says with a sigh as he places the vehicle in park.

"I'm going to go talk to my dad," I inform him.

He clasps my thigh in a soft but dominating grip. "If you get the feeling that he plans to kill me, give me a heads up. I'm more than willing to face what's coming my way, but I at least want to be prepared."

I laugh but stop when I see the seriousness in his eyes. I caress his face, loving the feel of his rough beard under my palm. My body is on fire for this man.

"That look in your eyes right now is exactly what got you fucked against an alley wall," he warns.

"Mmm," I purr.

"Stop." I snap out of my horny daze. "Packing my shit while you lay all of this at your father's feet is one thing. Doing it with a swollen cock is another."

"You have nothing to worry about," I offer, but he doesn't seem to think the outcome will be pleasant.

"Twenty-years-old or not, I'd kill any man that fucked my daughter and got her pregnant," he advises. "He's already been more forgiving by letting me work after he found out about the sex than I ever would've been."

"My back was as sore as my pussy after that night." My eyes flutter closed. "The brick was as unforgiving as your cock."

"Jesus," he hisses, mouth meeting mine in a brutal kiss before I can even open my eyes.

We're panting by the time he pulls away.

"I'm going to sneak in your room tonight." He swallows and nods. "Will you turn me away again?"

Doubt, uncertainty, and the memory of his rejection last time fill my voice.

"I doubt I'll still be here, baby, but you're welcome in my bed no matter where I lay my head down to sleep."

I peck his lips one last time, youthful glee filling me to the brim even when the news that I have to share with my father burdens me.

"See you in a little while," I promise as I climb out of the vehicle.

Less than five minutes later, I'm standing, heart racing at my father's office door. When I entered the house, my mother pointed in this direction and simply said, "He's waiting for you."

I raise my hand to knock, praying he's asleep, which is ridiculous, or on the phone. Hoping that he's busy and I'll have to wait just a few minutes longer.

"It's open," comes the gruff voice I've learned to despise over my many years of fucking up.

I turn the knob, ignoring the near sting of the metal against my palm, and push the door open.

"Close it." His gruff command is obeyed. "Have a seat."

I sit in the chair across from his desk. How do these same types of things being barked at me from Jameson make me wet, yet with my father only make me want to cower in fear?

I guess having the same response to my father would be inappropriate.

"How long are you home for this time, Georgia?"

He looks as exhausted as I feel. The sun set long ago, the second half of our trip spent in darkness and silence.

"It depends on how this conversation goes," I answer honestly.

"A threat?" He tilts his head, the same motion that a few years ago would have me quivering in my chair.

"No. I'm not a teenager any longer. I've lived in hell the last couple of years. I—"

"You chose that life. I never wanted that for you."

"I know that." He raises an eyebrow at me. "I know that *now*. I'm grateful to you and Mom. You don't have to put up with my shit. You don't have to continuously chase after me, trying to rescue me from myself."

"Parents do everything they can for their children. We love you. Taking off and leaving will never change that."

"I love you guys, too." I love the smile that tugs at the corner of his mouth and brightens his eyes. I don't say it often enough, not even close to as often as I feel it.

"You didn't fight Hound in coming back." I'm not surprised he's well aware of my agreement to return to New Mexico. "Is there a reason you're so agreeable to being here?"

Moment of truth.

"I'm pregnant."

He stops breathing.

"The baby is Jameson's."

I've never seen that color of red on my father's face in all my life.

It seems like a millennia before he releases a long, jagged breath.

"Hound's?" he finally says like Jameson and Hound could possibly be two different men.

He types something on his phone, and I crane my neck to try to see if it's the execution order Jameson is so sure is coming.

He waits, only looking up from his phone when the door opens. My mother's softly scented perfume hits my nose, wiping away all hope that Jameson has been called in here to face this with the Cerberus MC President right along beside me.

I can't look at her, not when she sits in the chair beside me, not when she clasps my hand in her lap, and especially not when the tears that have been threatening since my truth spilled from my lips, begin to fall.

"Your daughter is pregnant," Dad spits as if I may not stay that way for long.

My free hand protects the innocent life cradled there, and my head snaps up.

My mother gasps, her hand clenching mine even tighter.

"The baby is Hound's."

The grasp loosens, but I squeeze tighter, unable to lose her touch in the face of what comes next.

"A baby?" she whispers.

I nod, eyes evaluating my father's face, still unable to look at her.

"I'm not ashamed." I raise my head higher, my spine stiffening with the same steel I found in the Vegas bathroom earlier in the day.

"So you're keeping the baby?" Is that hope in my rigid father's voice?

"Yes," I answer.

My mother releases a breath in a long whoosh, relief evident in the gesture.

"And Hound?"

"He's on board with my decision."

"I'm not okay with you sleeping with my men."

Here it comes.

"I've only slept with Jameson." A knot forms low in my stomach, and I beg it not to start turning. Getting violently ill right now is the worst thing that can happen.

"I fired Grimlock a mere two months after he started working here your senior year," he reminds me.

"Okay?" I don't hide the confusion in my voice.

"I fired him because rumors of you two together spread through my club like wildfire."

I can't help the chuckle that slips out.

"That's why he was here one day and then gone the next?"

My father nods. "I don't like you sleeping with my men. It's dangerous. I can't take the risk that they think they can disobey orders because of their connection to you."

"Man," I correct.

He shakes his head. "What?"

"I slept with one man. I've only slept with Jameson. No others, not from this club. He's the only one." I take a long breath and release it slowly. "Ever."

"Really?"

I hate the disbelief in his voice. Hate that I'm going to have to explain the rumors that started in high school and ruined my reputation. How I fed those fires because people already had those opinions so why argue with them. It seems my parents aren't even immune to the talk of the town.

"I will stay as long as you'll have me." My mother begins to cry silently beside me. "So long as Jameson is still employed with Cerberus."

"No," my father hisses. "I can't have it. I didn't even want to keep him after Dallas, but Dominic talked me into it. This just cements that I should've followed my gut instinct in the first place."

"Yes, Sir," I say as I stand. My father has made my decision for me.

"Diego," my mother sobs as she catches my wrist on my way out. I look down at her. "Go take a nap, honey. I'll be up in just a few minutes."

I leave the room closing the door on the hushed voices of my parents arguing.

Chapter 23

Hound

I think waiting for the confrontation is worse than the actual confrontation itself. It's the anticipation. The worry about what will happen. The hundreds of scenarios you work through in your head are never what actually happens.

I'm not startled by the knock on my door. I'm not even surprised that it's both Kid and Shadow on the other side when I tug the door open. A show of force. It's exactly how I'd handle the situation.

"Kincaid wants to speak with you," Shadow says, his gruff voice not giving anything away.

I grab the straps of my two rucksacks and follow them from the room. It may seem overdramatic, but I could be walking toward my death, yet, even knowing that I trudge along with my head held high the short distance to the conference room. I don't miss that Kincaid is waiting for me in a room that leaves no chance of my seeing Gigi before I face him.

Smart.

It's also what I would've done.

Kid pushes open the right side of the double doors, but he doesn't follow me inside. He and Shadow turn, hands clenched down by their sides. The fact that they're both standing at attention isn't lost on me. It's another show of force, one of unity with their president.

I swallow thickly, but enter the room and close the door behind me. At the end of the table, Kincaid sits silently with his hands steepled, index fingers resting against his bottom lip. I step forward, and resisting the urge to salute him, I reach into my pocket and pull the lone key to my room down the hall from my pocket. Once within arm's length, I pass it to him.

"Room's clear, Mr. Anderson."

He accepts the key, turning it over and over in his palm. I take a few steps back, hands gripping my rucksacks so hard they begin to ache. Time stretches for what seems like hours before he speaks.

"Mr. Anderson?" He clears his throat. "Now you treat me with respect?"

When his eyes meet mine, the fury in them is enough to make my blood run cold. My eyes dart, looking for an escape. There's one way in, and one way out. The passage to safety is guarded by two of Kincaid's Marines, two of his closest friends, men so close Gigi considers them uncles.

"My intention was never to disrespect you, Sir." Dressed in civvies or not, this man deserves my respect, not only as the leader of the club I'm fixing to be booted out of, but also because he's my child's grandfather.

"Georgia is keeping the baby."

"Yes, Sir." This isn't news to me.

"And you plan to stick around?"

I nod. "I may not be a part of Cerberus any longer, but I'm not walking away from my child."

"Just your child?" I shake my head, but he continues before I can argue with his wording. "Do you plan to marry her?"

I shake my head and wait for him to come off of his chair and pummel my face with both fists. When he doesn't, I try to do my best to explain.

"This isn't the fifties, Sir. The last thing any of us need, including our unborn child, is to be brought into a loveless marriage."

At this he growls, so deep and so long in his throat, my life nearly flashes before my eyes.

"That's my daughter you're talking about," he hisses, and I reflect back on the way I responded nearly the same way last night when Gigi was saying horrific things about Izzy. I commend his restraint, the control over his instincts I wasn't man enough to have myself.

"Can you tell me that you loved every single woman you touched before you met Mrs. Anderson?" He narrows his eyes at me. That's just as scary as the growl. "I'm not saying I hate her, but I hardly know her. Standing here and confessing something to you that I never even considered telling her would be a lie. I'm not, by normal practice, a liar, Sir."

"My wife thinks you sticking around is a good idea." My burden lifts, if only a fraction of an inch. "I wholeheartedly disagree with her."

The burden increases tenfold.

"Georgia will leave if you leave." I nod, knowing it's true. I promised her that raising the child together is what I wanted. She's the one who suggested the awful idea of a three-bedroom apartment. "I let that factor into my decision about you."

Silence grows heavy between us once again. I can tell he wants me to ask, to plead, but it would only show weakness. He's both hoping for it, so he can prove himself right, and wishing against it because his daughter and I are having a baby whether he likes it or not, and needs me to be a man he can trust her and his grandchild with.

The moments stretch on, lasting an eternity in the already late hours of the night.

He clears his throat. "You still being a part of Cerberus changes nothing. You impregnating and dating my daughter doesn't give you any allowances the other men don't have."

My eyes snap from the front of his shirt where I've been staring at for what seems like hours to his eyes.

"Dating," my voice cracks, "Sir?"

"Dating," he affirms.

There are worse things than waking up to Georgia Anderson's body against mine.

I shake my head to clear the thought.

"You don't want to?" he asks questioning my physical response to thinking of his daughter naked and splayed out across my chest.

"I will," I agree so hastily I forget the last part. I swallow again. "Sir."

"Do you want to?" he asks again.

"Yes, Sir. I'd like nothing more than to date your daughter."

"She may run again." This is something I know about her.

"I'll chase her and our baby to the ends of the Earth."

He nods, the only physical approval he's shown other than his words.

"Maybe Dominic was right to vouch for you."

"Thank you, Sir." I step forward to thank him and shake his hand, but he just passes me the key to my abandoned room back.

"Rack up. You have shit to do tomorrow."

"A new mission?" Why I ask I have no idea. Being allowed to stay in Cerberus, the privilege of being this close to Gigi is more than I could've ever expected.

"Georgia has a doctor's appointment. Shadow is taking her."

"I'm taking her," I insist.

His eyes narrow at the challenge, but there's something else there, something akin to pride or expectation.

"So be it," he agrees.

Backing away, I open the door and step out into the hallway in one swift move. Shadow is as stoic as ever standing sentry over the room, but I don't miss the slight twitch of Kid's mouth as I walk past. I ignore the groups of guys, the ones I've spent numerous months with in foreign countries as they hover near the hallway door to the conference rooms. Those nosy fuckers are just as bad as teenage girls. I should know. Izzy prattles on relentlessly about the girls in her school.

I don't bother unpacking once I get inside my room. It's a simple task and can be completed in mere minutes. I hit the shower, scrubbing every inch of my body, preparing myself for Gigi's visit later. Her sneaking into my room will do nothing but anger Kincaid, even though I'm now *dating* his daughter, but he didn't lay out any ground rules, so I'm going to play ignorant to the fact that fucking her in his clubhouse will piss him off. Gigi is irresistible, and I promised her I'd never turn her away again. My promise to her is more important than any emotion her father could face with the news.

The damage has already been done, right?

I wait.

And wait.

And wait some more.

I wait until sleep drags me under and the erection that sprang up just thinking about my dark-haired girl deflates in desperate sadness.

Chapter 24

Gigi

"It's late," Mom says with a yawn when she finds me sitting on a stool at the breakfast counter.

"Couldn't sleep," I say and stare down at the uneaten peanut butter and jelly sandwich on the counter in front of me.

"Want some milk," she asks as she tugs the fridge door open.

"No thanks. Where's Dad?"

"At the clubhouse," she answers.

"Doing what exactly?"

She turns in my direction and frowns. "You know exactly what he's doing."

"Firing Jameson? Getting his guys to hide his body?"

She chuckles, but it's guarded as if she knows what Dad is capable of when he's protecting his family.

"I doubt he's going to kill that man."

"He wants to," I mutter.

"I'm pretty sure that's not the way your father was leaning when he headed over there." She places a cold cup of milk in front of me. I eye it with disinterest.

"Why are you staring at me?" I ask when I look up and find her leaning against the counter, arms crossed over her chest, and her eyes drilling holes into me.

"We only want what's best for you, Georgia. We want you to be happy."

"Is this when you tell me that marrying Jameson is what is best? It's what will make me happy?"

I don't know how to be a wife or a mother, but I can't deny the pain I get in my chest at the thought of having both.

She shakes her head, a soft smile playing at the corners of her mouth. "Marrying a man you don't love just because you're pregnant is the last thing you need. It's not a decision to be made lightly."

I spin the glass of milk around on the counter, concentrating on the ring of condensation it leaves behind as if it's the most interesting thing in the world. I usually run from serious conversations, opting to ignore anything that may resemble an adult choice.

"Marrying a man for anything less than being madly in love is a huge mistake." I look up to find her eyes distant, pain pulling at her previously smiling eyes. "You don't marry out of fear or some obligation to another person. Love. Love is the only reason you stand before your friends and God and say vows, commit to one person for the rest of your life."

I've heard Dad, Shadow, and Kid talking about Mom's first husband, the same man that came after her after abusing her during their entire relationship. He died for his efforts less than a hundred yards from where we are right now.

"I can see myself loving him," I confess.

I don't know if my appeal is merely sexual or if it goes deeper than that, but there has been a pull, low in my gut that confuses me whenever he's around.

"That's a start." The smile that was disappearing with her memories is renewed the moment the front door opens, and Dad appears in the kitchen.

He's not happy, but the black cloud of anger that rained down on all of us in his office earlier seems to have dissipated some.

"You need to eat," he huffs on his way to wrap his arms around Mom. "You're too skinny, and the baby needs the nourishment."

"How quickly you accept my delicate decision." I pick up my previously ignored sandwich and take a hearty bite.

"I'm a realist, Georgia. No matter how much I wish things were different, I can't ignore the truth of the situation."

"Different?" Irritation marks my tone enough that he leans in, head on my mother's shoulder, arms wrapped tight around her, and his eyebrow cocks up. "And exactly how do you wish my life was different?"

"I'd prefer you educated, married, and mentally, financially, and emotionally prepared. Parenting is hard even for those that plan on the children they conceive."

My mom's smile grows wider as she turns her head and kisses Dad on the jaw.

"Your dad struggled a little in the beginning. Two babies are a handful with everything else going on."

I've heard those stories as well. Only these were told around Thanksgiving tables and near the fireplace at Christmas. The stories of him coming to terms with being the father of not one, but two, little girls were told to family and friends in rooms filled with friendly taunting and laughs.

"I remember." I smile at both of them, so in love even after two decades, is something I've longed for for a while, although I'd never admitted it out loud.

"Blade made you a doctor's appointment for tomorrow. Thankfully, Dr. Davison had an opening, but it's first thing in the morning," Dad says nuzzling into Mom's neck.

Her cheeks flush, and I want to groan at the arousal he's building in her, but that's what kids do, and I'm no longer a child.

"Dr. Davison is old as the hills, and besides, he's a general practitioner. I think an OB/GYN is better suited for this situation. Don't you?"

"Dr. Camryn Davison, his daughter, is in her residency. I hear she's better than the OB she's working under."

The pride he has in his eyes for his friend's daughter hurts more than it should. I haven't seen it pointed in my direction since stealing home once at a softball game in middle school.

"Sounds good," I agree and laugh when shock runs across his face at my quick agreement.

I never give in that easy. Normal Gigi would argue, throw a fit about him running her life and making decisions for her, but I know, even though he may not be happy about my out-of-wedlock pregnancy, he'd never send me to a doctor he didn't have full faith in.

"I trust you, grandpa." I slide off of the stool, still unable to stomach the half-eaten sandwich and laugh again when he begins to look sick.

"Too soon, honey," my mother chides as I kiss them both on the cheek and head up to my room.

Maybe making Dad freak out means whatever sexual tension that was building between them will have faded away and they'll just go to bed. Although I'm exhausted, I know I'll sleep better in Jameson's arms. My skin tingles at the mere thought of his hands not just wrapped around me, but his hand wandering lower.

I shake my head.

"Soon," I mutter, kicking off my shoes and climbing under the warm sheets.

When I hear my mom giggle on their way upstairs, I groan and settle in, knowing they won't be going to sleep anytime soon.

I spend an hour staring up at the ceiling in my childhood bedroom, mind racing with worry and doubt. There's nothing I could be doing right this second to make things easier, but I'm still restless at the idea of being back in Farmington. I have no prospects. The only plan on my horizon is hanging out at my parents' house and growing a baby. The truth of the boredom I'm facing agitates me. I'm not an idle person. I'm not lazy. I can't stand being stagnant, just sitting around and not doing a damn thing.

Turning my head, I glance over at my dresser. Usually, when I'm dragged back home, I've got a suitcase and a stray bag or two. This time, I was honest with Jameson. There was nothing back at the apartment that I wanted to keep. The vacancy on the carpet across the room is unsettling as my itch to get up and do something claws at my skin.

It's how it has always been. I'm finicky and make decisions pretty quickly. It's why I just up and leave sometimes. I don't even have to be annoyed or pissed at my parents. Some days, I just feel like leaving.

I bite my lip at the thought of Jameson chasing me, hunting me down after I've left Farmington in my dust. Smiling, I turn to my left side, closing my eyes, and I let the fantasy of him finding me, punishing me for my insolence invades my mind. That thought, that idea carries me into sleep and keeps me warm all night long.

Chapter 25

Hound

She never came to me last night. I have no idea what happened in her house last night after her dad returned.

"You really know how to fuck shit up don't you?"

I turn to look at Scooter who is smoking just outside of the front door of the clubhouse.

"Clearly," I mutter, glancing to his cigarette and remembering a time when smoke in my lungs first thing in the morning was what I lived for.

I lick my lips unconsciously, and Scooter offers his pack in my direction.

"No thanks," I tell him and look over at the construction crew that's already milling around across the street.

"They work fast as hell," Scooter says, his eyes focusing across the street as well.

"Kincaid going to build you a house out back now that you're family and shit?"

"Not likely. I'm pretty certain I'll end up a casualty on our next mission. It'd be easier to explain than a corpse in the clubhouse."

He chuckles, but he's shaking his head. "If Prez didn't kill you in the moment, he won't do it later. Well..."

"What?" I turn back to look at him.

"He may if you fuck her twin and knock her up too."

I punch him in the arm hard enough to nearly knock him off the side of the small concrete porch.

"That shit's not funny. I have no intention of fucking her twin."

"Who's fucking whom?"

We both turn to see Gigi walking down the sidewalk toward us.

Scooter clears his throat, tosses his cigarette butt into the ashtray, and apologizes for his language before he turns and walks toward the garage.

"Hey." It's the best I can manage at the sight of her in a dress that hits the middle of her thighs and clings to the perfect globes of her breasts.

"I see you've made friends while I was gone." She smiles, but I can see the exhaustion playing near her eyes and the same pink on her cheeks she gets when she either gets sick or orgasms.

Betting that the glow is from morning sickness and not coming, I step closer to her.

"I missed you last night," I confess and wrap my arms around her. I press a soft kiss to her forehead before pulling my head back to look into her eyes.

"I fell asleep waiting for Mom and Dad to go to sleep," she says, her eyes beaming up at mine.

"What's that look for?"

A sheepish smile spreads across her beautiful face, the pink in her cheeks doubling.

"I dreamed about you last night," she confesses.

"Did you?" My cock thickens at the salaciousness in her eyes. "Dare I ask what this dream entailed?"

"Well," she says turning, breaking my hold on her, and walking toward the SUV we drove back from Vegas in yesterday. "There were ropes."

"I'm good with ropes."

"There was a ball gag."

"Not my style," I whisper in her ear as I tug open the passenger side door so she can climb inside. "I want to hear you whimper, moan, and come loud enough to make the neighbors bang on the wall."

Her breathing grows shallower, eyelids lowering.

"There were also nipple clamps and a butt plug."

My cock, ready for all of it, pushes against the zipper of my jeans. Since I go commando, I know I'll have indentions from the teeth in a line right down the length of it.

"We're going to the doctor's office," I remind her.

Her pretty white teeth clamp on her bottom lip as she fights a smile. "We can always stop off at the park. We have time."

I lean in close, her breath mixing with mine. "It's your first visit."

"It is," she agrees.

"I looked on the internet, and your first visit includes an exam," I inform her.

"Okay," she says watching my mouth and only half listening.

"We can stop at the park."

She nods, pink tongue sweeping across her lip. I can feel the echo of the action in the throb of my cock.

"Please," she begs. "I dreamed of you fucking me all night. I needed it so much, I fingered myself the second I woke up."

"Did you?"

I groan at the frantic nodding of her head. "And again in the shower."

So the flush on her cheeks wasn't from morning sickness.

"You have an exam in an hour."

"We have time," she urges.

"Then you'll be the one explaining to the doctor why my come is dripping out of you during your exam."

Fuck do I hate she has that damn exam.

Her eyes widen at realizing what a stop at the park will mean, and I can't help but laugh.

She shoves at my shoulder. "You asshole. You got me all hot and bothered, and now we can't do a damn thing."

"You're wet."

"So wet," she pants.

"We can take care of that."

I close her door and walk around to the driver's side, thankful there isn't a soul in sight to see the pole trying to escape my jeans.

***

"That smirk," she says with a quick shake of her head.

"You're beautiful after you come." I shift, not finding any comfort in the motion. My cock was ignored in the park when I lifted her off her seat of the SUV and forced her pussy to my mouth. She came twice, and I licked her clean, my dick going untouched the entire time. It seemed like a good idea at the time. I regretted it the instant we got inside the exam room, and she stripped naked only to cover her amazing body back up with a thin, paper gown.

"I could've sucked you off."

I groan and shift again.

"You'll get your chance," I promise just as a soft but authoritative knock hits the door.

"Come in," Gigi says, an expectant look on her face.

A female doctor, too damn young to have already gone through medical school walks in with a bright smile on her face.

"Hello, Georgia." She offers her hand, and my girl shakes it.

"Gigi, please," she corrects, her eyes narrowing at the doctor.

"Your dad called this morning. Gave me a little history. I noticed in your chart that it's been a few years since your last pelvic exam."

"Listen, Cam," Gigi begins, and I can tell she's suddenly irritated just by her tone.

"It's Dr. Davison, now," the professional says with such sharpness I recoil then dart my eyes to Gigi, fully expecting her to come off the table and claw the doctor's eyes out.

Instead, Gigi laughs. "You've been Cam all my life."

"Don't remind me," Cam says with a familiarity I'm just now catching onto. "Babysitting you is something I'd rather not remember."

"You were mean," Gigi says.

"You stuck bubble gum in my hair." Her arms cross over her chest, nose tilting up in defiance.

"You had your boyfriend over and ignored us. Ivy hurt herself in the bath because you were too busy sucking face with that Benelli boy!"

Cam closes her eyes and takes a deep breath. "That was ten years ago. Your parents forgave me, and you should too. I babysat you for several more years after that."

"Hi," I say standing and trying to diffuse the situation. I offer her my hand. "I'm Jameson Rawley."

"The father, I presume." She shakes my hand, full professional mask back in place.

"Let's get started." She turns back to Gigi like they weren't enemies years ago. "Yearly exams are vital for your health, Gigi."

"I know. I won't miss another one."

When Dr. Davison asks her to lie back for a breast exam, I nearly get up and walk out. The pictures marking the walls don't help either. Breasts, albeit rendered with an artist's hand, are everywhere. I look down at my hands instead.

"Please don't talk to my dad about me," Gigi says in a pleading voice. "I'm grown."

"Of course," Dr. Davison says.

The breast exam is complete, and I finally look up when Gigi covers her chest.

"Let me get the nurse for the next part. I'll be right back."

"You know her?" Why I ask I don't know. Clearly, they have a history.

She just nods, but I pay attention when her teeth strike her bottom lip. "I'm going to be imagining it's you when she slides her fingers inside of me."

"God damn," I hiss. "You need to stop."

There's a soft knock, and now two people dressed in scrubs make their way inside the already cramped room.

My throat is dry, and I only stare when the nurse tries to make casual conversation.

I'm hard as steel by the time Dr. Davison asks Gigi to lie back.

I'm leaking from my tip when the request is made for her feet to be placed in the stirrups.

I nearly come as Gigi moans when Dr. Davison inserts her fingers into my girl.

"Are you experiencing discomfort," the doctor asks, concerned.

"No," Gigi pants. "It's just a little weird with you being the one to do this."

Dr. Davison laughs. "I assure you. We're very professional here."

I'm not a ménage kind of guy. I can admit I've had my fair share of fucking several girls at once, but it wasn't something I ever sought out, rather something that just ended up happening. I sure as fuck don't want to share a second of Gigi's time, but her words and the knowledge that she's inappropriately turned on right now would bring me to my knees if I were standing.

"Is sex safe?"

I choke out a disbelieving cough.

The doctor laughs again. "That's the most asked question we get when a couple finds out they're expecting."

I fucking blush when she looks over at me, at least two fingers deep inside my girl.

"Sex is safe. I suggest lots of showers beforehand and no douching. Pregnant women's hormones are all over the place which makes you more prone to yeast and urinary tract infections."

"What about piercings?"

I can feel the heat creep up my chest to my face. She's fucking with me. I just know it. These are questions we can Google, yet she's asking them in a room with two women I don't know. I'm not a shy man, but their professionalism makes me uncomfortable.

Dr. Davison tries to cover a laugh with a quick cough. The older nurse just looks bored.

"You've got what?" Gigi looks over at me, and grins, knowing I'm going to paddle her ass later for this. "Four or five piercings."

"Seven, total," I correct.

Dr. Davison looks impressed, but it's the nurse's "Oh my," that earns Gigi another couple of slaps to her naked ass.

"Piercings are fine." Dr. Davison's voice is a little higher than it has been so far today. She gives me a serious look. "So long as they're taken care of, not infected, and clean."

"Of course," I respond.

Dr. Davison pulls off her latex gloves and tosses them to the used instrument tray before turning back to Gigi.

"Do you have any more questions?"

I watch Gigi's throat work on a swallow, and I try to prepare myself for what's coming. My palm is already warming, and I know I'm going to redden her ass before we even leave the parking lot.

Yet, all thoughts of distributing punishment fade away when her mouth opens.

Chapter 26

Gigi

"Will cocaine hurt the baby?"

I avoid Jameson's eyes even though I can feel the fire from them burning into the side of my face.

"Any drugs including cigarettes, excessive amounts of caffeine and some over the counter medications can be harmful to the fetus," Dr. Davison explains. "How often are you using? There are programs—"

"I haven't." I shake my head, the only thing I can think to do to keep the tears burning my eyes from falling. "The night..."

I look over at Jameson, but he's looking down at hands knotted together in anger, not in disappointment. His anger I can handle. Knowing he'll meet my eyes and I'll see the same disappointment that's been so familiar on my parents' faces will be unbearable.

"The night I conceived. I used cocaine that night. I haven't used since then."

I'm speaking to Cam, but my eyes stay on Jameson, begging him to look at me, praying he'll still want me. I wasn't going to say anything, but I vowed to be the best mother I can be, and I knew I'd worry relentlessly if I didn't know.

"Look at me." I feel Cam's hand on my shoulder. When I turn to face her, she pushes a tissue into my hand, and it's only then that I realize the tears have begun to fall. "Your baby will be fine. There's minimal risk so long as you don't use again."

I nod, and she continues.

"Is it something you're struggling with? There are programs I can refer you to."

I shake my head. "I'm okay. I haven't even thought about drugs in months. It was something I did to make my life easier. It made doing my job easier."

I look back at Jameson. His face is a passive mask, and I realize his indifference is much, much worse than disappointment.

"Okay," Cam says with one final rub to my back. "Are you taking prenatal vitamins?"

I shake my head. "They made me sick, and I couldn't keep them down."

"They're important. Try eating a few crackers and drinking some juice or ginger ale before even getting out of bed in the morning. According to your paperwork, you're nine weeks along. Morning sickness tends to ease up in the second trimester, so you only have a few more weeks to go."

"Thank you." I give her a weak smile.

She hands me a card from the front pocket of her white coat. "My cell number is on there. You call me if you have any questions. Tell your mom I said hi."

Thickness fills the air when Cam and the nurse exit.

"Jameson," I begin.

He stands, and I pray he'll walk up to me, comfort me, and tell me everything will be fine, but he turns toward the door. "I'll wait outside while you get dressed."

It takes twice as long to get my clothes back on as it did to take them off, even when I did it slowly to tease and taunt Jameson. I get sick, emptying my stomach into the trash, so overcome with worry that I can't even feel sorry for whoever has to deal with it. I swish my mouth with mouthwash I've been carrying in my purse since I get sick all the time.

When I finally make my way out of the room, Jameson is leaning right outside of the door. I can't speak. I don't even know what I would say to him, so I just walk past him and Dr. Davison who's standing up at a computer kiosk and typing in information. My dad will find out about the cocaine use if he wants. Blade can gain access to just about any database in the world. Farmington Women's Clinic would be child's play for him.

I feel his heat close, but not close enough as I step up to the business counter to make my next appointment.

"Your co-pay for the exam is thirty dollars," the nice receptionist says as she hands me a card for an appointment in a month's time.

"Co-pay?" I ask, but shake my head. Of course, my dad still has me on his insurance. That information would've been helpful when I sprained my knee on a new pole routine six months ago. Blade would've tracked me down, but I would've saved a couple thousand dollars. I would've left Dallas before Hound even showed up had I not had to use my savings to pay medical bills.

"I got it," Jameson says and hands cash over my shoulder.

"No," I tell him and reach into my purse for my own money.

"Now is not the time to test me," he growls in my ear.

I step out of the way, thanking the woman when she hands me a printed receipt.

"See you next month," she says with a bright smile before turning to help the next person behind me.

"Not likely," I mutter.

He doesn't touch me, doesn't say a word as we exit the doctor's office and make our way down the long hall of doors that lead to other practices.

I yelp in surprise when he pushes open the door to the family restroom and drags me inside. He doesn't even bother to flip on the light, but I can still see how angry he is in the glow of the red exit sign above the door.

"You planning on running?" I shake my head. A lie. It's my first instinct at his reaction to my confession in the exam room. "I'm pretty fucking sure that's exactly what 'not likely' meant."

I snap my head up, not realizing I said it loud enough for him to hear.

"I'll find you," he warns as his hands go first to the buckle of his belt, then the top button and zipper of his jeans. "I'll chase you clear across the world if I have to."

"I'm not running."

"Damn right you're not," he hisses as one hand strokes his now exposed cock and the other one presses down on my shoulder. "Get on your knees, Gigi."

I obey without second thought.

The second he presses the glistening tip of his cock against my lips, I moan, knowing this is the very first time I've had a dick in my mouth since Jordy convinced me to try to suck his in high school.

"Go slow," he groans. "Don't want you to chip one of those pretty teeth."

I open my jaw wider, but his invasion is still too much. My eyes water as he presses deeper without withdrawing. Breathing through my nose is nearly as unrelenting as his fist in my hair. It may be the hottest thing I've ever experienced.

"Fuck," he whispers on a pant when I gag. He pulls back an inch or so but then presses in again. "Close your mouth and suck or I'm going to fuck your throat."

I whimper, hating the choice because fuck if I don't want to experience both.

I tighten my lips around the shaft, sucking until my cheeks collapse. The unique feel of the metal against my tongue and my lips when he pulls out and pushes back in makes me wet. The saliva dripping from my chin goes ignored as his grip gets even more brutal in my hair.

"I'm not going to last," he grunts but doesn't slow the now driving force of his hips.

I press my palms against his tense thighs and relish the feel of the muscles jumping and flexing with his exertion.

"Swallow it all," he hisses just as his cock jerks in my mouth.

The first thick, salty burst makes me squeeze my watering eyes closed, and I try to focus only on his pleasure. Letting myself actually consider what I'm doing would probably make me puke, so I push it to the back of my mind, sucking and swallowing until he slips free of my mouth.

"Don't," he snaps when I raise the back of my hand to my mouth to clear away some of the mess.

He flips the light switch, and we both squint at the sudden illumination of the room. When I can focus again, I see him staring at me, cock still half mast, and hanging from the opening in his jeans. His chest rises and falls in harsh breaths, but he's looking at me differently. Different from the way he watched me while I danced on stage the first day we met. Different from the way he focuses on my face when I come. And thankfully, different from the way he looked at me when Cam left the exam room after my confession.

There's danger in his eyes and damned if my body isn't begging him to do his worst.

"Please," I beg, standing so I can get closer to him.

"You need something?"

His thumb sweeps over the corner of my mouth before dipping inside. I toy with it against my tongue, the tang of his orgasm renewed in my mouth.

I nod and squirm, shifting back and forth in my ballerina flats.

"No." One simple word. An order he expects me to obey without questions.

I watch, mouth hanging open at the rejection, as he tucks himself back into his jeans and washes his hands.

"I'm wet," I purr, running my hands over the muscled expanse of his back.

"I know," he says as he dries his hands. "You'll wait."

"I don't want to," I huff, arms crossed over my chest for emphasis.

"You won't get another chance to come until you've taken your punishment."

"Punishment?" I laugh at the absurdity of his words, all the while my pussy clenching against the soft satin of my panties. "For what?"

"For those orgasms I gave you at the park." He turns facing me with a damn paper towel and runs it under my eyes. "For those comments and the striptease in the exam room, but more importantly for letting me fuck you in an alley while you were high on coke."

"Dr. Davison said the baby will be fine."

"I know he will." I smile at his insistence that he's having a son. "But that doesn't negate the fact that you were a virgin and made the decision to no longer be one while you weren't at a hundred percent capacity to make fucking decisions like that."

"I knew what I was doing," I argue. If anything, the coke made the sex in the alley even better. I would've called it euphoric, but every time he's rammed inside of me since has been just as good.

"Still isn't going to keep me from spanking your ass later."

He grabs my hand, flipping the lock on the door and pulling me back into the hallway. A mother with a toddler in a stroller and another baby strapped to her chest glares at us while tapping her mom sandals on the linoleum.

"That's not what the family restroom is used for," she hisses.

Jameson shrugs. "What can I say? She's insatiable."

We don't hear her response over my laughter as we make our way outside to the SUV.

Chapter 27

Hound

"So we're heading back to your room?" I love the eagerness in her voice. It almost makes me not want to make her cry with quick successive swats to her ass. Almost.

"Nope," I tell her and crank the vehicle. "We're going on a date."

I look over at her to find her beaming at me.

"A date?" The joy on her face, in her eyes is palpable. "Like you fingering me in a dark movie theater?"

My spent cock twitches in my jeans at the prospect.

"Like lunch. That's what people do when they date."

"We're dating now?" She huffs as she clicks her seatbelt in place.

I pull mine across my chest, never taking my eyes off of her.

"I bet my dad is going to flip over that." She turns her head in my direction with a mischievous look in her eyes. "Let's do it."

The only thing that's missing is a creepy laugh and her rubbing her hands together.

"It was your dad's idea." Her face falls.

"Really?" She shakes her head. "Not possible. He may have said it, but he can't possibly be okay with it."

"You don't like the idea?" I tilt my head and wait for her answer.

"That my dad is okay with us dating?" She laughs. "Not at all."

"Because you're only happy when you're fighting him?" That devilish smile is back on her lips. "What about us dating? You okay with that idea?"

She shrugs now, but the pink on her cheeks and gleam in her eyes betrays her apathy. "I'm okay with lunch, even though I'll probably just puke it up."

"Doctor said just a few more weeks," I remind her and put the SUV in drive.

***

"Is this okay?" I ask as I back the SUV into a parking spot.

She laughs. "You're just like my dad. He always backs in also."

I shrug. "Never know when you'll have to get away. Backing in now makes it easy to leave in an emergency later."

"Always the soldier," she mutters.

I climb out and make my way around the front of the vehicle, frowning when she opens her door and jumps out before I can open the door and help her down.

"This is a date. I'm supposed to open the door for you."

She huffs. "You just fucked my face in a bathroom at the doctor's office, and now you want to be a gentleman?"

I pin her to the door, leaning in close, the press of my hips against her stomach tantalizing in the heat of the sun.

"You have earned so many slaps on your ass. I may have to split it up over two days." Bending my knees, I press my thickening cock against the apex of her thighs.

"Yes, please," she says, eyes focused on my mouth.

"You forget," I say backing away. "You don't get to come until they're all done."

"You're a monster," she says exactly like the gingerbread man in Shrek when the king is taunting him with his broken-off legs.

I can't help the laugh that bubbles from my throat. "I love that fucking movie."

I grab her hand and usher her toward the door of the chain restaurant that's exactly like every other damn chain restaurant in town. It makes me wish for that taco bar I ate at with Rocker and Scooter on our way back from Denver last month.

"You like Shrek?" she asks softly as the hostess gathers menus for us. It's early, the lunch rush imminent but not in full swing.

"Don't tell Izzy. I make her think I hate all those kinds of movies, but in reality, most of my favorite movies are animated like that. Shrek, Minions, any Disney movie, except Frozen, that's where I draw the line."

"Will I get to meet her?" We sit across from each other in the booth the hostess guides us to.

"Thank you," I tell her accepting the menus she offers and orders our drinks. "Who?"

Gigi huffs again in agitation. "Izzy. Will I get to meet her?"

I haven't mentioned anything about Gigi or the baby to Izzy even though I've spoken to her twice since I found out about the pregnancy.

"Of course," I say and wait for the dread to settle in my stomach. It never does. "We're meeting up in a few weeks in Albuquerque. She'll be disappointed that I don't bring the bike because she likes to ride, but I think she'll be excited to meet you."

"And when you tell her about the baby? How do you think she'll respond?" We pull our hands back when a waitress walks up and places our Cokes on the table.

We haven't had a chance to look at the menu, but we both tell her cheeseburgers and fries.

When she walks away, and my attention is back on Gigi, I find her still waiting for an answer.

"I honestly don't know. I imagine she'll be shocked."

"Not upset?"

I shake my head. "Why would she be upset?"

She looks down at the table, wasting time not answering by rearranging the silverware roll and positioning her drink just right.

"I'd be upset if my parents told me they were having another baby." She shrugs. "She's not much younger than I am, just figured it would be the normal response."

"You spoiled little brat," I tease with a wide grin.

"You'd be upset if your mom got pregnant."

"Well," she says taking a moment to think it through. "Not now, but when I was younger? Absolutely. They had Ivy to dote on. My sister is a pleaser by nature. They were always so proud. Second place sucks. Third would be even worse. Third could mean they wouldn't have any love left over for me at all."

"It doesn't work that way." I reach for her hand, cupping it between both of mine. "When you told me you were keeping the baby, even before you made your mind up if I'm being honest, I knew I would love that baby just as much as I love Izzy."

"Your heart can only hold so much love," she says with sadness in her voice.

"Also false." I squeeze her hand until she looks up at me. "It just grows bigger or holds some in reserves until it's needed. Your parents don't love Ivy more than they love you. They're good people. Your dad is a good man. You're difficult. A pain in the ass on your best day, but that doesn't cancel love. I promise you."

She takes a moment before responding, and I don't know if she's accepting what I said or trying to think of a way to counter my truth.

"So what? You're Team Kincaid now?" She's grinning, and I feel the heaviness of the conversation drift away with her quip.

"I'm a man with one daughter and a son on the way. I know what it's like to love two kids so fiercely that I can't imagine loving anyone else." The sadness returns. "But then I think about it, and I know I could love twice as many kids just as much. If we had a second kid, if you're pregnant with twins I'd love them both, equally."

"Don't even fucking joke about shit like that," she hisses, and the smile on my face is so wide my cheeks ache.

"Twins are hereditary."

"My mom had IVF." She winks at me, maintaining the upper hand.

"Thank fuck," I say and sit deeper in the booth. "I was seriously freaking out at the possibility."

Her laugh is music to my ears, a calming salve to my injured ego. When I'd heard her mutter 'not likely' to the receptionist my blood ran cold. Getting her on her knees, my cock down her throat to show her who's in charge was my only thought.

"How about we get to know each other?" she asks.

I grin, finally letting myself believe that all of this is real. "What do you want to know?"

She's nervous as she picks at the cuticle of her thumb nail.

"Out with it, gorgeous."

"When will you tell Isabella?"

I smile, knowing how my oldest daughter is going to respond with the news and pull out my phone. I type out a quick text to her and frown when the phone immediately begins to ring.

"You're supposed to be in class," I say when the call connects rather than a normal greeting.

"It's gym class," she explains. "No one does anything but sit in the bleachers on their phones. What's this big news?"

Gigi rolls her lip between her teeth, chewing on it.

"I've met someone."

I hold the phone away from my ear as Izzy squeals like the teenage girl that she is.

The worry that creased Gigi's brow suddenly disappears, her lips turning up in a smile.

Was she worried Izzy wouldn't be happy? I should've explained to her long ago that Izzy has always wanted me to be happy, the point of near harassment to look for something long term.

"There's more," I begin when she finally calms down. "We're having a baby."

The squealing begins anew.

"I'm going to be a big sister!" Izzy screams to those around her.

I reach across the table and squeeze Gigi's hand before bringing it to my lips and kissing the tips.

"I'm so happy for you," Izzy says, voice softer. The emotion is clear, and I couldn't be happier to be the father of such a loving young woman.

"Thank you, Iz. Call me later this evening if you can and we can discuss it more."

"Love you, dad."

"Love you, sweetheart."

I put my phone back in my pocket.

"That went well," Gigi says with a bright smile.

"You were worried?" She shakes her head, but I can tell that's not the entire truth. "She's an amazing person. She'll love you."

I swallow, the words I've not even spoken rolling from my mouth easier than it should at this point.

"When she finds out I'm less than five years older than her, she may not be as happy as she is right now."

Shaking my head, I reject her words. "You'll see," I promise as the waitress begins to unload our plates from the serving tray.

We eat slowly, the burgers better than I anticipated, but maybe it's her company, her smile, and the way she's quick to laugh at stupid jokes that adds seasoning to the meal, making it the most palatable thing I've consumed in a while. Other than her pussy of course.

"Really?" I ask as we walk to the SUV, my hand on her lower back, my cock twitching with the innocuous touch.

"Seriously," she verifies. "My cousin Kaleb has named every one of his dogs after some sort of weapon. "They have Remington now. Their cat is named AK, but I think the kids named it that years ago. Mia was his first dog, his partner at the police department. She's gone now, but they had like fourteen years with her."

I hate the pain in her voice, but my heart sings at the compassion she has for the animal. Somehow this amazing woman thinks she's going to be a terrible mother, but knowing she gets upset over the death of a relative's dog says a lot about the person she is.

"Mia?" I say hoping to draw her out of her sadness. "Doesn't sound like any weapon I've encountered."

I open the door for her, looking down at her perky ass in her dress as she climbs up.

"Well, M-One-A," she corrects. "M1A."

"Oh," I say with clarity. "That makes sense now. Pretty clever name."

I cross in front of the vehicle as quickly as I can so we can continue our conversation.

Before she can ask me another favorite dish, color, or childhood memory, I turn to her the second I get inside with her. "I want to go to every single doctor appointment you have."

"Are you waiting for more confessions? I don't have any."

"No. I want to experience everything. The sound of the first heartbeat, the tiny black and white pictures. I want to be there the second they prove to you that my boy is in there."

"And if it's another girl?"

I sigh playfully and put the SUV in gear. "Then I'll have to buy a fuck ton more guns, won't I?"

Her laughter fills the cabin of the vehicle as I pull out into traffic. "You're going to be a great dad."

I stiffen.

"I mean," she begins.

"I know what you meant. I'm thankful that Izzy's stepdad is super protective of her. As bitter as I want to be about another man raising my daughter, she really lucked out in that department."

"That's good," she says.

I hate the silence that swarms around us. Gone is the teasing and laughing. Gone is the happiness that filled both of us while chatting at the restaurant.

"Give me your phone," I tell her as we pull into the gravel lot of the clubhouse.

She hands it over, and I type my cell number and send a quick text to my phone.

"Now you can reach me." I hand it back to her.

"We seem to be doing everything backward."

"We'll catch up." I kiss her on the cheek and hate the sound of the door when it closes me back inside alone.

Something catches in my chest when I watch her disappear around the corner toward her dad's house. I have a single room in a clubhouse with more than a handful of other guys. No real privacy. No real home.

"Her suggestion of a three-bedroom apartment doesn't sound so crazy," I mutter as I climb out of the SUV and head to the garage.

Chapter 28

Gigi

Me: I can't wait to spank your ass.

I stare down at the text Jameson sent from my phone inside of the SUV debating if going to him is what's best for me.

Do I want the promise he eluded to several times today? Fuck yeah, I do, but the mood changed into something dark and depressing after our incredible meal. That's not something I'm sure I can face again.

I sigh and climb out of my bed. My parents disappeared into their room over an hour ago with no peep, giggle, or other noises I refuse to examine. Yet, I stayed in my bed trying to talk myself into going to him.

Creeping down the stairs, I head out of the house and use the backdoor to the clubhouse. Thankfully unlocked, the door leads just off the kitchen to the hallway of rooms. When Ivy and I were brought home from the hospital, this is where we made our home. Until we were six and Dad finally broke down and had our house built, we roamed these halls with all the other kids.

I let myself into Jameson's room, locking the door securely behind me. I expect to see his sleeping form on his bed, and he's there, but he's sitting on the edge of the bed, in all his naked glory.

"I've been waiting for you." The low gruff of his voice sends shivers over my entire body, and I realize debating even coming here wasn't what I wanted at all. I wanted this, this man looking at me like he both loves and hates the sight of me.

"I wasn't going to come," I confess. "Afraid you wouldn't let me come and wondering if my entire night is only going to be filled with pain, my morning consumed by the aches you're sure to leave on my body."

"Yet here you are." He hasn't shifted, hasn't moved his body one single inch since I stepped inside, and his calmness makes me shiver harder.

"Yes," I pant.

"You have much to atone for," he says crooking his finger and drawing me closer. "All the lies. Running from me after Dallas, keeping the secret about my baby, the way you acted at the doctor earlier, but most importantly the idea in your head that you could ever run from me again."

"I want to run right now," I admit. "Will it hurt badly?"

"If I do it right."

I'm trembling, my knees barely strong enough to hold my weight when I finally make it within arm's reach.

"And if I do it right, you'll beg me not to stop, plead with me to redden your ass every day for the rest of your life."

I moan, not at the idea of him spanking me, but because the idea that he would be around every day turns me on more than anything.

"I want that."

I flinch, the anticipation of his touch incomparable to the actual feel of it on my hip.

"Strip," he directs as his hand falls away.

I scurry out of the same dress I wore to the doctor's office earlier.

"No panties?" The approval in his voice is enough to keep me from ever covering my pussy again.

I stand before him naked as the day I was born, eyes roaming over the taut flesh of his stomach, the rippling muscles of his arms as he runs his hands up and down his muscular thighs.

"I didn't want anything to get in your way." I'm nearly breathless, longing for him to put his hands back on me.

"You walked through a clubhouse full of horny bastards with my pussy bare?" The possession. God, I crave it. To be needed, to be wanted by this man is almost incomprehensible, but his words ring true deep down in a place I don't bother to examine often. "I think that only adds to my count."

"Oh God," I mutter.

"You're going to feel me all over for days," he promises. His hand runs up my bare thigh, over my hip, until his huge hand is testing the weight of my breast. "On your ass for being so petulant."

He twists my nipple until I cry out in either pain or pleasure, at this point I'm not even sure myself.

"Deep inside where I'm going spend the night fucking you. You'll beg me to stop; you'll think you can't take anymore." The tip of his index finger runs delicately down my sternum, a contradiction to his dark vows.

"I won't stop. I'll take what I need because whose pussy is this?"

His finger ghosts over my clit. My hips move seeking more pressure. It earns me a slap to the sensitive bud.

"Whose is it?" he growls nudging my legs further apart.

"Yours," I pledge.

"Remember that."

Next thing I know I'm slung over his lap, face buried in sheets that smell like him, ass on display.

The first smack comes out of nowhere, and like any other time I'm in pain, I try to scramble away from it. The hand pressed low on my back ensures I stay exactly where he's positioned me.

"Do I need to add more?"

I shake my head as his hand rubs over the injured flesh of my right ass cheek.

He smacks and rubs, three strikes and fifteen seconds of stinging massage, repeatedly for what seems like days.

Then, he's spreading my sore cheeks, the cool air in his room licking at the entrance to my body. I'm wet, embarrassingly so, and I didn't even know I was turned on. The cacophony of sensations leaves my head spinning.

I need more.

I never want to be hit again.

"So filthy," he praises, fingers sweeping through the slickness of my desire until they stop, toying with the virgin flesh of my anus. "Whose ass is this?"

"Mine," I argue at the unfamiliar burn as he dips the tip of his finger inside.

Three more strikes; fifteen more seconds of massage.

"Whose?" His finger begins to dip inside again.

"Y-yours," I hiss as he presses deeper.

"Not tonight." I moan when he pulls free. "But soon it will be."

My mouth is dry, the heavy breathing from my punishment and the unsure emotions running through my head have left me delirious, unsure of what's coming next, but knowing that I'll die without it.

"Hurt?" he asks gripping my abused ass cheek in his hand.

I wince, but the warmth of his hands and the sting combine until I'm panting and hoping he hits me again.

"Yes," I admit. "So good."

His dark chuckle turns me on, too.

"Knees and elbows," he commands releasing me and standing me up on wobbly legs. I scramble to mind him, arching my back, feet hanging off the edge of the bed.

He rams inside before I even realize he's positioned himself behind me. The intrusion of his cock and the metal lining the bottom of his shaft is sensation overload. I cry out, uncaring of who in the clubhouse may hear. There's no one that exists in this world but him and me.

"Fuck, your ass is so red." He drives his statement home by gripping my tender flesh and thrusting even deeper.

Howling when he grips a fistful of my hair and forcing my back to arch even deeper, I'm left as nothing more than sensation.

I come. I burst wide open, the darkness disappearing behind the bright flashes in my vision, yellows, and purples, pulsing in time with my release.

Then the sting of his hand on my already tender ass brings me back around.

"I. Didn't. Give. You. Permission." Each word is underlined with another slap to my ass and another brutal shove of his cock.

I come again.

He punishes me.

And I realize I could do this every second of every day for the rest of my life.

"You fucking bitch," he hisses as his cock kicks, and he starts to come.

I smile at both the pleasure he's found with my body and the words he said in awe rather than in a derogatory way.

His weight leans over my back, and I collapse, the cool sheets a needed relief against my sweaty skin.

"You weren't supposed to come," he mutters in my ear. Biting nips of his mouth on my shoulder is enough to stir my overused body until I'm squirming under him once again.

"Your fault," I say on a moan when his tongue sweeps out and licks the shell of my ear.

"You're making me hard."

He's still inside of me, hips moving his cock in and out in lazy strokes.

"You never went soft," I argue.

"I'm always hard around you."

I smile against the mattress.

Suddenly his weight is gone, and I'm being shifted to the center of his bed on my back.

He's back inside of me, chest to chest, mouth hovering near mine, a second later.

I realize as his breath becomes mine that we've never kissed. My tongue has never tasted or felt the roughness of his. And more than anything, more than breath or food or water, it's what I need to survive.

He's watching my mouth, and I pray he needs it as much as I do.

He doesn't lean in; he doesn't press his mouth to mine. He leaves me hanging, gasping, slowly dying in his arms as he hitches my leg up. I press my heel into his back, urging him harder, deeper because it doesn't matter that I'm slowly fading from the deficiency of his mouth, I can't imagine a kinder death than one where he's buried deep inside of me.

When my eyes flutter closed, then and only then does he resuscitate me. Only then does he press his soft but firm lips to my mouth.

The jolt of electricity, the renewed life force is an arrow down my body. It begins to pulse in my clit. My orgasm, another one I didn't get permission for, takes over, clenching and gripping around him while he takes over my mouth.

The lazy sweeps of his tongue don't match the now hurried thrusts of his hips. The soft words he whispers against my lips are a contradiction to the punishing grip of his hand on my ass as he angles my hips just right.

"Perfect," he praises just before he stills, the hot jets of his come coating my womb.

We lie, his weight held up by his strong arms. The kisses we share are calm and satiated.

"You're sleepy," he chuckles against my mouth, and I realize that I'm so dazed and exhausted that I'm sliding in and out of consciousness.

I grumble my dissent when he pulls back and leaves the bed, only waking enough to grumble at him when he begins to massage a soothing cream into the skin of my abused ass.

Chapter 29

Hound

When my eyes open the following morning, the sun is high in the sky, peaking around the side of the curtains and washing the amazing woman beside me in enough of its rays to make her glow. She breathes softly against my chest as one of my hands grip the ass cheek of the leg she has hitched high up on my own thigh. My other hand is resting on my stomach, but the backs of my fingers are nestled against her lower belly.

Emotion clogs my throat knowing that as she sleeps, our child grows, gets stronger, and readies himself to join us. I pull Gigi even closer when she takes a deep breath. She mumbles something incoherent when her stomach growls.

Wincing, she raises her head from my chest when my fingers flex against her ass.

"Ouch," she pouts.

I smile down at her. She's perfection personified, even with messy hair and breath that could use the aid of a toothbrush and mouthwash.

"I loved spanking you last night," I admit to her.

"I loved kissing you."

Jesus, the way she clamped down on me, coming when my mouth met hers. There was no greater feeling than that alone.

"I could tell." My cock is hard, part pure biology, part waking to a naked woman plastered to my side.

"Round three?" she asks with a delicate swivel of her hips.

Her stomach growls again, interrupting my agreement.

"I'll get you some crackers and juice." I try to pull away, but she clings harder to me.

"I'm not hungry." Her stomach cries out again.

"Lying to me will only get your sore ass spanked again." Another swivel of her hips, the heat and slickness of her pussy nearly burning my thigh.

"Mmm," she hums.

"The doctor said you need to eat before you get out of bed," I remind her. "So you don't get sick."

She smiles, sleepy but horny at the same time. "I have no intention of getting out of bed."

Her hand trails down my stomach making the muscles jump and beg for more attention. She gets dangerously close to my cock, and I know the tease of her fingers will be enough to make me ignore her hunger.

I grab her wrist but ease the rejection by brushing my lips against hers.

"Crackers and juice," I tell her against her lips before sliding off of the bed and pulling on a pair of jeans. I don't bother with the top button or shoes.

"Hurry back. As soon as I drink my juice, I'm going to drink your juice."

I ignore the twitch of my still half-erect cock and laugh as I walk out into the hall and close her inside of my room.

"Drink my juice," I mutter. The ridiculous and immature words still making me chuckle as I walk into the kitchen. I choke on them when I see Kincaid, Kid, Shadow, and a couple of the other guys drinking coffee at one of the long kitchen tables.

"What's so funny?" Scooter asks before popping a piece of biscuit in his mouth. "Gigi say something funny?"

Fuck. My. Life.

Kincaid's eyes narrow, and the second Shadow clears his throat, the guys, Scooter included, stand up and clear out.

"Grab a cup of coffee," Kincaid says. "Then have a seat."

I don't argue. I don't tell him that I'm only out of my bed because his naked daughter is hungry. I sure as fuck don't mention the two servings of juice she wants this morning.

"Yes, Sir," is all I mutter as I turn my back and pour coffee into the biggest cup I can find. I don't bother with cream or sugar, knowing bitterness is all I'll be able to taste anyway.

I sit across from him, facing all three members, Kincaid in the middle, Shadow to his right with a look of impassivity on his face. His eyes tell a different story. Kid is on Kincaid's left with a mischievous sparkle in his eye. Classic Kid.

"Morning," I mumble.

"Almost midday," Shadow corrects with a quick glance down at his watch.

"Late night?" Kid asks.

I choke and sputter on the sip of coffee I attempt to take.

Kincaid's eyes close, and his jaw ticks, muscles flexing as he clenches his teeth.

I ignore the taunt, praying it's the right direction. Most people would deny, but even though through omission, I've lied enough to the men of this club. The man sitting in front of me will be a part of my life for the foreseeable future, and I don't want to ruin that so early on.

"How did the doctor's appointment go yesterday?"

I look up at Kincaid. "It went well."

Do not think about the blowjob in the family restroom. Do. Not.

"Well?" He raises an eyebrow at me. "That's all I get?"

"Dr. Davison seems nice, knowledgeable. She confirmed that Gigi is nine weeks. She says her morning sickness should start to fade after she hits the second trimester."

"Her next appointment?"

I look from Shadow to Kid wondering why they're even here for this but then consider Kincaid may need them if I say anything that makes him want to jump across the table and choke the life out of me.

"In a month," I repeat from what I remember the receptionist telling her yesterday. "She's covered by your insurance."

He nods.

"I'd like to take that over."

Kid leans in but doesn't say a word, and I wonder if this is it. If requesting to take care of his daughter, asking her parents to give up that final hold on her is what will make him snap. Kincaid, however, doesn't look upset but contemplative.

"What does Georgia say about it?"

"I didn't ask."

Kincaid huffs a laugh. "That child—"

"Woman," I correct.

He rolls his bottom lip between his teeth before speaking again. "That *woman* has been bucking any type of authority, any person who makes decisions for her long before she ever hit puberty. What makes you think you can just do something like take over her health insurance?"

Because she's mine, and I'll spank her ass if she gives me any shit about it.

"It's a simple thing," I counter.

"For me it's simple. For you it's simple. For Georgia," he tilts his head, and I already know his train of thought.

"It's enough to make her run," I finish for him.

"Exactly," he confirms.

"Even still. I want that responsibility."

"Responsibility?" I hate the snark in Shadow's tone. "Now you want to be responsible?"

"The fuck is that supposed to mean?" If he even mentions the alley back in Dallas, I'll bust his fucking nose.

"Didn't get it right the first time you knocked up a chick in high school? Want a second stab at abandoning your *responsibility*?"

Izzy.

"There's more to the story than the information you think you have."

"I sure as fuck hope so," Shadow spits.

Annoyed, I cross my arms over my chest and sit back in my chair. Kincaid just looks on, not saying a word but I can tell he's curious about the rest of the story as well.

"You seem a little too invested, Shadow." His eyes narrow and I forget he's the club VP. I've got three ranks above his ass where it counts, seventeen years in the Corps compared to his four. "Upset Gigi is with a man that's not you?"

Kincaid is on his feet, rough palms against his best friend's chest as Shadow, furious, tries to push him out of the way to attack.

"She's like my daughter you piece of shit."

"Enough," Kincaid hisses, but Shadow only calms slightly. "Go."

Kid, already on his feet mumbles, "I'm sure as fuck glad I only have one son. Girls are too much fucking trouble."

"You wouldn't understand what it's like to take care of a child, yours or not," Shadow spits before he raises his hands in surrender. Kincaid, still between us, removes his hands. "She sure as fuck deserves better than you."

I nod because it's the truth. Gigi deserves to be worshipped, deserves to have everything laid at her feet. She sure as hell doesn't deserve to have her ass beat in the darkness and her mouth fucked in restrooms.

"I was out of line," I concede because all I see is protective fire and love in his eyes, not jealousy or his own sense of sexual ownership.

Shadow joins Kid who has been hovering at the entrance to the kitchen, and they leave. The front door slams, and it seems to bring Kincaid back to his senses.

"Has making friends always been hard for you?" He takes his seat, and I follow his actions.

"I usually do better on my own," I answer.

"We're a fucking team here, Hound. Pissing off your VP, sleeping with the President's daughter, getting her pregnant isn't winning you any awards in the club right now."

"I know." What else can I say?

"Tell me about Isabella Montoya." It's not a question. I knew the truth would come out. I never planned to hide it deliberately from him, but the fewer people who knew about my daughter, the easier it was to keep her safe.

I spend the next twenty minutes explaining all of the same things I confessed to Gigi just days ago. He nods at some parts, jaw clenching at others, but he never interrupts me.

By the time I'm done, my eyes are glistening with the renewed loss of Izzy, the pain always just under the surface.

"We, as a club, can help you fight for custody," he says when I sit back in my chair emotionally exhausted.

I shake my head. "She'll be eighteen next summer. Then she can make her own decisions."

"That stepdad of hers seems like a complete asshole."

I chuckle. "He fucking hates me that's for sure, but he's good to her. I think he despises me more because Gabby wouldn't let him adopt her. Izzy doesn't have my last name, but at least she doesn't have his."

"A small consolation for missing out on your child's entire life. I couldn't even fucking imagine." He twists the cold cup of coffee on the table in front of him. "I hated being away from the girls, even for short-term missions. It's why we expanded and brought new guys in."

"It was easier when I was overseas fighting. I could push missing her out of my mind. I could focus on the job."

"So much for juice and crackers."

We both snap our heads up at Gigi walking into the kitchen. I clear my throat, a natural response to the sway of her tits under her thin dress. She's rumpled, sexy as fuck, and it's clear she fell back asleep after I left the room.

"Hey, Dad." She gives him a quick wave before walking over to the coffee pot.

"Let me help you," I say standing from my seat. I pull crackers from the cabinet and hand them to her with a quick kiss on the forehead. "Take a seat. I'll grab you some juice."

"Ginger ale," she specifies. "I've already gotten sick."

"How are you feeling, sweetheart," Kincaid asks as she joins him at the table.

"Sore," she says with a chuckle as she sits.

I hold my breath, waiting for her to taunt her dad with our activities from last night.

"Getting sick every morning is like an ab workout for people training for a damn triathlon," she adds.

She winks at me when I hand her the ginger ale. See? Even Gigi can make adult decisions.

Chapter 30

Gigi

I roll my eyes at my mom when she gasps, clutching at the base of her neck like I've ruined her delicate sensibilities.

"What else was I supposed to do?"

Misty busies herself with pouring another glass of wine for my mom.

"You can always come home," Mom answers.

"I'm here, unmarried and pregnant."

"And if Hound didn't sweep you off the sidewalk? You think you would've walked into that clinic and just… ended things?"

"That's what I was there for," I mutter. The thought of aborting my baby less than a week after I had made that final decision makes me sick to my stomach now.

"You would've changed your mind," Misty says as she sits beside me at the dining room table. "I did."

"What?" My eyes snap in her direction.

"I was in the room, sitting on the table talking with a nurse about my options before I realized it wasn't what I really wanted."

"Griffin?"

She nods, swallowing, her throat working under the effort.

"I thought I had no way out, no other choice."

"But you did have a choice."

Just as I had.

"I did," she agrees. "I thought adoption was better. The baby would have a chance to thrive, have someone who loved him, put him first when I wasn't capable."

"Adoption?" I'm confused. This is the first time she's ever said anything about any of this. Griffin is a few years older than us, and he's always just been around. I don't have a single childhood memory without him, Josephine, Samson, and Delilah in it. I know Samson and Delilah were adopted, but I don't recall when they came to live with Jaxon and Rob.

I laugh at the thought. "So Shadow found out and made you change your mind?"

"I wish," she mutters.

"Even though I'd already found a wonderful adoptive couple, the moment I held Griffin for the first time, I knew there was no way I could give him to someone else. I snuck out of the hospital and came here."

I smile, imagining Shadow welcoming her with open arms. He's one of the most loving men I know aside from Dad and Uncle Dom.

"I bet he was excited. A son and you. All of you together."

My mom laughs. Well, it's more of an incredulous snort.

"Hardly," Mom says.

"Shadow welcomed Griff with open arms. He made Misty fight and claw for his attention, for his love." She shakes her head. "It was pretty tense around the clubhouse for months."

I look back to Misty to see her smiling. "He finally came around."

"What made him?"

Her lips form a flat line, and I can tell she doesn't want to tell me exactly what pushed him into action. Misty looks at Mom who just tilts her head as if saying, *"You started the story, might as well finish it."*

"I left. I packed mine and Griff's things while he was away. When he came home, he found out we'd left. Showed up at my new apartment like he owned me and demanded I come back."

I lean in closer and grin when she shrugs.

"What did you do?"

"Within twenty-four hours, she and Griffin were back at the clubhouse. They were madly in love and inseparable," Mom says.

Misty chuckles. "We didn't fall in love overnight. It was growing for months. He was a stubborn ass and just wouldn't consider it."

"It took you leaving for him to come to terms with it." I look past my mom at nothing in particular as I let the information soak in.

"I know that look," Misty says as she touches my arm. I look at her, a small smile playing on my lips. "What worked for us may not work for you."

"What?" I recoil, my head pulling back a few inches. "I'm not going to run to make Jameson fall in love with me."

"But you want him to?" Mom asks.

"I don't want to raise this baby alone," I tell her. "But love doesn't necessarily play into that, I guess."

"Do you love him?" Misty asks.

I shrug. "I don't know. I really like him, but I don't have much dating experience, so I don't really know."

I crave him. My body needs his. But my heart? Who the hell knows?

"It may be too soon just yet. You'll know when you do. You won't be able to think of anything else. It'll consume you until that's all there is." Mom has this faraway look in her eyes, and I know how much she loves my dad. I want that. One day I want to look exactly like her, so in love with another person, that joy is all I feel when I think about them.

"Sounds like prison," I mutter, not ready to let anyone know what my heart desires.

They both laugh.

"Just you wait," Misty says with a pat on the top of my hand. "It's all-consuming. It's not like prison at all. More like a cocoon. There's nothing better than waking up every morning knowing half of your soul is lying right next to you."

I picture waking up this morning in Jameson's arms. All consuming is right. It was unbelievable, but it wasn't my heart that was clenching with love, it was my clit throbbing in need. I may be young, but I know there's a difference between lust and love.

I'm totally in lust with Jameson Rawley.

"Your birthday is in a week and a half," Mom reminds me as she stands to grab the bottle of wine off the counter.

I watch, not saying a word as she tops both her and Misty's glasses off.

"Planning a kegger?" I finally ask.

"Hardly," Misty laughs.

"I'll be twenty-one."

"Then we'll let you buy the alcohol for the party," Mom teases.

"Savage," I mutter, even though it doesn't really upset me. I always preferred coke over booze anyway, even though the hangovers were pretty fucking similar.

"So you're okay with a small party in the clubhouse?" I roll my eyes again.

"Or no party," I murmur.

"We have to do something," she insists. "I just didn't know if you were planning on hanging out with your friends."

"Really? I don't have any friends left in town," I remind her. "Is Ivy coming home?"

"She can't. Has some internship she signed up for."

I frown. I'm always in Ivy's shadow, but the thought of spending our first birthday apart makes me sad. I blame it on fluctuating hormones, and plaster a fake smile on my face.

"Can you make it earlier than usual? The thought of having to be awake past ten entertaining people makes me exhausted just thinking about it."

"I remember those days." Misty stands from the table and carries her empty wine glass to the sink. "I was tired the entire time I was pregnant with both boys."

"Speaking of your son, where is Cannon? I haven't even heard him mentioned since I've been back."

Misty looks down at her watch as if she expects him any minute. "He's still at school."

I may be the only one from Cerberus that never had any intentions of college. Cannon is in San Diego at college.

"Is he doing well?"

Cannon was almost as wild as I was in high school, but the same rules didn't apply to him since he has a dick. The double standard was always a subject of contention for me.

"He's struggling," Misty says. "College is just one party after another for him. He's missing class, failing most subjects. Shadow has spoken with him, and things get better for a while, but I suspect they'll kick him out soon."

Mom rubs a hand over Misty's back, but she only looks down into her wine glass as if it holds the answers for her son's future.

"And Samson?" Changing the subject is all I can think to do. I have no advice to give on Cannon.

"Still in Denver working some sort of internship with Ian Hale," she advises. "He should be home for Thanksgiving."

"I've missed so much." She gives me a weak smile.

"But you're home now." She kisses my forehead before walking toward the door. "That's what counts. See you ladies later. Shadow is going to want dinner shortly."

"See ya," I say as Mom says, "Later."

"I guess Khloe is at school also?"

Mom stands at the sink, handwashing both wine glasses.

"Yeah. Kid is losing his mind because she's been moved up to advanced placement English."

"Why would that bother Kid?"

Mom laughs as if she's remembering some inside joke. "Well, it seems some of the high school boys find her attractive."

I nod my head with a smile. "I can see that. She's beautiful."

"She is," Mom agrees. "Kid is spitting nails, doing his best not to get arrested for beating up children at school."

"Geez," I huff. "Dad, Kid, Shadow...every one of them are like alpha Rambos."

Mom laughs hard. "Don't think for one minute that Hound isn't exactly the same way."

My thighs clench at the memories of just how controlling Jameson is.

Chapter 31

Hound

"He's trying to keep us apart," Gigi mutters from the bed as I grab clothes out of the dresser and shove them into my rucksack.

"It's just work," I counter. "I have to work."

"He knows my birthday is in a week, and he's making sure you're not here."

Her brow crinkles, and damn if she isn't adorable.

"You want to celebrate your birthday with me?"

She gives me a small, sad smile. "I just don't want to spend any time apart from you."

Her confession makes my pulse thrum in my ears.

"Not tired of me yet?" I stuff the last of my clothes in the bag and pull the cord to close it. "You'll miss me?"

Her head tilts, and she looks at me as if I'm an idiot.

"I'll miss your cock," she teases a few seconds later.

"Really?" I prowl toward her, arms on either side of her crossed legs. "You know I can deny you my cock even if I'm here."

Her breathing slows, growing erratic. "But you won't."

I nip at her bottom lip. "You know better than to challenge me."

Her delicate, pink tongue sweeps out to the injured flesh of her lip. "You know I like everything you give me."

The tips of her fingers run down my chest, still naked from our shower not long ago, to the button on my jeans.

"I think you cause trouble just so I'll spank your ass."

She smiles, soft and knowing. "You're a very smart man."

We've spent the better part of the last two weeks barricaded in my room, only leaving every once in a while to 'date.'

Her dad hasn't cornered me, but he still has that look on his face, as if he's tasting something nasty, when he sees us together. Shadow's attitude from the kitchen has disappeared, so I'm certain Kincaid has told him the story about Gabby and her parents and the true reasons I'm not a father to my daughter.

I've heard bits and pieces about his and Misty's story and the fact that she didn't tell him she was pregnant. He missed the doctor's appointments, feeling the baby kick, and his birth. Because of this, I know he has to have some apathy for my situation. Although he may feel bad for me, he hasn't extended any courtesy or offered more than a working relationship. The guys hang out in the garage, and I chill in my room with Gigi.

This next mission, the first since we arrived back from Vegas will be a test. I was able to get along with the Cerberus men on missions before, but I have no clue how things are going to go now.

Scooter and Rocker have at least been courteous, but I can tell they're keeping their distance, no doubt following their Prez's leadership.

"One more time before you leave?" Gigi all but begs.

I chuckle. This woman is insatiable, waking up with sex, not going to bed until I've come inside of her, not to mention the times I wake in the night with her mouth or hands on my cock.

"You're going to kill me," I mutter against her lips.

"I'm just trying to keep you young."

She moans, breathy and ragged when I slip my fingers under my t-shirt she's taken to wearing for bed. Her heated flesh against my fingertips, the feel of her tight cunt fisting my cock is going to be hard to go without.

"I'll let you come one more time," I concede. "But you don't get to come once while I'm gone."

"No promises," she pants against my mouth.

"Fine." I shrug and pull my hand from where it was cresting her entrance.

"No," she whines and reaches for me.

"If you plan to get yourself off while I'm gone, then you can just start today."

"It's not..." she sighs and crosses her arms over her chest, leaning and pressing her back against the headboard. "It's not the same. When I come alone, it's nothing like when I do it with you."

"I know," I agree because fuck if jacking off is anything like orgasming inside her mouth or pussy. I've only come with my hand on my dick once since we returned with news of her pregnancy, and even then I was edging her, teasing her as I refused to let her come.

"Please," she begs.

"Now or later?"

Her eyes narrow and damn I hate leaving her.

"Now," she decides.

I press my fingers back to her slit, toying with the bundle of nerves at the top. She whimpers, rolling her hips, begging me without words to enter her.

"I'll know if you masturbate, Gigi." I press the tips of two fingers inside. "And if you do, I'll make you wait months before you get off on my fingers..."

I press deeper, my middle finger rubbing over that spot that drives her crazy.

"Or my mouth." I lick inside of hers enough to tease her. "Or on my cock."

"You wouldn't," she moans.

"Try me and find out," I warn, before bending my head and biting her nipple through the t-shirt.

She's lost, giving in to her release. By the time her eyes focus, my mouth is on her, and I'm licking her through a second orgasm.

She's weightless, completely pliable, and begging me to stop when I'm done fucking her through a third and coming inside her.

"Remember what I said."

I kiss her again, knowing we're already on borrowed time.

"I'll miss you," I confess against her lips before turning to the bathroom to get cleaned up.

"You'll miss this pussy," she mutters, and I can tell she didn't say it for me to hear.

We've been inseparable for weeks, and yet she's still waiting for me to disappear, to toss her out and replace her. What the beautiful woman sitting on my bed doesn't realize, is for the first time in my life I'm not planning on my next chick to fuck, because she's the only one I can imagine fucking, now and in the foreseeable future.

"You, Georgia Leigh Anderson." I give her a solicitous smile. "I'll miss your pussy too, though."

One last kiss and I pull away, lingering against her mouth. Feeling the heat of her body will only make things worse later.

"The guys," she begins, but she's shaking her head when I look over my shoulder at her.

"What is it?"

"The guys look for women after the missions are done."

"Okay?" She's right. They normally stay one extra day and use it to do the paperwork wrap up and finding pussy is on the top of the list for most of the guys.

"Will you be, you know, looking for a woman?" If she were jealous, I'd be turned on, but the insecurity in her voice nearly guts me.

"Will you go out and look for someone to fuck while I'm gone?"

Her head snaps up. "Of course not!"

"Why not?"

"Because you're all that I want."

"Exactly," I tell her and walk out of the room.

Staying aloof and never really talking about the emotional side of what's going on with us is difficult. Yeah, we can mask what we're feeling with sex and depravity, but the heart side of things is always right there on the cusp. Well, it is for me. Unsure of how she feels about what's going on between us is what keeps my lips closed tight.

"About fucking time," Scooter complains when I walk down the front steps of the clubhouse.

"Listen, guys." I look over to see Kincaid, Shadow, and Snatch standing near an SUV. It's then that I notice that there are three, rather than the usual two, ready to leave. "This should only take us five days, six tops."

"They're going along with us?" I whisper to Scooter.

"Looks that way." He claps his hands, rubbing them together in excitement. "Working with those guys is the highlight of my fucking year."

"It was my understanding that they no longer did this sort of thing."

"Like I said," he repeats. "Highlight of my year."

"Children," Kincaid chides as he looks in our direction. "If I may continue?"

I shift my rucksack from one shoulder to the other and give him my full attention.

"This job is domestic. This isn't a rescue."

Scooter is all but bouncing around like an unmedicated child with ADHD.

"This is—"

"An assassination," I interrupt.

Both Shadow and Snatch look in my direction, but it's the hard look Kincaid gives me that makes me stand up straighter.

"I'm giving you a chance to opt out," Kincaid says, and no one moves. "Your dossiers are in the trucks. Load up."

I move in the same direction as Scooter and Rocker. They've been my men since our first mission.

"Hound," Kincaid says just before I lift my boot to climb inside the SUV. "You're with us."

Scooter snickers. "Like a visit to the principal's office." He laughs again. "Maybe he'll spank you like you spank his daughter."

"Fuck off," I hiss before turning back around and walking toward the Prez's SUV. "We need to get our own place." I mutter.

It's not the first time I thought it, but Gigi hasn't brought it back up, and I know I can't do it without her dad's permission. Hopefully, I'll get a chance to ask him during this trip. When I climb in behind Shadow who's driving and meet the tattooed stare coming from Snatch, I realize I may not get the opportunity.

I busy myself with the folder of information that was left in my seat.

"The President?" I ask. Knots form in my stomach.

"Ever met him?" Snatch doesn't even look at me when he speaks.

"I—" I release the folder and run a rough hand over the top of my head. "We served in Glein together, when all of that Carpathian shit was coming to a head."

"Fuck," Shadow says from the driver's seat.

"Yeah," I mutter. "Melwas Kocur is a piece of shit."

"That's putting it nicely," Snatch mutters on my right.

"I went to the boat with Colchester and Moore to save the kids while the fucking church burned to the ground. My best friend died outside of the church that day." I shake my head trying and failing to stop the flood of memories. "Severe food poisoning and a two-day hospital stay is the only thing that probably kept me alive in Badon. Colchester lost more than two-thirds of his men that night."

"He's our assignment."

My eyes snap to Kincaid. Surely I didn't hear him correctly.

"He's our Commander in Ch—"

"Keep reading," Kincaid orders.

I do, finding that my assumption is all wrong. We're not there to assassinate the President of the United States but prevent an attempt on his life.

I look up nodding. We've all carried out commands in the military, and even now as a former Marine, my service to God and country doesn't end. When I met Maxen Colchester, he wasn't the President but a Captain in the Army.

"Does this mean what I think it means?" There's only one way to get close to the President without causing questions and a media uproar.

Snatch smiles over at me, giving me his full attention this time.

"Yep." Kincaid chuckles. "We're gonna be Secret Service."

"Dream job?" Shadow asks looking at me in the rearview mirror.

"Hardly," I confess. "Don't get me wrong, they have a serious fucking job to do. I'm more of an action man myself, but I can admit that it's always been sort of a bucket list thing for me."

Protecting the President? What soldier wouldn't jump at that opportunity?

"This is the second time we've been called to do this. Once with Fitzgerald after Monica, and now with President Colchester," Kincaid informs.

"Wait," I say looking over at Snatch. I circle my face and point to his. "You just gonna stand in your black suit with all that ink and metal on your face?"

He laughs. "The jewelry has to come out. We can't have anything metal on our persons. We have to go through security before we suit up with Secret Service issued weapons. The tats will be covered up with theatrical makeup."

"That means," I begin.

"The metal is going to have to come out of your cock, too." Kincaid shakes his head at Snatch's information dump and looks out the window.

"Joy," I mutter as we near the airport housing the Cerberus private plane.

***

"He even kind of looks like a wizard," I mutter to Scooter as we stand in the background while Kincaid and Shadow speak with Merlin Rhys about the night's objectives. "Maybe because of his dark eyes?"

"I don't know what it is about him, but he doesn't look like someone I want to cross," Scooter replies.

"Definitely not," I mutter just as those dark eyes look from Kincaid in my direction. As if he's somehow looking into my soul, I can't break the hold he has on me.

I'm locked in his stare as he nods at Kincaid and walks past him, right in my direction.

"Lieutenant Rawley," Merlin says as he holds his hand out.

"Sir." I'm confused as to how he knows my name when I've never set eyes on this man before. He's some sort of adviser to the Party, so I'm certain it's his job to know everyone who has the chance of coming into contact with Colchester. I take his proffered hand, and a chill runs over my body at the contact.

"A moment of your time?" He tilts his head in the direction of a quiet corner.

I sidestep Scooter and turn in the direction Mr. Rhys indicates. Once in the abandoned corner of the room, he looks around, exhaustion crinkling the corner of his eyes.

"Mr. Anderson has your team's directions, and he'll go over those with you momentarily, but I need to speak to you about your expectations when the President dies tonight."

***

"Thank you for having me as your President," Colchester says as he concludes his side of the debate. "It's been the greatest honor I can imagine."

My eyes scan the crowd, searching for any sign of discord. I look in people's eyes, watch their hands, trying to find someone, anyone that is disgruntled or pissed about any of the men standing on the stage at my back.

I can't see the President, but his words echo in my ears. He sounds resigned, as if he knows what's going to happen tonight. Having this debate, knowing there is such a serious threat to his life or the life of the former Vice President is a stupid idea, but I'm not a politician, and those decisions are way above my pay grade, which is exactly what Merlin Rhys said when I informed him of my opinion during our conversation.

A man in the corner rolls his eyes at Colchester's words, but before I can inform Rocker, who's closest to him, there's a commotion to my right.

I'm moving the second I see the cameraman nearly knock over his camera, the dolly getting trapped around cords taped to the ground. I'm mere feet from him when he reaches into his pocket, like it's the most natural thing in the fucking world to pull out a utility knife in the presence of dozens of Secret Service and the President of the fucking United States.

Shadow is taking action as well as one other Service member. The camera crashes to the ground, a deafening sound, as people scramble and scream all around us. Once we get our hands on him, he's easier to wrestle to the ground than I presume a would-be assassin should be.

I stand once the cameraman is subdued, but as Shadow is talking into his mic, I hear a different kind of scream at my back. Turning, I see commotion erupt on the stage. The blood-curdling scream came from Greer Colchester, the First Lady.

"It was a diversion," I yell.

Kincaid, Shadow, and I swarm the stage along with several other Service members.

"Strength in the Mountains," the man under the President chants. The familiar Carpathian motto sends a shiver up my spine.

"There's strength here, too," Mr. President claims, and I've never felt prouder of a soldier in my life.

I notice a knife wound bleeding on his bicep, as the First lady and Embry Moore cling to him.

"The ambulance is ready. The paramedics are coming now," Kincaid says as he pushes in closer to the injured President.

It isn't until I slide in closer that I see the ceramic knife sticking out of Colchester's stomach. My blood runs cold even while my body acts. Kincaid grabs Embry Moore who looks like he can't decide between staunching the blood flow and cupping his President's jaw. The First Lady is sobbing uncontrollably and whispering to him.

The gurney arrives, and Colchester is lifted from the ground in less than ninety seconds after the attack. Mrs. Colchester clings to her husband, kissing him frantically before I pull her away. This wasn't part of my plan for tonight. Rhys told me to stay with Colchester no matter what, so after I grab her, I hand her off to another agent and go back to the President's side.

I see a flash of a fist, as Embry Moore tries to fight Kincaid who is wrapped around his front. The punch doesn't land, but it only takes seconds to get him under control and whisked away.

Protocol is protocol. We're trained to act, to ensure the safety of both of them, and even though going one way while President Colchester's bleeding body is pushed in a different direction is the last thing either of them wants, it's exactly what has to happen.

"This way," Mr. Rhys says as he directs paramedics who look more military than medical down a dark hallway.

They don't question the man. They act, just like everyone did on stage, just like we're all clearly trained to do. Seconds later the President's gurney is being pushed into the back of the ambulance.

"Hurry," Merlin urges when I go to step back.

Recognizing his intention, I climb in the back with them. I watch, stunned, as a man in scrubs works on Maxen Colchester. An IV is inserted, and blood from a bag begins to replace what's spilled both from his arm and stomach wounds. The guy in scrubs works, the paramedics providing him with help before he even asks for it. I'm stunned by the silence, confused why we're racing down dark city streets with no sirens, yet not having to slow once for traffic.

"We lost him," I hear Merlin say into a phone I didn't even know he'd pulled out. "Protocol says we head to the funeral home. He'll be cremated immediately. Those were his wishes. Thank you, Belvedere."

He ends the call and grasps the ashen hand of the President.

After no more than five minutes, the ambulance stops and the back doors are pulled open. I step out and take in my surroundings. A field hospital, one so advanced and equipped, it rivals many metropolitan ones I've been in.

The President, now with a solid heartbeat according to the machine connected to the gurney, is pushed further into the room where half a dozen medical staff wait, leaving Merlin and me alone.

He pulls an envelope from his pocket and hands it to me. "This is your debrief on what happened tonight."

I take it, but I'm too stunned to speak.

"Maxen thanks you for your service, both here tonight and in Glein."

I swallow. "I didn't think he remembered me."

"He remembers everyone. You were a Patriot then as you are one again tonight. You're the reason Cerberus was called in." And then he's gone.

Chapter 32

Gigi

"Thank you," I tell Khloe with a small smile on my face.

"That spray hose is the best thing ever. This version is much better than the one we had."

"Sweet."

I place the baby bath beside me as Mom hands me another gift. Why we're doing this in light of what happened a few days ago, I'll never understand.

Everyone has been upset, the news of the President's assassination making it to us before Cerberus even returned from DC. Those of us in New Mexico had no clue that is where the guys went, but we, along with the rest of the nation, watched in horror as a Carpathian rebel stabbed Maxen Colchester in the stomach, the wound becoming fatal on the way to the hospital.

"Happy Birthday," Mom says and kisses my forehead. "This is from Misty."

It's my birthday. Although twenty-one today, there is such a heaviness in the room and no one seems to want to address it. Jameson was with President Colchester when he took his last breath, yet he refuses to talk about it, citing it's club business and shit about national security. I pull apart the wrapping paper and look down at the gift in my lap.

"What in the world?"

Mom chuckles and comes back to stand beside me. "It's a breast pump."

"Okay?"

Misty laughs along with Mom, and it seems out of place even though a week ago things would've been different.

"Sometimes when you're new to nursing, you get sore. The pump will be a lifesaver."

"Actually, I'm not going to have a problem with sore nipples. The fuck," I hiss when Jameson pinches my thigh.

"You don't plan to breastfeed?" Misty asks. "I mean it's your choice, but your mom did, so I just figured you would."

"We," I turn my head to glare at Jameson as my thigh burns from his warning. "I haven't decided yet."

He kisses my cheek, not giving a shit that we're in the middle of the clubhouse. The first ring of people around us are the women, and the outer ring is filled with irritated Cerberus men, new and old, who've been forced, by my mother no doubt, to help me celebrate my birthday.

The real reason I earned a pinch on my thigh was that he knows me well enough, even after just a couple of weeks spending time together that I was going to blurt something about my sex life. He knew there was the possibility of mentioning the nipple clamps, or how I come so hard when he's fucking me as his teeth are nearly cutting into my puckered flesh.

I shift in my seat.

"She's uncomfortable," Dad advises the entire room. "Em, let her open those more private gifts while she's alone."

I'm not embarrassed but every one of his men are here and no doubt imagining my tits after the explanation of the pump. *He's* the uncomfortable one.

"Last one," Mom says and hands me a small box.

"That," Jameson says snatching the box from my hand. "Is for later."

Dad groans again, this time walking right out the front door. The other men follow as Mom, Misty, Khloe, and Aunt Mak start cleaning up.

"When are you going to let me have my gift?"

"Maybe never if you don't get out of this birthday funk you're in," he warns.

"I miss my sister," I confess. "This is our first birthday apart."

He looks confused. "You were on the phone with her for two hours earlier."

"I know." Standing from the chair, I begin to gather the gifts. "She's usually the sentimental one, yet I was the one crying about her not being here."

"You're hormonal," Aunt Mak says with a soft pat on my back as she takes the gifts from my hands. "It'll pass."

"About two months after the baby is born," Misty says.

"If she's lucky," Khloe mutters, and I know she's remembering the post-partum depression she struggled with for a while.

"That's not all that's bothering you," Jameson whispers in my ear as we make our way back to his room.

"I don't have any right to bitch about petty shit," I mumble and flop down on his soft bed.

"Never stopped you before," he teases as he props my feet on his lap, drops my flip flops to the floor and begins rubbing the soles.

"Before, the country wasn't in mourning. Before, I wasn't pregnant. Before the things that seemed petty to others weren't petty for me."

"Still." I moan when his thumb presses hard, working at the knot in my arch. "Tell me why you're upset."

"Every one of the gifts I got today was a baby gift."

"Okay." He keeps rubbing.

"It's my birthday, Jameson. Yet, they turned it into a baby shower."

"Ever think that the reason they got things for the baby now instead of later is because they're worried that you're going to take off again, and they want the baby to have the things it needs?"

"Well shit. I'm not going anywhere."

"I know that, but you've taken off too many times for them to believe that." Releasing my foot, he leans in and presses his lips against mine. "My gift isn't for the baby."

When he pulls away, my tongue licks against the tingle his beard left behind.

"No?"

He shakes his head, the playful twitch at the corner of his mouth making me narrow my eyes, suspicion growing low in my gut. I shake the box, smiling when it gives off an interesting rattle.

"Car keys?" I beam up at him.

"Fat chance. Open it and see."

I tug the ribbon and let it fall into my lap. I can't help but laugh when I take the top off.

"My dad would've killed you if I opened that out in the living room," I say with a chuckle.

"I have plans, devious plans for you tonight," he warns.

"And they include this?"

I look down again at the *gift*. The shiny butt plug looks innocuous nestled in tissue paper, but I know it's not. He's threatened to take me there, vowed that it will happen sooner or later, but he's not gone any further than the tip of one finger.

"I want you to wear it." He gives me a heated stare, and who am I to object? I nod, the corners of my mouth lifting into a smile to match his.

"We're going to Denver. You'll wear it on the drive."

I shift my weight on the bed.

"Denver?" He nods. "That's over seven hours away."

Without a word, he takes the plug from the box and disappears into the bathroom. When he comes back out, he's holding a small bottle of lube I've never seen before. It's not something we've ever needed before. I'm always wet and ready for him. It doesn't matter if we're teasing each other for hours or he just gives me a certain look. I always slicken for him, my body ready for him all the time.

"Turn over and pull your dress up."

I obey, gasping when he hitches my hips up forcing me to my knees. Wasting no time, he tugs my thong to the side. Fingers, already slick with the cold gel, sweep over my backside.

"Fuck," he mutters. "Seven hours is a long ass time."

"Forever," I agree and push back into the fingers he's pressing into me.

"I don't know that I can wait."

I hiss and try to scoot away when the cool metal of my gift brushes my anus.

"Settle down." His tone doesn't leave room for objection. That husky growl is just like when I'm riding him, and he's so close to coming but doesn't want to give into the explosion of pleasure just yet.

I yelp when his heavy hand slaps the crease where my ass meets thigh.

"I didn't move," I complain.

He ignores me. "Push back into it. Ah fuck, yeah Gigi just like that."

There's a burn that somehow is also pleasurable. I feel the toy slip into place, and the fullness is only a tease. I wiggle, adjusting to the intrusion, and groan when he taps on it.

"How does it feel?"

I begin to answer him, but then his fingers are in my soaked pussy, and I'm left speechless.

"Dammit," he grumbles. "There's no way I can wait."

I smile at the sound of his zipper.

"What about delayed gratification?" I tease.

"Never been good at it," he confesses before slamming inside of me.

"Oh, God," I cry.

I'm so full as the ring through his head taunts that spot deep inside, and the fullness of his cock presses against the thin layer of skin separating him from the plug.

I'm a writhing mess. He's everywhere, inside of me, fingers bruising my hips in his grasp, mouth biting at the delicate skin of my shoulder blades.

"You can come," he offers.

And I chuckle at the absurdity of his permission. As if I could prevent the orgasm that rushes through my body and explodes in a blinding light behind my eyes.

"Fuck, fuck, fuck," he chants before stiffening, buried to the base of his cock. I'm so full of him and the toy, I can easily feel each pulse of his dick during his release.

I whimper when he withdraws and purr like a happy little kitten when he cleans me with a warm washcloth.

"Not a chance," he whispers against my lips.

My eyes flutter open to find him leaning in close. "Just for a minute."

"You can sleep in the car," he offers. "We have an appointment."

Biting my lips when he helps me off of the bed, I can see both satisfaction and longing in his eyes.

"I think this is doing just as much for you as it is me."

I rock from one foot to the other, not having a damn clue how I'm going to leave this room and out of the front of the clubhouse without everyone knowing exactly what's going on.

"You have no idea."

Walking to the door, I stop just before my hand grabs the knob.

"What's wrong?" he asks as his hand sweeps down my back and over my ass coming dangerously close to my gift.

"I think I'll come before I make it outside."

"Your mom and dad are out there," he reminds me. "You really want to explain that?"

I walk, slowly and deliberately, and much to my embarrassment the guys that left the party earlier for cleanup are back inside. The entire Cerberus MC is here to watch my plugged walk of shame.

"You guys heading out?" Dad asks as we enter the living area.

"Yeah," Jameson answers, but I just ignore him, face scrunched in concentration as I walk to the door.

"She not feeling well?" Dad asks behind me.

"She's tired," Jameson says making my excuses. "I'll make sure she gets plenty of rest."

"Drive safe," Dad says as Jameson joins me, hand at the small of my back.

"No," I say as we come down the front steps and I see the Jeep waiting. "I'm not getting into that."

"Your dad thinks we're heading to Denver to have the seats reupholstered. We have to take it."

He opens the passenger side door.

"Jameson, this thing bounces all over the road."

He just stares into my eyes.

"I can hardly walk and keep it together."

Mirth takes over his smile, and I realize this vehicle is as much a part of his game as the plug is.

"Imagine how many times you'll come between now and Denver." He nips at my bottom lip. "Play along, and I may even make a half-way pit stop to fuck you again."

Chapter 33

Hound

"What is this place?" Gigi asks with her neck craned so she can see out of the side window.

I don't answer, rather just watch her, loving the pink blush on her cheeks from the drive over. I promised we'd stop once so I could take care of her needy pussy. We ended up stopping twice. The plug in her ass, the tiny whimpering noises she made relentlessly as we drove was enough to drive me mad.

"The Hale-ish Retreat and Spa?" She turns her head, looking at me over her shoulder. "I could use a massage."

"Maybe next time," I offer. "Tonight is going to go a little differently than you're thinking."

I adjust my cock behind its denim confines and climb out of the crappy Jeep. She has the passenger-side door open by the time I walk around the front.

"It's a spa," she whines. "I'm sure they specialize in massages."

"The spa is closed."

Confusion draws in her brow as I help her jump down from the seat.

"You've never heard any of the guys talking about this place?"

She chuckles. "Cerberus men aren't the type to get facials and hot stone rubdowns."

I smile, loving the innocence I'm going to command tonight.

"They don't go through the front door," I say as I reach down for her hand and walk around the corner of the building.

She sighs, pulling another smile to my lips. "This night is weird. Why are you making this weird?"

"It's only going to get weirder." I turn to face her, arms on her shoulders, so she knows to pay attention. "If you want to leave at any time, all you have to do is say the word."

"Yep, weirder." She tries to look over my shoulder at the nondescript door at my back, but I shift her again so she can look into my eyes.

"I need you to wear this." I pull a thin mask from my back pocket and begin to tie it around her head. It's soft and looks like a gorgeous monarch butterfly. "If it got back to Garrett or Alexa that I brought you here, your dad would probably gut me."

She gasps, eyes searching mine. "As in Garrett Hale?" I nod. "Oh, God."

My cheeks hurt with the size of my grin. "You know where you're at now."

She nods quickly, her throat working on a rough swallow. "I've always been curious about this place."

"So you have heard the guys talking about it?"

"Yes," she whispers.

I turn, grabbing her hand again and taking another step closer to the door. She doesn't budge.

"What's wrong?"

She shakes her head. "I don't..." Another thick swallow. "I can't have sex in front of people. Stripping is one thing, but this—"

My lips are on hers before she can say another word. I lick into her mouth, bite at her lips, all the while my hands are tight on her ass and grinding her on my rock-hard cock.

"I'd never share the sight of your pussy with another person," I pant against her mouth when I'm finally in control enough to pull away. "Trust me?"

She nods, and this time when I take her hand and pull her toward the door, she follows.

Having made an appointment last week, the sign in process is quick, and before long we're led into a wide-open room. I hold her against my chest as we stand just inside letting our eyes adjust to the dimly lit room.

The soft thump of music surrounds us, as does the heat and humidity of more than a dozen people in all stages of sexual activity.

"Wow," Gigi mutters.

"What do you think?" I ask with my head bent close to her ear. The shudder that runs down her spine is familiar. It's the same way her body reacts to mine when I look at her with need and desperation. For good measure, I dip my legs and press my erection against her, knowing it's rubbing against the plug in her ass. I started her out small but increased its size both times we stopped to quench my thirst for her pussy.

"I'm wet."

Two words, with enough power to make me nearly come in my jeans.

"Happy birthday." I kiss her temple and try to get my libido under control.

"No one's ever given me an orgy for my birthday before."

My grip on her middle tightens. "I sure as fuck hope not."

"Let's go to the room," I offer.

"Room?" She tilts her head to the side to look at me. "I want to watch."

"Believe me, gorgeous. You'll get to watch."

I direct her down a darkened hallway, thankful for the instructions I got in an email when I made the appointment. Nothing is less sexy than having to stop and ask directions when all you want to do is get naked.

I type in the passcode I was given, and the door opens with a soft beep.

"No," she says and stops no less than two feet inside of the room.

"They can't see us," I promise as we both look across the room and see another couple on the other side of a large window. "They want to be watched, but they don't want to see us. We want to watch but not be seen."

"Th-they can't see in here?" She hasn't moved, legs locked and refusing to get any closer.

Stepping around her, I wave my hands near the glass and try to get their attention.

"Look," I say motioning to a small TV in the corner. "All they can see is their reflection. They know there's a chance someone will be in this room, but they can't be one hundred percent sure."

She closes the distance between us until her palms are flat against the glass. The swipe of her tongue on her perfectly pink lip makes my cock jump.

"She looks like she's having a good time." Her words are breathy, arousal clear in the tone.

I crowd her, leaning over her back, every inch of my body I can manage touching some part of hers.

"We can turn the sound on, listen to her as he tongues her to orgasm."

She nods, almost erratically.

Leaning to the side, I grab the remote on the small table and hit the sound button. The woman's gasps fill the room. The man devouring her releasing guttural grunts as he feasts on his woman.

Gigi is entranced, squirming and needful as she watches the illicit show. Unable to wait another second longer, I tug down the zipper of her dress and pull it over her head. I hate that her breasts have been too sore to wear a bra the last week, but fuck if I don't love the sight of her gorgeous tits. The nipples, a shade or two darker than her stage days, are puckered and beading, reaching toward the glass and the other couple.

With a slight push of my hand against her back, I press until the tips of her breasts touch the cold glass. She hisses, but it turns into a moan matching that of the other woman as she orgasms.

"That's so fucking hot," she mutters.

I don't respond, too busy working her thong down her thighs. Instinctually, she arches her back and angles her ass out, presenting herself to me, exactly the way I like, only this time is different. This time the bright red jewel on the plug in her ass reflects the soft light in the room. It's my turn to swallow and breathe.

"Fuck," I grumble when two fingers sweep at her seam, finding it soaked and swollen for me.

"She's..." She doesn't finish her sentence, but I look around her, and I know immediately what she's seeing as the man pulls his mouth from the cunt he's been eating and spreads her legs even further.

"The plug in your ass is bigger," I say with a punctuated press of my erection against her ass.

"Your cock is much bigger. It scares me." Those are her words, but her ass is still pushing against me, rotating ever so often in a tiny circle.

"It will be uncomfortable at first, but by the time it's over, you'll be begging me for more."

My fingers roam down the front of her stomach, pausing briefly over my growing little boy before sliding through the slickness of her desire.

"I need you on the bed."

She nods but doesn't make to move there until I turn her shoulders in that direction. She goes, eyes never pulling from the action on the other side of the room. When she lies on her back, and her thighs fall open, I can feel my cock weeping in my jeans.

"We're going to mimic them," I inform her as I pull a small bottle of lube and a condom from my pocket before shedding my clothes.

"You missed the first step," she says petulantly referring to the oral.

"I've made you come several times today with my mouth," I remind her.

Fuck, the way she looked sitting on the steering wheel with her pussy right in my face. I'll never forget it.

"True," she agrees. "Better hurry."

I follow her eyes and see that the other woman is wrapping her mouth around his cock. I shake my head. "If you put your mouth on my cock right now, I'll come." I crawl up her body, licking at her knees, thighs, and tits on my way up. "And I'm coming in your ass tonight."

She whimpers with another delicious rotation of her hips.

"Stop." The unfamiliar voice throws me for a second before I turn my head and watch the man grip a pile of the woman's hair and pull her off his cock.

"Seems he's having the same problem," she says with a chuckle.

We watch, entranced as the woman is thrown to her back and the guy slams inside of her. Flexing my hips, I'm only a few seconds behind him, groaning when Gigi's cunt only opens enough to fit the head of my cock inside of her.

"Oh God," she pants. "So full."

With the larger plug in her ass, there's no way to sink all the way in without hurting her.

"Feel good?" She nods, but the glint in her eye tells me she's not exactly sure.

I press my thumb to her clit as the moaning of the couple fills the room around us.

"Can they hear us?" she whispers.

I shake my head, my hips moving, my cock looking for just one more inch of her glorious heat. I inch forward again when her mouth finds mine. I'm breathless when we break apart, shattered in her arms, and thinking about a future I haven't allowed myself to imagine in a very long time.

Her head tilts, and I utilize the opportunity to suck at the soft skin on her neck.

"Mmm. He's taking the plug out."

I turn my head to see the guy back on his haunches, thumb toying with the woman's clit as he works the plug from her body, so I do the same.

I press harder with my thumb when she whimpers as the largest part of the toy stretches the tight ring. With my hand still against her body, I tear the rubber open with my teeth and roll it down my cock.

She looks at me confused.

"The condom is for easier cleanup," I explain, working the bottle of lube open with my mouth and coating the tips of my fingers. I'm obsessed with the frown on her pretty face, knowing how much she loves my come dripping out of her. "Don't worry. Next time I fuck your ass, I'll fill you up."

Her bottom lip rolls between her teeth when I press my slickened fingers against her ass. It doesn't stop the moan when I dip two and then three fingers in her prepared opening.

"You ready?" I ask as I pull my hand from her pussy and add a thick layer of lube to my throbbing cock.

She nods, glancing quickly at the other couple. Either the guy is incredibly eager or anal sex isn't new for them because he's pounding away in her like his ass is on fire.

Her eyes widen when I press the tip of my cock against her. "Please," she begs. "Go slow."

"Of course," I say to calm her nerves. Now, I pray my body complies.

I lean over her, my mouth breathing in her shallow pants as I press deeper. When she tenses, I lick at her lips, grip her hips in assurance, and still my hips.

"Give it a second." I bite at her lip when she squeezes her eyes closed. "Look at me."

I watch her, search her eyes for the level of discomfort that will make me back away.

"More," she moans after an endless moment.

I give her what she asks for, sliding my aching cock forward another inch. When she doesn't tense up like the first time, I keep going, pressing into her, teeth grinding from the softness, from the heat, and from the grip she has encased my cock.

"All the way?" she asks with a quiver in her voice.

"Yeah, gorgeous. I'm all the way in." She nods, the sheen of tears forming on her lower lashes. "Is it too much?"

She nods at first, but then her head shakes back and forth.

"I have to move," I warn.

"Please," she begs again.

The first couple of slow thrusts are met with tense, tight muscles, but they evolve until she's pressing against me, meeting my movements with her own.

"You're mine." I push as deep as I can go. "Your beautiful mouth. This tight pussy."

Turning my hand face up, I push two fingers inside of her and stroke the front wall of her clenching cunt.

"This ass." I pull out and slam back in. "My baby inside of you. Every part of you belongs to me."

I lean forward, pressing my lips against her left breast as my hips surge and my fingers plunder.

"This amazing heart." I kiss the flesh, my lips trembling against her skin. "I own all of it."

"I'm going to cum," she hisses, but I knew this already. Her pussy clenches, her ass tightens, and her eyes roll back into her head.

"Mine," I grunt one final time before spilling inside of the condom.

I stay inside of her, fingers working in tandem with the flutters of her pussy as she comes down from her orgasm. It isn't until she whimpers, finally coming back to reality that I give in and drag myself out of her.

"Happy birthday," I whisper against the crown of her head as I pull her into my arms.

"Best. Birthday. Ever."

Chapter 34

Gigi

"Hey," I look up when something taps against my foot. "It's the holidays. You aren't supposed to be sad."

I look over at my twin and smile.

"I'm not sad." The response is immediate, but I know deep down it's a lie.

Jameson has been gone for last three weeks, and I haven't spoken to him in two days. The aura around my dad and Shadow is thick. I know something is wrong, but they won't speak to me about it.

All I get is "It's confidential club business."

"Well, you seem mopey. We should go to Jake's."

I roll my eyes at her. "Right. Sorry."

I watch as she tips her wine glass to her lips. Not drinking isn't a problem for me, but the torture of knowing I can't even if I wanted to is like sandpaper to my skin.

"How's my nephew doing?" I smile and look at her only to find her eyes focused across the room.

Griffin.

Of course, her attention is with him even though she's sitting and making small talk with me.

"They found out he has two heads. So it's more like Siamese twins than just one baby."

She smiles. "I bet he's going to be adorable."

"He has hooves like a zebra. Hurts really badly when he kicks."

"Sounds good," she says standing without warning and crossing the room.

I hear a chuckle on my other side, and I turn to find Lawson and Delilah cuddled up together. I'm hot with jealousy that they get to spend all of their time together.

"You know she doesn't hear or see anything else when he's within a fifty-mile radius," Lawson says with a huge grin.

"At least it's two heads," Delilah teases. "That's much better than two butts."

I grin, grateful for her attempt to lighten the mood.

"So," Delilah says leaning in closer to me. "You and Hound are like, together-together? I heard Misty talking to your mom, and Em mentioned that you haven't hardly been in your room at home."

My old reaction would've been to tell her to mind her own fucking business, but things have changed since I came home. Delilah, Ivy, and I spent the majority of the Thanksgiving holiday together. We shopped, hung out, and gossiped about everything. I felt closer to them than I have since junior high school.

"I miss him when he's gone. Dad won't let us share a room in his house, but for some reason, he doesn't mind me staying here." I blush but continue with my confession. "The bed smells like him, and I sleep better in his space than my own."

Delilah snorts, and I see Lawson tighten his grip around her shoulders.

"Some things are private," he hisses in her ear loud enough that I can hear him.

She shakes her head and kisses him on the cheek. When a familiar gleam hits her eyes, I know she's going to spill.

"When I went on a girl's trip with Ivy and a few girls from school during Spring break—" She pauses to laugh, and pink marks Lawson's cheeks. "I came home early and found him asleep with a body pillow. He'd put a thong and a bra on it."

Lawson groans, but refuses to make eye contact.

I laugh, low because I don't want to draw any more attention to him, but it's hilarious.

"That's not the best part," Delilah continues.

"I'm going to choke you with my cock later," Lawson warns.

My eyes widen, and now the pink is on Delilah's cheeks because we both know I wasn't supposed to hear *that*.

Jealousy hits me again. I'd give anything to be choked with Jameson's cock tonight.

She looks back over her shoulder at him, longing in her eyes. As if to seal the deal and guarantee the threat is carried through, she turns back in my direction.

She makes a motion toward her chest. "He had stuffed the damn bra cups with socks. I walk in, and he's passed out with this pillow Delilah gripped against his chest."

"I miss her when she's gone," he mutters.

"When's the wedding again?" I say changing the subject, so Lawson is more comfortable and also because I sleep in Jameson's shirts and sometimes his boxers just so I feel closer to him when he's gone.

Delilah beams as Lawson looks down at the sparkle of her engagement ring.

"October," they say in unison.

"That will make almost three years of being engaged. Why not sooner?"

"We want to get married here. That means graduating, and working around getting the new shop setup for Law." She grins in my direction. "We didn't want the stress of planning a wedding."

Lawson sighs. "I told you, planning shouldn't stress you out."

Delilah shakes her head, and I can tell this is an ongoing argument with them. Clearly, he wants her to have his last name now.

"The dress has to be perfect, the menu, the guest list. It's all very stressful when I want it to be perfect, and that's impossible with school."

He turns her face, the rough palm of his hand cupping her cheek with a delicate touch. Fuck, I miss Jameson.

"If it's you and me, beautiful, then it can be nothing but perfect."

I feel the hot tear roll down my cheek, and I attempt to dash it away with my hand before anyone notices.

"See," Delilah says. "You're so mushy, you're making her upset."

She winks at me, and I can't help but laugh. She knows better. She knows all about my intense feelings for Jameson. I've had several lengthy conversations with both her and Ivy about how much I care for him and how terrified I am that if I tell him exactly how I feel that our entire world will shift and change. Things are good right now. Well, when he's here they're good, and I'm not going to risk upsetting our new normal.

My phone rings, and I scramble to get it off of the table. The bump I'm sporting these days is small, smaller than it should be according to the doctor, but it still gets in the way.

I activate the call, but frown when Facetime doesn't activate fully.

"Hey, gorgeous."

I nearly cry when I hear his voice.

"I can't see you," I complain.

I walk out of the living room without a backward glance. I only feel rude for the briefest of seconds, because this man has all of my attention.

"You know how it is. Technology doesn't always work, but I can see you." I smile not giving a damn that my hair is a mess. "Now show me my little boy."

This happens every time he video calls. I tilt my phone and lift my shirt so he can see the evidence of his child.

"He's getting big." There's pride in his voice, but also an unexplained strain.

"You haven't called." God, I sound like a controlling bitch. I shake my head and try to keep the tears at bay. I'm overcome with relief and if I'm being honest, anger at his silence for the last several days.

"We..." He pauses and clears his throat. "It's been a mess over here."

Over here. That's where he always is. I never know if he's even in the US. Most trips, I know, take him out of America, but he never tells me, never gives me details, never talks about what he's done once he returns.

"I can't wait to hold you in my arms." Tears fall silently at his words. It's Christmas Eve. He was only planning on being gone two weeks. He was supposed to be here with me.

"Wh-when do you think that will be?" I'm needy, desperate to lay my eyes on him, feel his skin against mine, have him hold me through the night.

"Is now soon enough?"

By the time the words leave his mouth, the bedroom door swings open and he's there. He's standing in front of me, looking exhausted and sad, but he's still the most handsome man I've ever laid eyes on.

"Hi," I say suddenly shy as I swipe at my eyes with the sleeve of my sweatshirt.

He doesn't say a word as he crosses the room and wraps me in his arms. I don't care about a single thing other than this moment. My ears register the soft thud of my phone as it hits the carpet at our feet, but I can't be bothered to let go of him and find it.

"Fuck, I missed you."

I sob against his shoulder, feeling silly for the tears now that he's here. I don't usually cry in front of him, and when I do, I blame it on hormones. I haven't sobbed like this since the night he found me in Vegas, and I was struggling with the decision I had to make.

"I hate it when you're gone," I confess and hold him tighter.

"I know." He consoles me with the warm rub of his palms over my back before dropping to his knees, raising my sweatshirt, and pressing his warm lips to my stomach.

My fingers tangle in his hair, but he doesn't look up at me. His forehead is pressed against our growing child, and at first, I find it endearing, loving that he missed both of us, but then his shoulders shudder with his own sob.

He's never gotten emotional like this in front of me. I've seen irritated, lustful, angry, but I've never heard the wretched sound that just escaped his lips.

"Hey." I drop to my knees as well and wrap him in my arms.

"The girl." He shakes his head. "We couldn't save her."

I feel his warm palms flat against my stomach.

"We couldn't save the baby." Another sob, one that matches mine at this exact moment. "We were too late."

I hold him as he cries, as he tries to put himself back together. I hold him when he grows exhausted, and I don't even let him go when he gets heavy and pulls me against his chest on the hard floor.

Chapter 35

Hound

"Shhh," I whisper when Gigi mumbles something unintelligible as I scoop her off of the floor. "I got you."

I tug off her jeans, barely resisting the urge to slide her silk panties down her legs along with them. The sweatshirt, t-shirt, and bra come off next. Resisting the furl of her pink nipples is an exercise in fortitude that I nearly fail. One finger, one sweep of my skin against her delicate flesh is all I allow myself. I know I should at least pull a t-shirt over her head, but I leave her bare, needing the feel of her skin against mine. I cover her quickly knowing she'll be chilled without her clothes.

I want to wake her, to say things to her I've only said once before, but say them knowing I mean them this time. I know, without a doubt, that how I thought I felt for Gabby is nothing compared to the burn I have deep in my soul for Georgia Anderson.

I don't, however. I crawl into bed and pull her back against my naked front. I palm her growing belly and count my lucky fucking stars that they're both safe and in my arms.

***

The familiar tingle in my nuts forces me into semi-consciousness. I do my best to ignore it. Waking with a throbbing erection seems to be part of my daily schedule since Gigi started sleeping in my bed, and it's ten times worse when I'm away from her.

It's the chuckle that makes my eyes snap open, and the firm suction along my shaft that has me nearly coming off the bed.

Looking down, I find the most amazing woman curled over herself between my splayed thighs. She gives me her best attempt at a smile, but the thickness of the cock in her mouth impedes it.

"Eager this morning?" The darkness in the room means it's either earlier than morning or she finally got someone to put the blackout curtains up she was complaining about several days ago.

She releases me with a pop, her tongue tracing the veins along my shaft. "I heard Lawson threaten to choke Delilah with his dick. It made me crave your dick in my mouth."

I frown down at her. "He shouldn't be saying things like that loud enough for you to hear."

She shrugs, tongue never taking a break as it toys with each one of my barbells and flicks the ring in the head.

I cup her cheek, my emotions barely in check after my breakdown yesterday. It took a full day and a half before I could get my shit together to call her after we found Marisol dead, her unborn child brutally cut out of her and also dead by her side. I'd spoken with Kincaid. I knew she was fine, but I knew I had to be close to her, knew I had to be in this house, in this room, when I heard her voice again.

"I love you," I whisper. Her head begins to shake back and forth, throat bobbing up and down. "So fucking much."

Tears spring to her eyes. "Really? Me?"

"You."

"I love you, too," she says back after an agonizingly long minute.

There's too much distance between us, too much space and time. Three weeks is a long ass time to be so far away from a piece of your very own heart. I sit up, and in the next second she's on her back, and my mouth is covering hers.

We don't say another word. We let the room fill with our love as I fill her with my cock. Slight whimpers and an occasional grunt are the only sounds we make, but we never lose eye contact. I'm reluctant to even pull out of her after we climax together, but I'm exhausted, and the last thing I need is my arms giving out and falling on her.

She traces the back of my hand as it tickles over her stomach.

"Mom felt the baby kick yesterday."

My heart breaks a little. She's been feeling the movement for weeks, assuring me it would be soon that I would be able to feel it too. I'm almost bitter at the knowledge that someone else got to do that first.

"Another thing I've missed." She presses her palm against mine until my hand is flat against her skin. "I'm missing everything again."

"I'll talk to Dad. Ask him to keep you home."

"I have to work, Gigi." I fucking hate more than anything that I have to. "I can't get preferential treatment."

"He can find something for you to do here. I know you're good with computers," she bargains.

"I'm better in the field." I know it, and she knows it. Plus, Blade has the computer skills covered, except for the field stuff, which I'm already doing.

"I need you here," she mutters, her breath ghosting over my chest.

I squeeze her tighter and decide to change the subject.

"How did the doctor's visit go? How is my boy doing?"

I feel her tense, and an eerie chill settles over me.

"We did the sonogram." There's something off about her voice, and I know she's fixing to confirm some of the nightmares I've had over the last seventy-two hours.

"What else?" I hate the strain in my voice, but I'm already preparing myself for the worst.

The last couple of weeks have made it very apparent that things can go to shit at the drop of a hat, and I know deep down that I'm never supposed to be happy.

"Camryn says that I'm measuring small." I tense. "So she did some kind of special sonogram. The baby is perfectly fine."

I take a few deep breaths, trying to calm the fear that just won't release me.

"Are you sure? Please, tell me the truth."

"I am." She pushes up and looks down at me. "It's just..."

God, I can't take this. "Tell me. What's wrong with my son?"

"That's just it," she says with a twinkle in her eye. "You don't have a son. You're having another daughter."

"Excuse me?"

A wide smile spreads across cheeks still pink from her orgasm. "A girl. We're having a girl."

My throat goes dry, making swallowing difficult. "But she's healthy?"

She nods, searching my eyes and waiting for my reaction. What can I tell her? That I'm terrified? That I have no clue how to raise a daughter? So I opt to just speak the only truth I know. "I can't wait to meet her."

It's then, with the flex of my fingers against her stomach that my daughter decides to introduce herself to me. At first, it's a simple tremble, but then Gigi's tight stomach moves and I feel every bit of it against my hand. I stare down, in awe of it. The gift of life, a woman's ability to grow and nurture something from a handful of cells into a human being is nothing short of miraculous. This baby, this tiny little girl is half of me and half of her. The sting of tears behind my eyes is welcomed, even after my embarrassing breakdown last night.

"I hope she's nothing like me," Gigi confesses as her head lowers to rest on my chest again.

"I hope she's exactly like you." She snorts. "I hope she's fierce, resilient, able to speak her mind, and doesn't let people walk all over her."

"You won't be saying that when she's fourteen and thinking she's grown."

I pull her closer and kiss the top of her head. "There won't be a boy in a hundred-mile radius that will even speak to her."

She huffs.

"What?" I pull my head back and tilt her chin up. "I said I wanted her to be exactly like you. I never said I wasn't going to be ten times worse than your dad."

"I," she begins but pauses for a long minute. "I was so terrible to both my parents. Gave them such a hard time. Made them worry. I understand now because I know I'll do everything in my power to protect this baby, even if that means protecting her from herself."

"And that," I tell her before I brush my lips against hers, "is what parenting is all about."

"How long are you back for?" God, I don't even want to think about leaving her again. "Dad and Shadow were in the conference room all day yesterday, so I already know there's another job lined up. Is it your team? How long do we have?"

Her eyes grow dark and disappointed when she reads the look on my face. "I have to head out on Tuesday."

"Two days?" Tears form in the corners of her eyes. "We only have two days? How long this time."

"I don't know the details yet." I press my mouth to hers. "But let's not waste a second getting upset about it."

I press her to her back and tell her everything I'm feeling. I profess my love, my devotion, and we make plans for the future. Life is perfect for the first time ever. I can't help smile at knowing that there is actually a way for me to be happy. I never imagined I could have this. Never even let myself picture having a woman that loved me, yet here I am.

Chapter 36

Gigi

"Only two weeks left," Camryn says with a smile as she slips her gloves off of her hands.

"I'm not ready," I confess.

I knew Dad shouldn't have sent Jameson on this last mission. Both promised me it was a quick job, and he'd be home before I knew it.

"First-time parents never are," she cajoles. "But you'll know what to do when the time comes."

I've spent the better part of an hour asking her all of the questions I could easily research online, but I wanted to hear them from a professional, not a book or online chat rooms. I mean, I look at those too since I've become obsessed with all things childbirth.

"I want to see you next week," Camryn says before walking to the door. "Make sure you make the appointment before heading out."

I sigh, rolling off of the exam table and get my lower half redressed.

Kid is waiting for me in the parking lot, but the smiling man I've known all of my life is gone, having been replaced with a man filled with anxiety. He won't even look at me as he helps me inside of the SUV.

"We have to head back to the clubhouse," he informs me as he climbs inside and backs out of the parking space.

"I needed to grab a few things from Target," I whine, knowing he's probably in a pissy mood because Khloe is still getting hit on at school. There's been tension between those two since the spring semester started at her school.

"Not today," he says shutting down any rebuttal I might have had planned.

Pissed, I turn my head to look out the window and rub the tightening spot on my stomach.

The clubhouse is frantic by the time we get back there. The guys who didn't head out on the last job are running around. Shadow is barking orders, and there's a tension in the air that makes the hair on the back of my neck stand up. Something's wrong. I can feel it in my bones.

"How the fuck did that happen?" Dad bellows. The anger in his voice travels out of the open door to the conference room. "I won't calm the fuck down! I lost a man today, and you're telling me to calm down?"

No. No. No. No.

I arrow toward the conference room, standing in the doorway. I almost break at the sight of my dad with his head hung low, one hand clutching his cell phone and the other gripping the top of his shaved head.

"Daddy?" The one word is a guttural plea.

I just know my world is going to come crashing down around me by the devastated look on Dad's face.

I shake my head. "No, daddy. Please."

I'm a twenty-one-year-old woman, but I've turned into a child needing her father to make her world make sense again.

"We lost Catfish." He's broken, torn down, but that doesn't stop the relief I feel in my bones.

I'm a horrible person for being thankful that someone else, someone other than Jameson, is dead.

I clench my stomach, the tightness that's been present increasing to the point of excruciating pain.

"And Jameson?" I ask when the pain subsides marginally and look up to see the same wrecked look in Dad's eyes.

"It all went to shit."

The pain is back, and he forgets who's on the phone as he stands from the table and rushes to me.

"Jameson?" I ask again, his name the only word I can manage with the pain in my stomach.

"We need to get to the hospital," he says, the calm I remember from childhood taking over his voice. He does so well in chaotic situations, and today is no different. He places a soothing hand on my back before barking orders through the open door.

My pulse, pounding in my ears like a damn snare drum blocks out the conversation around me. It isn't until I'm scooped up in my dad's arms that I focus again.

"Where's Jameson?" I'm sobbing by this point.

"We need to focus on the baby, Georgia. You're in labor."

I shake my head. "I can't do this without him." I tremble, my hand gripping his t-shirt to the point my knuckles turn white. "He's supposed to be here!"

"Get Camryn Davison on the phone. I want her at the hospital by the time we get there." I hear a 'yes, Sir.' "And make sure they have a room ready for her. We're not spending a damn second in the waiting room."

I fight to get out of the SUV when Dad places me in the back seat and struggles to get the seatbelt around my swollen stomach. The tremble in his hands betrays his distress.

"You'll be fine." I turn to see Mom sliding in beside me. "You get to meet your daughter today."

Her eyes are swollen, and I know she's been crying. They're both lying to me.

"Just tell me," I beg, my own tears renewed as I watch her face.

She shakes her head, tears brimming and threatening to fall. "I don't know anything."

"Please," I beg. "Please don't lie to me."

I don't miss the relief in her eyes when the next contraction begins and demands all of my attention.

The hustle into the hospital is quick and seamless. Dad cradles me in his arms, much like he did when I was a kid and fell asleep on the couch watching TV. He doesn't have to bark orders here in public. The commands he made back at the clubhouse have been carried out perfectly. We go straight to a room, and Camryn is waiting for us.

"My phone," I hiss after I shed my clothes to get into a hospital gown, and she tries to take my clothes away. "The back pocket of my jeans."

I tap out a text, watching the screen with hope. The three little bubbles don't pop up. The device in my hand doesn't buzz or begin to ring.

"What the hell is going on? Where is he?"

My mom clears her throat. "I don't know."

"Where's Dad?" I push past her in the small bathroom and enter the room.

Camryn is there, waiting, but I can tell from the look on her face that she knows something I don't.

"Someone needs to tell me what's going on," I demand.

"You're going to have that baby a little early it seems," Camryn says with the nicest smile she can manage. She closes the distance between us and helps me climb into the bed. "I don't want you to worry. Two weeks early isn't huge, especially for a girl. Their lungs mature quicker than a boy's would."

Once I'm on the bed, nurses are all around me strapping monitors around my stomach.

My dad is gone for what seems like forever, and my mom won't look at me. She types away furiously on her cell phone and checks it every second when her fingers aren't flying over the keypad.

When Dad enters the room, his eyes find mine before they search for my mother. My whole life, he's looked for her first, as it is in his blood to make sure the other half of his soul is safe before worrying about others.

I swallow, shaking my head as he reaches my head. I've been demanding answers, begging everyone to tell me the truth, to tell me something. Now that the moment has come, I can't even look him in the eye.

"Georgia," Dad says softly.

I don't lift my eyes to his. I focus solely on the texture of the faded fuchsia blanket covering me.

"Please don't, Daddy."

The machines by my side beep, alerting me to another contraction. My epidural an hour ago has numbed the pain to the point it's my broken heart that is destroying me and not the child trying to be born while her father is...

I sob, refusing to think in my head what my heart is already feeling.

A gentle knock and Camryn entering the room keeps my dad from ripping my useless muscle from my chest.

"It's time, Gigi." Camryn stands at the end of the bed and pulls a sterile towel from the top of an instrument tray. She dons gloves and looks back at me. "Are you ready?"

I shake my head and earn a small smile from her lips.

"Diego, are you staying?"

It's then that I meet his eyes. They plead with me, much the same way mine did to him when I begged him not to make Jameson go on another mission. The way I looked each and every time he got orders after we started making plans for our future. My dad is the one responsible for the empty life, the single parenting I'll be forced to do. He doesn't get the right to stand there and cheer me on when he's the sole reason my world is crashing down around me.

"He's not welcome in this room." I expect him to argue, to insist that he's there for his little girl as she brings her own daughter into the world. He doesn't. He nods, kisses the back of my hand, and walks out.

"You have about a minute," Camryn says with her eyes on the monitor at my bedside. "Then I need you to push."

I lie back, not acknowledging my mom when she clasps my hand in her own. Normally warm, the coolness of her fingers is a shock to my system, but I don't respond to that either. My eyes trace imaginary patterns on the ceiling. I ignore the pain and Cam's voice instructing me to bear down.

I shake my head. "I won't do this without him."

Mom begs.

Cam rubs my calf giving me encouragement hinted with agitation.

I don't know how long it goes on. Seconds? Days? Years?

"Listen to me," my mother spits, yanking my chin and forcing me to look at her. "You have to push."

"Jameson," I sob. "I need him."

"You have to do this without him." Tears fill her eyes once again. "He'd want you to carry on."

Oh, God. That's as good as confirmation that he's gone.

"I don't want this without him."

"You're killing her, Georgia." I shake my head. I'd never do anything to hurt my daughter. "Her heart rate is all over the place. If you don't push, they're going to take you in for an emergency C-section."

I shake my head. "No."

I don't know what I'm denying. The loss of him, the fact my baby is in danger? Am I still refusing to push? I don't have a damn clue.

"Please turn that damn thing off," my mom snaps, but she's already reaching to my side.

It's only then I hear my cell ringing.

"Oh, thank God," she says as I see the facetime call from Jameson.

"Jameson," I sob when the video connects.

"We're having a baby today," he whispers as if talking too loud will ruin the moment.

"I need you here," I cry. "I can't do this without you."

"I'm here, gorgeous." I nod, conceding that this is the best I can get.

My adrenaline is through the roof, my entire body shaking uncontrollably. I hate myself for losing faith so quickly.

"Focus, Gigi." My eyes snap back to his. "Give Emmalyn the phone, so you can concentrate on getting my baby here."

I nod and do as he says.

"Head's out," Cam says.

She asks me to stop pushing, and it's only when my eyes flutter back to the screen that I take him in fully for the first time. His face is battered, covered in blood, and his voice, although soothing is low and weak. There are people around him, insisting he lie back.

"One more push," Cam urges.

"You can do it, gorgeous." I smile at his encouragement and bear down even though the medicine is strong enough to keep most of the pain away.

"She's here," Cam says.

There's a rush, nurses shuffling around.

The baby cries, the most amazing sound in the world.

"Amelia Kate," Jameson whispers. Her name on his lips is the second most beautiful thing in this world.

And it all shatters again when I hear the long beep of a heart machine. The same one you hear on TV when someone dies. Confused, I look over at my monitors, but nothing seems wrong. Amelia is still wailing, so I know she's fine.

When I look back, I watch Jameson's eyes roll back. There's a shuffle, the phone pointed at nothing.

"He's coding!" I hear before the call is disconnected.

Chapter 37

Kincaid

The look on my wife's face as she exits Georgia's room is one I haven't seen in a long time, so long, in fact, I can't recall if I've ever seen it before. She's sobbing, and her fists meet my chest repeatedly when she's close enough to make contact.

I crush her to my chest. Knowing how upset she must be if violence is her go-to response.

"Why would you do that?" Her voice has a frantic squeal to it, and I want nothing more than to make everything right for her. For Georgia. Hell, even for Hound because his well-being and the love he has for my daughter is what has kept her around so long this time.

"I had no choice," I begin to explain. "He refused to go into surgery before seeing her."

My beautiful wife shakes against my chest, the tremble in her small body almost enough to bring me to my knees.

"He coded just as Amelia cried, Diego. She was so upset they had to sedate her." Sobs wrack her body. "She didn't even get to hold her baby girl first."

I run my hand through her hair and try to soothe her. If I'm being honest, touching her soothes me, and I need it more now than ever before. I knew what was going on because I was on the phone with Rocker while Hound was on the phone with my daughter.

"Do you know anything else?" Em pushes against me until my arms relax and she's looking up in my eyes.

I sigh.

"Don't give me that *club business* bullshit. This is one time I won't back down without answers."

My gorgeous, stubborn queen.

"They were able to get his heart started back, but he's pretty fucked up. He was hit several times, and one round made it through his Kevlar. We won't know more until the surgeon comes out and gives an update."

"And where are they?"

I sigh again, but I won't deny her the information she's demanding. "Brazil."

"Have you made arrangements for Curt's family?" I hang my head at the mention of Catfish. He's been with us for a couple of years, but I didn't know him very well. He did a great job for the club and always gave a hundred percent in the field, but he's kept to himself, preferring to be alone when he was home rather than hang out with the other guys.

I shake my head. "I was so worried about Georgia. I haven't had the chance."

"She's fine," Em assures me. "Amelia is fine."

I clear my throat. Georgia and I have been butting heads since she was old enough to talk back, but the pain and disappointment in her eyes today was something new altogether.

"She hates me for putting him in that situation," I mutter.

"She doesn't hate you."

"If he doesn't make it," I begin but have to pause and release a shuttering breath. "She'll never speak to me again."

I let the heat of my wife's warm hand seep through my shirt over my heart. She's strength and faith where I'm the realist in the family. I know more than her what Hound is facing.

"He'll be fine," she assures me, and the calm in her voice almost makes me believe it, too. "But you have to go."

"Go?" I shake my head. "I'm not going anywhere. My place is here with my family."

"And I want you here, but Georgia needs you in Brazil. Your men need you. They lost a friend today."

"I've made arrangements for Shadow and Dom to head down. Plane leaves in an hour."

She takes a step back, her hand falling from my chest. "Georgia needs you to go to him because she can't. You're the only one she trusts to tell her the truth."

"I can't leave her. Can't leave you."

"I've got everything under control here." Reaching up on her tiptoes, she brushes her lips across my cheek. "Don't miss your plane."

I cling to her, not happy one bit about leaving her and Georgia here, but hating what I'm going to find when I step foot on Brazilian soil.

"I'll call you when we land," I promise, and walk away without looking back.

If I focus on the pain and fear she's trying desperately to hide, I'll never be able to leave her.

***

Thirteen hours later our boots are on the ground. Two hours after that, we're heading into the hospital. I hate the simplicity of the place. The smell, the grime clinging to the corners and along the walls are telling of just how different this place is compared to hospitals in the States.

Scooter is smoking a cigarette, tossing one away and lighting a new one as we approach. The tremble in his hands and the devastated look in his eyes make my gut clench. We spoke when we landed, but haven't had an update since.

"Hey," he says, face ashen and voice rough and filled with emotion. "They've started the paperwork to release Catfish's body."

I nod, fighting the urge to wrap him in a hug. He reminds me of Shadow's son Griffin, so young and having seen so much evil in his short life.

"And Hound?" Last I heard he was out of surgery, but the doctors refused to consider him stable since he coded twice during his operation.

He nods, swallowing thickly and refusing to meet my eyes. "He's hooked up to a vent. The break-through round hit him in his chest. By the time they were able to operate on his stubborn ass, the bullet had moved into his lung. He's holding on, but they won't let us back to see him with our own eyes."

"Fuck that," Shadow growls beside me. "Let them try to tell me I can't see one of my men."

Scooter gives a small smile and flicks his cigarette butt into the grass. "I was hoping one of you would say that."

"Where are the other guys?" I ask.

"Rocker and Grinch are inside." He hitches a thumb over his shoulder. "Davy and Dragon are with local authorities trying to sort this shit out."

All I have to do is look at Dom, and he's headed back to the SUV to help Davy and Dragon with the mess this failed mission has created.

"Let's go talk to the doctor," I urge as I walk past him.

He tosses his newly lit cigarette away.

"How's Gi-Georgia?"

"She's good. The baby is perfect."

"He refused to go into surgery. Refused to let them touch him with anything but monitors until he talked to her."

It may end up costing him his life.

"I would've done the exact same thing if it was Em," I say instead, knowing it's the truth. It's then that I realize Hound is the best thing to happen to my daughter. If he loves her as much as I love Emmalyn, there's no way I can do anything but give them both my blessing. Hell, I know he'd do anything in his power, including fighting with Satan or Saint Peter to get back to her.

Reassured, I slap Scooter on the back as we climb off of the elevator. "Now point me in the direction of this doctor that has no idea who he's refusing."

Chapter 38

Gigi

Trying to roll over only forces a pained gasp from my dry lips.

"Easy," I hear Mom say from beside me.

"I hurt," I grumble, hoping she can take the pain away just as she has all of my life.

"Childbirth is the most beautiful and most painful thing you'll ever go through." Her voice is soft; her hands warm on my shoulder.

"Amelia?" My eyes flutter open but slam shut against the brightness of the room.

"She's perfect," Mom assures me. "Waiting to meet you."

The reminder that I haven't met my daughter yet is like a knife to my heart. Both for the missed opportunity and the realization of what happened right after her birth.

"Jameson," I sob. It's not a question because I can feel in my soul that he's gone. There's an emptiness in my chest that only he was ever able to fill. That spot is now cold and desolate.

"Shh." The calming hand my mother runs in circles along my arm doesn't bring the comfort it did in childhood. This isn't a scraped knee or harsh words spoken on the playground by mean girls who want to hurt my feelings. This pain is real and so acute I can hardly catch my breath.

"Please calm down," my mother begs.

Calm isn't something I can manage, and I grow angrier at the ridiculous request.

"They'll sedate you again."

My breath hitches, head aching with misery I have no idea how I'll ever survive it.

"Please." I don't know what I'm begging for, but I'm certain that if she had the power to take it all away, she'd do it in the blink of an eye.

"Shhh." The hand, the circles, the energy so strong I know it's something only a mother can possess for a hurting child, is almost enough to settle me. Almost enough to make me believe everything will be okay.

Almost.

But, how can it? How can a day so beautiful be endured when it's also filled with tragedy? Filled with such loss that the good, the beautiful is dulled like a consolation prize.

"He promised me forever, but now he's gone."

Saying the words out loud gut me. Acknowledging my truth rips my soul to shreds.

"No, baby girl. He's not gone."

Her assurance does nothing for me. Lying only makes my anguish sharper, like razors on my skin.

"He's out of surgery," she continues. "He's hurt, but he's not gone."

I shake my head, hope the last thing I need. Hope is only going to make things worse, and in this moment I hate her saying the words. I hate my dad for putting us in this situation. I hate the world for taking away the only man I could ever love.

"I know you don't agree," my mother says, and it's only now that I realize she's walked away.

Chills run up my arm where her comforting touch was only seconds ago.

"Wires and a ventilator are better than her being sedated again because she thinks he's dead."

I open my eyes, head tilting to the side to watch my mother as she paces near the door. I've never heard her use that tone with anyone, much less my father who I assume she's speaking with.

"Now, Diego," she snaps before pulling the phone from her ear and hitting the end button.

Her phone chimes and the familiar sound of a Facetime call makes my heart rate spike.

I shake my head as she walks closer. She's holding the phone away from her chest as if it's a bomb she's terrified is going to detonate in her hands.

"They've labeled him critical stable," she warns. "He looks like hell, but he's not gone."

"This is a bad idea," my dad says from the other end of the call.

"Daddy?" I say as I reach for the phone.

When I turn it to face me, I'm met with the warm eyes of my father. His face softens, the angry, agitated look I expected nowhere on his face.

"Hey, baby girl." I'm comforted by the nickname, calmed by the kind baritone of his voice. "I hear I'm a granddad."

I nod, my voice getting stuck in my throat. I'm a mother, one who's not even met her daughter yet. I'm failing as a parent already, which only proves the things I've been telling Jameson for the last several months as reality sets in.

"I want you to know, before I turn the phone around, that it looks worse than it actually is."

I shake my head. "Please don't lie to me."

"He's holding on," Dad assures me.

"I can handle it," I lie. The tight smile I attempt fails as tears roll down my cool cheeks.

"I love you, baby girl."

His words echo in my ears as the phone shifts before landing on a man I hardly recognize. The beard is familiar, but his color is off. His size, once so huge and powerful, is diminished in the hospital bed. The cords and wires connecting to his ashen body are nothing like I imagined while preparing myself for this moment.

I begin to cry, my body shaking so hard I drop the phone. My mother, being the strongest woman I know, grabs the phone and holds it in front of me. I ignore the tremble in her hands that matches mine.

"Listen, Georgia."

I shake my head, unprepared to hear my dad make promises he's unable to keep. I can't bear assurances and empty words.

"Listen," he urges again. "Hear the beep?"

My sobs quieten as I try to focus on what he's referencing.

"That's his heart monitor," he explains as the consistent *beep, beep, beep* is heard through the phone. "It's strong, steady. He's in an induced coma because of the vent. His lung was punctured. He's not dying, baby girl. He's healing."

"H-he's going to live?"

"I have every faith that he will," Dad answers.

"Promise me, daddy." Tears brim my eyes again. "Please."

"Baby girl." I can hear the emotion in his voice, but I don't miss the fact that he never utters the words. He never tells me everything is going to be okay. How can he?

"Have faith," he urges.

"Leave your phone," Mom instructs.

I watch as the phone is propped against something.

"Love you, baby girl," Dad says before I hear the click of a door. Silence, other than the beep of his monitor and the rush of air every time the machine pushes air into my love's lungs, fills the room around me.

"I'm going to have the nurses bring Amelia in," Mom says as she lifts my hand and wraps my fingers around the phone.

"Thank you." I hope she knows the two words are meant for everything she's done.

My eyes close against the warmth I feel on her lips as she brushes them against my forehead, but then they focus back on the man in the hospital bed.

When the door clicks closed as my mother leaves the room, the begging begins. I beg him to live, to fight, to hold on for me, for Amelia. I make promises I'm not even sure I can keep, but have every intention of trying to manage. I promise to let him do dirty things to me. Swear he can punish me for missteps I haven't even committed yet if only he'll wake up.

He doesn't.

I know he's unable. After Dad's explanation, I know he's physically unable to fight against the drugs they have pumped into his body so he can get better, but that doesn't keep me from selfishly hoping he will. It doesn't keep me from watching him so intently that my eyes begin to hurt because blinking means losing a second of time with him.

A whimper from the doorway is the only thing strong enough to make me refocus. A nurse with a smile too bright for the situation pushes a small cart topped with a plastic basket into the room. Pink and wiggly is all I can see until Mom sidesteps the nurse and reaches inside to pull Amelia out.

I smile back at the phone, hoping the noise was enough to make Jameson wakeup.

"You're missing the most precious moment," I chide as if he's aware of his surroundings. "I know you hate missing this."

"Shh-shh-shh," Mom coos as she walks closer.

"I'll hold her twice as tight until you can have her in your arms," I promise.

I whimper right along with Amelia as Mom pulls the phone from my hand and replaces it with the most perfect angel I've seen.

"Don't," I say as I settle the little bundle in my arm and reach for the phone with my free hand.

"I'm just propping it up," she assures me as she rolls the table closer.

I watch the screen of the phone as she settles it against the pink water pitcher. I don't fight the smile that crests my lips when I split my time between watching the screen and looking down at the miracle we made.

"She's perfect," I whisper to Jameson as Amelia calms, her lips jutting out as she falls asleep.

"She's got his eyes," Mom says. "I imagine her chin is his as well, but I've never seen him without a beard."

"She's a mix of everything good from both of us."

Tears fall from my eyes transforming the spots on the blanket from light pink to fuchsia.

"I'll give you guys some time," Mom says after another brush against my head. She repeats the action to Amelia's tiny head before backing away. "I'm going to have to track down an extension cord and have Misty let Shadow know your dad will need to find one also."

"Thank you." I take a few seconds to look up at my mother. She nods, eyes still brimming with tears.

"There is a waiting room full of people waiting to see you and meet Amelia."

"I'm not ready," I tell her with my eyes back on my daughter.

"Let me know when you are." The softness in her voice is unexpected. I anticipated her telling me not to be selfish, to urge me to consider other people's feelings. "Ivy is chomping at the bit to get back here."

"She's here?" How long was I out?

Mom nods. "She jumped on the first plane. Isabella is out there as well."

I begin to tremble. "I want to see them both."

Mom glances back at the phone before her eyes meet mine again. "It will be hard for Isabella to see him like that. Maybe after you end the video?"

I shake my head. "The video stays until he wakes up."

"That could be days, Georgia." It doesn't come out as chastisement, only her acknowledging the length of time in case my hopes were up for immediate gratification.

"I know. You can explain to her, just like Dad did for me. She'll want to see him."

Mom nods even though she seems unsure.

"Give me ten minutes alone, and then you can send them back."

I don't bother to look at the door when it clicks softly behind my mother.

"Your sister and aunt are going to meet you soon," I tell Amelia's sleeping form.

My fingers trace the small pout of her lips, trailing down her tiny chin.

"Everything is going to be just fine."

My eyes sting as I lie to my daughter for the very first time.

Chapter 39

Hound

"Fuck." That's what I try to say, but even to my own ears I know it comes out as nothing but a garble before I start coughing.

My body hurts. Every fucking inch of it, as if I've been set on fire and then pelted with shards of glass.

"It's okay," a deep voice assures me.

I want to grab whoever it is by the throat for spewing shit he has no idea about. The pain radiates from every joint, every muscle. I cough, and the agony increases tenfold.

"Jesus," I hiss.

"You had a punctured lung," an unfamiliar voice says as harsh hands press down on my shoulders. It's only then that I realize I've been fighting. What, I'm not certain, but the only cognizant thought I can manage is to move, to get away from the fire burning over every inch of my skin.

"I'm burning," I scream. "Get me away from the flames."

"It's the morphine burning off."

"Hound." I stiffen at the sound of Kincaid's voice. "Calm the fuck down."

"Hurts," I mutter. "Make it stop."

A deep chuckle meets my ears "Don't be a pussy."

"Daddy!" I freeze at the sound of Gigi's voice.

I try to force my eyes open, but they don't budge, the heaviness of them too much to fight against.

Everything comes rushing back. The pleading in Gigi's eyes as I begged her to push, the first cries of my baby girl as she entered the world. The pain of losing a friend in a shitty country when the mission went to hell. The harsh burn as the bullet penetrated my vest.

"Daddy?" Her voice is pleading this time, her fear enough to calm me even with the scorching heat from my injuries.

"Keep talking to him, Georgia," Kincaid commands.

"Please," I beg as the hands holding me down loosen up.

"Our daughter is beautiful," Gigi assures me with a sob. "She has your gorgeous eyes."

I smile through the pain.

"Mr. Rawley?" It's the unfamiliar voice once again. It's marked with such a heavy accent, I know I'm still in South America. "I'm Dr. Cardoso. I need you to open your eyes."

I nod but wince when fire lights up my chest. Attempting to take a deep breath, an attempt to gain the strength and courage only leads to more coughing, heavier hands against my shoulders.

"I'm here, Jameson. Stay calm. Do it when you're ready." I want her hands on me. I want to spank her ass for traveling to this shitty country with my newborn daughter.

"Take it easy, Dad."

"Izzy?" What the fuck is she doing in Brazil?

I hate the harsh weakness in my voice. I know what I'm trying to say, but my ears only register a gruff jumble of sounds.

"Eyes," the doctor urges again.

I fight the pain. I fight the heaviness until my eyes open to the smallest of slits, only when I shift my head searching for Gigi and Isabella, all I find is Kincaid's smiling mug and the mocha latte skin of a man I've never seen before.

"Where?" I begin before I have to take a shallow breath and swallow past the sandpaper filling my mouth. "Where are my girls?"

"Still in New Mexico," Kincaid says before holding up his phone. "They're safe."

My eyes open wider, taking in the gorgeous sight of Gigi, holding our daughter and Izzy sitting beside her, so half of her is in the frame.

"Hey, gorgeous," I whisper, my voice gaining strength at the sight of her.

She smiles wide even though tears mark her cheeks and her shoulders jerk with sobs.

"I've missed you," she finally manages.

"How I—"

"Almost two weeks," Kincaid says.

I look at him over the top of the phone before dropping my eyes back down to the screen. It's then that I notice the background. She's in my room in the clubhouse. Baby things we've collected surround her, lining the walls to the point that moving around in there is an impossibility.

"You deserve a castle, not a tiny room," I muse, more to myself than anyone in particular.

"Yes, she does," Kincaid agrees, but with humor rather than irritation in his voice.

"Why are you here?" I ask him, my eyes fluttering with exhaustion already.

"You've met my daughter, haven't you?" He smiles. "I was on a plane down here before I met my granddaughter. I knew she wouldn't have it any other way."

"Good man," I whisper.

"We've had you on video since the day Amelia was born," Izzy says, playfulness marking her tone.

Gigi smiles, a nod of her head confirming. "Why are you so obsessed with me?"

She laughs, and the sound washes over me, precious enough to make some of the pain in my body dissipate.

"Because I love you. I miss you, and I need you to get better so you can come home and do the nighttime diaper changes like you promised."

"I can't wait," I answer honestly.

"You owe me a million dollars in data usage," Kincaid adds from my bedside.

I smile, wondering if he knows about the bonus Merlin had deposited in my bank account after shit went down in D.C. months ago. I'd offer it gladly if seeing me, even in a comatose state calmed even an ounce of Gigi's fear.

"So sleepy," I pant. "Hurts so badly."

"He needs his rest," the doctor says. "Mr. Rawley, I'm going to give you pain medicine in your IV. You need to rest."

I shake my head. Sleep, although I can tell it's what I need, is the very last thing I want. I know the deed has been done as my pain numbs to something more bearable and my eyes grow even heavier.

"Love you," I whisper before darkness beckons me and I give into the call.

***

"Goddammit," I grumble as Kincaid's strong arms help ease me off of the bed.

It's been days since I first woke, but even with threats of violence, Dr. Cardoso won't release me until I can walk on my own and am able to get the spirometer up to the fucking smiley face and hold it there for five seconds. He's an evil bastard, and I know he's been sent to do nothing but fucking torture me.

"Today's the day," Kincaid says in an unfamiliar timbre.

"Since when did you go all soft and nice," I hiss, but make it to standing.

"I miss my fucking wife," he complains. "And Georgia says I can't leave until we can make that fucking plane ride together."

I chuckle, the pain not as acute in my chest.

"I can ride on a fucking plane. Let's just leave today." I try for conspiratorial, but the words rush out with over-exertion just from fucking standing near my bed.

"And have your lung collapse mid-flight?" he growls. "I promised her I'd deliver you safely, not some fucking corpse, but if you could speed up your recovery, that'd be awesome."

"Doing my best here, Gramps."

His grip tightens on my arms. "I told you not to fucking call me that."

"Make you feel old?"

"Says the guy who can't get up and take a piss without coughing up a lung and taking a two-hour nap afterward."

He's such an asshole, but for some reason, I'm smiling.

"I can't wait to get home. Can't wait to hold my baby girl. Can't wait to press my lips against your baby girl. Feel her skin against my lips."

I wince when his fingers dig into me. "I'll fucking drop you right now," he threatens.

I laugh, not only at getting a rise out of him, but realizing we've already made it to the bathroom. It's taken half the time it did yesterday. The day before that he had to practically carry me in here.

"Wanna give me a hand?" I ask.

"Fuck no," he grumbles, but doesn't back away completely, still afraid I'll fall from the exhaustion I've always felt when I make it this far.

"Gigi would hold my cock if she were here," I tease, but the growl he releases makes me wonder if I took things too far.

"Say one more thing like that about my daughter, and you won't have a cock to hold."

I laugh when I hear him mutter 'asshole' as he closes me in the small bathroom.

Even though I know he's pissed, he's waiting outside of the door when I pull it open.

"I'm ready to go home," I lament as he helps me back into the bed.

He clears his throat, and I expect him to rage on me once I'm settled on the mattress, but I look up to find softness in his eyes I've only ever seen when he looks at Emmalyn.

"I wanted to say thank you."

"For making you feel old?" I smile, trying to lighten the mood.

"For living. For loving my daughter more than I ever could've asked for." Emotion clogs his throat, and he clears it twice before talking again. "Georgia would've never forgiven me if you didn't survive."

"I could never leave her. Couldn't leave Amelia or Izzy either. I had no other choice. Surviving was the only choice I had."

"You have my blessing." He smiles at me. It's weak but not in a bitter way. It's a smile I imagine I'd have when the day comes with either Izzy or Amelia when I have to trust their heart and happiness to another man.

"So I'm getting married now?" I joke, but warmth wraps around me at the thought of his daughter having my last name.

"I don't think Georgia will have it any other way."

I smile, trying to hide the fact that I'd proposed to Gigi shortly after I told her I loved her the first time, but she refused. She slapped me and told me that there was no way she was marrying me when she was a 'fat cow.' Her words, not mine. I spanked her ass until it was bright red for insulting herself while my child grew in her womb. She came four times that night, and I never broached the subject again.

"Well, there's only one way to find out, and it starts with that." I point to the spirometer on the side table.

Kincaid smiles and hands over the device that holds my future in its little plastic grasp.

"Get to work, Hound. I need my wife." I smile at him before my lips hit the mouthpiece. "Say one dirty word about my daughter, and I'm on the next plane out of here without you."

"I wasn't," I argue, but my smile never leaves my mouth.

"You were, too." His words are harsh, but the twitch in his lips tells me he wants to smile. "I can't handle it."

"She's a grown woman," I remind him. "She's a mother."

"I still can't handle it." His head shakes.

I laugh as he backs a few feet away from the bed.

"You have to let her grow up." Getting him worked up over Gigi is the second-best thing to seeing Gigi on video chat.

"Yeah?" His grin grows. "So now would be a good time to tell you about Izzy's boyfriend?"

"Bullshit," I hiss. "She's too fucking young."

"Then I won't tell you that he's been to the clubhouse several times."

I groan when I sit up straight in the bed. My body is so fucking tight from lying here for weeks.

"Or that he stays the night, on the couch of course."

"I'll fucking kill you." The gleam in his eye is unreadable.

"You'll have to catch me first." He angles his head toward the forgotten spirometer in my hands.

His chuckle as he leaves and the little, yellow piece of plastic floating in the spirometer is all I can hear.

Chapter 40

Gigi

"Where have you been!" I snap as soon as Facetime connects.

I frown down at the blacked-out screen and feel bad for waking Amelia with my raised voice. I cradle her, rocking her gently until she sighs and falls back asleep.

"That's a silly question, gorgeous. Where else would I be?"

I love hearing his voice, but hate that I can't see his face. This last week, reception has been spotty at best and more than a few of our video calls have been just a black screen when I wanted nothing more than to see his bearded face.

"You haven't called all day," I grumble. It's now after midnight, but that doesn't matter. He's been upset he's missed so much the last couple of weeks, he has me call when I wake up at night and nurse. He wants me to call when I bathe Amelia, when I miss him. That means I'm constantly calling. Dad warned me that he needs his rest to gain his strength so he can come home, but he insists I call him. Who am I to deny him?

"I've been resting." Only now do I hear the exhaustion in his voice.

"That's it," I say with renewed energy. "I'm coming to Brazil. Amelia is three weeks old now, and I read online about people who travel with newborns all the time. We'll be fine."

He chuckles, the sound warming me and sounding closer than it has in weeks.

"I miss you," I complain.

"Going to Brazil would be a waste, Gigi."

"I need to be with you," I argue. "I need to hold you, kiss your lips, and trim that out of control beard."

He laughs again. "You love my beard."

"I love everything about you. Going to Brazil is what I need." I look down at our sleeping daughter. "Amelia needs to meet her daddy."

"You sure you're willing to put her in my arms?" I nod, a lone tear rolling down my cheek. "I hear you're spoiling her by holding her all the time."

"Babies are supposed to be cuddled." I trace her lips.

"She looks so good in your arms." I smile wide, grateful that even though I can't see him, that he can see us.

"She'd look even better in yours," I counter.

"You sure?"

I jerk my head up at the shuffling sound near the door, and my breathing stops. Worn, a little tattered, but still as handsome as ever, Jameson is watching me from the open doorway.

"You're here?" Sobs wrack my body as I sit, unable to make my body cooperate and go to him.

"I'm here."

He doesn't bother with his phone as it drops to his feet when he closes the distance that's been between us for far too long.

All but collapsing he falls to the bed, back against the headboard.

"You're here," I repeat, stunned but happier than I've ever been.

I turn to him, head resting against his hard chest as I cry. Every second since he's been gone has felt like a million years. It's been a lifetime since I could touch the warmth of his body, feel his heart beating in sync with mine, that I honestly never thought I'd be able to feel those things again.

Amelia wiggles between us before the room fills with her shrill cries. I move back, allowing her room and giving Jameson the chance to see his daughter unaided by technology for the very first time.

I rock her, trying to calm her as his rough finger trails softly down her tiny cheek.

"She's beautiful." I nod in agreement. "She looks like you."

Fingers trace over her full head of hair, and my tears are renewed as she blinks up at him, instinctively knowing that her family is together and safe.

"You should've told me you were coming home," I complain. "I would've cleaned up. Would've bathed."

Personal hygiene and trying to impress people with my looks hasn't even been a consideration since being discharged from the hospital. At first, I was exhausted, from childbirth and wondering if Jameson was going to survive. After he woke up, I focused on him and taking care of Amelia. I'm exhausted, and even though I've had multiple offers of help from others, I've refused every one, knowing this is something I had to do on my own, if only to keep my mind and my hands busy.

His fingers tilt my chin up, bright green eyes finding mine. "You're beautiful." He watches my mouth, and that familiar tingle that's been absent for so long returns with a vengeance. "So beautiful."

A harsh breath rushes through my nose when his lips meet mine. Everything is apparent in his kiss. Love, lust, and a longing I'm suffering right along with him is evident in the grip of his fingers when his arm wraps around my back.

"Don't cry, gorgeous." His fingers sweep my cheeks, but they're only replaced by new ones.

"I've missed you so much." I've said it so many times in the past weeks, but it's only now, confessing it against his lips that the words aren't accompanied by a pain in my chest.

Amelia wiggles again, getting upset that she doesn't have his undivided attention.

"You're as needy as your momma," he coos down at her.

I laugh, a genuine laugh that fills the room for the first time since I came home. "You have no idea."

"You're here." We both look up to see Izzy standing in the doorway.

He opens his arms to her, and she runs right into them, apologizing when he winces.

With eyes squeezed tight, he holds her, rocking her back and forth in his embrace as she sobs into his neck. I look down at Amelia, giving them a moment when I see a tear break free from the corner of his eye.

"All of my girls are here." He clears his throat, but the emotion doesn't leave his face when Izzy pulls back and sits near his feet on the bed. He glances at all of us, spending long moments looking all of us in the eye before he focuses on Izzy. "Tell me about this boy that's been hanging around?"

"Huh?" Izzy looks as confused as I feel.

"The boy that followed you here from Arizona." She tilts her head to the side before her brows furrow, and she glances over at me.

"There's no boy, dad."

"Kincaid said—" He sighs before turning his eyes up to the ceiling. "I'm going to kill him."

"I'm so confused," I mutter.

His laugh fills the room even though it's not as strong as I remember. "Don't worry about it, gorgeous."

He presses a soft kiss to my forehead.

"I'm going to go back to sleep," Izzy says giving us each a hug and planting a soft kiss on Amelia's head. "I'll see you in the morning."

She lingers near the door, never taking her eyes off of her dad as if she's afraid he's going to be gone by the time she wakes.

"Get some rest, Iz. We'll see you in the morning."

She nods, trusting him and closes the door on the way out.

"I can't believe her mother let her come."

I don't respond, but it doesn't take long before I have to face the hot glare I feel on the side of my face.

"Don't look at me like that," I mutter when I face him. "She's eighteen now. She completed her last classes online. Passed every test. I urged her to go back home, but she refused."

"Gabby knows where she's at?"

I remain silent.

"Gigi?" I remain silent. "You may still be healing, but I will pink your ass."

At just the suggestion, my skin warms as if he's already taken his large hand to my ass. I bite my lip as I look up at him, and almost smile when his eyes heat.

"We'll get to that later," he promises. "Does Gabby know where she's at?"

"She knows that she's safe, but Izzy has been worried that they would come get her, so she turned off her cell phone and refused to give them the information."

He growls, but the warning doesn't do what he hopes because I'm not chastised, merely turned on with the anticipation of his wrath.

"She's still going to college in the fall," I say to appease him. "She just wants to spend the summer here."

"Damn right she's going to college," he mutters.

His irritated voice startles Amelia causing her to begin to cry.

"Oh, baby girl," he coos. "Don't cry."

"I imagine she's hungry," I explain when his soothing words don't calm her.

He watches with rapt attention as I lower the neck of my nightgown and raise her to my breast.

"So beautiful," he praises as his fingers toy with the curly hair at the nape of her neck.

I smile up at him, his eyes switching between the two of us like he can't go a second without seeing either of us.

"Marry me," he whispers.

"You ask now?" I try for irritated, but the light reflecting in his bright eyes makes it impossible. "While your daughter is nursing and my legs haven't seen a razor for the better part of a month?"

He smiles. "Marry me, and I'll shave you tomorrow so you can thank me."

"Thank you?" I squeak. "Thank you for what?"

He's given me everything, including the precious life that's suckling at my breast, but petulant has always been my thing, and I don't intend to change now.

"Thank me for the life I'm going to provide for you. Thank me for the orgasms I may allow you to have."

I narrow my eyes. "May allow?"

He smiles wide. "And I'll thank you in return." He kisses my lips, but it's only a sweeping brush. "I'll thank you for all the babies you're going to give me. Thank you for making the house I'll build a home. I'll thank you every day for loving me, for making me the happiest man in the world. Marry me."

"On one condition," I barter. I smile when his eyebrow rises. The look he's giving me says he's left no room for compromise. "You can't deny my orgasms."

His head shakes back and forth. "Everything I just said, and that's what you focus on?"

Cupping his cheek with my free hand, I focus on his lips for a long minute before looking up in his eyes. "You'll love me, provide for me, and give me more babies even if I don't marry you. I'll make our house a home, and I'll love you until the day I die even if we don't marry, but orgasm denial is brutal, and I won't sign on the dotted line unless you promise."

"How about," he says inching his mouth closer to mine. "How about, I promise not to let you go to bed at night without letting you come?"

I tilt my head, already knowing he can tease me all day long, torture me, tie me up so I can't finish myself off. Hell, he's done it before. But the one time, he put me to bed with my body on fire and my orgasm just out of reach, was one of the most brutal things I ever suffered. Waking up to his mouth and soul-clenching orgasm made it worth it, but it's not something I want to ever happen again.

"Deal," I breathe.

He kisses me again, tongue searching and sweeping against mine until I'm breathless when he pulls away. "I'm still going to pink your ass for taking so long to answer."

"I can't wait," I whisper against his lips.

We both look down at our beautiful daughter, and for the first time in my entire life, I feel complete.

***

I scrunch my eyes against the noise.

"Baby girl," the hiss from the door way echoes around the room again. "Psssst."

I roll my head, face rubbing on Jameson's chest hair. Snuggling deeper, I didn't realize how much I missed his touch and the warmth of him in my arms. I missed all of him. I smile, running my hand down his abs to the thickness of his cock. Even in his sleep he's virile and ready for me.

"Georgia Leigh!"

My head snaps to the door as I jerk my hand away and Jameson jolts under me. Amelia begins to whimper in her bassinet.

My dad, brow furrowed stands in the open doorway, but there's a soft smile playing at his lips.

"I haven't had the chance to hold her yet." He tilts his head in Amelia's direction. "It's almost noon. I've been waiting for you to wake up."

I clear my throat, embarrassed that my dad caught me touching Jameson's cock. "Give me ten minutes and I'll bring her out to you."

Still asleep, Jameson flexes his hips, no doubt searching for the warmth of my palm.

Dad's smile fades away completely. "I'll give you five."

The door closes softly behind him, and my body shakes from a chuckle coming from Jameson's chest. "So I guess a blow job is out of the question."

I swat at his stomach. "Maybe later."

Pulling me closer with his lips against my temple, I allow a few more seconds in his embrace.

"I bet just the feeling of your lips wrapped around me would be enough," he bargains.

My hand wanders from the crisp hairs on his chest, past his navel to the thickness straining against the cool sheets. "Maybe the first time," I coo. "But I'm going to take my time with you. Remind you why you love me."

He groans when my soft fingers trace the throbbing vein along his erection. "I don't need a reminder for that."

Pouting when I get out of the bed, he watches with hooded eyes as I tug off my nightgown and get dressed. By the time I'm out of the bathroom, he's already changed Amelia's diaper and redressed her.

"You're a natural," I tell him, running my hand down his cheek.

"She's perfect." He holds her close, kissing her forehead and sniffing the top of her head.

"Dad's waiting," I remind him. "Why don't you jump in the shower? I may be able to get him to watch her for an hour or so while I take care of that tent in your pants."

Laughing, he hands her over, but doesn't move away until I'm thoroughly kissed and breathless.

"Can't wait," he whispers in my ear, slapping my ass as I walk away.

I find Dad sitting at one of the kitchen tables drinking a cup of coffee. The second I cross the threshold his hands are out, fingers flexing in a demanding action for me to turn her over.

I watch, unshed tears brimming my eyes as my father does exactly what Jameson did just moments ago. He kisses her and breathes in her scent right from that delicate spot on the top of her head.

"I didn't understand my childhood and why you and Mom were so protective of us until her," I confess. "I want to wrap her in bubble wrap and hide her from the world."

"I still want to wrap you in bubble wrap," he says without taking his eyes off of Amelia. "And I want to do the same for her."

"I was horrible growing up. I fought you at every turn. Did things just to upset you, when all you were trying to do was make sure I was safe." I lean my head on his shoulder and look down at my amazing little girl. "I pray she's less like me and more like Ivy."

He turns, kissing the crown of my head. "You turned out just fine."

I swallow thickly, the emotions that I've been bombarded with in the weeks since giving birth are right on the edge, the slightest things making me tear up. Today is no different.

"I got lucky. Jameson and Amelia are the best things that could've happened for me."

He shifts, holding Amelia close to his chest and wrapping his arm around my shoulder. "I feel the same about you girls and your mom. Now I have this precious little one to protect, and I couldn't be happier. It gives me purpose."

"I'll take all the help I can get." My life has made a complete one-eighty in the last year. The old Georgia Leigh Anderson would've told him to fuck off and let me raise my daughter how I see fit. Now, as a mother, I know that there isn't a thing I wouldn't do to keep my family safe. Motherhood doesn't allow for stubbornness and digging your feet in just to spite others.

"She looks tiny compared to you, grandpa."

I look up, smiling as Jameson makes his way into the kitchen.

"Can't believe your ugly ass made such a cute little girl, Hound," Dad teases back. "Good thing Amelia looks like her mother."

I expect Jameson to argue, but instead he leans in kissing my lips and looks over at my dad. "I couldn't agree more."

I breathe in the familiar smell of his skin straight from the shower. He didn't towel off completely and there are still droplets of water clinging to the tips of his hair and the back of his neck.

"Think you can keep an eye on her for an hour or so?" Jameson must be more eager than I am if he's asking this of my father.

My dad looks between us before narrowing his eyes at the man by my side.

"No." I pull my head back, shocked at his answer.

Jameson chuckles beside me. "Cockblocker," he mutters but there's laughter in the word.

Something in their relationship has changed over the weeks they were in Brazil together. The tension that existed before is no longer around.

"Come on," Jameson whispers in my ear before tugging on my hand to help me stand.

"He said no," I hiss at him as we get closer to the doorway.

"He wouldn't let go of her right now if I had a gun to his head," he assures me.

Looking over my shoulder at my dad, I find him smiling and looking down at Amelia as if nothing else in the world matters. His phone rings. It startles me to the point of jumping, but he, calm as ever, just shifts so he can pull the ringing device from his jeans.

"Kincaid," he snaps when the call connects.

I watch as his brow furrows with whatever news he's receiving on the other end. The set of his shoulders goes from relaxed to rigid.

"He did what?" His jaw ticks, and before I can go to them, Jameson is already pulling Amelia from his arms. He releases her immediately before standing from the table.

"I appreciate your discretion in the matter." He nods, even though the guy on the other line can't see him. "I'll let Morrison know."

Shadow?

My dad ends the call.

"Oh God," I whisper. "Has something happened to Griffin?"

My heart is thudding, crashing against my ribs so fast my hands are already trembling.

"Tell me he's not dead," I beg, unable to respond to Jameson's arm around my shoulder.

"He's not dead," Dad answers as he storms toward the back door leading to the houses. "But he may be after Shadow is done with his ass."

I hear him mutter something about selling drugs on base before the door snaps shut with a bang. Amelia begins to cry hysterically, and as much as I want to follow him to get the details, my duties and responsibilities rest solely on the little girl currently throwing a fit in my arms.

Cerberus MC Continues with Griffin next!

Newest Series
Cerberus MC
Gatlinburg, TN Chapter
Hemlock: Cerberus TN Book 1
Ace: Cerberus TN Book 2

Standalones
Crowd Pleaser
Macon
We Said Forever
More Than a Memory

Cole Brothers Series
Love Me Like That
Teach Me Like That

Blackbridge Security
Hostile Territory
Shot in the Dark
Contingency Plan
Truth Be Told
Calculated Risk
Heroic Measures
Sleight of Hand
Controlled Burn
Cease Fire
Crossing Borders

Cerberus MC

Kincaid: Cerberus MC Book 1
Kid: Cerberus MC Book 2
Shadow: Cerberus MC Book 3
Dominic: Cerberus MC Book 4
Snatch: Cerberus MC Book 5
Lawson: Cerberus MC Book 6
Hound: Cerberus MC Book 7
Griffin: Cerberus MC Book 8
Samson: Cerberus MC Book 9
Tug: Cerberus MC Book 10
Scooter: Cerberus MC Book 11
Cannon: Cerberus MC Book 12
Rocker: Cerberus MC Book 13
Colton: Cerberus MC Book 14
Drew: Cerberus MC Book 15
Jinx: Cerberus MC Book 16
Thumper: Cerberus MC Book 17
Apollo: Cerberus MC Book 18
Legend: Cerberus MC Book 19
Grinch: Cerberus MC Book 20
Harley: Cerberus MC Book 21
A Very Cerberus Christmas
Landon: Cerberus MC Book 22
Spade: Cerberus MC Book 23
Aro: Cerberus MC Book 24
Boomer: Cerberus MC Book 25
Ugly: Cerberus MC Book 26
Bishop: Cerberus MC Book 27
Legacy: Cerberus MC Book 28
Stormy: Cerberus MC Book 29
Oracle: Cerberus MC Book 30
Newton: Cerberus MC Book 31

Ravens Ruin MC
Prequel: Desperate Beginnings
Book 1: Sins of the Father
Book 2: Luck of the Devil
Book 3: Dancing with the Devil

MM Romance
Grinder
Taunting Tony

Westover Prep Series
(bully/enemies to lovers romance)
One-Eighty
Catch Twenty-Two

Lindell
Back Against the Wall
Easier Said than Done
With a Grain of Salt

Made in the USA
Columbia, SC
30 June 2024

37904609R00391